ACCLAIM FOR THE HELEN TRILOGY BY PRESTON AND CHILD

TWO GRAVES

"A good thriller forces the reader to finish the book in one sitting. An exceptional thriller does that plus forces the reader to slow down to savor every word. With TWO GRAVES, Preston and Child have delivered another exceptional book...The gothic atmosphere that oozes from the pages will envelop the reader...Pendergast is a modern-day Sherlock Holmes, quirks and all...The mystery tantalizes, and the shocks throughout the narrative are like bolts of lightning. Fans will love the conclusion to the trilogy, and newcomers will seek out the authors' earlier titles."

—Associated Press

"Pendergast—an always-black-clad pale blond polymath, gaunt yet physically deadly, an FBI agent operating without supervision or reprimand—lurks at the dark, sharp edge of crime fiction protagonists."

—*Kirkus Reviews*

"A lavish story and one that takes the time for some skillful vignettes and characterizations."

—*Charlotte Observer*

"Preston and Child's high-adrenaline thriller wraps up the trilogy...with a bang...[An] intelligent suspense novel."

—*Publishers Weekly*

"TWO GRAVES provides readers exactly what they would expect from a Preston and Child novel—thrills, high adventure, treacherous plot twists, and well-researched scientific intrigue. The story is never predictable, and Pendergast is a multi-layered personality who keeps you guessing throughout."

—BookReporter.com

"The action is constant and starts with a bang."

—*RT Book Reviews*

"Another fast-paced murder mystery that crosses the country, dips into Mexico and then wallops Manhattan hotels. It's the perfect holiday gift for that thriller-genre lover in your life."

—*Asbury Park Press*

COLD VENGEANCE

"Before you even open the cover of a Preston and Child book, you know you're in for a good, if chilling, even thrilling time."

—*Asbury Park Press*

"[Preston and Child are] still going strong...Such is the talent of our authors that we happily follow their characters...all over the globe, from the moors of Scotland to the loony bins of New York City; the recipe is mixed well with a dash of assassins here and a soupcon of Nazis there, a couple of traitors and some really fascinating secondary characters...*Cold Vengeance* is a hot hell of a fun read."

—Examiner.com

"4½ stars! Top Pick! Preston and Child continue their dominance of the thriller genre with stellar writing and twists that come at a furious pace. Others may try to write like them, but no one can come close. The best in the business deliver another winner."

—*RT Book Reviews*

"Douglas Preston and Lincoln Child have outdone themselves once again, and with *Cold Vengeance* at the #1 spot on the *New York Times* bestseller list, it's proof this is without a doubt the best in the entire series."

—**GoodReads.com**

"5 stars! This fast-paced series continues to provide the reader with many twists. What you thought you knew from prior Pendergast novels may not necessarily be true."

—**TheMysteryReader.com**

FEVER DREAM

"This is no dream; it's the authors' best book in years."

—*Library Journal* **(starred review)**

"A thrill a minute."

—*San Jose Mercury News*

"[One of the] summer's best beach books."

—*Newark Star-Ledger*

"Preston and Child up the emotional ante considerably in this thriller featuring brilliant and eccentric Pendergast...Once again, the bestselling authors show they have few peers at creating taut scenes of suspense."

—*Publishers Weekly* **(starred review)**

TWO
GRAVES

TWO GRAVES

DOUGLAS PRESTON

&

LINCOLN CHILD

GRAND CENTRAL
PUBLISHING

NEW YORK   BOSTON

Copyright © 2010 by Splendide Mendax, Inc. and Lincoln Child
Excerpt from *White Fire* copyright © 2013 by Splendide Mendax, Inc. and Lincoln Child

Translation of *Der Erlkönig* from the German by Edgar Alfred Bowring

Grand Central Publishing
Hachette Book Group
237 Park Avenue
New York, NY 10017
www.HachetteBookGroup.com

Grand Central Publishing is a division of Hachette Book Group, Inc.
The Grand Central Publishing name and logo is a trademark of Hachette Book Group, Inc.

The Hachette Speakers Bureau provides a wide range of authors for speaking events. To find out more, go to www.hachettespeakersbureau.com or call (866) 376-6591.

The publisher is not responsible for websites (or their content) that are not owned by the publisher.

Printed in the United States of America

Originally published in trade paperback by Hachette Book Group
First oversize mass market edition: July 2013

10 9 8 7 6 5 4 3 2 1
OPM

*Lincoln Child dedicates this book
to his daughter, Veronica.
Douglas Preston dedicates this book
to Forrest Fenn.*

Before you embark on a journey of revenge,
dig two graves.

—CONFUCIUS

PART ONE

6:00 PM

THE WOMAN WITH THE VIOLET EYES WALKED slowly beneath the trees of Central Park, hands deep in the pockets of her trench coat. Her older brother walked beside her, his restless eyes taking in everything.

"What time is it?" she asked, yet again.

"Six o'clock precisely."

It was a mild evening in mid-November, and the dying sun threw dappled shadows over the sweeping lawn. They crossed East Drive, passed the statue of Hans Christian Andersen, and ascended a slight rise. And then—as if possessed by the same thought—they stopped. Ahead, across the placid surface of Conservatory Water, stood the Kerbs Memorial Boathouse, toy-like, framed against the vast ramparts of the buildings lining Fifth Avenue. It was a scene from a picture post-card: the small lake reflecting the blood-orange sky, the little model yachts cutting through the still water to the appreciative cries of children. In the gap between two skyscrapers, a full moon was just appearing.

Her throat felt tight and dry, and the necklace of freshwater pearls felt constricting around her throat. "Judson," she said, "I'm not sure I can do this."

She felt his brotherly grip on her arm tighten reassuringly. "It'll be okay."

She glanced around at the tableau spread before her, heart beating fast. A violinist was sawing away on the parapet before the lake. A young couple sat on one of the boathouse benches, oblivious to everything but each other's company. On the next bench, a short-haired man with a bodybuilder's physique read the *Wall Street Journal*. Commuters and joggers passed by in small streams. In the shadow of the boathouse itself, a homeless man was settling down for the night.

And there *he* stood before the lake—a slender figure, motionless, dressed in a long pale coat of exquisite cut, blond-white hair burnished platinum by the dying light.

The woman drew in a sharp breath.

"Go ahead," Judson said in a low voice. "I'll be close by." He released her arm.

As the woman stepped forward, her surroundings vanished, her entire attention focused on the man who watched her approach. Thousands of times she had imagined this moment, spun it out in her mind in all its many variants, always ending with the bitter thought that it could never happen; that it would remain only a dream. And yet here he was. He looked older, but not by much: his alabaster skin, his fine patrician features, his glittering eyes that held her own so intently, awakened a storm of feeling and memory and—even at this time of extreme danger—desire.

She stopped a few feet from him.

"Is it really you?" he asked, his courtly southern drawl freighted with emotion.

She tried to smile. "I'm sorry, Aloysius. So very sorry."

He did not reply. Now, all these years later, she

found herself unable to read the thoughts that lay behind those silver eyes. What was he feeling: Betrayal? Resentment? Love?

A narrow scar, freshly made, ran down one of his cheeks. She raised a fingertip, touched it lightly. Then, impulsively, she pointed over his shoulder.

"Look," she whispered. "After all these years, we still have the moonrise."

His glance followed hers, over the Fifth Avenue skyline. The buttery full moon rose between the stately buildings, perfectly framed against a pearlescent pink sky that graded upward into deep, cool violet. His frame shuddered. When he looked back at her, a new expression was on his face.

"Helen," he whispered. "My God. I thought you were dead."

Wordlessly, she slipped a hand through his arm and—without giving it conscious thought—began to walk around the lake.

"Judson says you're going to take me away from... from all this," she said.

"Yes. We'll return to my apartment at the Dakota. And from there, we'll head to—" He paused. "The less said about that, the better. Suffice to say, where we're going, you'll have nothing to fear."

She tightened her grip on his arm. "Nothing to fear. You have no idea how good that sounds."

"It's time to recover your life." He reached into the pocket of his jacket, drew out a gold ring set with a large star sapphire. "So let's start at the beginning. Do you recognize this?"

She flushed as she looked at it. "I never thought I'd see it again."

"And I never thought I'd get the chance to replace it on your finger. That is, not until Judson told me you were still alive. I knew, I *knew*, he was telling the truth—even when nobody else believed me."

He reached over, caught her left forearm lightly, lifting it as if to place the ring on her finger. His eyes widened as he took in the stump of her wrist, a scar running along its upper edge.

"I see," he said simply. "Of course."

It was as if the careful, diplomatic dance they had been engaged in suddenly ended. "Helen," he said, his tone now with an edge. "Why did you go along with this horrific scheme? Why did you conceal so many things from me? Why haven't you—"

"Let's please not talk about that," she interrupted quickly. "There were reasons for everything. It's a terrible story, a *terrible* story. I will tell it to you—*all* of it. But this is not the time or place. Now, please—place the ring on my finger and let's leave."

She raised her right hand, and he slid on the ring. As he did so, she watched his gaze move past her, to the scene beyond.

Suddenly he stiffened. For just a moment he stood there, her hand still in his. Then, with apparent calm, he turned toward the spot where her brother was standing and gestured for him to join them.

"Judson," she heard him murmur. "Take Helen and get her away from here. Do it calmly but quickly."

The fear that had just started to recede spiked hard in her breast. "Aloysius, what—"

But he cut her off with a brief shake of his head. "Take her to the Dakota," he told Judson. "I'll meet up with you there. Please go. *Now.*"

Judson took her hand and began walking away, almost as if he had anticipated this.

"What is it?" she asked him. No reply.

She looked over her shoulder. To her horror, she saw

that Pendergast had a pistol out and was pointing it at one of the model yachtsmen. "Stand up," he was saying. "Keep your hands where I can see them."

"Judson—" she began again.

His only response was to quicken his stride, pulling her along.

Suddenly a shot rang out behind them. "*Run!*" Pendergast cried.

In an instant the tranquil scene fell into pandemonium. People scattered amid screams. Judson yanked her harder, and they broke into a run.

A stutter of automatic weapons fire cut through the air. Judson's hand jerked away from her own, and he fell.

At first she thought he had tripped. Then she saw the blood gushing from his jacket.

"Judson!" she cried out, halting and bending over him.

He lay on his side, looking up at her, twisting in pain, his mouth trying to work. "Keep running," he gasped. "Keep—"

Another clatter of the automatic weapon, another line of whistling death drawn through the grass as bullets thudded into the earth, and Judson was hit again, the impact flipping him over onto his back.

"*No!*" Helen screamed, leaping away.

The chaos swelled: screams, the crack of gunfire, the tread of fleeing people. Helen was aware of none of it. She fell to her knees, staring in horror at his open but unseeing eyes.

"Judson!" she cried. "*Judson!*"

A few seconds may have passed, or more—she had no way of knowing—and then she heard Pendergast calling her name. She looked up. He was running toward her, his pistol drawn, firing to one side.

"Fifth Avenue!" he cried. "Run to Fifth Avenue—!"

Another gunshot rang out, and he, too, was knocked to the ground. This second shock roused her. She leapt to her feet, her trench coat wet with her brother's blood. Aloysius was still alive and had managed to get back on his feet, taking cover behind a bench, continuing to fire at the couple who, just moments before, had apparently been interested only in making out.

He's covering my escape.

Wheeling around, she took off at top speed. She'd get to Fifth Avenue, lose the gunmen in the teeming crowds, then make her way to the Dakota, meet up with him there...Her panicked thoughts were interrupted by another fusillade of shots, more screaming of panicked people.

Helen ran on, hard. The avenue lay ahead, beyond the stone gates of the park. Just fifty feet to go...

"Helen!" She heard Pendergast's distant cry. "Look out! To your left!"

She glanced left. Under the darkness of the trees, she could see two men in jogging outfits, sprinting directly for her.

She swerved away, toward a grove of sycamores off the main path. She glanced over her shoulder again. The joggers were following—and they were gaining fast.

More shots rang out. She redoubled her efforts, but the heels of her shoes kept sinking into the soft earth, slowing her down. Then she felt a terrific impact against her back and was thrown to the ground. Someone grasped the neck of her trench coat and hauled her roughly to her feet. She struggled, crying out, but the two men pinned her arms and began dragging her toward the avenue. With horror, she recognized their faces.

"Aloysius!" she cried at the top of her lungs, looking back over her shoulder. "Help! I know these people! *Der Bund*—the Covenant! They'll kill me! Help me, *please*—!"

In the dying light, she could just make out Pendergast. He had struggled to his feet, bleeding freely from the gunshot wound, and he was limping toward her on his one good leg.

Ahead, on Fifth Avenue, a taxi idled at the curb, waiting—waiting for her and her abductors.

"Aloysius!" she screamed again in despair.

The men pushed her forward, opened the cab's rear door, and flung her inside. Bullets ricocheted off the tempered front window of the cab.

"*Los! Verschwinden wir hier!*" one of the joggers shouted as they tumbled in after her. "*Gib Gas!*"

Helen struggled fiercely as the taxi pulled away from the curb, trying with her one good hand to claw her way to the door. She got the briefest glimpse of Pendergast, in the gloom of the park. He had fallen to his knees, still looking in her direction.

"No!" she cried as she struggled. "*No!*"

"*Halt die Schnauze!*" barked one of the men. He drew back his fist and punched her in the side of the head—and darkness came rushing over all.

+ Six Hours

A DOCTOR IN WRINKLED SCRUBS STUCK HIS head into the waiting room of the Lenox Hill ICU. "He's awake, if you'd like to talk to him."

"Thank God." Lieutenant Vincent D'Agosta of the NYPD stuffed the notebook he'd been examining into his pocket and stood up. "How is he?"

"No complications." A note of irritation crossed the physician's face. "Although doctors always make the worst patients."

"But he's not—" D'Agosta began, then fell silent. He followed the doctor into the intensive care unit.

Special Agent Pendergast was sitting up in bed, attached to half a dozen monitoring machines. An IV was in one arm, and a nasal cannula was fitted to his nostrils. His bed was strewn with medical charts, and he held an X-ray in his hand. Always very pale, the skin of the FBI agent was now like porcelain. A doctor was bending over the bed, in intense conversation with his patient. Although D'Agosta could barely hear Pendergast's replies, it was clear the two men were not exactly in agreement.

"—*Completely* out of the question," the doctor

was saying as D'Agosta approached the bed. "You're still in shock from the gunshot wound and loss of blood, and the wound itself—not to mention the two bruised ribs—will require healing and ongoing medical attention."

"Doctor," Pendergast replied. Normally, Pendergast was the quintessence of southern gentility, but now his voice sounded like ice chips rattling on iron. "The bullet barely grazed the gastrocnemius muscle. Neither the tibia nor the fibula was touched. The wound was clean, and no operation was required."

"But the blood loss—"

"Yes," Pendergast interrupted. "The blood loss. How many units was I given?"

A pause. "One."

"One unit. Due to damage to the minor tributaries of the Giacomini vein. Trivial." He waved the X-ray like a flag. "As for the ribs, you said it yourself: bruised, not broken. The costae verae five and six, at the heads, approximately two millimeters from the vertebral column. Being true ribs, their elasticity will aid in quick recovery."

The doctor fumed. "Dr. Pendergast, I simply cannot permit you to leave this hospital in your condition. You of all people—"

"On the contrary, Doctor: you cannot prevent it. My vitals are within acceptable norms. My injuries are minor, and I can tend to them myself."

"I will note on your chart that you are leaving the hospital against my express orders."

"Excellent." Pendergast flipped the X-ray like a playing card onto the nearby table. "And now if you'll excuse me?"

The physician took one final, exasperated look at Pendergast, then turned on his heel and left the room, followed by the doctor who had admitted D'Agosta.

Now Pendergast turned to D'Agosta as if seeing him for the first time. "Vincent."

D'Agosta quickly approached the bedside. "Pendergast. My God. I'm so sorry—"

"Why aren't you with Constance?"

"She's safe. Mount Mercy redoubled their security measures. I had to..." He paused a moment to control his voice. "To check up on you."

"Much ado about nothing, thank you." Pendergast removed the nasal cannula, slid out the IV needle from the inside of his elbow, then detached the blood pressure cuff and pulse oximeter. He pulled back the sheets and sat up. The movements were slow, almost robotic; D'Agosta could see the man was driving himself by a sheer iron will.

"I hope to hell you aren't really planning to leave."

Pendergast turned to look at him again, and the fire in his eyes—fierce coals in an otherwise dead face— shut D'Agosta up immediately.

"And how is Proctor?" Pendergast asked, swinging his legs over the side of the bed.

"He's fine, they say. Considering. A few broken ribs where the impact of the shot hit his bulletproof vest."

"Judson?"

D'Agosta shook his head.

"Bring me my clothes," Pendergast said, nodding toward the closet.

D'Agosta hesitated, realized it was useless to protest, and brought them over.

With a wince, Pendergast stood up; swayed almost imperceptibly for a second; then steadied himself. D'Agosta handed him his clothes, and he drew the curtain.

"Do you have any idea what the hell happened back there in the park?" D'Agosta said to the curtain. "It's all over the news, five people dead, homicide's going crazy."

"I have no time for explanations."

"Sorry, but you're not getting out of here without telling me what happened." He took out his notebook.

"Very well. I will speak to you for the length of time it takes me to get dressed. And then I *am* getting out of here."

D'Agosta shrugged. He'd take what he could get.

"It was a carefully planned—*exceptionally* carefully planned—abduction. They killed Judson and kidnapped my wife."

"*They?* Who?"

"A shadowy group of Nazis, or Nazi descendants, called *Der Bund*."

"Nazis? Jesus, why?"

"Their motives are obscure to me."

"I need details of exactly what happened."

Pendergast's voice came from behind the curtain. "I went to meet Judson and Helen at the boathouse, to take Helen and hide her from this group. Helen arrived at six, as agreed. I quickly became aware that we'd been set up. One of the model yachtsmen was acting suspicious. He didn't know the first thing about boats, and he was nervous—sweating in the chill air. I drew on him and told him to stand up. That precipitated it."

D'Agosta took notes. "How many were involved?"

A pause. "At least seven. The yachtsman. Two lovers on a park bench—they killed Judson. A would-be homeless man, who shot Proctor. Your CS people have probably already reconstructed the sequence of the firefight. There were at least three others: two joggers, who kidnapped Helen as she was trying to escape, and the driver of the ersatz cab they forced her into."

Pendergast emerged from behind the screen. His

usually immaculate suit was a mess: the jacket was covered with grass stains, and the lower part of one trouser leg was torn and crusted with dried blood. He stared at D'Agosta as he straightened his tie. "Good-bye, Vincent."

"Wait. How the hell did this...this *Bund* learn about your meeting?"

"A most excellent question."

Pendergast grabbed a metal cane and turned to leave. D'Agosta caught him by the arm. "This is nuts, you walking out of here like this. Isn't there something I can do to help you?"

"Yes." Pendergast plucked the notebook and pen from D'Agosta's hand, opened the notebook, and quickly scrawled something. "This is the license plate of the cab Helen was abducted in. I managed to get all but the final two numbers. Put all your resources into finding it. Here's the hack number, too, but my guess is it's meaningless."

D'Agosta took back the notebook. "You got it."

"Put out an APB on Helen. It might be complicated, as she's officially dead, but do it anyway. I'll get you a photograph—it will be fifteen years old, use forensic software to age it."

"Anything else?"

Pendergast gave a single, brusque shake of his head. "Just *find that car*." And he stepped out of the room without another word, limping down the hall, accelerating as he went.

+ Twenty-Two Hours

As D'Agosta drove west away from Newark, he felt as if he were stepping back in time to when he'd been a beat cop at the Forty-First Precinct of the old South Bronx. The dilapidated shops, the shuttered buildings, the ravaged streets—all were a reminder of less happy days. He drove on as the view outside the windshield grew steadily grimmer. Soon he reached the heart of the blight: here—in the midst of the densest megalopolis in America—entire blocks lay empty, their buildings burnt shells or piles of rubble. He pulled over at a corner and got out, service piece where he could get to it quickly. But then he saw, amid all the decay, a single building—standing like a lonely flower in a parking lot—with lace-curtained windows, geraniums, and brightly painted shutters: a spot of hope in the urban wasteland. D'Agosta fetched a deep breath. The South Bronx had come back; this neighborhood would, too.

He crossed the sidewalk and started across a vacant lot, kicking aside bricks. Pendergast had beaten him here: he could see the agent at the far end of the lot, beside the burned-out remains of a taxi, speaking to a uniformed police officer and what looked like a small

CSI team. Pendergast's Rolls-Royce was parked at the corner, spectacularly out of place on these impoverished streets.

Pendergast gave D'Agosta a curt nod as he approached. Other than the shocking paleness, the FBI agent now looked more like his old self. In the late-afternoon light, his trademark black suit was clean and pressed, his white shirt crisp. He had traded the ungainly aluminum cane for one of ebony, topped by a handle of carved silver.

"...Found it forty-five minutes ago," the beat cop was telling Pendergast. "I was chasing some twelve-year-olds who'd been boosting copper wire." He shook his head. "And here was this New York taxi. The license matched the one on the APB, so I called it in."

D'Agosta turned his attention to the taxi. It was little more than a husk: the hood was gone, the engine cannibalized, the seats missing, dashboard scorched and partially melted, steering wheel broken in two.

The head of the CSI team approached from the far side of the vehicle. "Even before the vandals got to it, this was almost useless as evidence," he said, pulling off a pair of latex gloves. "No paperwork or documentation. It was vacuumed and wiped down, all fingerprints removed. They employed a particularly aggressive accelerant. Anything the perps didn't take care of, the fire would have."

"The VIN?" D'Agosta asked.

"We've got it. Stolen vehicle. Won't be of much use." The man paused. "We'll haul it back to the warehouse for a more thorough examination, but this smells like a professional cleanup job. Organized crime."

Pendergast took this in without replying. Although the agent remained utterly still, D'Agosta could feel a sense of desperation, of ruthless drive, radiating from him. Then, abruptly, he drew a pair of latex gloves from a coat pocket, snapped them on, and approached the vehicle. Crouching over it, wincing briefly with pain, he circled once, then twice, spidery fingers running lightly over the scorched metal, glittering eyes taking in everything. As the others watched, he peered carefully into the engine space; the passenger compartment, front and back; the trunk. Then, as he began a third revolution, he pulled some small ziplock bags, a few sample tubes, and a scalpel from his pocket. Kneeling beside the front fender, his face creasing momentarily with the effort, he used the scalpel to scrape some shavings of dried mud into one of the bags, which he then sealed and returned to his pocket. Rising, he completed the third circuit, more slowly this time. Stopping at the right rear tire, he knelt again and—using a pair of forceps—plucked several small pebbles from the treads of the tire and placed them in a second bag. This, too, quickly disappeared into his pocket.

"That's, uh, evidence," the cop began.

Pendergast rose and turned toward the cop. He said nothing, but the cop took a step backward under the force of the FBI agent's stare.

"Right. Keep us in the loop on that," the cop muttered.

Still Pendergast skewered the man with his stare. He looked at the CSI team, each in turn, and then finally at D'Agosta. There was something accusatory in his gaze, as if they were guilty of some unnamed offense. Then he turned and began walking in the direction of the Rolls, limping slightly, using the cane for support.

D'Agosta scrambled after him. "What's next?"

Pendergast did not stop walking. "I'm going to find Helen."

"Will you be . . . working officially?" D'Agosta asked.

"Do not concern yourself with my status."

D'Agosta was taken aback by his cold tone.

"Carry on with the official homicide and kidnapping investigation. If you uncover anything of interest, let me know. But remember also: this is my fight. Not yours."

When D'Agosta stopped, Pendergast turned, his voice softening as he laid a hand on his arm. "Your place is here, Vincent. What I have to do, I must do alone."

D'Agosta nodded. Pendergast turned away again and opened the car door, simultaneously raising his cell phone to one ear. As the door closed, D'Agosta could hear him speaking into the phone: "Mime? Anything? Anything at all?"

+ Twenty-Six Hours

HORACE ALLERTON WAS PREPARING TO ENJOY his favorite activity—a relaxing evening with a cup of coffee and a good scientific journal—when a knock sounded at the front door of his neat Lawrenceville bungalow.

He put down his cup and glanced at the clock with a frown. Quarter past eight: too late for a friend to be calling. He picked up the magazine, *Stratigraphy Today*, and opened it with a quiet sigh of contentment.

The knock came again, more insistent.

Allerton's eyes rose from the magazine to the door. Jehovah's Witnesses, maybe, or one of those annoying kids who went door-to-door, selling magazine subscriptions. Ignore them and they'd go away.

He had just started in on the magazine's lead article—"Mechanical Stratigraphy Analysis of Depositional Structure," a promising evening's reading indeed—when he glanced up and had the shock of his life. A man in an elegant black suit, face as white as Dracula, stood in the center of his living room.

"What on earth—?" Allerton cried, leaping up.

"Special Agent Pendergast. FBI." A shield and

identification card appeared out of nowhere, shoved into his face.

"How, how did you get in? What do you want?"

"Dr. Horace Allerton, the geologist?" the agent asked. His voice was cool but with an underlying shimmer of threat.

Allerton nodded, swallowed.

Without a word, Pendergast stepped over to a chair, and now Allerton noticed the limp and the silver-headed cane. The geologist sat back guardedly in his own wing chair. "What's this all about?"

"Dr. Allerton," the FBI agent began as he took a seat, "I've come to you for help. You are known for your expertise in analyzing soil composition. And I've taken particular note of your knowledge of glacial deposition."

"And?"

The agent reached into his pocket, took out two sealed plastic bags. He laid them both on the coffee table, separating them.

Allerton hesitated, then bent forward to examine them. One was filled with a sample of micaceous clay mingled with soil, the other with small broken pebbles of porphyritic granite.

"I need two things. First, I would like a distribution map of the type of clay found in sample one."

Allerton nodded slowly.

"The pebbles in sample two are the product of a gravel crusher, are they not?"

The geologist opened the bag and slid the pebbles into his hand. They were rough, sharp, the edges unworn by time, weathering, or glacial abrasion. "They are."

"I want to know where they came from."

Allerton glanced from one bag to the other. "Why

come to me at this time of night, sneaking in like this? You should make an appointment, see me at my Princeton office."

A faint tremor passed over the FBI agent's sculpted face. "If this were merely an idle request, Doctor, I would not have troubled you at such a late hour. A woman's life is at stake."

Allerton put the bags down beside his coffee cup. "What exactly is the, uh, time frame you had in mind?"

"You are known to have a small but quite fine mineralogy laboratory in your basement."

"You mean...you mean you want these analyzed *now*?" Allerton asked.

In response, Pendergast merely leaned back in his chair, as if making himself comfortable.

"But that could take hours!" Allerton protested.

Pendergast continued to fix him with a level gaze.

Allerton glanced at the clock. It was now eight thirty. He thought of his magazine, and the article he'd been looking forward to. Then he glanced again at the FBI agent in the opposite chair. There were dark smudges beneath the man's pale gray eyes, as if he had not slept in a long time. And the look in those eyes made him most uneasy.

"Perhaps if you told me why you needed these particular analyses?"

"I will. They were recovered from a car that had evidently spent some time driving over a crushed-gravel road and a muddy driveway. I need to find that location."

Allerton scooped up the samples and rose. "Wait here," he said.

As an afterthought, he took his cup of coffee with him to the basement.

+ Thirty Hours

MIDNIGHT. PENDERGAST SAT IN HIS ROLLS-ROYCE outside the house of Dr. Allerton, engine idling.

He had been fortunate: the particular type of granite outcropped in only one area that also contained a gravel pit. This pit was owned by the Reliance Sand and Gravel Company, located just outside Ramapo, New York. They ran a large gravel-crushing operation that supplied an area covering a significant portion of Rockland County. Using his laptop to visit the Reliance website, Pendergast had been able to map the approximate geographic range of Reliance's customer base, which he duly marked on an atlas of Rockland County.

Next he turned to Allerton's analysis of the mud. It was largely composed of an unusual type of clay, identified as a weathered micaceous halloysite, fortunately not common to the region, although—according to the geologist—somewhat more so in Quebec and northern Vermont. Allerton had given Pendergast a map of its geographic distribution, copied from an online journal.

Pendergast compared this with the distribution region he had marked for the gravel. They intersected in only one area, somewhat less than a square mile in extent, north and east of Ramapo.

Now Pendergast opened Google Earth on his laptop and located the coordinates of that square mile of overlap. Zooming in to the program's maximum resolution, he examined the terrain. Much of it was heavily wooded, situated along the border of Harriman State Park. A suburban neighborhood took up another section, but it was a recent development and all the roads and driveways appeared neatly paved. There were some dirt roads and houses scattered elsewhere, as well as a few farms, but they showed no areas that looked graveled. Finally he spied a structure that looked promising: a large, isolated warehouse. The place had a long driveway; a small adjacent parking area that showed up in a mottled pale hue that looked very much like gravel spread over muddy ground.

Shutting off the laptop, Pendergast stowed the computer and pulled away from the curb with a screech of rubber, heading for the New Jersey Turnpike.

Ninety minutes later, he parked the Rolls off to the side of the road, half a mile past the Rockland County Solid Waste facility, on a wooded stretch just short of the warehouse. Through the denuded trees, pale in the moonlight, he could make out the building, a single light burning before its heavy corrugated-metal door. For half an hour, he kept the structure under surveillance. Nobody came or went; it appeared deserted.

Taking a penlight from the backseat, but keeping it switched off, he slipped out of the car and approached the building through the trees, moving silently. He circled it cautiously. The lone window was painted black.

Turning the flashlight on, Pendergast knelt, wincing with pain. He took the gravel sample from his pocket

and, using the light, compared it with the gravel that
lined the driveway. The match was perfect. He reached
down and fingered a small sample of mud under the
gravel, spreading it between his thumb and forefinger.
Perfect as well.

Flitting across the open area around the warehouse,
Pendergast pressed himself against the corrugated wall,
then made his way around to the front, keeping low.
Externally it was decrepit, defunct, without signage of
any kind. And yet, for such a shabby building, the padlock on the lone door was expensive and new.

Pendergast hefted the padlock in one hand, let his
other hand drift over it in an almost caressing gesture. It did not spring open at once, yielding only after
manipulation with a tiny screwdriver and a bump key.
He pulled it free of the hasp, then—weapon at the
ready—opened the door just enough to peer through.
Darkness and silence. He slid the door open a little farther, slipped inside, and closed it behind him.

For perhaps five minutes, he made no movement
except to pan his flashlight around, examining the
floor, walls, and ceiling. The warehouse was almost
completely bare, with a concrete pad floor, metal walls,
empty shelves along the surrounding walls. It seemed
to offer no more information than the burned-out
taxi had.

He made a slow circuit of the interior, pausing now
and then to examine something that caught his attention; pluck a bit of something up here; take a photograph there; fill sample bags with almost invisible
evidence. Despite the apparent emptiness of the warehouse, under his probing eye a story began to emerge,
still little more than a ghostly palimpsest.

An hour later, Pendergast returned to the closed
door of the warehouse. Kneeling, he spread out a

dozen small sealed plastic envelopes, each containing a fragment of evidence: metal filings; a piece of glass; oil from a stain on the concrete, a bit of dried paint, a broken chip of plastic. His eye roved over each in turn, allowing a mental picture to form.

The warehouse had once been used as a vehicular pool. Judging by the age and condition of the oil spots on the floor, at one time it had seen fairly heavy use. More recently, however, only two vehicles had been stored. One—judging by the faint tread marks on the concrete floor, a Goodyear brand size 215/75-16—belonged to the Ford Escape that had been used as the getaway taxi. Spatters of yellow on one wall, as well as a reverse-image tracing of spray paint on a fragment of wood tossed into a far corner, indicated also that this was the spot where the Escape had been converted into a counterfeit New York City taxi—down to the paint job and fake medallion.

The other recent vehicle was harder to identify. Its tire print was broader than that of the Escape, and most probably a Michelin. It might well belong to a powerful European luxury sedan, such as an Audi A8 or a BMW 750. The faintest of paint scrapings could be seen against the inside of the warehouse door where this vehicle had recently come in contact; Pendergast carefully transferred them to another evidence bag with a set of tweezers. It was automotive paint, metallic, and of an unusual color: deep maroon.

And then, as he examined the paint, his eye noted—in the narrow channel of the sliding door—a tiny freshwater pearl.

His heart almost stopped.

After a moment, recovering, he picked it up with tweezers and stared at it. In his mind's eye, he could visualize—roughly twenty-four hours before—the taxi returning here. It would have contained four people: the driver, two men dressed in jogging suits, and an unwilling companion—Helen. Here she was transferred to the maroon foreign car. As they prepared to leave, there was a struggle; she tried to escape, forcing open the door of the car—that accounted for the scratch of paint—and in the process of subduing her, Helen's abductors snapped her necklace, scattering small pearls all over the passenger compartment and, no doubt, the floor of the warehouse. There would have been oaths, perhaps a punishment, and a hurried scuffle to pick up the explosion of pearls lying across the concrete.

Pendergast glanced at the tiny, lustrous bead held between the tips of the tweezers. This was the one they missed.

With Helen safely secured in the second car, the vehicles would have gone their separate ways, the counterfeit taxi to its fiery end in New Jersey, the maroon vehicle to...?

Pendergast remained, still kneeling, deep in thought, for another ten minutes. Then, rising stiffly, he exited the warehouse, padlocked it behind him, and walked noiselessly back to the waiting Rolls.

+ Thirty-Seven Hours

THOMAS PURVIEW WAS ALWAYS FASTIDIOUS about getting to his law office promptly at seven o'clock, but this morning someone else had been even more punctual: he found a man waiting in his outer office. He had the look of someone who had just arrived. In fact, it almost appeared as if he were about to try the door to the inner office, but of course Purview realized this was unlikely. As he walked in, the man turned, then limped toward him, one hand holding a cane, the other extended.

"Good morning," Purview said, shaking the proffered hand.

"That remains to be seen," the stranger replied in a southern accent. He was thin, almost gaunt, and he did not respond to Purview's professional smile. Purview prided himself on his ability to read the trouble in a new client's face—but this one was unreadable.

"Are you here to see me?" Purview asked. "Normally I require an appointment."

"I have no appointment, but the matter is urgent."

Purview stifled a knowing smile. He had never known a client who didn't have an urgent matter.

"Please step into my office. Would you care for some coffee? Carol isn't in yet, but it will only take me a minute to make."

"Thank you, nothing." The man walked into Purview's office, looking carefully around at the walls of books, the row of filing cabinets.

"Please have a seat." Normally, Purview enjoyed reading the *Wall Street Journal* between the hours of seven and eight in the morning, but he wasn't about to turn away a prospective client—especially not in this recession.

The man took a seat in one of the several chairs in Purview's spacious office, while the lawyer seated himself behind the desk. "How can I help you?" Purview asked.

"I'm looking for information."

"What kind of information?"

The man seemed to recollect something. "Forgive me for not introducing myself. Special Agent Aloysius Pendergast, FBI." He reached into his coat pocket, removed his ID, and placed it on Purview's desk.

Purview looked at the ID without touching it. "Are you here on official business, Agent Pendergast?"

"I am here on the investigation of a crime, yes." The agent paused to once again glance around the office. "Are you familiar with the property located on Two Ninety-Nine Old County Lane, Ramapo, New York?"

Purview hesitated. "It doesn't ring a bell. Then again, I've been involved in a great many real estate transactions in Nanuet and the surrounding area."

"The property in question consists of an old warehouse, now empty and by all appearances abandoned. Your address is listed for the LLC that holds the deed to this property, and you are the attorney of record."

"I see."

"I want to know who the real owners are."

Purview considered this for a moment. "I see," he repeated. "And do you have a court order requiring me to produce those records for you?"

"I do not."

Purview allowed the faintest smile of lawyerly superiority to settle over his features. "Then surely you, as a federal officer, know that I can't possibly violate attorney-client privilege by giving you that information."

Pendergast leaned forward in his chair. The face remained disturbingly neutral, unreadable. "Mr. Purview, you are in a position to do me a very large favor, for which you will be handsomely rewarded. *Ecce signum.*" Reaching into his pocket again, he withdrew a small envelope that he laid on the desk, taking back his ID at the same time.

Purview just couldn't help himself; he thumbed open the envelope and saw that inside was a brick of hundred-dollar bills.

"Ten thousand dollars," the agent said.

An awful lot of money for simply furnishing a name and address. Purview began to wonder what this was about: drugs, maybe, or organized crime. Or perhaps a sting? Entrapment? Whatever it was, he didn't like it.

"I doubt if your superiors would look very kindly upon your attempt at bribery," he said. "You can keep your money."

Pendergast waved this away like a pesky fly. "I'm offering you a carrot." He paused significantly, as if refraining from mentioning the other half of that equation.

Purview felt a shiver. "There's a due process for everything, Agent, ah, Pendergast. I'll assist you when I see a court order telling me to do so—and not before. Either way, I won't take your money."

For a moment, the FBI agent did not reply. Then, with the faintest of sighs—whether of regret or irritation it was impossible to say—he plucked the money off the table and returned it to the inside pocket of his black suit. "I am sorry for you, then," he said in a low voice. "Please listen carefully. I am someone for whom time is in extremely short supply. I have no inclination, and no patience, for bandying the finer points of law. You are proving yourself an honest man: good for you. Shall we find out just how . . . *courageous* a man you are? Allow me to assure you of one thing: you *will* give me those records. The only question is how much mortification you'll have to endure before doing so."

In his entire adult life, Thomas Purview had never allowed himself to be intimidated by anyone. He had no intention of starting now. He stood from his desk. "Kindly leave, Agent Pendergast, or I shall call the police."

But Pendergast showed no signs of standing. "The records for the warehouse in question are relatively old," he said. "At least two dozen years old. They are not available in digital format—I've checked. However, *so* much other information is. It flies through the virtual ether, Mr. Purview—one only has to reach out and snag it. And I have a resource, a talented resource, who is exceptionally good at such snagging. He has furnished me with another address I think we should discuss. In addition to Two Ninety-Nine Old County Lane, I mean. It's an address of particular interest."

Purview picked up his phone and began dialing 911.

"One Twenty-Nine Park Avenue South."

The hand paused in midair.

"You see, Mr. Purview," Pendergast went on, "it isn't only statements and records that are available on the Internet. Images are available, too. Security camera images, for example—if one knows how to access them."

Pendergast reached into his suit, pulled out a notebook. "Over the last few hours, my, ah, *resource* has sent a worm across the backbone of the Net, using pattern-recognition software to search for images of your face. He found them in—among other places—the security cameras at that particular address."

Purview remained very still.

"Which shows you in the company of one Felicia Lourdes, Apartment Fourteen-A. A lovely girl, young enough to be your daughter. And you do have several. Daughters, I mean. Correct?"

Purview said nothing. He slowly replaced the phone.

"The security images are of the two of you embracing passionately in the elevator. How touching. And there are quite a few of these images. It must be true love, is it not?"

Again, silence.

"What was it Hart Crane said about love? It is 'a burnt match skating in a urinal.' Why do people take such risks?" Pendergast shook his head sadly. "One Twenty-Nine Park Avenue South. A very good address. I wonder how Miss Lourdes can afford it. Given her position as a paralegal, I mean." He paused. "The person who would find this address to be of particular interest is, of course, your wife."

Still, silence.

"I am a desperate man, Mr. Purview. I will not hesitate to act on this immediately if you do not comply. Indeed, in that case I will be forced—in the unfortunate parlance of our times—to 'escalate.' "

The word hung in the air like a bad smell.

Purview thought for a moment. "I believe I'll step out of my office now for a fifteen-minute walk. If, during that time, somebody were to break in and rifle my files—well, I would have no knowledge of said person or said act. Especially if the files in question were left seemingly undisturbed."

Pendergast did not move as Purview picked up his *Wall Street Journal*, stepped out from behind the desk, and walked toward the door. As he reached it, he turned. "By the way, just so you don't make a hash of things, try the third cabinet, second drawer down. Fifteen minutes, Agent Pendergast."

"Enjoy your walk, Mr. Purview."

+ Forty Hours

FOR THE PAST FORTY HOURS, SHE HAD BEEN blindfolded and kept constantly on the move. She had been bundled into the trunk of a car, the back of a truck, and—she guessed—the hold of a boat. In all the furtive shuttling from place to place, she had grown disoriented and lost track of time. She felt cold, hungry, and thirsty, and her head still ached from the savage blow she'd received in the taxi. She had been given no food, and the only liquid offered her had been a plastic bottle of water, thrust into her hand some time back.

Now she was once again in the trunk of a car. For several hours they had been driving at high speed, apparently on a freeway. But now the car slowed; the vehicle made several turns; and the sudden roughness of the ride led her to believe they were on a dirt road or track.

Whenever she had been transferred from one make-shift prison to another, her captors had been silent. But now, with the road noise reduced, she could hear the murmur of their voices through the vehicle. They were speaking a mixture of Portuguese and German, both of which she understood perfectly, having learned them before either English or her father's native Hungarian. The talk was faint, however, and she could make out very little beyond the tones, which seemed angry, urgent. There seemed to be four of them now.

After several minutes of rough travel, the car eased to a halt. She heard doors opening and closing, feet crunching on gravel. Then the trunk was opened and she felt chill air on her face. A hand grabbed her by the elbow, raised her to a sitting position, then pulled her out. She staggered, knees buckling; the pressure of the hand increased, raising her and steadying her. Then— without a word—she was shoved forward.

Strange how she felt nothing, no emotion, not even grief or fear. After so many years of hiding, of fear and uncertainty, her brother had appeared with the news she had long dreamed of hearing but had resigned herself would never come. For one brief day she had been afire with the hope of seeing Aloysius again, of restarting their lives, of finally living once more like a normal human being. Then in a moment it was snatched away, her brother murdered, her husband shot and perhaps dead as well.

And now she felt like an empty vessel. Better to have never hoped at all.

She heard the creak of an opening door, and she was guided over a sill and into a room. The air smelled musty and close. The hand led her across the room, apparently through a second door and into an even mustier space. A deserted old house in the country, perhaps. The hand released its grip on her arm, and she felt the pressure of a chair seat against the back of her knees. She sat down, placing her remaining hand in her lap.

"Remove it," said a voice in German—a voice she instantly recognized. There was a fumbling at her head, and the blindfold was pulled away.

She blinked once, twice. The room was dark, but her long-blindfolded eyes needed no period of adjustment. She heard footsteps recede behind her, heard the door close. Then, licking dry lips, she raised her eyes and met the gaze of Wulf Konrad Fischer. He was older, of course, but still as powerful looking and as heavily muscled as ever. He was seated in a chair facing her, his legs apart and his hands clasped between them. He shifted slightly, and the chair groaned under his massive build. With his penetrating pale eyes, his dark tan, and his closely trimmed thatch of thick, snow-white hair, he exuded Teutonic perfection. He looked at her, a cold smile distorting his lips. It was a smile Helen remembered all too well. Her apathy and emptiness were replaced by a spike of fear.

"I never expected to receive a visit from the dead," Fischer said in his clipped, precise German. "And yet here you are. Fräulein Esterhazy—forgive me, Frau Pendergast—who departed this earth more than twelve years ago." He looked at her, hard eyes glinting with some combination of amusement, anger, and curiosity.

Helen said nothing.

"*Natürlich*, in retrospect I can see how it was done. Your twin sister—*der Schwächling*—was the sacrificial pawn. After all your protests, your sanctimonious outrage, I see how well you have learned from us, after all! I almost feel honored."

Helen remained silent. The apathy was returning. She would be better off dead than living with this pain.

Fischer peered at her intently, as if to gauge the effect of his words. He took a pack of Dunhills from his pocket, plucked one from the box, lit it with a gold lighter. "You wouldn't care to tell us where you've been all this time, would you? Or whether you've had any other accomplices in this little deception—beyond your brother, I mean? Or whether you've spoken to anyone about our organization?"

When there was no response, Fischer took a deep drag on the cigarette. His smile broadened. "No matter. There will be plenty of time for that—once we get you back home. I'm sure you'll be happy to tell the doctors everything...that is, before the experiments begin."

Helen went still. Fischer had used the word *Versuchsreihe*—but that word meant more to her than simply "experiments." At the thought of what it meant—at the memory—she felt a sudden panic. She leapt to her feet and ran headlong toward the door. It was a mindless, instinctive act, born of the atavistic need for self-preservation. But even as she charged the door, it was opened, her captors standing just beyond. Helen did not slow, and the force of the impact knocked two of them back, but the others seized her and gripped her hard. It took all four to restrain her and drag her back into the room.

Fischer stood up. Taking another deep drag on the cigarette, he regarded Helen as she struggled silently, fiercely. Then he looked at his watch.

"It's time to go," he said. He glanced again at Helen. "I think we had better prepare the hypodermic."

+ Forty-Four Hours

THE KNOCK CAME AT HALF PAST TWO IN THE afternoon. Kurt Weber put down the bottle of sweet tea he'd been drinking, dabbed at the corners of his mouth with a silk handkerchief, turned off his computer monitor, and walked across the tiled floor to answer it. A quick look through the eyehole indicated a respectable-looking gentleman.

"Who is it?"

"I'm looking for the Freiheit Importing Company."

Weber replaced the handkerchief in his breast pocket and opened the door. "Yes?"

The man stood in the hallway: slender, with piercing silver eyes and blond hair so pale, it was almost white.

"May I have a minute of your time?" the gentleman asked.

"Certainly." Weber opened the door farther and motioned the man to a seat. Although the man's suit was plain—simple black—it was of beautiful material, exquisitely tailored. Weber had always been something of a clotheshorse, and as he moved back behind his desk, he found himself unconsciously adjusting his own cuffs.

"Interesting," the man said, glancing around, "that you conduct your business in a hotel."

"It was not always a hotel," Weber replied. "When it was built in 1929, it was called the Rhodes-Haverty Building. When it became a hotel, I saw no reason to bother relocating. The view of Atlanta's historic district from here is second to none."

He took a seat behind the desk. "How may I be of service?" The visit, of course, was almost certainly a mistake—the "importing" Weber did was for a private client only—but this wasn't the first time people had called on him. He had always made a point of being polite with such callers, to give the impression his was a legitimate business.

The man sat down. "I have just one question. Answer it, and I'll be on my way."

Something in the man's tone made Weber hesitate before replying. "And what question is that?"

"Where is Helen Pendergast?"

This is not possible, Weber thought. Aloud, he said: "I have no idea what you're talking about."

"You are the owner of a warehouse in down-state New York. It was from this warehouse that the operation to abduct Helen Pendergast was put into motion."

"You aren't making any sense. And since it appears you have no business to conduct, I'm afraid I shall have to ask you to leave, Mr. . . . ?" As he spoke, Weber very casually opened the center drawer of his desk and placed his hand inside.

"Pendergast," the stranger said. "Aloysius Pendergast."

Weber drew out his Beretta from the desk, but before he could aim it, the man, seemingly reading his mind, lashed out and slammed the pistol from Weber's grasp. It went tumbling across the floor. Covering Weber with his own weapon, which had appeared from nowhere, the man retrieved the Beretta, put it in his own pocket, and returned to his chair.

"Shall we try again?" he asked in a reasonable voice.

"I have nothing to say to you," Weber replied.

The man calling himself Pendergast hefted the weapon in his hand. "Are you truly not attached to your own life?"

Weber had been very carefully trained in interrogation techniques—both how to administer and how to resist. He had also been schooled in how one of superior blood and breeding should conduct himself before others. "I'm not afraid to die for what I believe in."

"That makes two of us." The man paused, considering. "And what is it, exactly, that you believe in?"

Weber merely smiled.

Pendergast glanced around the office again, his gaze finally returning to Weber. "That's a rather nice suit you're wearing."

Despite the big Colt trained on him, Weber felt perfectly calm, perfectly in control. "Thank you."

"Is that by chance a Hardy Amies, my own tailor?"

"Sadly, no. Taylor and Merton, just a few doors down Savile Row from Amies."

"I see we share a fondness for fine clothes. I would imagine our mutual interest extends beyond just suits. Take ties, for instance." Pendergast caressed his own. "While in the past I've usually favored handmade Parisian ties, like Charvet, these days I prefer Jay Kos. Such as the one I'm wearing at present. At two hundred dollars, not cheap, but in my opinion worth every penny." He smiled at Weber. "And who makes your ties?"

If this was some novel interrogation technique, Weber thought, it was not going to work. "Brioni," he replied.

"Brioni," Pendergast repeated. "That's good. Well made."

Suddenly—again with speed that more resembled an explosion than movement—Pendergast shot up from his chair, leapt over the desk, and grabbed Weber by the throat. Dragging him backward with shocking strength, he threw up the sash of the nearest window and propelled the struggling Weber into it. In terror Weber grasped the window frames on both sides. He could hear the traffic on Peachtree Street twenty stories below, feel the updraft.

"I love the windows in these old skyscrapers," Pendergast said. "They actually open. And you were right about the view."

Weber clung desperately to the sides of the window, gasping with terror.

Reaching around with the butt of his gun, Pendergast smashed the fingers of Weber's left hand, breaking bones, then pounded on his right. With a cry, Weber felt himself shoved backward into open space, his arms flailing uselessly, his legs still hooked over the windowsill. Pendergast prevented his fall by grabbing his tie, holding him out at arm's length from the window.

Frantically Weber pressed his calves against the sill, choking and fighting to maintain a grip.

"A man should always know his wardrobe—and his wardrobe's limitations," Pendergast went on, his voice still light and conversational. "My Jay Kos ties, for example, are made of Italian sevenfold silk. As strong as they are beautiful."

He gave Weber's tie a rough jerk. Weber gasped as one leg began to slip from the sill. He scrabbled to regain his footing. He tried to speak, but the tie was choking him.

"Other manufacturers sometimes cut corners," Pendergast went on. "You know, like single stitching, only two folds." He gave the tie another tug. "So I want you to *be sure of* the quality of your tie before I ask you my question again."

Jerk.

With a harsh sound, Weber's tie began to rip. He stared at it, crying out involuntarily.

"Oh, dear," Pendergast said, disappointed. "Brioni? I don't think so. Perhaps you've been deceived by a forgery. Or you've been cutting corners, lying to me about your haberdashers."

Jerk.

The tie was now torn halfway across its fat end. From the corner of his eye, Weber could see a crowd gathering below, pointing upward, distant shouts. He felt his head start to swim. Panic overwhelmed him.

Jerk. Rip.

"All right!" Weber screamed, scrabbling at Pendergast's hand with his own broken and twisted fingers. "I'll talk!"

"Make it quick. This cheap tie isn't going to last much longer."

"She's, she's leaving the country tonight."

"Where? How?"

"Private plane. Fort Lauderdale. Pettermars Airport. Nine o'clock."

With a final, brutal tug, Pendergast pulled Weber back into his office.

"*Scheiße!*" Weber cried as he sprawled across the floor, in a fetal position, cradling his ruined hands. "What if my tie had torn completely?"

The man's smile simply widened. And suddenly Weber understood—this was a man as far on the edge as a person could be while remaining sane.

Pendergast withdrew a step. "If you're telling the

truth, and I recover her without incident, you don't have to worry about seeing me again. But if you have deceived me, I'll pay you another visit."

In the act of turning toward the door, Pendergast stopped. He loosened his own necktie, unknotted it, threw it toward Weber. "Here's the real thing. Remember what I said about cutting corners." And with a final, cold smile, he slipped out of the office.

+ Forty-Five Hours

PETTERMARS AIRPORT. PENDERGAST HAD JUST under six hours to go seven hundred miles.

A quick check of the local airports showed no feasible commercial flights and no chartered planes available on such short notice. He would have to make the trip by car.

He had flown into Atlanta and taken a cab from the airport. He would need to rent a vehicle. Locating a specialty rental agency a few blocks down Peachtree, he selected a brand-new storm-red Mercedes-Benz SLS AMG. He contracted for a one-way trip to Miami, with full insurance coverage, at a staggering price.

Even though rush hour had not yet begun, the notorious Atlanta traffic was already choking the freeway interchanges. Merging onto I-75 south, Pendergast quickly pressed the accelerator to the floor, passing through a construction zone at high speed by sticking to the right-hand shoulder. As he had hoped, the ear-shattering roar of the Mercedes's ferocious 563-horse engine attracted attention and helped clear the way for him. He blasted along the shoulder at close to a hundred miles an hour until he passed a speed trap.

Excellent.

A Georgia state trooper came shooting out from behind an embankment, sirens wailing and lightbar flashing. Pendergast pulled over so fast the cop almost rear-ended him. Even before the trooper could call in the license plate, Pendergast was out of the car with his shield held high, striding toward the trooper's vehicle and motioning with his hand to lower his window.

Reaching the vehicle, Pendergast pushed his shield inside. "Federal Bureau of Investigation, New York office. I'm on an emergency mission of the highest priority."

The trooper looked from Pendergast, to the shield, to the Mercedes, and back again. "Um, yes, sir."

"I had to improvise the car. Listen to me carefully. I'm on my way to Pettermars Airport, outside Fort Lauderdale, by way of Interstates Seventy-Five, Ten, and Ninety-Five."

The state trooper stared at him, struggling to keep up.

"I want you to radio ahead and authorize my rapid and unrestricted passage along this route. No stops. And no escorts—I'll be traveling too fast. My vehicle is somewhat recognizable, so this should not be a problem. Understand?"

"Yes, sir. But our jurisdiction ends once you leave Georgia."

"Have your commanding major call his counterpart in Florida."

"But perhaps the FBI's New York office—"

"As I said, this is an emergency situation. There's no time. Just do it."

"Yes, sir."

Pendergast sprinted back to his car and laid a hundred yards of rubber getting back up to speed, leaving the state trooper sitting in a blue cloud.

By four o'clock Pendergast was past Macon, arrowing due south. Cars, road signs, scenery passed by in brief smudges of color. Suddenly, coming around a bend, he saw a line of red brake lights ahead: two semis were driving abreast, crawling up a hill, the one on the left trying to pass the one on the right by inching ahead up the rise, slowing everyone behind—a despicable act on a two-lane freeway.

Driving once again on and off the shoulder, flashing his lights, Pendergast passed the series of cars until he was directly behind the left-hand truck. It studiously ignored the blasts of his horn and the flashing of lights—if anything, it seemed to slow a little, out of spite.

The freeway curved to the right, and—as often happened—the truck in the slow lane began to drift into the shoulder. Pendergast used this opportunity to move himself back into the left-hand shoulder. As he anticipated, the trucker in front of him moved left as well, to block his passage. This was his chance. He decelerated slightly, then—switching the transmission into manual mode—he yawed abruptly right into the gap created between the two trucks, using his paddle shifters to scream from fifty miles per hour to ninety in three seconds, darting past the trucks and shooting forward onto the empty freeway ahead. He was rewarded by twin angry blasts of air horns.

He drove on without stopping, occasionally moving into the left or right shoulder to pass vehicles, honking and flashing his lights at the more recalcitrant drivers, sometimes terrifying them into changing lanes by coming up behind them at high speed and not braking until the last possible moment. By five thirty he was past Valdosta and crossing the border into Florida.

He knew that the most direct route was

problematic—heading as it did through Orlando and its tangle of clogged, tourist-filled interchanges—so instead he turned east on I-10, making for the Atlantic coast. It was a less-than-satisfactory alternative, but it was nevertheless the one with the greatest probability of success. At Jacksonville, he turned south again onto I-95.

Outside Daytona Beach, he stopped for gas, flinging a hundred-dollar bill at the surprised attendant and screeching off without waiting for change.

As the evening lengthened, the traffic on the freeway began to thin, and the long-haul trucks drove faster. Pendergast dodged between them—top down, the night wind helping to keep him awake—pushing the vehicle harder. Titusville, Palm Bay, and Jupiter shot past, mere blurs of light. As he came into Boca Raton, he activated the GPS system and punched in his destination.

He had covered the distance at an average of one hundred and twenty-five miles per hour.

Pettermars Executive General Airport was located ten miles west of Coral Springs, carved out of the eastern flanks of the Everglades. As he approached it through the sprawling Fort Lauderdale suburbs, Pendergast could make out a small tower, a set of wind socks, the twinkle of runway lights.

Five minutes to nine. The airport runway came into view, beyond a ragged field of switchgrass. A single-engine, six-seater propeller plane was warming up outside the closest hangar.

Pendergast pulled in front of the FBO with a squeal of brakes, sprang from the car, and ran as fast as his limp would allow into the low, yellow-painted building.

"Where is that plane headed?" he asked the lone

airport administrator behind the desk, pulling out his shield. "It's an FBI emergency."

The man hesitated only a moment. "They filed a flight plan to Cancun."

Cancun. Probably a false destination. However, it indicated the plane was headed south, over the border.

"Any other flights scheduled for this evening?"

"A Lear, incoming from Biloxi in ninety minutes. Is there something I can help you with—?"

But the administrator was talking to an empty room. Pendergast had disappeared.

Exiting the FBO, Pendergast ran back to the Mercedes and slipped inside. The plane was moving toward the runway now, its engine rumbling. A security fence surrounded the hangar and the taxiway; its set of chain-link gates was closed. There was no more time: Pendergast aimed the car at the gates and stamped on the accelerator. With a roar, the vehicle shot forward, taking out the gates and sending them tumbling onto the tarmac.

The airplane was just beginning to lumber down the runway, slowly picking up speed. Pendergast drew level with it and looked into the cabin. The pilot was striking: tall and very muscular, with a deep tan and perfectly snow-white hair. The person sitting in the copilot's seat glanced out the window at the Mercedes. It was one of the joggers who had apprehended Helen in Central Park. Recognizing Pendergast, the man quickly drew a gun and fired out the window.

Pendergast sheared away from the shot, then swerved in close to the wing, placing himself in the shooter's blind spot. As he adjusted the car's speed to match that of the aircraft, he briefly considered circling in front to cut it off—but that might easily lead to the plane losing control. Helen was on board. Instead he edged the car even closer to the wing, still pacing it. Opening the door, he waited, his body tense—and then launched himself from the moving car onto the right landing gear assembly. His timing was just a fraction off target and he slid down the struts, feet dragging for a moment on the tarmac; with a mighty heave he pulled himself from the humming asphalt to a more secure position, wincing from the pain of his injured leg.

The plane was rapidly accelerating, moving upwards of thirty knots, and the wind whipped at his hair and clothes. Pendergast hoisted himself up the gear assembly until he was directly beneath the wing. He leaned forward, taking his gun from its holster. He could just make out the form of the jogger in the copilot's seat; any view of the other passengers was blocked by the wing.

The end of the runway was in sight now, with nothing but switchgrass and swamp beyond; the pilot appeared to be having trouble compensating for the extra weight and drag. Pendergast leaned forward still farther. The jogger stuck his head out the window, peering back into the darkness, looking for him. Just as the plane became airborne, Pendergast took careful aim and—extending himself almost horizontally from the landing gear—shot the man full in the face.

The man screamed as his head snapped back. His body spasmed violently, involuntarily; the door flew open and the body tumbled outward, smacking into the tarmac like a side of beef just as the plane lifted off. Then the plane was airborne, skimming over the marsh below. The wheels would come up at any moment.

Pendergast thought quickly. The plane was already thirty feet above the ground. He holstered his gun, balanced himself on the horizontal landing strut beside the wheel, pulled a fountain pen from his pocket, and stabbed into the tiny flap of the fuel sump at the bottom of the cowling. Then—just as the hum of the wheel hydraulics began—he timed himself for a leap from the landing gear. Keeping himself at the correct entry angle, he hit the marsh with a terrific splash, plunging into the water and underlying mud.

+ Fifty-Three Hours

PENDERGAST SAT ON A STEEL STANCHION AT the end of Pettermars Airport's runway 29-R. The night was dark and starless, and the only illumination came from the parallel lines of runway lights that led off toward the horizon. The fall from the plane had reopened his gunshot wound. He had managed to stem the flow of blood and done his best to rinse the foul mud away. It would need closer medical attention and antibiotic treatment, but right now he had more important things to do.

Over his shoulder, several hundred feet in the air, another light slowly became visible: an approaching plane. It resolved into a set of running and warning lights. A minute later, a Learjet 60 hurtled past some twenty feet over Pendergast's head, its reverse thrusters screaming as it prepared to land, the wake turbulence of the jet's passing hurling up a violent cloud of dust.

Pendergast took no notice.

He had searched the body of the jogger, which had come to rest hidden in the tall grass at the end of the runway. Nothing. There had been a flurry of activity on the airfield triggered by his bashing down of the gate.

The police had come, searched the area, impounded the Mercedes, and gone. They had found neither him nor the body.

Now everything had returned to normal; all was quiet. He rose and, keeping well within the darkness of the grass, circled the airstrip to an ancient pay phone at the gas station on the airfield road, which—miraculously—worked. He put in a call to D'Agosta.

"Where are you?" came the voice from New York.

"Not important. Put out an APB on a Cessna 133 single-engine plane, call letters November-eight-seven-niner-foxtrot-Charlie. It was heading into Mexico with a flight plan for Cancun, but it will be forced to land within a—" he thought a moment—"two-hundred-mile radius of Fort Lauderdale, due to a slow leak in the fuel line."

"How do you know it has a leak?"

"Because I introduced it. A hollow plastic tube, wedged into the fuel sump. There's nothing they can do in the cockpit to reverse it."

"You've got to tell me what the hell's going on—"

"Call me back at this number when you get a hit."

"Wait, Pendergast, Jesus—"

Pendergast hung up. He left the lighted area of the phone booth, retreating to the darkness of a vacant lot overgrown with palmettos. He lay down on the ground—the loss of blood had made him weaker—and there he waited.

Thirty minutes later he heard the phone ring. He got up, made it to the booth, his head spinning. "Yes?"

"We got a hit on that APB. The plane landed maybe ten minutes ago at a tiny strip outside Andalusia, Alabama. Tore up the landing gear, too."

"Go on."

"They must have called ahead, because a van was

waiting. There was only one person on the field, a guy drinking coffee in the hangar. He saw a bunch of people bundle into the van, then they hauled ass, heading in the direction of the—" a pause—"Conecuh National Forest. Ditched the plane, left it right there on the runway."

"Did the onlooker get the plates of the van?"

"Nah. It was dark."

"Alert the Alabama Highway Patrol. And put out an APB at all the border crossings—they're headed into Mexico. I'll call you later. My cellular phone is out of commission."

A reluctant pause. "You got it."

"Thank you." Pendergast hung up.

He sat perhaps another ten minutes, still motionless, in the humid darkness. Then he dialed another number.

"Yo," came the high, breathy voice of Mime, the reclusive hacker of questionable ethics whose only contact with the outside world was Pendergast himself.

"Anything?"

"Dunno. It's not much. I was hoping to get more before I called you..." His high voice paused dramatically, teasingly.

"I have no time for games, Mime."

"Right," said Mime hastily. "I've been listening in on the electronic eavesdropping of our friends in Fort Meade—monitoring the monitors, you might say." He chuckled. "And they *do* scrutinize domestic calls and e-mails, you know, despite protests to the contrary. I isolated a piece of cell phone chatter that I think is from this group you call *Der Bund*."

"Are you sure?"

"Impossible to be one hundred percent sure, my man. The transmissions are encrypted, and all I was able to figure out was that they're in German. Cracked a few proper nouns here and there. According to the government's triangulation of the cell signal, it's been moving fast across central and northwestern Florida."

"How fast?"

"Plane-fast."

"When?"

"Seventy minutes ago."

"That must be the plane that just landed in Alabama. What else?"

"Nothing except for a brief unencrypted burst in Spanish. That burst mentioned a place: Cananea."

"*Cananea*," Pendergast whispered. "Where is that?"

"A town in Sonora, Mexico...in the middle of nowhere, thirty miles south of the border."

"Sketch me a picture of the town."

"My research indicates it has a population of thirty thou. It was once a huge mining center—copper—and it was the site of a bloody strike that helped launch the Mexican Revolution. Now it hosts a couple of maquiladora factories on the north side and that's about it."

"Geographic situation?"

"There's a river that starts in Cananea and flows north over the border into Arizona. Called the San Pedro. One of the few north-flowing rivers on the continent. It's a major route for smuggling drugs and illegals. Except that the surrounding desert is brutal. That's where a lot of those would-be immigrants die. The border along there is apparently remote as hell, just a barbed-wire fence—but it's got sensors and patrols up the wazoo. Plus a tethered blimp that can see a cigarette on the ground in the dark."

Pendergast cradled the phone. It made sense. Deprived of their plane, and anticipating the APB border alerts, Helen's captors would have had to find a clandestine way to cross the border into Mexico. The Rio San Pedro corridor south to Cananea was as good as any.

That would be his last chance to intercept them.

He left the telephone booth—staggered, his head still spinning—and found himself forced to sit down abruptly in the dirt. He was weak, he was exhausted, he was losing blood, and he had not slept or taken nourishment in more than two days. But this sudden weakness went beyond the physical. His mind, his entire being, was wounded.

He forced himself to examine his shattered psychological state. What he now felt for Helen—whether or not he still loved her—he did not know. He had believed her dead for twelve years. He had reconciled himself to that. And now she was alive. All he knew for certain was that if he had not insisted on seeing her again, if he had not bungled their assignation so badly, Helen would still be safe. He had to reverse that failure. He had to rescue her from *Der Bund*—not only for her preservation, but for his own. Otherwise...

He did not let himself think about the *otherwise*. Instead—summoning every last reserve of strength—he rose to his feet. He had to get to Cananea, one way or another.

He limped toward the parking lot of the airfield, bathed in sodium lights. A single car was parked there: an old tan Eldorado. No doubt owned by the airport administrator.

It appeared the man would be doing him another favor.

+ Eighty-Two Hours

PENDERGAST PULLED THE SMOKING, BATTERED Eldorado into a gas station outside the tiny town of Palominas, Arizona. He had covered the twenty-two hundred miles without rest, stopping only for gas.

He got out, steadying himself by leaning on the door. It was two AM, and the immense desert sky was sprinkled with stars. There was no moon.

After a moment, he went into the convenience store attached to the gas station. Here he purchased a map of the Mexican state of Sonora, half a dozen water bottles, some packages of beef jerky, cookies, some potted meat product, a couple of dish towels, bandages, antibiotic ointment, a bottle of ibuprofen, caffeine tablets, duct tape, and a flashlight. All these went into a doubled-up plastic grocery bag, which he took back to the car. Sitting in the driver's seat once again, he studied the map he had bought, committing its features to memory.

He left the gas station and drove eastward on Route 92, crossing the San Pedro River on a small bridge. Past the bridge, he turned right on a dirt ranch road heading south. Driving slowly, the car bumping and scraping along the rutted track, he moved through scrubby mesquite and catclaw thickets, headlights stabbing into the crooked branches. The unseen river lay to his right, outlined in black by a dense line of cottonwood trees.

About half a mile from the border, Pendergast drove the car off the road into a thicket of mesquite, forcing it in as far as it would go. He turned off the engine, exited the car with the grocery bag in hand, then listened in the darkness. A pair of coyotes howled in the distance, but otherwise there was no sign of life.

He knew this was an illusion. This stretch of the Mexican-U.S. border, separated by only a five-strand barbed-wire fence, bristled with sophisticated sensors, infrared video cameras, and downward-looking radar, with rapid-response Border Patrol teams mere minutes away.

But Pendergast was unconcerned. He had an advantage few other smugglers or border crooks had: he was going south. Into Mexico.

Tying up the grocery bag in his suit jacket, he fashioned it into a crude haversack, slung it over his shoulder, and began to walk.

The movement of his injured leg caused it to start bleeding again. He paused, sat down, and spent a few moments unbandaging the wound by flashlight, smearing fresh antibiotic ointment into it, then binding it up again with clear bandages and the dish towels. He followed this by swallowing four ibuprofen and as many caffeine tablets.

It took him several minutes to get back on his feet. This would not do: he had a long way to go. He chewed some beef jerky and took a drink of water.

By keeping off the dirt track, away from the river, he hoped to avoid the various electronic traps and sensors. The huge tethered blimp that hovered unseen in the night sky overhead may have noted his presence, but as he was moving south, he hoped it would not trigger a response—at least, not yet.

The night air, even in summer, was cool. The coyotes had ceased howling; all was silent. Pendergast moved on.

The road made a ninety-degree turn to parallel a barbed-wire fence—the actual border. He crossed the road—certain he had now set off various sensors—arrived at the fence, and within seconds had cut the strands and forced his way to the Mexican side. He limped off into the darkness, crossing a vacant expanse of pebbled desert, dotted with catclaw.

Not much time passed before he saw headlights on the American side. He kept going, angling toward the cottonwoods along the river, moving as fast as he could. Several spotlights flicked on and the pools of light speared the desert night, scouring the landscape until they fixed on him, bathing him in brilliant white.

He kept going. A megaphoned voice echoed over the field, speaking first English and then Spanish, ordering him to halt, to turn around, to raise his hands and identify himself.

Pendergast continued on, ignoring this. There was nothing they could do. They could not pursue, and it would be fruitless to call their counterparts on the Mexican side. Nobody cared about clandestine traffic headed south.

He angled toward the line of cottonwoods along the river. The spotlights followed him for a while, with more desultory megaphoned commands, until he entered the trees. At that point they gave up.

Hidden within the protective canopy, he sat down to rest on the banks of the shallow creek of the San Pedro. He tried to eat, the food like cardboard in his mouth; he forced himself to chew and swallow. He drank some more water and resisted the impulse to unwrap his freshly blood-soaked bandages.

He estimated that Helen and her abductors would cross the border around the same time or perhaps shortly ahead of him. It was remote, barren desert country, covered in greasewood and mesquite, riddled with unmarked dirt roads used by illegal aliens and smugglers of guns and drugs. *Der Bund* would certainly have arranged for transportation on the Mexican side, along one of these dirt roads leading to Cananea, thirty miles south of the border. They would be traveling this web of improvised roads, and he would have to catch them before they reached the town—and the paved roads that led away from it. If he did not, his chances of ever finding Helen dropped to almost nil.

Standing again, he limped down the mostly dry bed of the river, once in a while splashing through stagnant pools of inch-deep water. He might, even now, be too late.

About half a mile south, through the thin screen of trees, he spied distant lights. Moving to the embankment, he peered out and saw what appeared to be a lonely ranch, sitting by itself in the vast desert plain. It was occupied.

The moonless night provided cover for his approach. Soft yellow lights shone in the windows of the main adobe building: an old whitewashed structure surrounded by broken-down corrals and ruined outbuildings. The gleaming, late-model SUVs parked outside, however, indicated the place was now being used for something quite different from cattle ranching.

Pendergast approached the parking area at a partial crouch. He saw the momentary glow of a cigarette and noted a man at the front door of the house, watching the vehicles and the approach road, smoking and cradling an assault rifle.

Drug smugglers, without doubt.

Keeping to the dark, Pendergast circled the house. Parked to one side was a motorcycle: a Ducati Street-fighter S.

Moving now with exquisite care, Pendergast approached the house from its blind side. A low adobe wall separated the scrub desert from the dirt yard. He crouched at the wall and, with a cat-like movement, hopped over it and darted across the dirt yard, pressing himself against the flank of the house. He waited a moment for the stabbing pain in his leg to recede. Then, reaching into his pocket, he removed a small but exceedingly sharp knife and continued along to the corner.

He waited, listening. There was the murmur of voices, the occasional cough of the man smoking outside. After a moment, he heard the man drop the cigarette butt and grind it out with his foot. Then came the flick of a lighter, the faint glow of indirect light over the dark yard, as a fresh one was lit. He heard the guard inhale noisily, breathe out, clear his throat.

Pressed against the corner, Pendergast felt in the dirt, picked up a fist-size rock. He tapped it softly against the ground, then waited. Nothing. He scraped the rock in the dirt, making a somewhat louder noise.

Around the corner, the man fell silent.

Pendergast waited, then scraped again, a little louder.

Silence still. And then the low, furtive crunch of footfalls. The man approached the corner of the building, paused. Pendergast could hear his breathing, hear the faint rattle of his rifle as he moved it into position, getting ready to charge around the corner.

Slowly, Pendergast lowered himself into a deeper crouch, controlling his pain, waiting. The man suddenly whipped around the corner, rifle at the ready; in an instantaneous movement Pendergast sprang up, the tip of his knife severing the flexor tendon of the man's right index finger as he simultaneously knocked the rifle upward and brought the rock down hard on the man's temple. He went down without a sound, out cold. Pendergast detached the rifle—an M4—and slung it over his shoulder. He crept up to the Ducati. The key was in the ignition.

The beastly, skeletal-looking bike had no saddlebags, and he slung the improvised haversack over his shoulder, next to the M4. Once again, keeping low and to the shadows, he crept around to the three SUVs parked in the dirt lot and worked the point of his knife into a tire of each one.

He moved back to the Streetfighter, slid onto the seat, and pressed the ignition. The massive engine immediately roared to life, and—without wasting even a second—he kicked the shifter down out of neutral, eased off the clutch, and cranked the throttle wide open with a violent twist of his right hand.

As he laid a huge spray of dirt tearing out of the driveway, pushing the RPMs up past eight thousand while still in first gear, he could see in his rearview mirrors the drug dealers boiling out of the ranch house like bees, guns drawn. He briefly squeezed the clutch and kicked the bike up into second as a fusillade of shots sounded. The lights of the SUVs fired up as they started the engines, then more shots and cries of vengeance...and then all was behind him, disappearing into the dark night.

He continued south, working his way up through the motorcycle's gears, tearing across the vacant desert. He had to intercept them before Cananea...

He urged the Streetfighter on ever faster as the immense night sky, studded with stars, wheeled overhead.

+ Eighty-Four Hours

WELL BEFORE DAWN, HE SAW A FLICKER OF RED in the immense desert blackness—the taillights of a vehicle moving fast through the distant brush. It was off to the southwest. Five miles farther south, he could see the glow of the town of Cananea.

Veering off, he cut across the open desert until he intersected one of the parallel tracks to the east. The vibration of the bike on the rough road, the slashing of brush against his legs, had shaken loose his bandage, and he felt blood creeping down his leg, the drops hissing on the hot muffler. He fished out another quartet of ibuprofen tablets and popped them into his mouth.

The vehicle was now invisible in the brush somewhere on his right. He raced along, the lights of Cananea growing in intensity. According to Mime, the first thing they would encounter would be several small maquiladora factories north of the town. Paved roads ran from the factories into town, where they joined a major highway. He could not let them reach one of those paved roads. He had to catch them in the desert.

He accelerated further as the glow in the southern sky brightened, allowing him to increase his speed.

Cananea was now only two miles off. Figuring he was about even with the unseen vehicle, Pendergast swerved to the west, tearing across the empty landscape, the bike leaping ditches and popping through brush. In another minute he saw the vehicle's lights virtually due west, running parallel, and he was close enough to see that there were actually two vehicles, one behind the other—Escalades, by the look of them. They were moving fast, but not nearly as fast as he.

They had not yet, apparently, seen his headlight.

He unslung the M4 with his left hand and, keeping his right hand on the throttle, steadied the rifle across the handlebars, bracing it against his side. He checked to make sure it was in fully automatic mode.

But now the vehicles had seen his lights: they began to veer away from him, going off-road, crashing through the sparse brush.

They were too late. He was moving faster, he was nimbler, and off-road the big SUVs could not accelerate well. Coming in at an angle, he aimed the bike for the gap between the two vehicles and darted into it, braking hard in order to match their speed. The maneuver allowed him to identify the occupants of both vehicles, and it took only a moment to pick out Helen's frightened face in the back window of the second. A man leaned out of the first and fired ineffectually at him with a handgun; Pendergast gunned the Ducati's powerful engine and pulled away, accelerating alongside the first vehicle while letting loose with the M4, raking the car at chest level as he accelerated past. The SUV veered off, went into a skid, and then flipped, rolling over and over before bursting into a fireball.

The second vehicle had braked rapidly and was now far behind. Applying sharp pressure to the rear brake, Pendergast brought the Streetfighter into a power slide, throwing up a huge curtain of dirt, ending up with his back to the town, facing the Escalade. He waited to see what the vehicle would do.

Instead of stopping to fight, it veered off farther and went lurching over the rough plain, tearing through the low creosote bushes, heading for the paved road at the edge of town. A steady sound of futile gunfire came from the vehicle, punctuated by flashes of light.

Pendergast gunned the Ducati, fishtailing into a ninety-degree turn and then accelerating after them.

He rapidly caught up, keeping to the south in a flanking maneuver, forcing the vehicle into an easterly trajectory, away from the factories and the town. But the road to the nearest factory, lined with sodium lights, was approaching fast.

More shots rang out from the vehicle, kicking up dirt to one side of him. A man was aiming out the back window with a handgun. But the Escalade was lurching so violently that Pendergast was in little danger of being hit. He accelerated the bike, again tracing a track behind and parallel to the Escalade. He eased the rifle into position once more. More futile shots came from a man leaning out the window.

Pendergast swerved into a converging trajectory and goosed the bike, eking out one last burst of acceleration, bringing himself alongside the car and letting loose with a burst aimed low and front, taking out a front tire. At the same time, a fusillade of gunfire from the car struck the Ducati, breaking its chain and sending the bike into a slide. Pendergast rapidly worked the front and rear brakes to avoid going into an uncontrollable spin. As his speed abruptly dropped, he leapt off into a creosote bush before the bike tumbled into a narrow ravine.

Immediately he rose with the rifle, aimed, and fired

again at the receding car. The Escalade was already slewing about on the burst tire, and the shot took out the rear wheel on the same side, the SUV fishtailing to a stop. As it did so, four men leapt out and knelt down by the car, unleashing a steady fire.

Pendergast threw himself to the ground and—as the bullets kicked up dirt all around him—aimed carefully. His superior weapon took out first one man, then another, in rapid sequence. The remaining two retreated out of sight behind the vehicle and stopped shooting.

Unfortunate.

Pendergast rose and, running as fast as he could— barely more than a shambling limp—charged. He kept up a continuous fire as he did so, making sure his shots went high. Suddenly both figures appeared at one side of the vehicle; one was dragging Helen with a gun pressed to her head, and the other—the tall, muscular, snowy-haired man who had piloted the plane—was crouching behind, using the others as protection. He did not appear to be armed—at least, he was not firing.

Once again Pendergast threw himself down and aimed, but he did not dare fire.

"Aloysius!" came a thin scream.

Pendergast aimed afresh. Waited.

"Drop your weapon or I will kill her!" came a sharply accented cry from the man using her as a human shield. The three figures were backing up now, away from the Escalade, the white-haired man keeping behind the other two.

"I will kill her, I *swear*!" the man screamed. But Pendergast knew he wouldn't. She was his only protection.

The man fired at Pendergast twice, but the handgun, at a distance of a hundred yards, was inaccurate.

"Let her go!" Pendergast cried. "I want her, not you! Let her go and you can walk away!"

"No!" The man gripped her desperately.

Pendergast slowly stood, letting his rifle fall to one side. "Just let her go," he said. "That's all. There will be no problems. You have my word."

The man fired another shot at Pendergast, but it went wide. Pendergast began limping toward them, rifle still held to one side. "Let her go. That's the only way you'll get out of here alive. Let her go."

"Drop your gun!" The man was hysterical with fear.

Pendergast slowly laid his gun down, stood up, hands raised.

"Aloysius!" Helen wept. "Just go, *go*!"

The man, dragging Helen backward, fired at Pendergast again, missing him. He was too far away—and too panicked to shoot straight.

"Trust me," Pendergast said in a low, measured voice, his arms held out. "Release her."

There was a moment of terrible stasis. And then, with an inarticulate cry, the man abruptly threw Helen to the ground, lowered his pistol, and fired point-blank into her body. "Help *her* or chase me!" he cried, turning and running.

Helen's scream pierced the air—and then, abruptly, cut off. Taken completely by surprise, Pendergast rushed forward with an inarticulate cry and within moments was kneeling beside her. He saw instantly that the shot was fatal, blood flowing rhythmically from a hole in her chest—a bullet to the heart.

"Helen!" he cried, voice breaking.

She grasped him like a drowning woman. "Aloysius...you must listen..." Her voice came as a gasped whisper.

He bent down to hear.

The hands clutched tighter. "*He's* coming...Mercy... Have *mercy*..." And then a gush of blood stopped her speech. He placed two fingers against the carotid artery in her neck; felt the pulse flutter in her very last heartbeat, then cease.

After a moment, Pendergast rose. He limped unsteadily back to where he had dropped the M4. The white-haired man appeared to have been as surprised as Pendergast by this development, because only belatedly had he started to run, following the shooter.

Pendergast knelt, raised the weapon, and aimed it toward his wife's murderer, a fleeing figure now five hundred yards distant. In a curious, detached way he was reminded of the last time he had gone hunting. He sighted in the figure, compensated for windage and drop, then squeezed the trigger; the rifle bucked and the man went down.

The white-haired man was a powerful runner; he had already overtaken the killer and was now even more distant. Pendergast took aim, fired at him, missed.

Taking a slow breath, he let the air run out, sighted in on him, compensated, and fired at the man a second time. Missed again.

The third attempt clicked on an empty magazine even as the man disappeared into the vastness of the desert.

After a long moment, Pendergast put the gun down again and walked back to where Helen's body lay in a slowly spreading pool of blood. He stared at the body for a long time. Then he got to work.

+ Ninety-One Hours

THE SUN STOOD HIGH IN A SKY WHITE WITH heat. A dust devil whirled across the empty expanse. Blue mountains serrated the distant horizon. Scenting death, a turkey vulture rode a thermal overhead, turning lazily in a tightening gyre.

Pendergast dropped the last shovelful of sand onto the grave, slapped it down with the flat of the rusty blade, and smoothed the sand into place. It had taken him a long time to dig the hole. He had gone deep, deep into the dry clay. He did not want the grave disturbed by animal or man.

He paused, leaning on the shovel, taking shallow breaths. The wound in his leg was once again bleeding freely from the exertion, soaking through the last of his bandages. Beads of sweat, mixed with the mud, trickled down his expressionless face. His shirt was torn, slack, brown with dust; his jacket shredded, his pants ripped. He stared at the patch of disturbed ground, and then—moving slowly, like an old man—bent down and took hold of the rude marker he'd fashioned from a board he had taken from the same abandoned ranch house where he'd found the shovel. He did not wish it to be too obviously a grave. He took the knife from his pocket and scratched, in an unsteady hand:

H.E.P.
Aeternum vale

Limping to the head of the grave, he pressed the sharpened base of the marker into the earth. Taking a step back and raising the shovel, he took careful aim, then brought the head down onto the marker's top with a bone-jarring impact.

Whang!

. . . He was sitting before a small fire, deep in the heavily wooded flanks of Cannon Mountain. On the far side of the fire sat Helen, dressed in a plaid flannel shirt and hiking boots. They had just completed the third day of a week's backpacking trip through the White Mountains. Beyond a glacial tarn, the sun was going down—a ball of scarlet fire—highlighting the peaks of the Franconia Range. Faintly, from far below on the mountain, rose voices and snatches of song from Lonesome Lake Hut. A pot of espresso sat on the fire, its aroma mingling with the scents of wood smoke, pine, and balsam. As Helen turned the pot on the fire, she glanced up at him and suddenly smiled—her unique smile, half shy, half assured—then set two tiny porcelain espresso cups on the firestone, one beside the other, with a neat precision that was totally her own . . .

Pendergast swayed, gasping with the effort of the shovel's blow. He wiped one unsteady forearm across his brow. Mud and sweat smeared the tattered sleeve of his suit. He waited, standing in the blazing heat of the sun, trying to catch his breath, to summon the final dregs of his strength. Then, once again, with a gasp of effort, he lifted the shovel. The weight of it caught him off balance and he staggered back, fighting to steady himself. His knees started to buckle, and before he tottered yet again he brought the shovel head down onto the marker with all the strength he could muster:

Whang!

> . . . *London, early fall. The leaves on the shade trees lining Devonshire Street were kissed with yellow. They were walking toward Regent's Park, having just exited Christie's. Rising to a dare of Helen's, he had just bought at auction two works of artwork he'd loved at first sight: a seascape by John Marin, and a painting of Whitby Abbey that the Christie's catalog had listed as being by a "minor Romantic painter" but that he thought might be an early Constable. Helen had smuggled a silver flask of cognac into the auction, and now—as they crossed Park Crescent and headed into the park proper—she began to quote in a full voice the poem "Dover Beach" for all to hear: "The sea is calm to-night. The tide is full, the moon lies fair . . ."*

He had dropped the shovel without realizing it. It lay across his shoes, askew, the point half buried in the loose soil. He knelt to pick it up, then quite abruptly fell to his knees; he reached a hand out to steady himself but it slipped and he collapsed to the ground, the side of his face in the dirt.

It would be easy, remarkably easy, to stay like this, lying here above Helen's body. But he could hear the slow *drip, drip, drip* of blood onto the sand and he realized he could not let go until the work was complete. He raised himself to a sitting position. After a few minutes, he felt just strong enough to stand. With supreme effort, using the shovel as a crutch, he stood—first the left leg rising, then the right. The pain in his injured calf had gone away; he felt nothing at all. Despite the fierce glare of the sun, darkness was creeping in around the periphery of his vision: he had but one more chance to set the marker permanently in the ground before he lapsed into unconsciousness. Taking a deep breath, he grasped the handle of the shovel as hard as he could, raised it with shaking hands, and—with a final spark of strength—swung it down against the headpost.

Whang . . . !

. . . A warm summer night, the trill of crickets. He and Helen were sitting on the back veranda at Penumbra Plantation, tall glasses in their hands, watching the evening fog creep in from the bayou, glowing in the moonlight. The mists rolled first over the marshy verge, then the formal garden, then the carpet of grass leading up toward the big house; they eddied about the lawn, tendrils licking at the steps like a slow-motion tide, whitened to ghostliness by the orb of the moon.

On a wheeled server nearby sat a pitcher of iced lemonade, half full, and the remains of a plate of crevettes rémoulade. From out of the kitchen came the scent of grilling fish: Maurice was preparing pompano Pontchartrain for dinner.

Helen looked over at him. "Can't it just stay like this forever, Aloysius?" she asked.

He took a sip of lemonade. "Why not? Our entire life lies ahead of us. We can do with it what we like."

She smiled, glanced skyward. "Do with it what we like . . . Promise on the moonrise?"

Gazing in mock solemnity at the amber moon, he put a playful hand across his breast. "Cross my heart."

He stood in the middle of that vast, empty, brutal, and alien desert. The darkness crept deeper across his vision, as if he were looking down a dark tunnel, the end of which was moving farther and farther away. The shovel slipped from his nerveless fingers and clattered to the stony soil. With a last, half-audible sigh, he sank to his knees and then—after a swaying pause—fell across the grave of his dead wife.

PART TWO

1

ALBAN LORIMER ENTERED THE LOBBY OF THE Marlborough Grand Hotel in New York City, his pale eyes hungrily taking in the polished acres of red Italian marble, the discreet lighting, the whispering wall of water cascading into a pool of blooming lotus flowers, the vast hushed space milling with people.

He paused in the center of the atrium, energized by the early-morning bustle around him. He focused on random individuals and followed their trajectories across, around, in, and out of the lobby. Many were heading toward the line at the Starbucks kiosk, from which wafted the heady scent of brew and bean.

New York City...

His smooth hand stroked the lapel of his wool pinstriped suit, his thin but powerful fingers enjoying the give and texture of the expensive wool. He had never worn such a suit before. His shoes were also of the finest quality, and he had groomed himself with care to look his very best, as if he were about to have the interview of his life. And it *was* an interview of sorts: today was an important day, a red-letter day—rather hastily put together and arranged, of course, but essential nonetheless. He breathed deeply. How wonderful it was, what a lovely feeling of security, to be well dressed, with money in your pocket, standing in a hotel lobby in the greatest city in the world. The only thing that marred his appearance was the small white bandage covering his left earlobe, but that of course could not be helped.

Coffee? Maybe later.

With a final smoothing down of his suit front, Alban strode across the lobby marble toward the banks of elevators, entered one, and pressed the button for the fourteenth floor. He glanced at the brand-new Breitling watch he had been given, which he was so pleased with: seven thirty-one AM.

There were others in the elevator, most carrying enormous cups of coffee. Alban wondered at the size of these coffee cups. People in New York seemed to drink large amounts of coffee. He himself preferred coffee in what his people called the Italian style, strong, short, and black. He was also surprised and even mildly shocked that so many tourists to New York City did not dress properly. Even here, in this beautiful and expensive hotel just off Fifth Avenue, they dressed as if they were picking up their children at the playground or going for a jog, in warm-up suits, running shoes, sweatshirts, or jeans. But few of them could actually be contemplating a run, given their physical condition, many of the men with hanging guts and the women slab-sided and heavily made up. He had never seen so many people in poor physical condition. Then again, he was forgetting: this was the common herd.

He exited at the fourteenth floor, took a left, and walked briskly down the hall, taking each dogleg at an easy pace until he reached the far end of the corridor, where an emergency door led to a staircase. He turned and looked back down the hall. There were eight room doors on the right, eight on the left. In front of about half of them, a wake-up newspaper had been folded and placed. Some guests took the *Times*, others the *Journal*, and a few *USA Today*.

He waited, hands clasped in front, all his senses now on alert. He was utterly still. He knew that, from the time he had entered the hotel to this point, his image had been recorded on hidden security cameras. The idea pleased him not a little. Later, looking at those images, people would say things like, *What a superior fellow he is!* and *What taste he has in clothes!* They would all be very, very interested in him. His picture might even be in the papers.

Right now, however, in the particular place he stood, the camera recording that stretch of corridor was directly over his head, and he was in its blind spot.

Still he waited. And then, at the precisely necessary moment, he began walking back down the hall with a purposeful step. At the very moment he came to the door of Room 1422, it opened and a woman in a bathrobe bent down to pick up the *Wall Street Journal*. Without altering his pace or making any sudden movements, he veered into her, pushed her into the room, at the same time whipping his right arm around her neck and squeezing so tightly she could make no noise. With his left hand he gently closed the door and did the chain.

She struggled mightily as he dragged her into the center of the carpeted room. He enjoyed the flexing of her muscles as she fought him; enjoyed the heaving of her diaphragm as she tried to make a sound; enjoyed the twisting of her torso as she attempted to shake him off. She was a fighter, athletic, not one of those fat old women in the elevator. In this he was lucky. Her age was perhaps thirty, with agreeably blond hair, no wedding ring. Her bathrobe became undone in the struggle, allowing him to see her as God had made her. He continued squeezing her, tightening the choke hold until she got the message and ceased her struggle.

Then he loosened his hold just slightly, enough so she could breathe but not enough for her to scream. He allowed her to draw in a gasp of air, then another, before tightening once again.

They stood there, locked together, her back pressed to his chest, as she trembled all over and finally began to collapse, her legs buckling in sheer terror.

"Stand up straight," he commanded.

She obeyed, like the good girl she was.

"This will only take a moment," he said. He needed to do it, he wanted to do it, but something in him also wanted to prolong this exquisite moment of power over another human being, this basking in the vicarious thrill of her terror. It was surely the most wonderful feeling in the world. It was certainly his favorite.

But it was time to get down to business.

With a certain regret, he removed a small, specially sharpened penknife from his pocket. He reached out to the side and, in a quick, almost ritualistic gesture, deftly inserted the blade into her throat. He held it there for a loving, lingering moment, listening to the gargle of her pierced windpipe. Then he made a quick lateral motion that severed both the windpipe and the carotid artery, exactly as one would stick a pig. As her body began to spasm he quickly released her and skipped back while she fell forward, away from him, the blood erupting in a controlled direction. It would be wrong to get blood on his suit—very wrong. They would disapprove.

She fell facedown on the rug, not too hard, the kind of *thump* that those directly below might ascribe to an overturned piece of furniture. Alban waited, watching with great interest until the death struggle had ceased and the body bled out.

Again he checked his watch: seven forty AM. *Schön*.

Kneeling, almost as if in prayer, he took a small leather-wrapped bundle from his pocket, unrolled it on the rug, and laid out his few essential tools. Then he began to work.

He would be enjoying that Starbucks doppio in the lobby by eight.

2

... ONCE AGAIN, THE MISTS CLEAR, AND THE man smiles. He thumbs the safety off his handgun and takes aim.

"Auf Wiedersehen," he says. His crooked smile widens as he savors the moment.

The young woman, her hand still in her bag, finds what she needs, grasps it. "Wait. The...the papers. I have them."

A hesitation.

"The papers from...from Laufer." She recalls a name she glimpsed on one of the papers, plucked out of her memory at random.

"Impossible! Laufer's dead." The man, the Nazi, appears taken aback, the cruel confidence on his face changing into alarm, uncertainty.

Her fingers close around some of the papers, curling them up and partially crushing them, and she lifts them from her handbag, just enough to show the black swastika on the letterhead.

Taking an impatient step forward, the man reaches out to snatch them. But hidden in their wrinkled folds, curled around it, lies her can of Mace, which she scooped up as she gathered the papers together. As he glances down, reaching for the bundle, she lets fly with a blast directly into his face.

The man topples backward with an inarticulate cry, the pistol dropping to the floor as his hands fly to his face, the papers scattering. Snatching them back up, she kicks the gun aside and sprints for the door, running through the altar-like room beyond to the staircase and hurtling down to the second floor, taking the steps three at a time, the heavy knapsack like a millstone around her shoulders. This is where it starts to happen: the feeling of drifting, of heaviness in her legs, of semi-paralysis. From upstairs she hears harsh words, German, guttural, the tread of heavy feet.

She runs past the counterfeiting room, past the bedrooms, hearing always behind her the sound of the man's pounding feet. She races down to the first floor, gasping from exertion, still strangely slowed as if by molasses and fear, but manages to reach the front door, grasps the handle.

Locked. And all the first-floor windows are barred.

As she turns back, a gun goes off behind her, the round taking a hunk out of the door frame. She flings herself into the sitting room, slipping behind a large display case that stands away from the wall of the room as if in preparation for being removed. Pressing her back against the wall for support, gripping the wainscot rail, she raises her feet and cocks her legs; a second later the man enters and she kicks forward with both legs, heaving the case down onto the man. He leaps to one side as crockery, pewter, books, and glass come crashing, again in slow motion; the man only partially escapes being crushed, the top edge of the falling case catching his knee, knocking him to the floor with a howl of fury.

Leaping over the case, she runs from the dining room.

Another shot rings out and she suddenly feels the tug in her side, with a flowering of heat so scorching that the pain of it almost brings her to her knees.

She half runs, half falls down the narrow staircase to the basement, tears past the heap of books, leaps onto the chair she had placed earlier, wriggles out the opening in the window. She hears the thud of footsteps overhead: the man is on the move again, but the tread slower, heavier, favoring one leg.

She thrashes through the ailanthus trees to the rickety table pushed up against the eight-foot brick wall, scales it, kicks it away as she leaps over, landing in her friend Maggie's backyard.

Here she pauses. All is quiet. Still, she must keep moving. She enters the back patio and then Maggie's kitchen, closing the door softly behind her and leaving the lights off.

One AM: Maggie wouldn't be back from work yet. She examines her side, bleeding profusely, and is relieved to find the round only grazed her skin.

Quickly she moves through the dark, silent apartment to the front door. Then—carefully, very carefully—she cracks it and peers out. East End Avenue is quiet, a few cars passing by beneath the soft streetlights. She darts out, closes the door behind her, and scurries northward, scanning the avenue for taxis, her side hurting, shoulder aching under the weight of the knapsack. Not a cab in sight.

And then it happens. Just like all the times before: the screeching of brakes, the slam of a door, the clatter of running feet.

"Halt!" comes the harsh cry. "Hände hoch!"

Another man is running toward her, gun in hand.

With a muffled cry of frustration and despair, she ducks into the closest open doorway: an all-night delicatessen. Even at this late hour it's full of people, standing at the order counter and helping themselves to the self-

serve salad bar. She flies through, knocking down stacks of canned goods, overturning the salad bar and flinging the slippery contents to the ground—anything to slow the man's advance. The deli erupts in cries of protest. She runs into the back kitchen, charges through an open doorway in the right wall, tears down a short corridor, and bursts into another kitchen, larger and dark: apparently, this second, adjoining building houses a more formal restaurant. She darts into the silent restaurant—past the tables set with white tablecloths, ready for the next day's diners—unlocks the front door, and finds herself back on East End Avenue, fifty feet from where she started.

She looks around wildly. Still no cabs. It will be only a matter of minutes, maybe seconds, until the Nazi reemerges. Sweeping the scene, her eye catches something in the greenery of Carl Schurz Park on the far side of the avenue: a brick wall, with a closed gate beside it, and—beyond—the yellow bulk of a large, Federal-style building.

Gracie Mansion.

Sprinting across the avenue, she clambers up the crosspieces of the gate and reaches the top of the brick wall. She knows the current mayor doesn't live here, disdaining the mansion for his own ultra-luxurious apartment—but it will still be well guarded.

Glancing over her shoulder, she sees the second Nazi emerge from the delicatessen. He catches sight of her, breaks into a run.

Cursing her slowness, she slides down the far side of the wall and makes for the mansion. It is dark inside, with floodlights bathing the exterior. She runs toward a uniformed cop standing at one corner of the building.

"Hey, Officer," she says, trying to control her breathing, shifting her backpack to cover the bloody patch under her arm, "Can you tell me how to get to Times Square?"

The cop stares at her like she's a madwoman.

She positions herself between the mansion and the policeman. "I got lost and I'm trying to find my way back to my hotel. Can you help me?"

Behind the cop, she sees the second Nazi, peering over the brick wall, staring at them.

The officer frowns at her. "Miss, do you have any idea where you are?"

"Umm...Central Park?"

The officer now looks convinced she's high on drugs. "This is a restricted area. And you're trespassing. I'm afraid you'll have to come with me."

"Okay, Officer."

She walks alongside the cop as he leads the way toward the front of the house. Glancing back, she sees that the Nazi has disappeared. Still, she now has to get away from the cop—she can't risk having her name entered into the official record. She waits until they are near the mansion's east front. The cop opens the gate with his key, escorting her toward his squad car. She drifts back, lagging. And then, abruptly, she breaks for the line of trees standing along the edge of the park.

"Hey!" the cop shouts. "Come back here!"

But she doesn't come back. She runs, and runs, through the trees, the deserted streets, the dark avenues, runs until she thinks her heart will explode...

Corrie awoke with a muffled cry. For a moment she was confused, disoriented, with no recollection of where she was. Then she saw the scuffed walls around her, saw the closed door directly in front of her, smelled the odor of old shit, and her memory came flooding back. She had fallen asleep in a stall in the ladies' room of Penn Station. She had been dreaming again...that same hideous, awful, extended dream, the dream that was not a dream—because it *had* happened, exactly that way, two weeks earlier.

She shook her head, trying to dispel the fog of fear. Two weeks had gone by. Nothing had happened. Surely she was safe.

She stood up. Her knees protested the movement. Her butt was asleep from sitting on a toilet seat for six hours. At least the bullet graze had healed and her side was no longer sore. Exiting the stall, she washed her face and hands, brushed her teeth and combed her hair with the toiletries she'd purchased in a Duane Reade. She examined herself in the mirror. Two weeks on the street, and a bit of art, had turned her into a filthy, homeless drug addict, for sure.

It was six PM, and Penn Station was bustling— exactly as she'd hoped. For the last two weeks, she had never moved except as part of a crowd. Her eyes roved everywhere, checking for anyone who might be shadowing her, on the alert in particular for that cruel face with the smoked glasses. She had become a street person, hiding in subway stations and churches, sleeping on park benches and highway underpasses, eating Big Macs retrieved from the Dumpster behind McDonald's after closing time. It was clear enough that she had stumbled across some kind of powerful, organized Nazi group or conspiracy. That was the only explanation for the safe house, for all the apparatus and paperwork— and for the dogged determination with which the men had chased her. They knew she had stolen papers.

Maybe she was overly paranoid, but it seemed likely they would go to any lengths to find and kill her.

She could have gone to the police. But that would have required an explanation of her B&E: a felony that would have ended her career in law enforcement before it even began. And they might not believe her, or the

Nazis might have split. Who would believe that Nazis were operating out of a house in twenty-first-century Manhattan?

She had tried to reach Pendergast several times, with no luck. The mansion on Riverside was shut up tight. As she readjusted the now-familiar weight of the knapsack on her shoulder, she reminded herself how important it was to get in touch with him. The papers were important, she felt sure, although having no German of her own she could not be certain.

She'd kept discreet watch on her own apartment building several times and seen no signs of suspicious activity. She was confident they hadn't found out who she was.

But it wasn't over. One way or another, she had to get these papers into Pendergast's hands, tell him about the house. The Dakota apartment would be her next stop.

She made her way down to the Eighth Avenue subway. The station was packed, and a train was just arriving. She hung back, at the far end of the platform, waiting for the train to disgorge its passengers and take on the hordes. She waited longer still, until the train had left the station and the exiting riders had departed, for the surface or for the commuter trains to Long Island and New Jersey. For a few moments, the station was empty. Glancing around one final time, she sat down on the edge of the platform, lowered herself carefully onto the track bed, and then—walking in the path of the quickly dwindling train—vanished into the darkness of the tunnel.

3

LONG AGO, DETECTIVE LIEUTENANT VINCENT D'Agosta had learned to be late to any appointment at the M.E. building on East Twenty-Sixth Street. He had found out the hard way that there were distinct disadvantages to being early, most of which involved arriving while an autopsy was still ongoing and thus being compelled to witnesses the final stages, which were inevitably the worst. They'd told him he would eventually get used to it.

He hadn't.

This one, he knew, would be more challenging than most. A young IT consultant down from Boston on a business trip, butchered and dismembered in a New York luxury hotel, security feeds showing a killer who looked like a model, with a victim who was equally attractive. The nature of the crime—which had all the hallmarks of a random killing for pleasure, perhaps involving a libidinous component—guaranteed strong public interest. Even the *Times* had run a story.

At a certain level, while he hated to admit it to himself, he was not displeased to be here. The zone captain had assigned the case to him, making him squad commander. It was his crime, his baby.

He passed through the doors containing the famous phrase, TACEAT COLLOQUIA. EFFUGIAT RISUS. HIC LOCUS EST UBI MORS GAUDET SUCCURRERE VITAE. "Let conversation cease. Let laughter flee. This is the place where death delights to help the living." And this made him think, with some satisfaction, how well things were going in his own life. His heart injury was just about fully healed, his relationship with Hayward was on track, his ex-wife was out of the picture, he was in regular touch with his son, and his unreliable employment history and disciplinary letters were now firmly in the past. The only unsettled issue was Pendergast and the man's pursuit of his kidnapped wife. But if anyone could take care of himself, it was the FBI agent.

His mind returned to the case at hand. It was more than an opportunity; it marked a crossroads in his career, a new beginning. Perhaps even the first step on his path to captain.

With this in mind he entered the main corridor of the M.E. building, flashed his shield at a nurse by way of greeting, signed in, and headed for Autopsy 113. He gowned up outside, then entered the room—to find that his timing had been perfect.

The dismembered body lay on a gurney. On a second gurney next to it, arrayed in rows with military precision, were the missing pieces, large and small, that had been cut from the corpse, along with Tupperware containers holding the various organs removed by the pathologist in the course of the autopsy.

The forensic pathologist was weighing the last one to be removed from the body cavity—the liver—and transferring it to its own container.

Arrayed around the body were two people from his freshly assembled team: Barber, the precinct-assigned investigator; and the guy from latent prints with the funny name he couldn't recall. Barber was in fine form, his usual cheerful self, his baby-brown eyes taking in everything. The guy from latents—what the hell was his name?—had the face of a man with big news. It irritated D'Agosta that neither looked the slightest bit queasy. How did they do it?

He tried to avoid dwelling on the details, keeping his eyes moving, not coming to rest on any particular item. Under the circumstances, he actually felt pretty good: that morning, to the annoyance of his girlfriend, Laura, he had turned down his favorite breakfast—challah bread French toast—along with orange juice and even coffee, satisfying himself with a tall glass of Italian mineral water.

A murmur of greeting, nods. He didn't recognize the gowned-up forensic pathologist, who was still reporting data into a headset. It was hard to see much of her, but he could tell she was young and strikingly good looking, with lustrous black hair pulled back— but very tense, brittle.

"Doctor? I'm Lieutenant D'Agosta, squad commander," he said to her by way of greeting.

"Dr. Pizzetti," she replied. "I'm the new forensic pathology resident."

Nice. Italian. A good omen. The "new" part explained her nervousness.

"When you have a chance, could you fill me in, Dr. Pizzetti?" he asked.

"Of course." She began tidying up the corpse, dictating the last of her observations. It lay on the gurney like a loosely assembled human jigsaw puzzle, and she now straightened some of the pieces that had become displaced during the autopsy, returning the corpse to a semblance of human shape. She shifted some organs, fixed lids on a few still-open Tupperware containers.

And then her assistant spoke to her in a low voice and handed her a long, evil-looking needle.

D'Agosta felt himself go rigid. What was this? He hated needles.

Pizzetti bent over the head. The cranium was already open, the brain removed. Wasn't it over? What the hell was she doing?

As he watched, she reached down, opened the corpse's eye with her thumb, and inserted the needle.

D'Agosta should have looked away quicker, but he didn't, and the sight of the needle sliding into that bright blue staring eye tightened his stomach in the most unpleasant way. Usually they took samples of ocular fluid for toxicology tests at the beginning of the autopsy—not at the end.

D'Agosta pretended to cough into his mask, still looking down and away.

"We're almost done, Lieutenant," said Pizzetti. "We just needed one more tox sample. Didn't get enough the first time."

"Right. Fine. No problem."

She ejected the needle into a medical waste bag and handed the syringe, filled with a yellowish orange fluid, to her assistant. Then she stepped back and glanced around the room. She peeled off her fouled gloves, tossed them into the red-bag waste, pulled down her mask, and unhooked her headset. Her assistant handed her a clipboard.

She *was* tense. D'Agosta's heart softened for her: young, a new resident, probably her first high-profile case. Worried about making a mistake. But from what he could see spread out in front of him, she'd done a fine piece of work.

She began the briefing with the usual litany: height, weight, age, cause of death, distinguishing marks, old scars, health, morbidities, pathologies. Her voice was pleasant although tight. The latents guy was taking notes. D'Agosta preferred to listen and retain by memory; note taking often caused him to miss things.

"Only one wound contributed to death: the one to the throat," she said. "No tissue under the fingernails. Prelim tox tests all negative. No sign of struggle."

She went on with a meticulous description of the depth, angle, and anatomy of the single stab wound. *This was an organized, intelligent killer,* D'Agosta thought, as he heard how efficient the fatal wound had been in exsanguinating the body, silencing the victim immediately and causing her to bleed out very quickly, all with one thrust with a razor-sharp, double-bladed knife about four inches long.

"Death," she concluded, "occurred within thirty seconds. All the other cuts were made postmortem."

A pause.

"The body was dismembered using a Stryker saw, perhaps one very much like the one beside me." She pointed to a saw mounted on a rack next to the body. "The Stryker has a wedge-shaped blade that moves back and forth at high speed, driven by compressed air. It is specifically designed to cut through bone but to stop instantly when encountering soft tissue. It is also designed not to cause any spraying of bone or fluids as it cuts. The perpetrator's use of it appears to be expert. *Unusually* expert." She paused again.

D'Agosta cleared his throat. The bolus in his stomach hadn't gone away, but at least it wasn't threatening to erupt. "So the perp might be an M.E. or orthopedic surgeon?" he asked.

A long silence. "It's not my place to speculate."

"I just want an off-the-cuff opinion, Doctor. Not a scientific conclusion. I won't hold you to it. How about it?" He tried to speak gently, so she wouldn't feel threatened.

Another hesitation. D'Agosta started to get a clearer idea of why she was so tense: she might be wondering if the murderer was a colleague. "It seems to me the person who did this had professional training." It came out in a rush.

"Thank you."

"The perpetrator also used surgical tools to cut the flesh down to the bone—the precision is remarkable—retractors to draw away the flesh—we documented the marks—and, as I said, used the Stryker to cut the bone. All the cuts were done very precisely, with no slips, no mistakes, much as a surgeon would in an amputation. Except, of course, the vessels weren't tied off or cauterized."

She cleared her throat. "The body was dismembered symmetrically: one cut three inches below the knee, one three inches above, one two inches above the elbow and another two inches below. And then the ears, nose, lips, chin, and tongue were removed. All with surgical precision."

She indicated the body parts, laid out on the second gurney positioned next to the corpse. The ears, nose, lips, and other small bits and pieces had been washed and looked like waxwork fakes, or parts from a clown kit.

D'Agosta felt the knot in his stomach tighten, a burning rise in his throat. Christ, even that glass of mineral water had been a mistake.

"And then there was *this*." Pizzetti turned and indicated an eight-by-ten print tacked to a corkboard, along with many others taken at the crime scene. D'Agosta had already seen this at the scene, but still he braced himself.

Written on the stomach of the victim was a message traced in blood. It read:

Proud of me?

D'Agosta looked at the guy from latents. What *was* his name? It was now his turn, and D'Agosta could tell from the gleam in his eye that he had something to say.

"Yeah, ah, Mr.—"

"Kugelmeyer," came the quick, eager response. "Thank you. Well. We got practically a full series off the body. Right and left thumb, right and left index, right ring, some partial palms. And we got two beauties right from that message there, in the victim's blood, no less, written with the *left* index finger."

"Very good," said D'Agosta. This was more than good. The killer had been shockingly careless, allowing himself to be recorded by half a dozen security cameras, leaving his prints all over the crime scene. On the other hand, the crime-scene unit hadn't been able to recover much from the scene itself: no saliva, semen, sweat, no blood or other bodily fluids from the perp. Naturally they had a lot of hair and fiber—it was a hotel room— but nothing that looked promising. No bite marks on the body, no scratches, nothing yet that would yield the killer's DNA. They had swabbed many of the latents, however, hoping to pick up some stray DNA, and they were confident the lab would succeed in this.

Pizzetti went on. "There was no sign of sexual activity, penetration, sexual violence, or molestation. The victim had just taken a shower, which made recovery of potential evidence from the body easier."

D'Agosta was about to ask a question when he heard, behind him, a familiar voice.

"Well, well, if it isn't Lieutenant D'Agosta himself. How are you, Vinnie?"

D'Agosta turned to see the hugely imposing figure of Dr. Matilda Ziewicz herself, chief medical examiner for New York City. She stood there like a linebacker, a cynical smile on her red-lipsticked mouth, her bouffant blond hair covered by an oversize cap, her specially sized smock bulging. She was brilliant, imposing, physically repellent, sarcastic, feared by all, and extremely effective. New York had never had a more competent chief M.E.

Dr. Pizzetti tensed up even more.

Ziewicz flapped a hand. "Carry on, carry on, don't mind me."

It was impossible not to mind her, but Pizzetti made an effort, resuming her rundown of all the preliminary results, relevant or not. Ziewicz listened with great attention and then, as Pizzetti continued, clasped her hands behind her back and made an excruciatingly slow turn around the two gurneys, the one holding the body and the other all the parts, examining them with redly pursed lips.

After several minutes, she issued a low *hmmmm.* And then another, with a nod, a grunt, a mumble.

Pizzetti fell silent.

Ziewicz straightened up, turned to D'Agosta. "Lieutenant, do you recall, these many years ago, the museum murders?"

"How could I forget?" It was the first time he had encountered the formidable woman, back in the days before she'd been appointed chief M.E.

"I never thought I'd live to see a case as unusual as that one. Until now." She turned to Pizzetti and said, "You've missed something."

D'Agosta could see Pizzetti freeze. "Missed... something?"

A nod. "Something crucial. Indeed, the very thing that lifts this case into..." She gestured toward the sky with a plump hand. "The stratosphere."

A long, panicked silence followed. Ziewicz turned to D'Agosta. "Lieutenant, I'm surprised at you."

D'Agosta found himself more amused than challenged. "What, you glimpse a claw in there somewhere?"

Ziewicz tilted her head back and issued a musical laugh. "You are very funny." She turned back to Pizzetti while everyone else in the room exchanged puzzled glances. "A good forensic pathologist goes into an autopsy with no preconceptions whatsoever."

"Yes," said Pizzetti.

"But you did come in here with a preconception."

Pizzetti's visible panic mounted. "I don't believe I did. I had an open mind."

"You tried, but you did not succeed. You see, Doctor, you *assumed* you were dealing with something—a single corpse."

"Respectfully, Dr. Ziewicz, I did not. I've examined each wound and I specifically looked for substituted body parts. But each part goes with the others. They all match up. None were switched with any other corpse."

"Or so it seems. But you did not do a *complete* inventory."

"An inventory?"

Ziewicz moved her ponderous bulk over to the second gurney, where pieces of the face had been rinsed and laid out. She pointed to a small piece of flesh. "What's this?"

Pizzetti leaned forward, peering. "A piece of...the lip, is what I assumed."

"Assumed." Ziewicz reached out, selected a set of long tweezers from a tray, and picked up the piece with great delicacy. She placed it on the stage of a stereo zoom microscope, switched on the light, and stepped back, inviting Pizzetti to look.

"What do you see?" Ziewicz asked.

Pizzetti looked into the scope. "Again, it seems like a bit of lip."

"Do you see cartilage?"

A pause. Pizzetti poked at the bit of flesh with the tweezers. "Yes, a tiny fragment."

"So I ask again: what is it?"

"Not a lip then, but . . . an earlobe. It's an earlobe."

"Very good."

Pizzetti straightened up, her face a mask of tension. Ziewicz seemed to expect more, however, and so after a moment Pizzetti stepped over to the gurney and examined the two ears lying like pale shells on the stainless steel.

"Um, I note that the ears are both present and undamaged. The lobes are not missing." Pizzetti paused. After a moment, she went back to the stereo zoom and stared once more into the eyepieces, poking and prodding the earlobe with the tip of the tweezers. "I'm not sure this belonged to the perpetrator."

"No?"

"This earlobe," said Pizzetti, speaking carefully, "does not appear to have been torn or cut off in the process of struggle. Rather, it appears to have been removed surgically, with care, using a scalpel."

D'Agosta remembered a small detail from the surveillance tapes he had spent hours watching, and it sent a shock through his system. He cleared his throat. "I will note for the record that the surveillance tapes indicate the perp had a small bandage over his left earlobe."

"Oh, my God," Pizzetti blurted into the stunned silence that followed this announcement. "You don't think he cut off his *own earlobe* and left it at the scene of the crime?"

Ziewicz gave a wry smile. "An excellent question, Doctor."

A long silence developed in the room, and finally Pizzetti said: "I'll order up a full analysis on this earlobe, microscopics, tox tests, DNA, the works."

Her smile broadening, Dr. Ziewicz peeled off her gloves and pulled down her mask, tossing them in the waste. "Very good, Dr. Pizzetti. You have redeemed yourself. A good day to you all, ladies and gentlemen."

And she left.

4

Dr. JOHN FELDER WALKED UP THE FRONT STEPS of the rambling gothic mansion. It was a brilliant late-autumn morning, the air crisp, the sky a cloudless blue. The mansion's exterior had recently been given a thorough cleaning, and the aged bricks fairly shone in the sunlight. Even the black bars on the ornate windows had been polished. The only thing, it seemed, that had not been cleaned was a bronze plaque, screwed into the front façade: MOUNT MERCY HOSPITAL FOR THE CRIMINALLY INSANE.

Felder buzzed the front door and waited while it was unlocked from within. The door was opened by Dr. Ostrom himself—director of Mount Mercy. Felder ignored the chilly frown that gathered on Ostrom's face. The man was not happy to see him.

Ostrom took a step back, allowing Felder to slip inside the building. Then he nodded to a waiting guard, who immediately relocked the door.

"Dr. Ostrom," Felder said. "Thank you for allowing this visitation."

"I did try to reach Pendergast in order to secure his approval," Ostrom told him. "However, I've been unable to contact the man, and I could think of no sound reason to deny your request any longer, given your position—technically, anyway—as court-appointed psychiatrist." He led Felder to a far side of the waiting area and lowered his voice. "However, there are some ground rules you must agree to abide by."

"Of course."

"You must limit your visit, and any future visits, to ten minutes."

Felder nodded.

"You must not unduly excite the patient."

"No, certainly not."

"And there is to be no further talk of any extracurricular—"

"Doctor, *please*," Felder interrupted, as if even the mention of such a subject was painful.

At this, Ostrom looked satisfied. "In that case, come with me. You'll find that she occupies the same room as before, although we have elevated the level of security."

Felder and Ostrom followed an orderly down a long corridor, lined on both sides by unmarked doors. As he walked, Felder felt a shiver run down his spine. Barely two weeks had passed since this very building had witnessed the greatest shame and humiliation of his professional life. Because of him, a patient had been allowed to escape Mount Mercy. No, not to escape, he reminded himself: to be kidnapped, by a man posing as a fellow psychiatrist. At the thought, Felder's cheeks flamed afresh. He himself had bought the whole deception, hook, line, and sinker. If it hadn't been for the patient's quick restoration to Mount Mercy, his career would have been jeopardized. As it was, he'd been given a one month mandatory leave of absence. It had been a near miss, an extremely near miss. Yet here he was, back again. What drew him to this patient like a moth to a flame?

They waited while the orderly unlocked a heavy steel door, then they proceeded down another endless, echoing passage, stopping finally before a door identical to all the others, save that a guard stood before it. Ostrom turned to Felder.

"Do you wish me to be in attendance?" he asked.

"Thank you, that won't be necessary."

"Very well. Remember: ten minutes." Ostrom unlocked the door from a key on a heavy chain, then opened it.

Felder stepped inside, then waited as the door was shut and locked behind him, letting his eyes grow accustomed to the dim light. Slowly, the features of the room grew sharper: the bed, table, and chair, all bolted to the floor; the bookcase, now stuffed with old volumes, many leather-bound; the plastic flowerpot. And there, behind the table, sat Constance Greene. There was no book or notepaper before her; she was sitting up quite straight, composed and erect. Felder suspected she had perhaps been meditating. Whatever the case, there was no idle, daydreamy quality in the deep, cold eyes that met his gaze. Unconsciously, Felder caught his breath.

"Constance," he said, standing before the table, hands clasped together like a schoolboy's.

For a moment, the woman did not answer. Then she nodded slightly, her bobbed hair swaying. "Dr. Felder."

Felder had been thinking about this moment for two weeks now. And yet just hearing that low, antique voice seemed to scatter his carefully prepared thoughts. "Listen, Constance. I just wanted to say...well, that I'm so very sorry. Sorry for everything."

Constance looked at him with her disquieting eyes but did not reply.

"I know what pain and suffering—and mortification—I must have caused you, and I need you to understand something: that is the *last* thing, the very last, I would ever want to inflict on a patient." *Especially a patient as unique as yourself,* he thought.

"Your apology is accepted," she said.

"In my eagerness to help you, I let down my guard. I allowed myself to be deceived. As, in fact, we all allowed ourselves to be deceived."

This last bit of face-saving elicited no response.

He added a solicitous note to his voice. "Are you feeling well, Constance?"

"As well as could be expected."

Felder winced inwardly. For a moment, silence settled over the small room as he considered what to say next.

"I made a mistake," he said at last. "But I've learned from that mistake. Remembered something, actually. It's a maxim we were taught in medical school: there are no shortcuts to effective treatment."

Constance shifted slightly in the chair, moved her hands. For the first time, Felder noticed the bandage on her right thumb.

"It's no secret that I've taken a particular interest in your case," he went on. "In fact, I think I can safely say that no one is more sympathetic to or understanding of your condition than I am."

At this, a brief, cold smile appeared. "*Condition,*" she repeated.

"What I am asking you is whether we can pick up the treatment where we left off, start work again in the spirit of—"

"No," Constance interrupted. Her voice was muted, but there was nevertheless such a ring of iron to it that Felder was immediately chilled.

He swallowed. "I'm sorry?"

She spoke quietly but firmly, without once taking her eyes from his. "How could you even think of continuing your so-called treatment? Because of your lack of judgment, I was abducted and assaulted. Because of your overwhelming eagerness to involve yourself professionally with a patient you perceived as exotic, I was held captive and nearly perished. Do not insult my intelligence by making me complicit in your failure. How could you expect me to ever trust you again—and isn't trust the fundamental requirement for therapeutic treatment? That is, of course, assuming I need therapeutic treatment—an offensive presumption on your part."

As quickly as the passion had come, it was gone. Felder opened his mouth, then closed it. There was nothing to be said.

Into the silence came a knock. "Dr. Felder?" Ostrom's voice sounded from the other side of the door. "Your ten minutes is up."

Felder tried to say good-bye but found he couldn't even manage that. He inclined his head slightly, then turned toward the door.

"Dr. Felder," came Constance's quiet voice.

Felder turned back.

"It is possible I have spoken too harshly with you. You may visit me from time to time, if you wish. But you must come as an acquaintance only—not as a doctor."

Felder felt a sudden, overwhelming relief—and gratitude. "Thank you," he said, wondering at his own rush of feeling as he stepped out into the relative brightness of the hall.

5

D'AGOSTA HAD COMMANDEERED THE MAIN conference room of the Detective Bureau at One Police Plaza. After the autopsy, he made the mistake of drinking three doppios and downing two crumb cakes at the Starbucks in the lobby, and now something was going on in his stomach that did not seem related to normal digestion.

Twelve fifty-five PM. Christ, it was going to be a long day. The problem was, despite the progress they'd made, he had a bad feeling about this case. A very bad feeling. Once again, he wondered where the hell Pendergast was. He'd love to just run the evidence by him, for an informal opinion. This case was right up his alley. Proctor, fresh out of the hospital and back at the Riverside Drive mansion, had heard nothing. Constance knew nothing. No one answered the phone at the Dakota apartment, and Pendergast's cell phone was apparently still dead.

D'Agosta shook his head. No point in worrying— Pendergast often disappeared without notice.

Time to go. D'Agosta gathered up his file and laptop, rose from his desk, and left the office, heading for the conference room. Over thirty officers had been assigned to the case, which put it in the middling range of importance. The highest-profile cases might have more than double that number. But it was still a lot of damn people, many of whom would have something to say. So much for his afternoon. Still, such meetings had to happen: Everyone had to know what everyone else knew. And it was a fact of life that, no matter how much you cajoled or threatened, you just couldn't make a cop sit down and read a report. It had to be a meeting.

He arrived at a few minutes past one and was glad to see everyone was already there. The room was restless, with a palpable sense of anticipation. As the rustling died away, D'Agosta heard an ominous growl in his gut. He strode up to the podium that stood on the stage beside a projection screen. They were flanked by wheeled whiteboards. As his eyes swept the room, he noticed Captain Singleton, the chief of detectives. He was sitting in the front row, next to the assistant chief for Manhattan and several other top brass.

His stomach lurched again. Laying his file on the podium, he waited a moment for silence, and then spoke the words he'd been rehearsing.

"As most of you know, I'm Lieutenant D'Agosta, squad commander." He gave the group the briefest rundown on the homicide, then consulted the list of names he'd drawn up. "Kugelmeyer, Latents."

Kugelmeyer strode to the podium, buttoning his hideous brown Walmart suit as he did so. D'Agosta placed a finger on his watch, gave it a subtle tap. He had threatened everyone with serious harm, even death, if they went over five minutes.

"We got an excellent series of latents from the corpse and the room," Kugelmeyer said quickly. "Fulls and partials, right and left, and palms. We ran them through all the databases. Negative. The perp, it seems, has never been printed."

That was it. Kugelmeyer sat down.

D'Agosta glanced around the room again. "Forman, hair and fiber?"

Another quick report. This was followed by a dozen others—blood spatter, footwear, microscopics, victimology—each following the other with military precision, much to D'Agosta's satisfaction. He tried to avoid glancing at Singleton, despite being eager to gauge the man's reaction.

One thing D'Agosta had learned about meetings like this was to create a little bit of drama by saving the best for last, knowing this would keep everyone awake and paying attention. And in this case, the best was Warsaw, the video geek from the forensic investigation division who specialized in analyzing security videos. While he was officially a detective, Warsaw looked more like a scruffy teenager, with his slept-on hair and pimples. Unlike the others, he didn't wear a suit, even a bad one, but rather skinny black jeans and T-shirts with heavy-metal logos. He got away with it because he was so good.

He was also a bit of a show-off. He came bounding up to the podium with a remote in hand; the lights dimmed.

"Hello, everyone," Warsaw began. "Welcome to the perp show gag reel."

That got a laugh.

"The Marlborough Grand has the latest in digital security, and we got beautiful, and I mean *beautiful*, footage. We got the perp from the front, back, side, above, below—HD all the way. Here are the high-lights, edited down to, ah, five minutes. Your folders have a selection of still shots taken from the footage, which is as we speak being shared with various other luxury hotels and—very soon—with the *Times*, *Post*, and *Daily News*."

The movie began, and it was just as good as Warsaw promised. The excerpts showed the perp—his left ear bandaged—in the lobby; on the elevator; walking down the hall; walking up the hall; pushing into the victim's room. And then it showed excerpts of the man leaving more or less the same way, unhurried, unruffled, unconcerned.

D'Agosta had seen the excerpts before, but they chilled him all over again. Most killers, he knew, could be divided into two broad groups, disorganized and organized. But this man was so cool, so methodical, that he almost deserved a category of his own. And once again D'Agosta felt deeply bothered by this. It just didn't fit. Didn't fit at all.

The clip ended, there was a smattering of applause. To D'Agosta's mild annoyance, Warsaw hammed a bow and left.

D'Agosta returned to the podium. It was now two thirty. So far, everything had gone like clockwork. His stomach rumbled again—it was starting to feel like he'd swallowed a bottle of hydrochloric acid. He had saved the very last bit, the earlobe, for himself. Squad commander's prerogative.

"We don't have DNA yet on the extra body part recovered from the crime scene—the earlobe," he began. "But we do have some prelims. It belongs to a male. The condition of the skin indicates an age under fifty—that's as close as we can get. It's almost certain that the presence of the earlobe was not a result of a struggle at the crime scene. Rather, it seems to have been carried to the crime scene and deliberately placed there. It also appears the earlobe was removed from its ear some hours prior to the time of the homicide—and it was removed not postmortem, but from a body still alive—no surprise, since as you can see from the video the perp is most definitely alive and kicking.

"We know what the perp looks like, and soon all of New York City will know. He's striking, with his ginger hair, expensive suit, good looks, and Olympic-athlete physique. We got prints, hair, clothing fibers, and soon we'll have his DNA. We've ID'd the Charvet tie, and we're close to IDing his suit and shoes. Looks like we're one step away from nailing the guy."

D'Agosta paused, made a decision to say it.

"So—what's wrong with this picture?"

It was a rhetorical question and nobody raised their hand.

"Is the guy really this stupid?"

He let the question hang for a long moment before continuing. "Look at the guy in the video. Can he really be the complete and total idiot he seems? I mean, there are simple steps he could have taken to disguise or alter his appearance, to evade the cameras at least in part. He didn't have to stand stock-still in the middle of the lobby for five minutes while the entire staff noticed him and the cameras shot B-roll from four angles. He's not a guy trying to blend in. We got psych working on it, figuring out what makes the guy tick, what motivates him, what the message on the body means, what the earlobe left at the scene means. Maybe he's crazy and wants to be caught. But it strikes me the guy seems to know what he's doing. And there's no way he's stupid. So let's not assume this case is anywhere near being in the bag, despite all we've got."

A silence. There was another thing bothering D'Agosta, but he chose not to mention it, because it might sound a little strange, and anyway he didn't know quite how to articulate it. It had to do with the timing of the attack. The camera caught it all. The guy was strolling down the hall, and—just as he was about to pass the door of the victim's room—she opened it to get the paper. The timing had been perfect.

. . . Coincidence?

6

K<small>YOKO ISHIMURA WALKED SLOWLY DOWN THE</small> hallway, whisking the polished wooden floor ahead of her with a traditional hemp broom. The hall was spotlessly clean already but Miss Ishimura, out of long practice, swept it anyway, day in, day out. The apartment—three apartments, actually, which had been combined into one by the owner—was shrouded in a close, listening silence. The traffic noise from West Seventy-Second Street barely penetrated the thick stone walls here, five stories above the street.

Returning the broom to the nearby maid's closet, she took a felt cloth, walked a few steps farther down the hallway, and passed into a small room with Tabriz and Isfahan carpets on the floor and an antique coffered ceiling above. The room was full of beautifully bound illuminated manuscripts and incunabula, stored within cases of mahogany and leaded glass. Miss Ishimura polished first the cases, then the glass, and then, with a separate special cloth, the volumes themselves, carefully passing it over the ribbed spines, the head caps, the gilded top edges. The books, too, were already clean, but she dusted each one nevertheless. It was not simply from mere force of habit: when Miss

Ishimura was anxious about something, she found solace in the act of cleaning.

Ever since her employer had returned home four days ago, without warning, he had been acting strangely. He was already a strange man, but this new behavior was exceedingly disturbing to her. He spent his days in the sprawling apartment, clothed in silk pajamas and one of his English silk dressing gowns, never speaking, staring for hours at the marble waterfall in the public room, or sitting in his Zen garden for the better part of a day, in an apparent stupor, unmoving. He had stopped reading newspapers, stopped answering the telephone, and ceased communicating in any way, even with her.

And he ate nothing—nothing. She had tried to tempt him with his favorite dishes—mozuku, shiokara—but everything went untouched. More disturbingly, he had begun taking pills. She had surreptitiously noted the names on the bottles—Dilaudid and Levo-Dromoran—looked them up on the Internet and was horrified to find they were powerful narcotics, which he showed every evidence of abusing in larger and larger quantities.

At first, it had seemed to her that he was wrapped in a deep, almost unimaginable sorrow. But as the days passed, he seemed to physically collapse as well, his skin turning gray, his cheeks slack, his eyes dark and hollow. As he sank increasingly into silence and apathy, she felt that, rather than sorrow, there was no feeling left in him at all. It was as if some terrible experience had burned all emotion from him, hollowed him out, leaving him a dry, ashen husk.

A small blue LED began to flash beside the door. For Miss Ishimura, who was deaf and mute, this was the signal that the phone was ringing. She walked over to a corner table where a telephone sat and examined the caller ID. It was Lieutenant D'Agosta, the policeman. Calling again.

She stared at the ringing phone for perhaps five seconds. Then—on impulse—she picked it up, despite express orders to the contrary. She placed the receiver in one of the TTY machines she used and typed a message: *You wait, please. I will call him.*

She exited the room, then passed down the long hallway, turned when it doglegged, continued down a second hallway, then stopped and rapped quietly on a *shoji*—a rice-paper partition serving as a door—pulling it back after a moment and stepping inside.

The room beyond contained a large Japanese *ofuro* bathtub built of blond hinoki wood. Agent Pendergast reclined within the tub, only his head and narrow shoulders rising above the steaming, high-walled surface. Bottles of pills and French mineral water were arrayed in lines, like sentinels, behind him. Naked, his appearance shocked her even more: his face dreadfully gaunt, and his pale eyes dark, almost bruised. A copy of T. S. Eliot's *Four Quartets* sat on the wide tub edge beside a heavy, gleaming straight razor. She had noticed him absently stropping the razor, sometimes for hours, in the bath, until its edge sparkled wickedly. The bathwater was tinged the palest rose—the bandage on his leg injury must be leaking again. He had done nothing about it, despite her urgent entreaties.

She handed him a note: *Lieutenant D'Agosta*.

Pendergast merely looked at her.

She held out the phone and mouthed a word. "Dozo."

Still he said nothing.

"Dozo," she mouthed again, with emphasis.

At last, he told her to engage the speakerphone in the wall. She did so, then stepped back deferentially. She could not hear, but she could read lips with complete perfection. And she had no intention of leaving.

*   *   *

"Hello?" came the voice, tinny and thin through the speakerphone. "Hello? Pendergast?"

"Vincent," Pendergast replied, his voice low.

"Pendergast. My God, where have you been? I've been trying to reach you for days!"

Pendergast said nothing, merely reclining farther into the bath.

"What's happened? Where's Helen?"

"They killed Helen," Pendergast replied in a flat, expressionless, terrible voice.

"*What*? What do you mean? When?"

"In Mexico. I buried her. In the desert."

There was an audible gasp, then a brief silence, before D'Agosta spoke again. "Oh, Jesus. *Jesus*. Who killed her?"

"The Nazis. A shot to the heart. Point-blank range."

"Oh, my God. I'm so sorry, *so* sorry. Did you . . . get them?"

"One got away."

"All right. We're going to get the bastard. Bring him to justice—"

"Why?"

"Why? What do you mean, *why*?"

Agent Pendergast raised his eyes to Miss Ishimura, and with a small twirl of his right index finger indicated that she should hang up the phone. The housekeeper—who had been intently watching his lips during the brief exchange—came forward after a short hesitation, pressed the OFF button, stepped backward across the slate floor of the bath, and then very quietly shut the *shoji*, leaving Pendergast once again alone.

Now she knew what the problem was. But it did not help her at all. Not at all.

7

BALANCING THE SMALL METAL SERVING TRAY of drinks in one hand, Vincent D'Agosta opened the sliding door and stepped out onto the apartment's microscopic balcony. There was just enough room for two chairs and a table. One of the chairs was occupied by Captain Laura Hayward. One lovely leg was crossed over the other, and she was perusing the pathology report D'Agosta had brought home with him. Traffic noise drifted up from First Avenue, and, though still very warm considering it was the last day of November, there was a pronounced bite to the air: this was probably the last time they'd share the balcony until spring.

He set the tray of drinks down on the table and Hayward glanced up from the grisly photographs, apparently undisturbed. "Mmm, those look good. What are they?"

D'Agosta handed one of the glasses to her. "Try it and see."

Hayward took a sip, frowned, then took a second, smaller sip. "Vinnie, what is this?"

"An Italian spritz," he said as he sat down. "Ice, Prosecco, dash of club soda, Aperol. Garnished with a slice of some blood oranges I picked up from Greenwich Produce in Grand Central on the way home."

She took another sip, then set the glass down. "Um." She hesitated. "I wish I could say that I liked it."

"You don't?"

"It tastes like bitter almonds." She laughed. "I feel like Socrates here. Sorry. You went to a lot of trouble." She took his hand, gave it a squeeze.

"This is a popular drink."

She picked up the glass again and held it out at arm's length, examining the gauzy orange liquid. "It reminds me of Campari. You know it?"

"You kidding? My parents drank it back in the day, when they lived in Queens and were hoping to pass for Manhattan."

"Thanks anyway, Vinnie my love, but I'll take the usual, if you don't mind."

"Sure." He took a sip of his own glass, decided he'd take his usual, as well. Stepping through the open door and heading into the kitchen, he put the glasses in the sink and got two more drinks: for himself, a frosty Michelob; for her, a glass of the flinty but inexpensive Pouilly-Fumé they always kept in the fridge. Carrying them back out to the balcony, he sat down again.

For several minutes, they remained in silence, taking in the heartbeat of New York City, quietly savoring each other's company. D'Agosta shot a covert glance at Hayward. For the past ten days or so, he'd been planning this evening down to the minutest detail: the meal, the dessert, the drinks—and the question. Now that he was healthy, now that his job was on track and his divorce just an unpleasant memory, he was finally ready to ask Laura to marry him. And he was fairly confident she'd say yes.

But then things had sort of come undone. This

bizarre murder, which was guaranteed to suck up all his time. And especially the freakish news about Pendergast.

He'd gone ahead with the dinner. But now was not the time for the proposal.

Hayward glanced again at the report, flipped through the pages. "How did the big meeting go this afternoon?"

"Good. Singleton seemed to like it."

"Are the DNA results back yet?"

"No. That's the slowest goddamn lab in town."

"Interesting how the killer made no attempt to disguise himself or to avoid the security cameras. It's almost like he's daring you to find him, isn't it?"

D'Agosta took a sip of his beer.

Hayward peered at him. "What is it, Vinnie?"

D'Agosta sighed. "It's Pendergast. I finally reached him this afternoon on the phone. He told me his wife was dead."

Laura put down her drink and looked at him in shock. "Dead? How?"

"The people who kidnapped her. They shot her in Mexico—apparently to distract Pendergast, to allow themselves to get away."

"Oh, my God..." Laura sighed, shook her head.

"It's just a horrible tragedy. And I'd never heard him like that before. He sounded like—" D'Agosta paused. "I don't know. Like he didn't care. Like he was *dead*. And then he hung up on me."

Hayward nodded sympathetically.

"I'm worried about his state of mind. I mean, to lose her like that..." He took a deep breath, looked down at his beer. "I'm bracing myself for a reaction."

"What kind of reaction?"

"I don't know. If the past is any guide, maybe an

explosion of violence. The guy's so unpredictable. Anything could happen. I feel like I'm witnessing a slow-motion train wreck."

"Maybe you should do something."

"He made it obvious he doesn't want any sympathy, any help. And you know what? For once, I'm going to honor his wishes and not interfere."

He lapsed into silence.

For a moment, Hayward did not answer. Then she cleared her throat. "Vinnie, the man's hurting. I never thought I'd hear myself say it, but maybe this is the one time you *should* interfere."

He glanced up at her.

"Here's how I see it. Pendergast has never failed before. Not like this. I mean, he was so completely, utterly intent on discovering the truth about what really happened to his wife. It was a quest that almost got you killed. It almost got me gang-raped. And then, when he started to believe she was still alive after all . . ." Hayward paused for a moment. "Here's the thing: deep down, I don't think he ever *believed* he would fail. You know Pendergast, you know how he works. This is the thing he wanted more than anything, more than any of those cases of his—and now it's finished. Done. He's failed. I can hardly imagine what he's feeling." She paused. "You say he's going to erupt into violence. But if that's the case, why isn't he out there, on fire to catch her killers? Why isn't he breaking down our door, enlisting your aid?"

D'Agosta shook his head. "Good questions."

"I think he's in total despair," said Hayward. "I'm sure of it."

They settled into silence. D'Agosta sipped his beer moodily.

Finally, Hayward stirred again. "Vinnie, I'm saying

this against my better judgment. But what Pendergast might need to draw him out of this is a really good case. And you know what? There's one right in front of us." She tapped the pathology report.

D'Agosta sighed. "I appreciate what you're saying. I really do. But this time...I'm not going there. It's just not my place, butting in." And he glanced over the table at her, smiled a little wistfully, then let his gaze settle on the façades across First Avenue, burnished pink and gold by the setting sun.

8

ALBAN LORIMER WAS PLEASANTLY SURPRISED BY the lobby of the Vanderbilt Hotel. It was quite different from the Marlborough: a smaller, quieter, more intimate space. A huge urn of fresh flowers dominated the hushed confines of the lobby, which was arranged more like an elegant living room. There were plush carpets, deep comfortable sofas and chairs arranged around ebony tables topped with glass. The walls were of dark oak paneling and the fixtures of handblown glass, Victorian perhaps.

He took a seat at a small table in the lobby. A waiter came by and asked him if he would care for tea. Alban thought a moment, looked over the evening tea menu, and said yes, he would very much care for a pot of tea, preferably an Assam or some such mild blend, prepared English-style in the pot, with whole milk and sugar. He was very particular with his order and made sure the waiter paid attention to it, and to him, while he gave it.

The waiter went off while Alban made himself comfortable, absorbing the feel of the place. The first thing that struck him was that the clientele here seemed different. Whereas the Marlborough Grand had been just that—grand—this hotel felt more like a quiet, upper-class club of wealth and privilege, catering to locals and their guests.

The differences intrigued him. Did each hotel have its own personality? The Marlborough Grand was like a young blonde with flash and style, a bit loud, maybe even vulgar, but pretty, sexy, and fun. The Vanderbilt appeared in his mind's eye like a distinguished, gray-haired gentleman of taste and breeding: handsome, charming, but a trifle dull. He wondered which one he preferred. It was hard to say. He didn't have enough experience.

He was looking forward to visiting other hotels in New York City and making a study. He would create a complete character, a person, for each hotel. It would be fun.

As he waited for his tea, he smoothed one hand over his suit front. The bandage on his right index finger bothered him. It itched. But there was nothing he could do about that now. At least he felt secure, knowing he looked different enough from the person whose crisp, clear picture had been in all the papers. The clearer the picture, of course, the less he had to change his appearance. Funny that no one seemed to realize this irony. But of course, it might be that the police *did* realize that. One had to be careful.

Now he was Mr. Brown. His hair was brown. His eyes were brown. His skin, while not exactly brown, was olive. Only his clothing was not brown—he didn't care for brown suits—but rather gray, and it was Brooks Brothers from shoes to tie. He had never heard of Brooks Brothers until today: it was a New York clothier whose suits were banal enough to help him fit in even better. Although it had turned somewhat colder overnight, the cashmere cap he wore, pulled down over his ears, might still look a little strange. Perhaps some people thought he was a cancer victim, covering up his loss of hair.

Two large, shaped pieces of beeswax, stuck between his upper molars and cheek, rounded out his sharp cheekbones and gave him a broader, friendlier, and perhaps somewhat dumber-looking face. And, of course, he had altered his walk by paring down the heels of his new shoes to make the outside of the heel lower than the inside by three-eighths of an inch—which had the effect of changing the rhythm of his stride. He had been instructed that the way a person walked was one of the key characteristics used by identity specialists.

The tea was excellent, as he knew it would be. He left a couple of fresh, crisp bills on the table, and as he rose he pressed his left hand on the glass tabletop, letting his fingers grip the side, where the waiter was less likely to clean.

He strolled to the elevator, got on, and pressed the sixth-floor button. Exiting, he strolled to the end of the hall—again finding a blind spot beneath an unobtrusive security camera—and settled in to wait. The hall was not as long as that in the Marlborough, and he feared the wait might be a long one. But no: just five minutes later he started back down the hall again, walking fast this time, and then as the maid rounded the corner, carrying a pillow, he slowed his pace, arranging his face into a warm smile. He intercepted her halfway down the hall and held out his hands, eyes twinkling.

"Say, that pillow is for me, isn't it? Room Six Fourteen?"

"Yes, sir."

"Thank you." He took the pillow, gave the woman a five-dollar bill, and turned, heading toward Room 614. As he walked, he gave the pillow an inquisitorial squeeze. Firm, shape-retaining foam. It seemed the individual in Room 614 didn't like the drowning sensation caused by soft, overstuffed goose-down pillows. Something they had in common.

He went to the door of Room 614 and gave a polite double rap. In response to the standard query— delivered in a gruff male voice—he said: "Your pillow, sir."

The door opened. Alban held out the pillow and, as the man within reached for it, started forward abruptly, giving the surprised man a little push inside and instantly silencing him with a hammerlock around his throat, shutting the door gently with his free hand. This one hardly struggled, not at all like the woman, and when he did it was a sorry, feeble sort of effort. He was older, fatter, softer, yielding. Alban pushed him into the center of the room. The man made a few half-hearted attempts to punch around and behind, but a sharp tightening around his throat soon caused him to stop. Alban could feel the man's knees starting to tremble, from fear or perhaps lack of oxygen. The man's thin greasy hairs—combed over a dimpled bald patch, reeking of lime tonic—were right under Alban's nose, and it angered him. This was not nearly as much fun as the woman. It lacked a certain challenge, perhaps even flair. He would have to remember that.

He loosened his grip, and the man drew in a ragged, gasping, desperate breath. "What do you—?"

Alban tightened his grasp again. He did not want any discussion.

As the man began to struggle once more, Alban said, in a friendly tone, "Shhhh, everything's going to be all right if you cooperate." The man stopped. Amazing how they believed you. Nevertheless, he kept his arm around the man's neck—just in case.

He positioned the man, braced himself, then removed the penknife, keeping it well out of the man's field of view. He extended his arm far to the right—then swung it in fast, sticking it deep into the throat with a sharp twist, just as he had done a hundred times before, practicing for the most part on pigs; then he heaved the man forward while simultaneously jumping back.

A huge razzing spray of blood and exhaled air erupted forward, but not a drop touched Alban. The fall was louder and heavier this time and gave Alban a certain unease, reminding him that his technique might still need refining. He checked his watch, waited out the man's death spasms, then took out his tools and quickly went to work.

Yes, he thought, puffing a bit at the effort, he was looking forward to his little personal study of New York City hotels and the individual characters he would mentally fashion of each one.

9

THE WING OF THE HOTEL HAD BEEN CORDONED off, all the guests moved. The hotel manager, a high-strung young man, had actually been carted away, having had some kind of a nervous breakdown. That was something new in Lieutenant D'Agosta's experience. The press was barricaded on Fiftieth Street outside and, even up on the sixth floor, D'Agosta could hear the faint commotion below and see the lights of the squad cars shining up into the window through gauzy curtains. Or maybe that was just dawn finally breaking after a long, long night.

D'Agosta stood in the bedroom area, booties over his shoes, watching the last of the forensic unit as they wrapped up the crime scene. More than eight hours had passed since the murder. The body had been removed from the hotel room, along with the extra finger they found with it: the first joint of the right index finger. The carpet held a bloodstain three feet in diameter, and the opposite wall was sprayed crimson, as if from a hose. The room carried the characteristic iron smell of violent death, along with an undercurrent of the various chemicals employed by the forensic unit.

Captain Singleton had arrived half an hour before for the wrap-up. On the one hand, D'Agosta was grateful for the support: when the chief of detectives showed an interest, things really got done. On the other hand, he couldn't help but feel that the man's sudden presence might be a vote of no-confidence. This second killing had catapulted the case to the top of every late-night news broadcast in the city, pushing the five-victim gun battle in Central Park completely out of the public consciousness. And, let's face it, he and Singleton hadn't always been best of chums: some years ago, in a disastrous case D'Agosta had been involved in with Pendergast, Singleton had been a stickler for the rules when D'Agosta came up before a disciplinary hearing. But in Singleton's defense, the captain had always tried to give him a fair shake. So why—considering how much he respected the man—did D'Agosta feel a prickling of resentment at Singleton's appearance now? Maybe it was because the captain had refused a police backup when a worried D'Agosta had approached him, off the record, about the boathouse meeting between Pendergast and Helen. "Nazis here, in New York?" he'd told D'Agosta. "That's ridiculous—even for Agent Pendergast. I can't deploy an entire squad on a whim." D'Agosta—whom Pendergast had sworn to silence anyway—hadn't pushed it. And now Helen Pendergast was dead.

"*Happy Birthday*," Singleton murmured, repeating the message they'd found written in blood on the victim's corpse. "What do you make of that, Lieutenant?"

"We've got a real psycho on our hands." The messages—and the extra body parts—had been kept back from the press.

"We certainly do," said Singleton. He was tall and slender and well groomed, in his late forties but still with a swimmer's physique. His carefully clipped salt-and-pepper hair was rapidly turning to white, but he seemed to retain a certain restless, springy manner that made him seem younger. One of the most decorated cops on the force, he was famous for his hard work and apparent lack of need for sleep. Unlike most detectives, he dressed well, favoring expensive, tailored suits. There was something about him that always made one want to go the extra mile. He was the sort of man who did not discipline through fear or a raised voice; rather, he would just seem "disappointed." D'Agosta would rather be screamed at for half an hour by another captain than suffer a minute of Singleton's grave and disappointed countenance.

"I've been thinking about it," said Singleton, with the tone D'Agosta knew meant a difficult or controversial piece of advice was coming up. "The psychological aspects of this case are extraordinary. We're outside the bell curve of the usual deviant pathology here. Don't you think, Lieutenant?"

"I agree." D'Agosta remained noncommittal. He wanted to see where Singleton was going with this.

"We know the earlobe was removed several hours before the first killing. Now the M.E. tells us the fingertip was also removed several hours before *this* killing. We've got the first security tapes showing a bandage on his earlobe, and now the new tapes show he's wearing that peculiar cap and a bandage on his finger. What kind of a killer would cut himself up like that? And what do these messages mean? Whose birthday is it, and who's supposed to be proud of him? And finally: Why is a so obviously organized and intelligent killer so sloppy about his identity?"

"I'm not sure he is sloppy," D'Agosta said. "Notice how different he looked in the security feeds this time."

"And yet he left fingerprints behind. He doesn't mind us knowing it was him, post facto. In fact, the body parts would seem to imply he *wanted* us to know."

"What bothers me is the way he stopped the maid," D'Agosta said. "In the interview, she insisted that he knew about the pillow and the room number that requested it. How could he know that?"

"He might have an inside contact," Singleton said. "Someone working the front desk or the switchboard. These are all angles you'll have to look into."

D'Agosta nodded glumly. He really wished Pendergast were here. These were exactly the kind of questions he might be able to answer.

"Do you know what this suggests to me, Lieutenant?"

D'Agosta braced himself. Something was coming. "What, sir?"

"I never like having to say this. But right now, we're out of our depth. We need to bring in the FBI's Behavioral Science Unit."

D'Agosta was surprised. And then he wasn't surprised. It was a logical step with a serial killer like this, who presented an extreme and perhaps unique pathology.

He found Singleton gazing at him earnestly, looking for agreement. This was also new to D'Agosta. Since when did Singleton ask for his opinion?

"Chief," he said, "I think that's an excellent idea."

Singleton seemed relieved. "You realize, of course, that the men and women aren't going to like it. For one thing, there's no element in these crimes requiring FBI involvement—no evidence of terrorism or interstate links. And you know how obnoxious the FBI can be—*will* be. But in all my career, I've never seen a killer quite like this. The BSU has access to databases and research far beyond what we've got. Still, it's going to be tricky getting our people with the program."

D'Agosta was well aware of how poorly the NYPD worked with the FBI. "I understand," he said. "I'll talk to the squad about it. As you know, I've worked with the FBI before. I don't have any personal issues with them."

Hearing this, Singleton's eyes flashed. For a minute, D'Agosta feared he might bring up Pendergast. But no—Singleton was too tactful for that. Instead, he simply nodded.

"As chief, I'll make the initial contact with Quantico and then pass things along to you. That's the best way to proceed, especially with the FBI, who are sticklers about rank."

D'Agosta nodded. Now he really wished Pendergast was here.

For a while, they watched in silence as the fiber guy moved slowly across the floor on his hands and knees, tweezers in one hand, going over square after square of the grid laid down with strings. What a job.

"I almost forgot," Singleton said. "What were the results of the DNA test on the earlobe?"

"We still haven't gotten them back."

Singleton slowly turned toward D'Agosta. "It's been sixty hours."

D'Agosta felt the blood rushing to his face. Ever since the forensic DNA unit had been shifted out of the M.E.'s office and made into its own department—with Dr. Wayne Heffler as director—they had been impossible to deal with. A few years ago, he and Pendergast had had a run-in with Heffler. Ever since, D'Agosta suspected that Heffler had made a point of holding up his lab results just long enough to piss off D'Agosta but not so long that he himself got into hot water.

"I'll get on it," said D'Agosta evenly. "I'll get on it immediately."

"I'd appreciate it," said Singleton. "One of your responsibilities as squad commander is to kick ass. And in this case, you may have to, ah, put the toe of your boot right up inside, if you get my meaning."

He gave D'Agosta a friendly pat on the back and turned to leave.

10

THE TAXICAB PULLED UP TO THE SEVENTY-
Second Street entrance of the Dakota, stopping opposite the doorman's pillbox. A uniformed man emerged
and, with the gravitas of doormen the world over,
approached the cab and opened the rear door.

A woman stepped out into the early-morning sunlight.
She was tall and sleek and beautifully dressed. The white,
broad-brimmed hat she wore set off her freckled face,
deeply tanned despite the lateness of the season. She paid
the driver, then turned toward the doorman.

"I'll need to use your house phone, if you please,"
she said in a brisk English accent.

"This way, ma'am." And the doorman led her down
a long, dark passage beneath a portcullis to a small
room facing the building's interior courtyard.

She picked up the phone, dialed an apartment number. The phone rang twenty times without answer. The
doorman waited, eyeing her. "There's no answer, miss."

Viola eyed the doorman. This was someone who
could not be pushed around. She offered a sweet smile.
"As you know, the housekeeper is deaf. I'll try again."

A reluctant nod.

Another twenty rings.

"Miss, I think that's enough. Allow me to take your name."

She rang again. The doorman was now frowning, and she could see he was getting ready to reach over and press the ENGAGED button.

"Please, just a moment," she said, with another brilliant smile.

Even as the doorman's hand was reaching over to cut her off, the phone was finally answered.

"Hello?" she said quickly. The hand withdrew.

"May I know the reason for this damnable persistence?" came the monotonal, almost sepulchral voice.

"Aloysius?" the woman asked.

A silence.

"It's me. Viola. Viola Maskelene."

There was a long pause. "Why are you here?"

"I've come all the way from Rome to speak to you. It's a matter of life and death."

No response.

"Aloysius, I appeal to you on...on the strength of our past relationship. Please."

A slow, quiet exhalation of breath. "I suppose you must come up, then."

The elevator whispered open to a small landing, with maroon carpeting and walls of dark, polished wood. The single door opposite was standing open. Lady Maskelene walked through the doorway and then stopped, shocked. Pendergast was standing inside, wearing a silk dressing gown of muted paisley. His face was gaunt, his hair limp. Without bothering to shut the door, he turned away wordlessly and walked over to one of the room's leather sofas. His movements, normally brisk and economical, were sluggish, as if he were moving underwater.

Lady Maskelene closed the door and followed him into the room, which was rose-colored with the sparse decoration of a few ancient, gnarled bonsai trees. Three of the walls held a scattering of impressionist paintings. The fourth was a sheet of water, falling over a slab of black marble. Pendergast took a seat on the sofa, and she sat down beside him.

"Aloysius," she said, taking his hand in both of hers, "my heart breaks for you. What an awful, awful thing. I'm so terribly sorry."

His eyes looked through her rather than at her.

"I can't even begin to imagine how you must feel right now," she said, pressing his hand. "But the one thing you mustn't feel is guilt. You did everything you possibly could—I know you did. What happened was beyond your power to prevent." She paused. "I wish there was something I could do to help you."

Pendergast freed his hand from hers, closed his eyes, and tented his fingertips on his temples. He seemed to be making a huge effort to concentrate, to bring himself into the moment. Then he opened his eyes again and looked at her.

"You mentioned a life at stake. Whose?"

"Yours," she replied.

This did not seem to register at first. After a moment or two, Pendergast said, "Ah."

There was another silence. Then he spoke again. "Perhaps you'd care to explain the source of your information?"

"Laura Hayward contacted me. She told me what had happened, what was going on. I dropped everything and flew from Rome on the very next plane."

She couldn't stand the dull way he was looking at her—looking past her. This was so unlike the courtly, collected, nuanced Pendergast she had first met at her villa on Capraia—the man under whose spell she had fallen—that she could not bear it. A terrible anger rose in her heart at the people who had done this to him.

After a hesitation, she took him in her arms. He stiffened but did not protest.

"Oh, Aloysius," she whispered. "Won't you let me help?"

When he still did not respond, she said, "Listen to me. It's fine to grieve. It's *good* to grieve. But this—shutting yourself up here, refusing to speak to anyone, refusing to see anyone...it's no way to handle this." She held him tighter. "And you *must* deal with it—for Helen's sake. For my sake. I know it will take time. That's why I'm here. To help you through your grief. Together we can—"

"No," Pendergast murmured.

Surprised, she waited.

"There will be no *handling* it," he said.

"What do you mean?" she asked. "Of course there will. I know it seems utterly hopeless right now. But given time, you'll see that—"

He sighed with something like impatience, some of his self-possession returning. "I see that it is necessary to enlighten you. Will you come with me?"

She looked at him for a moment. She felt a flicker of hope, even relief. This was a flash of the old Pendergast, taking charge.

He rose from the sofa and led the way to an almost invisible door set into one of the rose walls. Opening it, he started down a long, dim hallway, stopping at last at a paneled door that was standing ajar. Pushing it wide, he stepped in.

Viola followed, glancing around curiously. She had been in Pendergast's Dakota apartment before, of course, but never in this room. It was a revelation.

The floor was covered in antique wood planking, very wide and beautifully varnished. The walls were clad in historic textured wallpaper of an exceedingly subtle design. The ceiling was painted as a blue trompe l'oeil sky in the style of Andrea Mantegna. There was a single display case, containing numerous strange things: a piece of lava, twisted and dark; an exotic lily of some kind, pressed within a sealed case of clear plastic; a stalactite, its end roughly broken off; what appeared to be a piece from a wheelchair; several mangled bullets; an antique case of surgical instruments; various other items. It was an eccentric and even bizarre collection, whose meaning was perhaps clear only to Pendergast himself.

This must be Pendergast's private study.

But what most caught her eye was the Louis XV desk that occupied the middle of the room. It was made of rosewood, with gilt edging and fantastically complex inlays. Its surface was empty save for three items: a small glass medical container with a rubber top; a hypodermic syringe; and a silver dish that held a small white pyramid of some fine powdery substance.

Pendergast took a seat behind the desk. There was only one other chair in the room: an ornate fauteuil pushed up against the far wall. Viola placed it before the desk and sat down as well.

For a moment, they sat in silence. Then, with a wave of his hand, Pendergast indicated the items on the desk.

"What are those, Aloysius?" Viola asked, fear rising in her heart.

"Phenylcholine para-methylbenzene," he said, pointing at the white powder. "First synthesized by my great-great-grandfather in 1868. One of the many odd potions he developed. After initial private, ah, trials, it remains to this day a family secret. It is said to confer upon the user a state of complete and utter euphoria, offering total negation of care and sorrow, along with, supposedly, a unique intellectual epiphany, for a period of twenty to thirty minutes—before inducing irreversibly fatal, and painful, renal failure. I have always been curious to experience its initial effects, yet until now never have—for self-evident reasons."

Speaking about the objects on the desk seemed to rouse a degree of energy in Pendergast. His bruised-looking eyes shifted to the small medication bottle. "Hence, this." He picked it up and showed it to her, the colorless liquid within shifting slightly. "A mixture of sodium thiopental and potassium chloride, among other compounds. It will induce unconsciousness, then stop the heart—well before the unpleasant side effects of the para-methylbenzene manifest themselves. While still providing enough time to give me a modicum of peace and, perhaps, even diversion before the end."

Viola looked from Pendergast, to the objects on the desk, then back to Pendergast. As the implications of what he was saying became clear, a feeling of dread and horror swept over her.

"Aloysius, no," she whispered. "You can't be serious."

"I am deadly serious."

"But..." She fell silent as her throat closed up involuntarily. *This can't be happening, it just can't be happening...* "But this isn't you. You have to fight this. You can't take the...the coward's way out. I won't let you."

At this, Pendergast put his hands on the desk, rose slowly to his feet. He walked to the door, held it open for her. After a certain hesitation she rose and followed him as he turned and walked back down the corridor, through the hidden doorway, and into the reception room. It was as if she were in a bad dream: She wanted to stop him, she wanted to sweep those hateful things off the table and dash them to the ground. And yet she could not. So deep was her shock that she felt herself powerless to do anything. *It's a matter of life and death*—her own words now returned, torturing her with their irony.

Pendergast said nothing more until they had reached the door leading to the elevator. Then, at last, he spoke again. "I thank you for your concern," he said, his voice strangely faint and hollow, as if coming to her from a great distance. "And for the time and effort you have taken on my behalf. But now I must ask you to return to Rome."

"Aloysius—" she began, but he raised a hand for silence.

"Good-bye, Viola. You would do well to forget me."

Viola realized she was crying. "You can't do this," she said, her voice trembling. "You simply *can't*. It's too selfish. Aren't you forgetting something? There are people, many people, who care about you. Who love you. Don't—*please* don't—do this to them. To us." She hesitated and added, in an angrier tone: "To *me*."

As she spoke, something seemed to flicker in Pendergast's eyes—a faint spark, like the glow of an ember encased in ice—before vanishing again. It came and went so quickly she could not be certain she'd seen it at all. Maybe it was a trick of the tears that filled her own eyes.

He took her hand, gave it an almost imperceptible pressure. Then, without another word, he opened the front door.

Viola looked at him. "I won't let you do this."

He looked at her briefly, even kindly. "Surely you know me well enough to realize that nothing you or anyone can do will change my mind. And now it is time for you to go. It would be highly distressing to both of us if I were forced to have you shown out."

She continued to look at him, pleadingly, for another minute. But his gaze had gone far away once again. At last she turned away, her entire body shaking. Sixty seconds later, she was once more walking across the interior courtyard, legs like rubber, without the faintest idea of where she was headed, the tears coursing freely down her cheeks.

Pendergast stood in the reception room for a long time. Then—very slowly—he made his way back to his private study; seated himself behind the desk; and—as he had been doing for numberless hours—once again began to contemplate the three items arrayed before him.

11

AFTER LEAVING SINGLETON, D'AGOSTA HEADED
straight downtown. *Fucking Heffler*. He was going to
wipe the floor with that son of a bitch. He was going to
cut the man's balls off and hang them on a Christmas
tree. He remembered the time he had visited Heffler
with Pendergast, and how Pendergast had ripped him
a new one. That had been fun. He, D'Agosta, was—he
decided—going to "do a Pendergast" on Heffler.

With these pleasant thoughts in mind, he pulled up
at the forensic DNA unit on William Street, an annex
to New York Downtown Hospital. He glanced at his
watch: eight AM. He had checked with the duty officer
and learned Heffler had been in the office since three.
That was a good sign, although D'Agosta wasn't quite
sure what it meant.

He heaved himself out of the unmarked car, slammed
the door, and strode through the glass entranceway of
the William Street building. He passed by the recep-
tionist, holding out his badge. "Lieutenant D'Agosta,"
he said loudly, without slowing down. "I'm here to see
Dr. Heffler."

"Lieutenant, the sign-in sheet—?"

But D'Agosta continued on to the elevator, punching the button for the top floor, where Heffler had installed himself in a cushy, oak-paneled corner office. Stepping out of the elevator once again, he found there was no secretary in the outer office—too early. D'Agosta breezed through and flung open the door to the inner office.

And there was Heffler.

"Ah, Lieutenant—" the director began, rising abruptly.

D'Agosta hesitated a moment. This was not the Heffler whom D'Agosta was familiar with: the glossy, supercilious prick in a thousand-dollar suit. This Heffler was rumpled, tired, and had the look of a man who had recently been called on the carpet.

He launched into his rehearsed speech anyway. "Dr. Heffler, we've been waiting over *sixty hours*—"

"Yes, yes!" Heffler said. "And I've got the results. They just came in. We've been working on it since three this morning."

A silence. Heffler's manicured fingernails eagerly tapped a file on his desk. "It's all right here. And please allow me to apologize for the delay. We've been understaffed—these budget cuts—you know how it is." He flashed D'Agosta a look that hovered somewhere between sarcasm and a simper.

Hearing all this, D'Agosta felt the wind go right out of his sails. Someone had already gotten to Heffler. Was it Singleton? He paused, took a breath, and tried to shift down. "You have the results on both homicides?"

"Absolutely. Please, Lieutenant, sit down. I'll go over them with you."

Grudgingly, D'Agosta took the proffered chair.

"I'll just summarize, but please feel free to interrupt if you have questions." Heffler opened the file. "The DNA sampling was excellent, the team did a great job.

We have solid DNA profiles from hair, latents, and of course the earlobe. All match to a very high degree of certainty. We can confirm that the earlobe did indeed belong to the perpetrator."

A page turned. "For the second homicide, we also have solid DNA profiles from hair, latents, and the fingertip. Again, all three match each other and the DNA profiles from the first homicide. The finger and earlobe came from the same individual—the killer."

"How certain are the results?"

"Very certain. These were excellent profiles with abundant, uncontaminated material. The possibility of this being coincidence is less than one in a billion." Heffler was already starting to recover some of his own self-assurance.

D'Agosta nodded. This was nothing new, really, but it was good to have confirmation. "Did you run it against the DNA databases?"

"We did. Against every database we have access to. No hits. That isn't surprising, of course, since the vast majority of people don't have their DNA in any database."

Heffler closed the report. "This is your copy, Lieutenant. I've transmitted the master file electronically to the chief of homicide, the homicide analysis unit, and the central investigation and resource division. Is there anyone else who should get it?"

"Not that I can think of." D'Agosta rose, picked up the file. "Dr. Heffler, when Captain Singleton called you, did he mention we also wanted mtDNA analysis?"

"Well, no, because Captain Singleton didn't call me."

D'Agosta looked Heffler in the face. Somebody had definitely kicked this son of a bitch in the ass, and he wanted to know who. "*Someone* must have called you."

"The commissioner."

"The commissioner? You mean Tagliabue? When?"

A hesitation. "At two o'clock this morning."

"Oh, yeah? What did he say?"

"He informed me this is a very important case and that even the slightest problem might be, ah, career ending."

A beat.

And now Heffler smirked. "So good luck, Lieutenant. You have the results you wanted. You've got quite a killer on your hands—let's hope you don't have a . . . problem."

The smile indicated he very much hoped the opposite.

12

AT FIRST GLANCE, THE LIBRARY AT MOUNT Mercy Hospital for the Criminally Insane looked like the typical reading room of any gentlemen's club: dark, polished wood; baroque fixtures; discreet lighting. Closer examination, however, revealed certain unique differences. The wing chairs and wooden refectory tables were immovable, having been screwed to the floor. No sharp objects or heavy, blunt implements were to be seen. The magazines being browsed by the inmates all had their staples removed. And at the room's single entrance stood a muscular man wearing an orderly's uniform.

Dr. John Felder sat at a small round table in a far corner of the library. He was fidgeting with his hands, clearly nervous.

There was movement at the entrance, and he glanced over quickly. Constance Greene stood in the doorway, accompanied by a guard. She looked around, saw him, and came over. She was dressed modestly, in a white pleated skirt and a blouse of the palest lavender. In one hand she held a letter; in the other, an airmail envelope.

"Dr. Felder," she said in her courtly voice as she sat

down across from him. She placed the letter inside the envelope and turned it facedown on the table, but not before Felder noticed that the letter seemed to contain only one word. It was in a strange script, Sanskrit or Marathi or something similar.

He looked from the letter to Constance. "Thank you for seeing me," he replied.

"I did not expect you to return so soon."

"Neither did I. I beg your pardon. It's because..." He stopped, glanced around to make sure they were not being overheard. Despite being reassured, he lowered his voice. "Constance, I'm finding it very difficult to get on with things, knowing that...that you don't trust me."

"I don't understand why that should vex you. I'm simply an ex-patient—no doubt one of many."

"I'd like to find some way I could make it up to you." Felder was unused to talking about his feelings, especially to a patient, and he felt himself flush with both embarrassment and shame. "I don't expect to treat you in the future—I respect your wishes in that regard. It's just that I wish...well, that I could somehow compensate for what happened...for what I did. Make it right. So you could trust me again."

These last words tumbled out in a rush. Constance looked at him, her violet eyes cool and appraising. "Why is this important to you, Doctor?"

"I..." He realized he didn't really know why. Or hadn't examined his feelings closely enough to see.

For a long moment, the table was silent. Then Constance spoke. "Some time ago, you told me you believed I was, in fact, born on Water Street in the 1870s."

"I did say that once, yes."

"Do you still believe it?"

"It...it seems so bizarre, so difficult to comprehend.

And yet I have found nothing to contradict you. In fact, I've found independent evidence to support what you say. Also, I know you're not a liar. And when I examine the clinical issues—*really* look at them—I wonder if you suffer from any psychotic condition at all. You may be emotionally troubled, true, and I'm sure there's some past trauma that continues to haunt you. But I just don't believe you're delusional. And I increasingly doubt if you even threw your child off that ship. Your note to Pendergast seemed to indicate the baby was still alive. I feel like there's something going on here, some ruse or perhaps larger plan, which has yet to be uncovered."

Constance went still.

When she said nothing, he continued. "All circumstantial evidence, of course—but highly persuasive. And then, there's *this*." He extracted his wallet, opened it, and pulled out a small piece of paper. He unfolded it and passed it to Constance. It was a photocopy of an old newspaper engraving, depicting an urban scene of dirty-faced children playing stickball on a tenement street. Standing to one side was another child, thin and frightened, broom in her hand. She was an almost photographic likeness of a young Constance Greene.

"It's from the *New-York Inquirer*, 1879," Felder said. "It's titled *Guttersnipes at Play*."

Constance stared at the engraving for a long time. Then she brushed it gently, almost lovingly, with her fingertips before folding it again and handing it back to Felder. "You keep this in your wallet, Doctor?"

"Yes."

"Why?"

"I, ah, consult it from time to time. Trying to unravel the mystery, I suppose."

Constance continued to regard him. It might have been Felder's imagination, but he thought that the look in her eyes softened. After another moment, she began to speak.

"Back when that engraving was made," she said, "newspaper illustrations were done by artists in the field. They would make pen-and-ink drawings, pencil sketches, charcoal—whatever—of things they felt colorful or newsworthy. They would submit their artwork to the newspaper, where professional engravers would reproduce it in a form that could be printed."

She nodded again at the folded paper, still clasped in Felder's hand. "I recall when that drawing was made. The artist was illustrating a series of articles on the tenement districts of New York. He did that sketch and then, I suppose taken by my appearance, he asked to paint my portrait. My parents were already dead, so he asked my older sister. She agreed. When the work was finished, he gave her his preliminary pencil sketches for the portrait by way of payment."

"Where are those studies?" Felder asked eagerly.

"Long gone. But in gratitude, my sister gave him a lock of my hair in return. Gifts of such locks were very common then. I recall the artist putting the snippet of hair into a small envelope and pasting it to the inside of his portfolio cover."

She paused. "The name of the artist was Alexander Wintour. If you could find his portfolio, perhaps the lock might still be inside. It's a long shot, I admit. But if you did, and the portfolio hadn't been disturbed, a simple DNA test would prove what I say: that I am almost a century and a half old."

"Yes," Felder murmured, shaking his head. "Yes, it would." He wrote down the artist's name on the back of the picture, folded it up, and slipped it back into his wallet. "Thank you again for seeing me, Constance." He stood up.

"Certainly, Doctor."

He shook her hand and exited the library. For the first time in days, he felt a spring in his step, a feeling of renewed vigor in his limbs.

And then, on the front steps of Mount Mercy, he paused again.

Why was Constance doing this? She had always seemed supremely indifferent as to whether people believed her or not. Something had changed.

But what? And why?

13

D'AGOSTA CHECKED HIS CELL PHONE, SAW THAT it was sixty seconds before one o'clock. If what he'd heard about Special Agent Conrad Gibbs was true, the man would be arriving on the dot.

D'Agosta felt uneasy. Most of his previous experience with the FBI had been through Pendergast, and he realized this was probably worse than no preparation at all. Pendergast's methods, operation, and mentality were alien if not hostile to standard FBI culture.

He gave a once-over to the coffee from Starbucks and the dozen doughnuts from Krispy Kreme, laid out on the little sitting area in his office, and then a final glance at his watch.

"Lieutenant D'Agosta?"

And there he was, standing in the door. D'Agosta rose with a smile. His first impression was good. True, Special Agent Gibbs was a product of the mold: buttoned down and by the book, handsome, chiseled, an off-the-rack suit covering his trim physique, his brown hair cut close, his thin lips and narrow face tanned from his past assignment in the Florida Panhandle—D'Agosta had gone out of his way to check up. At the same time, he had an open, pleasant look about him, and the humorless demeanor was far better than a wiseass or better-than-thou attitude.

They shook hands and D'Agosta found Gibbs's grasp firm, not crushing, brief and to the point. He walked around his desk and led the agent to the sitting area, where they both sat down.

They opened with some pleasant chitchat about the weather and the differences between New York and Florida. D'Agosta asked about the agent's last case, which he had concluded with great success—a run-of-the-mill serial killer who scattered the pieces of his victims in the dunes. Gibbs was soft-spoken and clearly intelligent. D'Agosta appreciated the former quality a great deal. Aside from making him easier to work with, it would go a long way with his squad—although, to be sure, most of his squad members were loudmouthed in the typical New York sort of way.

The only problem was, as Gibbs went on about his case, he was starting to sound suspiciously long-winded. And he wasn't eating anything…while D'Agosta was just about dying for a Caramel Kreme Crunch.

"As you probably know, Lieutenant," Gibbs was saying, "down in Quantico we maintain a comprehensive database of serial killers as part of the National Center for the Analysis of Violent Crime. We define a serial killer as follows: a perpetrator who targets strangers, who has killed three or more people, for motives of psychological gratification, usually with a consistent or evolving signature in each killing."

D'Agosta nodded sagely.

"In this case we only have two killings, so it doesn't meet the definition—yet. But I think we all agree there's a high probability of more to come."

"Absolutely."

Gibbs removed a slender folder from his briefcase. "When we first heard from Captain Singleton yesterday morning, we did a quick-and-dirty run-through on our database."

D'Agosta leaned forward. Now things were getting interesting.

"We wanted to find out if there were any other serial killers who left pieces of their own body at the scene, who had the right M.O., et cetera." He laid the folder on the coffee table. "Granted, these are preliminary findings, but we can keep this between ourselves. I'll summarize, if you don't mind."

"Of course."

"We have an organized killer here. Very organized. He is educated, has money, and is comfortable in luxury surroundings. The dismemberment M.O. is not as uncommon as you might think—dozens of serials fit that profile—but usually such killers take away body parts. This one doesn't. In fact, he *leaves* his own body parts at the scene—something completely unique."

"Interesting," said D'Agosta. "Any thoughts on that?"

"The head of our forensic psychology unit is working that angle. He believes the killer identifies with the victim. He's essentially killing himself serially. He is someone full of self-loathing who was almost certainly abused sexually and psychologically as a child, told he was no good, better off dead or not born, that sort of thing."

"That makes sense."

"The aggressor appears normal on the surface. Since he has no inhibitions and will say anything to get what he wants, and very convincingly, he can be charming and even charismatic. Underneath, however, he is a deeply pathological individual, utterly lacking in empathy."

"Why does he kill?"

"That's the crux of the matter: he almost certainly has libidinous gratification."

"Libidinous? But no semen was found and there doesn't seem to be a sexual component. And his second victim was an older man."

"Correct. Let me explain something. Our database is built on what we call aggregates and correlations. What I'm telling you about this killer is based on a high degree of correlation with dozens of others with a similar profile and M.O. It's also based on interviews with over two thousand serial killers who answered questions about why and how they did what they did. It's not infallible, but it's pretty damn close. Everything points to this killer getting a sexual charge out of what he's doing."

Still doubtful, D'Agosta nodded anyway.

"To continue: The crimes had a sexual gratification component. That gratification comes from sexual excitement generated by two things: a feeling of control and power over the victim, and the presence of blood. The sex of the victim is less important. The lack of the presence of semen may only mean the killer did not climax or did so clothed. The latter is common."

D'Agosta shifted in his chair. That doughnut wasn't looking quite so appetizing now.

"Another commonality is that this type of serial homicide involves a large ritual component. The killer receives gratification from killing in the same way, in the same sequence, using the same knife, and inflicting the same mutilation to the corpse."

D'Agosta nodded again.

"He has a job. Probably a good one. This type of killer only operates in an environment he knows well, and so we may find that he is either an ex-employee or, more likely, a former guest of both hotels."

"We're already running the guest lists and employee lists against each other, and against a description of the perp."

"Excellent." Gibbs took a deep breath. He certainly was a talker, but D'Agosta wasn't about to stop him. "His expertise with a knife is high, which means he may use one in his profession or simply be a knife aficionado. He has a lot of self-confidence. He's arrogant. This is another prime characteristic of this type of killer. He thinks nothing of being caught on security videos; he taunts the police and believes he can control the investigation. Hence the messages left behind."

"I was wondering about those messages—if you had any specific theories, I mean."

"As I said, they are taunting."

"Any idea who they're directed at?"

A smile spread over Gibbs's face. "They aren't directed at anyone in particular."

"*Happy Birthday*? You don't think that was directed at anyone?"

"No. This type of serial killer mocks the police, but doesn't as a rule single out individual investigators, particularly in the beginning. We're all the same to him—the faceless enemy. The birthday is probably generic or might refer to any anniversary—perhaps even that of the perp himself. Something you also might look into."

"Good idea. But isn't it possible these messages might be directed at someone who isn't a cop?"

"Highly unlikely." Gibbs patted the folder. "There are a few other things in here: the aggressor was probably abandoned by his mother; he lives alone; he has poor relationships with the opposite sex or, if he is homosexual, with his own sex. Finally, something happened very recently that set him off: rejection by a lover, loss of a job, or—this is most likely of all—the death of his mother."

Gibbs sat back with a satisfied expression on his face.

"That's your prelim?" D'Agosta asked.

"We'll refine it considerably as we feed in more information. The database is extremely powerful." Gibbs looked D'Agosta in the eye. "I have to say, Lieutenant, you certainly have done well bringing us this problem. The BSU is the best in the world at this. I promise, we'll work closely with you, tread lightly, respect your people, and share everything on a real-time basis."

D'Agosta nodded. You couldn't ask for more than that.

After Gibbs had left, D'Agosta sat in the armchair for a long time. As he chewed thoughtfully on the Caramel Kreme Crunch, he thought about what Gibbs had said concerning the killer and his motive. It made sense. Maybe too much sense.

God, he could really use Pendergast right now.

He shook his head, polished off the doughnut, licked his fingers, and with a supreme act of will shut the box.

14

D'AGOSTA BLEW OFF THE DOORMAN BY FLASH-
ing his badge and walking right on past the pillbox,
not even making eye contact, the man hurrying behind
with a "Sir? Sir? Whom are you visiting?" D'Agosta
called out Pendergast's name and apartment number
loudly and headed for the interior courtyard.

The elevator operator proved to be a little more
stubborn, requiring an overt threat about obstruction
of justice before he reluctantly closed the old-fashioned
grillwork doors and ascended to Pendergast's suite of
apartments.

D'Agosta had been in the Dakota many times before,
and he was usually struck by the scent, a mixture of beeswax polish, old wood, and a faint overlay of leather. Everything about the place was genteel and old-fashioned, from
the polished brass of the elevator knobs and trim, to the
hushed carpeting, to the lovely travertine walls with their
nineteenth-century sconces. He noticed very little of this
now. He was sick with worry about Pendergast. For days
he'd been waiting for the shoe to drop, waiting for the
pressure cooker to explode. Nothing. And that was probably worse than any explosion.

The doorman had called up, of course, so when D'Agosta pressed the buzzer the intercom came quickly to life.

"Vincent?"

"I need to talk to you. Please."

A long, long silence.

"On what subject?"

There was a strange quality to Pendergast's voice that gave D'Agosta the creeps. Maybe it was the electronic rasp of the intercom.

"Could you let me in?"

Another odd pause.

"No, thank you."

D'Agosta took this in. *No, thank you?* He sounded bad. He recalled Hayward's advice and decided to give it a try.

"Look, Pendergast, there's been a couple of murders. A serial killer. I really need your advice."

"I'm not interested."

D'Agosta took a deep breath. "I won't take up more than a minute or two. I'd like to see you. It's been a while. We need to talk, catch up, I need to find out what's been going on, how you're doing. You've had a terrible shock—"

"Pray leave the premises and do not bother me again."

His voice sounded even more cold, stilted, and formal than usual. D'Agosta waited a moment, and then said gently, "That's what I'm not going to do. I'm going to stand here, annoying you, until you let me in. I'll stay here all night, if necessary."

That finally got through. After a long moment, the locks began turning, one after the other. The door opened slowly, and D'Agosta entered the foyer. Pendergast, dressed in a black dressing gown, had already turned his back and uttered no greeting. D'Agosta followed him into the reception room, the one with the bonsai trees and the wall of water.

Moving listlessly, Pendergast turned and seated himself, folding his hands in front, and raised his head to look at D'Agosta.

D'Agosta froze. He couldn't believe what he saw. The man's face was collapsed, gray, his normally silver eyes as dull and heavy as old lead. His clasped hands were shaking, ever so slightly.

He launched in gamely. "Pendergast, I just wanted you to know how sorry I am about Helen's death. I don't know what your plans are, but I'm one hundred percent behind you—however you want to go about nailing the bastards."

There seemed to be no reaction whatsoever to this.

"We need to get a...ah, death certificate, determination of homicide. We'll need to exhume the body, go through the legal crap with Mexico. I'm not sure what's involved, but you can bet we'll expedite the hell out of it. We will get her a decent burial in the States. And then we'll launch an investigation hammer and tongs—FBI, of course, they'll back up one of their own. There's NYPD involvement, too, and I'll make damn sure our resources are deployed, big-time. We will get those scumbags, I guarantee it."

He stopped, breathing heavily. Pendergast's eyes were lidded; he seemed to have gone to sleep. D'Agosta stared. This was even worse than he thought. As he looked at his old friend and partner, a terrible realization dawned on him, hitting him like a shock of high voltage.

"Jesus Christ. You're using."

"Using?" Pendergast murmured.

"On drugs."

A drawn-out silence.

D'Agosta felt a sudden welling of anger. "I've seen it a thousand times. You're on drugs."

Pendergast made a small gesture with his hand. "And?"

"And? *And?*" D'Agosta rose from his chair. He flushed. He had seen so much bullshit, so much death and murder and ridiculously pointless suffering caused by drugs. He hated drugs.

He faced Pendergast. "I can't believe it. I thought you were smarter than this. Where are they?"

No answer. Just a grimace.

D'Agosta couldn't stand it. "Where are the drugs?" he asked, his voice louder. When Pendergast didn't respond, he felt rage take over. He was standing by the bookshelves and pulled a book off a shelf, another. "Where are the drugs?" He knocked one of the bonsais with the back of his hand, sweeping it off its table. "*Where are the drugs?* I'm not leaving here until I have them. You fucking *idiot!*"

"Your working-class expletives have lost their charm."

At least this was a flash of the old Pendergast. D'Agosta stood there, shaking, and realized he had better get a handle on his anger.

"This apartment is very large, and most of the doors are securely locked."

D'Agosta felt crazy. He struggled to maintain control. "Listen, about Helen. I know what a horrible tragedy—"

At this Pendergast interrupted him, his voice cold. "Do not mention Helen's name or what happened. Ever again."

"Right. Okay. I won't, but you can't just...I mean..." He shook his head, truly at a loss for words.

"You mentioned you needed help with a murder

case. I have told you I'm not interested. Now, if there's nothing else, may I ask you to leave?"

Instead, D'Agosta sat down heavily, put his head in his hands. Maybe the murder investigation would be the thing Pendergast needed to snap him out of this, although he doubted it. He rubbed his face, raised his head. "Let me just tell you about the case—okay?"

"If you must."

D'Agosta smoothed his hands down over his legs, took a couple of breaths. "Have you been following the papers?"

"No."

"I have a summary of the case here." D'Agosta removed the three-page brief he had printed out earlier and handed it to Pendergast. The agent took it and scanned it perfunctorily, his eyes dull, unresponsive. But he didn't hand it back right away; he continued looking at it, flipping the pages. Then, after a moment, he started from the beginning and began reading again, this time more closely.

When he looked up, D'Agosta thought he caught a gleam of something in the agent's eyes. But, no—it was his imagination.

"Um, I thought the case was sort of up your alley. We've got this special agent from the BSU assigned. A fellow named Gibbs. Conrad Gibbs. You know him?"

Pendergast slowly shook his head.

"He's got a lot of theories. All very pat. But this case...well, it seemed custom-made for you. I've got a binder here with the preliminary crime-scene analysis, lab reports, autopsy, forensics, DNA—the works." He slipped it out of his briefcase and held it up, questioningly. When there was no response, he laid it down on a table.

"Can I count on your help? Even if it's just an informal opinion?"

"I regret I won't have time to look through this material before I leave."

"Leave? Where are you going?"

Pendergast rose, ponderously, his black dressing gown cloaking him like a figure of the grim reaper himself. That gleam D'Agosta imagined he saw had certainly been a figment of his hopes: the eyes were duller than ever.

Pendergast offered D'Agosta his hand. It was as cold as a dead mackerel. But then it unexpectedly tightened and, in a much warmer voice, if strained, Pendergast said: "Good-bye, my dear Vincent."

Pendergast closed the door to his apartment. He walked toward the door leading out of the reception room, but paused, then turned, hesitating. His face betrayed an extreme inner turmoil. Finally, he seemed to make a decision. He walked over to the table, picked up the thick binder, and flipped it open, beginning to read.

For two hours he stood there, stock-still. And then he laid it down. His lips moved and he spoke a single word.

"Diogenes."

15

THE 1959 ROLLS-ROYCE SILVER WRAITH PURRED up the northern reaches of Riverside Drive, the glow of the streetlamps and traffic lights reflecting off its polished surfaces. Passing 137th Street, it slowed, then turned in to a driveway bordered by a tall wrought-iron fence, its gate standing open. Moving past barren ailanthus and sumac bushes, the vehicle came to a stop beneath the porte cochere of a large Beaux-Arts mansion, its marble-and-brick façade rising four stories into the gloom, mansard roof topped by a crenellated widow's walk. There was a flicker of lightning overhead, followed by a growl of thunder. A cold wind swept off the Hudson. It was only six PM, but early December in New York City was already under cover of night.

Agent Pendergast got out of the car. In the dim light, his face was pale, and even in the chill air it was beaded with sweat. As he stepped toward an oaken door set into the pillared entrance, there was a rustle in the shrubbery at the rear of the carriage drive. He turned toward the noise to see Corrie Swanson emerge from the gloom. She looked inexpressibly dirty, her clothes creased and muddy, her hair matted, her face smudged.

A torn, frayed knapsack hung from one shoulder. She glanced both ways, like a skittish colt, then darted up to him.

"Agent Pendergast!" she said in a hoarse whisper. "Where have you been? I've been freezing my ass here for days waiting for you! I'm in trouble."

Without waiting to hear more, he unlocked the door and ushered her inside.

He closed the heavy door, then snapped on a light, revealing an entryway with a polished marble floor and walls of dark velvet. He led the way into a long, refectory-like space of carved gothic fixtures, and then beyond to a large reception hall, lined by glass-fronted cabinets. Proctor, Pendergast's chauffeur, stood stiffly in a bathrobe, leaning on a crutch, apparently roused by the sound of their entrance.

"Proctor, please have Mrs. Trask run a bath for Miss Swanson," Pendergast said. "And have her clothes washed and pressed, please."

Corrie turned toward him. "But—"

"I'll await you in the library."

Ninety minutes later, feeling renewed, Corrie walked into the library. The room was dark, and no fire had been laid on. Pendergast was seated in a wing chair in a far corner, motionless and almost invisible. There was something about his presence—a restless stillness, if such a thing were possible—that gave her an odd feeling.

She took a seat opposite him. Pendergast sat, his fingers tented, his eyes half closed. Feeling unaccountably nervous, she hurried into her story. She told him about Betterton, his accusations and theories about Pendergast, the yacht, and her crazy decision to break into the house on East End he had mentioned to her.

While she spoke, Pendergast had seemed distant,

almost as if he wasn't listening. But the mention of the house seemed to catch his attention.

"You engaged in breaking and entering," he said.

"I know, I know." Corrie colored. "I'm stupid, but you already know that . . ." She tried to laugh and found no corresponding amusement—or even reaction—in him. Pendergast was weirder than usual. She took a deep breath and went on. "The place looked like it'd been deserted for years. So I broke in. And you won't believe what I found. It's some kind of Nazi safe house. Stacks of *Mein Kampf* in the basement, old radio equipment, and even a torture room. Upstairs it looked like they were packing up to leave. I found a room full of documents in the process of being shredded."

She paused, waited. Still no reaction.

"I rifled through the documents, thinking they might be important. A lot of them were covered with swastikas and dated back to the war. Some were stamped STRENG GEHEIM, which I later found out means 'top secret' in German. And then I saw the name Esterhazy."

At this, Pendergast woke up. "Esterhazy?"

"Your late wife's maiden name, right? I learned that researching the website."

An incline of the head. God, he looked awful.

"Anyway," she went on, "I stuffed as many documents as I could into my knapsack. But then—" She paused. The memory was still so fresh. "A Nazi caught me. He tried to kill me. I sprayed the mother with capsicum and managed to get away. I've been scared shitless and on the run ever since, living in shelters and hanging out in Bryant Park. I haven't been in my apartment, I haven't been at school. All this time I've been just trying to *reach* you!" Quite suddenly, she felt herself on the verge of tears. She forced them back roughly.

"You wouldn't answer the phone. I couldn't stake out the Dakota, those doormen are like the KGB."

When he did not respond, she reached into her knapsack, pulled out the sheaf of papers, and put them on an end table. "Here they are."

Pendergast did not look at the papers. He seemed to have gone far away again. Now, with her spike of anxiety ebbing, Corrie looked at him more closely. He was shockingly thin, even gaunt, and in the dim light she could see the bags under his eyes, the paleness of his skin. But most surprising of all was his demeanor. While his movements were usually languid, you nevertheless had a sense that it was the languor of a cat: a coiled spring, ready to strike out at any moment. But Corrie did not have that sense now. Pendergast seemed unfocused, detached, barely interested in her story. He seemed little concerned by what had happened to her, the danger she had put herself in for his sake.

"Pendergast," she said. "Are you all right? You look...sort of funny. I'm sorry, but you do."

He waved this away as he might a fly. "These so-called Nazis. Did they get your name?"

"No."

"Did you leave anything behind that might lead them to your identity?"

"I don't think so. Everything I had was in this." And she nudged the knapsack with her foot.

"Any indication that they've been tracking you?"

"I don't think so. But I stayed underground. Those guys were freaking *scary*."

"And the address of this safe house?"

"Four Twenty-Eight East End Avenue."

He fell silent for a minute before rousing himself to speech once again. "They don't know who you are. They have no way of finding you, short of happening upon you by accident. That is of course unlikely, but we shall reduce the likelihood even further." He glanced at her. "Is there someplace you can stay? With friends, perhaps? Somewhere out of town?"

Corrie was shocked. She'd just assumed that Pendergast would take her in, protect her, help her deal with the situation. "What's wrong with here?"

There was a protracted silence. Then Pendergast let out a deep, shuddering breath. "Without going into detail, the fact is that, at present, I am simply incapable of looking after your well-being. In fact, I am so preoccupied that I could actually pose a threat to your safety. If you rely on me, you place yourself in grave danger. Besides, New York City is the one place you stand a chance, however small, of coming in contact with these people. Now: is there anyplace else you can go? I can guarantee that you'll get there safely, and have sufficient funds—beyond that, you will be on your own."

This was so unexpected that Corrie felt herself in a kind of daze. Where the hell could she go? Her mother was still in Medicine Creek, Kansas, of course—but she swore she'd die before she ever set foot in that shit hole again.

"My father lives near Allentown," she said, dubiously.

Pendergast—whose expression had once again turned distant—returned to her. "Yes. I do recall your mentioning that. Do you know where he lives?"

Already Corrie was regretting bringing up her father. "I have his address. I haven't seen him since he skipped out on my mom, what, fifteen years ago?"

Pendergast reached over, pressed a small button beneath the end table. A minute later, Proctor was standing in the doorway to the library. Even with the crutch, he looked immensely powerful.

Pendergast turned to him. "Proctor, please call our

private livery service. I would like them to take Miss Swanson to an address she will give them outside Allentown, Pennsylvania. Provide her with three thousand dollars and a new cell phone."

Proctor nodded. "Very well, sir."

Corrie looked from Pendergast to Proctor and back again. "I still don't believe it. You're just telling me to turn tail and run?"

"I've explained that necessity already. You'll be safer with your father, especially given that you've had no recent contact with him. You need to stay away for at least a month, perhaps two. Use only cash—no credit or debit cards. Destroy the SIM card, throw away your old cell phone, and don't transfer the contacts except by hand. Contact me—that is, Proctor—when you plan to return."

"What if I don't want to go stay with my loser dad?" Corrie fumed.

"These people whose safe house you invaded, who you robbed of highly incriminating documents, are not to be underestimated. You do not want them to find you."

"But..." This was unreal. She started to get mad. "What about school?"

"Of what use will school be to a dead person?" Pendergast said evenly.

She stood up. "Goddamn it, what's going on with you?" She paused, looked at him more closely. "Are you sick?"

"Yes."

Even as he spoke, she realized the sweat was streaming down his brow. Jesus, he really *was* sick. It explained a lot. She struggled to overcome her irritation. She had been so terrified these past few weeks, and maybe Pendergast was right to want her to hide.

"I'm sorry." She sat down abruptly. "I just don't like the idea of running away. Who are these people and what the hell is going on?"

"I'm afraid that information would put you in greater danger."

"Let me stay and help with whatever's troubling you." She managed a smile. "We made a good team once."

For the first time, he seemed affected. "I appreciate the gesture," he said in a low, even voice. "Truly, I do. But I require no help. At this moment, in fact, all that I require is solitude."

She remained in her seat. She'd forgotten what a pain in the ass Pendergast could be.

"Proctor is waiting."

For a moment, she just stared. Then, without another word, she got up, picked up her knapsack, and strode out of the library.

After Corrie had left, Pendergast sat, motionless, in the darkened room. Ten minutes later, he heard the distant sound of a door closing. At this, he rose and walked over to one of the bookshelves. He pulled out a particularly large and hoary old volume from it, which produced a muffled clicking sound. The entire bookshelf swung away from the wall. Behind it stood a folding brass gate that opened onto a solid maple door: the hidden service elevator to the mansion's basement. Pendergast stepped in, pressed a button, and rode the elevator down to the basement. Getting out, he progressed through long and secret corridors to an ancient stairway, hewn from the living rock, that corkscrewed down into darkness. Descending this staircase to the mansion's vast and rambling sub-basement, he made his way through a series of dimly lit chambers and galleries, perfumed with the scent of ages, until he came to a room full of long tables covered with modern laboratory equipment. Turning up the light, he strode over to a device that looked like a cross between a fax machine and a modern cash register. He sat down before the machine, turned it on, and pressed a button on its side. A wide tray in its front panel popped free. Inside were a number of small, squat test tubes. Taking one out, Pendergast held it between thumb and forefinger. Then—plucking a lancet from his jacket pocket—he pricked his other thumb, took a blood sample, placed it into the test tube, inserted it in the machine, pressed a series of buttons, and settled down to wait.

16

DR. FELDER CROSSED SEVENTY-SEVENTH STREET, rounded the corner onto Central Park West, climbed a short set of broad steps, and walked into the dimly lit confines of the New-York Historical Society. The austere Beaux-Arts building had recently undergone an extensive renovation, and Felder looked around the public entrance curiously. Although the galleries and library had been subjected to a painstaking twenty-first-century face-lift, the institution as a whole seemed firmly rooted—or perhaps mired—in the past, as the hyphen in its name New-York made abundantly clear.

He approached the research information desk. "Dr. Felder to see Fenton Goodbody."

The woman at the desk consulted her computer screen. "Just a minute. I'll call him."

She picked up a phone, dialed. "A Dr. Felder to see you, Mr. Goodbody." She hung up. "He'll be right down."

"Thank you."

Ten minutes passed. Felder had ample time to examine the entrance hall in its entirety before Mr. Goodbody appeared. He was tall, bespectacled, heavyset, and florid, in perhaps his early sixties. He wore a hairy tweed suit with a matching vest.

"Dr. Felder," he puffed, wiping his palms on the vest before shaking hands. "Sorry to keep you waiting."

"No problem."

"I hope you don't mind if we make this quick? It's already half past eight, you know, and this evening we close at nine."

"That should be fine, thank you."

"In that case, follow me, if you please."

Goodbody led the way past the research desk, along an echoing passageway, through a door, down a narrow staircase, along a second, far more institutional passageway, and then into a large room whose walls were completely covered by metal shelving stuffed to bursting with material: large archival boxes, yellowing papers tied up in dusty ribbons, rolled documents, volumes bound in crumbling leather, accordion files labeled in copperplate script. Felder looked around, his nose itching. He had heard stories of the historical society—of its endless, almost uncatalogable collections of documents and artwork—but this was the first time he had set foot inside.

"Now let me see." Goodbody took a scrap of paper from his pocket, removed the glasses from his nose, folded them, put them in his jacket pocket, held the scrap of paper an inch from his eyes. "Ah, yes. J-14-2140." He put the paper back in his pocket, removed the spectacles, polished them with the fat end of his tie, and seated them assertively back on his nose. Then he strode over to a far wall. Felder waited while the older man searched, first high, then low, without success.

"Now, where in blazes...I was just looking at them...Ah! Here we go." Goodbody reached over, seized a stack of oversize sheets, and brought them to a nearby desk. They were awkwardly held together by loose covers tied with string. Beaming at Felder, Goodbody dropped the assemblage lightly onto the wooden surface. A puff of dust arose.

"So, Dr. Felder," Goodbody said, indicating a chair set before the desk. "You're interested in the work of Alexander Wintour?"

Felder nodded as he took a seat. He could feel a four-alarm allergic reaction building in his nose. He didn't want to open his mouth until the dust had settled.

"Well, you will probably be the first. I doubt anyone besides myself has examined these since they were originally donated. Following your query, I was able to dig up some information on the man." Goodbody paused. "Just what is your doctorate in again? Art history?"

"Ah, yes, that's right," Felder said quickly. He hadn't given any thought to what his cover story should be—or even considered he might need one. The lie had come quickly and thoughtlessly, and now he was stuck with it.

"Then if you'll show me your credentials, we'll be all set."

Felder looked up. "My credentials?"

"Your research credentials, yes."

"I, ah, I'm afraid I don't have them with me at present."

Goodbody looked surprised and pained. "Don't have your credentials? Oh, dear. Oh, dear, that is a shame." He paused. "Well, I can't leave you here by yourself. With the collections, I mean. Rules, you understand."

"There isn't any way for me to . . . examine these?"

"I shall have to stay with you. Remember, half an hour's all we can allow, I'm afraid."

"That will do." Felder wasn't especially eager to stay any longer than necessary.

His guest's compliance seemed to restore Goodbody's equanimity. "Well, then! Let's see what we have." He untied the string, removed the cover. Beneath was a sheet of heavy, textured paper, its surface almost entirely obscured by dust.

"Stand back!" Goodbody said. He fetched a deep breath, then blew laterally across the sheet. A gray mushroom cloud arose that briefly obscured the archivist.

"As I said, I did come across some material on Wintour," came the disembodied voice of Goodbody. "Notes in the accession files dating back to when this donation was accepted. It seems he was the lead illustrator for the *Bowery Illustrated News*, a weekly periodical published in the final decades of the nineteenth century. That's how he earned his living. But what he really wanted was to be a painter. It seems he was fascinated by the lower classes of Manhattan."

The dust had cleared again, and Felder could make out the image on the paper. It was a painting, oil by the look of it, of a young boy sitting on the front steps of a brownstone. He held a ball in one hand and a stick in the other, and he was looking straight out of the frame with a somewhat truculent expression.

"Ah, yes," Goodbody murmured, glancing down at it.

Carefully, Felder turned it over and placed it to one side. Beneath was another painting, this one of a large storefront, the label R & N MORTENSON WOODEN & WILLOW WARE above it. Four children were leaning out the lower course of windows, again with rather sullen expressions on their faces.

Felder turned to the next. A boy, sitting in the back

of what appeared to be a brewer's wagon. The street beneath was very uneven, full of rubble and broken stoneware. On the verso, somebody—probably Wintour—had scrawled WORTH & BAXTER STREETS, 1879.

Several similar paintings followed. They were mostly studies of young men and women, framed by lower-class Manhattan backgrounds. A few showed men at work or children at play. Others were more formal portraits, either head-and-shoulders or full-length poses.

"Wintour was never able to sell his work," Goodbody said. "After his death, his family—despairing of disposing with them any other way—offered everything to the society. We couldn't accept the sketches, studies, and albums—space considerations, you understand—but we took the paintings. He was, after all, a New York artist, if a minor one."

Felder was looking at a painting of two boys playing hoops before a storefront whose banner read COOPER'S GLUE. BY THE BARREL. AT HIS PRICES. He wasn't surprised Wintour had not had more success selling his work: by and large, the paintings were rather mediocre. It wasn't the settings, he thought, so much as a sort of artistic indifference, a lack of vitality in the faces and the poses.

He turned to the next sheet—and was utterly transfixed.

There, staring out at him, was Constance Greene. Or rather, Constance Greene as she would have looked at around six years of age. This time, Wintour had risen to the level of his subject matter. It was similar to the engraving Felder had seen in the newspaper, *Guttersnipes at Play*, only infinitely more life-like: the turn of the eyebrows, the faintly pouting lips, the drape of the hair, were unmistakable. Only the eyes were different. These eyes were quintessentially child-like: innocent, a little frightened perhaps. Not at all like the eyes that had looked into his own in the reading room at Mount Mercy that very morning.

"Now, *that* one is quite nice," Goodbody said. "Quite nice indeed. A candidate for display, perhaps?"

Hurriedly, as if waking up from a trance, Felder turned the page. He didn't want Goodbody to see how powerfully the portrait had affected him—and for some obscure reason he didn't like the idea of it being put on public display, either.

He moved rather quickly through the rest, but there were no more of Constance, and there was no lock of hair to be found.

"Do you know where I might find more of his work, Mr. Goodbody?" he asked. "I'm particularly interested in the albums and sketches you mentioned."

"I'm afraid I have no idea. Our records indicate his family lived in Southport, Connecticut. Perhaps you might try there."

"I'll do that." Felder stood up, wobbling slightly and catching his balance on a shelf support. The portrait had thoroughly shaken him up. "Thank you so much for your time and effort."

Goodbody beamed. "The society is always happy to help art historians in their research. Ah: it's just nine o'clock now. Come—let me escort you back upstairs."

17

THE LIBRARY IN THE RIVERSIDE DRIVE MAN-
sion was cold and dark, the dead ashes of the fireplace
heaped with unopened mail. A long table that normally stood in one corner had been dragged into the
middle of the room and was now piled with printouts
and photographs, some of which had fallen to the floor
and been trodden on. An oaken panel at one end of the
library stood open, exposing a flat-screen monitor on
which an endless loop played, over and over, of a man
standing in the lobby of a hotel.

Pendergast moved restlessly around the room, like a
caged animal, pausing sometimes to stare at the monitor, at other times stopping to lean over the disordered
papers on the table, shuffling them about, examining one or another and then tossing it back into the
heap with an impatient gesture. It was a strange colla-
tion of documents, mostly fluorescent photographs of
gel electrophoresis plates, covered with shadowy lines
and wavering squiggles of DNA molecules, like blurry
photographs of the spirits of the dead. He picked up
one, then another—held them side by side, his hands
trembling—and then let both fall back into the heap.

Straightening up, he walked across the library to a small wheeled sideboard covered with bottles, poured himself a glass of Amontillado, drank it down in one gulp, filled the glass again, the liquor slopping over the rim, and drank that down as well.

Once again he began pacing. He wore no jacket—it lay slung across a chair. His tie was pulled down, his shirt rumpled. His pale blond hair was damp, and his face was covered with an unhealthy sheen of sweat.

The clock on the mantelpiece chimed out midnight.

Another turn brought him back before the bottle of Amontillado. He poured the glass, raised it to drink, but—after a moment's hesitation—put it back down, untasted, with such force that it broke the stem, spilling the pale amber liquid.

He ignored this and resumed pacing, pausing a moment before the fireplace, where he jabbed at the dead ashes with a poker, mixing the freshly strewn letters with the dead coals.

Next, he stopped in front of the monitor and made a sustained effort to watch. Picking up the remote, he jabbed repeatedly at it with his spidery fingers, paging through the video frame by frame, peering intently at the man in the dark suit entering, standing, and leaving the lobby. He moved closer to the screen, his gaze lingering especially on the face of the man, his bearing, the way he walked, gauging his height and weight. Another impatient jab and a new video came on, this one of the same man—or was it?—striding confidently down the hallway of a different hotel lobby. Pendergast watched the two videos again and again, in slow, fast, and stop motion, zooming in, zooming out, in an endless loop of lobby-corridor-lobby-corridor, before at last tossing the remote onto a chair and moving back to the sideboard.

He took up another delicate glass with a trembling hand, spilling the sherry as he poured it, and drank it down as well, seeking to dull the edge of withdrawal with the effects of alcohol, even though he knew he was only prolonging the agony.

Another turn around the room, and then he stopped. A large, muscular figure had appeared in the door, holding a silver tray. His face, in shadow, was entirely unreadable.

"What is it, Proctor?" Pendergast asked sharply.

"If there's nothing else, sir, I'm going to bed."

Proctor waited for instructions, but when Pendergast said nothing he vanished a little painfully into the gloom. As soon as he was gone Pendergast resumed his pacing, his obsessive watching and rewatching of the videos, his repeated checking of the documents on the table.

In midstride, abruptly, he stopped and turned. "Proctor?" he said, not in a loud voice.

The shape materialized again in the doorway. "Yes?"

"On second thought, bring around the car, if you please."

"May I ask where we're going?"

"One Police Plaza."

When Vincent D'Agosta was immersed in a particularly complex case, he found the hours from midnight to two to be an ideal time to gather his thoughts, reorder his files, and—most important—set up the corkboard he used as a way to arrange evidence in space and time, to connect the dots of the case. The corkboard covered half a wall, and over the years had become a bit shabby looking, but it was still serviceable. Now it was one in the morning and D'Agosta was standing before it, affixing a stack of index cards, photographs, and Post-it notes to the board with pushpins and connecting pieces of string.

"Ah, Lieutenant. One o'clock and still hard at work, I see."

D'Agosta turned to see Special Agent Conrad Gibbs leaning on the open door frame, a smile on his face. D'Agosta tried to tamp down the bubbling spring of irritation he felt at the interruption. "Good evening, Agent Gibbs."

They had established a formal, strictly professional relationship, which suited D'Agosta just fine.

"May I?" Gibbs gestured himself an invitation to enter.

D'Agosta couldn't think of a way to say no. "Sure, come on in."

Gibbs strode in, hands behind his back. He nodded at the corkboard with his nose. "Now, that's a blast from the past. We used to do that sort of thing years ago, when I was at Quantico. We've switched over to computers. In fact—" Gibbs smiled—"I've recently started mapping cases on my trusty iPad." He tapped his leather briefcase.

"I prefer the old-fashioned way, I guess," said D'Agosta.

Gibbs examined the corkboard. "Nice. Except I can't read your handwriting all that well."

D'Agosta told himself Gibbs was just trying to be friendly. "The good sisters at Holy Cross never could beat good handwriting into me, I'm afraid."

"Too bad." Gibbs didn't seem to see any humor in this. Then he brightened. "I'm glad I found you here at this late hour. I just came up to drop something off." He laid his briefcase on top of the mess on D'Agosta's desk, flipped the latches, opened it, and took out a fat binder. Without a word, but with a face tinged with pride, he proffered it to D'Agosta.

D'Agosta took it. The cover was emblazoned with

the seals of the FBI and Behavioral Science Unit, and read:

The Federal Bureau of Investigation
Behavioral Science Unit

and

The National Center for the Analysis of Violent Crime
Behavioral Analysis—Unit 2

**THE HOTEL KILLER:
A PRELIMINARY ASSESSMENT**

Profile & Modus Operandi

Threat Assessment Perspective

"That was fast," said D'Agosta, hefting the report. "So you're calling him 'the Hotel Killer'?"

"You know how we are at the FBI," said Gibbs with a little laugh. "Always got to have a name for everything. The papers have given him a variety of names—we picked the most suitable one."

D'Agosta wasn't sure the hotel industry, or the mayor for that matter, was going to like the nickname, but he said nothing. He was going to get along with the FBI if it was the last thing he did.

"We're throwing our full resources at this case," Gibbs said. "Because, as you'll see from that assessment, we believe the Hotel Killer is just getting started and that the killings are likely to accelerate. On top of that, we're dealing with an exceptionally sophisticated and organized perp. This case is big now, but it's going to be huge if we don't stop him."

"Is this my copy?"

"It surely is. Happy reading."

As Gibbs turned to go, he almost collided with a gaunt, spare figure in black that had strangely materialized in the door frame.

D'Agosta glanced up. Pendergast.

He looked like a real, honest-to-God zombie. There was no other way to describe him: the clothes hanging on him like a death shroud, the eyes bleached almost to whiteness, the face hollow and cadaverous.

"Excuse me," said Gibbs distractedly, trying to pass. But instead of letting him go, Pendergast moved to block him while extending his hand, a thin but ghastly smile forming on his death-mask features.

"Supervisory Agent in Charge Gibbs? I am Special Agent Pendergast."

Gibbs stopped dead, quickly gathering his wits. He took Pendergast's hand. "Good to meet you, Agent Pendergast. Um, or have we already met?"

"No, alas," said Pendergast. His tone of voice alarmed D'Agosta, it was so unlike him.

"Well, well," said Gibbs. "And what brings you here?"

Pendergast stepped into the office and silently pointed at the fat binder in D'Agosta's hands.

At this, Gibbs became confused. "You're...assigned to the Hotel Killer case? I'm sorry, this is quite a surprise—no one informed me."

"No one informed you, Agent Gibbs, because I have not yet been assigned to the case. But I will be. Oh, yes: I most certainly will be."

Gibbs's confusion seemed to deepen, and he seemed to struggle to maintain a professional demeanor at unwelcome news. "I see. And your department and area of expertise are...what, if I may ask?"

Instead of answering, Pendergast laid a pseudo-friendly hand on Gibbs's shoulder. "I can see, Agent

Gibbs, that you and I are not only going to be colleagues working hand in glove, but we are also going to be *good* friends."

"I look forward to it," said Gibbs uneasily.

Pendergast patted Gibbs on the shoulder, and—D'Agosta thought he saw—gave it the slightest of pushes, as if propelling the man toward the door. "We shall see you tomorrow, Agent Gibbs?"

"Yes," said Gibbs. He had recovered his equanimity, but he was clearly put out, and his face was darkening. "Yes, we shall. And then I would be glad to exchange credentials with you, hear about your background, and properly liaise our two departments."

"We shall *liaise* until you are surfeited," said Pendergast, turning his back on Gibbs in a gesture of dismissal. A moment later Gibbs left.

"What the fuck?" said D'Agosta, his voice low. "You just made a big-time enemy…What's gotten into you?"

"What the *fuck* indeed," said Pendergast, the foul word sounding unnatural in his mouth. "You asked me to be involved. I am involved." He plucked the report from D'Agosta's hands, flipped through it in the most cursory manner, and then casually dropped it into the trash can beside D'Agosta's desk.

"What is that charming word you are so fond of employing?" he asked. "Bullshit. Even without reading it, I can tell you that report is pure, unadulterated bullshit, still warm from the cloaca in which it formed."

"Um, why do you say that?"

"Because I *know* who the killer is. My brother, Diogenes."

18

THE MAN CALLING HIMSELF ALBAN LORIMER SAT
back on his haunches and wiped one leather-gloved
hand across his forehead. He was breathing heavily—
dejointing a body of this size with the relatively small
tools at hand was hard work—but he was in good shape
and he relished the exertion.

This one had been the best yet. The hotel—the
Royal Cheshire—was glorious indeed, with its sleek,
beautifully understated lobby clad in whites and blacks.
It had a very intimate feel, which made his job more
difficult but at the same time more of a challenge. The
hotel's personality was a little harder to describe than
the first two. A member of the peerage, perhaps, the
product of a great many generations of breeding and
refinement, with money and style but without the least
need for vulgar display. This particular fifteenth-floor
suite was tasty indeed.

And the young woman—he'd made sure it was a
young woman—had proven most satisfactory. She had
struggled valiantly, even after he'd opened her throat
with the penknife. In turn, he'd rewarded her efforts by
taking particular care this time around, arranging the

body parts into a likeness of Leonardo da Vinci's *Vitruvian Man*, with various organs arranged at the compass points of the circle and the pièce de résistance laid carefully on the forehead. Now he fetched a deep breath, dipped a gloved finger into the fresh blood ponded beneath the body, wrote the brief message across the bare midriff—tickle, tickle!—then wiped the fingertip dry on a clean section of carpeting.

Alban wondered if *he* had guessed who was committing these murders. It was, after all, such a delightful irony...

Suddenly he looked up. Everything was silent—and yet he instantly understood he had only a second or two to act. Quickly, he collected his tools, rolled them up into the leather bundle, stood, darted out of the suite's bedroom into the living area, then ducked into the bathroom, hiding behind the door.

A moment later there came the click of the room's lock disengaging and the creak of the door opening. Alban heard the muffled sound of footsteps on the carpeting.

"Mandy?" came a masculine voice. "Mandy, honey, are you here?"

The footsteps receded, moving across the living area toward the bedroom.

As quietly as possible, Alban tiptoed out of the bathroom, opened the room door, stepped out into the hallway—and then, after a moment's hesitation, nipped back into the bathroom, hiding behind the door once again.

"Mandy...? *Oh, my God!*" A sudden shriek came from the bedroom. "No, no, *no!*" There was a scuffling, thudding sound, as of a body falling to the floor on its knees, followed by gasping and choking.

"Mandy! *Mandy!*"

Alban waited, as the crying from the bedroom dissolved first into hysteria, then cries for help.

The door to the suite burst open again. "Hotel security!" came a gruff voice. "What's going on?"

"My wife! She's been murdered!"

More thudding footsteps retreating past the bathroom, followed by a gasp, a sudden burst of talk into the radio, more tiresome cries of horror and disbelief from the bereaved husband.

Now Alban crept out of the bathroom, scurried silently to the door, opened it, stepped out—paused—then closed the door softly behind him. Walking easily down the hallway to the elevator bank, he pressed the DOWN button. But then, as the floor indicator above the elevator showed it beginning to rise, he stepped away again, moved farther down the hall, opened the stairwell door, and descended two flights before emerging again.

He looked down the empty hallway with a smile and headed in the direction of the elevator.

Two minutes later, he was walking out the service entrance of the hotel, hat brim low over his eyes, gloved hands deep in his trench coat pockets. He began sauntering casually down Central Park West, early-morning sun setting the pavement agleam, just as police sirens began sounding in the distance.

19

CORRIE SWANSON STOOD ON THE PORCH AT the shabby front door of a sagging duplex at the corner of Fourth Street and Birch in West Cuyahoga, Pennsylvania, a run-down dying suburb of the city of Allentown. There had been no answer to her numerous rings, and as she gazed up and down the street—lined with crappy twenty-year-old pickup trucks before identical duplexes—she realized it was exactly the kind of place she imagined her father calling home. The thought depressed her enormously.

She pressed the buzzer again, heard it sounding inside the empty house. As she glanced around once more, she saw curtains moving in the attached house, and across the street a neighbor had paused while bringing out the garbage and was staring at the black Lincoln Continental that had brought her.

Why was the damn driver waiting? She tried the door, shook it in impatience.

Leaving her suitcase on the porch, she went back to the car. "There's no need for you to hang around. You can go now."

The driver smiled. "Sorry, Ms. Swanson, I have to

see you into the house. If no one's home, I'm supposed to call for instructions." He even had his cell phone out.

Corrie rolled her eyes. This was unbelievable. How was she going to get rid of this guy?

"Don't call yet. Let me try again. Maybe he's asleep." It was entirely possible the bum *was* asleep, or maybe just passed out drunk. Then again, even though it was Saturday, he might be at work—if he still had work, that is.

She went back, tried the door again. The lock was crap and she had her tools in her bag. Blocking the view of the door with her body, she fished out the tools, inserted them into the lock, wiggled them around, and in less time than she expected felt the give of the pins. The door opened.

She pushed in with her luggage and shut the door behind her. Then, pulling the blinds apart and standing at the window, she waved to the driver, gave him a fake smile and a thumbs-up. The driver responded with a wave of his own, and the black car eased from the curb and went on down the street.

Corrie looked around. The front door opened directly into a living room that, to her surprise, was neat and clean, if a little shabby. Setting down the suitcase, she flopped onto a ratty sofa and exhaled.

The depressing nature of her situation just about overwhelmed her. She should never have agreed to this proposal. She hadn't once seen her father in the fifteen years since he'd walked out. She could forgive him for that—her mother was a psycho—but what she couldn't forgive was the fact he'd made no effort to keep in touch with her, write her, call her. No birthday or Christmas presents, no card on her graduation from high school, no phone call, not one, during the many times she was in trouble—nothing. It was a mystery why her memories of him were of a warm, funny, kind father who took her fishing—but then she was only six when he skipped town, and any loser bum could seem funny and kind to a needy, unloved kid.

She looked around. There wasn't much personality in the place, but at least there were no empty liquor bottles, no trash baskets overflowing with crushed beer cans or old pizza boxes lying about. It just didn't look like anyone had been there in a while. Where was he? Maybe she should have called.

This was so fucked up. She almost felt like crying.

She heaved herself off the sofa, wandered into the bedroom. It was small but tidy, with a single bed and a well-thumbed copy of *Twelve Steps and Twelve Traditions* sitting on the bedside table. The room had two closets. Idly, without much curiosity, she opened one of them. Jeans, chambray work shirts, and a couple of cheap-looking suits hung on wire hangers. Closing the door, she went to the second closet. This was strange: the shelves were full of packages wrapped in brown paper, dozens of them, of all different sizes, carefully, almost lovingly, stacked cheek by jowl with bundles of letters, bright oversize envelopes that could only be holiday or birthday cards, and numerous post-cards held together by rubber bands. She peered at a few. They were all addressed to her: Corrie Swanson, 29 Wyndham Parke Estates, Medicine Creek, Kansas. They seemed to be arranged in chronological order, going back more than a dozen years. Every stamp or postmark on every package bore a cancellation sticker, and every single one had been marked with an official-looking message: RETURN TO SENDER.

Corrie stared at the contents of the closet for a minute, scratching her head. Then she exited the bedroom, went out the front door, and knocked on the duplex next door. More motions of the curtain, then a tight voice.

"Who is it?"

"Corrie Swanson."

"Who?"

"Corrie Swanson. I'm Jack Swanson's daughter. I'm here..." She swallowed. "On a family visit."

A muffled noise that could have been a grunt of surprise, then the sound of locks turning. The door opened and a squat, unpleasant-looking woman stood in the doorway, hammy arms folded, face the texture of a Brillo pad. A smell of cigarette smoke exuded from the room behind her. She looked Corrie up and down with a narrow eye that lingered on her streak of purple hair. "Jack Swanson's daughter? I *see*." More scrutiny. "He's not here."

"I know that," said Corrie, struggling to keep the habitual sarcasm out of her voice. "I'm just wondering where he is."

"He left."

Corrie swallowed another sharp reply and managed to say, "Do you know where he's gone and when he might be back?" She bestowed a fake smile on the harridan.

More scrutiny. Judging by her facial grimaces, the woman seemed to be considering whether or not to tell her something important. "He's in trouble," the woman finally said. "Ran out of town."

"What kind of trouble?"

"Stole a car from the dealership he worked at, used it to rob a bank."

"He did what?" She felt genuine surprise. She knew her father was a loser, but the impression she had accumulated over the years of him—filtered through the bitterness of her mother's invective—had been that of a charming rogue who cut corners, slept with too many women, a get-rich-quick schemer who couldn't hold a real job and whose best moments in life were spent bellied up to the bar, telling jokes and stories to his admiring friends. A criminal he was not.

Of course, a lot could have changed in the fifteen years he'd been gone.

As she considered this, she thought that—perhaps—this wasn't such a bad thing after all. She could live in his house and not have to deal with him. Provided he'd paid his rent. But even if he hadn't, the rent on a dump like this wouldn't be much, and Pendergast had given her three thousand dollars.

"Robbed a bank?" Corrie couldn't help but give the lady a shit-eating grin. "Wow. Good old Dad. Hope he made away with a bundle."

"You may think it's funny, but I assure you *we* do not!" And with that the woman pressed her lips together and firmly shut the door.

Corrie retreated to her half of the house, shut and locked the front door, and once again flopped down on the sofa, kicking up her feet and lying back. To avoid any unpleasantness, she would have to be proactive, inform the cops she was here, contact the landlord, make sure the rent, power, and water were paid up. Once again, she told herself it was better that her loser father was on the lam. This way, she wouldn't have to deal with his bullshit.

Still, somewhere deep inside, she felt thwarted. Disappointed. Sad, even. She had to admit that, despite everything, she wanted to see him—if only to ask him straight out why he had abandoned her, why he had left her at the mercy of a mother he knew full well to be a horrible drunken bitch. There had to be an explanation for that—and for all those letters and packages stashed in his closet. Or at least, that's what she hoped beyond all hope.

She realized she was thirsty and went into the kitchen, turned on the tap, let the rusty water run until it ceased being lukewarm, filled up a glass and drank it down. So he was on the run. Where would he have gone?

And even as she asked the question, she realized she knew the answer.

20

FELDER HAD NEVER BEEN TO SOUTHPORT, CON-
necticut, before, and he found himself unexpectedly
charmed. It was an attractive, sleepy harbor town in
otherwise bustling Fairfield County. As he turned off
Pequot Avenue onto Center Street, heading for the historic district, he thought one could do a lot worse than
to live in a place like this.

It had a quintessential New England atmosphere.
The houses were mostly Colonials, early twentieth century by the look of them, with white clapboards and
picket fences and manicured grounds dense with trees.
The town library was impressive as well—a rambling,
Romanesque structure of dressed stone with whim-
sical details. The only blot on the town's escutcheon
seemed to be an old mansion a few doors from the
library, a dilapidated Queen Anne pile straight out of
The Addams Family, complete with gaping shutters,
loose slates, and a weed-choked lawn. The only thing
missing, he thought wryly as he drove by, was a grinning Uncle Fester in an upper window.

His spirits rose again as he entered the village proper.
Pulling into a parking space across from the yacht club,

he consulted a handwritten note, then—with a spring in his step—crossed the road to a cheery, one-story wooden frame building overlooking the harbor.

The interior of the Southport Historical Museum smelled pleasantly of old books and furniture polish. It was stocked with a variety of nicely preserved antiques, and appeared deserted save for a well-coifed woman of a certain age—also nicely preserved—who sat in a rocking chair, doing needlepoint.

"Good afternoon," she said. "Is there anything I can help you with?"

"As a matter of fact, yes," Felder replied. "I was wondering if you could answer a few questions."

"I'd be happy to answer what I can. Please have a seat." The woman indicated a rocking chair across from hers.

Felder sat down. "I'm doing some research into the painter and illustrator Alexander Wintour. I understand that his family came from this area."

The woman nodded. "Yes, that's true."

"I'm interested in his work. Specifically, his sketchbooks. I was wondering if they still exist, and whether you could give me a lead on where I should start searching for them."

The woman placed the needlepoint carefully in her lap. "Well, young man, I can tell you with some assurance that they almost certainly do exist. And I know where you can find them."

"That's very good to hear," Felder said, feeling a little thrill course through him. This was going to be easier than he had hoped.

"We know quite a bit here about the Wintour family," the woman went on. "Alexander Wintour never really reached the top shelf, you might say. He was a good illustrator with a fine eye, but not what you would call a real artist. Still, his work is interesting from a historical point of view. But I'm surely telling you what you already know."

She smiled brightly.

"No, no," Felder hastened to assure her. "Please go on."

"As far as the family went, his brother's son—his nephew—made an excellent match. Married the daughter of a local shipping magnate. Alexander, who never married, moved out of the Wintour family bungalow on Old South Road and into his nephew's much grander residence nearby."

Felder nodded eagerly. "Go on."

"This shipping magnate was an avid collector of literary memorabilia—books, manuscripts, the odd lithograph, and in particular epistolary material. It's said he obtained the complete collection of Albert Bierstadt's correspondence from his 1882 trip across California, including dozens of sketches. He also managed to procure a series of love letters written by Grover Cleveland to Frances Folsom, before she became his wife—he was the only president ever to have a wedding in the White House, you know."

"No, I didn't know," Felder said, leaning in a little closer.

"Well! And then there are the letters Henry James sent to his editor at Houghton Mifflin during the writing of *The Portrait of a Lady*. Really, a most impressive collection." She folded her hands over the needlepoint. "In any case, Alexander Wintour died young. He never married, and his sister was said to have inherited much of his artistic output, beyond a collection of paintings that were donated to, I believe, the New-York Historical Society. The albums and notebooks must have been passed on to her son. The son and his wealthy wife had only one child of their own—a daughter, Alexander's grandniece. She's still alive and living here in Southport. We at the museum have little doubt that Wintour's sketchbooks are still in her library, along with her grandfather's collections of letters and manuscripts. Naturally, we would dearly love to have them, but..." The woman smiled.

Felder practically clasped his hands together in excitement. "This is wonderful news. Tell me where she lives, please, so I can call on her."

The woman's smile faded. "Oh, dear." She hesitated a moment. "Now, that's a bit of a problem. I didn't intend to get your hopes up."

"What do you mean?"

The woman hesitated again. "I told you that I knew where you could *find* the sketchbooks. I didn't say you'd be able to *see* them."

Felder stared at her. "Why not?"

"Miss Wintour—well, not to put too fine a point on it, but she's been an odd one ever since she was a little girl. Never goes out, never has company, never sees anyone. After her parents died, she remained shut up in that house. And that *dreadful* manservant of hers..." The woman shook her head. "It's a tragedy, really, her parents were such pillars of the community."

"But her library—?" Felder began.

"Oh, many people have tried to gain access—scholars and the like, you know, the Henry James and Grover Cleveland letters in particular have historical and literary importance—but she's turned everyone away. Every last one. A delegation from Harvard came down expressly to examine the Bierstadt letters. Offered a tidy sum, so people say. She wouldn't even let them in the front door." The woman leaned forward, touched the side of her head with a fingertip. "Batty," she whispered confidentially.

"There isn't...*anything* I could do? It's terribly important."

"Frankly, it would be a miracle if she let you in. I hate to say it, but I know of quite a few scholars and others who are waiting—" she dropped her voice—"for a time when she won't be around any longer to block access."

Felder stood up.

"I'm sorry I can't be more helpful."

Felder sighed. "I've come all the way up from the city. As long as I'm here, I might as well try to see her."

A look of pity came over the woman's face.

"Can you tell me where I can find her house, please?" he asked. "There's no harm in knocking on her door, is there?"

"No harm, but I shouldn't get my hopes up if I were you."

"I won't. If I could just have the address—" Felder took out his handwritten note, preparing to jot it down.

"Oh, you won't need that. You can't miss it. It's that big mansion on Center Street, just down from the library."

"Not...not the one that's falling apart?" Felder asked, his spirits sinking farther still.

"The very one. Dreadful how she's let the family estate go to rack and ruin. A real eyesore to the community. As I said, quite a few around here are waiting..." Her voice trailed off decorously as she picked up her needlepoint again.

21

DR. JOHN FELDER DROVE—SLOWLY, VERY slowly—down Center Street, the dead December leaves skittering and whirling in his wake. He kept his head low, as if not wanting to look much past the dashboard of his Volvo. The dejection he felt seemed quite out of proportion to the disappointment he had just experienced. He realized he'd allowed himself to believe this one trip to Connecticut might already be the end of his quest.

It was still possible. Anything could happen.

The houses slid by, one after the other, with their crisply painted fronts and well-tended plantings, mulched and protected for winter. And then the prospect ahead seemed to darken, as if a cloud was passing over the sun...and there *it* was. Felder winced. He took in the wrought-iron fence, topped with pitted spikes; the dead, frozen weeds covering the front yard; the dreary mansion itself, with its too-heavy gabled roof beetling over the dark and discolored stone of the façade. He half imagined he could make out a huge crack, running, Usher-like, from foundation to roofline; all it would take was a puff of wind from the wrong direction to bring the whole thing shivering down into perdition.

He pulled over, killed the engine, and got out of the car. As he pushed the gate open with a hollow groan, red grains of rust and chips of black paint came off on his hands. He made his way up the cracked and heaving concrete walkway, trying to think of what to say.

The problem was, Felder realized, that although he was a psychiatrist by profession, he wasn't any good at manipulating people. He was a terrible liar and easily gulled himself—as recent events had made painfully obvious. Should he continue the academic ruse he'd used at the historical society? No—if old Miss Wintour had turned away a delegation from Harvard, she wouldn't have anything to do with a lone scholar who'd misplaced his credentials.

Maybe, then, he should play on her family pride, tell her he wanted to resurrect her great-uncle's artistic reputation from lonely obscurity. But no—she'd had plenty of opportunity to do that herself already.

What on earth was he going to say?

All too soon he reached the front steps. He mounted them, the mortared stones tilting treacherously beneath his feet. A massive black door stood before him, scuffed, the paint crazed and flaking. Set into it was a large brass knocker in the shape of a griffin's head. It glared at Felder as if it were about to bite him. There was no doorbell. Felder took a deep breath, grasped the knocker gingerly, and gave it a rap.

He waited. No response.

He gave the knocker a second rap, a little harder this time. He could hear the echo of it reverberating hollowly through the bowels of the mansion.

Still nothing.

He licked his lips, feeling almost relieved. One more

try—then he'd leave. Taking firm hold of the knocker, he rapped with severity.

An indistinct voice sounded within. Felder waited. A minute later, footsteps could be heard echoing across marble. Then came the rattling of chains, the sliding of locks badly in need of oil, and the door cracked open.

It was very dark inside, and Felder could see nothing. Then his gaze drifted downward and he spotted what appeared to be an eye. Yes, he was sure it was an eye. It looked him up and down, narrowing with suspicion, as if perhaps believing him to be a Jehovah's Witness or Fuller Brush man.

"Well?" a small voice demanded from out of the dark.

Felder's jaw worked. "I—"

"Well? What is it?"

Felder cleared his throat. This was going to be even harder than he'd expected.

"Are you here about the gatehouse?" the voice asked.

"Excuse me?"

"I said, are you here about renting the gatehouse?"

Seize the opportunity, you fool! "The gatehouse? Ah, yes. Yes, I am."

The door closed in his face.

Felder stood on the top step, perplexed, for a full minute before the door opened again—wider this time. A diminutive woman stood before him. She was dressed in a fox fur, slightly moth-eaten, and—bizarrely—a broad-brimmed straw hat of the kind one might take to the beach. An expensive-looking black leather purse hung from a narrow arm.

There was a shifting in the darkness behind her, and then the entire doorway seemed to move. As it resolved into the light, Felder realized the shape was a man. He was very tall—at least six and a half feet—and built like a linebacker. His features and complexion made Felder believe he might be from ancient Fiji, or perhaps the South Sea Islands. He wore an odd, shapeless garment with an orange-and-white batik pattern; his hair was cropped very close to his head; crude but remarkably complex tattoos covered his face and arms. He looked pointedly at Felder but did not speak. *That must be the manservant*, Felder thought. He swallowed uncomfortably and tried not to stare at the tattoos. All that was missing was a bone in the nose.

"You're lucky," the woman said, pulling on a pair of white gloves. "I was about to stop running the advertisement. It seemed like a good idea—after all, who wouldn't be honored to rent such a place?—but then again, one doesn't understand the modern mind. Going on two months now in the *Gazette*—waste of good money." She walked past him, down the steps, and then turned back. "Well, come along then, come *along*."

Felder followed as she led the way through the dry weeds, rattling in the winter wind. From what the woman at the Southport Museum had implied, he'd expected Miss Wintour to be a superannuated, withered crone. But instead she appeared to be in her early sixties, with a face that reminded him vaguely of an aging Bette Davis—well maintained, even attractive. She had an accent to match—the kind associated with the North Shore of Long Island in better days, where his own family came from, only rarely heard anymore. As he walked, he was all too aware of the hulking manservant trailing silently behind them.

"What is it?" she asked out of the blue.

"I'm sorry," he replied. "What is what?"

"Your name, of course!"

"Oh. Sorry. It's . . . Feldman. John Feldman."

"And your profession?"

"I'm a doctor."

At this, she stopped to look back at him. "Can you furnish references?"

"Yes, I suppose so. If it's necessary."

"There are formalities that must be seen to, young man. After all, this isn't just *any* gatehouse. It was designed by Stanford White."

"Stanford White?"

"The only gatehouse he ever designed." Her look turned suspicious again. "That was in the advertisement. Didn't you read it?"

"Ah, yes," Felder said quickly. "Slipped my mind. Sorry."

"Hmpf," the woman said, as if such a fact should be seared into one's memory. She continued wading through the dead grass and weeds.

As they rounded the rear edge of the mansion, the gatehouse came into view. It was of the same dark stone as the main building, guarding an entrance—and driveway—that apparently no longer existed. Its windows were cracked and hazy with grime, and several had been boarded up. The two-story structure did have graceful lines, Felder noted, but they were overcome by shabbiness and decay.

The old woman led the way to the building's only entrance—a door, held shut with a padlock. Interminable fishing in her purse produced a key, which she fitted to the lock. Then she pushed the door open and waved at the interior with a flourish.

"Look at *that*!" she said proudly.

Felder peered inside. Thick motes of dust hung in the air, almost choking the sunlight struggling through the windows. He could make out dim shapes, but nothing else.

The old woman—apparently irritated that he hadn't dissolved into rapture—stepped inside and flicked on a light switch. "Come in, come in!" she said crossly.

Felder stepped inside. Behind them, the manservant stopped just within the doorway—he barely fit—and stood there, arms crossed over his barrel chest, blocking the exit.

A single bare bulb struggled to life high overhead. Felder heard the skittering of mice, disturbed by their entrance. He looked around. Heavy cobwebs hung from the rafters, and a riot of discarded jetsam from a long-gone era—perambulators, steamer trunks, a dressmaker's mannequin—filled much of the space. Dust rose in small puffs with each step he took. Greenish gray mold dappled the walls like the rosettes of a panther.

"Stanford White," the woman repeated proudly. "You'll never see another like it."

"Very nice," Felder murmured.

She swept a hand around. "Oh, it naturally needs the touch of a duster here and there, nothing that can't be done of an afternoon. Five thousand a month."

"Five thousand," Felder repeated.

"Furnished, and cheap enough at the price, I should say! The furnishings are not to be moved about, however. Utilities aren't included, of course. You'll have to pay for coal for the furnace. But the building's built so well you probably won't even be needing heat."

"Mmmm," said Felder. It couldn't be much above freezing.

"Bedroom and bath are upstairs, kitchen is in the next room. Would you like to see them?"

"No, I think not. Thanks anyway."

The woman looked around with no small amount of pride, blind to the dust and grime and mold. "I'm very particular about who I allow on the premises. I won't tolerate any licentious behavior or guests of the opposite sex. This is an historic structure, and of course I have a family name to protect—I'm sure you understand."

Felder nodded absently.

"But you seem a nice enough young man. Perhaps—we shall have to see—you can take tea with me, certain afternoons, in the front parlor."

The front parlor. Felder recalled what the woman at the Southport Museum had said: *A delegation from Harvard came down. Offered a tidy sum. She wouldn't even let them in the front door.*

He realized Miss Wintour was looking at him with an expectant frown. "Well? I'm not out here for my health, you know. Five thousand a month, plus utilities."

Incredibly, as if somebody else were speaking the words, Felder heard himself answer. "I'll take it."

22

D'AGOSTA HAD SEEN A LOT OF REALLY SICK SHIT
in his life—he'd never forget those two dismembered
corpses up in Waldo Falls, Maine—but this took the
cake. This was the goriest scene yet in a string of exceptionally gruesome murders. The young woman's body
had been stripped and splayed out on its back, dismembered limbs forming something like the face of a
human clock, a corona of blood spread out like a sun-
burst beneath it all, various organs arrayed around the
edges like a goddamn still life. Then there was the little
toe—the *extra* little toe—that had been lovingly placed
on the victim's forehead.

All this was capped by the message finger-painted
onto her torso—TAG, YOU'RE IT!

The M.E., forensic units, crime-scene units, latents,
and the photographer had all done their work, collected their evidence, and gone. That had taken hours.
Now it was his turn—his and Gibbs. D'Agosta had to
admit, Gibbs had been pretty good about the wait. He
hadn't flashed his shield and elbowed his way in,
the way other feds of his experience had done. Over
the years, the homicide division had tried to lay down

guidelines about the brass intruding into crime scenes, interrupting the work of the specialists, and D'Agosta took those rules very seriously. He didn't know how many times he'd seen a crime scene messed up by some honcho wanting a photo shoot, or showing his political friends around, or just pulling rank for the sake of it.

The room was hot from the bright lights and there was a bad smell in the air, the stench of blood, fecal matter, and death. D'Agosta took a turn around the corpse, his eye roving over every little detail, burning it into his memory, deconstructing and reconstructing the scene while keeping it free flowing. It was another meticulous killing, planned and executed with the precision of a military campaign. The scene exuded a feeling of self-confidence, even arrogance, on the part of the killer.

Indeed, as D'Agosta took it all in, he had a sense of déjà vu; there was something about this crime scene that reminded him of something else, and as he rolled that thought around in his mind he realized what it was. It had the look and feel of a museum diorama— everything highly crafted and set in its place, designed to create an impression, an illusion, a visual impact.

But of what? And why?

He glanced over at Gibbs, who was crouching on his heels, examining the writing on the torso. The arrayed lights cast his multiple shadows across the crime scene. "This time," he said, "the perp used a glove."

D'Agosta nodded. An interesting observation. His opinion of Gibbs went up another notch.

He was frankly more than a little dubious that Pendergast's brother was behind this. He saw no connection whatsoever between the M.O. of this killer and what Diogenes had done in the past. As for motive, unlike Diogenes's previous killing spree, this time he had no discernible motive to kill these randomly selected victims. The figure he had seen on the security tapes, while he was approximately the right height, weight, and build, did not move in that smooth fashion he recalled of Diogenes. The eyes were different. Diogenes did not strike him at all as the kind of psycho to start dismembering himself and leaving the parts at the crime scenes. Finally, there was the little matter of his alleged fall into a Sicilian volcano. The only witness to it was absolutely convinced he was dead. And she was a damn good witness—even if more than a little crazy herself.

Pendergast had refused to tell him why he believed the killer was his brother. All in all, D'Agosta felt this strange idea of Pendergast's was a product of his deep depression over his wife's murder, combined with an overdose of drugs. In retrospect, he was sorry he had tried to bring Pendergast into the case—and he felt damned relieved the special agent had not shown up at this crime scene.

Gibbs rose from his long assessment of the corpse. "Lieutenant, I'm beginning to think we might be dealing with two killers. Perhaps a Leopold and Loeb sort of partnership."

"Really? We only have one person on videotape, one set of bloody footprints, one knife."

"Quite right. But think about it. The three hotels all have extremely high security. They're crawling with employees. In each case our killer has gotten himself in and out without being surprised, stopped, interrupted, or challenged. One way to explain that is if he had an accomplice—a spotter."

D'Agosta nodded slowly.

"Our killer does the wet work. He's the magnet of our scrutiny. He's the guy waving at the camera saying, *Hi, Ma, look at me!* But there's a partner out there, somewhere—who's just the opposite. Who's invisible, who fades into the woodwork, who sees and hears all. They have no contact during the commission of the crime, except that they are secretly and continuously in communication."

"Via an earpiece or some similar device."

"Exactly."

D'Agosta liked the idea at once. "So we look for this guy. Because he's got to be on our security tapes."

"Probably. But of course he'll be very, very carefully disguised."

Suddenly a long shadow, emerging from the bedroom, fell across the corpse, startling D'Agosta. A moment later a tall figure in black emerged, backlit, his blond-white hair a bright halo around his shadowed face, making him look not like an angel but like some ghastly revenant, a specter of the night.

"Two killers, you say?" came the honeyed drawl.

"Pendergast!" said D'Agosta. "What the hell? How'd you get in here?"

"The same way you did, Vincent. I've just been examining the bedroom."

His voice was not exactly friendly, but at least, thought D'Agosta, it had a steeliness behind it that had been lacking during their last encounter.

D'Agosta glanced at Gibbs, who was staring at Pendergast, failing to control the disapproval on his face.

Another step forward and the bright light fell athwart Pendergast's face, raking it from the side, chiseling his features into marble-like perfection. The face turned. "Greetings, Agent Gibbs."

"The same to you," said Gibbs.

"I trust we have liaised to your satisfaction?"

A silence. "Since you mentioned it, no, I haven't yet had confirmation of your role in the case."

A *tsk-tsk* sound from Pendergast. "Ah, that FBI bureaucracy, so very dependable."

"But of course," said Gibbs, hardly able to disguise his ill will, "I always welcome the assistance of a fellow agent."

"Assistance," Pendergast repeated. He suddenly was in motion, moving around the corpse, bending quickly, examining articles with a loupe, picking up something with tweezers that went into a test tube, more rapid, almost manic movement—and then he had completed the circuit and was face-to-face with Gibbs again.

"*Two*, you say?"

Gibbs nodded. "A working hypothesis only," he said. "We're obviously not at the point where we can draw conclusions."

"I'd love to hear your thoughts. I'm terribly interested."

D'Agosta felt a certain uneasiness at Pendergast's choice of words, but he kept silent.

"Well," said Gibbs. "I don't know if the lieutenant has shared with you our provisional report, but we see this as the work of an organized killer—or killers—who operate in a ritual fashion. I'll get you the report, if you don't have it."

"Oh, I have it. But there's nothing like hearing it—how does the quaint saying go? Straight from the horse's mouth. And the motive?"

"These types of killers," Gibbs continued evenly, "generally kill for reasons of libidinous gratification, which can be satisfied only by the exercise of extreme control and power over others."

"And the extra body parts?"

"That is unique in our experience. The hypothesis our profilers are developing is that the aggressor is overwhelmed with feelings of self-loathing and worthlessness—perhaps due to childhood abuse—and is acting out a sort of slow-motion suicide. Our experts are working from that conjecture."

"How fortunate for us. And the message, *Tag, you're it?*"

"This type of killer often taunts law enforcement."

"Your database has an answer for everything."

Gibbs didn't seem to know how to take this, and neither did D'Agosta. "It is a very good database, I'll admit," Gibbs went on. "As I'm sure you know, Agent Pendergast, the joint NCAVC/BSU profiling system includes tens of thousands of entries. It's based on statistics, aggregates, and correlates. It doesn't mean our killer *necessarily* fits the pattern, but it does give us something to follow."

"Yes, indeed. It gives you a trail to follow deep into the wilderness, at least."

This rather strange metaphor dangled, D'Agosta trying to figure out exactly what it was Pendergast meant. A tense silence enveloped them as Pendergast continued gazing at Gibbs, his head slightly tilted, as if examining a specimen. Then he turned to D'Agosta and seized him by the hand. "Well, Vincent," he said. "Here we are again, partners on a case. I want to thank you for—how should I put it?—helping save my life."

And with that, he turned and strode out the door at a swift pace, black suit coat flapping crazily behind him.

23

LIEUTENANT D'AGOSTA SAT, SLUMPED FORWARD, in Video Lab C on the nineteenth floor of One Police Plaza. He'd left the scene of the third murder just an hour before, and he felt like he'd gone fifteen rounds with a prizefighter.

D'Agosta turned to the man working the video equipment, a skinny dweeb named Hong. "Fifteenth-floor feed. Back sixty seconds."

Hong worked the keyboard, and the black-and-white image on the central monitor changed, going backward rapidly in reverse motion.

As he watched the screen, D'Agosta mentally went over how the crime had gone down. The killer had forced his way into the room—once again, based on the Royal Cheshire security tapes, he'd seemed to know just when the door was going to open—and dragged the unfortunate woman into the bedroom of the hotel suite. He'd killed her, then proceeded with his ghastly work. The whole thing took fewer than ten minutes.

But then the woman's husband had returned to the suite. The killer had hidden in the bathroom. The man discovered the body of his wife, and his frantic cries were overheard by a hotel security officer, who entered the suite, saw the body, and called the police. The killer escaped in the resulting confusion. All this had been corroborated by the security tapes, as well as by the evidence found in the suite and by the statements of the husband and the detective.

It seemed straightforward enough. But the devil— the really weird shit, actually—was in the details. How, for example, did the killer know to hide in the bathroom? If he'd been disturbed in his bedroom work by the click of the front door lock, there was no way he could have made it to the bathroom in time without being seen by the husband. He must have hidden himself *before* the key card was swiped through the lock. He must have been alerted by some other cue.

Pretty damn clear the guy had an accomplice. But where?

"Start it right there," D'Agosta told Hong.

He watched the corridor video for perhaps the tenth time as the husband entered the suite. Five seconds later, the front door opened again and the killer— wearing a fedora and a trench coat—stepped out. But then—against all logic—he ducked back inside the room a second time. A few moments later, the hotel dick rounded a corner and came into view.

"Stop it for a moment," D'Agosta said.

The problem was, there was no accomplice in the hall to see the guy come. The hall was empty.

"Start it up again," he said.

He watched morosely as the hotel detective disappeared into the room, alerted by the husband's shouts. Almost immediately the killer stepped out again and headed for the elevator bank. He pressed the DOWN button, waited a minute, and then—as if changing his mind—walked the rest of the way down the hall, exiting through the stairwell door.

Moments later, the elevator doors opened and three men in suits stepped out.

"Stop," D'Agosta said. "Let's see the feed from the thirteenth floor. Begin at the same time index."

"Sure thing, Loo," said Hong.

They had already reviewed the tapes of the fourteenth floor—at that particular moment there had been several cleaning ladies at work, their carts blocking the corridor. Now D'Agosta watched as the killer emerged from the stairwell onto the thirteenth floor. He strode over to the elevator bank, pressed the DOWN button again, and waited. He let one elevator go by, then pressed the button again. This time, when the doors opened, he stepped inside.

"Stop," D'Agosta said.

He had been through this again and again. Where was the accomplice? In several instances, there was nobody around to observe, and in other situations, where there were people who might be spotting, he could find no physical matches between them. Nobody could turn himself from an old, stooped gentleman of eighty into a fat Dominican cleaning lady in fifteen seconds. Unless the killer had half a dozen accomplices.

This was seriously, seriously weird.

"Lobby camera," D'Agosta muttered. "Same time index."

The image on the monitor jittered, then came into focus again, showing a bird's-eye view of the hotel's discreet and elegant lobby. The elevator doors opened, and the killer emerged—alone. He began to walk toward the main exit, then seemed to reconsider, turned, and sat down in a chair, hiding his face behind a newspaper. Seven seconds later a uniformed man—

hotel security—went running past. Immediately afterward the killer got up, and—instead of heading for the main exit again—made for an unmarked door leading to the service areas. Just before he reached it, the door opened and a porter emerged. The killer slipped in as the door was closing again—he hadn't even needed to extend an arm.

D'Agosta watched as the form was obscured by the closing door. Other cameras had shown him going out an exit in the hotel's loading zone. Repeated viewings of the lobby and other video feeds again showed no sign of a possible partner in the murders.

Hong stopped the video of his own accord. "Anything else you'd like to see?"

"Yeah. Got any Three Stooges reruns?" And D'Agosta pushed himself wearily to his feet, feeling even older than when he'd first come in.

But as he was leaving, he was suddenly struck by an idea. The accomplice *didn't need to be in all those places*. If he had access to the live video feeds, he would have seen everything D'Agosta had. And could have warned the killer accordingly. So he was either someone in the security department itself, or someone who had hacked into the CCTV system and was diverting a private feed for himself, in real time—perhaps, if those cameras were networked, even over the Internet. In that case, the accomplice might not even be in New York City.

With this brilliant stroke in mind, D'Agosta immediately began thinking about how to exploit it.

24

THE CABIN DIDN'T BELONG TO HER FATHER AND
never had. Jack Swanson wasn't really the kind of person who actually owned things. He talked his way into
borrowing them, took them over, and then over time
acted as if they were his own. As was typical of Jack,
he had somehow stumbled across the run-down tar-
paper shack years ago, in timberland owned by Royal
Paper on the New Jersey side of the Delaware Water
Gap. The story Corrie heard was that he'd made friends
with some Royal Paper executive he'd met on a fishing
trip, who apparently agreed that if Jack wanted to fix
the place up he could stay there whenever he wanted as
long as he kept a low profile and didn't make a nuisance
of himself. Corrie was sure the transaction involved
many beers and fishing stories, and a big dose of her
father's apparent charm. The cabin had no heat, water,
or electricity; the windows were broken and the roof
full of holes; and nobody seemed to mind that Jack
went up there, slapdashed the shack into something
barely habitable, installed himself as its proprietor, and
used it as a base for occasional fishing trips to nearby
Long Pine Lake.

Corrie had never seen the place, of course, but she knew it existed, because her mother complained bitterly when she discovered that his "fishing cabin on the lake in New Jersey" did not actually belong to him when it came time to divide up their (nonexistent) assets in the divorce.

The cabin, Corrie felt sure, was where her father had holed up. He didn't own it, so officialdom couldn't trace him there. And she was pretty sure news of his seamy little bank robbery would not likely have traveled very far from Allentown, certainly not up into the little hamlets about the Worthington State Forest of New Jersey.

How many Long Pine Lakes could there be in that area? According to Google Maps there was only one, and Corrie sure as hell hoped it was the right one as she got out of the horribly expensive cab she'd hired from the bus stop in East Stroudsburg, which had taken her to a country store known as Frank's Place in Old Foundry, New Jersey, the closest commercial establishment she could find to Long Pine Lake.

Counting out a hundred and twenty bucks, she paid off the cabdriver, then sauntered into the store. It was just as she'd hoped, one of those cramped places selling fishing lures, bait, cheap rods, coolers, boating supplies, bundles of firewood, Coleman fuel, and—of course—beer. An entire wall of beer.

Just her father's kind of joint.

As she walked up to the counter, a silence fell among the beer-guts hanging out around the cash register. No doubt it was her purple hair. She was tired, she was irritated, and she was not happy to have spent a hundred and twenty dollars on a cab ride. She really hoped these good old boys weren't going to give her a hard time.

"I'm looking for Jack Swanson," she said.

More silence. "Is that right?" came the eventual response from the apparent self-appointed clown of the group. "What...Jack knock you up or something?" The man guffawed and looked to his friends, left and right, for approval.

"I'm his daughter, you mentally defective asswipe," she said in a very loud voice that reached to the farthest corners of the store and brought a sudden hush to the place.

Now the laugh came from the friends. Beer-Gut colored deeply, but there wasn't much he could do. "She got you that time, Merv," said one, a little less simian than the others, nudging his pal.

She waited, arms crossed, for an answer.

"So you're the kid he's always talking about," the less simian one said, in a friendly tone.

This business about her father always talking about her surprised Corrie, but she didn't show it. She didn't even look at Merv, who was clearly hugely embarrassed. "So—you all know my father?"

"He's probably up at his cabin," the nicer one said.

Bingo, thought Corrie. She'd been right. She felt a huge relief this hadn't been a wasted effort.

"Where's that?"

The man gave her directions. It was about a mile up the road. "I'd be happy to give you a ride," he said.

"No thanks." She hefted the knapsack and turned to leave.

"Really, I'd be happy to. I'm a friend of your dad's."

She had to stop herself from asking him what he was like. That wouldn't be the way to go about it—she had to find out for herself. She hesitated, gave the man a once-over. He looked sincere, it was freezing outside, and her knapsack weighed a ton. "All right. As long as Perv, I mean Merv, here doesn't tag along." She gestured at Beer-Gut Number One.

This elicited laughter.

"Come on, then."

She had him drop her off at the spot where a shortcut trail to the cabin left the main road. It was just a steep track in the pinewoods, which started out in a big puddle of mud she had to skirt around. She had what looked like a half-mile walk to the cabin, and as she went along the track—now and again crossing one of the switchbacks of Long Pine Road—she felt herself start to unwind, to really relax, for the first time in ages. It was a typical early-December day: the sun was shining through the branches of the oaks and pines, dappling the ground around her, and a smell of resin and dead leaves hung in the air. If ever there was a great place to hide from the cops—or Nazis, for that matter—this was it.

But as she thought about her father, and what she would say to him, and he to her, her stomach began to tighten up again. She could hardly remember him physically, had no real idea of what he looked like—her mother had thrown away the scrapbook of pictures of them together. She had no idea what to expect. So, he was now a bank robber? God, he might be an alcoholic or a drug addict. He might be one of those criminals full of whining self-pity and justification, blaming everything on bad parents or bad luck. He might even be shacked up with some horrible sleazy bitch.

And what would happen if he were caught, and there she was living in the cabin with him? She had already looked up the federal statute on the web, 18 USC § 1071, which required them to prove she'd actually harbored or concealed him and had taken steps to prevent his discovery or arrest. Just living with him wasn't enough. Still, how would it affect her future law enforcement career? It sure as hell wouldn't look good.

In short, this was a stupid idea. She hadn't really thought it through. She should have stayed back in his house where she was perfectly safe, and let him live his own life. She slowed, stopped, shrugged off the knapsack, and sat down. Why had she ever thought this was a good idea?

What she really should do now was turn around and go back to Allentown, or rather West Cuyahoga, and forget all about this bullshit. She rose, slung the knapsack back over her shoulder, and turned to leave. But then she hesitated.

She had come too far to run away. And she wanted to know—*really* wanted to know—about those letters in the closet. The postmaster at Medicine Creek was about as dumb as they came... but she didn't think he was *that* dumb.

She turned around and trudged on. The shortcut trail left the road for good, went around a bend, and there, in front of her in a sunny clearing, was the shack, all by itself, no other buildings even remotely nearby. She stopped and stared.

It was not charming. Tar paper had been tacked on with irregular strips of wood. The two windows on either side of the door were curtained but broken. Behind and through the oaks she could see an outhouse. A rusted stovepipe poked up through the roof.

The yard in front, however, was neat, the grass trimmed. She could hear someone moving inside the house.

Oh, God, here we go. She walked up to the door and knocked. A sudden silence. Was he going to bolt out the back?

"Hello?" she called, hoping to forestall that.

More silence. And then a voice from inside. "Who is it?"

She took a deep breath. "Corrie. Your daughter. Corrie."

Another long silence. And then suddenly the door burst open and a man tumbled out—she recognized him immediately—who enveloped her in his arms and just about crushed her.

"Corrie!" he cried, his voice choking up. "How many years have I prayed for this! I knew someday it would come! My God, I prayed for it—and now here it's happened! My Corrie!" And then he dissolved into great hiccuping gusts of sobbing joy that would have embarrassed her if she hadn't been so completely flabbergasted.

25

INSIDE, THE CABIN WAS SURPRISINGLY COZY, neat, and even charming in a beat-up, rustic sort of way. Her father—she called him Jack, unable to bring herself to say *Dad*—showed her around with no little amount of pride. It consisted of two rooms: a kitchen-living-dining area, and a tiny bedroom just big enough for a rickety twin bed, bureau, and washstand. There was no plumbing or electricity. An old Franklin stove supplied heat. An upright camping stove on legs, supplied by bottled gas, was used for cooking, and next to it an old soapstone sink was set up on two-by-fours, its drainpipe simply dumping water onto the ground under the floorboards. Drinking water came in plastic jugs lined up by the front door, filled, he said, at a spring half a mile from the cabin.

Everything was in its place, clean, and orderly. She noted no liquor bottles or beer cans anywhere. Red paisley curtains added a cheery note, and the rough wooden kitchen table was spread with a checked table-cloth. But what surprised Corrie the most—although she didn't mention it—was a large cluster of framed photographs that dominated the wall above the table, all of her. She had no idea so many childhood and baby pictures of her even existed.

"You take the bedroom and get settled in," Jack said, opening the door. "I'll sleep on the sofa."

Corrie didn't argue with him. She dumped her knapsack on the bed, and rejoined her father in the kitchen. He was standing over the stove.

"Are you staying for a while?" he asked.

"If that's okay."

"*More* than okay. Coffee?"

"Oh, my God, yes."

"It ain't French press." He laughed and dumped some coffee grounds into an enamel pot filled with water, stirred it, and put it on to boil.

So far, after the initial effusive greeting, both of them had somehow refrained from asking questions. Although she was dying to—and she knew he must be, too. It seemed neither one wanted to rush things.

He hummed as he worked, brought out a carton of doughnuts, and arranged them on a plate. She suddenly remembered that humming habit of his— something she hadn't thought of in fifteen years. She examined him surreptitiously as he bustled about. He was thinner and seemed astonishingly shorter, but that must be because she'd grown up. No man could shrink from giant size—which is what she remembered—to a measly five foot seven. His hair was thinning, with one jaunty tuft that stuck out from the top; his face was deeply scored but still strikingly handsome in a kind of sparkling, cheerful, Irish way. Even though he was only a quarter Irish, the other parts being Swedish, Polish, Bulgarian, Italian, and Hungarian. "I'm a mutt," she remembered him once saying.

"Milk, sugar?" he asked.

"Got cream?"

"Heavy cream."

"Perfect. Lots of heavy cream and three spoonfuls of sugar."

He brought the two steaming mugs over, set them down, and took a seat. For a moment they drank in silence and Corrie, realizing she was famished, ate one of the doughnuts. The birds were chirping outside, the late-afternoon light came dappling in through the rustling leaves, and she could smell the forest. It suddenly seemed so perfect she began to cry.

Like a typical man, Jack leapt up in a complete panic. "Corrie! What's wrong? Are you in trouble? I can help."

She waved him back down and wiped her eyes, smiling. "Nothing. Just forget it. I—I'm kind of stressed out."

Still all aflutter, he sat down and went to put his arm around her, but she shied away. "Just...hold on a moment and let me kind of get used to this."

He withdrew the arm all in a rush. "Right. Of course." His extreme solicitude touched her. She blew her nose, and there was an awkward silence. Neither one wanted to ask the other the first question.

"You're welcome to stay here long as you like," Jack finally began. "No questions asked, free to come and go as you please...Um, do you have a car? I didn't see anything."

She shook her head. And then she said, without really meaning to: "They say you robbed a bank."

A dead silence. "Well," he said, "I didn't."

Immediately, Corrie felt something go cold inside her. Already he was lying to her.

"No, really, I didn't. I was framed."

"But you...*ran.*"

He smacked his head, shaking his tuft of hair. "Yeah,

I ran. Like a damn idiot. Totally stupid, I know. But I didn't do it. Please believe me. They've got all this evidence, but it's because I was framed. It happened like this—"

"Wait." She held up a hand. "*Wait.*" She didn't want to hear any more lies—if in fact they were lies.

He fell silent.

She took a long drink of her coffee. It tasted wonderful. Grabbed another doughnut and took a big soft bite. *Stay in the moment.* She tried to relax, but the real question she wanted to ask, the one she'd been avoiding, kept coming back again and again to her mind, and so she finally swallowed and asked it.

"What's up with all those packages and letters in your closet?"

Jack stared at her. "You saw them?"

"What went on, exactly? Why did you just leave and...never call? For fifteen years?"

He looked at her, surprise and sadness mixing on his face. "Duette wouldn't let me call you, said you didn't want to talk, and...and I understood that. But I sent you something just about every week, Corrie. Presents, whenever I could afford them. As you grew older, I tried to guess what you might be into, what you might like. Barbie dolls, children's books. Every birthday, I sent you something. Something nice. And when I couldn't afford to send gifts, I sent you letters. I must have sent you a thousand letters—telling you what I was doing, what was going on in my life, giving you advice for what I guessed might be going on in your own. And it all came back. Everything. I figured Duette stopped it. Or maybe she'd moved and left no forwarding address."

Corrie swallowed. "So why did you keep on sending me things when you knew I wouldn't get them?"

He hung his head. "Because someday I hoped to be able to give them to you myself—all of them. In a way, they're kind of like a diary; a diary of my life, and—this may sound strange—of *your* life, or your life as I imagined it. How you were growing up. What your interests were. If you'd started dating. And…" He paused, embarrassed. "Having those letters and packages around, even though they'd been returned…well, after a while it almost felt like having you around, too. In person." Another pause. "I'd always hoped you'd write me, you know."

When she saw the closet full of letters and packages, Corrie had guessed—in fact, hoped—that this would be the explanation. But the last thing had never occurred to her: that, all the time she was waiting to hear from her dad, he'd been waiting to hear from her. "She said that you refused to pay child support, that you shacked up with another woman, couldn't keep a job, spent your time drinking in bars."

"None of that's true, Corrie, or at least…" He colored. "I did spend way too much time in bars. And there were…women. But I've been clean and sober for nine years. And I tried to pay child support when I could, I really did. Sometimes I went without eating to send her a check."

Corrie shook her head. Of *course* what her mother had told her all these years wasn't true. How could she have been so dense as to believe it—believe her lying, embittered, alcoholic mother? She suddenly felt horribly thickheaded and stupid. And guilty—for fifteen years of thinking bad thoughts about her father.

And yet her overwhelming feeling was one of relief.

"I'm sorry," she said.

"For what?"

"For not realizing all that. For…being so *passive*."

"You were just a kid. You didn't know."

"I'm twenty-two years old. I should've figured this out a long time ago."

He waved his hand. "Water under the dam."

She couldn't help smiling. "*Over* the dam."

"I never was any good at sayings and speeches. But I do live by a philosophy, and it's a good one."

"What's that?"

"Forgive everyone everything."

Corrie wasn't sure that was going to be her philosophy—at all.

He finished his cup, rose, picked up the pot. "More coffee?"

"Please."

He poured them each another mug, sat down. "Corrie, I do want to tell you about this so-called bank robbery. I was framed by someone at work, I don't know who. I'm pretty sure it had something to do with their scamming the customers, overcharging them on the financing. That's how they make their money, you know—on the financing. Problem is, they all do it. Except for one—Charlie, the only decent guy there."

"But you *ran*," she said again.

"I know. I've always done stupid, impulsive things. I figured I could hide up here while figuring out the truth. But obviously I don't even have a phone here, and I had to toss my cell phone, because they'll use it to track me. So now I've no way to investigate—and by running I've made myself look guilty as hell. I'm stuck here."

Corrie looked at him. She wanted to believe him.

"I'm not stuck here," she said. "I could investigate."

"Come on," he said, laughing. "You? You don't know the first thing about being a detective."

"Yeah? For your information, I'm studying law

enforcement at the John Jay College of Criminal Justice, I'm getting straight A's, and back in Medicine Creek I worked as the assistant to one of the country's top FBI agents on a famous serial killer case."

His eyes widened. "Oh, no. My daughter, a *cop*?"

26

THE MAN APPEARED SO SUDDENLY IN THE DOOR-
way of Madeleine Teal's office cubicle that she literally
jumped. He was a very strange-looking man, dressed in
black, with a pale face and gray eyes, and he radiated a
restlessness bordering on agitation.

"My, you gave me a start!" she said, pressing a hand
to her ample bosom. "Can I help you?"

"I've come for Dr. Heffler."

Now, that was a strange way of phrasing it—he did
look more than a little like the grim reaper—but the man
did have a mellifluous voice with a charming southern
accent. She herself came from the Midwest, and the various New York accents still grated on her nerves.

"Do you have an appointment?" she asked.

"Dr. Heffler and I are old buddies."

Old buddies. Somehow the way he said it didn't sound
right. Nobody would use the word *buddy* to describe Dr.
Wayne Heffler, who was a pretentious, pseudo-upper-class,
condescending twit, as far as Teal was concerned. She had
known plenty of Hefflers in her long career, but he was
truly the worst: one of those types whose highest pleasure
was found in reviewing the work of subordinates, with the

sole purpose of finding fault and pointing it out in front of as many people as possible. Meanwhile, he neglected his own work and left others to scramble to cover for him, knowing they would be blamed if something went wrong or fell through the cracks.

"And your name, sir?"

"Special Agent Pendergast."

"Oh. As in FBI?"

A singularly disturbing smile spread over the face of the special agent as a marble hand slipped inside his suit coat and withdrew a wallet, opened it to display a shield and ID, then gently closed it and reinserted it into the folds of black wool. With a not-displeasing sense of anticipation, Madeleine Teal pressed the intercom button and picked up the phone.

"Dr. Heffler, there's an FBI agent named Pendergast here to see you, no appointment, says he knows you."

A short pause. "Pendergast, did you say?"

"Yes, Doctor."

"Send him in."

She hung up. "You may go in."

But the agent didn't move. "Dr. Heffler may come out."

Now, this was different. She got back on the phone. "He wants you to come out."

"You tell that son of a bitch that if he wants to see me, I'm here, in my office—otherwise send him away."

She felt a gentle tug. Pendergast's arm had snaked up and was gently grasping the phone. "May I?"

She released the phone. No one could fault her for not opposing an FBI agent.

"Dr. Heffler? Agent Pendergast."

She couldn't hear the reply, but the cricket-like chittering that drifted from the earpiece indicated a raised voice. Heffler was arguing.

This, thought Madeleine Teal, *is going to be good*.

The FBI agent listened patiently, then responded. "I have come for the mtDNA results on the Hotel Killer."

More irritated chittering out of the mouthpiece.

"What a shame." He turned and smiled at her, an apparently genuine smile this time, as he handed her back the telephone. "Thank you. Now—which way is the laboratory where the mtDNA work is performed?"

"It's down the hall to the right, but...no one's allowed in there unescorted," she said, lowering her voice.

"Ah, but I won't be unescorted. Dr. Heffler will be escorting me. Or at least, he will be shortly."

"But—"

Pendergast, however, had his cell phone out and was making a call even as he walked out the door, turned right, and headed down the hall. Almost as soon as he'd vanished, Madeleine Teal's phone rang and she picked it up.

"Dr. Heffler, please," came the voice. "Mayor Starke."

"Mayor Starke?" Unbelievable. It really was him, calling personally. "Yes, sir, just a moment." She put the call through. It lasted less than thirty seconds. Then Heffler came bursting out of his office, face red. "Where'd he go?"

"Down the hall to the lab. I told him—"

But Heffler had already taken off down the hall at an undignified jog. She had never seen the man so put out, so frightened, and—she had to be honest with herself—she enjoyed it immensely.

The Rolls pulled up at the porte cochere of the mansion at 891 Riverside Drive. Agent Pendergast instantly alighted, a slender manila folder under his arm. It was late in the day and a chill wind was coming off the Hudson, tugging at his suit and stirring his pale blond hair. Dry leaves skittered along the pavement and blew around the house as the heavy oaken door opened to swallow his dark figure.

Winding his way swiftly through the dim corridors, Pendergast reached the library. It remained untidy, the refectory table stacked with papers, spilling to the floor. The section of bookcases revealing the flat-panel remained open. He moved briskly to the rear of the library, where a swift flick of his wrist at some invisible mechanism caused another section of shelves to swing open, revealing a small work space with computer and monitor. Without bothering to sit down, Pendergast began typing on the keyboard, the screen leaping to life. He pulled a compact disk out of the manila folder, scattering papers in his haste. He fed the CD into the computer and rapped out additional commands, reaching a log-in screen. When he filled out the password, a stark black-and-white welcome page came into view:

DOCTOR'S TRIAL GROUP
mtDNA DATABASE

Homo sapiens haplogroup mitochondrion
Polymorphisms and mutations

THIS IS A CONFIDENTIAL DATABASE.
UNAUTHORIZED USE STRICTLY FORBIDDEN.

More machine-gun typing followed, and then the screen displayed a rotating wheel. A moment later a single, small result popped into view. Pendergast, still standing, stared at the result for a full five seconds— and then he staggered. Stepping backward, he wobbled for a moment, then dropped unceremoniously to his knees.

27

SPECIAL AGENT PENDERGAST ENTERED HIS
Dakota apartment and walked into the reception room.
There he paused, irresolutely, listening to the whisper
of water over stone. After a moment, he stepped over
to a small Monet painting and straightened it, back and
forth, although it was already perfectly aligned against
the rose-colored wall. Next, he moved to a twisted bonsai tree, picked up a tiny pair of hand-forged clippers
that lay on the table beside it, and carefully snipped off
a few new shoots of growth. His hand trembled slightly
as he did so.

That done, he paced the room restlessly, pausing to
rearrange the lotus petals that floated in the base of the
fountain.

He had something he must do, but the prospect of
doing it was almost unbearable.

Finally, he stepped over to the flush door that led into
the apartment proper. Opening it, he walked down the
length of hallway, passing a number of doors. He nodded to Miss Ishimura, who was resting in her sitting
room, reading a book in Japanese, and soon reached
the end of the corridor, where the hallway made a

ninety-degree turn to the right. Pendergast opened the first door to the left after the turn and stepped into the room beyond.

The walls on either side were lined floor-to-ceiling with recessed mahogany bookshelves, each filled with eighteenth- and nineteenth-century leather-bound books. The wall before him was taken up by a deep window embrasure of polished mahogany, with two banquette seats facing each other, fitted with plush cushions. Between these lay a large picture window overlooking the intersection of Central Park West and Seventy-Second Street. Beyond lay the broad vastness of Central Park, its trees bare and stark in the winter sun.

He closed his eyes, let his body relax, and carefully regulated his breathing. Slowly, outside existence began to fall away; first the room, then the apartment, the building, the island, then the world itself, in an ever-widening circle of orchestrated oblivion. The process took fifteen minutes to complete. When it was done, he held himself suspended in the close darkness, waiting for absolute emptiness, absolute calm. When he had achieved it, he slowly opened his eyes—not physically, but mentally—slowly, slowly.

The small room was revealed in all its detailed perfection. But it remained empty.

Pendergast did not allow himself the luxury of surprise. He was highly skilled in the art of Chongg Ran, an ancient Himalayan mental discipline that he had taken years to master. It was rare for him to fail to achieve *stong pa nyid*—the State of Pure Emptiness. Clearly, there was resistance lurking somewhere in his mind.

He would need to take more time—much more time.

Once again, he regulated his breathing, allowing his heart rate to slow to forty beats a minute. He let his mind go blank, to still the inner voice, to let go of his hopes and desires, to forget even his purpose in coming to this room. For a long moment, he lingered again, weightless, in empty space. Then—infinitely more slowly this time—he began building a perfect model of Manhattan Island in his mind, starting with his apartment and moving outward. He went first room by room, then building by building, and then—with loving attention—block by block. Pendergast knew the topography of Manhattan as well as any living person, and he allowed himself to linger on every structure, every intersection, every obscure point of architectural interest, in a harmonious mental braid of memory and reconstruction, assembling every detail into a whole and holding it, in its entirety, in his mind. Step by step the great mental construction was made, expanding until it was bordered by the Hudson River to the west and the Harlem River to the east, Battery Park in the south and Spuyten Duyvil in the north. For a long, long moment he held the entire island in his head, its every feature existing simultaneously with every other in his mental reconstruction. And then—after assuring himself of its perfection—he vaporized it in a one-second flick of the mind. Vanished. Extinguished. Nothing remained but darkness.

Now, in his mind, he opened his eyes again. Five hours had passed. And Helen Esterhazy Pendergast was sitting in the window seat across from him. Of all the rooms in the Dakota apartment, this had been Helen's favorite. She had not been especially fond of New York, and this tiny den—cozy with books and the smell of polished wood, the view of Central Park spread out before it—had been her particular retreat.

Of course, Helen was not there in the literal sense; but in every other way she existed: everything in Pendergast's mind that touched on her, every memory, every tiny detail, was part of that mental construct, so much so that she could be said to have assumed a quasi-autonomous existence.

Such was the beauty and power of Chongg Ran.

Helen's hands were folded in her lap, and she was wearing a dress he well remembered—black satin, with pale coral-colored stitching traced along the low neckline. She was younger—about the age she had been at the time of the hunting accident.

Accident. The irony of it was that it *had* been an accident—only not in the way he'd believed these many years.

"Helen," he said.

Her eyes rose to meet his briefly. She smiled and then looked down again. The smile caused him to flinch in pain and grief; and the scene wavered and almost flew apart. He waited until it stabilized, until his heart slowed back down.

"There is a serial killer loose in the city," he said. He could hear the quaver in his own voice, along with a formal tone uncharacteristic of his usual exchanges with his wife. "He has killed three times. Each time, he left a message. The second message was *Happy Birthday.*"

There was a silence.

"This second killing took place on *my* birthday. Because of that—and certain other elements of the murders—I began to suspect they were the work of my brother, Diogenes. This seemed to be confirmed when I compared my DNA with that of the killer and learned that we were, in fact, closely related. Close enough to be brother-to-brother."

He stopped, checking to see the impact these words were having on his wife. But she continued to look down at the hands clasped in her lap.

"But now I've had a look at the mtDNA results as well. And they've shown me something else. The killer isn't related to me alone. He's also related *to you*."

Helen looked up. She either could not, or would not, speak.

"Do you remember that trip you made to Brazil? It was about a year before we were married, and you were away a long time—almost five months. At the time, you told me you were on a mission for Doctors With Wings. But that was a lie—wasn't it? The truth was that...that you went to Brazil in order to secretly bear a child. *Our* child."

The words hung in the air. Helen returned his gaze, a stricken look on her face.

"I think I even know when the child was conceived. It was on that first moonrise we shared—two weeks after we met. Wasn't it? And now...now you've left me to come to terms with the fact that I have not only a son I do not know, a son I've never met—but a son who is also a serial killer."

Helen dropped her eyes once again.

"I've also seen documents that indicate your family— and, in fact, yourself and your brother, Judson—were involved in eugenics experiments that date back to the Nazi regime. Brazil; John James Audubon; Mengele and Wolfgang Faust; Longitude Pharmaceuticals; the Covenant, *Der Bund*—it's a long, ugly story that I'm only beginning to piece together. Judson explained a piece of it to me once, not long before he died. He said: *What I've become was what I was born to be. It's what I was born* into—*and it's something beyond my control. If you only knew the horror that Helen and I have been subjected to, you'd understand.*"

He paused, swallowed.

"But the truth is that I *don't* understand. Why did you hide so much from me, Helen? Your pregnancy, our child, your family's past, the horrors Judson spoke of—why didn't you let me help you? Why did you keep our child apart from me all these years—and in so doing perhaps allow him to become...what he has now become? As you surely knew, those tendencies are a dark strain in my family going back generations. The truth is, you never, ever mentioned him until your own dying words to me: *He's coming*."

Helen refused to look at him. She was clenching and unclenching the hands that lay in her lap.

"I'd like to believe you weren't complicit—or, at least, merely tangentially complicit—in your sister's death. I'd also like to believe Emma Grolier, as she was known, was already dead, mercifully euthanized, when *you* learned of the plan. I certainly hope that was the case. It would certainly have made the whole arrangement easier to swallow for you.

"But why did she have to die for you in the first place? I have been thinking about that for a long time now, and I believe I understand what happened. After learning about the Doane family tragedy, and the cruel way they were used, you must have threatened Charles Slade and Longitude—and by extension *Der Bund*—with exposure over the Audubon drug. So the decision was made, in turn, to kill you in order to keep you silent. Correct?"

Now Helen's hands were trembling.

"Judson, your own brother, was tasked with the job. But he couldn't do it—and the very assignment was, no doubt, what made him secretly break with the Covenant. Instead he devised a way, an *elaborate* way, to keep you alive. He knew that your damaged twin sister had a terminal illness—I've just today been able to glean that much of her medical history from the public record. So he arranged for that hunting accident with the Red Lion—planning to substitute your twin sister's body for yourself. He told his minders about the blank cartridges in your gun; told them you'd be taking lead on the hunt. *Der Bund* was satisfied by that. He'd found a lion that would drag you away without harming you, but would also maul your sister's body on command. And Judson kept the plan from you until the night before—didn't he? That's why you seemed out of sorts that final evening in Africa—he was there near the camp, along with the lion's handlers and Emma's recently deceased corpse. He called you out and explained the whole scheme. Only it didn't go quite as expected; the lion didn't exactly stick to the plan, and you lost a hand as it dragged you away. Good thing your sister's body was, right afterward, sufficiently devoured as to allow Judson to leave your own hand—and the ring—behind as even more evidence proving your death. My word—the presence of mind he must have had."

Pendergast shook his head bitterly. "What a fiendishly complex arrangement—but it *had* to be complex, to keep from arousing my suspicions. If what happened had not seemed absolutely, utterly an act of nature, I would not have rested until learning the truth—just as I am not resting now."

A moment of terrible silence.

"But again—why didn't you simply come to me, that night in the hunting camp? Why didn't you let me help you? Why, why did you shut me out?"

He paused. "And there's something else—something I have to know. Do you love me, Helen? Did you ever love me? I always felt in my heart that you did. But now,

234 DOUGLAS PRESTON & LINCOLN CHILD

learning all this—now I can't be certain. I'd like to believe you first met me simply for access to the Audubon records, but that you then, unexpectedly, fell in love with me. I'd like to believe that your pregnancy was a mistake. But am I wrong in so thinking? Was our marriage just a contrivance? Was I an unwitting pawn in some grand design I don't yet understand the full extent of? Helen, *please* tell me. It is...it is a kind of agony for me, not knowing."

Helen remained stock-still. A single tear welled up in one eye, then trickled down her cheek. It was an answer of a kind.

Pendergast looked at her, waiting, for a long time. Then, with a barely perceptible sigh, he closed his eyes. When he next opened them, the room was once again occupied only by himself.

And then faintly, from somewhere in the front of the apartment, he heard a deeply muffled scream.

28

JUMPING TO HIS FEET, PENDERGAST EXITED THE reading room and sprinted down the hall toward the reception area, following the sound of the scream. As he approached, he could hear a growing commotion, several loud voices mingling with Miss Ishimura's unintelligible, high-pitched expostulations—and the sound of someone groaning and babbling.

He swept through the flush door into the reception room and was greeted by an extraordinary sight. A doorman and the head of Dakota security—a man named Franklin—were holding up between them a skinny young man, hardly more than a boy, dressed in jeans and a torn work shirt. His hair was matted, his entire body was covered with soot, and he smelled. One ear was wrapped in a bloody bandage, and there were grimy bandages on a hand and a foot. The boy was clearly half out of his mind, hardly able to stand, his eyes rolling in his head, murmuring incoherently.

Pendergast turned to the head security officer. "What the devil?"

"I'm sorry, Mr. Pendergast, but the boy, he's been hurt, he's in trouble."

"I can see that. But why have you brought him here?"

The security officer looked confused. "I'm sorry?"

"Mr. Franklin, why have you brought this boy here, to my apartment, of all places? He needs to go to a hospital."

"I know that, sir, but since he's your son—"

"My *son*?" Pendergast stared at the bedraggled boy in total amazement.

The head of security stopped, then restarted, all in a panic. "I just assumed, given what he said..." He again hesitated: "I hope I haven't done anything wrong, bringing him up here."

Pendergast continued to stare. All mental functions had ceased and he was overwhelmed by a feeling of unreality, as if the world had suddenly become flat, cartoonish. As he took in the boy's features—the hair, light blond beneath its mantle of soot; the silvery blue eyes; the narrow, patrician face—his sense of paralyzing astonishment only deepened. He could not move, speak, or think. And yet everyone in the room was waiting for him to say something, to act, to confirm or reject.

A groan from the boy filled the empty silence.

This seemed to jolt Franklin. "Forgive me, Mr. Pendergast, but we'll take care of it if you'd prefer, call the police or an ambulance. If he is your son, I thought you might wish to handle it yourself...not involve the authorities...." His voice trailed off in confusion.

Pendergast's lips moved, but no sound came out.

"Mr. Pendergast?" The head of security stood there with the doorman, each still holding the boy by one arm.

Another long silence seemed to solidify in the room as everyone waited, the whispering sound of the waterfall sliding down the marble becoming unnaturally loud.

Finally, it was the diminutive Miss Ishimura who reacted. She stepped up to Franklin and gestured vigorously at him. Her gestures were very clear: the security personnel were to lay the boy down on the leather sofa in the middle of the room. They did so, easing him into a supine position, while Miss Ishimura fetched a pillow and put it under his head. The movement seem to rouse the boy from his stupor. As he lay there, his eyes focused, roamed the room—and then fixed on Pendergast.

He raised his head, the pale eyes glittering, staring. "Father..." he gasped in strongly accented English. "Hide me..." Even this small exertion seemed to exhaust the boy and his head fell back, the eyes unfocusing, the lips moving in an unintelligible murmur.

Pendergast blinked. His vision cleared somewhat and his eyes, now very dark, traveled once again over the boy, his observant mind coming alive to many small details: the location of the bandages; the youth's height, frame, carriage, and facial features. As the mental lock slowly released itself, the full dimension of what he was seeing seeped into his consciousness: the resemblance to Diogenes; the even stronger one to himself and Helen. And, unbidden, the security videotapes that he had watched endlessly began to loop through his mind.

A sentence formed in his head. *This is my son—the Hotel Killer.*

"Mr. Pendergast," said Franklin, "what should we do? Should we call the police? This boy needs medical attention."

My son—the Hotel Killer.

Reality returned in a blinding flash. Pendergast was

suddenly all action, springing to the side of the boy, kneeling. He grasped the boy's hand—it was burning hot—and felt for a pulse. Rapid and thready. He had a high fever and was delirious. The self-amputations were probably becoming infected.

Pendergast rose, turned. "Thank you, Mr. Franklin," he said quickly. "There is no need to call the police. You have done well. I'll get him a doctor right away."

"Yes, sir." Franklin and the doorman exited the apartment.

Pendergast turned to his housekeeper, who watched his lips attentively. "Miss Ishimura, please get me bandages, a basin of hot water, antibiotic cream, washcloths, and scissors, and bring them into the Red Room."

Miss Ishimura went off. Pendergast slipped his arms under the boy and lifted him up—he was shockingly thin—carried him into the inner apartment, and laid him on a bed in a cool, disused bedroom that faced the inner courtyard of the Dakota. The boy began babbling, shivering violently. Pendergast pulled off and, where necessary, cut away his filthy clothes, then inspected his wounds, starting with the ear. The earlobe was gone, in a way that all too clearly matched the piece left with the first corpse. It was an ugly-looking wound, with an incipient infection. The missing finger was in still-worse shape, the bone end exposed, and the amputated toe had opened up and was bleeding badly. The boy appeared to have walked a long way on the injured foot.

Miss Ishimura arrived with the basin and washcloth, and Pendergast wiped the boy's face. The gesture brought the boy once more back into reality. "Father..." the boy said, "help..."

"I'm here," said Pendergast. "It's all right. You're safe now." His voice came out as a croak. He rinsed the washcloth and patted the face dry. Now Miss Ishimura returned with a tray of bandages, antibiotics, and other medical supplies.

"Not my fault...*bitte, mein Gott, bitte*, do not give me up..."

Pendergast gently washed the injured finger, cleaning the wound and applying antibiotic ointment and a fresh bandage. He next worked on the toe, which was in the worst shape, continuing to ooze blood despite all he did, but he washed and bandaged it all the same, wrapping it in a gauze cloth. As he worked, the boy moaned and turned restlessly, murmuring over and over, "Not my fault..."

When Pendergast was finished, he stood up. For a moment the room spun around, and Miss Ishimura grasped his arm and steadied him. She led him, almost like a child, out of the room into the hallway, signaling to him that she would take over, that he was not to concern himself with the boy any longer, that he was to go into his study and rest.

Nodding wordlessly, he walked down the hall to his study. He shut the door and leaned against it momentarily to steady himself, to try to bring order to his thoughts. He made his way to his habitual chair, eased himself down, closed his eyes, and fought—with a supreme effort of will—to bring his stampeding emotions under control.

Gradually, he was able to return his heart rate and respiration to their normal rates.

This was a problem, like any other. It must be thought of in that way: a problem.

My son—the Hotel Killer.

He picked up the telephone and dialed a number.

"Dr. Rossiter? Aloysius Pendergast here. I require a house call from you in my apartments at the Dakota. A sick boy, with several open wounds from amputated digits. There is a need for surgery, and, as always, I'll ask that you perform your services with complete discretion..."

29

CAPTAIN LAURA HAYWARD STRODE BRISKLY down the central corridor of PS Thirty-Two, heading for the school's auditorium. There had been a rash of hate crimes against homeless people that fall—beatings, robberies, even a case in which a destitute man had been set afire by rowdy teenagers in Riverside Park—and Hayward had been tasked by the commissioner with raising schoolchildren's awareness of the plight of the homeless and the reality of life on the streets. *Homeless people are people, too*, was her message. Over the past few weeks she had spoken at half a dozen schools, and the reception had been gratifying. She felt she was making a real difference. It was something she enjoyed doing—and she knew a great deal about it. The subject of her master's thesis had been the social structure of an underground homeless community in New York City, and she had spent months observing them, experiencing their lives, listening to their problems, trying to understand their histories, motivations, and challenges. In recent years she'd been too busy with standard police work to put her M.A. in sociology to much use, but now it seemed perfect preparation for what she was doing.

Rounding the corner, she was surprised to run into D'Agosta, walking her way.

"Vinnie!" she said, refraining from kissing him as they were both on duty. "What are you doing here?"

"Looking for you, actually," he said. "I was in the neighborhood. There's something we need to talk about."

"Why couldn't we have talked at breakfast?" she asked. He looked troubled—and a little guilty. There was something on his mind; she'd been aware of it for the last few days. But with things like that, you could never hurry him—you just had to wait until he was ready to open up. And then you had to seize the opportunity before he changed his mind.

She glanced at her watch. "I'm due to give that presentation in ten minutes. Come on, we can talk in the auditorium."

D'Agosta followed her down the hall and through a set of double doors. Beyond was a 1950s-era space, with a balcony and a wide stage, and it reminded Laura of her own high-school auditorium, with its pep rallies and fallout drills and all-school movie events. Already it was half full with students. They took seats in the rear.

"Okay," she said, turning to him. "What's up?"

For a moment he didn't speak. "It's Pendergast," he finally said.

"Why am I not surprised?"

"I'm worried sick about him. He's gone through about as rough a patch as a person can hit and now he's acting strange—even for him."

"Tell me about it," Hayward said.

"After his wife died, he retreated to his apartment and I'm pretty sure was getting into self-medication, if you know what I mean—hitting the hard stuff."

"What stuff?"

"I don't know which drugs, exactly, but I had the terrible feeling it was a calculated form of self-destruction—a run-up to suicide. I followed your advice and gave him the Hotel Killer case portfolio to chew over. It—seems to have unhinged him. He went from being totally apathetic to complete obsession with the case. He showed up at the third murder scene, got himself credentialed up, and now he's become the bane of Agent Gibbs's existence. I'm telling you, he and Gibbs are headed for a wreck. I've got to believe it's because Pendergast is feeling so devastated that he's antagonizing Gibbs. I mean, I've seen him needle people, get into their faces—but there was always a reason for it before."

"Oh, Jesus. Maybe my idea wasn't so hot after all."

"I haven't gotten to the worst part."

"Which is?"

"His theory of the crime. It's bizarre, to say the least."

Hayward sighed. "Let me hear it."

Another hesitation. "He believes the Hotel Killer is his brother, Diogenes."

Hayward frowned. "I thought Diogenes was dead."

"That's what everyone thought. The thing is, Pendergast won't tell me *why* he thinks his brother is the murderer. It seems so preposterous. I really worry that his wife's death has scattered his marbles."

"What's his evidence?"

"None that I know. At least none that he's shared with me. But I honestly don't see it in any case. The M.O. is totally different; there's nothing that links this case to his brother. And a quick-and-dirty search of the databases indicates his brother really did vanish and is presumed dead. This is crazy."

"So what does Singleton think of this theory?"

"That's the other thing." Even though they were alone in the back of the auditorium, D'Agosta lowered his voice. "Pendergast doesn't want me to tell anyone about this theory. I can't mention it to Gibbs, to Singleton—to anybody."

Hayward looked at him, opened her mouth to say, *Why haven't you told me this before?* But then she reconsidered. D'Agosta looked so troubled. And the fact was, he *had* told her—and was now obviously searching for her advice. And, ironically, it had been her idea to bring the case to Pendergast to begin with.

"The thing of it is, I know that if there *is* information this might be Diogenes—even if it seems like crazy information—he and I both have an obligation to pass it on. There's always a chance it might help the case. But...I promised him." He shook his head. "Christ, I'm really in the weeds about this."

Gently, she took his hand. "Vinnie, it's your duty to turn over all evidence, all information, even the crazy stuff. You're the squad commander."

D'Agosta didn't reply.

"I know Pendergast is your friend. I know he's been through a terrible ordeal. But this isn't about friendship. It's not even about what's best for your career. This is about catching a dangerous killer who's likely to kill again. Vinnie, you *have* to do the right thing on this. If Pendergast really has hard information, you've got to get it out of him. And when you do, you have to turn it over. It's as simple as that."

D'Agosta looked down.

"And as far as he and Gibbs are concerned, that's FBI business. You let them sort it out. Okay?" She gave his hand a harder squeeze. "I've got to give that talk now. We can speak more tonight."

"Okay."

She stopped herself from kissing him, then stood up. As she gave him one final look before heading to the podium, she was dismayed to find he appeared just as conflicted as before.

30

IT WAS NOON. THE DOCTOR HAD COME AND gone, the room was silent and dark, the curtains drawn, the boy—bathed and cleaned of soot—was asleep. A shadowy figure sat in a corner of the small, spare room, unmoving, his pale face like a ghostly apparition floating in the dimness.

The boy stirred, turned, sighed. He had been asleep for eighteen hours. One hand lay on the covers, shackled, with a chain attached to the metal bed frame.

Another sigh, and then a gleam appeared in the darkness—the gleam of an open eye. The boy turned again, restlessly, and finally raised his head. He looked around and his attention fixed on the figure in the corner.

For a long time they looked at each other in the darkness, and then the boy spoke in a whisper. "Water?"

The figure rose silently, left the room, and returned with a glass of water and a straw. The boy reached for it, the movement of his arm stopped by the chain. He looked at it, surprised, but said nothing. Pendergast held the glass for the boy, who drank.

When he was done, his head sank back to the pillow. "Thank...you."

His voice was weak, but no longer raving. His mind had returned to rationality. The fever was down, the antibiotics taking effect. The long sleep appeared to have done him good.

Another long silence ensued. And then the boy held up his wrist, the one with the chain on it. "Why?" he asked.

"You know why. What I want to know is—why you have come here."

"Because . . . you are Father."

"Father," Pendergast repeated, as if the word was foreign to him. "And how do you know this?"

"I heard . . . talk. Of you. Pendergast. My father."

Pendergast did not reply. Finally, the boy stirred again in the bed. "Do they . . . know I am here?" He spoke hesitantly, with a strange accent, part German but softened by the mellifluous roundness of what sounded like Portuguese. His face, now clean, was so pale and delicate that blue veins could be seen within it. Dark circles lay like bruises under his eyes, and his thin hair was plastered to his skull by sweat.

"If you are speaking of the police," said Pendergast, voice cold as dry ice, "I have not informed them. Not yet."

"Not the police . . ." said the boy. "*Them*."

"Them?"

"The others. My . . . my brother."

This was met with another profound silence, and then Pendergast said, in a strange voice: "Your brother?"

The boy coughed, tried to sit up. "More water, please?"

Removing his .45 and laying it out of reach, Pendergast went over to the boy, helped prop him up against the headboard with some pillows, and gave him another sip of water. This time the boy drank greedily, finishing the glass.

"I am hungry," he said.

"You will be fed in good time," said Pendergast, resuming his seat and sliding the .45 back into his suit. "Now: you were speaking of your—brother?"

"My brother."

Pendergast stared at the boy impatiently. "Yes. Tell me about this brother."

"He is Alban. We are...twins. Sort of twins. He is the one doing the killing. He has been cutting me. He thinks it *lustig*. Funny. But I escaped. Did he follow?" Fear had crept into his voice.

Pendergast rose, his slender figure like a wraith in the dim room. He paced to the curtained window, turned. "Let me understand," he said, voice low. "You have a twin brother who is killing people in New York City hotels. He's kept you a prisoner and has been cutting off your body parts—an earlobe, a finger, and a toe—and leaving them at the crime scenes."

"Yes."

"And why did you come to me?"

"You are...Father. Are you not? Alban...spoke of it. He talk of you a lot with others. They do not think I listen. Or that I understand."

Standing very still, Pendergast did not say anything for a long time. And then he stepped back to the chair and eased himself into it, almost as if he was in pain. "Perhaps," he said, passing a pale hand across his brow, "you should start at the beginning. Tell me everything you know. Where you were born, under what circumstances, who your brother Alban is, and what he and you are doing here in New York."

"I will try. I not know much."

"Do your best."

"I was born in...Brazil. They call the place Nova Godói."

At this, Pendergast froze. "Your mother was—?"

"I never met Mother. Alban was the good twin. I... bad twin."

"And your name?"

"I have no name. Only good twins get names. I... Forty-Seven."

"What are these good twins and bad twins? What does it mean?"

"Not know how it works. Not exactly. Good twins get all the good stuff, bad stuff go into bad twins. Good twins go to school, have sports, have training. They eat good food. We...work the fields."

Pendergast slowly rose from his seat, a shadow growing in silent amazement. "So the town, Nova Godói, is full of twins?"

The youth nodded.

"And your twin, this Alban: he's the one doing the killing?"

"He...loves it."

"Why is he killing?"

The boy shrugged.

"And you escaped? How?"

"They think I am more stupid than I am. I fooled them, got away." This was followed by a brief hiccuping sob. "I hope they do not follow me."

"Where were you held?"

"It was...under the ground. There was a long tunnel, old, very cool. They kept me in...giant oven, cold, big as a room. Bricks dirty, floor dirty. Big metal door. Last time...they forget to lock it."

"And?"

"I ran, just kept running."

"How did you find me?"

"I heard them say you live in fancy place. Dakota place. So I asked. A stranger told me, helped me, put me in yellow car. Gave me those." And he pointed to a few wadded bills Miss Ishimura had removed from the pocket of his jeans.

He fell silent. Pendergast slid his hand into his pocket, removed a key, and unlocked the shackle from the boy's wrist. "I'm sorry," he said. "I misunderstood."

The boy smiled. "I care not. I . . . used to it."

Pendergast pressed a button beside the door, and a moment later Miss Ishimura came in. Pendergast turned to her and spoke briskly. "Could you kindly prepare a full American breakfast for our guest? Eggs, sausage, toast, orange juice. Thank you."

He turned back to the boy. "So someone put you in a taxicab? How long was the ride?"

"Very long. Pass many, many autos."

"What do you remember of it? Did you cross any bridges, go through tunnels?"

"We crossed a big bridge over a river." He shook his head at the memory. "So many buildings, so tall."

Pendergast immediately picked up a house phone. "Charles? The cab that brought the boy. I need its hack number. Go through the building's security videos and get it to me right away. Thank you." He hung up, turned back to the boy lying on the bed, looking so lost, so confused, so vulnerable.

"Let me see if I understand what you've told me," he said. "You and your brother are twins, born and raised in Brazil. You are apparently part of some program. As part of this, he got all the desirable qualities, the good genetic material, somehow leaving the unwanted material to you, in a manner of speaking. Is that it?"

"They say we are dumping ground. Garbage."

"And you each get a number. You're Forty-Seven."

"Forty-Seven."

"So there must be a lot of you."

The youth nodded. "Could you open curtains? Please? I want to see light."

Pendergast went to the window and slid open the curtains, letting in the long yellow light of early winter, coming in low over the slate roofs, dormers, gables, and turrets of the famous apartment building. The boy turned gratefully toward the light, which fell on his pallid face.

In a gentle voice, Pendergast spoke. "The first thing is that you should have a name. A real name."

"I do not know what to call myself."

"Then I will name you. How do you like... Tristram?"

"I like it fine. And shall call you... Father?"

"Yes," said Pendergast. "Yes. Please do call me..." He struggled to get the word out. "Father."

31

CORRIE STOOD AT THE FAR END OF THE PARKING lot of the Joe Ricco Chevrolet-Cadillac dealership, rows of new cars and trucks glittering in the chilly sunlight. Times were tough, especially in the Allentown area, and she had just been given the bum's rush, hustled out the door of the dealership as soon as they realized she was a job seeker, not a buyer.

She was mightily annoyed. She had had her hair done at a local salon. It had been hell getting the purple out, and in the end they'd had to dye it black and cut it shoulder length, with a little flip. It gave her a 1950s retro look that she sort of liked, but it was still way too conservative for her taste. A tailored gray suit, low pumps, and a touch of makeup completed the transformation of Corrie the Goth into Corrie the Yuppie. It had made quite a dent in Pendergast's three thousand.

Fat lot of good it had done her.

In retrospect, she realized it was unrealistic to think she could get a job selling cars when she had no experience beyond a year of college. She should have applied for a position as a clerk-assistant or janitor or something. Now it was too late. She would have to figure out some other way to get in close to the dealership, find out what was really going on.

As she was standing there, wondering what to do next, a voice behind her said: "Excuse me?"

She turned to see an older couple, well dressed, friendly.

"Yes?"

"Are you available to help us?"

She looked around and was about to say that she didn't work there, but something stopped her. Instead, she said: "Of course." She bestowed on them a dazzling smile and offered her hand. "I'm Corrie."

"Sue and Chuck Hesse," said the man, shaking her hand.

She wasn't sure where this was going, but what the heck?

"Welcome to Joe Ricco Chevy-Cadillac," said Corrie.

"I've just retired from the university and we're looking for something comfortable and elegant," the man said.

She could tell right away that the professor was going to do all the talking—but she suspected, looking at the quiet, alert face of the wife, that the decision was going to be hers. They seemed like a nice couple. The man was even wearing a bow tie, which Corrie had always considered a sign of friendliness. She had the stirrings of an idea.

The only problem was that she knew nothing whatsoever about cars.

"We've been looking at sedans," said the man, "trying to decide between the CTS Sport and the CTS-V. Could you help us do a comparison?"

Uh-oh. Corrie offered another smile, and leaned toward them. "Um, I have a confession to make."

The man raised his bushy eyebrows.

"You're my first customers. And…well, I don't believe I'm very clear on the differences myself."

"Oh, dear…" said the man, looking around. "Is there another salesperson we could work with?"

"Chuck," said the wife in a stage whisper, "didn't you hear her? We're her first customers. You can't do that!"

God bless you, thought Corrie.

"Oh, yes. I didn't think of that. No offense intended." The professor became flustered in an endearing way.

"I'll do my best," said Corrie. "I really need the experience. And I could sure use the sale. I've been here three days on trial so far, and…" She let her voice trail off. "I don't know how much longer they'll keep me."

"I understand," said the man. "Of course, we're not going to buy anything today."

"Maybe you could show me where the sedans are?" Corrie asked. "We could look at them—and learn—together."

"They're this way." The ex-professor immediately took charge, leading them across the capacious lot to several rows of gleaming, handsome four-door cars in various colors. He seemed to know the lot quite well. He paused at one in red, laid his hand on it.

"Do you like that one?" Corrie said. She felt like an idiot but didn't know what else to say.

"It's not bad."

"If you don't mind my asking, what, ah, do you like about it? I need to learn these things if I'm going to sell them."

The man launched into an enthusiastic recounting of its features and handling, mentioning a "laudable" review he'd read in the *New York Times*, or maybe it was in *USA Today*. He spoke of the transformation of GM from a dinosaur into an innovative company, competing with Toyota and Honda on their own turf, a real American success story. Their quality was now second to none. As Corrie listened intently, giving him an encouraging smile, he gave her various selling tips, ticking them off on his fingers. Corrie had always looked at Cadillacs as being fuddy-duddy cars for old-sters, but apparently they were now a hot item.

"So," Corrie asked, when the man paused, "why's the V sedan almost twice as much as the Sport? I mean, I don't see a lot of difference."

Oh, but there was a big difference, the man said, his bow tie wagging. And he proceeded to enumerate the differences with professorial clarity, Corrie again hanging on to every word. She was amazed at how much research the man had done. *But then again,* she thought, *he was a professor.*

Twenty minutes later, Corrie led the couple into the main salesroom and looked around for the manager who had interviewed her—or, rather, had declined to inter-view her. And there he was, Diet Coke in hand, brown suit and all, talking to two other salespeople, laughing salaciously about something. They quieted down as she approached. The manager looked at her with squinty eyes but wisely didn't say anything.

"I want to tell you," boomed the professor, "that your new salesperson did a bang-up job selling us that red CTS-V sedan out there. Now, let's talk turkey on the price and get this deal done!"

Corrie stood there, wondering just what the heck was going to happen now, but the manager was a cool customer. Without batting an eye, he gestured to one of the salespeople to get the paperwork started, then shook the couple's hands, congratulating them on their taste and style, and praising Corrie for her fine work as if she actually were a salesperson.

He finished up with a pat on Corrie's back and a friendly, "If you'd care to step into my office, we'll talk in a moment."

Corrie stepped in and waited in trepidation. In half an hour the manager came back, settled behind his desk, sighed, clasped his hands together, and leaned forward. "What the hell do you think you're doing?"

"I sold a car for you, didn't I?"

He stared at her. "BFD. I sell half a dozen cars a day."

Corrie rose. "I was just trying to show you what I could do. If you don't like it, fine. Keep the commission and I'll walk out of here and never bother you again." She got up in a huff.

"Sit down, sit down." The manager seemed to be cooling off. "Okay, I'll admit, I'm impressed. Mr. and Mrs. Bow Tie have been in here a dozen times, and I was pretty sure they were just tire kickers. In thirty minutes you sold them a seventy-one-thousand-dollar car. How'd you do it?"

"That's my secret."

He stared at her. He didn't like that answer at all. "You want a job here? You learn some respect."

She shook her head. "I've got a system, and if your salespeople want to learn it, they can trail me while I work." She gave him an arrogant smile. The manager was clearly a first-class asshole, but an intelligent and predictable one who knew which side his bread was buttered on. She figured he might appreciate a brash go-getter.

"Well, well," he said. "All right. We'll try you out for a week. We need a girl salesperson, don't have one. No salary, commissions only, no benefits, you work as an independent contractor, cash under the table. Don't report your taxes because we sure as hell won't. And you'll work with a partner at all times. Agreed?"

"Agreed."

He stuck out his hand. "Joe Ricco Junior."

"Corrie Swanson."

They shook hands. "You related by any chance to Jack Swanson?" Ricco asked casually.

"No. Why?"

"Because it's his job you're replacing."

"Never heard of him. Swanson's a common name. You know, like the TV dinners?"

"You're not of *that* family, are you?"

She blushed. "Well, don't tell anyone. I like people to think I have to work for a living."

Ricco Junior looked impressed. Very impressed.

32

THE BOY SAT AT THE TABLE EATING TOAST WITH butter and jam. Never in his entire life had he tasted anything so wonderful. And the sausages the Oriental woman had given him—many times had he watched his brother eat sausages, but he had never enjoyed one himself, only salivated at the aroma, imagining how they must taste. As he chewed, slowly, savoring the incredible sweetness of the jam, he thought of his new name: Tristram. It sounded strange to him, and he repeated it in his head, trying to get used to it. *Tristram. Tristram.* It seemed almost a miracle, having a name of his own. He never thought it would be possible. And yet now he had one, just like that.

He took another bite of toast and glanced at his father. He was scared of his father: the man seemed so cool, so remote—almost, in that way, like *them*. But Tristram also sensed his father was an important man, and a good man, and he felt safe with him. For the first time in his life, he felt safe.

Another man entered the room. He was powerful, muscular, silent. Like the ones that so often punished him. Tristram watched him warily out of the corner of his eye. He was used to watching, observing, listening—while never seeming to do so. They would *correct* him if they thought he was listening or looking. Long ago he had learned to hide such habits, along with everything else about himself. The less they noticed him, the better. To be ignored was always his goal. Others had not been as careful as he. Several of those others had died. Caution was the key to survival.

"Ah, Proctor, have a seat," his father said to the man. "Coffee?"

The man remained standing, his movements stiff. "No, thank you, sir."

"Proctor, this is my son, Tristram. Tristram, Proctor."

Startled, Tristram raised his head. He wasn't used to being singled out, named, introduced like this to strangers. Such things usually came before a beating— or worse.

The man gave him the faintest of nods. He seemed uninterested. That suited Tristram fine.

"Were you followed?" his father asked.

"I expected as much, sir, and noticed as much."

"We need to get Tristram up to the Riverside Drive mansion. That's the safest place. Use the apartment's back passage, of course. I've arranged a decoy car. I believe you know what to do."

"Naturally, sir."

"Let's not waste any time." Then his father turned to him. "Finish your brunch, Tristram," he said in a not-unkind voice.

Tristram stuffed the rest of the toast into his mouth and gulped down the coffee. He had never eaten such delicious food, and he hoped that wherever they were going it would be as good.

He followed his father and the other one down many winding passageways, stopping at last at an unmarked wooden door. His toe began hurting, but he worked hard to disguise his limp. If they thought he was too damaged, they might leave him behind. He had seen it before, many times.

They stepped into a space that contained nothing except a coiled rope and a padlocked trapdoor in the floor. Pendergast unlocked the padlock, opened the door, and shone the flashlight down. Tristram had seen such dark holes before—had been in many of them—and fear suddenly spiked within him. But then, in the light, he was able to make out a small room below, with a dresser and a sofa and a series of strange machines lined up along a table, wires leading away from them.

His father dropped one end of the ladder down into the room below, then handed the flashlight to the man named Proctor. "Keep the boy close as you make your way through the back passage. When you ultimately emerge from Twenty-Four West Seventy-Second Street, make a careful surveillance. If you can get away without being seen, do so. You'll find a 1984 Honda Civic from Rent-A-Wreck parked at curbside. I shall meet you at the mansion in a few hours."

Pendergast turned to the boy. "Tristram, you'll go with Proctor."

The boy felt another surge of fear. "You not come?"

"He'll keep you safe. I'll join you shortly."

The boy hesitated for a moment. Then he turned and followed Proctor down the rope ladder with a feeling of resignation. He needed to do what they said, exactly what they said. Perhaps—as in the past—it would keep him alive.

Two hours later, Proctor sat with the boy in the large, dimly lit library of 891 Riverside Drive, awaiting Pendergast's arrival. Proctor had always seen himself as a soldier doing his duty, and that's how he thought of this assignment—even if it was chauffeuring a strange boy, Pendergast's son, no less. The boy was the spitting image of his father physically—but in his demeanor and behavior, a polar opposite. Nothing had been explained to Proctor, and he required no explanations. And yet, of all the surprises he had experienced in Pendergast's employ—and there had been many—this was the greatest.

The boy had initially been uncommunicative, anxious, and uncertain. But once they were within the mansion, and it was clear he could trust Proctor, Tristram began to open up and—within half an hour—was exhibiting an almost overwhelming curiosity. He asked, in his clumsy, strongly accented English, about everything: the books, the paintings, the rugs, the objets d'art. In so doing, the boy revealed a remarkable, even amazing, ignorance of the world. He had never seen a television set. He did not know what a computer was. He had never listened to the radio, knew nothing about music except for a few Germanic tunes like "The Horst Wessel Song." Proctor came to understand the boy had never eaten in a restaurant, never gone swimming, never played a game, never been hugged, never had a pet, never tasted ice cream, never met his mother, never ridden a bicycle—and apparently never eaten a hot meal until this morning. It was as if his personality was only just now starting to form, after years and years of dormancy, like a flower being hit by light for the first time. There had been a few flashes of rebelliousness and spunkiness, a dash of bluster, that came and went; but for the most part the boy was full of trepidation—fearful of being captured, anxious about offending, afraid to stand out in any way. He seemed beaten down, passive. Proctor wondered where in the world the boy had come from and under what bizarre circumstances he had been raised.

The double doors to the library opened, and Pendergast entered quietly.

Immediately, Tristram stood up. "Father!" he said.

Pendergast stepped back almost defensively. "It's fine, Tristram, you may remain seated." He turned to Proctor. "What news?"

The boy sat down again quietly.

"This time I don't believe we were followed," Proctor answered. "I've activated all the security measures."

Pendergast nodded. He turned to Tristram, then sat down in a nearby chair. "I need to know more. More about the place you grew up—Nova Godói."

Tristram screwed his face up. "I try."

"Describe it to me, please."

Tristram looked confused. "Describe?"

"What is it? A building, a town, a crossroads? What does it look like? How do you get to it?"

"I understand. But I not know much—they keep us, the bad twins, under guard. We not go anywhere." A sudden worried look crossed the boy's face, as if he was afraid of disappointing his father with his lack of knowledge.

"Just tell me what you know. What you've seen."

"It is town. Deep, deep in jungle. No road. Only way in is by river, or—" And here he imitated the motion of a plane's wings with his hand. "Town is on edge of lake."

"Lake," Pendergast repeated.

"Yes. In middle of lake is . . . the bad place."

"Tell me about the bad place."

"*No!*" Tristram was on his feet again, agitated. "No, no. Bad twins, like me, get taken to the bad place. They do not come out again."

He was so agitated that Pendergast said nothing for

several minutes, giving the boy time to calm down. "Who lives in the town, Tristram?" he asked at last.

"The workers. The good twins."

"And where do you live?"

"In the hole," the boy said simply. "With the others like me. The ones with numbers."

"What do you do during the day?"

"We work. In the fields. And sometimes we are taken. For...tests." He shook his head violently. "No talking about the tests."

"This town," Pendergast said. "Is it guarded?"

The boy nodded. "Soldiers. Many soldiers."

"Who do the soldiers answer to? How is the town led? Is there a governing council—a group of people in charge?"

Tristram shook his head. "One man."

"What is his name?"

"F...Fischer." Tristram barely whispered the word, as if merely to speak it was dangerous.

"What does he look like?" Pendergast asked.

"He is tall. Older than you. *Stark, kräftig*—strong, like him." Tristram pointed at Proctor. "His hair is white, all white."

Proctor was surprised at the effect this description had on Pendergast. The agent shuddered, then turned away.

"This town," he said in a strange voice, back still to them. "Does it have any other unique aspects to it?"

Tristram frowned. "Aspects? What you mean, aspects?"

Pendergast turned back. "Is there some way it might be different from other towns? A way for someone to recognize it, say, from a distance."

"Yes. It has..." And the boy raised both his arms, drawing his hands around in a circle, then tenting them together.

"I'm not sure I understand," Pendergast said.

Tristram made the gesture again, then sighed loudly, frustrated at not getting his meaning across.

Pendergast stood up again. "Thank you, Tristram. You have been most helpful. Now, listen: right now I have to try to prevent your brother from killing any more people."

Tristram nodded.

"As long as I'm doing that, I can't stay here with you."

"No!" The boy rose again.

"You must remain here. They're looking for you."

"I not afraid of them!"

Proctor looked at the boy. Brave words, and obviously well intended—but the greater likelihood was that, at the first knock on the door, he'd turn tail and hide behind his father.

"I know you mean well," Pendergast said gently. "But right now, you need to go to ground."

"Go...to ground?" the son repeated.

"Go into hiding. This house has places for that: where you can hide, safe from any attack, any threat."

A flash of anger distorted the boy's fine features. "Hide? In hole? I will not do such thing! I have been in hole too long!"

"Tristram. You took a big risk in escaping. You came to me. Now you must trust me." Pendergast took the boy's hand. "You won't be in any hole. Proctor will be with you. And I will visit as often as I can."

The youth's face had flushed red. He hung his head, clearly angry but holding his tongue.

Pendergast took Proctor aside. "You know where to put him."

"Yes, sir."

"And Proctor? I wonder if I could impose on you to

use this time—this enforced, ah, seclusion—to educate Tristram a little."

Proctor looked at Pendergast. "Educate him?"

"Talk with him. Let him practice his English. Be a companion—he's obviously in desperate need of socialization. He knows nothing of the outside world. Read books with him—novels, histories, whatever interests him. Listen to music, watch movies. Answer his questions. Show him how to use a computer."

Proctor stiffened at the thought of 'babysitting the boy. "Yes, sir," he said in a tight voice.

Pendergast turned, addressed Tristram. "I have to go now. You're in good hands with Proctor. I'll be back tomorrow. Tristram: I want you to recall everything you can about your childhood, growing up, how you lived, where you lived, what its layout was, who was with you—*everything*—and be prepared to tell me about it when I come tomorrow. We're going to have a long talk."

For a moment, the boy continued to hang his head. Then, with a sigh, he nodded sullenly.

"Good-bye, Tristram." Pendergast gave him a long, penetrating look. Then, nodding to Proctor, he turned and left the room as silently as he had arrived.

Proctor glanced at the boy. "Come on," he said. "I'll show you to your new room."

He led the way toward a row of bookshelves. The boy followed a little unwillingly. He seemed to have lost his eager curiosity.

Proctor glanced at the rows of books, found the title he wanted, grasped it, and pulled it away from the wall. With a click, the entire bookcase swung away, revealing an elevator beyond.

"*Scheiße*," murmured Tristram.

They entered the elevator, and Proctor pressed the

button for the basement. Once there, Proctor led the way through the maze of dimly lit stone passageways, heavy with verdigris and efflorescence. He kept the pace brisk, not allowing the youth to stop and look into any chambers whose contents he might find unsettling.

"My father does not like me," Tristram said in an unhappy tone.

"He's just doing what's best for you," Proctor replied gruffly.

They stopped at a small, vaulted room, completely empty except for a shield carved into one wall, depicting a lidless eye over two moons, one crescent, the other full, with a lion couchant beneath—the Pendergast family crest. Proctor approached it, pressed it with both hands. The stone wall behind swung away, revealing a circular stair that sloped down sharply into darkness. Tristram's eyes widened but he said nothing.

Snapping on a light, Proctor descended the stairs into the sub-basement, Tristram following. Reaching the bottom, they moved through a short passage leading to a vaulted space that seemed to stretch on as far as the eye could see.

"What is this place?" Tristram asked, looking around in wonder.

"This building used to be an abbey," said Proctor. "I believe the monks used this sub-basement as a necropolis."

"Necropolis?"

"Burial ground. Where they buried their dead."

"They *bury* the dead?"

Proctor refrained from asking what they did with the dead where Tristram came from.

He led the way past ancient laboratories; past rooms full of glass bottles, stored on row upon row of shelving; past rooms full of tapestries and ancient art. Proctor had never liked these moldering underground spaces, and he moved swiftly. The boy followed, looking left and right, eyes wide. At last Proctor led him down a side passageway to a small but well-furnished bedroom with an adjoining bath. There was a bed, a table and chairs, a row of books, and a dresser with a mirror set atop it. The space was as clean and as pleasant as the subterranean atmosphere—with its faint odor of ammonia and ancient decay—could permit. It sported a stout wooden door with a well-built lock.

"This is your room," he told Tristram.

The boy nodded, looking around. He seemed pleased.

"Can you...read?" Proctor asked, glancing at the books, the thought suddenly occurring to him.

"Only the good twins are supposed to read. But I taught myself. Just a little. But only German."

"I see. Well, if you will excuse me, I'll get you some things, be back in half an hour."

"What did you say is your name?"

"Proctor."

The boy looked at him, smiled a little shyly. "Thank you, *Herr* Proctor."

33

ALOYSIUS PENDERGAST BROUGHT THE ROLLS TO a halt at the corner of Bushwick Avenue and Meserole Street in Brooklyn. This was—according to the cab company's records—where the taxi had picked up the fleeing boy. It was an old, mostly abandoned industrial neighborhood that had just started to see the invasion of creative pioneers. But it still retained the rawness of graffiti, trash, boarded-up buildings, and the hulks of burned-out cars. The street scene was a mixture of derelicts, hipsters, and sketchy-looking young men.

Pendergast was conspicuous in his black suit as he stepped out of the Silver Wraith, locking the door behind him. Hands in his pockets, he strolled down Meserole Street. It was midafternoon, a brilliant but warmthless sun blasting the pavement. Several blocks ahead of him rose an old nineteenth-century brewery complex, covering almost an acre of ground. A huge square stack for the hops kiln rose above it, with the name VAN DAM still visible on it, along with the date of its founding: 1858.

A brewery. Tristram had, without knowing it, described just such a place: the long underground tunnel where the casks were stored; the huge brick kiln where the hops were dried. This, undoubtedly, had been the site of his incarceration and the site that his captors, Alban and no doubt his Nazi handlers, had been using as a base of operations—for whatever it was they were planning.

Pendergast approached, scrutinizing the building carefully. It was, even in this benighted corner of Brooklyn, a prime piece of real estate, and it had accordingly been securely boarded up with galvanized tin and plywood. Two ancient, massive industrial metal doors blocked what had once been the main entrance. These doors had been bolted shut, and the pedestrian door set into one of them was not only chained and padlocked, but also welded closed with two pieces of rebar.

Pendergast walked on, examining some of the smaller, secondary entrances set into the crumbling brick façade along the street, all of which were more or less impregnable. As he paused at one door, examining its frozen lock, he heard a voice behind him.

"Got any money, friend?"

Pendergast turned to see a rail-thin youth, undoubtedly a heroin addict, staring at him with hollow, hungry eyes.

"As a matter of fact I do." Pendergast delved into his suit and brought out a twenty-dollar bill. A spark ignited in the man's dead eyes, and he reached out with trembling fingers.

"I want to break into this building," said Pendergast, twitching the bill out of reach. "How?"

The man stared at him, his mouth open. "You a thief?"

"Insurance adjustor."

A hesitation as the man tried to think. "Can't get in there, that I know of."

"Yes, but if I *were* to try to break in—how would I?"

Another desperate effort to think. "I'd go 'round the back, where the railroad tracks are. Climb the fence."

Pendergast twitched the bill back toward the man, who snatched it and then set off down the street at a fast wobble. "Don't get caught," he called over his shoulder.

Pendergast walked to the far end of the block and followed the complex around the corner, where it ended in a disused railroad yard, stacked with rotting containers and old machinery, surrounded by a chain-link fence.

In a single, bat-like motion, Pendergast grasped the fence, vaulted the top, and dropped down onto the far side. He paused a moment to smooth down his suit. Then, moving among the containers and chest-high weeds, he followed a set of railroad tracks to the back of the brewery, where the tracks disappeared into the complex behind another set of industrial metal doors. As he approached, he noted that a number of the weeds had been bruised, broken, or otherwise recently disturbed by the passage of people and objects. The soft ground away from the tracks showed signs of footprints.

He followed the faint marks of disturbance across the railroad yard, away from the tracks and toward a small door set into the massive brick façade. Reaching the door, he found it as old and massive as the others, but not welded, and with freshly oiled hinges and a new brass lock of a model he did not recognize.

The lock proved to be a challenge, requiring the full set of his tools and skills. It also, unfortunately, caused quite a bit of noise, as several of the pins had to be sheared off with brute force.

Finally the lock yielded, but Pendergast did not open the door immediately. He waited, .45 drawn, for almost ten minutes. And then, flattening himself behind the door, he nudged it open with his shoe. It swung silently at first, then stopped with a loud groan of metal.

Silence.

Five more minutes passed. Pendergast ducked inside, diving to the floor, rolling, and taking cover behind a brick knee wall.

More silence. No one had shouted an alarm; no one had opened fire.

He waited, letting his eyes adjust to the gloom. He was in a vast space, illuminated by scattered holes and cracks in the roof, which let in brilliant pencil-beams of sunlight. Motes drifted through in slow cadences. The air smelled faintly sweet, earthy.

This was clearly the storage and loading area for the brewery, as the train tracks ran through the space, with loading docks and rotting cranes arrayed alongside. Where the tracks ended an old railroad car listed, its wheels off the rails, roof rusted and partially caved in.

Between him and the car was about thirty feet of open ground.

With a sudden burst of speed, Pendergast flitted across the space, then took cover behind the railcar. From this new vantage point he could see the door he had just come through, as well as a large, arched door at the far end of the open space. Debris littered the dusty, concrete floor, and in that dust he could see recent footmarks.

Edging along the railcar, he ducked across another open space, flattened himself behind one pillar, then another, and a moment later scurried up to the arched door. It was shut but not locked.

Reaching into his pocket, Pendergast turned on a small LED flashlight, held it against his .45, then spun around and—raising his weapon—burst through the door, panning across the space.

It was not a room at all, but the long, cool tunnel that had evidently once been used for storing beer, attested to by several stacks of rotting barrels and countless old mold-blown beer bottles.

Pendergast's sense of puzzlement deepened. They should be here, waiting for him. They would have guessed he'd be coming. And yet he could see no sign of them.

A few moments brought him to the far end of the tunnel and a second archway. Beyond that, he could see another vast, open space, speckled with fragments of sunlight, with the great hop kiln dominating one corner.

His light showed footprints all over the floor now, clustering around the massive riveted iron door of the kiln, which stood ajar. Above, a metal catwalk ran around the walls, just beneath the arched ceiling.

Creeping along the wall, Pendergast reached a point where he could look up to the catwalk. By now his eyes had fully adjusted to the gloom, and he could see that the catwalk was empty.

He continued moving against the wall, toward the great door to the kiln. He approached it from the far side, weapon drawn; then skipped past the door frame, coming at it from the other side, pulling it open while using it as a shield against potential fire.

But there was nothing save the loud groan of rusty iron, and when he shone the light around the interior of the hop kiln, nobody was there.

The walls were blackened with soot and the floor was strewn with food trash. A bucket sat in the corner. Shackles had been driven into the walls, and on the scorched brick floor underneath were some small stains of blood. A filthy blanket with no mattress lay rucked up in the corner. Some old bloody bandages had been tossed in another corner. Clearly, this had been Tristram's temporary prison.

Pendergast sorted through the trash with meticulous care, once in a while retaining something in a test tube or ziplock bag. But he found nothing of interest.

Back in the large space, he began to explore the area thoroughly. In an alcove he found the spot where Alban had presumably been living: a cot, an empty steamer trunk, a clean bucket. He searched the area, but it had been carefully cleaned out.

They'd known he was coming—and had abandoned the hideout.

In another alcove was a raw plywood table, on which sat a hot plate, a ten-dollar coffeemaker, and a mug. Shining the light low to the ground, Pendergast traced the web of footprints in the dust and dirt, hither and yon, and followed them as best he could, looking for other areas that might have been used. When that yielded nothing, he mounted the rickety metal stairs to the catwalk and traversed it, looking for hidden spaces. Nothing.

Once again, Pendergast searched Alban's alcove. He next inspected the table. The raw, unsealed top was splattered with coffee stains and rings. He held his flashlight at one edge of the table and began shining it at various raking angles across the surface. On the fourth try, the beam illuminated some faint writing marks in the soft plywood top. There was one mark in particular that had been written with pressure and underlined twice. Laying the light on the table, Pendergast removed a piece of paper and pencil from his suit and placed the paper over the marks, rubbing it ever so lightly with the side of the pencil. Slowly, bits and pieces of a scattering of letters materialized. On a separate piece of paper, Pendergast jotted them down, leaving blank the letters that were too faint to make out. He tried rubbing in several directions, each time getting a slightly different take on the letters, until he had five of the eight.

BE _ _ _ EST

He examined the rubbing with a loupe, examined the table itself, and was finally able to add another letter.

BE _ A _ EST

He stared at the piece of paper for a long time. And then, with one swift motion of the pencil, he completed the word:

BETATEST

34

DR. JOHN FELDER SAT, A LITTLE DEJECTEDLY, in the main room of the Wintour gatehouse. He had spent hours and hours restoring it to a modicum of livability—washing down the walls and floor with bleach, sweeping away the cobwebs, dusting all the surfaces, and dragging the clutter up into a tiny crawl space under the roof—and now he was able to sleep at night without imagining things crawling over his face and hands. He'd brought in just a few items: an air mattress and sleeping bag, a few sticks of furniture, a laptop, a space heater, books and groceries and a hot pot—the kitchen was too terrible to contemplate—and it hardly felt like home.

Again and again, as he toiled, he'd asked himself: *Why am I doing this?* But the fact was, he already knew the answer.

He got up from the lone chair and walked over to the window. It had been cleaned of grime and, through the last dying light of evening, afforded a good prospect of the Wintour mansion—cloaked in gloom, the brick walls straining under the too-large roof, the innumerable black windows like missing teeth. The day before, he'd been invited in for afternoon tea, and he'd found that the inside was just as creepy as the outside. Everything looked like a time capsule from the 1890s: the straight-backed, uncomfortable chairs with their lace antimacassars; the tiny wooden tables set with doilies, little glass figurines, ancient tchotchkes. The carpeting was dark, the wallpaper was dark, the walls were of dark wood, and it seemed as though no light could ever brighten the echoing spaces. Everything smelled faintly of mothballs. It wasn't dusty, exactly—and yet Felder was aware of a constant desire to scratch his nose. The old, evil house seemed to be watching and listening as they sat in the dreary front parlor, Miss Wintour alternately heaping invective on the town fathers or lamenting how much better the world had been when she was a girl.

It was past eight: dark enough now so that he could not be seen if he toured the grounds. He bundled himself warmly in his jacket, opened the door, stepped out, and shut the door quietly behind him. As he walked through the tangle of wintry, frozen undergrowth, the house seemed to follow his progress, glaring at him.

He had decided the old woman was not in any way demented—just highly eccentric. And she was as sharp and prickly as a thistle—the one time he had brought up the subject of her library, in as tactful and offhand a way as possible, she'd practically jumped on him, demanding to know the reason for his interest. It was all he could do to steer the conversation in another direction, smooth down her suspicion. But he had learned its location: beyond a set of pocket doors that were always kept closed and locked. He knew, because he'd seen the room through the mansion's windows by day: row after row of bookshelves, stuffed full of treasures both known and unknown.

He approached it now, very quietly, through the tall grass. Despite the light of the moon, the library windows were rectangles of unrelieved black. The house had no security system—he'd noticed that right away. But then, it didn't need one.

It had Dukchuk.

Dukchuk was the towering, always-silent manservant who opened the front door; who brought the tepid, watery tea; who stood behind Miss Wintour's chair while she spoke, his unreadable gaze on Felder. The man's tattoos gave him nightmares.

He returned his attention to the library window. It might well be unlocked—he'd noticed that the windows of the front parlor were. It would be just like Miss Wintour to have four extra locks on the front door but none on the windows. Still, there was Dukchuk. The fellow looked as if he might have his own, extralegal way of dealing with encroachers. Felder knew he would have to be supremely careful if . . .

If what? Was he really thinking what he was thinking?

Yes, he was. He realized now there was no way on earth old Miss Wintour would ever willingly show him the library. If he was going to get in, if he was going to find that portfolio, he would have to find another way.

He licked his lips. Tomorrow night was forecast to be overcast, moonless. Then—he would do it then.

35

PENDERGAST STOOD IN THE WORKROOM OF HIS sprawling apartments in the Dakota. The room was devoid of any decor or ornamentation, anything that would distract or hinder the most intense concentration. Even the color of the walls and the stain of the wooden floor were a cool gunmetal gray, as neutral as possible. The windows overlooking Seventy-Second Street were closed and tightly shuttered. In one corner sat a tall pile of yellowing documents: the papers that Corrie had brought him from the Nazi safe house. The only furniture was a long, oaken table that ran the length of the room. There were no chairs. The table was covered by police reports, SOC data, photographs, FBI profiles, forensic analyses, and other paperwork, all devoted to a single subject: the Hotel Killer murders. Committed by his son, Alban.

His son. Pendergast was finding this fact to be a most disruptive influence on his deductive processes.

He paced quickly back and forth along the length of the table, glancing at first one document, then another. Finally, with an exasperated shake of his head, he strode over to an audio player, set flush into one wall, and pressed the PLAY button. Immediately the low, sonorous strains of the *Ricercar a 6* from Bach's *Musical Offering* began to emerge from hidden speakers.

This was the only piece that was ever heard in this room. Pendergast did not play it for its beauty—but for the way the complex, intensely mathematical composition settled and sharpened his mind.

As the music continued, his pacing grew slower, his study of the documents strewn across the tabletop more ordered and nuanced.

His son, Alban, had committed these murders. Tristram said that Alban loved killing. But why journey all the way to New York from Brazil to commit them? Why leave the body parts of his own brother at the murder sites? Why scrawl bloody messages on the corpses—messages that could only be meant for Pendergast himself?

BETATEST. Beta test. There was clearly a method, a governing purpose, behind these killings. And Pendergast himself was meant to discover it. Or, perhaps, to *try* to discover it. Nothing else made sense.

With Bach's delicate, fantastically intricate counterpoint weaving softly in the background, Pendergast looked at the data afresh, forming a logical counterpoint of his own, mentally comparing times, dates, addresses, room numbers, external temperatures, ages of victims—anything that might point to a method, or a sequence, or a pattern. This process continued for ten, then twenty minutes. And then—abruptly— Pendergast stiffened.

Bending over the table, he rearranged several pieces of paper, examined them again. Then, plucking a pen from his pocket, he wrote a series of numbers across the bottom of one of the sheets, double-checking it against the documentation.

There was no mistake.

He glanced at his watch. Moving like lightning, he darted down the hall to his study, plucked a tablet computer from the desk, and typed in a query. He examined the response—cursed softly but eloquently in Latin under his breath—and then picked up a telephone and dialed.

"D'Agosta here," came the response.

"Vincent? Where are you?"

"Pendergast?"

"I repeat: where are you?"

"Heading down Broadway, just passing Fifty-Seventh. I was going to—"

"Turn around and come to the Dakota as quickly as you can. I'll be waiting at the corner. Hurry—there's not a moment to lose."

"What's up?" D'Agosta asked.

"We'll talk in the car. I just hope we're not too late."

36

D'AGOSTA DROVE LIKE HELL DOWN PARK AVENUE through the evening traffic, emergency lights flashing, once in a while goosing his siren at the sons of bitches who wouldn't pull over. Pendergast's phone call out of the blue, the almost manic urgency in the agent's voice, had unnerved him. He wasn't sure if Pendergast was cracking up or actually on to something, but he'd spent enough time around the man to realize he ignored Pendergast's requests at his own peril.

Now, as they tore southward toward the Murray Hill Hotel, D'Agosta looked sideways to examine Pendergast. The transformation the special agent had undergone since his wife's death covered the spectrum—from apathy, to a drug-induced stupor, and now this: a diamond-hard glitter in the man's eyes, his entire being bursting with coiled-spring tension and fanatical energy.

"You say another murder's about to be committed?" D'Agosta began. "Can you fill me in here? How do you know—?"

"Vincent, we have very little time, and what I have to say is going to seem strange to you, if not mad."

"Try me."

The briefest of pauses. "I have a son whom I never knew existed. His name is Alban. He's the killer—not Diogenes, as I had previously suspected. Of this there is no doubt whatsoever."

"Whoa, now, just wait a minute, Jesus—"

A short gesture from Pendergast silenced D'Agosta. "These killings are directed specifically at me. The precise motive is as yet unclear."

"I find it hard to—"

"There is no time for detailed explanations. Suffice to say that the addresses of the hotels, and the times of the killings, follow a pattern, a sequence. The next term in this sequence is twenty-one. And there's only one Manhattan hotel with twenty-one in its address—the Murray Hill, at Twenty-One Park Avenue. I've already checked."

"This is—"

"And have you noticed the times of the killings? It's another pattern, a simpler one. The first was at seven thirty in the morning. The next at nine PM. The third one, once again at seven thirty AM. He's alternating times. And it's almost nine now."

They tore through the Helmsley Building tunnel and around the viaduct, wheels squealing. "I don't buy it," D'Agosta said as he struggled to straighten the car. "An unknown son, this pattern of yours . . . it's frigging nuts."

Pendergast made a visible effort to control himself. "I know how strange it must seem. But at least for the time being, I must insist on your full and complete suspension of disbelief."

"Disbelief? That's an understatement. It's totally crazy."

"You'll find out soon enough. We are here."

D'Agosta angled the unmarked car and came to a screeching halt in front of the hotel. Unlike the three previous luxury hotels, this one was old and faintly seedy, its brown-brick façade streaked with soot. Leaving the car parked in the loading zone, D'Agosta got out but Pendergast was already ahead of him, flying into the lobby, his FBI badge out. "Security office!" he cried.

The concierge came stumbling out all in a panic, and in response to Pendergast's barked instructions led them past the lobby desk into a small inner office with a wall of CCTV screens. A security officer on duty leapt to his feet as they burst in.

"FBI," said Pendergast, waving the shield. "How many lobby tapes do you have online?"

"Um, one," the officer said, totally flummoxed.

"Back it up half an hour. *Now.*"

"Yes, um, yes, sir, of course." The poor guard lumbered about as fast as he could. Fortunately, D'Agosta noticed, it was a recent and modestly advanced system, and the man seemed competent. Within a minute the feed was playing in accelerated motion. D'Agosta watched the monitor, his skepticism growing. This was ridiculous: the Hotel Killer would never pick a dump like this to work in. It didn't match the M.O. He shot a covert glance at Pendergast: the wife's death had clearly touched him even more than was obvious.

"Speed it up," Pendergast said.

The man complied. They watched as figures flitted across the lobby with rigid intensity.

"*Stop!* That's him."

The security video stopped, then proceeded in real time. It showed a nondescript man walking casually into the lobby, pausing, adjusting his tie, then moving toward the elevators. D'Agosta felt his gut contract. The way the man moved, looked—it *was* him.

"Fuck," he muttered.

"Switch to the elevator cam," Pendergast said.

They followed the man's progress to the fifth floor, where he got out, walked down the hall, and waited. Then, just as a woman came around the corner, he started up again, following her down the hall, until they passed out of view of the camera. The running time stamp indicated this had taken place just three minutes before.

"Oh, Christ," D'Agosta said. "Christ. He's got another one."

"Back up the tape five seconds." Pendergast pointed at the image of the woman, turning to the concierge. "Do you recognize her? What's her room number? Quickly, man!"

"She checked in today." The concierge stepped back to the front desk, tapped the keys of the registration computer. "Room Five Sixteen."

Pendergast turned back to D'Agosta. "Stay here," he murmured. "Monitor these feeds. When he comes back into view, follow his every movement. I'm going after him. And remember—tell no one of my son."

"Whoa," D'Agosta said. "Hold on just a minute. Tell no one? Pendergast, I hate to say this, but I think you're way out of line—"

"*Tell no one*," Pendergast repeated firmly. And then in a flash he was gone.

Pendergast bounded up the five flights of stairs and ran down the hall to Room 516. The door was shut, but a single shot from his .45 blasted off the lock and he kicked the door open.

He was too late. In the small room, the woman he'd seen in the video lay on the floor, obviously dead but not yet dismembered. Pendergast hesitated only a moment, his silvery eyes darting all around, taking everything in. Then, leaping over the still form, he threw open the bathroom door. The window at the end of the narrow bath was shattered, opening on a fire escape. Pendergast vaulted through the window onto the fire escape and looked down, in time to see a young man—*Alban*—clambering down the last flight of the escape, climbing through the bottom hatch, and dropping to the ground.

Pendergast raced down the fire escape, three steps at a time, following Alban with his eyes as the youth ran down Park Avenue and disappeared around the corner of Thirty-Fifth Street, heading east, toward the river.

Pendergast ran after him. When he rounded the corner of Thirty-Fifth, he could see Alban almost two blocks east, silhouetted in the streetlights, tearing along at a tremendous speed—a phenomenal runner. Pendergast continued, but by the time he reached Lexington the now-tiny figure of Alban had already crossed Second Avenue and was running alongside St. Vartan Park. Realizing he would never catch him, Pendergast nevertheless continued on, at the least hoping to see where his son would go. The fleeing, barely visible figure passed First Avenue and ran toward FDR Drive, leaping a chain-link fence and climbing over a cement barrier and out onto the drive, where he dropped out of sight into the darkness.

Pendergast sprinted past St. Vartan Park, crossing First Avenue against the light. He hit the chain-link fence, clambered over it, vaulted the cement barrier, and ran out onto FDR Drive, dodging cars amid a sudden chorus of horns and screeching brakes. He made it to the far side and stopped, looking both ways, but he could see nothing: Alban had vanished into the night. The East River stretched out in front of him, the Hunter's Point ferry terminal lay on his right, the Queensboro Bridge on his left, atwinkle with lights. Directly in front of him two vacant, ruined piers stood out in the East River, extending from a decaying, rip-rapped riverbank below a broken-up quay, much of it reclaimed by a riot of undergrowth, old cattails, cane, dry reeds, and brambles—everything withered and brown in the wintry moonlight.

There were many, many places to disappear into, and Alban was gone. He clearly knew the lay of the land and had worked out his escape ahead of time. It was hopeless.

Pendergast turned and walked along the shoulder of the FDR Drive toward a pedestrian walkway five blocks south to recross the highway. But as he walked, he saw a figure out of the corner of his eye—a man, a young man, standing on the first ruined pier, illuminated from behind by the dim light of the bridge.

It was Alban. His son was looking directly at him. And—as Pendergast stopped and stared—he raised his hand and gave a little wave.

Immediately Pendergast vaulted over the railing of the drive and landed on the embankment below, clawing his way through the overgrowth. He came out on the broken cement quay only to find that Alban had once again vanished.

Sensing he must have headed up the embankment, Pendergast sprinted northward. And in a moment he saw movement ahead—Alban, running out on the second ruined pier, where he stopped halfway, turned, and waited, arms crossed.

As he ran, Pendergast drew his .45. To reach the second pier, he was forced around a row of ruined bollards and through more undergrowth, during which he again temporarily lost sight of Alban. Just as he came to the foot of the pier and emerged from the vegetation, he felt a stunning blow to his leg and was pitched forward, and—even as he was falling—felt a second blow to his hand, which sent the .45 flying. He rolled and tried to rise, but Alban anticipated the maneuver and slammed Pendergast's head down with his knee, pinning the agent to the cement.

And then, just as quickly as he'd been pinned, he was released. Pendergast leapt to his feet, ready to fight.

But Alban did not come after him. He merely stepped back, arms once again crossed.

Pendergast froze, and they stared at each other, like two animals, each waiting for the other to make the first move.

Then Alban suddenly relaxed. "*Endlich*," he said. "Finally. We can have a heart-to-heart...father to son...something I've been looking forward to for a long time." And he smiled rather pleasantly.

37

THEY LOOKED AT EACH OTHER THROUGH THE semi-darkness, not moving. Pendergast stood, catching his breath, only now realizing that he had never been quite so thoroughly and rapidly overcome in his life. Alban had entirely surprised him, the way he had stopped as if to wait for Pendergast to catch up, and then—in the space of mere seconds—set up an ambush and followed it through with remarkable success.

Keeping his eyes on his son, he brushed himself off, waiting for Alban to speak, waiting for his opportunity. He still had a backup sidearm and several other weapons on his person. Alban would not escape him now.

"Amazing, isn't it?" said Alban. "Here we are, face-to-face." His voice was cool, mellifluous. Unlike his brother, he did not have the trace of an accent, yet he spoke with the slight over-preciseness of one to whom English was a second language. "I was destined to meet you. As are all sons to meet their fathers."

"What about their mothers?" Pendergast asked.

This question did not seem to surprise Alban. He continued. "The test has reached a crucial phase. Allow me to compliment you, by the way, on solving my little riddle. And to think I doubted you would. I apologize."

"You like to talk," said Pendergast. Out of the corner of his eye, he could see the glint of the .45 in the weeds about ten feet to his left.

Alban laughed. "Yes, I do." He took a step to his right, then another, effectively blocking Pendergast's approach to the gun. Although he was only fifteen, he seemed much older—tall, extremely fit, strong, and whippet-fast. Pendergast wondered if the youth had been trained in the martial arts. If so, he did not believe he could best him in a physical contest.

"Why are you—?"

"Killing? Like I said, it's a test."

"Tell me—"

"About the test? It's simple. At least in part, it's to see who's the better man: you or me." He held out his hands toward Pendergast, turned up his palms. "Like you, I'm unarmed. Here we are, evenly matched. It's not quite fair since you're old and I'm young. So I'm going to give you a handicap."

Pendergast could feel his moment arriving, a window in which he could act. He prepared himself mentally, choreographing his actions in his head. But then, mere seconds before he made his move, one of Alban's extended hands jerked into Pendergast's jacket and—in one astonishing blur of movement—removed his backup sidearm. It happened so quickly that by the time Pendergast reacted, Alban was already in possession of the weapon.

"Oops." Alban examined it—a Walther PPK .32—and snorted. "Now, this is a side of you I wouldn't have guessed. A romantic, aren't we, Father?"

Pendergast took a step back, but even as he did so Alban stepped forward, keeping the distance between them a close five feet. He continued holding the Walther, his thumb on the safety.

"Why this test?" asked Pendergast.

"Ah! That really is the heart of the matter, isn't it? Why pit me against you? What a strange thing! And yet, so *much* depends on it—" But suddenly Alban stopped and stepped back, his arrogant self-assurance wavering.

"Is that why you're—"

"Calling this the *beta* test? Yes." After a moment, Alban relaxed, smiled again. Then he removed the magazine from the Walther, slid out the rounds with his thumb, one at a time, leaving just one in the magazine. He slid the mag back into place, racked the final round into the chamber, and thumbed off the safety. He handed the gun back to Pendergast, butt first.

"There. Your handicap. One round in the chamber. Now the advantage is yours. See if you can capture and take me in. With a single round."

Pendergast aimed the pistol at Alban. He would not—*could* not—kill him, not at present: his need to know his son's motive, his relation to *Der Bund*, was very great. But the boy was so strong and fast that he could escape, even now, simply by running.

A bullet in the knee would be necessary.

With the faintest flickering movement he dropped the muzzle and fired, but Alban moved so fast—even before Pendergast seemed to have started his own move—that the bullet missed, just nicking the cloth.

Alban laughed, reaching down, poking his finger through the hole in his trousers, wiggling it. "Close! Whew. But not good enough. What is the expression? This time, I *bested* you."

He took a quick step back, reached down into the weeds, and picked up Pendergast's .45. "Do you know the Goethe poem 'Der Erlkönig'?"

"In translation, yes."

"*Schön!* By heart?"

"Yes."

"Excellent. Here's what's going to happen. You're going to turn your back, close your eyes, and recite it. The first three stanzas should be sufficient. No—considering we're in relative darkness, I'll be even more sporting and make it only the first two stanzas. And then you can come looking for me."

"And if I cheat?"

"I'll shoot you." Alban's pale eyes twinkled. "Of course, I could just shoot you right now, and that would also be cheating. We *Pendergasts* do not cheat." Another pleasant smile. "Do you want to play?"

"I have more—"

"I think I've answered enough questions. Now: do you want to play?"

"Why not?"

"If you open your eyes early, it means you're a cheater; I shoot; you die."

"You'll merely outrun me. This is no challenge at all."

"It is true I could outrun you. But I won't do that. Instead, during your recitation, which should take no longer than ten seconds, I'm going to hide. And you will have to find me however you can—by intelligence, by stealth, by tracking, by deduction—it's up to you. So! Turn your back and let's begin."

Pendergast heard the soft click of the safety on the Les Baer being thumbed back. He immediately turned around and began to speak in a clear, loud tone:

Who rides there so late through the night dark and drear?
The father it is, with his infant so dear . . .

292 DOUGLAS PRESTON & LINCOLN CHILD

At the end of the second stanza, he quickly turned and scanned the deserted piers.

Alban was gone. The Les Baer lay in the weeds a few yards away.

Three hours later, Pendergast finally gave up searching.

38

"Damn it to hell," Lieutenant Vincent D'Agosta muttered as he stood in the hallway of the Murray Hill Hotel. Even in the corridor he could hear the shouts and electronic blarings of the press down on the street, along with a chorus of sirens, cars honking, and miscellaneous New York City noise. Hours had passed since the killing, but the media only got thicker. Traffic on Park Avenue was gridlocked from the hotel all the way to the MetLife Building, no doubt the rubbernecking effect at work. The hotel throbbed with the *thwap thwap* of helicopters above, their spotlights sweeping the building. And Pendergast had disappeared.

What was it about New Yorkers and crime? They loved it, they ate it up. The *News* and the *Post* had been running screaming headlines for days on the Hotel Killer. And now this. God forbid the crime rate should drop to zero; most of the papers in the city would go bankrupt.

Brilliant white light poured out into the hall from Room 516, and D'Agosta could see the occasional shadows of the figures still working in there. Gibbs was inside as well. It was complete bullshit that the man had been given access during the evidence-gathering phase—top brass were supposed to be kept out. But this time he'd insisted on going in, despite D'Agosta's demurral. Christ, he himself, the squad commander, hadn't been in there since the initial discovery.

"Hey, what's with the fucking Coke?" he bellowed at a latents specialist passing down the hall. "You know there's no eating or drinking at the scene!"

The man, immediately cowed, ducked his head in abject submission, turned, and hustled away down the hall, carrying the frosty can, not daring to sip from it.

D'Agosta could see some of the other detectives hovering around the corridor exchanging glances. All right, so he was pissed and showing it. He didn't give a shit. The whole thing with Pendergast had freaked him out, the way he'd disappeared like that. Just vanished. Along with the perp. And this crazy theory about it being his son...and yet, he'd called it right on the button: date, time, and place.

D'Agosta had been on a lot of strange trips with Pendergast, but this was the strangest of all. He was well and truly shaken up. On top of that, his not-so-old chest wound was giving him a hard time. He felt in his pocket for some Advil, popped a few more.

"Hey, who gave you permission to waltz in here like you owned the place?" he shouted at a white-coated forensic specialist just ducking in under the crime-scene tape. "Log in, for shit's sake!"

"Yes, Lieutenant, but you see I did log in. I was just visiting the men's room—"

His attempted smile was cut off by D'Agosta's shout. "Log in again!"

"Yes, sir."

D'Agosta turned back and abruptly saw Pendergast. The man's gaunt figure had materialized at the far end of the hall. As he approached, walking swiftly, D'Agosta's gut tightened with apprehension. He had to talk to him, find out more about this bizarre business of the alleged son.

He was shocked by the look on Pendergast's face: it fairly blazed with hard, dazzling intensity. He looked almost mad. And yet the eyes were absolutely clear.

"Where'd you go?" D'Agosta asked.

"I chased the killer to the river. He escaped at the piers."

"You . . . *chased* him?"

"He had just left the room when I arrived, by the fire escape. There was no time. I engaged in pursuit."

"And you're sure he's . . . your son?"

Pendergast stared at him. "As I said earlier, that information remains strictly between us."

D'Agosta swallowed. The intensity of Pendergast's stare unnerved him. "If you've got information, I mean, we've got to share it . . ." he began.

The look on Pendergast's face became distinctly unfriendly. "Vincent, I am the only person who can catch this killer. Nobody else can. In fact, their attempts would only make things worse. Therefore, we must keep the information to ourselves. At least for now. Do you understand?"

D'Agosta couldn't bring himself to answer. He did understand. But withholding information—especially the possible identity of the killer? You couldn't do that. Then again, it seemed a completely crazy idea that the killer was Pendergast's son—that he even *had* a son. The man was cracking up. Maybe they *should* with-hold it.

He had no idea what to do.

"Well, well, if it isn't Agent Pendergast." And here came

Gibbs, striding out of the hotel room. He approached, hand extended, the phoniest of smiles on his face. Pendergast took the hand.

"You look like you've been in a rumble," said Gibbs with a chuckle, looking over Pendergast's muddied suit.

"Indeed."

"I'm curious," said Gibbs, "how you and the lieutenant managed to get to the crime scene just, what, minutes after the perp arrived? The lieutenant said it was your idea, something about a number sequence?"

"Fibonacci," Pendergast said.

Gibbs frowned. "Fibonacci? Who's Fibonacci?"

"Leonardo Fibonacci," said Pendergast, "a medieval mathematician. Italian, naturally."

"Italian. Right."

"I examined the numerical evidence of the killings and discovered that the addresses of the hotels follow a pattern: Five East Forty-Fifth Street, Eight West Fiftieth Street, Thirteen Central Park West. Five, eight, thirteen. That is part of the Fibonacci sequence, each number being the sum of the previous two. The next term in the sequence would be twenty-one. I discovered there was only one Manhattan hotel at a twenty-one address—the Murray Hill, at Twenty-One Park Avenue."

Gibbs listened, head bowed, arms crossed, still frowning.

"The times of the killings follow a simpler sequence, alternating between seven thirty in the morning and nine in the evening. It's a sign of arrogance, like showing his face to the security cameras—as if we're so beneath contempt, he doesn't even have to try to hide his work."

When Pendergast fell silent, Gibbs rolled his eyes. "I can't argue about the times of death. But all that about the Fib...the Fib...that's got to be one of the most far-fetched ideas I've ever heard."

"Yeah, well," said D'Agosta, "it seems to have worked."

Gibbs took out his notebook. "So, Agent Pendergast, when you got here, what happened? The lieutenant tells me you just disappeared."

"As I was telling Lieutenant D'Agosta, I went directly to the room, found the bathroom window open. The perpetrator was descending the fire escape. I gave chase and pursued him to the river, where I lost him in the area of the old piers."

Gibbs took a few notes. "Get a good look at him?"

"No better than the security cameras."

"You can't tell me anything else?"

"I'm afraid not. Except that he's a fast runner."

D'Agosta could hardly believe it: Pendergast really was withholding evidence. It was one thing to talk about doing it; quite another to actively do it. Not only that, but Pendergast was doing so in an investigation D'Agosta himself was in charge of. He was finding it increasingly difficult not to take Pendergast's flippant attitude toward the rule of law personally.

Gibbs slapped his notebook shut. "Interesting that he chose a dump like this. It shows his M.O. is evolving. That's a common trait of this type of serial killer. He first kills in environments where he feels safe, then branches out, gets more daring. Pushes the envelope."

"You don't say," said Pendergast.

"I *do* say. In fact, I believe this is significant. He killed first in the Marlborough Grand, the Vanderbilt, the Royal Cheshire. Five-star hotels all. It suggests to me the perp comes from a wealthy, privileged background. He starts off where he's comfortable, then, as his confidence grows, he gets more daring, goes slumming, so to speak."

"He chose this hotel," Pendergast spoke mildly, "for

one reason only: because it is the only one in Manhattan with a twenty-one in its address. It has nothing to do with his background or his 'slumming' habits."

Gibbs sighed. "Special Agent Pendergast, how about if you stick to your own area of expertise and leave the profiling to the experts?"

"And which experts might that be?"

Gibbs stared at him.

Pendergast glanced at the open door of Room 516; at the shadows of those working within, still silhouetted upon the opposite wall of the corridor by the bright crime-scene lights. "Do you know Plato's Allegory of the Cave?" he asked.

"No."

"You might find it enlightening in the present situation. Agent Gibbs, I've thoroughly examined your forensic profile of the so-called Hotel Killer. As you say, it is based on probabilities and aggregates—the assumption that this killer is like others of his type. But the truth is, this killer is completely outside your bell curve. He does not fit any of your assumptions or conform to any of your precious data. What you are doing is not only a colossal waste of time but an actual hindrance. Your puerile analysis is badly sidetracking this investigation—which may well be the killer's intention."

D'Agosta stiffened.

Gibbs stared at Pendergast, and then spoke in measured tones. "From the beginning, I've wondered what the hell you were doing on this case. What your game was. We at the BSU have looked into your record, and we're not impressed. I've seen all kinds of unusual stuff in there—mysterious leaves of absence, inquiries, reprimands. It's amazing to me you haven't been cashiered. You speak of a hindrance. The only *hindrance* I see here is your interfering presence. Be warned, Agent Pendergast—I won't stand for any more of your games."

Pendergast inclined his head in silent acquiescence. There was a silence—and then he spoke again. "Agent Gibbs?"

"Yes, what now?"

"I note blood on your left shoe. Just a spot."

Gibbs looked down at his feet. "What? Where?"

Pendergast stooped, rubbed a finger along the edge of the sole, brought it up red. "Unfortunately, the shoe will have to be taken up as evidence. I'm afraid a report will need to be made of your error at the scene of the crime. Alas, it's obligatory, as the lieutenant will confirm." Pendergast waved his hand, calling over a CSI assistant with evidence bags. "Special Agent Gibbs will give you his shoe now—pity, as I note it's a handmade Testoni, no doubt a painful loss for Mr. Gibbs, considering his modest salary."

A moment later, D'Agosta watched as Gibbs stomped down the hall in one shoe and one stockinged foot. Funny—he himself hadn't noticed any blood on the agent's shoe.

"One has to be so careful at a crime scene these days," Pendergast murmured at his side.

D'Agosta said nothing. Something was going to happen, and it wasn't going to be nice.

39

It was a cold, gray, drizzly Monday morn-
ing, the cars lined up on the lot like blocks of wood,
dull in the dull light, streaming rivulets of water down
their flanks. It was just past eleven but already it was
shaping up to be a terrible day for selling, which was
just perfect as far as Corrie was concerned. She'd
retreated with the other salespeople into the lounge,
where they were all drinking bad coffee and shooting
the breeze, waiting for customers to show up. There
were four other salespeople in the lounge—all men. Joe
Ricco and his son Joe Junior weren't around, and the
salesmen were in a relaxed mood.

Corrie had gotten to know them over the past two
days, and they were all first-rate, top-drawer assholes.
All except Charlie Foote—the man her father had
mentioned. He was younger than the rest, a little shy,
and for the most part he didn't join in the asinine frat-
house banter. He'd graduated college, unlike most of
the others, and he was the best salesman of the group;
something about his gentle voice and understated, self-
deprecating manner seemed to work like a charm.

One of the older salesmen had the floor and was finishing up a tits-and-ass joke, which Corrie laughed hard at. She took a sip of her coffee, added another container of fake cream to try to drown out the burnt taste, and said, "Weird, isn't it, that I replaced a salesman with the same last name."

She directed her statement to the salesman who had made the joke. His name was Miller. He was a real comedian, and Corrie had been forcing herself to laugh at all his lame jokes. She had even passed on a hot customer to him, pretending to need guidance, and then let him keep the sale. In return, Miller had sort of taken her under his wing, no doubt hoping to get lucky. He was already starting to make comments about a bar he went to after work that served killer margaritas. She wouldn't disabuse him of the pathetic notion she might sleep with him—at least, not until she had a chance to cash in her chips.

"Yeah," said Miller, lighting up even though he was only supposed to do that outside. But Joe Ricco smoked and so no one objected. Miller was a beefy, crew-cut redhead with triple rolls around his neck, a beer belly, wide lips, and a pug nose. The look was somewhat mitigated by his expensive suit. They all dressed well. Gone were the days, she thought, of the fast-talking salesman in plaid polyester.

"What was he like?" Corrie asked. "Jack Swanson, I mean."

Miller exhaled. "Asshole."

"Oh, yeah? So that's why he was fired?"

Miller guffawed. "Nah. The guy robbed a bank."

"*What*?" Corrie feigned shock.

"Miller, take it easy, we're not supposed to talk about that at work," said another salesman, a guy by the name of Rivera.

"Fuck it," said Miller. "There's no customers around. She'd hear about it eventually."

"Robbed a bank!" Corrie interjected, eager to keep the thread of conversation going. "How?"

Miller seemed to find this funny, too. "The guy's an idiot. He can't sell cars worth shit, makes no commissions, so one day he borrows an STS off the lot, drives to the local Delaware Trust, goes in, and robs the damn place."

More laughter.

"How do they know it was him?" Corrie asked.

"First, the car came from our lot, like I said, our dealer plates. Second, he's wearing his usual crappy suit—which we all identified. And Ricco himself saw the guy driving it off."

Nods all around.

"Third, they find a hair of his on the headrest."

"Open and shut," said Corrie. She felt glum. This was going to be a bitch and a half—assuming her father really was innocent in the first place.

"Not only that, but they found his fingerprints on the piece of paper the guy handed to the cashier."

This was beginning to sound just a little too convenient. "And now he's in jail?"

"Naw. The guy disappeared. They're still looking for him."

Corrie let a beat pass. "So how was he an asshole?"

Miller took another drag, exhaled into his nose while looking at her. "You're interested, aren't ya?"

"Yeah. I mean, we do have the same name."

A nod. "Like I said, he couldn't sell worth shit. And . . . he wouldn't get with the program."

"Program?"

"We do business a certain way around here."

"Should I know about this program?"

Miller stubbed out the cigarette and rose, looking toward the showroom floor, where a couple of people had walked in and were folding their umbrellas. The man was holding a manila file folder. "You're going to find out right now. On a crappy day like today, everyone who walks in is a buyer. Follow me." He winked at her, his eyes roaming over her tits.

As they approached, Miller greeted the couple in a low-key way, speaking softly. He introduced Corrie as a salesperson in training and asked their permission for her to be involved. It was a nice technique and they said yes. "She might get her first commission out of this," said Miller. "Could be a red-letter day for her. Right, Corrie?"

"Right!" said Corrie brightly.

Corrie looked the two over. The man was almost certainly a doctor, with very little time, used to making quick decisions. His wife, thin and nervous, dressed in track clothes, wanted a black Escalade. With no preliminaries, the husband launched into a carefully prepared spiel. He had spent hours on the Internet. He had actually identified the car on the lot that he wanted. It had a long list of optional equipment, which he had printed out; he knew the invoice price and was willing to pay two hundred dollars above it. If they weren't able to make a deal now, on the terms he named, he was ready to move on to another dealer, the one in the next town, who had an almost identical vehicle on his lot. And another thing: he didn't want any of that fabric protection or rust-proofing or other rip-offs like that. Just the car.

The doctor halted, puffing slightly. This was probably as stressful for him as an emergency room code, Corrie thought. She wondered just how Miller was going to handle it.

To her surprise, Miller didn't seem put out. He didn't launch into negotiations or try to counter the man. On the contrary, he complimented the doctor on his research, expressed the opinion that he himself appreciated the opportunity of concluding a quick and efficient transaction, even if there was little profit in it. A sale was a sale. Of course, he wasn't sure it would be possible to sell the car at that rock-bottom price, but he would check with the owner of the dealership. Did the doctor intend to pay cash or finance?

The doctor would finance. Ten thousand down, the rest on time.

Miller got the good doctor's Social Security number and other financing details. He deposited the doctor and his wife in the luxury waiting room with cups of coffee while he went back to his cubicle, Corrie trailing behind. She watched over his shoulder as he checked the doctor's credit rating on the computer and began writing up the offer.

"Don't you have to ask Mr. Ricco?" she said.

"I don't need to ask him shit," said Miller.

"Are you really going to let them have the car for what he's asking?"

Miller grinned. "Sure."

"So how can you make a profit? I mean, two hundred bucks seems hardly worth it."

Miller continued to write, then signed at the bottom with a flourish. "There's more than one way to skin a cat," he said.

"Like how?"

"Watch and learn."

She followed him back into the waiting room. He flourished the papers. "We're all set," he told the couple. "The boss, Mr. Ricco, approved it, although it took quite a lot of pushing. Between you and me, he wasn't very happy. But as I said, a sale's a sale and on a lousy day like today we're lucky to make any sales at all.

Only one thing, though: your credit rating didn't quite qualify for the most competitive financing rate. But I still got you an excellent rate, almost as sweet, the very best possible under the circumstances—"

The doctor frowned. "What do you mean? My credit's not good?"

Miller gave him an easy smile. "No, not at all! You have quite a good credit rating. It's just not in the absolute top tier, that's all. Perhaps you were late with a mortgage payment or two, maybe you carried over that credit card debt from one month to the next without paying the minimum. Small stuff. Believe me, I got you the very best rate possible."

The doctor's face flushed and he glanced at his wife, who looked put out. "Have we been late with a mortgage payment?"

Now it was her turn to redden. "Well, I was late by a week some months ago—you remember when we were on vacation?"

The doctor frowned, turned to Miller. "So what's the rate you got us? I won't pay anything exorbitant."

"It's just three-quarters of a percentage point higher than the best rate. I also was able to stretch it out to seventy-two months, to keep your monthly payments down."

Miller named the monthly payment, which did indeed seem reasonable to Corrie, especially for a loaded, eighty-thousand-dollar Escalade. She began to wonder how they made money selling cars at all.

In twenty minutes, the good doctor and his wife were driving off the lot with their new car, and as soon as they were gone Miller began wheezing with laughter. He retreated to the staff lounge, refilled his coffee cup, eased his stout frame down. "Just sold Dr. Putz an Escalade," he announced to the assembled group. "Two hundred dollars over invoice. Putz was determined to make a crackerjack deal. So I made him a crackerjack deal."

"I'll bet," said one of the others. "Credit problem, right?"

"Right. I told him his credit wasn't quite up to snuff... and he financed at seven and a half percent over seventy-two months!"

Laughter, shaking heads all around.

"I don't get it," Corrie said.

Miller, still chuckling, said: "The profit built into that financing deal is, what, eight thousand dollars? That's how we make our money—financing. That's the first lesson in selling cars."

"Eight thousand *profit*?" she asked.

"Pure, unadulterated profit."

"How does that work?"

Miller lit up, inhaled a massive lungful, kept talking while the smoke dribbled back out. "Before he came in here, old Dr. Putz obviously spent a lot of time checking Edmunds, but he failed to check the most important thing: his own credit rating. Jacking up his rate by three-quarters of a percentage point over seventy-two months on seventy thousand is over three grand alone. And that's on top of a jacked-up rate to begin with. Shit, if he'd gone to his bank before he came in here, he could've borrowed that money at five and a half percent, maybe less."

"So that wasn't true—that his credit rating wasn't good?"

Miller swiveled his head around. "You got a problem with that?"

"No, no," she said hastily. Out of the corner of her eye she saw Charlie rolling his eyes, a look of annoyance on his face. "I think it's just fine," she repeated.

"Good. 'Cause your predecessor, old Jack, he just didn't get it. Even when he sold a car, which was hardly ever, he'd give them the true best rate. Then, when we called him on it, the son of a bitch threatened to go to the attorney general. Report the dealership."

"That sounds serious. What would've happened?"

"It's not exactly an uncommon practice. Anyway, it didn't come to that, because the dickhead went off and robbed a bank. Solved our problem for us!" He turned and stared at Charlie. "Right, Charlie?"

"You know I don't like that way of doing business," said Charlie quietly. "Sooner or later, it's going to come back and bite you."

"Don't pull a Jack on us," said Miller, his voice suddenly not so friendly.

Charlie said nothing.

Another couple came into the dealership.

"They're mine," said another salesman, smacking his hands together and rubbing them. "Seven and a half percent, here we come!"

Corrie looked around. It was now as clear as day. One of them had framed her father to stop him from going to the AG.

But which one? Or . . . was it *all* of them?

40

THE ALARM BELLS HAD BEEN GOING OFF EVER since D'Agosta got the message that Glen Singleton wanted to see him. And now, as he entered the captain's outer office, the alarms rang even louder. Midge Rawley, Singleton's secretary—normally so gossipy—barely looked up from her computer terminal as he approached. "Go right in, Lieutenant," she said without making eye contact.

D'Agosta walked past her into Singleton's private office. Immediately, his fears were confirmed. Sure enough—there was Singleton, behind his desk, nattily dressed as usual. But it was the expression on the captain's face that made D'Agosta's heart sink. Singleton was perhaps the most straightforward, honest man D'Agosta had ever met. He hadn't the least hint of guile or duplicity—what you saw was what you got. And what D'Agosta saw was a man struggling with a very thorny problem.

"You wanted to see me, Captain?" D'Agosta asked.

"Yes." Singleton glanced down at a document that lay on his desk. He scanned it, turned a page. "We're in the midst of a situation, Lieutenant—or at least, *you're* in the midst of it."

D'Agosta raised his eyebrows.

"As squad commander for the Hotel Killer murders, you appear to be caught in a turf war. Between two FBI agents." He glanced down again at the papers on his desk. "I've gotten my hands on a formal complaint Agent Gibbs has just made against Agent Pendergast. In it, he cites lack of cooperation, freelancing, failure to coordinate—among other grievances." He paused. "Your name comes up in the complaint. Comes up more than once, in fact."

D'Agosta did not reply.

"I called you in here, privately, for two reasons. First—to advise you to stay out of the crossfire. This is an FBI matter, and, believe me, we don't want to get involved."

D'Agosta felt himself stiffening, as if at a cadet review.

Singleton glanced back down at the document, turned yet another page. "The second reason I called you in was to learn anything special about this case that you might know. I need you to share with me the relevant information—*all* the relevant information. You see, Lieutenant, if the shit hits the fan and this thing escalates into World War Three, I don't want to be the one who gets blindsided."

"It's all in the report, sir," D'Agosta said carefully.

"Is it? This is no time to take sides, Lieutenant."

A silence settled over the office. At last, Singleton sighed. "Vincent, we haven't always seen eye-to-eye. But I've always believed you were a good cop."

"Thank you, Captain."

"But this is not the first time your association with Pendergast has become a problem. And jeopardized my good opinion."

"Sir?"

"Let me be frank. Based on his report, Agent Gibbs seems to believe Pendergast is withholding information. That he isn't sharing everything he knows." Singleton paused. "The fact is, Gibbs is deeply suspicious about Pendergast's actions regarding this latest murder. And I don't blame him. From what I've seen in this document, there's not even a hint of standard law enforcement protocols being followed here. And there seems to be a lot of unexplained, ah, *activity* going on."

D'Agosta couldn't meet Singleton's disappointed gaze. He looked down at his shoes.

"I know that you and Pendergast have a history. That you're friends. But this is one of the biggest serial murder cases in years. You are the squad commander. This is yours to lose. So think a minute before you answer. Is there *anything* else I should know?"

D'Agosta remained silent.

"Look, Lieutenant. You went down in flames once before, almost destroyed your career, thanks to Pendergast. I don't want to see that happen again. It's obvious Gibbs is bound and determined to crucify Pendergast. He doesn't care who gets caught up in the collateral damage."

Still D'Agosta said nothing. He found himself recalling all the times he'd stood shoulder-to-shoulder with Pendergast: against that terrible creature in the natural history museum; against the Wrinklers, deep beneath the streets of Manhattan; against Count Fosco and that bastard Bullard in Italy; and, more recently, against Judson Esterhazy and the mysterious *Bund*. And yet, at the same time, he could not deny his own doubts over Pendergast's recent behavior and motives, even his concern for the man's sanity. And he couldn't help but recall Laura Hayward's words: *It's your duty to turn over all evidence, all information, even the crazy stuff. This isn't about friendship. This is about catching a dangerous killer who's likely to kill again. You have to do the right thing.*

He took a deep breath, looked up. And then, as if from far away, he heard himself say: "Pendergast believes his son is the murderer."

Singleton's eyes widened. "Excuse me?"

"I know it sounds crazy. But Pendergast told me that he thinks his own son is responsible for these killings."

"And . . . you believe this?"

"I don't know what to believe. Pendergast's wife just died under terrible circumstances. The man's come as near to cracking up as anyone I've ever seen."

Singleton shook his head. "Lieutenant, when I asked you for information about this case, I wanted *real* information." He sat back. "I mean, this sounds ridiculous. I didn't even know Agent Pendergast had a son."

"Neither did I, sir."

"There's nothing else you want to tell me?"

"There *is* nothing else I can tell you. It's like I said—everything else is in my report."

Singleton looked at him. "So Pendergast withheld information. And you've known about this for how long?"

D'Agosta winced inwardly. "Long enough."

Singleton sat back in his chair. For a moment, neither man spoke.

"Very well, Lieutenant," Singleton said at last. "I'll have to think about how best to address that."

Miserably, D'Agosta nodded his understanding.

"Before you go, let me give you one last piece of advice. A minute ago, I told you not to get involved in this. Not to take sides. And that's good advice. But the time may come—and, based on what you've just told me, it may come sooner than I expected—that all of us will be forced to take a side. If that happens, you *will* come down on the side of Gibbs and the BSU. Not on the side of Pendergast. Frankly, I don't like the man, I don't like his methods—and this business about his son makes me think he's finally gone off the deep end. Is that clear, Lieutenant?"

"Extremely clear, sir."

"Good." Singleton looked down and turned the report over on his desk, signaling that the meeting was at an end.

41

PROCTOR MOVED QUIETLY THROUGH THE library, his eyes scanning the books. He was not a bookish person, and almost all the titles were unknown to him. Many were also written in foreign languages. He had no idea how to "educate" anyone, let alone a strange, weak boy the likes of Tristram. But an assignment was an assignment, and Proctor knew his duty. He had to admit the boy was easy to care for. His needs were modest, and he was grateful for every kindness, every meal, no matter how simple. At first—based on his broken speech and strange ways—Proctor assumed he was mentally defective, but that had clearly been a misjudgment; the boy was catching on very fast.

His eye stopped at a title he recognized: *Rogue Male*, by Geoffrey Household. A good book. A very good book.

Proctor placed his finger on the spine, slipped the book out, then paused to listen. The housekeeper had the night off. The mansion was silent.

. . . Or was it?

With an easy motion, he tucked the book under his arm and turned, his eye taking in the dim library.

It was cold—Proctor did not bother with a fire when Pendergast wasn't around—and most of the lights were off. It was nine o'clock in the evening, and a bitter winter night had settled in, the wind sweeping off the Hudson.

Proctor continued to listen. His ears could now pick up the sounds of the house, the deep, muffled moan of the wind, the faint ticks and creaks of the old mansion; the scent was as usual, beeswax polish, leather, and wood. And yet he thought he'd heard something. Something quiet, almost below audibility. Something from above.

Still moving casually, Proctor strolled to the far end of the library and slid open a small oak panel, exposing a computer security pad and LCD. It was green down the line, the alarms all set, doors and windows secure, motion sensors quiescent.

With the punch of a button, Proctor temporarily deactivated the motion sensors. Then he strolled out of the library into the reception hall, through a marble archway, and into the so-called cabinet—several rooms that had been arranged by Pendergast into a small museum, its displays taken from the seemingly endless collections of Pendergast's great-grand-uncle, Enoch Leng. In the center of the first room stood a small but vicious-looking fossilized dinosaur, all teeth and claws, surrounded by case after case of bizarre and other-worldly specimens, from skulls to diamonds, meteorites to stuffed birds.

He moved easily, smoothly, but inside he felt anything but easy. Proctor had an internal radar, honed by years in the special forces, and at the moment that radar was going off. Why, he did not know—there was not one thing he could put his finger on. Everything seemed secure. It was instinct.

Proctor never ignored his instincts.

He climbed the stairs to the second floor. Skirting the moth-eaten, stuffed chimpanzee with no lips, he scanned the doors up and down the hall. All closed. His eyes rested momentarily on the painting of a deer being torn apart by wolves, then moved on.

All was well.

Returning to the first floor, he went back to the library, reactivated the motion sensors, picked up *Rogue Male*, sat down in a chair strategically positioned toward a mirror on a far wall that allowed him a view out of the library and across the entire reception area.

He opened the book and pretended to read.

As he did so, he maintained his senses on highest alert—especially his sense of smell. Proctor had a supernaturally keen sense of smell, almost as good as a deer's. It was not something most humans anticipated, and it had saved his life more than once.

Half an hour passed without one thing to arouse his suspicions. He realized it must have been a false alarm. But—never one to make assumptions—he closed the book, yawned, and walked over to the secret bookcase entrance to the elevator that descended into the basement. He rode the elevator down and walked along the narrow basement corridor of undressed stone, the walls covered with niter, damp, and lime.

He turned a corner, pressed himself noiselessly into a recess, and waited.

Nothing.

Slowly, he inhaled, his nose testing the currents of air. But there was no human smell in it, no strange eddies or unexpected warmth; nothing but the chill damp.

Now Proctor began to feel a little foolish. His isolation, his unaccustomed role as protector and tutor, had put him on edge. Nobody could be following him. The bookcase entrance had closed behind him and had clearly not been reopened. The elevator he had taken remained in the basement; no one had called it back to the first floor. Even if someone were on the first floor, they could not possibly have followed him into the basement.

Gradually, under these thoughts, the feeling of alarm began to subside. It was safe to descend to the sub-basement.

Stepping down the corridor to the small stone room, he pressed on the Pendergastian crest. The hidden door opened. He stepped through and waited until it snugged back shut again. Then he descended the long curving staircase and began making his way through the many strange rooms that made up the sub-basement, full of glass bottles, rotting tapestries, dried insects, medicines, and other bizarre collections of Enoch Leng. He hurried to the heavy, iron-banded door that opened into Tristram's quarters.

The boy was waiting for him patiently. Patience was one of his great virtues. He could sit still, unmoving, with nothing to do, for many hours. It was a quality Proctor admired.

"I brought you a book," Proctor said.

"Thank you!" The boy rose and took it with eagerness, looking at it, turning it over. "What's it about?"

Proctor suddenly had a twinge of doubt. Was this really the right book for someone whose brother was a serial killer? That hadn't occurred to him before. He cleared his throat. "It's about a man who stalks and tries to kill a dictator. He's caught and escapes." He paused. His description didn't make it seem very interesting. "I'll read you the first chapter."

"Please!" Tristram sat down on the bed, waiting.

"Stop me if there are any words you don't understand. And when I'm done, we'll talk about the chapter. You'll have questions—be sure to ask them." Proctor settled into a chair, opened the book, cleared his throat, and started to read.

"I cannot blame them. After all, one doesn't need a telescopic sight to shoot boar or bear . . ."

Suddenly, Proctor felt something behind him: a presence. He spun and leapt up, clapping his hand on his weapon, but the figure vanished back into the darkness of the corridor even before his hand had touched the gun. But the image of the face he'd seen was engraved on his mind. It was the face of Tristram—only keener and more blade-like.

Alban.

42

SUPERVISORY SPECIAL AGENT PETER S. JOYCE'S
office was one of the more cluttered in the big building at 26 Federal Plaza. The shelves were filled with
books about American history, the criminal justice system, and nautical lore; the walls were decorated with
photos of his weather-beaten thirty-two-foot sloop, the
Burden of Proof. Joyce's desk, however, was completely
bare, like the deck of a ship cleared for an approaching gale. The office's lone window looked out into the
Lower Manhattan night—Joyce was a confirmed night
owl, and he always saved his most serious work of the
day for the last.

There was a soft knock at the door.

"Enter," Joyce said.

The door opened and Special Agent Aloysius Pendergast came in. He shut the door quietly behind him,
then stepped forward and slipped into the single chair
placed before Joyce's desk.

Joyce felt a twinge of annoyance that the man had
seated himself before being asked, but he covered it up.
He had more important things to say.

"Agent Pendergast," Joyce began. "In the three years

since I was transferred to the New York field office, I've tolerated your, shall we say, *unconventional* behavior as an agent—often against the advice of others. I've run interference for you on more than one occasion, backed up your methods when others have wanted to call you on the carpet. I've done this for a variety of reasons. I'm not a stickler for protocol. I'm no lover of the FBI's fondness for bureaucracy. I'm more interested in results—and you've rarely disappointed in that regard. You may be unconventional, but you're damn effective. Your military experience is highly impressive—at least from what I've seen of the nonclassified reports in your folder. And there is an extremely complimentary appraisal in your folder, written by the late Michael Decker, one of the most decorated and honored agents in recent memory. I've frequently thought back to that appraisal when complaints of your behavior have crossed my desk."

He sat forward, put his arms on the desk, and tented his fingers. "But now, Agent Pendergast, you've done something that I can't ignore, and that I can't tolerate. You have stepped way, *way* over the line."

"Are you referring to Agent Gibbs's formal complaint?" Pendergast asked.

If Joyce was surprised by this, he didn't show it. "Only in part." He hesitated. "I'm no friend of Agent Gibbs or the BSU. His assertions about your freelancing, your failure to coordinate, deviating from standard procedure, not being a team player, don't really concern me." He made a dismissive motion. "But his other charges are more serious. Your involving yourself in this case without waiting for official authorization, for example. You of all people should know that Gibbs is only on the case because the New York City police specifically asked for help from the BSU. You're

not affiliated with Behavioral Sciences—your business
with this case is obscure, and your efforts to have yourself assigned to it have seriously ruffled some feathers
around here. Yet even that, I might have been able to
overlook—but I can't overlook your most egregious
infraction."

"Which is?" Pendergast repeated.

"Withholding information of critical relevance to
the case."

"And may I ask what that information is?"

"That the Hotel Killer is your own son."

Pendergast went rigid.

"Gibbs suspected you were withholding information, Agent Pendergast. The NYPD confirmed it. When
they first heard you suspected your son to be the killer,
early this afternoon, they did not take it seriously. They
thought you were...well, non compos mentis. But of
course they were duty-bound to follow up. Comparison of the Hotel Killer's DNA with yours—which
we have on file, as you know—has verified it." Joyce
sighed. "This information—information of absolutely
crucial importance—you withheld from the investigation. There can be no possible justification. It not only
looks bad, it *is* bad. This goes far beyond conflict of
interest. It verges on a criminal charge of aiding and
abetting."

Pendergast did not reply. He looked back at Joyce,
an unreadable expression on his face.

"Agent Pendergast, I have no idea how your son got
involved in this, or why, or how you learned of it, or
what you were planning to do about it. You're clearly in
an intolerable personal position, and for that you have
my deepest sympathy. But let me be frank with you:
your actions in this matter have been unethical at best
and illegal at worst."

Joyce let this hang in the air a long moment before continuing.

"As you know, when it comes to disciplinary action, we have a fixed bureaucracy in place. As a first-line supervisor, I can't even give you a slap on the wrist. So I sent a report to the Office of the Special Agent in Charge–New York Division, detailing your offenses and recommending immediate termination."

Another pause.

"The SAC's office dropped it right back in my lap. They wouldn't touch it. So this morning I resubmitted the report, this time to the Office of Professional Responsibility."

Joyce sighed. He gave Pendergast a sidelong stare, as if trying to evaluate a Japanese puzzle box. "Ordinarily, the OPR boys would have been all over you like stink on shit. There would be interrogations, they'd be calling witnesses, a decision would be made, a punishment would come down. And you'd be put through the wringer while the process ground on. Instead, what happens? Within an hour, I get a response: 'Thirty days off the street.'"

Joyce shook his head. "That's it. Instead of five to ten in Leavenworth, you get thirty days off the street: a month without pay. And since your annual FBI salary is—what, a dollar-a-year honorarium?—I doubt that's going to sting very much." He raised a speculative eyebrow. "I don't know who your guardian angel is, Special Agent Pendergast, but I'll tell you this: you're one charmed son of a bitch."

The room fell into silence. At last, Joyce shifted in his chair. "Is there anything you'd like to add?"

Pendergast shook his head almost imperceptibly. "I would say you've articulated the situation admirably, Supervisory Special Agent Joyce."

"In that case—take your thirty days. And stay far, *far* away from this case." Turning away from Pendergast, Joyce plucked *Cruising Boats Within Your Budget* from a shelf behind him, placed it on his desk, and began to read.

43

PROCTOR WHEELED BACK TO TRISTRAM, WHO was sitting on his bed, white-faced. "Stay here," he said. "I'll lock you in. You'll be safe in this room." He stepped out, locked the door securely, and then raced down the stone corridor, flattening himself against the wall just before the hallway opened on to the nearest sub-basement room.

He took out his .45, racked a round into the chamber, flicked on the laser sights. Then he took a moment to clear his head, get a feel for the tactical situation. He pushed away all surprise, all pain from his bruised ribs, all speculation about how the youth could have gotten in—and focused on the problem at hand.

The killer meant to lure him out into the sub-basement proper. Alban wanted him to follow. Just as clearly, that was the course of action he must take. There was no other. He could not allow the young man—now inside the security of the house—any freedom of action. He had to track him down. Alban meant to ambush him—he was sure of that. So he had to be unpredictable. He had to develop a strategy.

And he had to understand why Alban hadn't killed him outright, when he'd clearly had the chance.

All these thoughts occurred in a split second.

Eyeing the ground, Proctor looked for traces of Alban's passing, but was unable to tease out the youth's marks from the welter of fresh footprints in the dust. He took a deep breath and, after a moment, spun around the corner and covered the room with his weapon. A single, naked lightbulb, hanging from a wire that ran the length of the sub-basement, illuminated the room, casting deep shadows. Cases along the walls displayed a motley collection of stuffed reptiles.

The room appeared to be empty.

With a quick movement he darted across the floor and took cover behind an old case that lay on its side, rusting halberds spilling out. From that vantage point he scoured the room as best he could. He did not need to hurry. The killer wasn't trying to escape—the killer was stalking him just as surely as he was stalking the killer.

After ascertaining that the room was empty, Proctor darted to the far end and flattened himself against the archway that led into the next chamber, back in the direction of the staircase leading upward. This was filled with shelving, not just along the wall but also running across the middle, loaded with glass bottles in different colors, filled with strange and bizarre objects, dried insects, lizards, seeds, liquids and powders. There were many places to hide among those complicated rows of shelves, many places in which to set up an ambush.

A pity, what he would have to do.

Proctor carried a Beretta Px4 Storm with a 9 + 1 magazine, but he always carried two extra twenty-round magazines on his person: fifty rounds in all. He had a phobia of running out of ammunition. It had never happened to him, and it never would.

He slipped out the ten-round magazine, inserted one of the twenties. It significantly increased the weight of the weapon, but it was necessary for what he was about to do.

Unpredictable…

Suddenly Proctor surged under the archway, firing repeatedly into the rows of shelves as he sprinted down the length of the room, shooting ahead first to one side and then to the other. The result was a roar of sound and a chaotic storm of glass as the expanding rounds tore through multiple rows of shelves, fragmenting as they went, blowing the shelving to smithereens. The noise in the confined space was deafening. Anyone hiding among the shelves would be, at the very least, blinded by flying glass and quite possibly struck by fragmenting bullets. Such a person would be unable to return fire accurately.

Proctor continued running into the next chamber, maintaining a withering fire, blowing hundreds of glass bottles into glittering showers as he ran.

The twenty rounds carried him through to a third chamber, a smaller space filled with cases of stuffed birds. Here, the magazine empty, he took cover behind a heavy oaken case that projected from one wall. Crouching, he held his breath and listened with great intensity.

The residual sounds from the shoot-up echoed through the sub-basement: liquids draining, glass falling, an occasional crash. The stone floor behind him was now covered with thousands of glass shards. Nobody could walk over it—nobody—without making a sound. If the killer were behind him, he would not be able to follow without making his presence known.

Still he waited. Gradually the after-sounds of destruction died away, leaving the monotonous *drip*,

drip of liquids and a foul compound odor of alcohol, formaldehyde, dead animals, and dried insects.

He knew that the next room was also stuffed with display cases, offering many hiding areas. The cases, he recalled, were loaded with ancient tools and antique devices. Proctor had no idea why Enoch Leng had assembled these bizarre collections, nor did he care. All he knew was that—most likely in one of the ancient rooms ahead—his adversary was also waiting.

Proctor waited a very long time. Often success came from simply outwaiting one's adversary. Eventually they would move. And then, *bang*.

But this time, silence reigned. The adversary did not show himself.

While it was possible the killer was in one of the rooms he'd already passed through, dead or gravely wounded, Proctor somehow doubted it. His gut told him that Alban was in one of the rooms that lay ahead.

Waiting.

Proctor removed the empty magazine and inserted the second twenty-round box. In that moment he heard the crunch of a footfall on glass.

Spinning, astonished the killer was behind him, he quickly moved to a more defensible position in an alcove against the mortared wall.

He waited again, listening intently. The entire floor of the previous room was covered with shattered glass. It was not possible to move without making noise—or was it?

Ever so slowly, he crept up to the edge of the stone arch, listening. But there was no more sound. Could it have been something falling onto the glass?

The uncertainty began to eat away at Proctor. He had to see, to find out. In a burst of speed, he launched himself back through the archway, racing down the center of the room, again firing to the left and right. He saw a flash of movement to his far right, behind a row of shattered bottles, and he fired at it repeatedly through the shelves before taking cover in an alcove along the far wall.

Pressing himself into the space, he listened again. He must have hit the killer, or at least sprayed him with flying glass. He would be injured, perhaps blinded, frightened, disoriented.

. . . Or was this just wishful thinking?

Another loud crunch of glass, an unmistakable footfall.

Bursting from the alcove, Proctor ran, firing again in the direction of the sound, through the already-broken bottles, sending up a kaleidoscopic spray of glittering shards, additional shelves crashing down, beakers spraying their contents. But as he raked the area from where the sound had come, he realized there was nobody. Nothing. He kept running until he reached the far end of the chamber, taking cover in a corner, staring wildly about.

Abruptly, a pebble arced through the air, hit the lightbulb, and the room was plunged into darkness. Proctor immediately fired in the direction from which the pebble had been launched, the light from the adjacent room streaming in and providing a little illumination.

He lowered the gun, breathing hard. How many rounds did he have left? He normally kept count, but this time he had lost track. He'd fired twenty, plus at least fifteen more. Which left perhaps five in this magazine and ten in the final magazine.

His nightmare—running out of ammo—was starting to come true.

As he crouched in the black corner, he realized his

strategy had been a failure. He was dealing with an adversary of tremendous foresight and skill.

He would need a new strategy. The killer probably expected him to continue on, to keep probing, searching, as he had been doing. So instead he would now turn around and retrace his steps. He would force the killer to come to him.

Creeping along the wall, he reached the doorway to the next room. Light streamed through from its single bulb. This room, too, had been full of bottles, and the floor was covered with glass. He now faced the same problem he had posed his adversary. He could not move without making noise.

Maybe. Crouching, he slipped off his shoes. Keeping low, he inched around the archway into the next room in his stockinged feet, keeping to the deep shadows behind the shattered cases. Slowly, slowly he moved, in complete silence, ignoring the broken glass that cut into the soles of his feet. Between each step he paused, listening.

He heard a brief intake of breath, to his right, behind a massive row of broken shelves. Unmistakable. The killer must also be moving in stockinged feet.

Did the killer see him? Impossible to know.

Unpredictable—that's what he had to keep in mind.

He erupted into sudden, furious motion, running straight at the long, tall row of shelves, slamming into them and heaving them over, the shelving falling against the next row and the next, like dominoes, the already-broken and shot-up frames crashing down like a house of cards, trapping the person within in a storm of broken glass, chemicals, specimens, and twisted shelving.

As he stepped back, he felt a sudden blow to his arm and his .45 went flying. He spun, swinging his fist around, but the black figure had already flitted aside, slamming him in the ribs and sending him sprawling onto the glass.

Proctor rolled and was up in one swift motion, the jagged neck of a broken beaker in his hand. The killer jumped back, picking up his own piece of jagged glass. They circled each other warily.

Proctor, an expert with a knife, lunged, but the killer skipped aside and slashed at him, cutting his forearm. Proctor swept back and managed to rip the killer's shirt, but the killer once again—with supernatural speed—turned and avoided the main thrust.

Never in his life had Proctor seen anyone move so fast or anticipate so well. He advanced on the killer, slashing again and again, forcing him to retreat but scoring no hits. The killer backed against a table, dropped his shard of glass, and picked up a heavy retort. Proctor pressed his advantage, advancing and slashing. But then suddenly, as if from nowhere, the killer—who feinted back again as if once again in retreat—twisted around in the most extraordinary movement and slammed the retort against the side of Proctor's head, the heavy glass shattering and sending Proctor to the floor, dazed.

In a flash the killer was on top of Proctor, pinning him, the jagged glass of the retort pressed into his throat, right up against his carotid artery, with just enough pressure to cut the skin but go no deeper.

Proctor, dazed, stupefied in shock and pain, could not believe he had been bested. It did not seem possible. And yet he had been defeated—at the very thing he was most skilled in.

"Go ahead," he said hoarsely. "Finish it."

The killer laughed, exposing gleaming white teeth. "You know perfectly well that if I wanted to kill you, you'd already be dead. Oh, no. You have a message to deliver to your master. And I have a brother who needs...attending to."

As he spoke, a long arm snaked out and removed the key to Tristram's room from Proctor's pocket.

"And now, good night."

A sudden, stunning blow to the side of Proctor's head caused the world to shut down in darkness.

44

IN THE APARTMENT OVERLOOKING FIRST AVE-
nue, lieutenant Vincent D'Agosta paced restlessly. He
threw himself down on the living room couch, turned
on the television, ran aimlessly through the channels,
then turned it off again. He got up, walked to the sliding door, and looked out over the darkened balcony.
He went to the kitchen, opened the refrigerator door,
took out a beer, thought better of it, replaced it and
closed the door.

Every few minutes he glanced toward the phone,
then glanced away again.

He knew he should join Laura in bed, get some
sleep, but he also knew sleep just wouldn't come. In
the fallout that followed his meeting with Singleton,
he'd been given a so-called command discipline and
relieved of the squad commander post on the hotel
killings—as Singleton had pointed out, he was damn
lucky not to have fared worse, no thanks to Pendergast. The thought of getting up in the morning and
going back to his desk and picking up the pieces of half
a dozen piece-of-shit crimes was almost more than he
could stand.

He looked over at the phone again. He might as well get it over with—he'd never feel easy until he got it off his chest.

He sighed, then picked up the phone and dialed Pendergast's cell.

It was answered on the third ring. "Yes?" came the cool southern drawl.

"Pendergast? It's me. Vinnie."

There was a pause. When the voice sounded again, it had dropped several dozen degrees in temperature. "Yes?"

"Where are you?"

"In my car. Driving home."

"Good. I thought you'd still be awake. Listen, I just wanted to say... well, how sorry I am about what happened."

When there was no answer, D'Agosta struggled on. "I didn't know what to do. I mean, I was squad commander, it was my duty to report any and all possible evidence. Singleton was coming down hard on me—I was backed into a corner."

Still no reply. D'Agosta licked his lips. "Look, I know you've gone through a lot these past several weeks. I'm your friend, I want to help any way I can. But this... this is my job. I had no choice. You've got to understand."

When it came, Pendergast's voice was as brittle, yet as steely, as he'd ever heard it. "Even one with the meanest comprehension would understand. You betrayed a confidence."

D'Agosta took a deep breath. "You can't take it like that. I mean, we're not talking about the sanctity of the confessional here. Withholding the identity of a serial killer, even if it is your own flesh and blood—that's illegal. Trust me, better it came out now than later."

No response.

"They took me off the case. And you—let's face it—you were never on it to begin with. Let's put that all behind us now."

"My son—as you so kindly pointed out—is a serial killer. How, precisely, am I supposed to put that behind me?"

"Then let me help you. On the side. I'll still have access and I can pass developments on to you. We've worked that way before—we can do it again."

Once again, Pendergast was silent.

"Well? What do you say?"

"What do I say? What I say is this: exactly how much longer am I to be burdened with self-serving justifications and unwanted offers of assistance?"

D'Agosta felt the full force of this, and the unfairness of it all, coming suddenly to a boil. "You know what *I* say?" he shouted. "Fuck you!" And he slammed down the phone.

45

As soon as Pendergast entered the mansion he sensed something was wrong. There was a watchful silence in the air, an unnatural stasis—and a faint, strange odor. A quick check showed that all the alarms were on and green, the locks un-tampered-with, everything in its place.

Nevertheless, Pendergast moved fast through the echoing corridors to the library. It was cold, dark, and silent, the fireplace dead, no sign of Proctor.

Swinging open the bookcases, he took the elevator to the basement, raced along the subterranean passageway to the secret door, opened it. Now the smell hit him like a wall—the commingled stench of formaldehyde, ethanol, and myriad other liquids, powders, and unguessable concoctions. He drew his .45 as he raced down the curve of the staircase.

He emerged through the archway into the long string of underground chambers that made up the sub-basement, ran through the first half dozen, then stopped abruptly. The rooms ahead—stretching off one after another, connected by stone arches, illuminated by a string of lightbulbs—presented a scene of destruction. Everywhere glittered shards of colored glass and shattered bottles lay amid puddles of smoking liquids. Specimens were strewn everywhere, shelving lay upended and shattered upon the stone floor, and the cases along the walls were peppered with large-caliber bullet holes.

"Tristram!" he cried as he began to run.

He flew through the vaults, his shoes crunching on a carpet of glass, turned a corner halfway down the series of chambers, came to his son's room, jammed his key in the lock, then turned it and wrenched open the door.

A body lay on the floor, covered with a sheet. Stifling a gasp, Pendergast rushed to it and pulled the sheet back—to uncover Proctor, his face covered with blood. He quickly felt the pulse in his neck: strong. The chauffeur was alive but unconscious. Pendergast made an examination of Proctor's body, determining he was merely battered, with a nasty gash on his head that had bled copiously and was clearly evidence of a concussion.

Going to the connecting bathroom, he rinsed a cloth in warm water and returned, gently cleaning Proctor's face and the cut on his head. The effort began to revive the man, and he tried to sit up, almost fainting as a result. Pendergast eased him back down.

"What happened?" Pendergast asked, quietly but urgently.

Proctor shook his head to clear it, then groaned at the resulting pain. "Alban...took Tristram."

"How in God's name did he get in?"

Another shake of the head. "No idea. Thought I heard...a noise."

"When did this happen?"

"About a quarter...to ten."

It was now past eleven. Pendergast leapt up. There was no indication Alban and his victim had left the house—the alarms had been green. And yet more than an hour had passed since the attack.

"I'm going to leave you here while I track them," he said.

Proctor waved a dismissive hand as if to say, *Don't worry about me.*

Sidearm at the ready, Pendergast performed a quick search of the room. Going through the mess of papers on Tristram's desk, his attempts to write in English, he found a striking drawing of a mountain, with a note indicating it was a gift to his father. This discovery caused a painful twinge. But he pushed the feeling away as best he could, took the drawing, and left the room, locking the door behind him.

He examined intently the marks in the dust of the side passage, but this close to Tristram's room there were too many confusing footprints to bring any order to. He returned to the main corridor, continuing on as swiftly as he could while still maintaining vigilance, examining the riot of ruin that covered the floor. Passing through several more chambers, he came to the old laboratory of Professor Leng. The confrontation had not extended this far—the lab was relatively in order. Old soapstone tabletops were covered with beakers, retorts, titration apparatuses. He looked around carefully, then made his way noiselessly along the walls to the open door leading to the next and final room. It was full of weapons, both ancient and relatively modern: swords, maces, rifles, blackjacks, grenades, flails, tridents.

Here Pendergast paused, fishing a small LED light from his pocket and exploring the room with it. Nothing appeared to be missing. At the far end, he stopped. There were fresh marks before an unobtrusive door in the wall.

The security alarms had been green. The motion sensors had not been triggered. The mansion was exceedingly well wired against intruders—except for the basement and sub-basements, accessible only through the hidden elevator and secret door, which because of their bizarre layout and almost limitless extent could not be properly wired for security. Indeed, attempting to have done so might actually have compromised that secret section of the mansion. But this was all speculation, because no intruder could find his way into them.

Pendergast stared at the closed door. Unless...was it even possible?

He quickly opened the door, which led to a crude stone passageway and a descending staircase, constructed from a natural crevasse in the schist bedrock. A strong smell of mold and damp rose from below. Heading down the long series of rude steps, he came to an ancient stone quay alongside a watery tunnel— the lair of the river pirate who had owned an earlier house near the site of the mansion. Normally, an old rowing skiff was upturned on the quay—but now it was gone. Fresh splashes and puddles of water on the stone edges of the quay attested to the fact the boat had been recently launched.

Pendergast knew the smuggler's tunnel led to the Hudson River. It was so well concealed, and the passage from it to the sub-basement so carefully barred and locked, Pendergast had always believed the rear tunnel entrance to be undiscoverable and impregnable. He now realized this had been a foolish oversight. With an hour's head start, Alban and his hostage would be gone—and impossible to trace.

He half sat, half collapsed onto the stone floor of the quay.

46

DR. JOHN FELDER STEPPED OUT OF THE GATE-
house and closed the door silently behind him. As the
calendar had promised, it was a moonless night. The
Wintour mansion had no exterior lights—Miss Wintour was too miserly to buy any more lightbulbs than
absolutely necessary—and the ancient pile was a vast
obscure shape rising before him, black against black.

He took a deep breath, then began pushing his
way through the knee-high tangle of dead weeds and
grasses. It was a cold night, close to freezing, and his
breath smoked the air. The mansion, the street, the
entire town of Southport seemed cloaked in silence.
Despite the darkness, he felt horribly exposed.

Reaching the main building, he pressed himself
against its chill flanks and paused, listening. All was
silent. He moved slowly along the exterior wall until he
came to the large bow window of the mansion's library.
The library boasted three sets of casement windows.
Moving even more slowly now, Felder peered into the
closest casement. Utter blackness.

Retreating slightly, he pressed his back to the stone
façade and peered around. There was nothing, not even

the hush of a passing car, to break the stillness. This side of the mansion was at right angles to the street, hidden from view by a wall of ancient arborvitae planted along the inside edge of the wrought-iron fence. He could not be seen.

Nevertheless, he stood in the lee of the library windows for a long time. Was he really going to do this? As he'd sat in the gatehouse that evening, hour after hour, waiting for midnight, he'd told himself he wasn't really planning anything wrong. He'd simply be appropriating the portfolio of a second-rate artist who nobody cared about, least of all Miss Wintour. In fact, he wouldn't even be appropriating it. He was simply borrowing it. At the end of the day, he could just mail it back to her anonymously. No harm done...

But then he'd come back to reality. He was planning a burglary. Breaking and entering. That was a crime, a misdemeanor or perhaps even a felony, punishable by jail time. And then his thoughts went to Dukchuk—and jail seemed a preferable alternative to getting caught by him.

His feet were going numb from the cold and the lack of movement, and he shifted position. Was he really going to do this? Yes, he was—in another minute. Or two.

He reached into the pocket of his jacket, checking its contents. A Maglite, a screwdriver, a scalpel, a tin of 3-In-One oil, a thin pair of leather gloves. He took another deep, shuddering breath; licked his lips; looked around yet again. Nothing. It was utterly black; he could barely make out the library windows against their heavy frames. The mansion was as silent as a tomb. Another moment of hesitation—then he plucked the gloves from his pocket, pulled them on, and stepped up to the nearest window.

Pressing close to the casement, he took out his flashlight, and—shielding its beam with his glove—turned it on and examined the center post where the two vertical sections of the window met. Damn—the espagnolettes had been twisted into place, the hinged levers effectively locking this pair of windows. Flicking off the light and taking another look around, he moved on to the next casement and examined it. Again, the handles that opened the windows had been twisted into a horizontal position. He couldn't get in without breaking the glass, reaching in, and turning the handle himself—unthinkable.

With a sensation that seemed half disappointment, half relief, he moved on to the last casement, hooded his light, and glanced in. The handle of the first matched window was securely in place. But the beam of his light revealed that its mate was slightly ajar, the espagnolette having broken off and been left unrepaired, the place where it had been fastened to the metal framing now just a hole.

Snapping off his light, Felder moved on, into the shadow of the far side of the bow window. Once again he waited, looking around and listening carefully. But there was nothing.

He realized his heart was pounding painfully in his chest. If he didn't do this now, he'd lose his nerve. Turning resolutely back to the final casement, he slipped the screwdriver into the thin space between the window edge and the frame, then applied gentle pressure. The gap widened with a squeak of protest. Felder stopped, took the lubricating oil from his pocket, applied it to the rusty hinges, tried the screwdriver again. Now the window moved silently. In a moment the gap was large enough for him to insert his fingers. Gently—gently—he pulled the window wide.

He put the oil and screwdriver back into his pocket. All remained still. Summoning his courage, he placed his hands on both sides of the window frame and raised his foot onto the sill, preparing to pull himself in. Then he hesitated. For a moment, he saw himself as if from a distance. It suddenly seemed ridiculous, even preposterous, what he was doing. A thought flashed through his head: *If my med-school professors could see me now.* But he was too nervous for such contemplations to last. Taking a fresh hold on the frame, he pulled himself up and, with one quick effort, was inside the room.

The library was almost as chilly as the night outside. Shielding the flashlight, Felder swept it briefly around the room, taking in the positions of the various pieces of furniture. It wouldn't do for him to tumble over a chair. The space was decorated similarly to the front parlor: prudish high-backed chairs, a few low tables covered with lace cloths on which were set various pieces of display china and pewter. The room was dusty, as if it had not been used in a long time. The walls on both sides were covered floor-to-ceiling with bookshelves, set behind cases of leaded glass.

He glanced around again, memorizing the location of the furnishings. Then, snapping off the light, he walked as quickly and as quietly as he dared across the room to the pocket doors. Here he stopped, placing his ear to the doors and listening intently.

Nothing.

Heart beating still faster, he turned back to face the library. He had no idea where to start. The shelves were stuffed with thousands of books, leather storage boxes, bundles of ancient manuscripts tied in decaying ribbons, and other material. The prospect of spending hours searching, fearing discovery at any moment, was intolerable.

He braced himself with thoughts of Constance. Then, turning to his left, he crept over to where the wall of bookshelves seemed to start, next to the pocket doors. Hooding his flashlight again, he snapped it on, long enough to see a row of tall, leather-bound books staring back at him, their ribbed spines glowing faintly in the light. They were the works of Henry Adams, in four volumes.

He walked a little way down the wall of shelving, then paused and flicked the light on again, briefly. On the shelf in front of him sat maybe half a dozen small wooden boxes of intricate workmanship, beautifully dovetailed and varnished. Paper labels were fixed to each, curling away slightly from the wood as the old glue dried. A note had been handwritten on each box in faded ink: *Bierstadt, Vol. 1. Bierstadt, Vol. 2.*

The Bierstadt correspondence. The goal of the Harvard delegation that had made a futile pilgrimage here. No doubt worth a fortune...

Felder turned off the light and took a quick step back from the shelves. Was that a noise?

He stood, motionless, for a long moment, listening intently. But there was nothing. He turned and glanced toward the pocket doors. There was no light shining beneath them.

Nevertheless, he took a few anxious steps toward the relative safety of the open window.

He paused again to listen for a good sixty seconds before returning his attention to the shelves. He raised his flashlight, again partially covering it with his hand, and briefly directed the shielded beam to the shelves in front of him. A huge, folio-size volume sat on the shelf at eye level, surrounded by smaller sets of books with matching gilt spines. It was Goethe's *Faust*, and it was a beauty, its leather binding stamped and tooled into fantastical shapes...

Felder jerked so violently he almost dropped the flashlight. Was he just hearing things in his extreme agitation? Or had that not been a footstep, a tread on the carpeting in the hall outside the library, a tread almost as stealthy as a cat's?

He glanced nervously toward the pocket doors. Still no light shone beneath them—all was black as pitch. He swallowed, then turned back to the shelving, preparing to take another look.

And then, something—he did not know what, exactly—prompted him to turn around again, move directly to the open window, slip out of it to the ground, and close it silently behind him, thanking God he had thought to bring the oil.

He stood there in the black of night, trembling slightly. As his heart rate subsided, he began to feel sheepish. It was just his imagination playing tricks on him. There had been no noise; there had been no light. If he let himself fall victim to every fit of the jitters, he'd never find that portfolio. He turned back toward the window. He'd let himself back in, get a better sense of the layout of the books . . .

Abruptly, the pocket doors to the library were thrown back. The violence with which they opened was just as terrible as the silence with which they moved. Felder shrank away from the window in dread. He could see a huge figure standing in the doorway, framed against the faintest of light from the hallway beyond. It was a man, clothed in a strange, shapeless garment. A long, curved wooden club was grasped in one hand, its cruelly carven length terminating in a croquet-ball-size sphere.

Dukchuk.

Felder stood in the darkness outside the library window, staring through the glass, rooted to the spot with terror. The manservant looked carefully around the room, his bald and dimly shining head moving with the slow deliberation of a great beast, taking in every square inch of the room. And then he closed the pocket doors again, swiftly and silently. The house fell still once again—leaving Felder's heart pounding furiously in his chest.

Recovering his wits, Felder retreated to the gatehouse as quickly as he dared. But even before the awful tingle of fear had completely faded, he sensed something else—a spark of hope. Because he had just realized something.

Adams. Bierstadt. Goethe. The books in the Wintour library were arranged in alphabetical order.

47

CONSTANCE GREENE SAT QUITE STILL IN THE
paneled fastness of Room 027, located on the first basement level of the Mount Mercy Hospital for the Criminally Insane. Room 027 had once been the site of the
hospital's Water Treatment room, a curative therapy
instituted by Bradford Tuke, one of Mount Mercy's
earliest alienists. While the cleats for the manacles had
long ago been removed from the walls, the perceptible dip in the carpeting in the room's center revealed
where the large floor drain—now filled with cement—
was located.

The room was now normally used for private psy-
chiatric sessions between doctors and low-threat-level
inmates. It was comfortably furnished. Still, while the
chairs and tables were not bolted to the floor, there was
a distinct lack of either sharp or blunt objects. The door
was not locked, but a brace of guards was stationed
directly outside.

The only other occupant of the room was Special
Agent Pendergast. He was pacing slowly back and
forth, his step uncertain, his face extremely pale.

Constance watched him for a while, and then her

gaze fell to the stacks of police reports, grainy black-and-white stills from security video cameras, forensic analyses, and DNA reports that were neatly arranged on the desk before her. She had read and taken in everything, her mind retaining all the details in their enormous complexity. The information had then been subjected to a meditative practice known as *Tsan B'tsan*, that most demanding of the arts of Chongg Ran, an ancient mental discipline from Bhutan whose subtleties were known to less than half a dozen people in the Western world—two of whom occupied that room.

During the state of *Tsan B'tsan*, Constance had come to an unexpected revelation.

After several minutes, she looked back at Pendergast, still pacing slowly across the floor.

"I think it would be best if we reviewed the events that have brought us to the present state," she said, quietly and coolly. "Your wife, Helen Esterhazy, the descendant of a Nazi doctor, was the product of a genetic experiment involving twins, organized by a group calling itself *Der Bund*, the Covenant. Twelve years ago, when she threatened to reveal the experiments, they arranged to have her killed. But in an elaborate ruse perpetrated by her own brother, Judson, she survived and her defective twin, Emma, died in her place. Recently, when *Der Bund* realized Helen was still alive, they kidnapped her from your intended safekeeping—and then killed her."

Pendergast's pace slowed even further.

"Your wife gave birth—early in your marriage, and unbeknownst to you—to twin boys. These were the product of *Der Bund*'s ongoing experiments in eugenics and genetic manipulation. One son, named Alban, was developed into a highly intelligent, aggressive, and remorseless killer, an example of Teutonic perfection as visualized by

Nazi ideology. The other son, whom you named Tristram, comprises what is left from their joint gene pool, and thus by necessity is Alban's opposite: weak, timid, empathic, kind, and guileless. Both were brought here, to New York, as some kind of beta test, the purpose of which is unknown beyond the fact that it involved Alban's serial killing of guests in hotel rooms and leaving messages intended for you. So far, am I correct?"

Pendergast nodded without looking at her.

"Tristram escaped to you. Last night, Alban found him and kidnapped him in turn, spiriting him away—as Helen Esterhazy was spirited away, not so long ago."

Somehow, this direct, factual recitation, devoid of emotion, seemed to clear the charged air of the room. Pendergast's expression eased somewhat, grew less distraught. He stopped in his pacing and looked at Constance.

"I cannot put myself in your place, Aloysius," Constance went on. "Because you and I both know that—*had* I been in your place, had this happened to me—my reaction would have been of a rather more . . . harsh and impulsive nature than yours. However, the fact you have come to me like this tells me a great deal. I know you must be tormented by the tragic way your wife's kidnapping ended. And I sense this cruel twist of fate—your son, the son you never knew you had, being taken in such a similar manner—has paralyzed you. You don't trust your own judgment. Had you decided on a plan of action, you would not be here now, with me."

Still Pendergast gazed at her. Finally, he sat down in a chair across the table.

"You are entirely correct," he said. "I find myself in a paradox. If I do nothing, I will never see Tristram again. If I go after him, I might precipitate his death—just as I did my wife's."

Neither spoke for several minutes. At last, Constance shifted in her chair. "The situation to me is clear. You have no choice. This is your child. For too long now, this contest of yours has been waged tangentially, along the periphery of your true adversary. You *must* attack the nerve center—the homeland, the viper's nest—directly. You must go to Nova Godói."

Pendergast's gaze dropped to the papers on the table. He took a deep, shuddering breath.

"Recall my own child," Constance went on. "When we learned of the threat posed to him, we didn't hesitate to act. Even if it meant my being accused of infanticide. You must act now, decisively—and with violence."

His eyebrows rose.

"Yes: *violence*. Great and decisive violence. That is sometimes the only solution. I discovered that for myself..." Her voice trailed off into silence, filled by the ticking of an antique clock.

"I'm sorry," he said, his voice low. "In my preoccupied state I didn't think to ask about your own child. You should have heard something by now."

"I received the sign just five days ago. He's finally in India now, away from Tibet, deep in the mountains above Dharamsala—safe."

"That is good," Pendergast murmured, and the silence fell once again. But even as Pendergast began to rise from his chair, Constance spoke again.

"There's something else." She swept a hand in the direction of the photographs and paperwork. "I sense something unusual about this Alban. Something unique in the way he perceives reality."

"What is it?"

"I'm not sure. He somehow sees...somehow knows... *more* than we do."

Pendergast frowned. "I'm not sure I understand."

"I don't fully understand it myself. But I feel he has some power, like an additional sense—one that in normal human beings is undeveloped or absent."

"Sense? As in a sixth sense? Clairvoyance or ESP?"

"Nothing as obvious as that. Something subtler—but perhaps even more powerful."

Pendergast thought for a moment. "I obtained some old papers, taken from a Nazi safe house on the Upper East Side. They pertain to the Esterhazy family, and they make mention of something called the *Kopenhagener Fenster*."

"The Copenhagen Window," Constance translated.

"Yes. The documents reference it frequently, but never explain it. It seems to have to do with genetic manipulation, or quantum mechanics, or perhaps some combination of the two. But it's clear that the scientists working on the Copenhagen Window believed it held vast promise for the future of the master race. Perhaps it is related to the power you mention."

Constance did not answer. In the silence, Pendergast clenched, then unclenched, his fingers. "I'll follow your advice." He glanced at his watch. "I can be in Brazil by dinnertime. I'll finish this, one way or another."

"Take extreme care. And remember what I said: sometimes violence is the only answer."

He bowed, and then raised his head again, fixing her with glittering, silvery eyes. "You should know this: if I cannot bring Tristram back with me, safe and sound, I will not return. You will be on your own."

The detached, almost oracular expression faded from her face, and a faint flush rose in its place. For a long moment the two simply looked at each other across the table. Then, at last, Constance raised one hand and caressed Pendergast's cheek.

"In that case, I wish you a tentative good-bye," she said.

Pendergast took the hand, squeezed it gently. Then he rose to leave.

"Wait," Constance murmured.

Pendergast turned back. The flush on her face deepened, and she looked down, not meeting his eyes.

"Dearest guardian," she said in a tone almost too low to be heard. "I hope . . . I hope that you find peace."

48

CORRIE STOOD OUTSIDE THE DEALERSHIP. IT was three o'clock in the morning, on a night as dark as sin, the air ten degrees below freezing. The ugly sodium lights blasted the rows of parked cars with a sickly yellow glow, glittering on the frost that rimed the windshields. They hadn't given Corrie any keys to the dealership, but she had managed to swipe Miller's when he left them around—which he did all the time, sending him into a fit of rage, searching and searching, cursing, kicking trash cans, and generally displaying his assholery in full bloom.

Corrie had expended a lot of research—and thinking—on the scam the salesmen were all so proud of. It turned out to actually be pretty common, known as a credit cozen. Miller had been right in saying it was widespread among dealerships, and rarely prosecuted. The more she thought about it, the more she realized that the only people at the dealership who would be threatened by such exposure would be the owners, not the salesmen. That meant the Riccos, Senior and Junior. If her dad had made good on his threat to blow the whistle, they were the ones with the most to lose.

Corrie decided to focus her attention on father and son.

Keeping well outside of the gaudy pool of illumination, she circled the dealership and came up to the building from behind, where the service and repair operations were located. There were still some area lights here, but the spot was hidden from the road; behind the dealership were only large cornfields, now rows of dry winter stubble.

She darted past the area lights and came up to the back of the building. There she slipped on a pair of latex gloves and waited. The place was empty, with no evidence of a night watchman or private security.

Or at least, none that was visible.

She crept around to the side entrance to the showroom. She tried the keys, found the right one, and entered.

Now—to keep the alarm from going off.

Earlier in the day, she had scoped the place out, noting the alarm keypads next to each door. That afternoon she had "accidentally" leaned on the keypad, pressing the red alarm button, setting it off and causing Miller to rush over and punch in the reset code. Which she had carefully noted. Now, as the warning light blinked on the pad and the LCD screen counted down, she pressed in the code. The light turned green.

The plate-glass windows of the showroom let in plenty of light from the lot—almost too much. Keeping to the shadows, she crept over to the Riccos' small suite of offices—where the two men, offices side by side, shared a secretary in an anteroom.

The door wasn't even locked.

She slipped inside and moved to Ricco Senior's office. A row of fake wood filing cabinets lined the back wall. She took out the small pry bar she had brought, inserted it into the edge of the top drawer, and applied pressure. The drawer opened with a jerk and a snap of cheap metal.

The drawer rolled out to reveal a deep row of files—hundreds, it seemed. And this was one drawer out of twenty. Now that she thought about it, she had no targeted idea of what she was looking for. Proof of the credit-cozen scam? She already had that. What she would start with, she decided, would be her father's personnel file. Beyond that, she would simply look through the files on a fishing expedition.

The first drawer contained only sales files. She flipped through them, forced open another drawer, then another. God, what a lot of paperwork.

After thirty minutes she finally arrived at the personnel files. They were in their own unmarked drawer, with nothing else. Flipping through them, she almost immediately came to SWANSON.

She hesitated, thinking. Even though it would be obvious the place had been broken into, she couldn't steal just his file—that would direct attention to him. No—what she'd do was steal a whole bunch of personnel files, along with some other random files. That way they wouldn't be able to pinpoint which file she was interested in.

She stuffed the SWANSON file into her shoulder bag and was starting to pull out other files at random when she suddenly heard a noise. The soft shutting of a door. Unmistakable.

She froze. She couldn't leave the little suite of offices by a back door—there was none. The only way out was through the big glassed-in showroom, bathed in light from the lot. Even as she waited, she heard another door shut and the click of footfalls on the polished granite floor of the showroom.

She silently closed all the file drawers, hoping they weren't too obviously mangled, slipped the pry bar into her shoulder bag, and retreated toward the back of the suite. Where?

The bathroom.

Easing open the door, she slipped in, bolted it behind her, and went into the stall, shutting and locking that as well. She climbed onto the toilet.

All was silent. Whoever was in the showroom wasn't likely to come into Ricco's office. And even if they did, they wouldn't come into the bathroom. Or would they? Too late, she realized she shouldn't have shut and locked the damn bathroom door. That would look suspicious, especially if they tried it and found it locked. She should have left the door partway open.

She started to sweat, the stupidity of her B&E sinking in. She had committed a serious crime—yet again. What was wrong with her? Was she a criminal at heart? Why did she take these crazy risks?

The click of footsteps came closer, and she heard the outer office door open. They *were* coming in. The footsteps now fell more softly on the plush carpeting of the outer office. She strained to hear.

A loud screech caused her to jump—the person had opened one of the jimmied filing cabinets. He slammed it rather loudly. Now the footsteps, brisker, moved through the suite of offices.

Suddenly there was a loud rattle of the bathroom door. A brief silence, then another, even more forceful attempt to open the door, with the muffled sound of a body pushing itself against it.

Who was it? Ricco? This was it. She was toast.

And now came a crash as the person hurled himself against the door, another crash, the splintering sound of wood—and light flooded into the bathroom.

A momentary silence. Corrie couldn't even breathe. Her heart was rattling in her chest like a rock being shaken in a tin can.

A quick footstep and the stall door was flung open so hard the flimsy latch went flying.

"You!"

Charlie Foote stood there, his pale face sweating. He was almost as frightened as she was.

"Let me explain—" Corrie began all in a panic.

Foote let out a long breath, held up his hand. "Please . . . get down off that toilet. You look ridiculous."

Corrie got down. He turned without a word and she followed him out of the bathroom. She could see the future parading before her eyes: the police arriving, her arrest, the discovery that she was her father's daughter, which in turn would lead to her father's arrest. Both of them convicted, sentenced to prison—maybe for years. It was the end of her career and her association with Pendergast . . . the end of her life, in fact, which she had only recently dragged up and out of the shit.

The train of thought was so awful that she staggered.

Foote caught her arm. "Easy." His voice was quiet. "Let's go into the lounge, where they can't see us from the street."

Corrie collapsed into the first chair she came to. Foote took a chair opposite her, elbows on his knees, staring at her.

"Please—" she began, ready to do anything, *anything*, to get out of this. But he shook his head and pressed her hand for quiet.

"Look, Corrie," he said. "I'm pretty sure I know what's going on."

She stared.

"You're Jack Swanson's daughter, right?"

She said nothing. This was worse than she thought.

Foote went on. "It's okay. Just calm down. I'm not going to rat on you. I already had my suspicions—the way you were always looking around, asking a lot of questions. And now, going through Ricco's office—you're trying to help your father, aren't you?"

Corrie said nothing.

"You may not look much like him, but I can hear his voice in yours. Corrie, I always liked your father. He and I were friends. I didn't—and don't—like what's going on around here, just as he didn't. Maybe he got a bum rap." He paused. "Is that what you think? Is that what this is about?"

Corrie looked at him. It was true, he'd always been polite to her, rather quiet, rarely joining in with the other salesmen's crude jokes. And she knew he was no fan of the credit-cozen scheme. Still, Corrie didn't know what to say. She was afraid to confirm or deny anything.

Foote nodded to himself. "Yeah. That *is* what you think—that he was framed. And you're here, breaking into the place, to prove it."

She was astonished at his perspicacity.

He reached over and gently grasped her bag, opening its flap. "And there it is: Jack's personnel file. Now I know I'm right." He mustered a wan smile. "You know what? You could use an ally. We can work together. Maybe I can help you—and clean this place up at the same time."

"You're not going to turn me in?"

He laughed, shook his head. "No way. But we'd better get out of here before Ricco Senior arrives. The old skunk sometimes comes in as early as five to do paperwork."

He held out his arm. Corrie almost felt like crying with relief. She staggered to her feet and caught it.

"I know an all-night diner where we can grab coffee and breakfast—and you can tell me all about your father and why you think he was framed." And he gestured toward the rear door of the dealership.

49

THE CABLE STREET DINER WAS LIKE A TIME WARP,
Corrie thought. No retro Hollywood chain could touch it.
It was perfect down to the broken jukeboxes at each table,
the bubbled linoleum floors and Formica tabletops with
their decorative peach and turquoise triangles, the flyspecked menus, and the bleached-blond waitresses belting
out the early-morning orders to the fry cooks in the back.

At least the coffee was strong.

Corrie went to the ladies' room, reached into her
pocket, and threw away the wadded ball of latex gloves
she'd worn when she broke into the dealership. She
wondered what old Ricco would say when he found his
files had been rifled. At least she could take the day off
so she wouldn't have to listen to him rant. Exiting the
ladies' room, she returned to the booth, drank coffee,
and listened to Foote. He was angry, and the more he
talked, the angrier he got.

"It frosts me," he was saying, "that those guys can't
make an honest dollar. I'm the number two salesman
there. And you know why? Because people sense that
I'm not a cheater. I don't *need* to run nickel-and-dime
scams to make money."

"I'm convinced they framed my father."

"The more I think about it, the more I think you may be right. Jack was a good guy. Not much of a salesman, but he had integrity. Hard to picture him robbing a bank."

A silence.

"So how *do* you make money if a guy wants a car two hundred bucks over invoice?" Corrie asked.

Foote sipped his coffee. "There are all kinds of honest profits in selling a car. Let's say you sell one for seventy grand. First off, you're going to get a three percent dealer holdback. That's not deducted from the invoice price, and it's twenty-one hundred bucks right there. Then you might get a spiff—that's a dealer incentive— worth another one to two grand. And on top of that there's a reasonable profit in *honest* financing. There's no need to jack up the rate."

He bit down on his toast with a crunch, his jaw muscles bulging.

"Anyway," he continued after another gulp of coffee, "the credit cozen isn't the only scam they pull. Sometimes they'll actually sell one vehicle and then, if the customer is old or inexperienced, and if he leaves for a while and comes back to pick up the car, they'll rework the paperwork and switch the car he bought with a cheaper one that looks the same. Twice I've seen salesmen fix up cars wrecked in a test drive and sell them as new. And the Riccos encourage it. Not directly—they're not that stupid—but with a wink and a nod, if you know what I mean."

Foote flagged down the waitress, ordered a second round of fried eggs. The man had an amazing appetite. He looked at her appraisingly across the table. "You absolutely *sure* your father didn't rob that bank?"

"He *didn't*," Corrie said, flaring up. "I'm sure, damn it!"

"Right, okay, I believe you."

Another silence.

"Maybe we could set a trap," Corrie said.

"I was just thinking along those lines myself." Foote finished his coffee, signaled the waitress over again, and pointed to the cup. "You know, maybe we could do more than just clear your dad's name. Maybe we could bring down the whole rotten operation in the process."

"How?"

Foote thought a moment. "We bring in a phony buyer. Wired up. Make sure Ricco himself handles the sale. Then we take the evidence to the police, get the place investigated. Once that happens, the cops will be a lot more receptive to the idea that your dad was framed."

Corrie thought back to her courses at John Jay. "A wire? Without a court order, I don't think that's admissible. The cops couldn't even act on it."

"What about your dad's alibi, then? Where was he when the bank was robbed?"

Corrie colored. "I never asked him about it. It didn't seem...right."

"He probably thinks he has a weak alibi, otherwise he wouldn't have run. But he may be mistaken in that. If his cell phone was on, that could track his location. Maybe someone saw him, saw his car. He may have used his credit card around the time of the robbery. Or maybe he was online with his computer at home. These days, there are a million ways to pinpoint someone's location at a particular moment. Jack might have an ironclad alibi and not even know it."

Corrie thought this over. It made sense.

"Is there any way to get hold of your father?" Foote asked.

"No. I have to go to where he is personally."

"I've got a car. We could go together."

Corrie looked at Foote. He was an earnest enough young man. But she didn't want to reveal her father's location to anyone—not even him. "Thanks, but I don't feel comfortable with that. I'll take tomorrow off from work and go see him. Then I'll give you a call."

"That's cool. Meanwhile, I've got a friend who I'm sure would be willing to wear a wire and expose those bastards. He's a professional actor, and he just loves stuff like this. I'll set it up. Maybe you're right, maybe the cops can't act on it—but it sure as hell will get their attention. If we let the DA hear it, *he* can get the court order."

"Thank you."

"Hey, listen, I like Jack. I'd like to help him. But I'm no knight in shining armor—this is for me, too. Getting rid of those lousy salesmen will give me a crack at more clients, maybe even get me my own dealership." He smiled. "But you need to find out about where your father was at the time of the robbery and call me. I'll bet you anything there's a way to prove he wasn't there."

50

Penelope Waxman sat, quite primly, on the uncomfortable straight-backed chair in the waiting room of the Polícia Militar station in Alsdorf, Brazil. It was a large room, painted yellow, with windows open to a pleasant breeze, a picture of the president on one wall, and—as in most of the official spaces she'd seen in Brazil—a crucifix hanging on another. A low wooden rail and gate bisected the room, separating the waiting area from the workers in the police station, busily filling out forms or typing on computer terminals. Occasionally a member of the police force, dressed in a blue shirt and red beret, would cross the room and disappear through a doorway.

Mrs. Waxman sighed and moved restlessly in her chair. She'd been living in Brazil for two years now, in a nice two-bedroom apartment in Brasilia—her husband was a textile exporter—but she had never grown used to the glacial pace at which official business was conducted. She'd been waiting over half an hour and so far hadn't yet even had the opportunity to file a report. The only way to speed it up in this country seemed to be by flashing a wad of money, but she had her pride and wasn't going to resort to that. She checked her watch: almost three PM. What on earth was taking so long? There was only one other person in the waiting room—the loud one.

It was really her husband's fault. He'd heard of this city, Blumenau, in the southern state of Santa Catarina, that was a near-perfect replica of an old Bavarian town. He'd dragged her down from Brasilia for a long weekend vacation. And she had to admit, Blumenau was a remarkable place. It *did* look exactly like a German city, plopped down, in all places, amid the rain forests and mountains of Brazil: it had beer halls, shops painted in festive colors, half-timbered buildings of white plaster and dark wood, ancient-looking gothic structures whose massive slate roofs—dotted with two or sometimes three layers of dormer windows—were as large as the façades below. And most of the townspeople were blond, blue-eyed, and pink-cheeked. In the streets, more German was spoken than Portuguese. Mr. Waxman, who was very proud of his own German heritage, was entranced.

But that was when the troubles began. Her husband hadn't had the foresight to reserve a hotel room in advance, and they arrived to find themselves in the middle of some gigantic German cultural festival. All the hotels were booked, and so the Waxmans were forced to find lodgings in the adjoining town of Alsdorf: a much smaller, much cheaper version of Blumenau, trying to capitalize on its neighbor's charms but, it seemed, without really succeeding. Its residents were generally poorer, less European in appearance, much closer to the indigenous population. And unlike Blumenau, Alsdorf seemed to have more than its share of crime. Just that morning, their traveler's checks had been stolen right out of the hotel room. Imagine, stealing traveler's checks! And so

364 DOUGLAS PRESTON & LINCOLN CHILD

her husband was now over in Blumenau, trying to get them replaced, while she was here in the Alsdorf police station, waiting to file a report on the theft.

Her thoughts were interrupted—yet again—by the other individual in the waiting area. He was once more launching into a long litany of complaints to the hapless woman behind the nearby desk. Mrs. Waxman gave him a sidelong, irritated glance. He was wearing a tropical shirt, bright and gaudy, and a wide-brimmed straw hat that would have been more at home on the head of a riverboat gambler. His linen pants were white, shapeless, and massively wrinkled. Given his pallid, even sickly, complexion, he was clearly a tourist—in short, the typical Ugly American, speaking English, the louder the better, assuming that everyone around should jump to their feet and do his bidding. He had fastened onto the woman in the office who spoke the best English.

"It's taking so *long*," he said in a whining, hectoring tone. "*Why* is it taking so long?"

"As soon as the officer in charge of processing forms can see you, he will," the woman replied. "If you had your passport, sir, it would go faster—"

"I *explained* that to you already. My passport was stolen. Along with my wallet, my money, my credit cards, and everything else that was in my pocket." He fell into a kind of lethargic, but still vocal, brooding. "My God. It's like something out of Kafka. I'll probably never get out of here. I'll wither and die, right in this very station—a victim of terminal bureaucracy."

"I am very sorry, sir," the woman said with almost saintly patience. "All of the officers are otherwise engaged. It is a busy day."

"I'll just *bet* it's a busy day," the man said. "I'll bet you anything petty thievery is the number one business in Alsdorf. I knew I should have stayed in Rio."

A member of the Polícia Militar emerged from a room in the back of the station and walked through the office, making his way across the waiting area.

The tourist leapt from his chair. "You! Hey, you!"

The police officer completely ignored him and disappeared out the front door.

He turned back to the secretary. "What is he, deaf?"

"He is busy on a case, sir," the woman said.

"Of course. Probably another pickpocketing. No doubt the guy who got me is out robbing more Americans."

The woman shook her head. "No. No pickpocketing."

"So what, then? What's so important that they can't see me? I'd like to know!"

The woman behind the desk did not respond to this. And rightly so, Mrs. Waxman thought. She had a good idea to give this obnoxious man a piece of her mind.

Now the tourist was peering out the front door again, looking in the direction the officer had gone. "Maybe it's not too late to catch up with him," he said, more to himself than anyone else. "I'll stop him, tell him my problem. He'd have to help me then."

The secretary shook her head. "He is much too busy."

"Too busy? Right, too busy drinking coffee and eating doughnuts!"

The woman, provoked at last, said rather crisply: "He is investigating murders."

Mrs. Waxman sat up in her chair.

"Murders?" the obnoxious tourist repeated. "What murders?"

But the secretary had clearly said more than she intended to. She merely shook her head again.

The tourist sat back in his chair, rolling his eyes. "Some local bar fight, no doubt. Meanwhile, I'm sitting in here, stripped of my identity in a foreign country. My *God*." A beat. "You said murders. More than one?"

The woman simply nodded.

"What, you got a serial killer on the loose or something?"

The woman gave away nothing beyond a firming of her lips. Suddenly the problem of the traveler's checks didn't seem so important to Mrs. Waxman. Murders? Maybe she should forget about the complaint, find her husband, and get back to Brasilia as soon as possible.

While she was considering this, an idea seemed to strike the obnoxious man. He sat up and fished around in the pocket of his shapeless linen pants, pulling out a wad of Brazilian reals. Then he leaned toward the low gate, in the direction of the secretary.

"Here," he said in a stage whisper that was still fully audible to Mrs. Waxman. "The pickpocket didn't get these. Give twenty reals to that officer in charge of, whatever, of forms processing. Maybe that will grease the wheels of progress."

The other office workers looked over at this. "I cannot do that, sir," the woman said quickly, frowning.

"Not enough, eh? Okay, I can play that game." The man pawed through some more of the crumpled bills, pulled out another. "Here. Fifty reals. Give that to him."

The woman shook her head again, more emphatically. "No bribes."

"No bribes? Who are you kidding? This is Brazil, right? I wasn't born yesterday, lady."

"There is no bribery of police in Alsdorf, sir," the woman told him in a firm, public voice, not without a tinge of pride. "The colonel doesn't permit it."

"Colonel?" the tourist asked, in a tone of deepest skepticism. "What colonel?"

"Colonel Souza."

"I don't believe it," the tourist replied. "What—are you looking for *more* reals? Thinking of splitting it with the officer yourself, are you?" He scoffed. "That's looking out for number one, all right."

"Sir, put your money *away*." The secretary finally seemed to have reached the limit of her patience. "Look—I will let you wait in the outer office. If I permit that, will you agree to wait in silence until your turn is called?"

The tourist looked at her suspiciously. "Will I be seen more quickly?"

"It is possible."

The man shrugged. "All right. Lead the way."

He stood up, and the secretary led him through the gate, past the worktables, and into an open doorway in the rear. A blissful silence reigned. Mrs. Waxman finally rose and, not even bothering to tell anyone, scurried out the door, looking for a cab to take her and her husband as quickly as possible out of the town of Alsdorf.

The tourist in the flowered shirt and shapeless linen trousers waited until the secretary had pointed him to a chair. Once her footsteps had receded, he quietly moved to the door, grasped its knob, and gently pushed it until it was almost closed. And then he turned and surveyed the outer office. It had a single table, surrounded by four chairs. Three of the walls were lined with filing cabinets. As he let his eye run along their length, the tourist smiled faintly.

A series of local deaths. A police chief who could not be bribed. This was proving to be promising indeed.

"Excellent," the man said in a dulcet southern accent far different from the one he had employed in the waiting room. "Most excellent."

51

ON BLUMENAU'S VILA GERMÂNICA, THE FESTIVE and brightly painted heart of German Village in the center of town, tourists could find a profusion of beer halls, beer gardens, and taverns. Many were jolly establishments, full of carousing patrons and faux-German wenches in gaudy costumes balancing numerous one-liter steins in their hands as they wound between the tables. But one or two of the drinking establishments were quieter, catering primarily to the locals; while still of remarkably authentic Bavarian architecture and interior design, they were darker inside, without the frantically convivial atmosphere of their neighbors.

One such place was the Hofgarten. Inside, it was low-ceilinged, with thick hand-hewn beams running just above the heads of the evening's patrons. Framed prints of German castles decorated the walls, and the daily menu was listed on chalkboards. Bavarian Brezen came free with each dinner order. A long bar ran around two sides of a central island, but many of the patrons seemed to prefer the deep wooden booths that lined the tavern's walls.

In one of the booths, a man sat reading a local paper.

He was short and barrel-chested, with powerful arms and a head that seemed ever so slightly too small for his body. His face was clean-shaven, with hair slicked back by brilliantine, and although his features were Brazilian, not German, they were nevertheless fine, with high cheekbones and an aquiline nose. He was drinking a stein of beer and smoking a short, slender cheroot.

He glanced up to see that a man had slipped into the booth, across from him. The movement had been so quick and silent, the stranger was already sitting comfortably by the time the smoker noticed him.

"*Boa tarde,*" the stranger said.

The man with the cheroot did not answer. He merely regarded the newcomer with the faintest of curiosity.

"May we speak in English?" the stranger continued. "My Portuguese is, alas, barely serviceable."

The other shrugged, then flicked the ash off his cheroot, as if he had not yet decided whether any speaking would, in fact, be taking place.

"My name is Pendergast," the stranger said. "And I have a proposition for you."

The other cleared his throat. "If you knew who I am," he said, "you would not be presuming to come to me with propositions."

"Ah, but I do know who you are. You are Colonel Souza, head of the Alsdorf Polícia Militar."

The colonel merely took another drag on the cheroot.

"I not only know who you are, but I know a lot about you. You were once a leader of the Batalhão de Operações Policiais Especiais—the most elite and prestigious high-speed unit of the Brazilian military police. The BOPE are both respected and feared wherever they go. And yet you left the BOPE—it *was* voluntary, wasn't it?—to become the head of the military police of Alsdorf. Now, I find

that very curious. Not to take anything away from Alsdorf, you understand—a charming village, in its way.
But it does seem like a remarkable step down from a
quickly rising career. You could have had your pick of
assignments in, say, the Polícia Civil or even the Polícia
Federal. Instead…" And Pendergast waved his hand,
encompassing the interior of the Hofgarten.

"You have been investigating my background," Colonel Souza replied. "I would suggest to you, *o senhor*,
that this is not a healthy line of work."

"My dear Colonel, I am merely setting the ground-
work for the proposition I mentioned. And have no
fear—it is not so much a business proposition as it is a
professional one."

This was met by silence. Pendergast let it deepen for
a minute before continuing.

"You also have a quality that seems almost unique
in this part of the world. You are immune to corruption. Not only do you refuse to accept bribes, but you
actively suppress them among your associates. This,
perhaps, is another reason you ultimately found yourself back in Alsdorf—no?"

Colonel Souza plucked the cheroot from his mouth
and ground it out in the ashtray. "You have outstayed
your welcome, my friend. Now I suggest you leave
before I have my men escort you out of town."

In response, Pendergast reached into the pocket of
his jacket, pulled out his FBI badge, and laid it open on
the table between them. The colonel inspected it carefully for a moment before looking back at Pendergast.

"You are out of your jurisdiction," he said.

"Very far out, I'm afraid."

"What is it you want?"

"I want your cooperation—in an undertaking that,
if successful, will greatly benefit both of us."

The colonel sat back, lit another cheroot. "I am listening."

"You have a problem. I have a problem. Let's talk first about yours." Pendergast leaned in slightly. "In recent months, Alsdorf has been troubled by a series of unsolved murders. Very unpleasant murders, too, based on the information that you've been withholding from the public."

Colonel Souza, as cover for his evident surprise, removed the cheroot, inspected it, replaced it once again.

"Oh, I've availed myself of your files," Pendergast said. "As I told you, my Portuguese is rather lacking, but it was more than sufficient to give me a good picture. The fact is, Colonel, there have been at least eight violent murders committed in and around Alsdorf in the last half year—and yet virtually no news of them has shown up in the local papers."

The colonel licked his lips. "Tourism is our life-blood. Such stories would be . . . bad for trade."

"Especially if news of the modus operandi were to leak out. Some of the murders seemed to be uniquely sadistic. Others were apparently done as quickly as possible—most frequently, by the application of a knife to the jugular vein. I have seen the photographs."

The colonel frowned but said nothing.

"And here's the part I find most hard to understand. There have been all these recent murders—but as far as I can tell, the Polícia Civil have done little about it."

The colonel's frown deepened. "They can't be bothered. Alsdorf is a poor town. It's beneath their interest. The deaths have all been among *camponês*. Peasants. Day workers from the mountains. Penniless drifters."

Pendergast nodded. "And so you are left with your

own Polícia Militar force to try to solve the murders—
with scant evidence to go on—all the while trying to
keep things a secret from the tourists and the townsfolk. As I said—a problem."

A barmaid came over, replaced the colonel's beer
stein with a fresh one, and asked Pendergast what he
wanted.

"I'll have what the colonel's having," he said in Portuguese, then switched back to English. "Let me ask
you a question. When you lie awake at night, thinking
about the case, thinking about who the killers might
be—where do your thoughts turn?"

The colonel took a sip of beer. He didn't reply.

"I think I know. Your thoughts travel upriver, into
the deep forests. To the place known as Nova Godói."

For the first time, the colonel looked at him with
genuine shock on his face.

Pendergast nodded. "There are many rumors about
the place, are there not? It has had an evil reputation for
more than half a century. Speculation about what goes
on there, about who lives there and what they do . . . let's
just say that plenty of whispering takes place among
the townsfolk of Alsdorf. Rumors of curious folks who
have made their way upriver to Nova Godói . . . never to
be seen again."

Pendergast's stein arrived. He looked at the beer but
did not touch it.

"There's something else I know about you, Colonel. It's true—you care about Alsdorf. You care deeply
about it. The fact that the civil police aren't interested
in these murders must stick in your craw. But the truth
is, you've been in the army. You were a decorated member of the BOPE. And I sense you are a man who—if
you saw your duty clearly—would not let bureaucracy,
or the chain of command, stand in your way. If you

knew what was going on at Nova Godói—if you knew they were responsible for these murders, *and for those not yet committed*—I believe that you would not hesitate to act."

Colonel Souza looked at Pendergast—a long, penetrating, speculative look. Then he nodded, almost imperceptibly.

"What do *you* know about Nova Godói?" Pendergast asked.

The colonel laid down the butt end of the cheroot in an ashtray, took a long draft from his stein. "It was said to have started as a mission, established centuries ago by the Franciscans, high in the mountains."

"And?"

He went on, reluctantly. "The good fathers were massacred by the local Indians, and so the mission was turned into a garrison for Portuguese soldiers, who eventually destroyed the *indígenas*. Then it became a plantation, which was abandoned in the 1930s. After the war, some German refugees settled there, as they did in many other areas of Brazil."

"What is its physical situation?"

"It's remarkably remote, almost impossible to reach, and then only by the *rio*. The German settlement is on the shores of a crater lake in the mountains. And in the middle of the lake there is an island, which is where the mission was built, and then the ancient fort." He shrugged. "The inhabitants keep completely to themselves. They use Alsdorf as their portal to the outside world, for news and supplies and the like, coming and going, but never interacting, even with their German compatriots." He paused. "They blend in as much as possible, try not to call attention to themselves. Beyond that, I can tell you nothing."

Pendergast nodded slowly. "It would be a dangerous

undertaking, along the lines of a military operation. And the civil police, of course, would be given no word of this—it would be undertaken by the men of your own Polícia Militar, and it would have to remain an undocumented action. The target will no doubt be well guarded and heavily defended: an attack force of at least a hundred men, preferably more, will be required. But you would not go in without a full briefing, without the benefit of a reconnaissance—which I will provide. As I implied, if we are successful—then this curse that has lain over Alsdorf would be lifted forever."

"So you are saying that the people in Nova Godói are responsible for the murders?" the colonel asked.

"That is exactly what I'm saying."

"And your evidence?"

Pendergast removed from the inside of his sports jacket several photographs from the crime scenes in New York. One by one, he laid them before the colonel, who perused them in silence.

"Yes, these are the same as the local killings," he said.

"These killings occurred in New York. I have traced the killer to Nova Godói."

"But why New York?"

"It is a long story, which I will be glad to tell you later. Now: do you need more evidence of what I say, or will this suffice?"

"It is sufficient," said the colonel, turning away from the pictures with disgust.

"There are a few conditions. Two young men are hidden somewhere within the Nova Godói compound. They are twins. Neither is to be harmed—I'll deal with them myself. I'll provide you with sketches."

The colonel looked back at Pendergast, saying nothing.

"There is one other. There will be a man in Nova Godói—a tall, powerfully built man with closely cropped snow-white hair. His name is Fischer. No one else is to touch him. He is mine and I will, again, deal with him."

A silence settled over the table.

"Those are my only conditions," Pendergast said. "Now—are you interested in hearing what I plan to do next?"

For a moment, the colonel remained silent. Then a slow smile spread over his features. "I find that I am very much interested, Agent Pendergast," he said.

52

THROUGH THE WINDOW OF THE LITTLE CABIN, Corrie could see an early-morning frost glittering on the ground and rimming the twigs of the surrounding beech trees. A weak sun struggled through the checked curtains, and the woodstove, well stoked, radiated a welcome warmth. Jack bustled over it, oiling a griddle. A pan of sizzling bacon sat nearby.

He glanced over. "Jack's special blueberry pancakes, coming up."

"Let me help," said Corrie, starting to get up.

"No, no!" Jack turned, his apron already smeared. He was not, she had to admit, much of a cook. But then, neither was she.

"*I'm* running the show, you just sit there." Without asking, he grabbed the coffeepot and refilled her mug.

"I don't like doing nothing."

He smiled. "Get used to it."

Corrie sipped the coffee. She had arrived by the afternoon bus the day before, making sure no one followed her, and had walked from Frank's Place all the way to the cabin. Her father had been ridiculously glad to see her. She had filled him in on the details of her investigation, and he was excited.

"So is it really true Charlie doesn't hustle the customers?" Corrie asked. While Charlie seemed convincing enough about other matters, she still found it hard to believe a car salesman could be scrupulously honest.

"Not that I ever saw," said Jack. "Old Ricco once had him into the office, left the door open, and was raking him over the coals for not getting with the program. Said it was 'hurting morale.'" Jack laughed. "Can you believe it? Honesty hurting morale."

"So why do they keep him on if he won't cooperate?"

"Charlie can really sell 'em." He ladled batter onto the griddle to the chorus of a friendly hiss.

One thing was starting to dawn on Corrie. Her father's problem wasn't dishonesty, but the opposite: a sort of inflexible, priggish honesty that bordered on self-righteousness. She'd learned from him that he'd been let go from a previous job—selling stereo equipment—because he refused to go along with certain shady sales tactics. In that job, too, he'd threatened to go to the Better Business Bureau. And he hadn't succeeded in selling insurance for similar reasons of punctiliousness.

She watched him as he bustled about the stove. She couldn't help wondering what she would have done in the same situation. Would she have gone along with the credit scam? Probably not, but she sure as hell wasn't the type to go running to the law over something as small as jacking up interest rates by a point or two. The credit card companies, banks, and mortgage companies pulled that sort of shit a million times a day. She probably would've just quit the job.

Once again, she wondered if she was really cut out for law enforcement. She simply didn't have the instincts of someone who took satisfaction in punishing wrongdoers. How did Pendergast do it?

Jack flipped the pancakes with a flourish. "Take a look at that."

They were indeed perfectly golden brown, the tiny wild blueberries leaking a delicious-looking purple stain. Maybe he was going to pull it off, after all.

"Real maple syrup to go with it," Jack said, lifting up the bottle. "So Charlie's got an actor friend who's going in there wearing a wire. I love it. I should've thought of that."

"It won't be admissible as evidence."

"Maybe not. But all they have to do is start poking around and asking questions, and the whole crappy business will come out. It's a good idea—really good."

Corrie's cell phone rang. She took it out. "That's Charlie now." She answered, putting the phone on speaker.

"Corrie," said Charlie breathlessly. "You won't believe this. It's unbelievable. We've nailed them. We don't need my friend after all. I've got the smoking gun—proof that they framed your father."

"What? *How?*"

"Yesterday, after you left, Ricco and the boys had a sales meeting. I was excluded. After the meeting, they all went over to the Blue Goose Saloon—to talk about the break-in, probably—leaving me to cover the showroom myself for the last hour of the day."

"And?"

"Old Ricco had gotten something out of his safe for the meeting and didn't shut it properly. Left it open just a crack. So I went in there—I just couldn't pass up the opportunity—and inside I found an envelope of cash, something like ten grand, with a note on it to a guy named Lenny Otero. Attached was a report from this guy Otero, all written in longhand, which detailed his expenses and fees for a certain 'project' he had recently completed."

"What project?"

"Framing Jack Swanson for bank robbery."

"It *said* that?" Corrie couldn't believe it.

"Son of a gun!" said Jack, leaping from his chair and smacking his fist in his palm.

"Who's that, your dad?" said Foote.

"Yeah. I've got the phone on speaker."

"Good. Anyway, it doesn't just come out and say it like that—not in so many words, of course. The report is written in a kind of oblique way, not naming names or anything, but when you read the whole note it's as clear as day. Otero even asks Ricco at the end to burn the report. This is a smoking gun—no mistake about it."

"That's fantastic!" Jack said. "What did you do with it?"

"I had to leave it in there—but I photographed it with my cell camera. I've got the pictures right in my pocket. So listen, here's what we need to do. We've got to go straight to the police, give them the pictures, and get them to raid that safe ASAP—I mean *ASAP*. The dealership opens at ten, that's in three hours. We'll just have to hope Ricco doesn't come in early today. Corrie, you and I have to take this to the cops right now, this morning, so they can get a warrant and search that safe. We know it's in the safe at least until ten o'clock. But if we wait much beyond that, God only knows, by eleven Ricco might have made the payment and burned the note and the safe will be empty."

"I understand," said Corrie. Jack was crowding her, his face tense.

"Listen, Corrie. I'll come get you. We have to go together—two of Ricco's employees will be better than one."

"Yes, but..." She thought fast.

"Just tell him where we are," said Jack. "You can trust him."

She shook her head.

"How far away are you?" Foote asked.

"A little over an hour by car, but—"

"That far? Shit. Look, I know you don't want to give away where your father's hiding, but we *can't* wait."

"All right. I'll meet you. There's a country store in Old Foundry, New Jersey, called Frank's Place. I'll be there in an hour."

"How will you get there if you don't have a car?"

"Don't worry about me, the cabin's not too far. I'll be there."

She hung up. Jack seized her and hugged her. "This is great!" he said. Then his expression changed suddenly as acrid smoke filled the small cabin. "Oh, no. I've burned the pancakes!"

53

THE DOCKS OF ALSDORF, SUCH AS THEY WERE,
lay alongside the Rio Itajaí-Açu, a broad, brown, odor-
ous river flowing out of the deep forested interior of
the southernmost provinces of Brazil. The docks were
a busy area, thronging with fishermen unloading their
catches in great wooden wheelbarrows, fish dealers
shouting and waving wads of money, ice mongers trun-
dling blocks, whores, drunks, and peddlers pushing food
carts loaded with soft pretzels, knockwurst, sauerbraten,
and—even more strangely—kebabs of tandoori chicken.

Amid these multitudes an odd figure made his
way—a stooped man dressed all in khaki, with a salt-
and-pepper Van Dyke beard, hair clamped down under
a Tilley hat. He was carrying a backpack bristling with
butterfly nets, bait-station setups, jars, traps, collecting
heads, funnels, and other obscure lepidoptery equipment. The figure was trying to get down to the landing
quays, pushing through the heedless crowds, his shrill,
querulous voice protesting in broken Portuguese as
he shoved his way toward a shack at the far end of the
floating quay, which sported a hand-painted sign reading ALUGUEL DE BARCOS.

*   *   *

Belmiro Passos, a skinny man in a T-shirt, shorts, and flip-flops, occupied the shack, eating a large soft pretzel and watching the figure approach. Behind Passos were boats—mostly battered Carolina skiffs with decrepit Yamaha engines—which he would rent to anyone for almost any purpose, legal or otherwise. His customers were primarily travelers going up- or downriver, visiting hard-to-reach villages, or fishermen whose own boats were out of order. Occasionally, Belmiro would rent to the rare adventure tourist, naturalist, or sport fisherman. As he watched the figure draw near, he immediately pegged him as a naturalist, and not only that but a butterfly collector, of which there were not a few who came to Santa Catarina State because of its varied and exotic butterfly population.

The agitated man finally broke free of the throngs of fishermen and came huffing over. Belmiro greeted him with a broad smile.

"*Yo...eu...quero alugar um barco! Alugar um barco!*" the man shouted, stammering over the words and mixing Spanish with Portuguese to create almost a new language.

"We speak English," said Belmiro quietly.

"Thank God!" The man shucked off his pack and leaned against it, panting. "My goodness, it's hot. I want to rent a boat."

"Very well," said Belmiro. "For how long?"

"Four days, maybe six. And I need a guide. I'm a lepidopterist."

"Lepidopterist?"

"I collect and study butterflies."

"Ah, butterflies! And where you go?"

"Nova Godói."

At this Belmiro paused. "That is very long way up

the Rio Itajaí do Sul, deep in the araucaria forest. It is a dangerous journey. And Nova Godói is private. No one go there. No trespass."

"I won't bother anybody! And I know how to deal with people like that." The man rubbed his fingers together to indicate money.

"But why Nova Godói? Why not go to Serra Geral National Park, which has many more rare butterflies?"

"Because the Nova Godói crater is where the last Queen Beatrice butterfly was sighted in 1932. They say it's extinct. I say it isn't, and I'm going to prove it!"

Belmiro gazed at the man. Fanaticism shone in his watery eyes. This could be quite profitable if handled correctly, even though he would probably lose a boat and perhaps even become involved in an unpleasant investigation.

"Nova Godói. Very expensive."

"I have money!" the man said, removing a fat roll of bills. "But, like I said, I need a guide. I don't know the river."

A slow nod. A guide to Nova Godói. Another problem. But not impossible. There were those who would do anything for money.

"How about you?" the man asked. "Will you take me?"

Belmiro shook his head. "I have a business to run, *doutor*." He didn't add that he also had a wife and children he'd like to see again. "But I find you a guide. And rent you a boat. I call now."

"I'll wait right here," said the man, fanning himself with his hat.

Belmiro went into the back of his shack, made a call. It took a few minutes of persuasion, but the man in question was one of those whose greed knew no bounds.

He came back out with a large smile. With what he planned to charge on this rental, he could buy two good used boats.

"I found you a guide. His name is Michael Jackson Mendonça." He paused, observing the man's unbelieving scowl. "We have many Michael Jacksons in Brazil, many here who loved the singer. It is a common name."

"Whatever," said the man. "But before I hire him, I'd like to meet this...ah, Michael Jackson."

"He come soon. He speak good English. Lived in New York. In the meantime, we finish our business. The cost of the boat is two hundred reals a day, *doutor*, with a two-thousand-real deposit, which I return when you bring boat back. That does not include Senhor Mendonça's fee, of course."

The fanatical naturalist began counting out the bills without even batting an eye.

54

CORRIE SWANSON LEFT THE CABIN AND TOOK
the shortcut over the ridgeline and down the switch-
back trail to the main road. She had left her father con-
sumed with anxiety, pacing about, issuing a constant
stream of unnecessary advice, warnings, and various if-
this-then-that predictions. His whole future depended
on her and Foote pulling this off—they both knew it.

The woods were cold and barren, the bare branches
of the trees knocking against each other in a rising wind.
A storm was coming, portending rain or, perhaps, even
sleet. She hoped to hell it would hold off until they could
go to the police and get them to raid the dealership. She
glanced at her watch. Eight o'clock. Two hours.

The trail came out on Old Foundry Road, and she
could just make out Frank's Place about a mile down
the road, with its dilapidated sign, the Budweiser Beer
neon flickering fitfully. She began walking toward it
quickly, along the shoulder of the road. As she drew
closer, she could see through the windows the early-
morning crowd already ensconced inside, drinking coffee and smoking cigarettes. She collected herself, then
pushed in through the creaking door nonchalantly.

386   DOUGLAS PRESTON & LINCOLN CHILD

"What can I do for you?" said Frank, straightening up and making a failing attempt to suck in his gut.

"Coffee, please."

She took one of the small tables and checked her watch again. Eight fifteen. Foote would be here by eight thirty at the latest.

Frank brought over the coffee with half-and-half and sugars. Three sugars and three half-and-halfs made the weak-ass coffee barely palatable. She gulped it down, shoved the mug out for a refill.

"Looks like weather," said Frank, refilling.

"Yeah."

"How're you and your dad getting on up there?"

Corrie tore three more sugars open at once, dumped in the contents, followed by the half-and-half. "Good." She kept her eyes on the plate-glass window that looked out across the parking area and gas pumps.

"Hunting season starts in a few days," said Frank, operating in friendly, advice-giving mode. "Lots of hunting up there around Long Pine. Don't forget to wear orange."

"Right," said Corrie.

A car pulled in, moving a little fast, and stopped with a faint screech. An Escalade Hybrid with smoked windows—Foote's car. She got up abruptly, threw some bills on the table, and went out. Foote opened the muddy passenger door and she slipped into the fragrant leather interior. Foote was dressed in his usual suit, immaculate, but nevertheless looking tense. Even before she could shut the door he was moving, pulling onto Old Foundry Road with a screech of rubber.

"I called the Allentown police," he said, accelerating. "Explained everything. They were skeptical at first, but I managed to turn them around. They're expecting us and are ready to get the ball rolling with a warrant if they like what I show them. Which they will."

"Good. Thank you."

"Don't thank me. I'm just protecting myself. And I think your dad got a bum rap."

He accelerated further, checking a radar detector clamped to his visor. They were flying down the country road, trees flashing by on either side. He headed into a corner, driving expertly, the wheels whispering a complaint of rubber as they took the turn.

"Oh, shit," said Corrie. "You just missed the turn for Route Ninety-Four."

"Damn, so I did." Foote slowed down and moved to the shoulder to pull a U-turn. He glanced over at her. "Hey, put on your seat belt."

Corrie reached around by the door to pull out the seat belt, fumbling for the latch, which had somehow slipped down in between the seats. As she did so, she felt a sudden movement behind her, turned partway, and felt a steel arm whip around her neck and a hand stuff a cloth into her face, choking her with the stench of chloroform.

But she was ready.

Hand tightening around a box cutter she'd kept hidden up her sleeve, she brought it up sharply, slicing deep into the meaty part of Foote's palm and twisting as she did so. Foote roared in pain, dropping the cloth as he grasped at his injured hand. Corrie twisted all the way toward him and brought the blade of the box cutter up against his throat.

"Gotcha," she said.

Foote did not reply. He was gripping his injured hand.

"Just what kind of an idiot do you take me for?" she said, pressing the edge of the blade deeper into his throat. "Maybe you fooled my dad with your working-class-hero bullshit. But not me. I had you pegged from the beginning. The only honest salesman on the lot, my ass. It was all just too nice and neat and convenient. And that crap about an itemized bill in the safe, for frame-up services rendered? Shit."

Quickly, before he could recover his wits, she felt through the pockets of his coat and pants, found a heavy-caliber revolver, pulled it out, and pointed it at him.

"So what the hell is really going on?" she asked.

Foote was breathing heavily. "What do you think? A scam. Something a lot sweeter than skimming off a few interest points here and there. I can cut you and your dad in."

"Like hell. My dad probably started to smell a rat—that's why you framed him." She gestured with the gun. "I know you must have figured out where his cabin is. You probably got here early, cased the joint, and saw me emerge onto the main road." She took a deep breath. "Now this is what's going to happen. You're going to drive up to the cabin. I'm going to have this gun trained on you the whole time. First, you're going to tell my dad the whole story. Then we're going to call the police. And you're going to tell them the story. Understand?"

For a moment, Foote remained motionless. Then he nodded.

"Okay. Drive slow. And no funny business, or I'll use this." The fact was, she'd never shot a gun in her life. She wasn't even sure the safety was off. But Foote didn't know that.

She kept well away from Foote, covering him with the handgun, as he eased off the shoulder onto Old Foundry Road, then made the turn onto Long Pine. Nothing was said as he made his way up the switchbacks.

A hundred feet from the turnoff to the cabin, she gestured with the gun again. "Stop here."

Foote stopped.

"Kill the engine and get out."

Foote complied.

"Now. Walk toward the cabin. I'll be right behind you. You know what'll happen if you try anything."

Foote looked at her. His face was exceedingly pale, with beads of sweat despite the cold. Pale and angry. He began walking toward the cabin, dead twigs snapping beneath his feet.

Corrie felt a hot rush of adrenaline coursing through her, and her heart was beating uncomfortably fast. But she'd managed to keep her voice calm, keep any quaver out of it. She kept telling herself she'd been in worse situations—a lot worse. *Just stay cool. Stay cool and this will all turn out all right.*

Just as they came up to the cabin door, Corrie heard the latch turn. The door opened suddenly, hitting Corrie in the wrist. With a cry of pain, she dropped the gun.

Her father stood in the doorway, looking from Foote to her and back again. "Corrie?" he asked, his face a mask of confusion. "I heard noises. What are you doing here? I thought you were going to town—"

Corrie leapt for the gun, but Foote was quicker. He grabbed it, shoving her roughly back at the same time. Jack Swanson stared uncomprehendingly at the gun as Foote raised it toward him. Just at the last moment, Jack leapt back into the wooded area behind the cabin, but the gun roared and Corrie could tell from the way her father's body twisted around that the bullet had hit home.

"You bastard!" she screamed, running at Foote, the box cutter raised. But Foote wheeled around toward her, slamming the butt of the handgun into her temple, and abruptly the world shut down.

She came to rapidly, her brain clearing. She had been hastily bound with plastic cuffs, hands and feet, and dumped unceremoniously in the backseat of Foote's car, where she was propped sideways.

She waited, unbearably tense, straining, listening. She had planned it all so carefully—and it had all unraveled in the space of fifteen seconds. What was she going to do now? What was going to happen? Oh, God, it was all her fault—she should have gone to the police instead of trying to handle it herself, but she was afraid they'd just arrest her father...

Then she heard more shots—two of them in rapid succession. And then silence. It was broken eventually by a gust of wind that started the tree branches swaying, knocking, knocking, knocking.

55

THE NATURALIST WAITED IN THE SHADE, REST-
ing on his pack, for Senhor Michael Jackson Mendonça
to arrive. The man eventually made his appearance,
with fanfare: a big, broad, brown, relatively young man
with a gigantic smile, long curly hair tied with a ban-
danna, wearing a sleeveless shirt, shorts, and flip-flops.
He bulled his way through the crowd, his loud, friendly
voice urging one and all to make way. He extended his
hand twenty yards before he even reached the naturalist, striding up and pumping the limp arm vigorously.

"Michael Jackson Mendonça!" he said. "At your
service!"

The naturalist retrieved his much-shaken hand as
quickly as he could. "I am Percival Fawcett," he said,
somewhat stiffly. At least Mendonça's English was near
perfect.

"Percival! May I call you Percy?"

This was permitted with another stiff nod.

"Good, good! I myself am from New York. Queens!
Twenty years in your great country of America. So ... I
hear you want to go to Nova Godói?"

"Yes. Although it seems that it may be difficult."

"No, not at all!" cried Mendonça. "It's a long journey, yes. And Nova Godói isn't a real town, a *public* town, that is. It's way up there in the forest. Off limits to outsiders. They're not friendly. *Not* friendly."

"I'm not in need of friends," said the naturalist. "I won't bother anyone. If there are problems, I can pay. You see, I'm on the trail of the Queen Beatrice. Are you familiar with it?"

Mendonça scrunched his face up in puzzlement. "No."

"No? It's the rarest butterfly in the world. Only one specimen was ever collected—it's now in the British Museum, specimen number 75935A1901." His voice took on a reverent tone as he recited the number. "Everyone assumes it's extinct . . . but I have reason to believe it's not. You see—" he was now waxing eloquent on his subject—"from what my research tells me, the Nova Godói crater is a unique ecosystem, with special conditions all its own. The butterfly lived there and nowhere else. And that crater hasn't seen a professional lepidopterist since the Second World War! So what do you expect? Of *course* no more have been sighted—because no entomologist has been there to see one! But now there is: *me*."

He fumbled in his pack and extracted a laminated photograph, showing a small brown butterfly pinned to a white card, with writing below it.

Mendonça peered at the image. "That is the Queen Beatrice?"

"Isn't it magnificent?"

"*Esplêndido.* Now we must talk about expense."

"That's the specimen in the British Museum. You can see it's sadly faded. The original is said to have a rich mahogany color."

"About the expense," continued Mendonça.

"Yes, yes. How much?"

"Three thousand reals," said Mendonça, trying to keep his voice nonchalant. "That includes four days. Plus cost of food and supplies."

"On top of the boat rental? Hmm. Well, if that's what it costs, that's what it costs."

"All up front," he added quickly.

A pause. "Half and half."

"Two thousand up front, a thousand when we arrive."

"Well, all right."

"When do we leave?" Mendonça asked.

The naturalist looked surprised. "Right now, of course." He began counting out the money.

The naturalist sat in the bow with his backpack, reading a book by Vladimir Nabokov, while Mendonça loaded the boat with a cooler of food, along with dry foodstuffs, a tent, sleeping bags, and his own modest kit bag containing a change of clothes.

In no time they were heading upstream, Mendonça at the tiller, the skiff cutting a creamy wake through the brown water. It was already late morning and Mendonça was thinking that they could reach the last town before the forest by nightfall. While there was no lodging there, they could at least get dinner and— especially—cold beer at a local *fornecimento*. They could camp in a field by the river. And there, he hoped to God, he could find out from someone how to get up the final leg of the Rio Itajaí do Sul to Nova Godói, a place that in truth he had never been to, although he had heard plenty of rumors about it.

As the boat moved up the river, passing various fishermen and river travelers, a nice breeze came over the water, cooling them and keeping away the mosquitoes. They passed the last few houses of Alsdorf, green fields coming into view, some planted with crops, others pastures for cattle. Everything was very neat and tended; that was how things were in southern Brazil. Not like chaotic, criminal-ridden Rio de Janeiro.

The naturalist put down his book. "Have you been to Nova Godói?" he asked pleasantly.

"Well, not exactly," said Mendonça. "But I know how to get there, of course."

"What do you know about the place?"

Mendonça gave a little laugh, to cover up his nervousness. He'd been afraid the man might start asking questions like this. While he didn't believe half the rumors he'd heard, he didn't want to frighten a customer off.

"I've heard some things." Mendonça shook his head, steering the boat past a group of fishermen hauling in a net.

"How many people live there?"

"I don't know. It's not a real town, like I said. It's on an old tobacco plantation, private property, closed to the public. It's a German colony of the kind that used to exist all around here, only much more remote."

"And it used to be a tobacco plantation?"

"Yes. Tobacco is one of our biggest agricultural products," said Mendonça proudly. To underscore this he removed a pair of cigars from his pocket, offering one to the naturalist.

"No, thank you. I don't smoke coffin nails."

"Ha, ha," said Mendonça, lighting his up. "You are funny." He puffed. "Tobacco. The plantation was abandoned in the 1930s. After the war, Germans arrived and a small settlement sprang up. They live up there and hardly ever come to town. The Germans down here don't like them, say they're Nazis." Mendonça laughed heartily.

"But you don't believe it."

"Here in Brazil, people think they see Nazis every-where. It's a national pastime. If there are five old Ger-mans in a town, everyone says, *They must be Nazis*. No—the people of Nova Godói just keep to them-selves, that's all. They are like a...what is the word?... like a cult. Outsiders not welcome. Not welcome at all."

Another big puff of cigar smoke, then another, leav-ing two clouds drifting behind the boat.

"Some people seem to think the murders in Als-dorf originate from Nova Godói," the naturalist said, offhandedly.

"Murders? Oh, you speak of the rumors going around town. People here are so provincial. You ask around in any town in Brazil, and they'll tell you the next town is all bad people. I lived in Queens, so I don't fall for that talk." He laughed again, making light of the rumors. He was surprised the naturalist had picked up as much as he had. No point in spooking the man until he had collected his final thousand.

"How about the *other* rumor? You know—that everyone up there in Nova Godói are twins?"

At this, Mendonça froze. He had heard that rumor, but it was a deep one, only whispered about. How in the world had the naturalist heard of it?

"I don't know anything about that," he said.

"Surely you do. They say the town is freakishly populated with twins, mostly identical. They say there have been experiments, genetic experiments. *Horrible* genetic experiments."

"Where did you hear this?"

"In a beer hall."

That seemed improbable. Mendonça felt a small chill. This naturalist was beginning to give him the creeps. "No, I don't know anything about that. It's not true." He cast about, hoping to change the subject.

"There's an old ruin up there, though. A fort. Do you know the history of that?"

"No."

"It was built by the Portuguese in the late seventeenth century." Among many of his other jobs, Mendonça drove a tour bus in Blumenau; he knew almost everything. "A group of Franciscan missionaries built a monastery on an island in the middle of the Godói crater lake and converted the Aweikoma Indians. Or at least they thought they did!" He gave a belly laugh. "One day the Indians rose up. They were tired of taking care of the monks' gardens. Killed them all. So the Portuguese military moved in, turned the monastery into a fortress, killed off or drove away the Indians. And when there were no more Indians, the soldiers left. Later, it was turned into a plantation."

"Why are there so many Germans in this region?" the naturalist asked.

"In 1850, the Brazilian government started a program of German colonization. You know about that? Germany was overcrowded and nobody had any land, and Brazil had land that needed settling. So Brazil offered any Germans who wanted to come free land in remote areas of the country. That's how Blumenau was settled, along with Alsdorf, Joinville, and several other cities in Santa Catarina. Thirty, maybe forty percent of our citizens here are of German descent."

"That is most interesting."

"Yes. The colonies were so isolated that they developed completely along German lines, with German language, architecture, culture—everything. That all changed completely in 1942, of course."

"What happened?"

"That is when Brazil declared war on Germany."

"I never knew that."

"Very few do. We joined with the Americans in World War Two. Brazil made it a law that these German colonists had to learn Portuguese and become Brazilian. Most of them did, but some in the remote areas did not. And a lot of Germans left Brazil to go back to Germany and fight for the Nazis. And then some came running back again, to hide from the Nuremberg courts. Or so people say. But that was a long time ago. They are all gone now. As we say in Portuguese, *água debaixo da ponte*: water under the bridge."

"No Nazis in Nova Godói?" The naturalist almost sounded disappointed.

Mendonça shook his head vigorously. "No, no! That's all a myth!" He underscored that with another series of vigorous puffs before jettisoning the chewed cigar stump overboard. Of course, the rumors about Nova Godói never seemed to end, all sorts of ridiculous, superstitious nonsense. But Mendonça had lived twenty years in Queens. He had seen the world. He knew the difference between rumor and fact.

The boat continued on at a steady pace, the fields now disappearing completely, the araucaria forest closing in, casting a pall of darkness over the brown river. And despite having lived in Queens, Mendonça felt a distinct chill of fear creep down his spine.

56

THE FIRST SHOT HAD CAUGHT JACK SWANSON IN the shoulder as he'd leapt for the cover of the shrubbery at the rear of the cabin. A second shot passed over his head.

He lay on the ground for a moment, stunned, listening to the nearby sounds of struggling, a grunt of effort. Then came the slamming of a car door. And with that, Jack was up and running into the woods. The sky was dark and a wind rattled the branches, shaking the dense thickets of mountain laurel that formed the understory.

He knew these woods. And the laurel, an evergreen shrub, made for perfect concealment. He charged into the laurel, bashing through the thicket, putting as much distance between himself and Foote as he could. When he felt he was deep enough, he dropped into a crouch and began moving laterally, zigzagging through the thickest stands, worming his way ever farther into the thicket. He already sensed, with growing relief, that he'd gotten away—Foote would never find him in this dense underbrush, riddled with low animal trails that formed many escape routes. But what had gone wrong? Why Foote? Foote was trying to help them . . .

A voice rang out.

"Jack!"

He froze. It was Foote.

"Jack! We need to talk!"

He stopped, crouched, breathing hard. Reality began to rearrange itself in his mind. It was true, then—it had to be true. Foote was part of the scam. Everything he'd told them was a lie. And now Foote had Corrie.

"Can you hear me, Jack? I've got your daughter! Hogtied in my car. So we've got a lot to talk about, right?"

Jack could hear Foote walking into the forest now, crunching through the thickets of mountain laurel. "Oh, *Jackie*! We need to *ta-alk*!"

Jack moved laterally, away from the line that Foote was taking into the woods. Christ, he had to think, to collect his thoughts.

Foote has Corrie.

That thought threatened to undo what little rationality he had managed to gather. What was he going to do? He couldn't run. Somehow he had to overcome Foote, save his daughter. Except that the bastard had a handgun, and he himself had nothing beyond a penknife. As he crouched, he realized with a certain sense of surprise, *I've been shot.* His shoulder was soaked in blood, his left arm dangling uselessly. Strange that there was no pain, only numbness. So he only had one arm, too.

What was he going to do?

Jack tried to think, but as he did so he could hear Foote getting closer, crashing through the brush.

He began moving laterally again, as silently as possible, keeping low and threading his way through the bushes. The gusts of wind covered his movements, masking both the sound and the motion of the brush caused by his passage.

"Jack, if you don't come out now, I'm going back to my car and I'm going to kill her. Do you hear me? Talk to me or she dies."

Fear and paralysis gripped Jack. His hand slipped into his pocket and brought out the penknife, flicked open the blade, tested it with his thumb. Dull.

"Talk to me!" Foote screamed.

Jack tried to make his mouth work. "All right. I'll talk."

He could hear Foote moving, triangulating on his voice. He shifted position, his mind racing. There had to be something. *Something.* He felt a stinging drop of icy rain, and another. The patter of rain—or was it sleet?—started to fill the woods.

"Listen, Jack. We'll work it out. Nothing's going to happen to you or your daughter if you cooperate. Okay?"

"Okay," Jack said. He heard Foote move closer, and he once again shifted his position, moving along a low animal trail into denser brush.

"Sure, I was involved in a scam," Foote went on in a soothing voice. "Not what you think. Not ripping off customers."

"What, then?"

"GMAC. The big boys. Get them to finance nonexistent car sales. Been working with the GMAC auditor, the guy who comes to the lot every month to count cars, punch in the VINs. It's a great scam and we make a *lot* of money. You'll get a nice cut of that."

Jack continued to move laterally.

"How does fifty grand sound? And I let your daughter go. It's all good."

He was continuing to move closer, slowly.

"So you framed me," Jack said.

"Yeah, it's true, I framed you for the bank robbery.

I'm really sorry, Jack. I couldn't have you going to the feds, triggering an investigation. Any investigation—even one about that stupid pansy-ass credit cozen—might have ultimately blown up in my face. You understand? Nothing personal."

A silence.

"Jack? I can't talk to the bushes. We need to talk face-to-face."

Foote was about fifty yards away, a long shot for a handgun. Jack stood up, immediately dropped back down as the shot rang out.

Foote came crashing toward him through the brush, firing again. Jack ran at a crouch, diagonally away, another shot pursuing him, snipping leaves and twigs off.

"Your daughter's dead meat!"

Jack continued on as fast as he could, weaving through the narrow gaps, moving in unexpected directions, the sleet and wind covering his tracks. But something happened, something snapped. The fear and paralysis vanished, replaced by anger. Searing, furious rage. The bastard had kidnapped his daughter, *bound* her, tried to kill him—and would surely kill them both at his first opportunity.

With the rage came a sudden clarity of mind. He could think again. And his thoughts were terrible indeed.

Foote, in his noisy pursuit, had lost track of Jack's position.

"Ha, ha, Jack. I wasn't aiming for you. Look, let's just talk. We can work this out, and you'll get your daughter back. Make it a hundred grand."

Jack recalled hearing the slamming of a car door after he'd been shot. It had been close to the house. No doubt that's where Corrie was being held. But where, exactly, was it?

Orienting himself, Jack began moving swiftly but stealthily through the densest part of the woods, making a loop around Foote, who continued to broadcast his position by alternately cajoling and making threats. Finally he heard the man say: "That's it! She's dead!" And then he heard him moving decisively through the forest.

Jack paused and picked up a pebble. With his good arm, he lofted it behind and to the side, where it rattled in some bushes. He could hear Foote stop, move quickly in that direction.

"Jack! I know where you are! One...two...three...!"

Jack used the man's movement and his loud voice as an opportunity to move quickly himself, once again laterally, but now in a new direction, based on where Foote seemed to be heading. Foote called out a few more times and then began to move as well—very fast—through the forest.

Jack picked up another pebble and tossed it, but it ricocheted off a tree—not as artfully placed as the other.

"Throwing rocks, are we? It ain't gonna work, asshole!"

Just keep yelling, thought Jack as he used the opportunity to sprint across an open area into another thicket. The sleet was coming down hard now, soaking him to the bone.

As he moved, he realized he was significantly behind Foote. He had to move faster. He threw another rock, which was answered by several shots aimed vaguely in his direction. He could indeed hear Foote continue pushing his way back toward the cabin, repeating his threats and describing in graphic detail what he was going to do to Corrie.

"I'm gonna do her brown, Jack—think about that! And then I'll strangle her, slowly!"

Jack sprinted at a crouch, scurrying through the laurel. The lashing of the storm allowed him to move almost at a run. He could hear Foote's yelling getting louder. He had to hurry, hurry.

Ahead, Jack saw an opening in the dark, cold forest—the track. Foote had stopped yelling. He pushed forward through the brush, keeping parallel to the road, as silently as possible, until he saw a dull gleam. There it was, parked pretty much where he thought it would be.

But Foote was closer to the car than he was—too close. The gun was visible in one bleeding hand. Foote was chuckling as he opened the rear door.

"Get ready, bitch," he said.

All the strength fled from Jack's limbs and he collapsed to the ground. This was it. He was too late. It was all over.

At that moment, something dark in color—one of Corrie's boots, followed by a jeans-covered leg—flashed out from the rear seat toward Foote. The boot caught him squarely in the crotch with a savage impact. Foote gasped in pain and staggered backward, dropping the gun.

In an instant, Jack was on his feet. In another, he was atop Foote, ignoring the gun in the grass, instead bringing the penknife down into the man's face with one smooth, swift motion, the blade going straight into his eye. The knife sank into the orb, the ocular jelly squirting out, the knife scraping against the thin bone in the back. Foote jerked and thrashed with an inarticulate roar, hands flying to his face. Jack fell on the gun, grabbed it, then trained it on Foote while the man lay rolling in agony, blood leaking between the hands gripping his face. Jack raised the gun, pointed it at Foote's head.

"No!" came the voice from behind him.

Jack turned. It was Corrie, lying in the backseat, hands tied behind her back.

"We need him alive," she said. "We need him to talk."

For a moment, Jack said nothing. Then, slowly, he lowered the gun. His eyes fell to her ankles. They were free, a pair of plastic cuffs lying scuffed and severed on the floor of the rear seat.

Corrie followed his glance. "There was a burr in the metal rail behind the driver's seat," she said.

And now Jack came forward. Wiping off the bloody penknife, he used it to cut through the plastic handcuffs. In another moment he was wordlessly hugging his daughter like he had never hugged anyone before in his life, the tears streaming down both their faces.

57

It was a cool morning after a night of rain, the mists drifting over the surface of the river, as they set off from the last town on the Rio Itajaí do Sul, the southernmost tributary of the Rio Itajaí.

Mendonça, in a foul mood and nursing a hangover, guided the boat upriver. The naturalist, Fawcett, resumed his seat in the bow, no longer reading his book but keeping a lookout for butterflies. Once in a while he would shout for Mendonça to slow down when he spotted a butterfly fluttering along the river's edge, and once he demanded that they actually chase a butterfly with the boat, with him leaning over the bow, swiping at the thing with his net until he caught it.

The last town on the river had been a sad, dirty, horrible little place called Colonia Marimbondo. While there, Mendonça had made careful inquiries about Nova Godói: where it was, how to recognize the landing place along the river. He had gathered most of his information at the local *cervejaria*, the central beer hall in the town, where he had been forced to spend his hard-earned money buying endless rounds to encourage the uncommunicative villagers to talk. What he had finally managed to squeeze out of them had unsettled him greatly. Most of it was no doubt superstition and sheer ignorance, but it badly unnerved him nonetheless.

They had set off early, just at dawn, the sound of the engine echoing off the wall of araucaria trees, dripping after a night of rain. Mendonça could feel the wetness gathering in his hair and beard and creeping through his shirt.

God in heaven, he couldn't wait for this to be over.

Around noon, they came around a broad bend in the river, and there, on the right-hand bank, stood a floating dock with a ramp leading up to a rickety wooden quay. Beyond the high riverbank lay a partially overgrown clearing in the forest, with several rusting Quonset huts and a ramshackle wooden warehouse. It was exactly as the villagers had described it.

"We have arrived," said Mendonça, eyeing the quay for signs of life. To his great relief, it looked abandoned.

He slowed the engine and angled the boat in, easing up to the dock, hopping out and tying it off. He stood on the dock as the naturalist, awkward as usual, hauled his pack out and transferred it to the dock, then got out himself, standing unsteadily and peering about.

"We have arrived," Mendonça repeated, mustering a smile. He held out his hand. "The rest of the money, please, *o senhor*?"

A pause. "Now, wait just a minute," Fawcett said, his beard wagging in sudden irritation. "We agreed: two thousand up front, and—"

"And one thousand *on arrival*," Mendonça finished for him. "Surely you remember?"

"Oh." The naturalist screwed up his face. "Is that what we agreed?"

"Yes, it is."

More grumbling. "You have to wait here until I come back. We agreed on a round trip, six days total."

"No problem," said Mendonça. "I wait. But you pay me now."

"How do I know you won't take off?"

Mendonça gathered himself up. "Because I am a man of honor."

This seemed to satisfy Fawcett, and he delved into his pack, fished around, extracted the wad of cash, and peeled off two five-hundred-real notes. Mendonça snatched them and stuffed them in his pocket.

The naturalist picked up his pack. "So where's the town?"

Mendonça pointed toward a four-wheel-drive track that crossed the clearing, passed by the huts, and disappeared into the forest. Beyond, the green canopy rose in hills, one after another, culminating in a volcanic caldera that disappeared into the low-lying clouds. "Up that road. About three miles. There's only one way to go."

"Three miles?" Fawcett frowned. "Why didn't you tell me this before?"

"I thought you already knew." Mendonça shrugged.

Fawcett fixed him with a scowling eye. "You wait for me. I'll be back in three days—seventy-two hours—by noon."

"I will stay with the boat, sleep in the boat. I have all I need." He grinned, lit a cigar.

"Very well." The naturalist struggled to get the pack on, adjusted the straps, and then began doddering up the muddy track, his figure appearing and disappearing in the drifting mists. As soon as he had finally vanished into the forest, Mendonça hurried down to the boat, fired up the engine, and cast off, heading back down the river toward Alsdorf as fast as he could go.

58

PENDERGAST HEARD, AT THE EDGE OF AUDIBIL-
ity, the sound of the boat engine as it moved down the
river, soon fading away. The trace of a smile crossed
his lips as he continued on. The jeep road wound its
way through the endlessly dripping forest, the strange
spiky branches of the araucaria pines heavy with drop-
lets. He trudged along, occasionally stopping to pursue a butterfly, as the road wound upward through the
dense forest in a series of broad switchbacks, mounting
higher and higher until it eventually reached into the
low-hanging clouds.

Half an hour later, the track leveled out as it arrived
at the top of a low ridge—the rim of an ancient volcanic
crater. From there it descended into the mist, the visibility now only a few hundred yards.

Pendergast peered closely at the crater. Then he
reached into his pocket and drew out a folded piece of
paper: the picture Tristram had drawn of a mountain—
the feature of Nova Godói he'd been unable to describe
in words. It perfectly matched the crater that now rose
up before him.

He made his way down, and as the trail once again

leveled out he came to two pillars of dressed lava rock on either side of the road, with a chain-link gate across and a rock wall extending on both sides out into the forest. Behind the gate stood a guardhouse. As he approached, two guards came tumbling out, rifles in hand. They cried out at him in German, pointing their rifles.

"I only speak English!" Pendergast cried, raising his hands. "I'm a naturalist! I'm here to look for butterflies!"

One of the soldiers, apparently the man in charge, stepped forward and switched into excellent English. "Who are you? How did you get here?"

"My name is Percival Fawcett," Pendergast said, delving into his pack and pulling out a UK passport. "Fellow of the Royal Society. I came here by boat up the river, I can tell you it was no easy trip!"

The guards seemed to relax somewhat, both putting up their rifles. "This is private property," the commander said. "You can't come in here."

"I've come halfway around the world," said Pendergast in a voice that combined a shrill pleading with a certain truculence, "to find the Queen Beatrice butterfly. And I will not be turned away." He pulled out a piece of paper. "I have letters of introduction from the provincial governor and another from Santa Catarina." He proffered the papers, which had been duly stamped, embossed, and notarized. "And I have a letter here from the Royal Society, urging cooperation with my important mission, and another from the Lepidoptery Department of the British Museum, endorsed by the Sociedade Entomológica do Brasil." More papers came out. "As you can see, mine is a mission of the utmost scientific importance!" His voice climbed in volume.

The commander took the sheaf of papers and rifled

through them, a frown disfiguring his keen, Nordic features. "We don't allow visitors for any reason whatsoever," he said. "As I told you, this is private property."

"If you refuse me entry," said Pendergast shrilly, "there will be a scandal. I will make sure of it. A scandal!"

This created a certain uneasiness in the guard's expression. He moved back and conferred with his subordinate. Then the commander went into the guardhouse and could be seen making a call on a radio. He spoke for some time, and then returned to the gate. "Wait here," he said.

A few minutes later a jeep came down the road, driven by a man in olive drab, with another man, in a uniform of solid gray, sitting in the backseat. The jeep stopped, and the man in the rear got out and stepped forward. Even though he wasn't exactly in a military uniform, he carried himself like a soldier.

"Open the gate," he said.

The guards rolled the gate aside. The man stepped forward, his hand extended. "I am Captain Scheermann," he said, with just a trace of a German accent, as he shook Pendergast's hand. "And you are Mr. Fawcett?"

"*Dr.* Fawcett."

"Of course. I understand you're a naturalist?"

"That's right," said Pendergast, his voice rising belligerently. "As I was telling these men, I've come halfway around the world on a mission of great scientific importance, endorsed by the governors of two Brazilian states as well as the British Museum and the Royal Society, in cooperation with the Sociedade Entomológica do Brasil"—he stumbled badly over the pronunciation. "I insist on being treated with courtesy! If I am turned away, I promise you, sir, there will be an investigation, a very thorough investigation!"

"Of course, of course," said the captain soothingly. "If I may—"

Pendergast went on, undeterred. "I am in pursuit of the Queen Beatrice butterfly, *Lycaena regina*, long thought extinct. It was last observed in the Nova Godói caldera in 1932. My twenty years of research—"

"Yes, yes," the captain interrupted, smoothly if a little impatiently. "I understand. There's no need for such excitement, no need for investigations. You're welcome to enter. We have our rules, but for you we will make an exception. A *temporary* exception."

A beat. "Well," said Pendergast. "That is most kind of you. Most kind! If there are expenses or fees—?"

The captain held up his hand. "No, no. The only thing we require is that you accept an escort."

"An escort?" Pendergast frowned.

"We're used to our privacy here, and some of our people might be startled by an outsider. You'll need an escort—mostly for your own comfort and safety. I'm sorry, but that is not open for negotiation."

Pendergast harrumphed. "If necessary, fine. But I will be moving about in the forest in all weathers, and he or she better be able to keep up."

"Naturally. Now, may I escort you to our town hall, where we can take care of the paperwork?"

"That's rather more like it," said Pendergast, climbing into the jeep as the captain held open the door. "In fact, that's capital. Just capital."

59

As they drove through the town, Pendergast peered about with evident interest at all that he saw. The drizzle was letting up slightly, the clouds lifting, and gradually the environs were coming into view. The village sported stuccoed buildings, and it spread across a grid of capacious streets along the shores of an emerald lake. While it could be no more than half a century old, it beautifully reproduced the architecture, cobbled streets, and general layout of an old Bavarian village, even down to the steep stone staircases rising up the shorefront, the hand-painted signs, the slate roofs and half-timbering of the larger public buildings.

The lakeshore itself was graced with long stone quays of neatly dressed stone, which led to a series of well-kept docks, wharves, and slips, on which crisply painted fishing boats and a few launches were tied up. Everything was cloaked in mist; the lake itself vanished into a drizzle of rain, its central island no more than a dim gray outline.

The town ended abruptly in a forest of immensely tall araucaria trees, mingled with pines and other subtropical species. The darkness, the fog, the dreary weather, and the untamed wall of forest formed a strange contrast to the town—so neat, clean, and so very European in character.

Perhaps because of the rain, the streets were eerily deserted.

In a few moments they arrived at the town hall, a half-timbered building done in faux-medieval style. The captain led the way into a spartan interior, with benches lined up as if for a town meeting, moving past them into a cluster of offices. Pendergast followed Scheermann into a large office in the rear of the building, its door open, with a broad picture window looking out over the lake. A fire burned in a brick fireplace. A vase of gorgeous red roses stood on a table. Behind a desk sat a roly-poly man in Tyrolean vestments, ruddy-cheeked and cheery-faced. And yet the man's blue eyes were utterly without expression, like small glass marbles reflecting back only the light that shone into them and nothing more.

"This is Bürgermeister Keller," said the captain. "Mayor of Nova Godói."

The mayor rose and extended a small, fat hand. "Looking for the Queen Beatrice butterfly, I understand!" he said genially. He, too, spoke perfect English. "I hope you find it."

The paperwork was time consuming, yet it was taken care of with great efficiency. Pendergast was given an official document, stamped and embossed, which he was told to keep on his person at all times. As they were concluding the arrangements, a thin man stepped into the office. He was about thirty-five, with a narrow head, a high-domed forehead that seemed to loom over his watery blue eyes, and a thick lower lip that also extended beyond the upper, giving his face a queer, caved-in look.

"And here is your escort," said the mayor. "His name is Egon."

"You are free to go anywhere you like, except out on the lake or to its island." The captain paused significantly. "You did not expect to go to the island, I trust?"

"Oh, no," said Pendergast. "The last QB was found on the mainland, along the shores of the lake. No need for water trips—I've had enough of that coming up the river!"

This little joke elicited a chuckle from the mayor. "Good. Egon will also show you to your evening's quarters. Egon, please see that the *Herr Doktor* receives every courtesy."

Egon nodded.

Pendergast bowed. "Thank you. Most kind, most kind indeed. But I shall not be needing evening quarters: the Queen Beatrice, you see, is best hunted at night."

They emerged back onto the streets as the sun finally broke free of the clouds, flooding the town with a weak light. Slowly the veil over the lake was drawn back, revealing the central island—a naked cinder cone topped by a grim fortress of ancient lava rock, black in color, its towers partly in ruins, battlements and crenellations broken and crumbling. A single ray of light pierced the gloom and illuminated the structure, and Pendergast could see, briefly—as the fugitive light passed over the old fort—the flash of something metallic hidden behind the massive walls.

The appearance of the sun had an unusual effect on the town. Suddenly, as if summoned, the streets filled with men and women going about their business with a remarkable fixity of purpose. It was almost like a movie set, many of the townsfolk dressed in vintage clothing from the late 1940s, the women with rolled bangs and tailored jackets or dresses, wide shoulders and hips, the men in dark baggy suits and hats, some smoking pipes. Others were dressed in more working-class outfits, jumpsuits and overalls, flat caps and straw boaters. All were handsome, and most sported classic Nordic looks—tall, blond, and blue-eyed, with chiseled cheekbones. They went about their business by bicycle, on foot, some with wheelbarrows and carts. But, Pendergast noted, no cars. The only vehicles were World War II—era jeeps driven by men in olive drab, always with an important-looking personage seated in the back, dressed in a gray uniform. These were the only people who seemed to have guns, and they were well armed indeed, packing high-caliber sidearms and, frequently, an assault rifle with an oversize magazine.

Many inhabitants stopped and stared at him, some gaping in surprise and some eyeing him with evident hostility. For the fact was, Pendergast, aka Dr. Percival Fawcett, stood out like a sore thumb. Which was precisely his intention.

Pendergast set off at a breakneck pace toward the quay, explaining loudly that the Queen Beatrice preferred the littoral zones and that its favored time of day was dawn, not sunset, but that one never knew. Egon seemed not to hear, following him with dogged persistence, never tiring, always keeping up.

The boats along the quay were beautifully maintained, and some were much larger than would normally be necessary for lake fishing. They included two big motorized barges, on which sat heavy machinery and exotic equipment of unknown function—again, far heavier than seemed necessary for a remote farming community. How such large vessels had been transported to this isolated lake could not even be guessed at. It was getting on toward evening, and the quay was a bustle of activity as fishermen began unloading the day's catch, which was then packed in ice and loaded into heavy handcarts. All was a picture of industry, hard work, and evident self-sufficiency—seemingly, a model society. Pendergast noted that the town did not appear to contain even a single bar or café.

"Egon, tell me: is this a dry town? Is alcohol consumption allowed?"

This question, Pendergast's first, received no answer from Egon, no acknowledgment that it had been heard.

"Well, then. Let us keep going."

Pendergast walked briskly along the quays. The poor weather finally lifted completely, giving way to a beautiful, even spectacular sunset, with the great orange globe of the sun dropping through vermilion layers of cloud on the far side of the lake, turning the water to fire, silhouetting the grim ruined fortress on its lonely island out in the middle of the lake.

Just beyond the far end of the quay was an unusual rock formation: three large stones, boulders actually, remarkably identical in size and shape, that rose up several feet above the surface of the water and were arranged in a roughly triangular pattern about ten yards apart. Here, Pendergast stopped and took a moment to look back at the town, sloping gently upward along the flanks of the old volcano. It was the very picture of orderliness, cleanliness, efficiency, and regulation. The buildings were beautifully maintained, freshly stuccoed in white, the shutters gaily painted in green and blue. Many of the buildings sported window boxes bursting with flowers. There was no trash, not even a gum wrapper, to be seen; no graffiti; no stray dogs—or, in fact, any dogs at all: no derelicts, drunks, or loafers; no street arguments, shouting, or excessive noise.

There were other things besides dogs and trash that seemed to be missing. While there were plenty of middle-aged and older people, there were no people infirm with age, no fat people, no one with physical defects. And, to his great interest, no twins.

It was, in short, a perfect little utopia, hidden in the depths of the Brazilian forest.

As night fell, lights came on in the island fortress, bright klieg lights that bathed the stone ramparts a brilliant white. In the quietness of twilight, as he stood on the quay, Pendergast could begin to hear sounds from across the water: the hum of generators, the clanking of machinery, the crackle of electricity, and, very faint, drifting across the dark lake, what might have been the screech of a bird—or, perhaps, a scream of agony.

60

BEYOND THE QUAY LAY A CURVE OF SHORE AND a pebbled beach. A quarter mile farther on, the forest began, a dark, spiky, seemingly impenetrable wall. The sky deepened as the sun dipped through the last layer of clouds and winked off in a swirl of light at the horizon.

Pendergast reached into his pack and removed a red light, turning to the imperturbable Egon and speaking in a hushed voice full of suppressed excitement. "My dear fellow, now we are coming to the time of the Queen Beatrice."

He set off down the beach, Egon following. Some small skiffs had been pulled up on the shingle, their nets draped out to dry. Farther along, the beach gave way to lava rock, and minutes later they arrived at the forest edge. The last of the light was dying against the island fortress, accentuating the brilliant illumination. Another distant cry—bird or human?—drifted over the water.

"Egon, you see that ruin over there?" Pendergast asked, pointing toward the fort. "Why is it all lit up? What's going on over there?"

Egon stared at him a moment, his eyes returning the

reflected glow from the fortress. And he spoke for the first time. "Agricultural research. Animal husbandry."

"Animal husbandry?" Pendergast shook his head. "Well, it's none of my business. We're for the forest." He delved into his pack and pulled out a flashlight. "Here's a red light for you. Don't use a regular flashlight, please—the QB is aversive to light. Follow me, stay close, and make no noise."

He handed Egon the red light and walked into the forest. The prickly branches of araucaria trees mingled with the thick understory to impede their way, everything still wet from the recent rains. But Pendergast, slender and nimble as a snake, moved with speed through the dark, dripping vegetation, shining his red light here and there, net in one hand, ready to strike.

"Keep up!" he whispered over his shoulder as Egon blundered along.

The ground began to rise. There were no trails in this part of the forest, no sign in fact that any humans ventured beyond the town. It had all the aspect of wilderness. And yet, for some inexplicable reason, it didn't feel quite right.

"There's one!" Pendergast suddenly cried out. "Do you see it? Oh, my God! I can't believe it!" And in a flash he was gone, whipping through the undergrowth, red light flickering, net waving frantically. Egon gave a shout from behind and began to pursue, crashing along.

Ten minutes later—from a heavy tree branch about thirty feet above the ground—Pendergast watched Egon stumble about in the forest, calling Fawcett's name and shining a powerful flashlight about, his voice strident and panicked.

Pendergast waited half an hour, until his escort had

moved his search farther south. Then, as silently and nimbly as a monkey, Pendergast descended from the tree. Placing a special hood on the red light, he moved swiftly northward, following the sloping ascent of land. For an hour he continued his rise until he came out on a narrow rim—the lip of an adjacent crater. Here he turned off the light. The trees had thinned out along the rim, giving him a view down into the broad bottom of the vast crater, illuminated by the light of a crescent moon. It was quite shallow, miles across, encompassing several thousand acres of tightly packed fields and pastures, taking advantage of the rich volcanic soil. This was the breadbasket of Nova Godói, clearly the former location of the old tobacco plantation, the crater forming an almost perfect microclimate for agriculture. At the far end of the crater stood a tight cluster of dead cinder cones, like black cylinders. Nestled up against them were agricultural sheds, greenhouses, barns, and silos. All was quiet among them, not a light to be seen in the velvety darkness.

A faint trail followed the rim, and he walked along it until he came to a second trail switchbacking down into the crater, steep at first, but soon leveling out as it approached the fields. In another moment he had reached the edge of the first field, a great spread of corn, quite still in the pale moonlight. Pendergast entered it and continued on at a swift, silent pace toward the far end of the crater—and the cluster of agricultural buildings.

Past the corn were other fields, bursting with a great variety of produce—tomatoes, beans, squash, wheat, cotton, alfalfa, and timothy, as well as rich pastures for livestock. Swiftly he passed through them all until he came out on the far side, where the buildings were.

He selected the first: a huge, flat-roofed metal warehouse. He found that its door was padlocked. A quick pass of his hand caused the lock to seemingly fall open. He pulled the door ajar and slipped into the interior, fragrant with the scent of machine oil, diesel, and earth. A quick flash of the hooded red light revealed rows of agricultural machinery—farm tractors, cultivators, ploughs, disk harrows, row planters, manure spreaders, harvesters, balers, backhoes, and loaders— all of old vintage but excellently maintained.

He moved through the building and out a door on the far side. To his right rose a barn, in which he could hear the soft lowing of milk cows. To his left stood a row of silos, and straight ahead a grid of greenhouses. It was a remarkable operation, an extraordinarily rich and productive farm, vast in size, impeccably run and maintained. And apparently deserted.

Pendergast scouted the edges of the greenhouses, their glass panes gleaming in the moonlight. Inside could be seen a profusion of flowers—flowers upon flowers. One greenhouse was bursting with exotic roses in every size, color, and shape.

At the far end of the greenhouses stood the dead cinder cones, steep and tall, their flanks covered with sliding volcanic ash. Pendergast skirted the base of the closest, and then stopped: there, built into the bottom of the cone, stood a narrow shed-like building, with no windows, its rear buried in the cinders.

He crept up to the door of the building and pressed his ear to it. At first he could hear nothing, but, over time, he picked up the faintest of sounds: movement, sighing, shuffling, perhaps even a cough.

This door was incongruously strong, of heavy wood banded and riveted with steel. The lock was sophisticated, but nothing that withstood Pendergast's efforts for more than sixty seconds. The door swung in on oiled hinges, the air exhaling a mephitic, offensive smell. All was dark.

Pendergast advanced, keeping the red light well shielded. The shed now revealed itself as merely an entrance, leading down into something built underneath or perhaps into the cinder cones. Before him was a shallow, broad staircase of well-worn stone. Pendergast paused at the top step, turning the red light off before beginning his descent. He could see a faint light from below—of a reddish hue—and as he proceeded the stench became stronger, the air redolent of unwashed bodies. Reaching the bottom of the staircase, he found himself in a long tunnel. In the darkness he could hear the sounds more clearly now. They were the sounds of shuffling, snoring, mumbling—the sounds of people. Many people.

With infinite care Pendergast crept forward in the darkness, keeping close to the nearest wall. The reddish glow came from two barred windows set in a pair of locked double doors at the far end of the tunnel. Keeping low, Pendergast slipped up to the doors, examined the lock, and listened. There was someone on the far side, someone passing back and forth: a guard. He listened, timing the guard's slow coming and going. At a safe moment, he rose and looked through the barred window.

A vast room greeted his eyes, illuminated in dull red light from strings of bare hanging bulbs. The room consisted of row upon row of crude wooden bunk beds extending into the gloom, stacked three bunks high, each with a single blanket wrapping up the form of a human being, faces sorrowful in restive sleep, while others moved about like ghosts, some going to or from a latrine along one wall of the room. Still others simply paced back and forth aimlessly, unable to sleep, their hopeless eyes reflecting the red light of the bulbs.

Everything Pendergast had not seen in Nova Godói was here: the deformed, the crippled, the ugly and squat, the weak, the aged—and, particularly, the infirm of mind. But what horrified him most of all was that he *recognized* some of these faces. Only hours before, he had seen some of the same faces in town, belonging to radiant, smiling counterparts—twins. Only these underground doppelgängers carried the strange and disturbing expressions of the mentally ill, the vacant of mind, the despairing and hopeless, their sinewy muscles, brown skin, and rough hands attesting to a lifetime of field labor.

At the far edge of his vision, Pendergast saw the guard turning. He was not of these people, he was one of the others: tall, handsome. His presence seemed unnecessary—these poor souls were in no condition to revolt, escape, or otherwise cause trouble. The look of resignation on their faces was universal and absolute.

Pendergast lowered his gaze from the window and made his way back down the tunnel and up the staircase. A few minutes later, he was breathing deeply—gasping even—the cool, fresh, aboveground air, the grotesque image of human suffering he'd just witnessed burned into his consciousness for all time.

61

THIS TIME, FELDER HAD STOOD IN THE DARK-
ness outside the library windows for over an hour, in
the freezing night, tense and fearful. The house looked
dead: no lights, no movement. And above all, no Dukchuk. Finally, reassured, trying to keep his courage up,
he opened the window and climbed in.

Leaving the window open in case he needed a
quick escape, he stood motionless in the chill room
for a long moment, listening. Nothing. Just as he'd
hoped.

He had taken every precaution. For the last few
nights, he'd kept watch on the library, surveilling it
from the safety of the arborvitae. All had been still.
The midnight near-encounter with Dukchuk must
have been a freakish coincidence, since the man didn't
seem to be in the habit of roaming the house at night.
The previous afternoon, Miss Wintour had asked him
in again for tea, and neither she nor her terrifying manservant had given the slightest indication that anything
was amiss. Nothing was suspected, it seemed.

But Felder knew he couldn't wait forever. He had
to act tonight—any more time and he'd lose his nerve

completely. As it was, Constance and Mount Mercy were beginning to seem far, far away.

He moved along the series of bookcases, feeling his way in the dark by touching the rippled surfaces of the doors' leaded glass. The W's would be near the end of the collection, putting Alexander Wintour's portfolio close to the pocket doors that led out into the main hallway. To his relief, those doors were firmly shut.

Felder paused at the second-to-last bookcase, listening, but the house was as silent as before. He pulled the Maglite from his pocket and, shielding it with care, flashed it over the books ahead of him. Trapp. Traven. Tremaine.

Snapping the light off, he moved on to the next and last bookcase. Once again, he hesitated, listening for even the slightest sound. Then he raised the flashlight, aiming it toward the upper shelves. Voltaire, in seven beautifully bound leather volumes—and beside them, a half dozen bundles of what looked like folded parchment, wrapped in crumbling crimson ribbon.

Keeping the flashlight beam on, he let it drift to the next shelf, then the next, and then trailed it laterally across the titles. Oscar Wilde's *Picture of Dorian Gray*. P. G. Wodehouse's *My Man Jeeves*. Both, apparently, first editions. And between them, three fat portfolios of black leather, plain and scuffed, with no title or markings.

Felder's heart began beating rather quickly.

Holding the Maglite between his teeth, he opened the glass case and eased the first portfolio from its shelf. It was covered in dust, and looked as if it hadn't been touched in a hundred years. He opened it carefully, almost afraid to breathe. Inside were dozens of what appeared to be rough sketches and preliminary studies for intended paintings. They were foxed, and faded, and quite similar in style to the ones he had seen in the historical society.

Felder's heart beat quicker.

He began leafing through the studies, fingers trembling. The first few were unsigned, but the third bore a signature in the lower right corner: WINTOUR, 1881.

He flipped to the back of the portfolio. There—attached to the inside rear edge with a narrow line of paste—was an envelope, brittle and yellowed. Taking the scalpel from his pocket, he cut the envelope free. His fingers felt numb and stupid, and it took him two attempts to open it.

There, nestled inside, was a small lock of dark hair.

For a moment, he just stared, with a strange mixture of emotion: triumph, relief, a little disbelief. So it was true, then—it was all true.

But wait—was it the *right* hair? There were two other portfolios. Might Wintour have collected hair from other girls? It seemed unlikely—but he had to check.

Sliding the envelope in his pocket, he put the portfolio back on the shelf and pulled down the next one, going through it rapidly. More sketches and watercolors. He felt his breath coming faster in his anxiety to get this done. There was no lock of hair in there. He pushed that back on the shelf and took down the third, flipping through it, in his haste tearing several pages. Again, nothing. He shut the portfolio and shoved it back on the shelf, but in his hurry he wasn't as careful as before and it made a dull *thump* as he over-pushed it into the back of the shelf.

He froze, his heart pounding. In the great cold silence of the house that small sound was like the crash of thunder.

Felder waited.

But there wasn't even the breath of sound in that frozen house. Slowly, he felt his muscles relax, his breathing slow. Nobody had heard a thing. He was just being paranoid.

He felt the envelope in his pocket; it gave out a dry crackling sound. Only then, as his fright subsided, did the full implications of his discovery sink in. All doubt was gone: Constance *really was* a hundred and forty years old. She wasn't crazy. She'd been telling the truth all along.

Strangely enough, this realization didn't shock him as much as he thought it would. Somehow, he already knew it was true: from the calm, matter-of-fact manner in which she'd always maintained her story; from the way she had been able to describe, in great detail, the contemporary appearance of 1880s Water Street; and from the essential honesty of her character. The fact was, this was what he *wanted* to believe, because—

With a crash of sound, the pocket doors of the library sprang open, revealing Dukchuk—dressed in his shapeless batik robe, holding the same cruel weapon Felder had seen before, staring at him with beady black eyes.

With a cry of fright Felder dashed for the window but Dukchuk was faster, leaping across the room and slamming the window shut, moving with a silence that was almost more terrible than a yell, displaying his teeth in a feral grin—and, for the first time, Felder noted they had been sharpened into points. With a scream Felder tried to defend himself but Dukchuk was on him, a tattooed arm whipping around his neck and contracting like a garrote, choking off Felder's cry.

Struggling madly, he felt a sudden, white-hot explosion of pain as the club violently impacted the side of his head. His knees gave way and Dukchuk flung him

down, striking his chest, the terrible blow knocking him to the ground, where he struggled, unable to
breathe.

A red mist rose before his eyes and he fought to
remain conscious, clutching his chest, until at last he
was able to suck in air with a huge gasp. As the mist
slowly dissipated and his vision cleared, Felder saw
Dukchuk standing over him in the faint light of the
hallway, massive tattooed forearms folded, his unnaturally small eyes like coals. Behind him stood the diminutive form of Miss Wintour.

"So!" Miss Wintour said. "You were right, Dukchuk. This man is nothing more than a common thief,
here under the pretense of being a lodger!" She glared
at Felder. "And to think of your nerve, drinking my tea
under my own roof, enjoying my kind hospitality, while
plotting to rob a weak, helpless old lady like myself of
my meager possessions. *Hateful* man!"

"Please," Felder began. He tried to rise to his knees.
His head throbbed, his ribs were undoubtedly broken,
and he tasted the metallic combination of blood and
fear in his mouth. "Please. I haven't taken anything.
I was just curious, I wanted to have a look around, I'd
heard so much..."

He fell silent as Dukchuk raised the club again men-
acingly. She would call the police; he'd be arrested; he'd
go to jail. It was the end of his career. What on earth
had he been thinking?

The manservant looked over his shoulder at Miss
Wintour, with a querying glance that carried the
unmistakable question: *What should I do with him?*

Felder swallowed painfully. This was it: the call
would go to the police, and all the ugliness would
begin. He might as well accept it. And start coming up
with a good story.

Miss Wintour glared at him a moment longer. Then she turned to Dukchuk.

"Kill him," she said. "And then you may bury his remains under the floor of the root cellar. With the others." She turned away and left the library without a backward glance.

62

DR. JOHN FELDER WALKED ACROSS THE MUSTY, faded carpeting of the old mansion, his movements slow, almost robotic. His head pounded; blood oozed from a cut on his temple, trickling down his neck; and his broken ribs grated on each other with each step. Dukchuk followed behind, occasionally prodding Felder in the small of his back with the club. The only sounds the manservant made were the swish of his tunic and the padding of his big bare feet on the carpet. The old lady had disappeared into the upper regions of the house.

Felder continued down the hallway without really seeing anything. This wasn't real, this couldn't be happening. Any minute now and he'd wake up on his uncomfortable little pallet in the carriage house. Or maybe—just maybe—he'd wake up in his own apartment back in New York, and this whole crazy trip to Southport would prove to have been nothing but a wild nightmare ...

And then Dukchuk prodded him again with the rounded end of his club, and Felder knew—all too clearly—that although this was a nightmare, it was no dream.

Still he could hardly believe it. Had old lady Wintour really given Dukchuk instructions to kill him? Was she serious or was it just an effort to scare him? This business of burying him in the root cellar with the others—what on earth could *that* mean?

He stopped. Ahead—in the faint, sickly electric light—he could make out a dining room, and beyond it what looked like a kitchen, with a door in its far wall leading out into the night—to freedom. But Dukchuk prodded him again, indicating with his club that Felder was to turn down another hallway to his left.

Now, as he resumed walking, Felder began to look around a little. Ancient, flyspecked lithographs lined the walls. Little china statuary sat on side tables here and there. But there was nothing, nothing that could conceivably be used as a weapon. He let his hands brush against his pockets as he walked. He could feel their contents: the screwdriver, the scalpel, the envelope with the lock of hair. The Maglite lay on the floor of the library, where he'd sprawled initially. The huge, nimble, muscular Dukchuk would just laugh at the scalpel and its one-inch blade. The screwdriver was a better bet: could he perhaps jam it into the man's chest? But the freak was so strong, so muscular—so *quick*—that he would never succeed. It would just make him mad.

It was hopeless. Worse than hopeless.

Dukchuk rapped on a closed door with his club, then gestured for Felder to open it. Felder turned the handle, his clammy hand sliding wetly over the white marble, pulled the door open. Beyond lay darkness. Dukchuk turned an old-fashioned knob on the wall and an overhead light came on, dangling from a wire. Ahead lay a rude set of stairs, leading down to the basement.

Felder felt his legs go wobbly with fear—fear that

had been buried under disorientation, pain, disbelief. This was for real. "No," he said, cringing back from the stairway. "No. Please. You can't do this."

Dukchuk poked him in the back with his club.

"I'll give you money," Felder babbled. "I've got a hundred and fifty, back in the carriage house. Maybe two hundred. We can go to the cash machine. It'll be our secret, she won't even have to know—"

Dukchuk jammed him in the back again, much harder. Felder teetered, catching the railing to keep his balance. Any harder and he'd be sent hurtling headfirst down the stairs.

"You can't kill someone like this. They know I'm renting the carriage house. The police will come looking, they'll tear the house apart." But even as he pleaded, he realized the police would do nothing of the sort. Who would believe a little old lady capable of cold-blooded murder? He'd rented the place under an assumed name, he'd told nobody he was staying here. Even if the cops came, they'd just knock on the door, ask a few polite questions, and go away.

Another hard jab.

He tried to swallow, felt himself gagging with fear instead. He took a step forward, then another, moving painfully down the steps like an old man. Dukchuk followed, keeping back several steps.

Time seemed to slow. Every step down into that basement was like a small agony. *Kill him. And then you may bury his remains under the floor of the root cellar.* Oh, God—oh, God, he really was about to die. Or was it still a sick, macabre joke, an effort to terrorize him? Somehow, he didn't think so.

He reached the bottom of the steps and stopped. It was chill and clammy, lit only by the bare bulb at the top of the stairs and a flickering, lambent light that came from a chamber to the left. A narrow hallway led ahead, with other, closed doors leading off from it.

This was it. He waited, bracing himself for the vicious blow to the head; for the blinding pain to explode in his brainpan; for the white light that would quickly fade to black. But instead Dukchuk prodded him ahead with his club.

They passed the open door on the left. Out of the corner of his eye, Felder saw tall, flickering candles; strangely painted linen hangings; small stone figurines arranged on plinths in a semicircle. Dukchuk's lair.

They were heading directly toward a closed door at the end of the hallway. As he stared at it, Felder's breathing began to quicken and he heard himself sobbing audibly. "Please," he murmured. "Please, please, please..."

They stopped at the end of the passage. Dukchuk motioned for him to open the last door. Felder reached for it, his hand trembling, his legs almost unable to hold him up. It took him three tries before he could grasp the handle with sufficient strength to turn it.

The door opened into darkness, the indirect candlelight revealing only faint shapes: apple barrels; boxes half full of rotting turnips and carrots; wooden shelving holding swing-top bale jars, many exploded, their dark and putrid contents sprayed across the undersides of the shelves above and dribbling down in congealed ropes.

The root cellar.

Felder heard his sobbing grow louder. It almost seemed like someone else was crying. Again, Dukchuk prodded him forward. But this time, Felder couldn't—or wouldn't—move. Instead, his hand slipped into his pocket, closed instinctively over the small envelope.

"Constance," he murmured. In this moment of supreme crisis, he realized all of a sudden—although he probably should have known it long before—that he was hopelessly in love with her. Maybe he had known it before—maybe he just hadn't consciously admitted it to himself. That's what this was all about. And now it was over. She would never know he'd found her lock of hair—nor would she ever know the price he'd had to pay for it.

Dukchuk prodded him again. And again, Felder remained where he stood, unable to move, on the threshold of the root cellar.

A vicious blow landed on his right shoulder, and Felder cried out, staggering forward. Another blow from the club caught him on the inside of the knee, and he crumpled to the ground, his head colliding with the earthen floor.

This was it.

Suddenly—it had something to do, he was sure, with the revelation of his feelings for Constance—he felt the fear recede. The feeling that replaced it was something like surprise—and anger. Surprise that this was the way he'd go out; that the last earthly sight he would ever see was the uneven, dusty floor; the huge plank-like feet of Dukchuk, turned partly away from him, their toenails black and ragged. And anger at the enormous unfairness of it. He had spent his life doing good, helping sick people, trying to be the best person he could be, earnest and kindhearted...and now was he to die the helpless victim of a crazy murderer?

The hand gripping the envelope felt something else press against it: something cold and straight. The scalpel. His hand released the envelope, closed over the blade. And—quite abruptly—Felder knew what he had to do.

In a single motion he pulled his hand from the pocket and—pinching the scalpel between his thumb and the knuckle of his middle finger, the index finger resting along its upper edge, as he'd been taught in dissection lectures at med school—slashed it with all the force he could muster through the massive Achilles tendon behind Dukchuk's nearest ankle.

There was a wet, sucking sound as the tendon— cleanly severed, its tension released—shot up like a fat rubber band and disappeared into the calf muscles of Dukchuk's leg. Instantly the man fell to his knees. His eyes widened, his mouth formed a perfect O, and for the first time the manservant uttered a sound: a deafening, calf-like bawl of pure agony.

Felder staggered to his feet, still grasping the bloody scalpel. Dukchuk howled a second time and clawed at Felder, but the psychiatrist jumped clear, at the same time slashing viciously at Dukchuk's hand, opening the palm like a ripe melon.

"You want some more, you son of a bitch?" Felder cried, astonished at his own rage. But Dukchuk was overwhelmed by pain, huddling on the floor now, clutching at his ankle, blood gushing from his hand, honking and bawling like a baby. He seemed to have forgotten all about Felder.

With a superhuman surge of strength, Felder swung around, reeled up the staircase, and staggered into the dining room, knocking over a chair in his progress. From somewhere upstairs he heard the old lady call down fretfully: "For heaven's sake, Dukchuk! Have your fun, but keep the noise down!"

Felder limped as fast as he could through the darkened kitchen. From below he could hear Dukchuk howling mindlessly, but the sounds were muffled now. Making for the rear door, he fumbled open the locks, threw the door wide. Ignoring the pain of his broken ribs and injured leg, he crashed through the overgrowth behind the mansion, reached the carriage house, entered just long enough to retrieve his case and keys, staggered over to his Volvo, got in, fired up the engine, peeled out onto Center Street, and drove away from the nightmare mansion with all the speed he could manage.

63

IN THE BRAZILIAN FOREST, NIGHT STILL REIGNED. Mists drifted through the dense trees and night blooming orchids. Pendergast made a silent beeline back to where he had left Egon and soon found signs of the man's blundering passage: broken branches, torn leaves, boot prints in the mossy floor. Following these signs, he moved swiftly until he could hear the man, still calling and wandering about. Pendergast made a long loop around him and came up from the opposite direction.

"Here I am!" he cried, waving his light about. "Over here!"

"Where were you?" Egon said, advancing on him with menace and suspicion, pointing the light in his face.

"Blast it, where were *you*?" Pendergast cried angrily. "I gave you specific instructions to follow, and you disobeyed! I've been wandering about, lost, for hours—and I missed a chance to capture that Queen Beatrice. I've half a mind to report you to the authorities!"

As Pendergast expected, Egon—steeped in a culture of authority and subordination—was instantly cowed.

"I'm sorry," he stammered out, "but you moved so fast, and then vanished—"

"Enough excuses!" Pendergast cried. "A night has been wasted. I'll let it go this time—but don't ever lose track of me again. I could have been killed by a jaguar or eaten by an anaconda!" He paused, fuming. "Let's go back to the town. You can show me to my quarters. I need some sleep."

They emerged into the town, wet and bedraggled, as dawn rose over the crater rim, casting a light that touched the bottoms of the clouds, blushing them coral. The crescent-shaped town came to clockwork life as the rays of sun invaded the cobbled streets: doors opening, chimneys smoking, streets filling with purposeful foot traffic. The island in the middle of the lake remained the same: black, grim, foreboding, issuing the faint sound of clanking machinery.

As they walked along the thronging streets, Pendergast once again noted, this time with a shiver of horror, that some of the faces he had seen in the underground ghetto had their mirror image among these handsome, busy people.

Egon led Pendergast to a small, half-timbered house adjacent to the town hall. Egon knocked and a woman answered in an apron, wiping her hands, the smell of baking bread issuing from the interior.

"*Herzlich willkommen,*" she said.

They entered to find two towheaded boys at a kitchen table eating bread with jam and soft-boiled eggs. They stopped and gaped at Pendergast with the same astonishment and curiosity the other townsfolk had displayed.

"Nobody speaks English," said Egon in his usual terse manner, ignoring the woman and her friendly greetings as he walked past her to a narrow staircase. He led the way up two stories to a cheerful garret with lace curtains, steeply pitched ceilings, and dormer windows looking back over town.

"Your room," he said. "You stay here until sunset. Then the woman give you dinner. I wait downstairs. Do not leave room."

"I'm to stay penned up here until sunset?" Pendergast cried. "Why, I only need four or five hours' sleep. I'd like to stroll through the town, see the sights."

"You stay here until sunset," Egon repeated truculently, shutting the door. Pendergast heard the key turning in the lock.

As Egon's footsteps retreated down the stairs, Pendergast perused the old-fashioned lock with a faint smile. Then he turned to his pack and collecting jars, unpacking the many specimens he'd collected on the river trip and in the forest that night, laying the butterflies out on spreading boards with flat-tipped tweezers, holding them in place with pinning strips. When he was done, he lay down on the made bed, fully clothed, and instantly went to sleep.

He awoke suddenly an hour later, hearing a knock at the door.

"Yes?" he said in English.

The tense voice of the hausfrau sounded on the other side of the door. "*Herr Fawcett, hier sind einige Herren, die Sie sprechen möchten.*"

As Pendergast rose from his bed, he heard the lock turning. The door opened to reveal half a dozen men in plain gray uniforms, all armed, their weapons drawn on him. They entered smoothly and swiftly in a well-coordinated operation, led by Scheermann, circling him on both sides. The operation was done with impeccable efficiency, leaving no possibility of reaction or escape.

Pendergast's eyes narrowed. He opened his mouth, as if to protest.

"Do not move," said Scheermann, unnecessarily. "Hands away from your sides."

Wordlessly, as Pendergast stood, hands extended, he was stripped, then dressed in a striped cotton gown and rude pants similar to the ones he had seen in the underground barracks. The guards led him down the stairs and pushed him into the street, weapons trained on him at all times, and he was paraded down to the docks. Strangely enough, the townsfolk paid him far less attention in his new prison garb than they had when he was wearing civilian clothes. This was clearly a sight they had seen before.

Nobody spoke. He was placed in the bow of a small barge, the guards forming a semicircle around him. With a roar from its steam engines, the barge moved slowly into the lake, leaving behind a boiling wake, heading in the direction of the gloomy fortress.

64

THE JOURNEY WAS SHORT. THEY LANDED AT A
stone quay; Pendergast was shoved forward, the soldiers prodding him with their rifles. Now the old fortress loomed directly above them, the crenellations of
its outer wall like black, broken teeth. They ascended
a cobbled road leading toward a massive iron gate; a
small door in the gate opened and they passed through.
The door clanged shut behind them.

An astonishing sight greeted Pendergast's eye.
The broken outer wall of the stronghold concealed
an internal structure retrofitted to the ruins and the
old stone foundations, which themselves had been
sturdily rebuilt and reinforced. It had a superstructure of poured concrete, streaked with damp and done
up in fascist monumental style, with smooth, massive
walls, broken only infrequently by tiny windows high
up along its flanks. A huge relief of the *Parteiadler* of
the Third Reich—an eagle clutching a swastika—was
carved into its side, the only adornment visible on the
otherwise blank walls and towers of this fort within a
fort.

Pendergast had paused to look around, and one of

the soldiers jammed a muzzle into his side. "*Beweg Dich!*" he barked.

Pendergast moved forward, through an outer courtyard to a door leading into the main fortress itself. Here were many more soldiers—some on guard duty, others polishing their weapons, others simply looking at Pendergast with sneering expressions. Mechanics hurried past, bent on unknown tasks.

Once inside the inner fortress, they moved upward, first through old stone corridors and staircases wet with damp and whited with niter, passing a few technicians and scientists in lab coats making their way down, until they emerged in the newer, upper portion of the fortress of concrete.

At the top of a circular staircase they came to an oaken door. The door opened into a suddenly spacious and airy room, high up, with glass windows providing splendid—if small—views over the rooftops of the fortress, across the lake, and reaching to the surrounding forests and mountains. It was a beautifully appointed office, the walls of dressed stone, a Persian carpet on the floor, a massive antique desk flanked by Nazi flags, with exquisite pieces of old silver and objets d'art carefully arranged along the walls. Behind the desk sat a remarkable-looking man, a specimen of Teutonic perfection: powerful and heavily muscled, with penetrating pale eyes, a dark tan, and a neatly trimmed thatch of white hair. He smiled.

Pendergast recognized the man instantly. Fischer.

"Very good, Oberführer Scheermann," he said.

The captain stiffened, clicked his heels. "*Danke, mein Oberstgruppenführer.*"

Fischer rose, plucked a Dunhill cigarette from a repoussé silver box, lit it with a gold lighter, and inhaled deeply, all the while keeping his eyes on Pendergast. Exhaling, he walked over and examined Pendergast, who remained motionless, surrounded by the guards with submachine guns. Fischer reached out with a powerful veined hand, caressed Pendergast's ersatz beard, then grasped it and tore it off. He circled Pendergast lazily, his smile growing.

And with that he extended his hand. For a moment, it seemed he might be offering to shake hands, but that turned out to be wrong: Fischer raised his massive palm and, with great force, slapped Pendergast across the face so hard it knocked him to the ground.

"Get those things out of his mouth," he ordered.

The soldiers kept their weapons trained on Pendergast while one of their number jammed the barrel of a Luger into the FBI agent's mouth, keeping it open while his fingers explored. A moment later he held his hand out to show Fischer what he'd discovered. In his palm lay some tiny lock-picking tools, several plastic theatrical cheek pieces used for altering one's appearance—and a small, glass ampoule filled with a clear liquid.

The soldier hauled Pendergast roughly back to his feet. Blood leaked from his nose. His eyes were the color of white paper.

"Now it is certain," the man said, staring at him. "It is indeed our Agent Pendergast. How good of you to make the long journey to us. My name is Wulf Konrad Fischer. I am the man who abducted your wife."

Another smile.

When Pendergast did not speak, Fischer went on. "I must say, your disguise was very good. I knew that a man like you would come looking for me—for *us*. And I assumed that, with your extraordinary abilities, you would eventually find me. What I didn't expect was your disguise. I had assumed you would sneak in and blend with the locals, or skulk in the forest. I didn't believe you would waltz in here, bold as brass. Your disguise was good, all that *Scheiße* about the Queen Beatrice. Very well done, the more so for being true. I commend you."

He inhaled on the cigarette, holding it vertical to prevent the ever-lengthening ash from falling.

"Where you slipped up was that little stunt with Egon. You see, Egon grew up in the forest; he knows the forest. For you to give him the slip—when I heard about that, I knew you were no naturalist."

Pendergast remained motionless.

"My colleagues and I were, shall we say, impressed by what you did on the *Vergeltung*. Of course, it was a great shock to learn that Helen Esterhazy was still alive. Although we very badly wanted to study her in vivo, you forced us to trim that loose end in a rather crude way. Still, we were at least able to perform a most revealing autopsy on her remains, which we quickly found in the makeshift grave you dug for her."

At this, there might have been a slight twitch beneath one of Pendergast's eyes.

"Oh, yes. We never allow a research opportunity to pass. We are scientists, first and foremost. For example, your spectacular and unexpected entry into our program—the *Vergeltung* again, and then your subsequent pursuit of Helen—was rather alarming. But, being scientists, we were able to adapt. We very quickly revised our plans so as to incorporate *you* into the final phase of our great work down here. We saw an opportunity and took it. And so: I thank you for your participation."

The ash had not yet fallen from the vertical cigarette. Fischer tilted it horizontally; the ash broke off, and then he took a moment to gently grind the butt into a chased-silver ashtray.

With a slender hand he picked up the tiny ampoule from where it had been placed on the desk along with the other things taken from Pendergast. He rolled it pensively between thumb and finger.

"I admire your courage. But you'll find that there was no need for this. On the contrary, we'll spare you the trouble."

He turned to the soldiers. "Take him to Room Four."

65

Room 4 lay in the bowels of the oldest part of the fortress. It was a tunnel-like space of massive basaltic blocks, with a floor of volcanic dirt and an arched ceiling. A single lightbulb hung from a wire. Pendergast was dragged in, prodded toward one wall at gunpoint, then chained hand and foot to a set of enormous iron ring-bolts set into the stonework, his arms and legs spread to nearly maximum extension.

Under the watchful eye of Scheermann, the soldiers made sure the chains were tight. Then, leaving him standing there, chained to the wall, they left the room, turning off the light and shutting behind them the massively thick iron door. A gleam of light briefly shone from a tiny Judas window set into the door, until that too was extinguished, the window shut and blocked.

Blackness reigned.

Pendergast stood in the humid darkness, listening. The soldiers remained outside, and he could hear their movements, the murmur of their voices. Beyond, he could make out nothing beyond a very deep rumble, the humming of large generators, and something else, something even deeper: perhaps the natural movement of magma beneath the not-so-extinct volcano. As if to underscore this, he felt a faint but discernible shuddering of the floor and wall, as if the entire fortress were trembling, ever so slightly, in response to the striking of a giant tuning fork in the earth beneath them.

In the darkness, Pendergast listened. And thought. Thought about what Fischer had said.

An hour passed. And then, Pendergast heard footsteps. There was a scraping noise as a heavy bolt was drawn back. A long cast of light as the door opened. Two figures stood in the doorway, silhouetted. They paused for a moment, side by side, and then separated as they came forward. The bare bulb in the center of the room went on. And standing before Pendergast were Fischer and Alban.

Alban. Alban, free from all disguises, makeup, and deception.

In actual features he looked like Tristram—only stamped into those features was a very different, even diametrically opposite, personality. Alban radiated supreme confidence, an easy charisma, only a trace of arrogance mingling with a sense of amusement. He carried himself with a calm air of discipline, a detachment from the world of sensuality, passion, and intuition.

He was, in many ways, more like Pendergast than Tristram was. Although—to his distress and dismay—Pendergast noticed that Alban had his mother's mouth and eyes. But the longer Pendergast gazed into that pale, angular face, with its high-domed forehead, blue-and-violet eyes, blond hair, and sculptured lips, the more he became aware something was missing. There was a hole, a huge hole, in this person, where his heart should have been.

Only then did Pendergast take in the rest of his son:

the clean, fresh-pressed work shirt and plain canvas trousers of a simple cut, the braided leather belt and sturdy, handmade leather boots. His clothes, curiously, contrasted strongly with the finely cut, expensive gray suit worn by Fischer, with his gold rings, watch, and lighter.

Finally, Fischer spoke. "May I have the pleasure, Agent Pendergast, of formally introducing you to your son Alban?"

Alban stood there, gazing at him. It was impossible to tell what was in those eyes of his, what emotion he might be experiencing, if any; he was so perfectly in control. "Hello again, Father," he said in a deep, pleasant voice, without the rough accent so apparent in Tristram's speech.

Pendergast said nothing.

There was a sharp rap on the door.

"Come in, Berger," Fischer said.

A small, very thin man with a blade-like face entered, carrying an old-fashioned doctor's bag in one hand and a folding table in the other. Behind him—being prodded forward by the butt of a submachine gun—was Egon. His hair was matted and stiff, and his face was white and creased with anxiety. A hunted look was in his eyes.

The guard closed the door, then stood in front of it, weapon at the ready. Fischer waited while Egon was bound to the wall in the same fashion as Pendergast. Then he turned back to the agent.

"You appear to be a man possessed of great scientific curiosity," he said. "In this respect, you are not unlike ourselves. So: Do you have any observations to make? Any questions? Because once we begin there won't be an opportunity for you to speak."

"Where is Tristram?" Pendergast asked. "Is he alive?"

"Tristram? So you have given *der Schwächling* a name. How nice. How domestic of you. If you're referring, as I assume, to Forty-Seven: naturally he's alive. He's carrying all of Alban's spare parts. For that reason, and that reason alone, he's a very important boy. Rest assured he is safely back in the fold. His moment of freedom undomesticated him somewhat, but he's been retamed and is now doing just fine." Fischer paused. "Actually, his kidnapping and return served three purposes. It brought him back to us, a future donor bank for Alban. We also knew that his kidnapping would draw you, like a moth to a flame. And at the same time, successfully spiriting Forty-Seven out from your own house, from under your own guardianship, would be a fitting end to the final phase of our work. Such admirable economy of action! How might you put that in English: killing three birds with one stone?"

"The final phase of your work," Pendergast said in a toneless voice. "You used that phrase earlier. I assume you refer to what you call the beta test?"

For a brief moment, Fischer seemed surprised. Then he smiled. "Excellent, excellent. Yes, I was referring to our beta test."

"What is it, exactly?"

"Surely you can guess the answer to that already. For more than half a century, we've been following in the footsteps of Doctors Mengele and Faust, continuing their great work on twins."

"Work that was started on helpless victims, held in concentration camps," Pendergast said.

"Work that began during the course of that unfortunate war, which we later carried here to Brazil. Work that is now complete—thanks in part to you."

"And the scientific principles involved?" Pendergast asked, coolly.

Fischer put a finger to his chin. "Simple in theory, exceedingly difficult in practice. Following conception, after the first mitosis, the two daughter cells are separated and begin to develop independently, creating the path toward identical twins. When the two embryos reach the morula stage, the really delicate work begins. We initiate a process of transferring genetic material between the embryos. In the good embryo, we augment the genetic material with the very best from the other embryo, swapping out the inferior stuff, which goes in turn into the bad embryo."

"But if they are identical twins," asked Pendergast, "how is there any difference between the two embryos?"

A smile illuminated Fischer's fine features. "Ah, Mr. Pendergast, you have precisely identified the central question our scientists have struggled with for years. The answer is this: The human genome carries three billion base pairs. Even among identical twins there are errors: bad copies, reversed sequences, and so forth. We augment that variation by slightly irradiating the unfertilized egg and sperm before union. Not so much as to create a freak; just enough to give us the variation we must have to swap genes. So instead of mixing and matching genes randomly, as nature does so crudely, we can build a man or woman according to careful specifications."

"And the 'bad' embryo?"

"Nothing is wasted. The bad twin develops into a baby as well. Your, ah, *Tristram* is a perfect example." Fischer chuckled. "He or she is raised for menial labor in the camps and fields, a useful and fulfilled member of society. *Arbeit macht frei*. And of course this bad twin, *der Schwächling*, is an excellent repository of organs and blood in case the good twin is damaged or requires a transplant. Naturally, these are isograft transplants, the most perfect kind, which cannot be rejected." He paused to light another cigarette. "The painstaking research, the refinement of the procedure, the perfection of the result—you can imagine it took years, *decades*, of careful work. It took many, many iterations, each one slightly better than the last."

"Iterations," Pendergast said. "In other words, sets of twins, intermediate steps in the process, that weren't yet up to your exacting specifications. Human beings to be liquidated."

"Not at all. You can see them every day in our village, living out useful and productive lives."

"You can also see their doppelgängers in your underground concentration camp."

Fischer cocked an eyebrow. "My, my, you were busy last night."

"And Alban? I assume he is the acme, the pinnacle, of your work?"

Fischer could hardly disguise his pride. "Indeed he is."

"Which means he himself is the beta test." Pendergast answered his own question.

"Yes. Dr. Faust volunteered his own family—a true man of science. The Faust-Esterhazy line proved exceedingly rich. But I must say the Pendergast line proved even richer. The union between you and Helen, accidental though it was, produced a most remarkable product. *Most* remarkable, exceeding all our expectations." Fischer shook his head. "We had allowed her parents to move to America and live there freely, raising their children. It was an early experiment to see how our subjects might function in outside society. It was a catastrophic failure. When Helen grew up, she went rogue on us. Her body had already been prepared to always bear twins—that was easy. When she accidentally got pregnant, she was forced to return here. Otherwise her fetuses would have died, without certain special treatments necessary for her to carry them to term. But she returned to Brazil more than eight weeks' pregnant, too late for the blastocyst cell treatment we'd developed here at Nova Godói. This forced us to try something new—a tricky and highly experimental technique of shifting genetic material between more developed fetuses. You'll appreciate this irony, Herr Pendergast, but it was the very lateness that led to our crowning success. We had always believed the genetic work had to be done early, no later than the first few weeks. And yet the delayed work on Helen's twins proved to be our breakthrough." Fischer paused. "Helen could never accept the fact that we would not let her take her children back to America. We had to keep them, of course. Even at such an early age, Alban was so promising."

Throughout this back-and-forth, Alban had been listening, a neutral expression on his face.

"This is your mother he's talking about," Pendergast said. "Doesn't that trouble you in the least?"

"Trouble?" Alban said. "On the contrary, what I feel is pride. Look at how easy it was to learn the location of your Central Park meeting place—from an employee of New York's own police department, no less!—and how quickly our people put a plan into effect."

This was followed by a brief pause.

"And Longitude Pharmaceuticals?" Pendergast asked. "What of them?"

"Merely one of many satellite operations loosely affiliated with our work," Fischer answered. "Our research was subtle, complex, and wide ranging; we had to draw from many sources. They are usually kept at arm's length—but when accidents occur, as they did at Longitude, certain unfortunate steps must be taken." Fischer shook his head.

"You mentioned that I was at least partly responsible for the successful conclusion of your work," Pendergast said. "That you incorporated me into its final phase. What precisely did you mean by that?"

"My dear Agent Pendergast, surely you must have guessed that by now. I've already referred to it: your attack on the *Vergeltung*, your dogged pursuit of Helen and us, her kidnappers. We had another final beta test for Alban in mind—but when you blundered into the picture, we turned what could have been a setback into an opportunity. We completely changed the parameters of the test—rather hastily, I might add. We decided to set Alban free in New York City. To prove that he could kill with impunity, even while revealing his identity to the security cameras. Leaving clues convincing you that the murderer was, in fact, your own son. That knowledge would give you, ah, sufficient motivation to catch him—don't you think? If the greatest and most intrepid detective, given every opportunity, cannot catch his own murderous son—wouldn't you say our beta test was a success? A complete, unmitigated success?"

Pendergast did not reply.

"And then Forty-Seven escaped and blundered his way to you. Once again, we turned misfortune to our advantage. We altered Alban's final mission. Instead of a fifth murder, he would kidnap Forty-Seven from *your own house*. A mission he executed flawlessly." Fischer turned to Alban. "Well done, my boy."

Alban nodded his acceptance of the praise.

"So now you've perfected your work on twins," Pendergast said. "You can produce a pair of them at will—one, a perfect killing machine, strong and intelligent and fearless and cunning. And, most important, perfectly free of any kind of moral or ethical constraint."

Fischer nodded. "Such *constraints*, as you put it, lost us the war, you know."

"And then you have the other twin, as weak as his sibling is strong, as lacking in natural ability as his counterpart is overflowing with it: slave labor and, if necessary, an unwilling organ bank. And so, having perfected this process, this ability to manufacture these diabolically perfect human beings—now that it's done, what are you going to do?"

"What are we going to do?" Fischer seemed taken aback by the question. "But surely that is obvious? The thing we have vowed—that we have *sworn*—to do ever since your armed forces stormed our cities, killed our leader, scattered our Reich to the four winds. Why would you think that our goal, Herr Pendergast, has varied one whit from that which it has always been? The only difference is, now—after seventy years of endless work—we are ready to set about achieving that goal. The final beta test is complete. We may now begin— what is the term you use?—the *roll-out*."

He dropped the cigarette to the dirt floor, ground it beneath his boot. "But this begins to grow tiresome." He turned to the man named Berger.

"You may proceed," he said.

66

BERGER—WHO HAD BEEN CHAIN-SMOKING throughout the conversation—now nodded almost primly. He set the folding table in place, placed the medical bag on it, opened it, and rummaged around inside. A moment later he removed a hypodermic syringe—a thick glass tube surrounded by a sheath of gleaming steel, with a long and cruel-looking needle attached. Bringing out a rubber-stoppered pharmaceutical vial containing a reddish liquid, he pushed the needle into it and then—carefully, without hurry—drew back the plunger until the hypo was nearly three-quarters full. He squeezed off a few drops of the liquid. Then he turned and approached Egon, syringe extended.

Throughout the conversation, Egon had been looking floorward, dangling from his manacles, like an animal resigned to his fate. But now, seeing Berger approach, he suddenly became animated. "*Nein!*" he shouted, struggling wildly. "*Nein, nein, nein, nein—!*"

Fischer shook his head in disapproval, then glanced over at Pendergast. "Egon failed to follow his explicit instructions: remain with you at all times. We see no point in rewarding failure here, Herr Pendergast."

Berger nodded to the guard. Putting his weapon to one side, the man came forward, grasped the luckless Egon's hair in one hand and his chin in the other, brutally forcing his head back. Berger approached, needle extended. He used it to gently probe various spots in the soft flesh beneath Egon's chin. Then, choosing one, he forced the needle—slowly, precisely—up into Egon's soft palate, inserting it right up to the needle hub. He depressed the plunger.

Egon's struggles grew hysterical. He screamed—or, rather, made a frightful gargling sound between his clenched teeth, as the guard kept his head locked.

Then—quite quickly—both Berger and the guard drew back. Egon slumped forward, panting, whimpering. Then his whole body stiffened. Veins began to stand out on his neck, blue and bulging. The network of veins quickly spread, like rivers finding new courses through fresh ground. They spread up to his face, down to his forearms, throbbing visibly. Egon began bucking against the restraints, making a strange *grrrrrr, grrrrrrr* sound. His spasms grew more violent, his face increasingly purple—until, with a violent eruption of blood from his nose, ears, and mouth, he collapsed, sagging against the restraints.

It was the most dreadful of executions.

With oddly fastidious motions, Berger returned the hypodermic and vial to his bag. Fischer had not even bothered to watch the proceedings. Alban had looked on, however, a glimmer of interest kindling in his blue-and-violet eyes.

Fischer turned back to Pendergast. "As I said, we were impressed by what you did on the *Vergeltung*. However, in the course of the proceedings, you caused us to lose many good men. Now that the beta test is complete, you are no longer necessary. In fact, you are a random element that needs to be removed. But before Berger continues with his work, you perhaps have a final observation, or a final question?"

Pendergast remained motionless, bound to the wall by the heavy chains. "I have something to say to Alban."

Fischer extended his hand in an offering gesture, as if to say, *Be my guest*.

Pendergast turned to Alban. "I am your father." It was a simple statement, spoken slowly, but pregnant with meaning. "And Helen Esterhazy Pendergast was your mother." He nodded toward Fischer. "Murdered by *this man*."

There was a long silence. And then Fischer turned to Alban, speaking in a condescending, almost fatherly tone. "Alban, do you have anything to say to that? Now would be an appropriate time."

"Father," Alban said, turning his eyes to Pendergast and speaking in a high, clear voice, "are you trying to provoke some sort of parochial family feeling? You and Helen Esterhazy merely donated sperm and egg. I was *created* by others."

"While your twin, your brother, is a slave laboring in the fields?"

"He's a productive member of society. I am happy for him. Everyone has his place."

"And so you think you're better than he is."

"Of *course* I'm better. Everyone here is created for his place and knows it from the beginning. This is the ultimate social order. You've seen Nova Godói. There's no crime. We have no depression, no mental illness, no drug addiction—no social problems whatsoever."

"Supported by a camp of slave laborers."

"You speak from ignorance. They have a purpose. They have all they need or want—except, of course, we can't let them reproduce. Some people *are* simply better than others."

"And you, being the best of all, are an Übermensch. The final, the ultimate Nazi ideal."

"I accept the label proudly. The Übermensch is the ideal human being, creative and strong, beyond the petty considerations of good and evil."

"Thank you, Alban," said Fischer. "That was most eloquent."

"The Übermensch," Pendergast repeated. "Tell me: what is the *Kopenhagener Fenster*? The Copenhagen Window?"

Alban and Fischer exchanged glances, obviously surprised and, perhaps, alarmed by the question. However, both men quickly mastered themselves.

"It is something you shall go to your grave in ignorance of," Fischer replied briskly. "And now, *auf Wiedersehen*."

A silence fell in the room. Pendergast's face was the color of marble. Slowly, his head drooped, and his shoulders sagged—a picture of despair and resignation.

Fischer regarded his captive for a moment. "It was a pleasure to meet you, Herr Pendergast."

Pendergast did not look up.

Fischer nodded to Berger and began walking toward the door of the cell. After a moment, Alban turned as well to follow him.

At the door, Fischer stopped, glanced back at Alban. A look of mild surprise came over his face. "I would have thought you'd like to witness this," he said.

"It makes no difference," Alban replied. "I have better things to do."

Fischer hesitated for a moment. Then he shrugged and exited the room, followed by Alban. The door clanged shut heavily behind them and the guard stepped over to take up position before it, submachine gun at the ready.

67

THERE WAS A BRIEF CHATTER OUTSIDE. THEN the door opened again. Three more guards came in: two bearing various chains and manacles, and another with an acetylene torch. Berger looked around. Now there were seven in the room: the four soldiers, himself, the prisoner—and the dead body of Egon.

Berger glanced at the corpse, its face still frozen in a ridiculous expression of agony, limbs stiff and angular, tongue protruding, thick as a kielbasa, streams of blood running down from the ears, nose, and mouth. He turned to the soldier on guard duty. "Get that out of the way," he ordered.

The soldier walked over and unshackled the iron clasps from Egon's wrists and ankles. Freed of the restraints, the corpse collapsed heavily to the ground. The soldier reached down, seized one raised claw, and hauled the body to a corner of the chamber, kicking it up against the wall.

Berger nodded at the prisoner named Pendergast, shackled to the wall. "Soften him up a bit," he told the soldier in German.

The soldier gave a slow, cruel smile. He approached

Pendergast—his arms and legs pinned to the stone wall—and over the course of several minutes administered a dozen vicious, methodical, well-placed blows to the face and, especially, the abdomen. Pendergast writhed against his restraints, and grunted with pain, but made no other sound.

At last, Berger nodded his approval. "Cover him," he said. The guard, breathing heavily, stepped back, picked up his submachine gun, and returned to his position near the door.

Following Berger's orders, the other three soldiers now approached. They freed Pendergast from the wall clasps, and the man fell to the ground. While the soldier with the machine gun kept a careful eye, two of the guards dragged Pendergast back to his feet, then fitted him with wrist manacles, a belly band, and leg hobbles consisting of two ankle cuffs. These were all welded in place by the guard wielding the acetylene torch. Finally, two six-foot iron chains were threaded from the manacles to the foot hobbles. When the restraints were all in place and the welds completed, the men glanced at Berger for further instructions.

"You may go," Berger told them.

The three turned toward the door.

"Just a minute," Berger said. "Leave the torch. I have a use for that."

The third guard placed the rucksack containing the acetylene torch and its two canisters on the floor. Then they left. The soldier with the submachine gun closed the door, then took up his position before it.

Berger pulled a short, metal-tipped quirt from his bag, then took a moment to observe the prisoner, take his measure. He was tall and thin, and clearly weak, his arms weighed down by the chains. His head hung down listlessly, his blond hair limp, blood streaming from his nose and mouth. His skin was gray and translucent, his spirit clearly broken. No matter: Berger would make him lively before the end—very lively.

"Before we begin," he said, "there's something you need to know. I was chosen for this task because you killed my brother on the *Vergeltung*. In our society, victims are always given the satisfaction of carrying out justice on the perpetrator. It is my right, and my duty, to punish you, and I accept the challenge with gratitude." He nodded at the body of Egon, crumpled up in a far corner like an oversize spider. "You will wish for a death as pleasant as his."

The man didn't seem to hear him, which raised Berger's anger a notch.

"Bring him forward," he told the soldier.

The soldier, propping his Sturmgewehr 44 rifle against the wall, approached Pendergast and pushed him roughly toward Berger. Then he moved back toward the door, picked up his rifle again, and resumed guarding the prisoner.

"Pendergast," said Berger, tapping Pendergast's chest with the quirt. "Look at me."

The bedraggled man raised his head. His eyes focused on Berger.

"First, you dig your grave. Then, you will suffer. And finally, you will be buried in it, perhaps alive, perhaps not. I haven't quite decided yet."

No sign of comprehension.

"Get that pick and shovel." Berger gestured toward the corner of the room.

The soldier underscored the order with a wave of his gun. "*Beweg Dich!*" he barked.

Slowly, the prisoner shuffled toward the far corner, the hobbles clanking awkwardly, the chains dragging.

"Dig here." Berger took his heel and scraped it along the floor, outlining a crude rectangle in the volcanic dirt. "Hurry! *Spute Dich!*"

As Pendergast began digging, Berger kept a safe distance, well beyond the swinging range of the tools. He watched the man lift the pick and bring it down painfully into the dirt, again and again, until he had broken up the top layer. He labored awkwardly, heavily encumbered with steel, and the short length of the chains greatly restricted the movement of his arms. When he slowed, Berger stepped forward and gave him a few brisk lashes with the quirt for motivation. Gasping with effort, the prisoner switched to the shovel and removed the loose dirt. At one point he laid the shovel down and mumbled that he needed to rest; Berger responded to that request with a kick that sent the man sprawling. That woke him up a bit.

"No stopping," Berger said.

The grave made slow progress. The prisoner worked doggedly, chains rattling against the cuffs, his face a mask of mental apathy and physical exhaustion. Here, thought Berger, was a man who knew he had failed; a man who wanted nothing more than to die. And die he would.

An hour dragged by, and finally Berger's impatience got the better of him. "Enough!" he cried. "*Schluss jetzt!*" The grave was only two and a half feet deep, but Berger had grown eager to move on to the next stage. The prisoner stood there, at the edge of the grave, waiting. Turning to the soldier, Berger said in German: "Cover me while I work on him. Take no risks. If anything happens, shoot him."

The soldier took a few steps forward, raising his weapon.

"Drop the shovel," Berger ordered.

The prisoner dropped the shovel and stood there, arms at his sides, head drooping, waiting for the end. Berger advanced on him, picked up the shovel, and—bracing himself—swung it against the prisoner's side. With a *thwack* the prisoner dropped to his knees, a look of pained surprise on his face. Placing the flat of his foot on the prisoner's chest, Berger gave him a push that sent him sprawling backward into the grave. Making sure the guard had a good bead on the prisoner, Berger stepped over and picked up the rucksack containing the torch and its heavy acetylene tanks. Holding its nozzle up like a candle, he snapped the torch on. It popped into life, an intense white light that filled the cell with harsh shadows.

"Ich werde Dich bei lebendigem Leib verbrennen," he said, leering at Pendergast and gesturing meaningfully with the torch.

He stepped back to the grave and looked down. The prisoner lay there, eyes widening in fear. He tried to sit up, but Berger planted his foot on the prisoner's chest again and stepped down, pushing him back. Keeping pressure on the foot, he leaned in and brought the needle-like flame toward the prisoner's face. It cast a ghastly light, turning the prisoner's eyes into gleaming points of fire. Closer and closer grew the flame. The prisoner struggled, trying to turn his face aside, first one way and then the other, but Berger pressed relentlessly with his foot, holding him in place, while the very edge of the flame began to sear the prisoner's cheek. Now he could see a gratifying terror fill the prisoner's eyes as the flame blistered the skin—

An extremely rapid and forceful—but slight—movement occurred; suddenly the prisoner seemed to contort himself in the strangest way, accompanied by a grinding *pop* of dislocating bone and sinew. Berger, starting back in surprise, saw, suddenly, the prisoner's hand rise. He felt the nozzle twitched out of his grasp, and an instant later a brilliant white light filled his field of vision. He pulled back, crying out, and was astonished to feel the cold bite of steel around the back of his neck, one of the prisoner's chains looping around and pulling him forward into the white light, closer and closer. It seemed to last forever—and yet it could have taken no longer than a second or two. The hissing spear of white drove like a needle into his mouth, nose, and then eyes; there was a sudden boiling and a soft, bubbly explosion, followed by pain to end all pain; and then all dissolved into white, white heat.

Pendergast fell back into the makeshift grave, yanking Berger's body on top of his own, using the hole and the body as cover while the soldier—having recovered from his surprise at this unexpected development—fired, the bullets kicking up dirt all along the rim of the grave. The depth was shallower than Pendergast would have liked, but it was enough. Still covered by Berger, he directed the needle flame of the torch to the chain that attached his left wrist to the steel belly band, slicing it away not at the wrist but at the band, leaving six feet of loose chain attached to his wrist. Bullets nicked and whined around him, several thudding into Berger's body with a sound like a hand slapping meat. With a sudden cry, Pendergast rose from the grave, flinging aside the body and swinging his arm around, wielding the now-free chain like a whip. It swung in an arc toward the ceiling, shattering the bulb.

As the room was plunged into darkness, he came forward, avoiding the soldier's panicked fire by staying low and moving in an arc diagonally and very fast. Meanwhile, he gave the chain another massive swing, wrapping it around the soldier's Sturmgewehr and wrenching it out of his hands, into his own. A single burst of the weapon dropped the soldier. Pendergast dove back into the grave just as the door burst open and the guard detail outside came pouring in, sweeping the room with fire. He waited until he was sure they were all within the room, and then—lying flat on his back in the makeshift grave—he raised the Sturmgewehr and raked them all with the weapon on full auto, emptying the massive box magazine in less than three seconds.

Suddenly all was silent.

Scrambling back out of the grave, Pendergast dropped the weapon and walked to the closest wall, stepping over still-twitching bodies. He took a deep breath, then another. And then, with all his strength, he slammed his shoulder against the wall, resetting the joint he had been forced to dislocate in order to get enough extra play with the chain to strangle Berger with it. Wincing at the pain, he waited until he was sure the shoulder was set properly and could be moved. He then grabbed the acetylene torch, switched it on, and used it to slice off his leg irons, belly band, and wrist cuffs, in his haste setting afire his shirt, which he pulled off while it was still burning. Throwing the rucksack containing the torch and tanks over his good shoulder, he looted a handgun, knife, lighter, wristwatch, flashlight, and a couple of box magazines from the corpses, scooped up the pick he'd used to dig the grave, grabbed the least bloody shirt he could find from one of the dead guards, and then charged out the door and sprinted down the tunnel beyond.

As he ran, slipping his arms into the shirt, he could already hear the commotion of shouted voices and the pounding of soldiers' boots echoing through the stone bowels of the old fortress.

68

COLONEL SOUZA AND HIS HANDPICKED FORCE of thirty men moved through the dense evergreen forests east of Nova Godói. He could see, through the breaks in the trees, the looming hills that marked the volcanic crater within which the town was located. He stopped to consult his GPS and observed, with satisfaction, that they were only a mile from the previously determined reconnoitering point on the crater rim.

All had gone according to plan. Their approach had been unobserved. The eastern forests were the densest and hilliest in the area. The lack of trails and any signs of hunting indicated this was, as hoped, a place not frequented by the residents of the town.

While thirty soldiers was a great many less than Pendergast had asked for, Souza had carefully considered the pros and cons of going in with a much larger force of less trained soldiers versus one of highly trained, fit commandos cherry-picked from his former group. He had settled on this as the perfect number. A lightning-fast commando-style assault was what the colonel had spent his earlier life training for, what he knew how to do—and what was more, it was clearly appropriate in this situation, against a limited force of fanatics. The men he had picked were proficient with their weapons, boasting exceptional tactical training and psychological preparation. His own son, Thiago, a superbly built, loyal, and intelligent young man, was acting as his aide-de-camp. Tactics were key; surprise was essential; to hit hard and fast the way to go.

The colonel smiled, thinking how the Internet had told them everything they needed to know. It was something he had never even considered until Pendergast had brought him detailed maps of the town and surrounding terrain, all created from Google Earth and overlaid onto standard topographic maps obtained from the Serviço Geológico do Brasil. These Americans with their technological ingenuity! The only essential information remaining was the internal layout of the fortress—and the actual numbers of men-at-arms in the enemy camp.

He felt sure Pendergast—with his clever plan of allowing himself to be captured—would obtain that information for him. The more time he had spent with the strange, pale gringo, the more impressed he had been. Of course, escaping from the Nazis was no sure thing—especially for a lone man. On the other hand, a lone man might well be the perfect strategy. Pendergast seemed to think so—he'd been willing to stake his life upon it.

The colonel's soldiers moved through the dripping forest in complete silence, shadows among the trees. The ground rose as they ascended the forested rim of the crater. At a certain point, Souza gestured for the soldiers to remain back while he went ahead with Thiago, his ADC. They were exactly on schedule, and he hoped Pendergast—given the unknown variables he would have to face—would be similarly efficient. Souza motioned for his squad to come forward. Moving with great caution, they came to an outcropping of rock. A convenient break in the trees afforded them a view of the village, lake, and island fortress.

The town lay below them, about a mile off, a half-moon of white and yellow stucco buildings with slate roofs arranged along the shores of the lake. Off to one side lay a large expanse of cultivated fields. The fortress itself sat half a mile offshore, to their northeast. It was built on a low cinder cone in the center of the lake, the lower ramparts of stone, with poured concrete forming the modern inner superstructure. This first glance gave the colonel a bad moment. A lot depended on the gringo.

Glassing the position of the fortress, he identified a shallow cove on the back side: an ideal place to land his forces, separated from the fortress by a ridge, protected and hidden. He examined it with minute care, memorizing every detail.

He consulted his watch. Fifteen minutes before the scheduled signal. He snugged himself down to wait in the shelter of the rocks and brush.

"Let the men have tea," he told his son. A moment later he and his men were enjoying hot thermoses of sweetened black tea with milk. The colonel sipped as he waited, occasionally gazing at the fortress with his binoculars. The sun was in just the right position—that had been carefully planned—and fortunately was not obscured by clouds. The weather reports were holding up nicely.

The tea tasted marvelous, and he enjoyed it slowly, taking the opportunity to light up a cheroot as well. He puffed at it reflectively. He had had his doubts about this mission, but those were behind him now. He had, he knew, two traits that were perhaps not always desirable in a public official: absolute integrity, with a hatred of bribes and corruption—and an instinct for finding his own solution to a problem, even if it meant operating well outside standard procedure. Both of these had seriously hurt his career, eventually landing him back— as Pendergast had so shrewdly observed—in Alsdorf. But Souza was now convinced that the only way to stop the murders in the town he'd sworn to protect, to lance the boil that was Nova Godói, was through extraordinary action. Pendergast, he sensed, was also one comfortable operating outside accepted practice. They had that much in common. Whatever the outcome, they were committed now. There was no longer any time for second-guessing—only for action.

Finally the moment came and he began to scrutinize the fortress steadily with the binoculars. And there it was: flashes of sunlight off a mirror. Pendergast had penetrated the fort according to plan.

The colonel felt an enormous sense of relief—not because he had doubted Pendergast's abilities, but because he knew, from his days with BOPE, that no matter how well one planned an operation, there were an unlimited number of ways it could go wrong.

The flashed message, in standard Morse code, was a long one. Very long. Grinding out the cheroot upon the rocky outcropping, Souza wrote everything down in his field notebook, word after word: a description of the fortress, a general layout of its passageways and tunnels, its strong and weak points, the size of the defending force, their weapons loadout—everything.

It was all good. Except for the fact that the defending forces, as best Pendergast could make out from his preliminary reconnaissance, numbered well over a hundred. That was considerably more than the colonel had assumed. Still, they would have the advantage of surprise. And according to Pendergast's information, they would have a clean line of attack, where the fortress's straightened quarters, passageways, and tunnels would minimize the defenders' advantage in numbers.

He sent Thiago back down to the group, and soon his men were moving down from the rim, spreading out, surrounding the town in preparation for a three-pronged assault—stage one of the attack.

69

SEEING THE DISTANT MIRROR FLASH OUT OF the green canopy of the forest, Pendergast knew that the colonel had received his message. Discarding the shard of mirror he'd appropriated from a barracks lavatory, he crept down from the ruined gun port halfway up the battlements of the old fortress. His reconnoiter had by necessity been incomplete, but he had nevertheless been able to identify the main ingress points, the defensive ramparts, the basic layout. What he needed to find now was the weakest, most vulnerable section of ancient curtain wall. The original plan he'd discussed with the colonel had been to find the fort's ammunitions cache, or central armory, and blow it up, opening a hole in the castle's outer wall; but he had been unable to do so. There were simply too many soldiers, swarming about like bees in an angry hive, for him to locate it.

No matter. He had the next best thing to an ammo dump in the small backpack slung over his shoulder: a brace of oxyacetylene tanks, nearly full.

Moving down an old spiral staircase, he paused to listen. The immense size of the fortress and its echoing passageways had proven a godsend, broadcasting the stomp of approaching boots. Indeed, Pendergast had been surprised at the blundering nature of the troops involved in the fortress's defense, their reactive thinking, their lack of strategy. It was the one detail that didn't feel quite right to him.

Still, he intended to take advantage of it as long as he could.

Moving still deeper into the older levels of the fortress, he found a tunnel that ran along the inside of the outer perimeter wall. He moved along it, briefly shining the flashlight on the masonry, testing the joints with the point of the purloined knife. The mortar was as rotten as wet soil, but the blocks here were well dressed and fitted together too tightly to be shifted. In some areas there were cracks in the masonry, but they were too small to be serviceable, and the masonry too stable for his purposes.

As he descended to the next level, pausing to listen from time to time, he passed a series of locked, stainless-steel doors set into the inner wall, relatively new doors retrofitted to what had probably once been the dungeons of the fortress, now apparently converted into laboratories. Several of the steel doors were wide open, lights still burning within the labs, giving every impression of having been hurriedly abandoned by the working scientists—perhaps at the sound of gunfire.

Just beyond the series of doors, he found what he was looking for. In the outer foundation wall, a series of large cracks ran upward in a broad radial pattern, with dislocated blocks along their margins. In some places, the cracks were as much as eight to twelve inches broad. The stone floor was similarly cracked. Most interesting. This cracking was not caused by the normal settling of the ground. Just the opposite. Rather, the radial pattern of the cracks implied that a resurgence of the volcano's caldera floor was taking place—creating massive

points of instability that seemed to run right through
the base of the twenty-foot-thick curtain wall.

Working fast with the knife, Pendergast first carved
away the rotten masonry around a displaced block along
the edge of the largest crack, then pried it loose with the
point of the pick. By working the block back and forth,
he finally managed to slide it out, leaving a gaping hole.
Reaching in, he was gratified to find that the interior
of the massive wall was traditional eighteenth-century
Spanish rubble-core construction, in which dressed
stone was used for the facing of the exposed walls, with
the large space between filled with loose stones and
dirt. Alternating with the knife and the pick, he managed to hollow out a cavity in the rubble large enough
to fit the twin cylinders of oxygen and acetylene. Carefully inserting them into place, he checked the wristwatch he had appropriated from one of the guards. If
all was going according to schedule, Souza's men would
at this moment be starting to invade the town, preparing to commandeer boats for the assault on the fortress
itself. According to the time line they had prepared, in
approximately twenty to thirty minutes several boats
would land at the island docks, making a diversionary
feint, while the boats filled with the main group of Souza's soldiers would meanwhile be landing in the cove
behind the fortress.

He therefore had fifteen minutes to wait. Now
would be a good time to examine the laboratories he
had passed earlier.

The first lab he came to was locked with a primitive
World War II–era mechanism that resisted the minis-
trations of his knifepoint for only a moment. He found
himself in a laboratory, not advanced by modern stan-
dards, but adequate for its purpose: the dissection and
autopsying of human remains.

But as he examined the space more closely, shining the flashlight around, he noted a small but telling difference between this room and a standard pathology lab, such as might be found in the basement of a hospital. No pathology lab he had ever seen required straps, cuffs, and other restraining devices.

It became clear to Pendergast that this lab was not for dissection; it was for vivisection.

Moving out of the room, Pendergast continued down the hall, shining his light into the open doors or the window insets of the closed ones. Most showed evidence of recent, active use. Several had not even been cleaned, with hair, blood, and bits of sawed bone still littering their gurneys. Much dreadful scientific work had been done here—and despite the apparent sudden abandonment, he nevertheless got the impression that a long-extended project had recently reached its culmination.

Something in one of the locked labs caught his attention. He stopped, peering intently through the window. Once again, he was able to defeat the lock in a matter of moments. The beam of his flashlight revealed a swatch of hair lying on a gurney. Other evidence—including dead insect larvae—indicated that the remains that had lain on this gurney had been in a state of decomposition.

Slowly, very slowly, he moved closer, shining his light on the hair. He noted that it had the precise auburn shade of Helen's hair; a color that had always reminded him of wildflower honey. Instinctively, he reached out to touch it—then managed to withdraw his hand before it made contact.

A plastic box stood on an organ table, and he went to it and—after a brief hesitation—removed its cover. Inside he found the remains of Helen's dress, buttons, some personal effects. As he gingerly reached inside and stirred the contents with his fingers, the beam of his light caught a flash of purple. He pushed aside a fragment of cloth to reveal a gold ring, set with a star sapphire.

Pendergast went rigid. For ten minutes, perhaps more, he did not move, simply staring into the box of personal effects. Then he took the ring and placed it in the pocket of his rough prison pants.

Leaving the room as silently as he had entered it, he paused for a minute, listening attentively to the distant drumming of feet, the hoarse bark of shouted commands. Then he quickly returned to the crack in the outer wall and the makeshift oxyacetylene bomb he'd placed within it, glancing at his watch. He was overdue to begin the detonation process.

70

COLONEL SOUZA WAITED WITH HIS MAIN BODY of men, hidden in the heavy forest at the edge of town. He had met with his returning scouts shortly before one PM, and things were exactly as he had hoped. The single road and three trails leading into the town were lightly guarded, but there did not appear to be patrols along the perimeter or elsewhere. The inhabitants did not expect an attack, especially one coming from a random part of the immense forests that encircled the town. They were living with a false sense of security—engendered, no doubt, by their extreme isolation.

The colonel, however, was taking no chances. He had set up a diversionary feint at the road gate, which would occur—he checked his watch—in exactly two minutes. There might be a large body of armed troops garrisoned in the town, ready for action at a moment's notice. One couldn't make assumptions.

His men, in full camouflage, waited in absolute silence. He had divided them into three *batalhões* of ten men each: Red, Blue, and Green, with one man from each squad assigned to the feinting maneuver.

The seconds ticked by. And then he heard it: automatic gunfire, punctuated with the louder, deeper explosions of grenades. The diversion had begun.

He raised his arm in a gesture of readiness as he listened intently to the diversion. There was return fire, but not as much as he expected, and it sounded scattered and disorganized. These Nazis, with their militarism and alleged martial brilliance, appeared to be flat-out unprepared.

Nevertheless, the colonel considered the possibility that they themselves could be made victim of a false display of weakness, lured by overconfidence into a deadly ambush.

The minutes ticked by as the diversion grew in sound, with additional explosions and gunfire issuing from his men, hidden in the forest outside the main gate. The response continued to sound anemic.

He adjusted his radio headset; watched the seconds tick down on his watch; and then abruptly lowered his arm. Instantly his men broke into movement, rushing forward. They burst from the brush at the edge of the clearing and began spreading out into three squads. The outbuildings of the town lay a hundred yards before them, across a muddy road and some garden plots: cheerful buildings with painted wooden shutters, flower boxes, and pitched roofs. His men crossed the road, trampled a vegetable patch. Two girls picking tomatoes dropped their baskets with a shriek and ran.

Souza's *batalhões*, now divided, streamed into the closest streets, the colonel leading the Blue unit and Thiago the Red. The key was a blitzkrieg tactic, racing down the streets with lightning speed and avoiding the kind of bunching that would favor a catastrophic grenade or RPG attack. They had to reach the harbor before any organized resistance could develop—a firefight in these narrow lanes was the last thing he wanted.

The colonel led his unit onward, the few pedestrians they encountered either freezing with surprise or fleeing in terror. As they drove deeper into the town, however, some unorganized gunfire began from house windows, rooftops, and side streets.

"Suppressing fire at will!" the colonel yelled into his headset.

His men began returning fire, shooting down the streets and up at the rooftops, and the scattered fire dropped away.

As they approached the central square and town hall, a more serious resistance developed. A band of young men, hastily armed but not in uniform, came piling into the square, taking position behind some horse-drawn carts. As Souza's three squads emerged into the open area of the plaza, gunfire erupted in front of them and from the intersecting streets.

"Red squad, maintain suppressing fire," the colonel ordered. "Blue, Green, keep moving!"

Thiago's Red *batalhão* took cover and unleashed a savage volley: a portable .50-caliber machine gun that swept the plaza with a murderous barrage, backed up by half a dozen well-placed RPGs. It had the desired effect, scattering and terrorizing the resistance; as soon as the square was clear the Red unit charged across it, following the other two squads into the narrow streets on the far side. Here the streets began sloping down toward the waterfront, and Souza could see vessels tied up along the stone and wooden quays.

He had already selected the two target boats during his binocular reconnaissance from the rim of the crater: a large, steel-hulled motorized barge and a sleek passenger transport vessel. But the incoming gunfire was starting again, not just from the rooftops but also from the harbor, enfilading the long streets leading down to the water. Suddenly a second group of men poured out of a side street along the quay, firing as they came.

"Counterattack!" the colonel cried, but already Thiago's machine gunner had let loose with the .50-caliber, dropping at least half a dozen of their attackers and routing the rest. A grenade went off close by, then another, blowing out a building façade and showering them with glass and masonry.

"Keep going!" the colonel cried, but the men needed no urging; the vanguard of the three squads peppered the streets ahead with small-arms fire and RPGs, the .50-caliber gunner bringing up the rear.

They came out along the broad quay, open from all sides. There was another scattering of fire, and one of the colonel's men grunted and staggered, but this defense was again answered with an overwhelming display of fire from the three squads, deafening in power, the RPGs plucking up targets and sending them sky-high with thunderous roars.

"Board the vessels!" Souza ordered.

The *esquadrões* boarded the two vessels according to their prearranged plan, cutting the hawsers from the bollards. The colonel's two nautical specialists took up positions in the pilothouses and started the engines as the rest of the men assumed defensive positions along the deck. In less than two minutes the boats had moved away from the docks and were heading into the lake, picking up speed, the squads maintaining a vicious suppressing fire aimed at the shore.

"Casualty report!" the colonel barked.

It came in quickly. The company's medic was treating two casualties, small-arms fire, neither one serious. Both men were still more or less in commission.

The colonel watched the shoreline recede with a huge feeling of relief. The operation had gone exactly to plan. If he had come in with a hundred men, they might still be caught up in the streets, with more wounded, more stragglers, and the inevitable idiot taking a wrong turn somewhere, getting lost, and having to be retrieved. They would have required more boats, more logistics, more opportunities for failure.

The sporadic fire from on shore died away as the boats began to move out of range, the heavy barge leading, his men now firing highly accurate rounds, keeping their opponents from regrouping and setting out in vessels in pursuit. The colonel took out a silk handkerchief, removed his helmet, and carefully mopped his face. Phase one was complete, with minimal casualties. With a certain reluctance he turned his attention forward, toward the dark island looming out of the water. He could make out no people, no movement. And as he examined the fortress rising above the black lava cinder cone, his sense of victory faltered somewhat. To his experienced eye it looked impregnable. Everything depended on the gringo. He did not like being dependent on the success of one person, no matter how capable—especially a person that he barely knew.

As he looked around, he found his men also regarding the fortress, their eyes dark and serious. They, too, were thinking his thoughts. The boats were now halfway across the lake, the island growing ever larger, the moment of truth coming closer.

He checked his watch. Again, everything depended on speed and surprise. The approaching boats were visible from the fortress, and no doubt the defenders on the island knew all about the attack in town. They had lost the element of surprise, which he of course knew would happen.

As he considered the situation, he began to reexamine their strategy. The idea of taking extra time to go around the island to assault the fortress from the cove behind was making less and less sense to him. What was it the British admiral, Lord Nelson, once said? "Five minutes make the difference between victory and defeat." And even more *a propósito*: "Never mind the maneuvers; go straight at 'em." The circling of the island would eat up not five but ten or more minutes, and present them with an uncertain shoreline and landing position. But directly ahead lay a beautifully open, empty, and undefended set of docks.

Yet again, he checked his watch. It was time for Pendergast's signal—past time. But there was nothing. And now uneasiness began to take hold of the colonel. It had been a mistake to rely on the man; a bad mistake. If they landed on the island before the signal, they had no hope of penetrating the fortress. It would be an exercise in futility. And returning to the town was no longer an option.

The signal was now five minutes late. And the island loomed ever closer. They were just coming into range of rifle fire. Souza spoke into his headset. "Halt the vessels! Come to a full stop!"

No one questioned the order, although he knew they were all wondering *o que diabos agora*. The barge slowed and stopped, with a quick backing of the engines; the transport, too, rumbled in reverse. The lake was calm, the sky clear. The town behind them smoked with a scattering of fires and dust kicked up from the brief battle. The island ahead remained dark and silent.

As they stood idle in the water, the sense of unease, of the possibility of impending defeat, seemed to spread across the barge. All eyes were on the colonel. He betrayed nothing of his own thoughts, nothing of his doubts. He kept his face studiously neutral, his gaze locked on the island. The boats drifted.

And then: a puff of smoke, followed by a gout of flame. A few seconds later, the sound arrived, a thunderous roar rolling across the water. A large section of the fortress's outer curtain wall came rumbling down from the bottom up, as if in slow motion, the stone blocks collapsing and tumbling down the slope, followed by the cave-in of reinforced concrete from above. A huge plume of dust rose up, leaving a gaping wound in the side of the fort.

Pendergast's signal. It wasn't what the colonel had expected—it was even better. And, it seemed, it had provided their route of entry.

"Full speed ahead!" the colonel cried into his headset. "Head for the docks!"

A shout went up from the men, a rousing cheer that matched the sudden roar of the diesel engines and the forward surge of the two vessels, heading straight for the undefended docks. As the boats closed in, the colonel cried: *"Estão prontos! Ataque!"*

71

FISCHER PUT DOWN THE RADIO AND ROSE AS Alban entered his office. He felt, as usual, a flush of pride as he faced the young man squarely, extending his hand. It was hard to believe that Alban was only fifteen years old. He looked twenty at least, six foot three inches tall, with finely chiseled features, sharp cheekbones, brilliant eyes shining beneath a noble brow, cropped blond hair, Michelangelo lips, white teeth—the face of a god. But most impressive of all was the air he projected: confidence without arrogance, charisma without show, manliness without bluster. One could only imagine what he would be like by the time he reached twenty-one.

Except that now, Fischer felt a small, nagging difficulty.

"You wanted to see mc, Herr Fischer?" Alban asked.

"Yes. I've learned that your father escaped from custody, killing Berger and a slew of guards in the process. And now it appears he's detonated some sort of improvised bomb, blown a hole in our defenses."

As he spoke, he watched Alban's face carefully for any display of incorrect emotion, but could find none.

"How did it happen?" Alban asked.

"*How* is not important, except that this is what results when a fool like Berger encounters a man like your father. Your father, Alban, is a truly formidable man. A pity he isn't on our side." When the boy remained silent, Fischer added, "And now a flotilla of armed Brazilian soldiers are about to land on the island."

"I will fight," said Alban immediately. "I'll defend the—"

Fischer made a small gesture of silence with his hand, instantly obeyed. "It's nothing our special brigade can't handle. In fact, it's already being handled. No, I've asked you here for another reason. I have a task for you. A special task."

Alban's face displayed attention, alertness. The one thing about Alban: it was hard to read his real feelings. Of course, that opacity was an essential part of his training, but still it made Fischer uneasy.

"The beta test is over. It was successful. But I must admit I was surprised that you did not wish to stay and witness your father's death. That shows...perhaps not weakness, but a lack of interest in the—shall we say—*finer* things? Precisely the values we have tried to inculcate in you, that we have raised you to appreciate. I say *lack of interest* because I would hate to think that— after all our careful work—any, shall we say, unmanly feelings played a role in your decision to leave the room. Had you been there, that fool Berger wouldn't have botched his right of vengeance so thoroughly."

"I apologize. I would have thought that, with all those soldiers in addition to Berger, nothing could have gone wrong."

"Something did go wrong—and all the soldiers are dead." Fischer paused to withdraw a cigarette from the silver box on his desk and light it. Alban remained respectfully at attention, his hands behind his back, waiting. Glancing at him again, Fischer couldn't help himself: he felt a surge of almost fatherly feeling for this fine young man. Which made the possibility of weakness all the more intolerable.

"And so now, Alban, your final task is this: I want you to track down your father and kill him. Just so there is no doubt—none—of what you can accomplish."

"Yes, sir," said Alban, without hesitation.

"It seems your father's explosive device has opened a hole in the defensive wall in old sector five, outside the pathology labs. So we know where he was just a few minutes ago. His ultimate aim is no doubt to find and rescue your twin. Finding and killing Herr Pendergast shouldn't be a difficult assignment, given your special abilities."

"I'm ready. I won't fail you."

"Good." He inhaled deeply, exhaled. "Report back to me when you are successful."

A sudden dull, muffled sound of gunfire penetrated the room, punctuated by the larger explosions of grenades and mortars. Fischer could see puzzlement enter Alban's eyes. "Don't concern yourself with that," he said. "They're only foolish locals. They will all soon be dead."

72

ESTÃO PRONTOS!" THE COLONEL CRIED AGAIN as the barge closed in on the dock, his men lining up along the port rail, weapons at the ready. The transport boat came sliding in behind, both engines roaring into reverse, the prop wash boiling out.

The boats contacted the fenders along the dock simultaneously, a perfect landing.

"Jump!"

The men charged out, leaping almost as one to the wooden planking, the second row readying themselves...

...A moment later, as soon as the docks were crowded with men, an enormous, shuddering explosion went off underneath. Fingers of fire thrust through the wooden planking, which heaved up and atomized instantly, engulfing the men. The colonel was blasted physically backward into the water. The side of the barge lifted up under the explosion, the metal-clad railing taking the brunt of the blast.

The shock of the water brought the colonel back to consciousness, his ears ringing, hair singed, uniform ripped. It all seemed so strange to him at first, returning as if from a long journey—and then he found himself in a boiling, watery mass of struggling men, the barge listing heavily to one side, the dock burning furiously, men screaming, body parts and blood everywhere.

Regaining his wits, he looked around and saw that the transport ship had been hit simultaneously. It, too, was listing heavily to one side, surrounded by dead and injured men.

The docks had been mined. Booby-trapped. And they had driven right into it.

He gasped, struggling in the water, but even as he tried to collect his wits, to think of a plan of action, he could hear automatic weapons fire from the shore and see gouts of water popping up all around. A deafening roar went off nearby, sending up a fresh plume of spray, and then another, with the rattle of gunfire continuing. The second stage of a devastating ambush.

Just beyond the docks, along the shore to the right, he saw some large boulders—potential cover. If they could only reach them...

"Men!" he screamed as he thrashed. "*Men!* Keep your weapons and dive! Dive! Move east toward the rocks! Stay underwater!"

He repeated the cry and then dove himself, swimming long and hard. This was an exercise they had undertaken in his BOPE days: an underwater swim with weapons.

He had to come up once, and then again, gulping air and plunging back down—each time to a peppering of fire. With his eyes open he could see the zipping of rounds through the water, leaving traceries of bubbles—but bullets, he knew, lost most of their deadly momentum after only twelve to fourteen inches of water.

Swimming hard, his lungs almost bursting, he

peered up and ahead through the green water. He could make out the murky outline of boulders: the underwater portion of the shoreline cover he was aiming for. He surfaced in the right spot, under the boulders, sheltered from the murderous fire pouring down from the direction of the fortress. Incredibly enough, other men—half a dozen at least, including Thiago, *graças a deus*—were surfacing around him, hauling themselves out. Rounds were striking the tops of the rocks, showering them with chips, but they were protected—for the moment.

A large explosion in the water just offshore reminded the colonel that the enemy had mortars and grenades, too, which would soon find them.

He pushed thoughts of the utter disaster out of his head. He had men; they still had fight; all was not lost.

Crouching behind the boulders, half in and half out of the water, he cried: "Regroup! Regroup!" He could see more soldiers in the water, swimming their way, some wounded, struggling. A few went down and did not come up again; others were crying out for help. There was nothing he could do except watch them get cut down and mortared, the ambushing troops finding their range.

Gasping, dazed by the sudden reversal in fortune, the colonel looked around. Six men and himself, crouching pathetically behind the rocks. They were terrified, paralyzed. He had to do something, take control, show leadership. He peered through a narrow crack in the rocks, took stock. The ambushers were firing from behind a volcanic ridge above the docks. To his right was a slide of black rocks; if they could cross the open ground and get behind those rocks, they would have cover moving laterally up the slope and around the curve of the island.

He looked about. "Listen!" He paused, then shouted. "*Filhos da puta*, listen!"

That roused them.

"We head upslope, then get behind that cover, there. *Now*. Follow my lead."

"What about covering fire?" Thiago asked.

"Too many attackers—and that would only warn them. We simply run like hell. On three ... One, two, *three*!"

They leapt over the boulders and ran diagonally across the slope of loose volcanic cinders. Immediately a barrage of fire erupted, but the ambushers had evidently not been expecting so soon a move and all seven made it behind the rockslide before the RPG volleys began. He could hear officers shouting orders in German.

"Keep going!" the colonel cried.

At a crouch, they kept on, angling diagonally up the slope and around the slight curve of the island. The fortress wall loomed far above them, rising ominously from the volcanic cinders, black and rough.

More fire came pouring in as they emerged from cover, the rounds kicking up the cinders all around them. A man to the colonel's left grunted with a thud of lead meeting flesh, a spray of blood and matter erupting from his chest, and he fell heavily onto the rocks.

They ran on and on, the bullets peppering the cinders around them. More orders shouted in German: "*Ihnen nach! Verfolgt sie!*" The colonel understood: the ambushers were in pursuit.

"Down!" he cried. "Drop and return fire!"

The men, so very well trained, spun and dropped almost as one into the soft cinders and let loose a withering fire from their own automatic weapons; the colonel was extremely gratified to see several of the pursuers go down, the rest quickly taking cover.

"Up!" he ordered. "Run!"

In a flash they were up again and running. And as they came around the slope, he saw—above them, about a quarter mile away—the ragged hole in the outer wall. They would have a far better chance within the fortress than out in the open, on the island.

"Head for that breach!" the colonel cried, pointing.

The men angled uphill, heading for the breach, but once again exposed to fire. If only they could reach the hole, *talvez...*

73

PENDERGAST, WEDGED INTO A BROKEN GUN PORT
in a half-ruined wall of the old fortress, had watched
the colonel's boats approach the docks. At first he had
believed it was part of the feint they had originally
planned; but then, in a horrific moment, he realized
the colonel had diverged from that plan.

He was headed straight for the docks.

Pendergast believed he understood the colonel's rea-
soning: speed was of the essence. He and the colonel had
discussed this line of attack, back in Alsdorf, and dismissed
it because of the danger, however small, of an ambush.
There was always the possibility that, at the sounds of the
attack on the town, the men in the fortress could move
quickly enough to arrange a trap—or arm a trap that was
already in place. The colonel had dismissed this possibility, but ultimately Pendergast's view had prevailed.

But, it seemed, not prevailed enough.

Pendergast watched the approach, his heart accelerating. It might work. Indeed, now he could also see
that the colonel had brought far fewer men than agreed
upon—with such a small force, surprise and speed
became essential.

492   DOUGLAS PRESTON & LINCOLN CHILD

If it worked, so much the better. But it was a risk—a huge gamble.

And then, at the first eruption of fire, the docks punched up into the air, the men blown back into the water, the two vessels lurching sideways—Pendergast felt the utter stillness of shock take over. All had instantly changed. He heard the distant rattle of automatic gunfire and saw, behind a sheltered ridge just below the castle walls, the faint flashes of muzzle flare. He couldn't see the ambushers from his vantage point, but he estimated they must comprise a moderate force—perhaps a hundred, a good portion of the fortress's complement—well trained and organized. As the smoke from the explosions on the dock began to clear, the full dimensions of the debacle sank in. Many of the invading force had been killed outright or badly wounded, and the survivors were being mowed down in the water. But the colonel himself seemed to have survived, along with a handful of his men. Pendergast watched as they made their way behind a screen of boulders along the shore; ran for more cover farther around the hill, losing a man on the way; and then completed the final dash toward the opening in the wall, during which another soldier was cut down. Four men and the colonel made it to the breach and immediately disappeared.

Five soldiers. And himself. Six against a fortress of well-armed, highly trained fighters who were genetically bred for ruthlessness and intelligence, on their own turf, defending their land, their town, their fortress—their very reason for existence.

As Pendergast considered the problem, he began to realize that there might not be any paths to success remaining. His only consolation was that the least predictable of all human activities was war.

Scrambling down from his perch, Pendergast sprinted along a tunnel, ducking into a side passageway when he heard the approaching sound of soldiers' boots. They went by and he flitted back out, descending a ruined staircase that headed into the foundations of the fortress. He could hear, echoing upward, the beginning of a fire-fight from within the walls: the defending soldiers were converging, no doubt, fighting the last of the colonel's men at the gap or just inside.

The sounds of firing grew louder as he reached the massive, sloping basement tunnel encircling the interior of the curtain wall. He heard boots behind him again and had just enough time to swing into an unlocked lab and close its door before they passed. More shoot-ing, bloody gargling screams. The Brazilians, at least, were putting up a remarkable fight.

He ducked back out into the passage and continued on until he came to a dogleg, beyond which a group of German soldiers was hunkered down, apparently pinned by fire from the Brazilians. The narrow tunnels, heavy stone walls, and endless alcoves and hiding places helped defray, at least to a degree, the Brazilians' severe disadvantage in numbers. Listening intently, Pender-gast surmised that the Brazilian soldiers must be in a highly defensible redoubt inside the wall itself, fighting hard but hemmed in on all sides. They were doomed unless they could break free.

Pendergast crept around the corner, waited for a loud explosion, and then—using the sound as cover—dropped one of the German soldiers with a shot to the femoral artery in the thigh, where the direction his shot had come from would not be as obvious. He waited again, took another opportunity to drop a sec-ond German. It was as he had hoped: the soldiers, not realizing they were taking fire from behind, retreated toward him in some confusion, thinking instead they were being exposed to fire from an unknown direction ahead. Pendergast quickly fell back into the lab to let them pass. He then moved out—now in front of the retreating group—and, rifling one of the bodies he had shot, retrieved several grenades and two full Sturm-gewehr magazines, all the while taking periodic cover as he was fired on by the panicked Brazilian troops.

Now rearmed, Pendergast made a loop back to the lab, wired all the grenades together, and tied a break-away knot around the spoon levers. Next, he searched around for a thin wire, and—finding one—pulled out the pins from all the grenades. With infinite care, he moved back into the tunnel, listening for the pauses between explosions and gunfire. At the correct moment, he sprinted down the tunnel, stopping at a point where the roof was webbed with cracks from the resurgent ground. Rolling a gurney out of an adjacent lab, he climbed onto it, affixed the bundle of grenades to the ceiling with a chock, and unrolled the thin wire he'd found in the lab from the breakaway knot holding the grenade levers. He shoved the gurney back into the lab and crouched in the doorway, listening again.

After a moment he let fly with several massive bursts from his gun. "*Sie sind hier!*" he shouted. "*Schnell!* Hurry, over here!"

He followed this cry with more bursts of gunfire. "Hurry!"

The German soldiers fell back rapidly toward him, crouching and firing as they retreated, crab-like.

Pendergast let loose another burst of automatic fire, then cried for help. "*Hilfe! Hilfe!*"

As they approached, Pendergast jerked the wire, releasing the spoon levers on the cluster of grenades—and then ducked into the lab, shutting the steel door behind him. A moment later, a massive explosion sounded in the hallway. The tiny window in the door blew out; the door itself was ripped from its hinges and flung into the room. Pendergast, crouching against the rear wall, stood up and dashed through the doorway into choking stone dust and plaster, running amid falling blocks as the tunnel partially unraveled and began to cave in around him. Still in choking dust, with visibility zero, he came up to the colonel's redoubt.

"Colonel, it's Pendergast!" he cried in English and then in Portuguese. "*Me ajude!*" And then: "Follow me—we have only a moment!"

He turned and ran back into the blinding dust, the colonel and his four remaining soldiers following.

74

PAST THE CAVE-IN, THE TUNNEL RAN IN A BROAD curve around the inside of the fortress's curtain wall, laboratories on the left, the massive wall itself to the right. It was the major route of movement along this lower level of the fortress: a dangerous place to be. The key, Pendergast decided, would be to go deeper still, where they might be able to escape into the labyrinth of underground passageways, dungeons, cells, and storage rooms. It was the area where Pendergast had initially been confined, but he had not explored it further during his quick reconnaissance of the fortress, believing it irrelevant.

Now it was most relevant. Indeed, it was their only chance.

Already he could hear a group of men running toward them, the clatter of rifles and the regular thud of boots echoing down the stone passageway. A laboratory door stood to their left, inset into a stone alcove, but it was locked and there was no time for Pendergast to pick it. With hand signals, he gestured for the colonel and his men to press themselves against both walls, drop to their knees, and level their rifles toward the approaching soldiers.

"Fire at will," he said quietly. The colonel repeated the command in Portuguese.

The footsteps grew closer, echoing around the curve of the tunnel. The small band readied themselves for a point-blank ambush.

In response to a barked order, the approaching soldiers halted, just out of sight. There was a sudden silence. A moment of electric intensity ensued—and then two expertly tossed grenades came bounding off the curved wall, hitting the floor and rolling toward the Brazilians.

Taken by surprise, Pendergast and the others leapt up in a flash, turning and throwing themselves back into the alcove of the laboratory door; the grenades went off simultaneously, an enormous pressure wave in the confined space slamming them backward. One of the Brazilians, not as fast as the others, was caught in the open and vanished in a cloud of blood, flesh, bone, and dust.

Shaking his head to clear it, Pendergast fired into the enveloping dust cloud. He could hear stones falling and realized the soldiers could not advance, at least not immediately, due to the blocks tumbling from the ceiling.

"Retreat!" he said, firing another blast into the dust.

The colonel and his three remaining men ran. Pendergast continued his suppressing fire until they were safely around the curve of the wall, then he followed. A few hundred yards past, he knew, lay a lateral tunnel; he had no idea where it went and was reluctant to chance it, but they now had no choice.

"To the right!" he called ahead. "*Direita!*"

They took the tunnel, leaving the dust-choked passage behind him. There was no lighting and the colonel's men pulled out flashlights to see what lay ahead.

The tunnel was old and disused, the stones encrusted with niter, the air dead and smelling of mold and decay. They came to an ancient oaken door, banded with rotten iron, wormy with age, which fell to a single blow from a rifle barrel.

Ahead, a circular stone staircase spiraled downward into foul darkness. Behind, they could once again hear the thud of boots.

The staircase had partially collapsed, and they slithered down the broken, tumbled, slimy stones until they arrived at the lowest level of the fortress. They raced down a long tunnel that began at the base of the stairway, the sound of their pursuers not far behind.

At length the tunnel branched, then opened into a large, domed space. At the center of this space was a most unusual sight: a freestanding steel cage about fifteen feet square, securely locked. It was not fixed to the ground: rather, it was constructed around what appeared to be a deep, natural fissure in the undressed floor of the fortress's sub-basement. Filling the fissure, and rising up to fill the cage as well, were countless boxes of weapons, grenades, shells, gunpowder casings, stamped with swastikas and warnings exhorting that the contents were very dangerous—SEHR GEFÄHRLICH. This appeared to be the central ammo dump of the fortress, located as a protective measure deep, deep within its bowels.

So their original plan, to detonate the ammo dump, would have been doomed to failure in any case: it was placed too deeply in the fortress to have blown open an entrance for the colonel and his men.

But there was no time for further examination, and they passed through the space into another passage leading out the far side.

Soon this passage came to a T, then branched again,

lined with rows of empty cells, the rotting remains of wooden doors lying on the damp ground. An ancient skeleton, streaked with copper salts, was chained to one wall. Water leaked down the walls, and puddles lay on the cindery floor, which—Pendergast noted—was most unfortunately preserving the footprints of their passage.

Now the grunt of running men, the thud of boots, grew ever closer.

"We've got to kill those men," the colonel said.

"An excellent suggestion," Pendergast replied. "Grenades, please."

He pulled out the last of his grenades, nodded to the colonel; as they ran, following Pendergast's lead, the colonel and his three remaining men all pulled the pins from their own grenades, keeping the spoons in position. As a corner in the tunnel loomed ahead, Pendergast gave a sharp nod; they released the spoons simultaneously as they dropped the grenades into the soft cinders, turned the corner, and threw themselves to the ground.

"How do you say it in English?" the colonel muttered. "Payback is a bitch."

"Douse all lights," Pendergast whispered in return.

Seconds later, multiple explosions ripped the tunnel directly around the corner, almost deafening them. Immediately Pendergast was on his feet, gesturing for the others to follow; they charged back around the corner, where confused, dim flashlight beams could be seen here and there amid falling rubble. They fired frantically into the massive dust cloud, aiming at the lights, the return fire ineffectual and chaotic.

In a few moments it was over. Their pursuers were dead, the dust was settling in the damp air. Turning on his own flashlight, Pendergast played it over the dead:

six soldiers in simple gray uniforms with only one small insignia in the shape of an Iron Cross. But the seventh, clearly the leader, was wearing an old Nazi uniform, the *feldgraue* field uniform of the Waffen-SS, with a few latter-day additions.

"*Babaca!*" the colonel said, kicking the body. "Look at that son of a whore, playing Nazi. *Que bastardo.*"

Pendergast briefly examined the uniformed officer, then turned his attention to the other dead: half a dozen fine-looking young men, ripped apart by the explosions and gunfire, their blue eyes staring sightlessly this way and that, mouths open in surprise, delicate hands still on their weapons. He bent down, retrieved another magazine and a spare grenade. The others similarly replenished their own supplies.

And then there was only silence, save for the slow cadence of dripping water. The smell of blood and death mingled with the muck, mold, and decay. But into the silence came the sound of rustling. The explosion had dislodged a section of the massive wall, and now insects, disturbed from their resting places, were slithering and crawling out, many falling from the ceiling—oily centipedes, white vinegaroons with spiked pedipalps, giant earwigs with greasy pincers, albino scorpions clacking their claws, furry leaping spiders.

With an oath the colonel brushed an insect from his shoulder.

"We must get out of here," Pendergast said. "Now."

Then something strange happened. One of the colonel's soldiers gasped, turned—and pulled a bloody throwing knife from his chest, staring at it in astonishment before collapsing to his knees.

75

COLONEL SOUZA, HEARING THE GASP, SPUN and fixed his light on the soldier. The man clutched the heavy blade in his own hand, staring at it with an expression of sheer amazement, before folding slowly to the ground.

"Take cover!" said Pendergast, dropping to a crouch.

Souza staggered up against the wall while Pendergast probed the passage with his light, examining the walls, the ceilings, the dark cells and rotten doors. Tendrils of mist drifted through the tunnel, illuminated in the thin beam. There was nothing but silence and the drip of water. The light played over the chained skeleton, a single wisp of long black hair still attached to its cranium.

"*Nossa Senhora,*" the colonel whispered, turning to Pendergast, their gazes meeting. Once again he found himself disconcerted by those pale eyes, which seemed almost to shine in the dark. He could feel his lower lip trembling, and he struggled to suppress it. He could not think, not yet, of how badly he had failed in this mission. His son, Thiago, had said nothing—nothing—since the disaster. He couldn't bring himself to meet the gaze of his son...but he could feel it. Yes, he could feel the pressure of the youth's eyes, the fear and censure, against the back of his neck, as if it were a tangible thing.

Crouching there, waiting for he did not know what, having no idea what they could possibly do now, he saw Pendergast move, reach out, and touch his fallen soldier's neck at the pulse. He waited a moment, then glanced over at the colonel with a faint shake of the head. It felt like another thrust of the knife. To lose these men, so many good men...but he couldn't contemplate that now.

Pendergast gently removed the bloody knife from the soldier's dead hand and examined it before sliding it into his own belt. Souza could see it was an old Nazi knife—an Eickhorn hewer—a heavy, thick blade, not easy to throw, but massive enough to split the breastbone on its way to the heart.

Again the colonel listened and again was surprised, even astonished, that he could neither hear nor see anything out there in the darkness. It was as if the knife had simply materialized in the man's chest.

No one said anything. There was a moment of stasis, and then Pendergast cautiously rose, breaking the terrible spell. Motioning the remaining men to follow him, he continued down the tunnel. The colonel covered the rear with his son, neither one looking at the other. He had somehow ceded command to this civilian, but he could not collect his wits sufficiently to reassert his role. With four men against a fortress of trained Nazi fighters, what could possibly come next? Once again, he pushed these terrible thoughts from his mind. Did Pendergast have a plan? The gringo was so silent, so strange.

The tunnel began to slope downward and the air

became increasingly fetid, foul smelling, the floor covered with water that gradually deepened as the slope continued, forcing them to wade. The mists thickened and their breath added more fog to the already-supersaturated air. The sound of their movement through the water echoed softly in the tunnel. At a certain point Pendergast gestured for a halt, and they stood in the tainted air, listening, but could hear no sound of anyone moving through the water behind them.

Still the tunnel continued, the water deepening. Dead, bloated insects floated on the surface scum, and on several occasions they passed human skeletons chained or partially walled into alcoves, dating back to the Spanish era, the bones eaten by time. Once a fat, white water moccasin glided by, paying them no attention.

Soon they came to a circular chamber, a confluence of tunnels. The water was now waist-deep. Here they paused while Pendergast appeared to examine the water for signs of a current, shining his light down and dropping a piece of thread onto the surface. But the thread just left a dimple; there was no movement, none at all, to indicate which direction they should go.

As Pendergast was about to turn away, the colonel saw the thread give a sudden spin; at the same time, the beam of his flashlight, penetrating the murky water, picked up a faint blur.

"Watch out!" he shouted, as simultaneously a cry came from the soldier behind him—*Thiago*. The colonel spun around, swinging his light frantically, but Thiago had vanished into the water. There was a violent thrashing below the surface, which ended almost as suddenly as it began. The colonel staggered over to where the murky water was still swirling; his flashlight revealed something under the water, rising, rising...A form surfaced, a dark cloudy stain spreading out from its neck, staining the water.

"*Meu filho!*" the colonel cried, seizing the body. "*Thiago! Meu filho!*" He turned the body of his son over and with an inarticulate cry lifted it, horror-struck as the head flopped back, the throat cut to the bone, the eyes staring wide. "*Bastardos!*" he screamed, dropping the body and lifting his rifle, his vision clouded with rage. He let fly a blast on full automatic, aiming into the darkness and sweeping it around, firing crazily into the water. The other soldier panicked as well, backing up and firing his weapon into the miasmic darkness.

"*Bastardos!*" Souza screamed again.

"Enough," Pendergast said, not loudly, but in a steel voice. "*Stop.*"

The colonel, feeling the cold grip of the man's hand on his shoulder, came to a jerking halt. He was shaking all over. "My son," he said in despair.

"He's playing with us," said Pendergast. "We've got to find a way out."

"He?" the colonel cried. "Who is *he*? Who is this man?" He felt another rage take hold and he screamed into the darkness: "Who are you? *Quem é você?*"

Pendergast did not answer. He pointed to the last soldier. "You. Bring up the rear." He turned back to the colonel. "Stay next to me. We must keep moving."

Souza followed Pendergast down a tunnel, chosen for reasons he did not know nor any longer care about. The American moved fast through the water, almost like a shark, slipping along, the colonel struggling to keep up. He saw Pendergast remove a grenade and yank out the pin, keeping it clenched in his hand, the spoon lever depressed.

They continued on until they reached another confluence of tunnels; another danger zone. And then all of a sudden, to the colonel's surprise, Pendergast turned and threw the grenade back down the tunnel they had just emerged from.

"Down!" he cried.

They threw themselves into the water as the explosion came, blasting down the tunnel in a wall of spray like a water cannon. After it passed, they could hear the echoes of it continuing to rumble this way and that through the labyrinthine passages.

Pendergast pointed to a tunnel.

"How do you know this is the way out?" the colonel gasped.

"It is the one without an echo," came the murmured reply.

The water deepened, but a stone walkway soon appeared partway along the tunnel wall, with stone steps leading up. Pendergast had chosen correctly: this was a route out, an old tunnel no doubt leading to the lake, a secret water passageway in and out of the fortress.

"*Agora eu esto satisfeito...*" A voice came suddenly out of the mists, echoing, distorted, horrible.

The colonel dropped, turned, and fired almost without thought, a truncated burst cut off as his magazine emptied. He continued depressing the trigger, screaming, "Who's there? Who is it?" His trembling voice echoed away among the mists.

The only reply was the single report of a gun out of the darkness; a brief flash of light; and the last of his soldiers dropped back into the water with a low gargling sound.

Pendergast crouched next to the colonel, using the stone quay as cover, his silvery eyes piercing the darkness.

Souza fumbled out the magazine, dropped it into the water, grabbed another from his rucksack, and with shaking hands tried to affix it into place. Pendergast reached over, placing a steadying hand on the gun as Souza finally got the magazine in place.

"Save your ammo," he said quietly. "This is what he wants."

"*Os fantasmas?*" said the colonel, shaking all over.

"Unfortunately, it's real."

With this enigmatic answer, Pendergast scrambled up the stone steps, the colonel stumbling after him, slipping as he climbed the slimy stairs to the narrow walkway, running along it and taking cover in an alcove.

"*Agora eu esto satisfeito...*" came the voice again out of the miasma, the sound like an ice pick into the colonel's ear. In the tunnel it was impossible to tell the direction; it came from everywhere and nowhere at once, a low but curiously penetrating voice.

"What does that mean?" Pendergast whispered.

"How horrible...it means 'satisfaction, fulfillment...'" Souza choked, his mind whirling. He could hardly come to grips with what had happened, what was still happening. It was a nightmare beyond anything he could have imagined.

"We've got to keep moving, Colonel."

Something about the agent's cool voice steadied him a little. Gripping his M16, Souza rose and followed Pendergast's fleeting form down the passage. They passed side pipes and tunnels, some of which were spewing black water.

Low laughter followed them. The colonel could not stand it. He felt everything crumbling again; his world was destroyed—and now this. How was this happening? Who was this devil?

"*Você está satisfeito, Coronel?*" came the voice, closer in the mists. Are you satisfied, Colonel?

It was as if the world suddenly flew away. Colonel Souza spun with a roar and ran back in the direction of the voice, a sound coming from his throat that wasn't entirely human, a bestial scream of rage, his finger locked on the trigger, the weapon on full automatic, the muzzle sweeping back and forth, the thirty-round magazine emptying into the mist.

A sudden silence fell as the magazine ran out. Souza stopped, almost as if waking up; stopped and waited, waited for the end, which he suddenly wanted more than anything else he had ever wanted in his life.

76

PENDERGAST, FLATTENED AGAINST THE WALL, heard the long, wild, sustained firing and the animalistic scream of the colonel as he charged down the walkway into the darkling mists, followed by a sudden silence. There was a moment of stasis as the sound echoed and died away in the tunnels: and then another single shot, not very loud, from a small-caliber weapon, broke the silence.

A moment later, he heard the colonel's body hit the water. And then he heard the voice again—the voice he knew so well.

"And now, Father, here we are. Just the two of us."

In the darkness, pressed against the wall, Pendergast said nothing.

"Father?"

Finally he felt able to speak. "What do you want?" he asked, slowly and evenly.

"I am going to kill you."

"And you really think you can do it? Kill your own father?"

"We shall see."

"Why?"

"Why climb Mount Everest? Why go to the moon? Why run a marathon? For me, this is the ultimate test of character."

A silence. Pendergast could formulate no response.

"You really can't escape me. You realize that, don't you?" The voice paused briefly. And then Alban said: "But first, a gift for you. Earlier, you asked about the Copenhagen Window. Would you like to know my secret? *Glance into the world just as though time were gone: and everything crooked will become straight to you.* Nietzsche, as I'm sure you're aware."

A knife flashed out of the darkness, like a bat on the wing, so fast and so unexpected that Pendergast could not quite dodge it. It struck his clavicle a glancing blow, little more than a flesh wound. He twisted away, fell and rolled, then was up and, after a quick sprint, took cover again, pressing himself into the next alcove, up against the wet, slimy wall. Even with the thrown knife, he couldn't pinpoint Alban's current location, the youth taking advantage of the peculiarities of the way sound echoed in the tunnels to disguise his position.

"You won't kill me, because you're weak. That's where we differ. Because *I* can kill *you*. As I just demonstrated. And I must say, that was an excellent evasion, Father. As if you sensed it was coming."

Pendergast noted a hint of pride in the boy's voice: that of a son impressed with his father. The weird sickness of it made it hard to focus. He felt the sting of the injury to his already-wrenched shoulder, felt the warm blood seeping through his wet shirt. A certain part of him—perhaps the greater part—did not care now whether he lived or died. He only hoped his son would shoot straight and true.

"Yes, it is true I could kill you now," the voice went on. "And, in fact, you're in my crosshairs as I speak.

But that wouldn't be right. I'm a man of honor and wouldn't just shoot you down like a dog. So I'll give you a choice. I shall count to ten. If you choose to die, do nothing, and on ten I will help you with your assisted suicide. If you wish to flee, to give yourself a sporting chance, you may do so."

Pendergast dove into the water, but not until the count had reached six.

Keeping underwater, he swam as fast as he could, the heavy rifle dragging him down. He stayed close to the wall, only coming up when he needed to gulp air. He heard several bursts of gunfire—Alban was true to his word and fired on ten—and could hear the bullets zipping underwater all around him. He wasn't moving fast enough, not nearly fast enough, and with a moment's regret he released the rifle. He swam with his eyes open but could see nothing. The water was cold and foul and full of dead things that bumped against him, and he felt more than once the slithering brush of a water snake. Ignoring all this, he kept going.

The tunnel made a broad curve and then—slowly, kicking hard under the water—Pendergast began to see the faintest light. He surfaced, noticed a gleam on the slick walls of the tunnel. The shooting had stopped. He continued, swimming on the surface. As he emerged from the tunnels into the lake, the light almost blinded him. It was still afternoon. He looked westward and saw that he was about half a mile from the opposite shore. He paused to glance behind him. Alban was nowhere to be seen, either at the mouth of the tunnel or anywhere on shore.

That, he knew, would not last long. The boy was surely coming after him.

He continued swimming, heading westward, toward the mainland.

77

ALBAN LISTENED FOR A WHILE IN THE DARK-
ness while the sounds of his father's swimming slowly
faded. The opening to the lake wasn't far; he would
reach it within a few minutes. His heart was beating
strongly and he could feel all his senses at their keenest
level of alertness, his mind running smooth and fast.
This was the most electrifying thing he had ever done,
strangely, unexpectedly thrilling. Now he understood
what Fischer had meant about appreciating the finer
things. A few years earlier, as a coming-of-age challenge, Fischer had sent him into the forest, armed only
with a knife, to kill a jaguar. That had been a remarkable experience. But this—hunting a man, and not any
man, but his own father—was the ultimate challenge.

Alban considered what his father would do next.
And the answer came easily: He would not remain on
the island, where he could do nothing and was completely outgunned and overwhelmed. He would swim
for shore. And he would swim due west, toward the
defectives' camp. Because he would be looking for his
other son, Forty-Seven. Alban's twin. The one who
now had a name: Tristram.

Tristram. Something about that name—the very existence of the name—deeply angered Alban.

Moving quickly, Alban jogged down the walkway to an obscure metal door in a side alcove. With a quick twist of a key in the well-oiled lock, he moved into a narrow tunnel that he knew led diagonally toward shore. A few moments later he emerged through another door into the light of afternoon, at a crumbling stone platform just above the lakeshore, surrounded by reeds. Pushing his way out of the vegetation, he climbed a few dozen feet up the side of the volcanic hill, his feet crunching on the cinders. Then he paused, turned, and surveyed the lake. Almost immediately his keen eyes spotted the figure of his father, swimming westward toward shore precisely as he had surmised.

He raised his rifle and examined his father through the magnification of the scope. He thought, idly, that despite it being a three-hundred-yard shot, in this windless and pleasant afternoon, given his superb marksmanship, it was an almost certain kill.

He lowered the rifle without firing, complimenting himself again on his strong sense of honor and justice. His father was a great man who would die a good death—not shot in the back from afar. The swim was about half a mile, and at the rate he was going with his wounded shoulder, it would take him at least fifteen minutes to reach the swamp on the far side. There was plenty of time to arrange for a more equal, more interesting contest.

Slinging his rifle over his shoulder, he hiked along the well-worn path circling the island. Within a few minutes a small landing came into view, to which were tied several outboard launches. Walking up to them, he looked them over, selecting the lightest and most maneuverable: a thirteen-foot fiberglass flat-bottomed skiff with a two-stroke engine. He leapt in, checked the gas, fired up the engine, and headed out into the lake.

The skiff slapped the water as it skimmed away from shore, with Alban standing at the tiller, peering ahead, feeling the lovely, cool air rush past. This close to the water it was hard to see his father, but he knew where he would be. And sure enough, as he approached the middle of the lake, he could see the man's faint movement in the afternoon light: the regularly moving arms, the splash of the feet, as he swam.

His father glimpsed him and dove. Alban slowed the boat, turning slightly to the south. With the dive and swim underwater, his father would change direction. But no: he wouldn't. That would be his surprise, to keep going in the same direction.

How long could he hold his breath?

An astonishing two minutes later—Alban could hardly believe it—he reappeared, just where Alban expected, along the same route almost a hundred yards closer to shore. Alban could swim a hundred and fifty yards underwater, but one hundred was still extraordinary, especially for a man his father's age.

Alban steered the boat toward the swimmer, closing the distance fast. Why not just run him over?

Why not, indeed? That would be sport. His father would dive, of course. And dive again. He goosed the engine to full throttle and aimed at the figure, sweeping toward him. His father dived at the last minute and Alban jammed the tiller around, carring the boat in a tight circle, aiming for where he knew his father would surface.

He didn't really expect to kill his father this way. But it would wear him out, exhaust him.

Best of all, it would be good sport—for both of them.

78

UNDERWATER, HIS EYES OPEN, PENDERGAST could see the boat make a tight turn on the surface and head in the very direction he had planned to take. But even as he saw this, and changed his plans yet again—hovering underwater and holding his breath—the boat changed its trajectory, slowing down even more, as if reading his mind.

Reading his mind? It seemed absurd...and yet even the most unusual hypotheses must be considered to explain the most unusual events. Pendergast was at the cusp of a revelation; he could sense it. A number of threads were twining themselves together in his hypoxic brain—the inexplicable nature of the killings in New York; the recent stalk in the fortress tunnels, with its uncanny display of second-guessing; Alban's pride-filled statement about his father's abilities; the youth's supreme self-confidence that Pendergast could not escape him. And then, the odd quotation from Nietzsche.

Something most unusual was going on. It *was* as if Alban was reading his mind.

But he needed air. *Now.* He rose straight up, burst

the surface, took a deep breath. And he saw Alban was heading away from him, swerving his boat and coming back around, a look of surprise and even consternation on the boy's face.

No, Alban wasn't reading his mind. It was something else. Pendergast recalled what Constance had said about Alban—something about a sixth sense, or perhaps an extension of one of the other five. The line from Nietzsche that Alban had quoted ran through his head, once, twice. What did it mean?

He kicked down under the surface about three feet and swam laterally, deliberately, toward shore. The boat above him swerved and made a loop, the whine of its engine filling his ears, then slowed and headed approximately toward the spot where he would have to surface for air. And yes, he would surface there; he would. That is what he would definitely do.

No, this was not a question of mind reading. Alban could not read a person's mind. He had some sort of unusual ability, but it was not that. It was both less than that, and more.

Pendergast, long before he needed air, abruptly shot to the surface after a split-second change of plans—and Alban, only twenty feet away but moving in the wrong direction, saw him, again surprised; he swerved the boat and jammed on the throttle. Pendergast waited, dove, and as the boat came overhead and moved in a tight circle he darted upward again, the Nazi hewer in hand, and rammed it into the hull as the boat passed overhead; the heavy blade cleaved the light fiberglass and he gave the knife a twist before the boat's forward motion wrenched it out of his hand. The propeller passed just inches over his head, buffeting him with turbulence, buzzing like a gigantic wasp.

Surfacing right behind the boat, he gulped air once,

then again, and kicked off for shore, swimming like mad. It would take Alban at least a few minutes to deal with the flood of water introduced by the leak, and he was already approaching the shoaling water near shore, a hundred yards from the beginning of the marsh grass and two hundred from thick cattails and swamp.

As much as he could, he swam underwater, making random changes in direction unexpected even by himself, often opposite to what his instincts told him, sometimes actually doubling back on himself. When he surfaced he could see Alban hunched over in the boat, working frantically to stanch the leak, but every time Pendergast rose for air he stood, shouldered his rifle, and cracked out a shot that smacked the water inches from Pendergast's head; turning and kick-diving down again, he heard several more shots zip past in the water.

His son was, without question, shooting to kill. That answered another important question that had been lingering in his mind.

He continued swimming, maintaining his erratic behavior but always trending toward shore. The boat was listing seriously now, but Alban had apparently blocked or stuffed the hole and was starting to bail, once in a while rising to take another shot when Pendergast surfaced. He was a superb shot: the only thing saving Pendergast was the afternoon sun lying low on the horizon, shining directly toward Alban and reflecting off the water in a blinding sheet.

Pendergast felt his feet brush the muddy bottom, and he swam until the water was waist-deep and he was at the edge of the marsh grass. Now he could wade, albeit awkwardly, keeping low. More shots came, but now distance and the surrounding cattails were in his favor, and then he was hidden by the thickening plants. Still, Alban continued firing—no doubt at the rustling of the vegetation disturbed by his passage. By slipping through the lanes of cattails, Pendergast was able to decoy his movements, reaching out and shaking stalks that were at a distance from him. But Alban quickly caught on to that, rounds ripping through on either side, snipping the cattails and sending up clouds of fluff.

The boat engine fired up and Pendergast redoubled his speed. He heard it approach, slapping through the reeds—and then there was a muffled sound as the propeller hit mud and the vessel grounded out.

A splash—Alban had jumped out and was pursuing him.

Thrashing through the cattails, Pendergast reached thick brush at the edge of the swamp, bulled through it, and continued on into the forest, shouldering past the heavy vegetation.

His son was superior to him physically and, perhaps, even mentally. No stratagem would shake Alban in this forest, a forest he knew well. Pendergast's only chance was to fully understand Alban's mysterious advantage—and use it against him.

The strange quotation from Nietzsche came into his mind yet again, unbidden:

Glance into the world just as though time were gone: and everything crooked will become straight to you.

That was when the revelation blossomed over him like a sunrise.

79

In his elegant office, Oberstgruppenführer Wulf Fischer indulged himself in another cigarette, offering one to his second in command, Scheermann. Fischer then lit it for the man, enjoying the reversal of roles; a gesture that demonstrated his own confidence and security, as well as the trust he placed in his captain.

He walked to the window that looked westward over the lake and raised his binoculars. He could see Alban's boat moving in circles, see the tiny swimming figure of Pendergast. If Alban had had any reluctance about killing his father, it did not seem to be in evidence now.

"This is charming. Take a look, Oberführer."

Fischer stepped aside and let his second in command gaze at the scene. He waited, inhaling the blended Syrian Latakia tobacco, grown and cured on their own farms, the finest in South America.

"Yes, most charming," Scheermann said as he lowered the glasses. "Alban seems up to the challenge. Very encouraging."

A silence. "We shall see if he is capable of the kill."

"I'm sure he will be, *mein Oberstgruppenführer*. His breeding and training were impeccable."

Fischer did not respond. The truth was, the true and final test had yet to take place. He inhaled smoke, let it stream from his nose. "Tell me: are there any survivors from the invading unit?"

"None. Five got into the fortress, but Alban and our soldiers seem to have killed them all. We found all five bodies."

"Any casualties among the Twins Brigade?"

"None. Although we lost a fairly large number of regular soldiers—upwards of two dozen. I'm still awaiting a final count."

"Regrettable." Fischer took back the glasses and peered through them again. It could almost have been two children playing in the lake, the boat moving in lazy circles, the swimmer diving and swimming under-water, coming up for air—everything, at that distance, appearing as if in slow motion. But now something happened: the boat appeared to have been holed, and Pendergast was swimming straight for shore.

Logic told Fischer that Pendergast was no match for his son—the son who carried all of his father's own best genes, enhanced, while unburdened of the delete-rious ones. And who had been trained from birth for this very sort of challenge.

"Quite a show," he said, keeping his voice confident. "The Romans in the Colosseum would be envious."

"Yes, Oberstgruppenführer."

That nagging feeling, however, that shadow of doubt, refused to go away, and as the contest on the water became prolonged the doubt only increased. Finally, Fischer spoke again. "I'm confident that Pen-dergast, if he reaches shore, will head for the defec-tives' camp. Alban will pursue, of course, but to be sure there are no problems, I want you to mobilize a group of our regulars and the Twins Brigade—now that they are warmed up—and transport them across the lake. I want them to act as a backup for Alban. Just in case. An insurance policy, you understand, nothing more." He tried to make it sound casual.

"Immediately, Oberstgruppenführer."

"On the double."

Oberführer Scheermann left with a crisp salute. Fischer turned back to the window, glassing the little drama on the lake. Alban was now standing in the boat, shooting—and missing. Granted, it was a highly difficult and precarious shot, in constant motion, unable to steady the weapon properly, the light the way it was.

Still . . .

80

As PENDERGAST SLIPPED THROUGH THE FOR-
est, he was well aware that Alban would be in pursuit,
despite the silence behind him. And, without doubt, he
would soon catch up.

As he glided forward, he considered his recent revelation. He thought he now understood Alban's unusual
ability. It was a quality that he himself, and others, possessed as well—but only vestigially, weakly. In Alban it
had been greatly enhanced. He had to be careful how
he deployed his realization; he had to wait for the right
moment, not let Alban realize he was aware of his special advantage: he could not afford to throw the surprise away at the wrong time.

He came upon a trail in the forest leading in the
direction of the defectives' camp. He sprinted along it,
pushing himself as hard as he could. The trail switch-
backed up a low rise, and within a few hundred yards
he crested the rim of the crater that enclosed the fields
and camp. He dropped down the far side, still running,
ignoring the switchbacks and descending at breakneck
speed straight down the steep slope.

He burst out of the vegetation edging the cultivated

land. A field of tall corn offered some cover and he darted into it, the rows running at a ninety-degree angle to his route of travel. He continued on, slowing only slightly, slipping and twisting between the rows of tall plants. But now he could hear his pursuer behind him, the rustle of his progress growing closer, always closer.

Pendergast turned ninety degrees and ran down a row of corn; then, as quickly as he could, he changed tactics, bashing through the rows, zigzagging from one to another. It was fruitless; there was no way to shake Alban and no way to ambush him. Alban was armed; he was not. This was not going to end well.

He saw light ahead and broke out of the far end of the corn. Still running, he crossed a field of bright cotton, the low plants affording no cover whatsoever. He could hear Alban running behind him, his breath coming hard. It had become a straight-ahead race now— and one he would lose.

Even as he realized he wasn't going to make the opening to the underground camp, he spotted the so-called defectives, streaming back in confusion from the far fields, dressed in ragged clothes, battered straw hats on their heads, tools and implements slung over their shoulders. It was a strange, silent, disorderly mob. Those in front paused, their mouths hanging open, astonished at the sight of the chase. He searched their milling ranks but could not make out Tristram.

At the same time, he heard, bizarrely, the sound of singing—a martial tune, no less. Looking to his right, he saw, streaming toward them from the direction of the docks, dozens of soldiers—the twins. There were around a hundred of them, the same number as the defectives: men and women, girls and boys, aged from perhaps fourteen to around forty, dressed in simple gray uniforms, sporting Iron Crosses—apparently the symbol of their new master race—led by several officers in crisp Nazi regalia. They were heavily armed, and as they approached they easily fell into formation, their voices bursting into song:

Es zittern die morschen Knochen,
Der Welt vor dem großen Krieg,

This was it, Pendergast realized. He could not outrun his son. He stopped, turned, and faced him.

A hundred yards back, Alban slowed to a trot, his face breaking into a smile as he approached. He unslung his rifle and fell back into a walk.

The soldiers approached.

Wir haben den Schrecken gebrochen,
Für uns war's ein großer Sieg.

But Alban didn't shoot him down. As he drew close, Pendergast saw, from the triumph in his eyes, that he wanted to draw it out, savor the moment of victory—not end it prematurely with a squalid shot. Indeed, now there was an audience. Now there was high drama, and a chance for Alban to prove himself: vindication in front of all.

It sickened Pendergast how well he understood his son.

Wir werden weiter marschieren
Wenn alles in Scherben fällt,

Supremely confident, Alban approached Pendergast, searched him, removing Pendergast's last weapon, a small knife. He held it up, tucked it in his own belt: a souvenir.

Now the marching soldiers came to a halt before them—young, beaming, rosy-cheeked, glowing with health and athleticism. Standing in rows, they finished their song:

Denn heute da hört uns Deutschland
Und morgen die ganze Welt!

The commander, Scheermann, dressed in a Waffen-SS uniform, strolled along the line of now-silent soldiers, turned and looked at Pendergast, and then at Alban. He walked around them in a slow circle.

"Well done," he said to Alban in perfect English. "He is the last one. I leave it in your hands."

"Thank you, *mein Oberführer*," Alban responded.

The boy turned to Pendergast with a smile. "Well, this is it, Father."

Pendergast waited. He looked over at the field hands, the slave twins, standing in a disorganized bunch, staring slack-jawed. They appeared not to have the slightest idea what was going on. The uniforms, the soldiers, the two groups of twins staring at each other across an unfathomable gulf of biology, of genetics . . .

Glancing from the soldiers to the enslaved field hands, Pendergast saw many of the same faces. Only where the defectives' faces were discouraged and hollow, the soldiers had the look of those who had found their place in the world and were supremely satisfied with it. This was how it should be. All was in order.

The horror of it closed off Pendergast's throat; he almost couldn't bear the knowledge that this was where his wife had come from, that she had been *bred* here, an early iteration of this vast eugenics experiment, stretching across at least three generations from the concentration camps of World War II to the forests of Brazil. Bred, no doubt, with the ultimate aim of creating a *true* master race, capable of establishing and maintaining a Fourth Reich, without the imperfections—mercy, compassion, shortsightedness—of their merely human forebears.

The idea was monstrous. Monstrous.

Scheermann, the Oberführer, said quietly: "Alban? We are waiting."

Alban took a step forward, his smile growing. With a brief glace at the Oberführer, he swung his fist and punched Pendergast in the side of the head with such force that it knocked the FBI agent to the ground.

"Fight," he said.

Pendergast rose, blood trickling from his mouth. "I'm afraid I can't give you that satisfaction, Alban," he said.

Another blow sent Pendergast sprawling again.

"Fight. I will not have my father die like a cowardly dog."

Again Pendergast rose, his pale eyes on his son. Again the fist swung hard. Yet again Pendergast went down.

A cry went up from among the ragged slaves. And now, out of nowhere, Tristram emerged.

"Stop it!" he shouted. "That's my father. And your father, too!"

"Precisely," said Alban. "And I'm glad you're here to see this, *Schwächling.*"

He turned and struck Pendergast again. "What a coward our father is. How disappointing!"

Tristram rushed at Alban, but with the utmost clumsiness; Alban deftly stepped aside while sticking out his foot—a schoolboy trick—and sent Tristram sprawling.

A manly laugh went up among the soldiers.

Pendergast got up from the dirt and stood silently, awaiting the next blow.

81

THE LAUGHTER DIED AWAY. ALBAN LOOKED down at his brother, lying in the dirt. Then he turned slowly back to Pendergast. Reaching down, he removed his sidearm, a Walther P38 that he had lovingly restored by hand. He felt the cool, heavy weapon in his hands. It had been given to him by Fischer when he turned ten, and he had replaced the original grips with elephant ivory he had carved himself.

His twin, Forty-Seven, sat up in the dirt, staring at the pistol.

Alban said, offhandedly: "Don't worry, *brother*, I've no intention of damaging my own personal blood and organ farm." He hefted the gun. "No—this one's for Father."

Der Schwächling rose to his feet.

"Go back to your own kind," Alban said. Meanwhile, the Nazi officers waited, expectantly. As did the brigade of superior twins. Waiting to see what he would do, how he—the one chosen for the beta test—would end this. This was the moment. *His* moment.

He would not make a mistake. Alban ejected the magazine to make sure it was full, then slid it back into place. With slow deliberation, holding his arm straight, he racked a round into the chamber.

His twin, however, did not move. He spoke in German, his voice loud and clear: *"Is this good?"*

Alban laughed harshly and, in return, quoted Nietzsche: *"What is good? All that heightens the feeling of power in man, the will to power, power itself."*

"That's sick," said his twin.

Alban waved as if at a pesky insect, highly conscious of his audience. The only one missing was Fischer. "What are you, Forty-Seven, but a bag of blood and organs—a genetic garbage dump? Your opinions are as meaningless as the wind in the trees."

This elicited another round of laughter from the soldiers. He couldn't help but glance at his father, who stared at him with those strange eyes. He seemed unable, now, to read anything in that look. No matter: it was irrelevant.

His twin—who clearly didn't know when to stop—spoke up again, but this time he spoke not to Alban, but to his own people. "You heard him. He called me and all of you *my own kind.* How much longer are we going to be treated like storage bags of blood and organs? How much longer are we going to be treated like animals? *I am a man.*"

And now a low murmur from the crowd.

"Don't strain yourself, *brother,*" said Alban. "If you want to see the power of will, watch this." He pointed the pistol at his father.

"Brother?" the twin cried, again addressing the crowd of defectives. "You hear that word? Can't you see how wrong this is? Brother against brother? Son murdering his own father?"

To Alban's mild surprise, the defectives responded. There was a sharp and growing murmur, more restless movement.

"Oh, ho!" Alban cried facetiously. "Speech, speech!"

This, to his relief, elicited a merry round of laughter from the soldiers. And he told himself it was, in fact, quite amusing, this crowd of pathetic imbeciles getting themselves all exercised with the pent-up frustrations and privations of many years. But he found himself shocked at the articulateness of Forty-Seven. That was not supposed to be allowed. And as he glanced around, he was unable to suppress an uneasiness developing in his forward-time sense, like an approaching storm. The ever-branching paths were narrowing, coming together and converging in his mind, leading toward a single future.

He looked back at his father, who was staring at him with glittering eyes. His finger moved to the trigger. It was time to get this over with.

"This is not right!" Forty-Seven cried out loudly, turning to the crowd. "Deep inside, you know it's wrong! Open your eyes! We are all brothers—sisters—*twins*! We share the same blood!"

The world-lines whipped and curled about in Alban's mind, a sudden five-alarm fire. He saw it, felt it: the great turning of the wheel. This couldn't be happening, not with their careful indoctrination, their years of planning and refining…and yet it *was* happening, and he could already begin to glimpse, like the ghostly image of an underpainting, how all this was going to end. The murmur of the defectives was growing into a hubbub, then into a roar, and the crowd moved tentatively forward, their hoes and shovels and scythes raised, some picking up rocks.

"*We can stop this!*" Forty-Seven shouted. "*Now!*"

Alban took a step back, the pistol leveled at his father. Oberführer Scheermann rapped out an order and the soldiers—lined up and heavily armed—raised their weapons.

"Go back to your fields!" cried the Oberführer. "Or we shall fire!"

But Alban knew that they would not—could not—fire on the defectives. Except for a handful of the latest iteration of twins—the best and most advanced, like himself—the others could not, if push came to shove, actually kill their siblings with their own hands. And if the Nazi officers, their minders, tried to shoot the defectives... It was all coalescing in Alban's mind with horrifying clarity. It would be the end of the program, the colony, an abrupt and shocking end to more than half a century of scientific research. The defectives, for all their hideousness, were essential. For the first time, he realized they were as essential to the project as he was. One could not exist without the other. Why had he not seen that before? Why had nobody seen that before? The whole plan had been based on a false hypothesis—a bluff. And now his own twin was calling that bluff.

This realization, this sudden reversal of fortune—unexpected and dreadful—left him stunned.

The crowd of defectives continued to jostle forward toward the line of soldiers, less tentative now, shouting, gesturing with their crude tools. Alban could feel the heat of their fury.

Now. He squeezed the trigger and fired at Pendergast.

But his father had anticipated it. Somehow, he had begun to move even before Alban fired, like a flash, incredibly quickly and unexpectedly—how did he do it?—evading the shot. Alban fired a second time but this shot was ruined by a volley of stones that came flying out of the crowd toward him, striking him and forcing him to fling up his arms in self-defense.

Pendergast had veered away and now lunged at him, launching himself in the air. Alban evaded with a pirouette, his father just striking him in the side. He fired again, but it was impossible to aim with the pelting rain of rocks and he was forced back, turning and hunching, his arms raised to protect his head. He could hear Scheermann crying an order to his regulars: *Fire over their heads!* With the lieutenants repeating it down the line, there came a massive volley of shots, and then another, like thunder.

It gave the defectives pause in their headlong rush. They halted in a kind of confused, chaotic milling, and the incipient fight abruptly turned into a standoff. Alban cast about and found his father, back up again, standing next to his twin, Forty-Seven, at the head of the crowd. Once again, he raised his weapon. But as he did so he saw in his mind the inexorable turning of the wheel, the crooked pathways of time growing straight... and he backed up, horrified by what he saw, as Pendergast stared at him with those terrible eyes. It was useless: every branch, every road of time led to a dead end, a checkmate at the end of every time line.

All at once he turned and fled, running through the line of soldiers, who parted to let him pass, as he knew they would. He needed to get to the lake and get a boat to the fortress, to find Fischer.

And to warn him of what was about to happen.

82

Pendergast watched Alban run, and he understood why. Alban's own gift had allowed him to see far enough ahead to—in essence—defeat himself. His genetically enhanced ability to sense just far enough into the future to carry out the Hotel Killings with such success, to elude his father's pursuit with ease, to kidnap his brother from the Riverside Drive redoubt, to survive and prevail in almost any imaginable confrontation—this gift had now turned against him. Knowledge of the future—even a brief, ten- or fifteen-second glimpse—turned out to be a double-edged sword with the keenest blade.

Meanwhile the standoff continued. Tensions were escalating to the breaking point: the defective twins were lined up on one side, furious, disorganized, raging; and on the other side was the Twins Brigade, lined up in disciplined ranks, silent but deeply rattled. And in the middle, the small cadre of Nazi officers who were only now realizing their dilemma as the two sets of twins, each about a hundred strong, faced each other in a standoff.

"Submit!" screamed Scheermann at the defectives.

"Go back to your camp!" He pointed at Pendergast. "Take that man into custody!"

Tristram, at the front of the crowd, cried out: "Touch my father, and we attack!"

A murmur of assent. The Oberführer hesitated. Pendergast waited. And then he saw the moment had arrived.

Without warning he strode toward the lines of twin soldiers and seized one by the collar of his uniform, as a teacher might seize a truant schoolboy.

"Stop him!" screeched Scheermann, removing his own sidearm, but in the standoff he seemed paralyzed to act, obviously surprised by the sudden, unexpected flight of Alban. Pendergast ignored him and dragged the astonished, passive soldier across the gap while with his other arm he snatched one of the defectives—the soldier's twin—by his ragged shirt, yanking him out, bringing the two men together.

"Meet your brother!" he cried at the soldier. "*Your own brother!*" He turned to the groups of twins facing each other. "All of you, right now—seek out your brothers and sisters! Your own flesh and blood!"

And he could see the eyes of the twins roving despite themselves, locking one after another on their opposites. There was a restless muttering, and the orderly lines of twin soldiers began to slacken, grow loose.

"That's enough," Scheermann said, raising his pistol toward Pendergast.

"Lower your pistol or we attack!" cried Tristram.

"You, attack? With hoes? You'll be slaughtered," Scheermann said contemptuously.

"Slaughter us—and there ends your grand experiment!"

Scheermann hesitated, his eyes darting along the line of ragged twins.

"These men—" Pendergast pointed at the Nazi minders—"they're your *real* enemy. Dividing brother from brother, sister from sister. They've turned you *all* into guinea pigs. But not them. *They* haven't participated. And *they* remain in charge. Why is that?"

The Oberführer's pistol hand was shaking ever so slightly. The seething crowd moved toward him. "Fire and you die!" came a voice, and another.

"Go back to your brigade, soldier," Scheermann said contemptuously.

The soldier did not move.

"Obey or face discipline!" Scheermann screamed, swiveling the pistol from Pendergast's head to point at the soldier.

"Lower your weapon," the soldier said slowly, "or we'll kill you all."

The commander's face was white. After a moment, he dropped his arm.

"Step back."

The Oberführer took a careful step back. Then another. Suddenly his arm flew up again, and he fired into the soldier's chest. "Attack the weak twins!" Scheermann screamed to the Nazi minders. "Fire at will! Destroy them!"

A roar of anger and dismay rose from the twins on both sides of the battle lines. There was a moment of terrible stasis. And then it was as if a dam had burst. The disorderly crowd of twins rushed the Nazi officers, their crude weapons raised.

Scheermann backed up, firing into the crowd, but he was immediately mobbed by the crowd of defectives, surging forward at a roar. There was a fusillade of shots from the soldiers and their commanding officers as the battle was joined, hand-to-hand, the Nazi officers firing every which way into the crowd at point-blank range, causing a dreadful slaughter. All was confusion, a fearful firefight erupting in the open field, soldiers struggling with the ragged defectives, the roar of automatic weapons, the clang of shovel and scythe against rifle, the screams of the wounded coming out of the fury of dust and blood.

"Brothers and sisters!" Tristram's voice rose up. "Don't murder your own kin!"

Something was happening. Many of the Twins Brigade were breaking ranks, changing sides, some throwing down their weapons and embracing their siblings—others turning their weapons on their officers. But a small cadre of latest-iteration twins remained with the Nazi officers, defending them furiously.

The chaos began to resolve itself and two sides emerged, fighting each other. The small group of loyalist twin soldiers and their Nazi officers were now outgunned and being forced to retreat, slowly, firing all the while, exacting a huge toll. The rest of the Twins Brigade who had turned were fighting alongside the defectives, more organized now, mounting a stronger attack and putting an end to the initial slaughter. The Nazis fell back into the cover of the cornfield, pursued by the main body of reunited twins. The battle raged on in the cornfield and a fire soon started, the flames leaping out of the dry stalks, a pall of smoke blanketing the scene, creating still more confusion.

Pendergast relieved a dead soldier of his sidearm, knife, and flashlight and headed into the corn toward the fiercest nucleus of fighting, battering his way through shattered cornstalks and heavy columns of smoke, looking for Tristram. He could hear the boy's voice in the thickest part of the action, calling, exhorting, urging his fellows forward—and it struck him to the core how much he had underestimated his son.

Now he circled fast around the Nazi officers and their rump of loyalist troops, retreating toward the lake. He swung around in a flanking maneuver and came up behind them, in their line of travel, crouching and waiting for them to come to him. As they did, Pendergast raised his gun, aimed at the Oberführer in the rear, as he anticipated, and brought him down with a single shot. He immediately came under heavy fire, the automatic weapons mowing down the corn around him; but the loss of their commander demoralized the retreating group, and after a moment of panic and confusion they broke and ran toward the lake, pursued by the others.

Continuing his one-man flanking maneuver, Pendergast moved eastward through the cornfields and into the forest. He bushwhacked his way to the top of the crater rim, where he stopped to reconnoiter. The retreating soldiers had arrived at the boats, and from his vantage point he could see what was happening: a group of them were hunkering down, making a stand while the rest loaded onto the vessels, scuttling the extras so they couldn't be followed. Another furious fight broke out as the vanguard of the pursuers, led by Tristram, reached the shore. But the Nazis and their remaining twin allies managed to cast off their boats and speed away from shore, leaving behind half a dozen wrecked and burning vessels.

The gunfire fell off and finally ceased as the vessels headed away from land, smoke drifting across the scene. The Nazis had gotten away and were now headed back across the lake to the fortress—to make their final stand.

83

WITH THE NAZIS ON THE RUN, THE RANKS OF defective twins—now swelled by the majority of their siblings—turned toward Nova Godói. Running along forest trails, they soon reached the town, streaming in. The well-swept streets were empty, the cheerfully decorated houses shuttered and dark. The townsfolk were hunkered down, some hiding, while many others appeared to have fled.

Reaching the central square, the groups of twins began to break into smaller parties, heading down the side streets, ready to engage in any mopping-up operations that might be necessary. Pendergast, following along, scanned the crowd and found Tristram. He went over to him. For a moment they looked at each other, and then they embraced.

"You need to establish a base of operations," he told his son in mixed German and English. "I'd suggest the town hall. Take the Bürgermeister and any other town officials into custody. Set up a strong defense in case of counterattack."

"Yes, Father," Tristram said. He was flushed and

breathing heavily, and a cut on his forehead was bleed-ing freely.

"Take great care of your own personal safety, Tris-tram. There may be plenty of Nazis still around, includ-ing rooftop snipers. You're a prime target."

"What are you going to do?"

"I have some unfinished business. At the fortress."

Pendergast began to turn away, then glanced back at his son. "I'm proud of you, Tristram," he said.

Hearing this, the boy flushed with confusion and even surprise. As Pendergast turned to go, he real-ized this was probably the first time anyone had ever praised him.

Leaving Tristram to secure the town hall, Pender-gast made his way by side streets to the village quay. There were some snipers, but without leadership, and in the growing dark they were ineffectual. The sun had set over the western ridge of the cinder cone, a streak of blood fading in the sky. Across the lake he could see the two boats with the remaining Nazi forces arriving at the island's shattered docks. He stared up at the cruel-looking lines of the castle, painted vermilion by the last rays of the dying sun.

The Nazis and the few remaining super-twins sym-pathetic to their cause had been soundly beaten and were in retreat. But there were still many enemy soldiers about; the Nazis retained their scientists, technicians, and laboratories; and their fortress remained a formida-ble redoubt, almost impregnable. They had been dealt a severe blow—but there was nothing to stop them from taking up their evil work again.

On top of that, Fischer was still alive.

For a long time, Pendergast stared across the lake. Then he walked down the quay, selected an inconspicu-ous and still-undamaged motor launch, jumped in, started the engine, and cast off, heading in the direction of the island.

The night was now so advanced that his little vessel vanished into the darkness of the lake. Keeping to a quiet speed, the engine purring and barely audible, he made his way across the lake, circling to the western side of the island. A few hundred yards from shore he cut the engine and rowed, using the flashlight, carefully hooded, to locate the tunnel from which he'd swum when escaping the fortress hours before. Finding the entrance, he rowed the launch into the stone passageway, then started the engine once again and threaded the labyrinth of watery passages until he felt the keel of the boat scrape against the stone of the floor. Beaching the craft, he continued on foot, passing the bodies of the colonel and several of his men, until he reached the large, domed space with the steel cage set into the center of its floor.

He paused, listening intently. Overhead, he could hear the faintest sounds of activity: the rhythmic tromping of boots, the faint bark of orders. But down here, in the lowest level of the fortress, all was quiet. He turned back to the ammunition dump contained within the steel cage, shining his light into it. It was a large and varied assortment of munitions and ammo: rolls of det cord and bricks of C-4, stacks of M112 demolition charges, 120mm tank gun cartridges, cans of precision-machined gunpowder, land mines, stacks of crates containing small-arms ammunition, cases of grenades, RPGs, mortars, .50-caliber machine guns, and even a brace of mini-guns with dozens of ammo boxes for each.

The large cage was securely locked, and it took Pendergast over five minutes, using improvised tools, to gain access. Once inside, he looked around more closely. As he'd noticed on his prior passage through this space, the Nazis had made use of a natural fissure in the old volcano to store their weapons. Despite the vast amount of shells, weapons, and casings visible within the cage, it was only the tip of the iceberg: an even greater amount of ordnance lay below the level of the floor, protected by the walls of the fissure itself. The Nazis had taken no chances that, in the event of an attack, a lucky shell hit from an invading force could accidentally touch off their magazine: it was buried deep in the lowest level of the fortress, its main bulk surrounded and shielded by protective volcanic rock.

It was also designed so that, if it did go off, the explosion would be severely confined by the natural rock. It would not destroy the fortress above.

Or would it? As he contemplated the arsenal, Pendergast remembered something else: the broad, fresh radial pattern of cracks he'd noticed in the curtain wall of the fortress. These were not cracks caused by the normal settling of an ancient wall; just the opposite. They had been caused by an upward heaving of the ground, an upsurge that had separated and dislocated the huge blocks along the castle's foundation. That indicated only one thing: a recent resurgence of the volcano's caldera floor by the upward movement of magma. Which meant the dead volcano was perhaps not so dead, after all.

As if on cue, a tremor—similar to the ones he'd noticed earlier—shook the floor ever so slightly beneath his feet.

The Nazis had been careful to safeguard their arsenal from any outside attack short of a tactical nuclear strike. However, in so doing, it was possible they had overlooked the possibility of an attack from *within*— an attack involving both high explosives . . . and Mother Nature. They were not, Pendergast thought with a faint smile, very good geologists.

Grabbing one of the canisters of black powder, he pierced it with his knife and poured the contents over the crates and boxes and powder kegs that made up the ammo dump. He emptied another canister over the weaponry, and then another, until the entire upper surface of the magazine was coated with a thick dusting of gunpowder. Then, taking two more cans, he slipped one under his arm while using the other to make a trail of powder away from the arsenal, out the open door of the cage and along the floor, headed back in the direction from which he'd come. Discarding the empty can, he opened the second and last, and continued the gunpowder trail, out of the domed area and down the narrow stone passageway.

The last of the gunpowder ran out and Pendergast put the can aside. Taking out his flashlight, he played it back along the narrow black trail he'd just made. It was approximately sixty feet long. He paused a minute, drew in a deep breath. Then, kneeling, he removed the lighter, held it to the end of the line of black powder, and flicked it on.

Immediately there was a spark, a puff of flame, and—with an angry hiss—the trail of powder began to burn, dissolving into a low cloud of smoke as it flared its way back toward the weapons cache. Pendergast turned and ran back down the branching passageways of the sub-basement.

He had just made it to the boat and was getting into it when a tremendous, earsplitting roar sounded behind him. This was followed by a second, and then a third, as a chain reaction of explosions began setting off more and more of the castle's cache of arms. Even at this distance, the force of the initial blast knocked him sprawling into the bottom of the boat; ears ringing, he got up, shoved off, started the engine, jammed it into full throttle, and headed out the escape tunnel at top speed, passing dangerously close to the stone walls as he followed the twistings and turnings of the passageway. Now the explosions were coming so fast they were no longer discrete blasts, but rather one constant fusillade of noise and fury, as the Nazi arsenal exploded with ever-increasing violence, the blasts moving deeper and deeper inside the fissure beneath the castle. The force of the explosions was shaking the very walls around him, and now stones, dirt, and nogging from the ancient ceiling were falling, collapsing with immense force into the water behind him, setting up a thunderous surge of water that pushed his boat forward.

He roared out of the mouth of the tunnel and into the open lake just as the entranceway collapsed into rubble behind him. Not stopping, not even slowing to look back, he goosed the throttle wide open and tore across the water in the direction of the town of Nova Godói. Not until he was halfway across the lake did he throttle down and glance back for a view of the castle.

The rumblings had ceased. The fortress remained standing, dark and silent, with only a thin trail of smoke coming from where the tunnel met the shore. He waited, the seconds ticking by, but still nothing happened. The exploding dump had evidently not been powerful enough to fracture the rock, to pierce down to the magma chamber underneath the cinder cone.

Still he waited. And then a shiver passed over the surface of the water. A low rumble reached his ears, almost below the audible range, a vibration he felt more in his bones than his ears. The surface of the lake shivered again, tiny wavelets kicked up, the rumble growing louder. Now the water was dancing crazily and he saw, along the very bottom of the massive wall encircling the fortress, a crack of red. Slowly it enlarged, moving horizontally, with small flares and puffs of steam, like the lid of some gigantic pressure cooker bulging up and about to explode.

A bright flash, and another. This was no man-made blast: it was too vast, too loud, and it came from too deep within the earth. The thunderclap struck him a moment later, almost bowling him over the side of the boat. Several vast and spectacular sprays of lava erupted into the night air, like giant fountains, with a screaming roar of releasing gas and steam. The bellowing explosions of thunder rolled across the lake like a physical force, shivering the surface of the water. As he stared, entire sections of the fortress—towers, ramparts, walls—seemed to come apart at the seams and rise, slowly, amid roiling clouds of fire and smoke separating into mushroom clouds.

He could make out tiny figures—some in uniform, others in lab coats, still others in coveralls—scrambling like ants down to the lake, diving in and piling into boats along the shore. Several other figures, their clothes aflame, like human firebombs, rose out of the eruption of rock, lava, and fire, trailing smoke.

As he watched, unable to tear his eyes from the sight, an additional huge staccato series of explosions shuddered the island with ugly cauliflowers of red and yellow. The fortress was now rent asunder, turning night into ghastly day. The blasts reached Pendergast a moment later, one after another, punches of overpressure pushing him violently back, skidding his boat across the now violently agitated surface of the lake. This led to one monumental explosion whose gout of fire and destruction engulfed the top half of the island, a vast storm of rocks, lava, and smoke that rose as the explosion accelerated, a raging upward column of destruction. And then there was a second, even

greater explosion, one so deep and muffled it seemed to
stir the mountains themselves. But this one wasn't an
explosion; rather it was an implosion: and Pendergast
saw the fractured, broken remains of the castle begin
to collapse in on themselves—slowly at first, and then
more and more quickly, until the vast ancient façade
crumbled in with an unearthly shriek. Pendergast saw
tongues of living lava shooting out from the rent maw
of the island, streaking upward in fiery tracers before
falling back down to the lake, dropping all around him
like bombs, sizzling and popping as they hit the water.

He revved up the engine again, heading toward
shore.

And then—with a final, convulsive blast that seemed
to shake the earth to its very core—the entire island
tore itself apart, hurtling house-size chunks of rock and
blocks of dressed stone thousands of feet into the air
with incredible violence, destroying many of the boats
of the would-be evacuees, the detritus arcing through
the night sky and falling as far away as the town of
Nova Godói, starting fires in the surrounding forest
and causing such a devastating rain of ruin that Pendergast found himself dodging a firing gallery of falling
rocks as he tore through the water at top speed in an
attempt to save his own life.

84

PENDERGAST PULLED THE LAUNCH ALONGSIDE
a wharf, leapt out, and ran along the quay. Several
members of the Twins Brigade were there, guarding
the docks, staring at the final destruction of the island.
The chaos from the final, dreadful explosion was settling down now, and in the lambent light of the erupting island he could see that half a dozen boats of various
sizes had escaped the final conflagration and were coming
across the lake toward the town. As he watched, one of
the boats—a small, sleek craft—approached the quay at
high speed. It held what appeared to be scientists or technicians in lab coats. The boat roared up against the quay,
slamming into the stone, and the occupants scrambled
onto land. They were glassy-eyed and stunned, several
with hair and eyebrows scorched, filthy with soot, cough-
ing and choking. They staggered up the quay toward the
town, saying nothing. The Twins Brigade watched them
pass but did not stop them. Instead they focused their
weapons on a second arriving boat, containing half a
dozen men in Nazi dress. They had also suffered from
the effects of the explosion, their faces blackened, uniforms singed. A few appeared to be injured.

As the boat approached the quay, the brigade took positions and began firing. For a minute, scattered, sporadic fire was returned by the Nazis in the boat; but the firefight was over almost before it had started. The Nazis threw down their weapons, raised their hands in surrender as the boat idled up to the quay. A detachment of twins led them away under guard.

Pendergast looked back over the lake, its black surface now a fiery reflection of the island, a gaping cone of boiling lava, only a few broken ramparts of the fortress remaining at the edges. A small skiff could be seen streaking over the water, approaching the quay at an oblique angle, keeping as much as possible out of the light of the flickering flames. Pendergast looked at it more closely. In it was a single man, seated in the stern, one hand on the tiller of the outboard. He was tall, powerfully built, with a thick shock of white hair that seemed to glow in the burning reflection of the ruined tower.

Fischer.

Pendergast drew his weapon and ran down the quay in the direction of the approaching skiff. But even as he did so, Fischer caught sight of him and gunned the motor, slewing sharply away from the quay, heading past it in the direction of the beach and the forest beyond. Pendergast fired once and missed; Fischer drew his own gun and returned fire, but from the moving boat the shot went wide. Pendergast stopped and took careful aim, this time punching a round into the outboard motor, which began to cough and sputter, billows of ugly black smoke rising into the ash-filled air. Fischer tried to turn the boat back away from shore, toward the center of the lake, but Pendergast fired a third time. Fischer staggered, grabbed his chest, and with a cry went over the gunwale of the boat into the water.

The burning boat drifted on while Pendergast ran past the end of the quay, to the pebbled beach opposite where Fischer's body had fallen into the water. Reaching the formation of three large, separated rocks rising from the water just beyond the quay, he leapt up on the closest, scanning the dark water for any sign of Fischer.

A shot rang out; Pendergast felt a sharp burning sensation, like a fiery slash of a knife, graze his left arm just below the knife wound in his shoulder. He fell back onto the slippery rock, barely managing to retain hold of his weapon, cursing himself for his lack of caution. When he was able to take cover and reconnoiter, he realized that Fischer must have himself taken cover behind one of the other three rocks: the one farthest into the lake.

Fischer's bullet had barely grazed Pendergast's arm, but nevertheless he could feel the warm blood began to trickle down toward his elbow.

Fischer's voice came from behind the rock. "It seems I've underestimated you," he said. "You've managed to make rather a mess of things. What do you plan to do now?"

"I'm going to kill you."

"One of us is going to die: but it won't be me. I am armed and uninjured. That little tumble over the side of the boat was an act, as perhaps you've guessed."

"You killed my wife. You must die."

"She belonged to us, never to you. She was *our* creation. Part of our great project."

"Your project is dead. Your labs, your base of operations, destroyed. Even your experimental subjects have turned against you."

"Perhaps. But nothing will kill our dream—the dream of perfecting the human race. It is the greatest—

the ultimate—scientific pursuit. If you think this is the end, you are sadly deluded."

"I greatly fear that *you* are the deluded one, *mein Oberstgruppenführer*," came a voice from behind Pendergast. He turned to see Alban approaching them from the direction of the forest. He was dripping wet, his shirt stained with blood, and one side of his once-handsome face had been dreadfully burned, pink and charred most horribly, the dermis fused in some places, in others the musculature and even bone showing. He held a P38 in one hand.

Alban leapt nimbly onto the third rock and stood there, outlined by the fiery island. Though he was burnt and wounded, he nevertheless moved with the same gazelle-like grace that Pendergast had noted so often before.

"I've been looking for you, Herr Fischer," he said. "I wanted to report that things have not gone exactly as you had planned." He nodded in the direction of the burning hulk of an island. "As you've probably noticed."

He tossed the pistol from hand to hand as he spoke and gave a strange chuckle. A fey mood seemed to be upon him. "Why don't you both come out from under those rocks you're hiding behind, stand up and face each other like men. The endgame will be an honorable one—correct, Herr Fischer?"

Fischer was the first to respond. Without speaking, he climbed up and stood on the rock. Pendergast, after a moment, did likewise. The three men, bathed in the infernal orange glow, faced each other.

Fischer spoke to Alban, his voice bitter. "I blame you even more than your father for this. You failed me, Alban. Utterly. After all I did for you, generations of genetic grooming and perfection, after fifteen years of the most exacting and careful upbringing—*this* is how you perform."

He spat into the water.

"And how *did* I fail, Herr Fischer?" His voice had a strange, new note in it.

"You failed the final test of your manhood. You had many chances to kill this man, your father, and did not. Because of that, the flower of our youth, the seed that was to sow the Fourth Reich, is scattered. I should shoot you down like a dog." Fischer's weapon briefly strayed toward Alban.

"Wait, *mein Oberstgruppenführer*. I can still kill my father. I'll do it right now. Watch me. Allow me to shoot him—and restore myself to your good graces." Alban raised his gun, aiming it at Pendergast.

For a long, freezing moment, the three men stood, points of a triangle, each on one of the three rocks jutting up out of the lake. Alban's gun was pointed at Pendergast. Pendergast moved his own firearm from Fischer and aimed it at his son.

For agonizing minutes Alban stood there, the two with their weapons pointed at each other, bathed in the hellish glow and thunder of the eruption on the island, the sound of sporadic gunfire in the town.

"Well?" Fischer said at last. "What are you waiting for? It's as I suspected—you don't have the guts to shoot."

"You think not?" Alban asked. Suddenly—quick as a striking snake—he swung his weapon around at Fischer and pulled the trigger. The round struck the man in the gut. He gasped, clutched his belly, and fell to his knees, dropping the gun.

"*You're* the failure," Alban said. "Your master plan was flawed—flawed fundamentally. You should never have allowed the defectives to live. I see that now. Having recourse to an organ bank was too high a price to pay for the filial bond you were never able to completely breed out. *You* failed, *mein Oberstgruppenführer*—and long ago, you taught me what the price of failure must be."

He aimed the gun again and shot Fischer a second time, square in the forehead. The back of Fischer's head detached from his body, dissolving in a mist of blood, bone, and brain matter; soundlessly, he fell backward, his body slipping off the rock and disappearing below the surface of the lake.

Pendergast saw that the slide of the P38 had locked back—his son's magazine was empty.

Alban, too, noticed this. "It would appear I'm out of ammunition," he said, snugging the weapon into his waistband. "It seems I won't be killing you, after all." Although it must have cost him dreadful pain, he nevertheless smiled crookedly. "And now, if you'll excuse me, I must be going."

Pendergast stared, only now managing to wrap his mind around what had just happened. He wondered how his son—despite the terrible burns, the wounds, the loss of everything—maintained his arrogant composure, his cocksure attitude.

"No words of farewell, Father, to your son?"

"You're not going anywhere," Pendergast said slowly, maintaining his weapon on Alban. "You're a murderer. Of the worst kind."

Alban nodded. "True. And I've killed more people than even you could imagine."

Pendergast aimed his weapon. "And now it is *you* who must die for your crimes."

"Is that so?" Alban issued a small laugh. "We shall see. I know you've figured out my unique temporal sense. Isn't that right?"

"The Copenhagen Window," Pendergast replied.

"Precisely. It's derived from the Copenhagen interpretation of quantum mechanics, of which you are no doubt aware?"

Pendergast nodded almost imperceptibly.

"The interpretation is the notion that the future is nothing more than an expanding set of probabilities, time lines of possibility, that continuously collapse into one reality as observations or measurements are made. It's the standard interpretation of quantum mechanics taught in universities."

"It would appear," Pendergast said, "that your mind has somehow become able to leverage this—to reach into the near future and see those branching possibilities."

Alban smiled. "Brilliant! You see, most humans have only a fleeting sense of the immediate future, perhaps a few seconds at most. You can see a car ahead slow at a stop sign, and you intuitively sense the probability that it will stop—or else continue on. Or you might know what someone is going to say moments before they say it. Our scientists recognized the usefulness of this trait over half a century ago, and set out to enhance it through breeding and genetic manipulation. I am the final product." There was evident pride in Alban's tone. "My sense of the branching probabilistic time lines is much more developed than in others. I can sense up to fifteen seconds into the future, and my mind can see the dozens of branching possibilities—as if through a window—and pick out the most likely one. It may not seem like much—but what a difference it makes! In a way, my brain can tune in to the wave function ψ itself. But it is not the same as *predicting* the future. Because, of course, according to the Copenhagen interpretation, there is no fixed future. And as you have so astutely realized, my ability can be stymied by sudden, illogical, or unpredictable behavior."

His smile, made gruesome by the dreadful burns, widened. "But even without making use of my special future sense, Father, I know one thing beyond any shadow of a doubt: *you can't kill me.* I'm going to walk away now. Into the forest. To stop me, you will have to shoot me dead—and that you won't do. And so, *auf Wiedersehen.*"

"Don't be a fool, Alban. I *will* kill you."

The youth spread his hands. "I am waiting."

A long silence ensued, and then Alban went on, almost jauntily. "With *Der Bund* gone, I'm free. I'm only fifteen—I have a long and productive life ahead of me. The world, as they say, is now my oyster—and I promise you it'll be a more interesting place with me loose in it."

And with that he leapt nimbly from the rock into the shallow water.

Pendergast followed him with his gun, blood dripping slowly from the fingers of his left hand, as Alban waded onto the beach and strolled up it. Pendergast remained unmoving, gun still aimed at his son, as Alban continued, in no apparent hurry, to the grassy verge of the shore, climbed the shallow embankment, and strolled into a field of grass, finally melting into the black and unbroken wall of trees at the forest's edge. Only then did Pendergast—ever so slowly—lower his weapon with a trembling hand.

85

IT WAS CHRISTMAS EVE AT MOUNT MERCY HOS-
pital. A small Douglas fir, freshly cut, stood in the waiting area near the guards' station, plastic trimmings
attached to its branches by discreet rubber bands. Deep
within the hospital, a recording of carols was faintly
audible. Otherwise, the vast and rambling mansion
was cloaked in a nostalgic silence, its resident murder-
ers, poisoners, rapists, arsonists, vivisectors, and social
deviants caught up in reveries of Christmases past: of
presents received, and—rather more commonly—of
presents inflicted.

Dr. John Felder walked down one of the interior
corridors of Mount Mercy, Dr. Ostrom at his side. Over
the last several weeks his broken ribs had mostly healed,
and the concussion he'd sustained had receded. The
only scar—the only external scar—that remained from
his ordeal in the Wintour mansion was from the cut on
his temple, now a scarlet, jagged line.

Ostrom shook his head. "What a strange case. I still
feel we've hardly scratched the surface."

Felder did not respond to that.

Ostrom stopped before a pair of double doors that—

like most at Mount Mercy—were unlabeled. A single guard stood outside.

"This is it?" Felder asked.

"Yes. If you need anything, call for the guards."

Felder extended his hand. "Thank you, Doctor."

"My pleasure." Ostrom turned and made his way back down the corridor.

Felder nodded to the guard, took a breath. Then he pushed open the doors and stepped inside.

Beyond lay the Mount Mercy chapel. It was an artifact from the days when the hospital had been a sanatorium for the very rich, and Felder, who had never seen it before, was amazed. It remained unchanged from its late-nineteenth-century zenith, when the numerous bequests of fearful, ailing patients had given the chapel's designers working capital a Medici would envy. It was a masterpiece in miniature, jewel-like and utterly perfect, the nave only six rows deep, with a single central aisle; and yet the builders had cleverly re-created the ribbed vaults of a gothic cathedral, and in so doing filled both the side walls and the curved ambulatory with delicate, vividly colored stained glass. In the late-afternoon light, the chapel's interior seemed almost drowned in color; the pews, the slender pillars, the other architectural features, were so dappled and painted with light as to be almost indistinguishable from each other. Felder took a hesitant step forward, and then another. It was like being inside an ecclesiastical kaleidoscope.

Felder advanced up the rows of pews, glancing left and right. All was silent—there was no one here. But then, as he approached the sanctuary, he noticed a tiny side altar off to the left. There, sitting on the single bench, was Constance Greene. She was motionless, camouflaged by the dappled half-light, and it took him a minute to make her out. He turned and approached her. She was leaning forward slightly, absorbed by the book she was holding up in both hands; her lips were just parted; her eyes were half shut, the long lashes giving the false impression that she was dozing. But Felder could tell she was quite alert, her eyes scanning the lines of the book intently. He wondered if perhaps it was a Bible. He tried to control the excessive pounding of his heart.

She turned, saw him. "Good day, Dr. Felder," she said.

He nodded. "May I join you?"

She smiled faintly, made room for him on the bench. As she closed the book, he noticed that it was not a Bible, but Petronius's *Satyricon*.

"It's been some time since you last came to visit," she said as he sat down. "How are you faring?"

"Well enough, thank you. And yourself?"

"The same. I hope that you won't find the holidays—"

"Constance," he interrupted. "Would you mind terribly if we dispensed with the formalities?"

She looked at him, surprised.

Felder reached into the breast pocket of his jacket. He took out two envelopes—one, old and faded; the other, fresh and new. He laid them in front of her, one after the other.

After a moment she took up the old envelope in both hands. Felder noticed her pupils dilate. Without a word, she opened it and looked inside.

"The lock of my hair," she said. She spoke in quite a different voice from the one she had used to greet Felder and inquire after his well-being.

Felder inclined his head.

Now she turned to him with something almost like excitement. "Where on earth did you find it?"

"In Connecticut."

Constance frowned. "Connecticut? But—"

Felder forestalled the question by raising his hand. "The less you know of the particulars, Constance, the better. For both of us."

Constance's eyes drifted to the scar on his temple. "When I suggested the existence of this lock, Doctor, it was not my intention that you should put yourself in any jeopardy to obtain it."

"I know that."

She slipped the lock out of the envelope, placed it in the palm of her hand. Glancing down at it, she traced a single fingertip along its brief extent with the gentlest of motions. In that strange aquarium of color and silence, her expression seemed to go far, far away. For many long minutes, she remained silent. Felder said nothing.

At last—quite abruptly—she collected herself. She returned the lock to its envelope and passed it back to Felder. "Forgive me," she said.

"Not at all."

"I hope you were not...unduly put out in its recovery."

"It proved an interesting experience."

Now Constance picked up the other envelope. It bore the return address of a laboratory in Saratoga Springs. "And what is this?"

"The DNA results on the lock of hair."

"I see." Constance's demeanor—which had grown more than usually informal—became more reserved. "And what does the report say?"

"Take a look at the envelope," Felder said. "You'll see that I haven't opened it."

Constance turned the envelope over. "I don't understand."

Felder took a deep breath. He felt his limbs begin to tremble, ever so slightly. "I don't need to read the results. I already believe you, Constance. Everything."

Constance looked from the envelope to him and then back again.

"I *know* how old you are—and how young you are. I don't need any DNA analysis to tell me that. I know you were telling the truth when you said you were born in the 1870s. I don't understand it—but I believe it."

Constance said nothing.

"I also know you didn't murder your child. No doubt you had a reason for the deception—and as soon as you feel able to tell it to me, we can proceed."

Something flickered in Constance's eyes. "Proceed?"

"With overturning your involuntary commitment. And getting the murder charges dropped." Felder moved a little closer. "Constance, you were sent here on my recommendation. I see now that was a mistake. You're not insane. And you didn't murder your child— that was a smokescreen. If you tell me where your child is, I will have it duly verified by the authorities. And then we can begin the process of obtaining your release."

Constance hesitated. "I . . ." she said, before stopping. She seemed uncharacteristically at a loss.

Felder had brooded, planned, dreamed about this moment. But now that it was actually happening, it seemed to take him by as much surprise as it took Constance. "I took a terrible risk obtaining that lock." He touched his scar. "This is the least of it."

He let that sink in.

"I had to know. It's not your fault, of course, but now that it's done, I want you to know that I'd do it again. I'd walk through fire for you, Constance. No— no, let me speak, please. I'd do it again because of . . ."

of my feelings for you. And it's not just because I've wronged you, by putting you in here. It's because of the way I've grown to feel about you. I want to undo the wrong and get you out of here, because it's my hope that by setting you free, by putting us on an equal basis, in time you can come to look at me, not as a doctor, but as...as..." He hesitated, more confused than ever. "And naturally at that point, because of professional ethics, I'll have to recuse myself as your doctor...if, of course..."

He finally fell silent, overwhelmed, and then, tentatively, reached out and took her hand. With trepidation, he looked up to meet her gaze. One glance was all it took. He looked down again and released her hand, feeling ill.

"Doctor," Constance said gently. "John. I'm touched— I am, truly, deeply. Your belief in me means more than I could put into words. But the truth is that I could never return the feelings you seem to have for me—for the reason that my heart belongs to another."

Felder did not look up. As Constance spoke, her voice had grown increasingly soft and troubled, until the final five words were just barely audible.

He thought back to that day in the Mount Mercy library, when Constance had first mentioned the existence of the lock; when she'd implied that his finding it, bringing it to light, would do more than simply vindicate her—for him it would be a lover's test, a way to prove the depth of his feelings, to wipe out the past with all its false steps and dubious medical observations. But he realized now it was all in his head, that she had implied no such thing. He had projected his own hopes onto what she'd been offering him: simply an opportunity to satisfy himself about the truth of her age. And only because he demanded it.

He felt Constance take his hand. He looked up to see her smiling at him. She had fully recovered, and her smile held its usual suspension of cool amusement and benevolent distance.

"I can't return your feelings, Doctor," she said, giving his hand a gentle pressure. "But there's something else I can do. I can tell you my story. It is a story I've not told to anyone else, at least not in its entirety."

Felder blinked. Her words were slow to settle in.

She went on. "I fear this story must remain between us. Are you interested?"

"Interested?" Felder repeated. "My God. Of course."

"Good. Then please consider this my gift to you." Constance paused. "After all—it is Christmas Eve."

86

THEY SAT, QUITE STILL, IN THE PROFUSION OF dappled light. Constance looked over Felder's shoulder, out into the main body of the chapel. The two envelopes, one old, one new, lay on the pew between them.

Constance began. "I was born at Sixteen Water Street, New York City, in the 1870s. Most likely it was in the summer of 1873. By the time I was five, both my parents were dead of tuberculosis. In 1878, my older sister, Mary, was confined to a workhouse—the Five Points Mission—and ultimately vanished. My brother, Joseph, died in 1880. This much you know.

"What you may not know is that my sister, Mary, was the victim of a doctor attached to the Five Points Mission, a surgeon of great skill who called himself Enoch Leng. Dr. Leng was a man with a singular ambition—to extend his own life span far beyond that of a normal human being. Before you judge him, however, I should explain that Dr. Leng was not trying to extend his life for selfish reasons. He was working on a scientific project—one that would take longer than a normal life span to complete."

"What scientific project?" Felder asked.

"The details of the project aren't necessary for my own story." Constance paused. "Now, here we come to the first of several grotesqueries. Dr. Leng's theories were unorthodox, as was his sense of medical ethics. His research led him to believe it would be possible to create a medical treatment—a formula or arcanum— for greatly prolonging life. The ingredients could be procured only from living human tissue, taken from a healthy young person."

"Good Lord," Felder murmured.

"As a specialist at a children's workhouse in the Five Points section of Manhattan, then New York's most notorious slum, Dr. Leng had no paucity of raw material. My own sister fell victim to his experiments—her mutilated corpse, along with dozens of others, was discovered in a mass grave about three years ago in Lower Manhattan."

Felder recalled coming across an article describing this discovery on one of his visits to the public library. It had been in the *New York Times*, written by that reporter—Smithback—the one who was later murdered. *So Mary Greene was Constance's sister*, he thought.

"I'm afraid a great many people fell victim to Dr. Leng while he was refining his technique. Suffice it to say that—in 1885—he succeeded in perfecting his arcanum."

"He found a way to prolong his life?"

"His technique centered on the bundle of nerves known as the cauda equina—I have no need of further anatomical explanation, you being a doctor. But yes: by increasingly subtle refinements, he did in fact succeed in creating an arcanum that would dramatically slow the aging process of the human body. By that time, I was a ward, living in his house."

"You—?" Felder began.

"After my sister vanished, I became—in the parlance of the day—a 'guttersnipe.' I had no family and lived in the streets, doing whatever it took to stay alive. I begged, I did cartwheels or swept the sidewalks free of filth for pedestrians, hoping for a penny. More than once I very nearly froze or starved to death. Many nights I slept within the shadow of the Five Points Mission, where Dr. Leng donated his services. One day the doctor stopped and asked my name. When I told him, I think he realized he was responsible for my situation—and for some unknown reason he took pity on me. Or perhaps not. At any rate, he took me into his mansion on Riverside Drive and used me as a guinea pig, administering the perfected arcanum, probably to test for side effects. And over time, strangely enough, he became fond of me. Why, I shall never know. He fed me, clothed me, educated me, and...continued to administer to me that same elixir that he gave himself."

Constance had been slow to utter these last words. For some minutes, the chapel fell into silence. The story was incredible, but Felder knew it was the truth.

At last, Constance resumed. "For many, many years, we lived a solitary, reclusive life in that mansion. I continued my courses of study in literature, philosophy, art, music, history, and languages, partly with the doctor's help and partly on my own, making free use of his library and scientific collections. Meanwhile, Dr. Leng continued his work. Around 1935, he achieved his second success. Using various chemicals and compounds that had been previously unavailable, he managed to synthesize an arcanum that no longer required... human factors."

"In other words, he stopped killing," Felder said.

Constance nodded. "As long as it prolonged his life,

he felt no special compunction against taking lives. However, as a scientist, it offended his sense of purity and aesthetic. Yes—he stopped killing. He no longer needed to. The arcanum we both continued to take was now purely synthetic. But his greater task remained incomplete. And so his scientific research continued until it finally stopped, rather suddenly, in the spring of 1954."

"Why 1954?" Felder asked.

A thin smile appeared on Constance's face. "Once again, that isn't germane to my story. But I will tell you one thing. Dr. Leng once explained to me that there are two ways to 'cure' a patient. The common way is by restoring him to health."

"What's the other?"

"Putting him out of his misery." The thin smile vanished. "In any case, with his work finally complete—or, more precisely, no longer necessary—Dr. Leng ceased to take the elixir. He lost interest in life, became even more reclusive, and began to age at a normal rate. But he gave me a choice. And I...chose to continue treatment.

"And so things remained for another fifty-odd years—until we were the victims of an unexpected and violent home invasion. Dr. Leng was killed, and I went into hiding in the deepest recesses of the house. Ultimately, order was restored, and the mansion passed into the hands of Leng's great-grandnephew: Aloysius Pendergast."

"Pendergast?" Felder repeated, hugely surprised.

Constance nodded.

Felder shook his head. It was too much to take in—too much.

"I watched Pendergast for many months before I finally revealed myself to him. He very kindly took me in as...as his ward." She shifted on the bench. "And there you have it, Dr. Felder—the story of my past."

Felder took a deep breath. "And—your child?" He couldn't help but wonder who the father was.

"I gave birth to my son in Gsalrig Chongg, a remote monastery in Tibet. Through a complicated process, the monks of the monastery recognized that my son was the nineteenth incarnation of one of Tibet's holiest rinpoches. This proved a great danger. The occupying Chinese authorities have been ruthlessly suppressing Tibetan Buddhism, especially the idea of the reincarnation of holy men. Back in 1995, when the Dalai Lama proclaimed a six-year-old boy as the eleventh incarnation of the Panchen Lama, the Chinese seized the boy, and he hasn't been seen since—perhaps murdered. The Chinese learned that my child had been proclaimed the nineteenth reincarnation of the rinpoche—and so they came to get him."

"So it was necessary to convince them that he was dead," Felder said.

"Precisely. I pretended to flee with the child and then throw him overboard, all as a diversion. My arrest was highly public, and it seemed to satisfy the Chinese. Meanwhile, my real child was being smuggled out of Tibet to India."

"So you brought a dummy aboard the *Queen Mary* and threw it overboard?"

"Exactly. A life-size doll. It went over the side in midpassage."

There was a brief silence before Felder spoke again. "There's something else I don't understand. Why did you send me after your lock of hair? I'd always assumed it was a..." Here he colored. "A labor of love. To exonerate myself, to prove myself to you. But you've made it clear that you—you have no feelings for me along those lines."

"Haven't you guessed the answer, Dr. Felder?" Constance replied. "Actually, I suppose there are two answers." She smiled slightly. "That day you came to visit me in the library here, I'd just learned my child had reached India safely. He's in Dharamsala, with the Tibetan government in exile, very well protected. Now he can grow up and undergo the proper training to fulfill his position as the nineteenth rinpoche, in absentia. Safe from the Chinese."

"So there's no longer a need to maintain this fiction that you murdered your child."

"Exactly. And as a result, there's no need for me to remain any longer in Mount Mercy."

"But to be allowed to leave, you'd have to be certified as compos mentis."

Constance inclined her head.

"Which meant convincing me of your sanity."

"That's correct. But there's also the second answer that I mentioned. By convincing you of my sanity, it would resolve the agonizing doubts in your own mind. If you knew I was speaking the truth, it would help you resolve the difficulties in my story—difficulties that I know have been wearing on you."

So she did care for him—in some manner or another. At the very least, she'd noticed his internal struggle and taken pity on him for it. In the silence that followed, Felder found himself—in light of all this new information—framing the arguments he would put forward for overturning Constance's commitment. He realized, with growing dismay, that nothing she'd just told him could be used as evidence. It would not even begin to stand up in a court hearing. He would have to find his own way through the legal maze—and the maze of demonstrating that the distant child in India was hers—but, he knew, he owed that to her . . .

and more. At least, proving the child was alive would be fairly straightforward—thanks to advanced DNA testing.

He still had so many questions to ask that he found himself somehow unable to frame even one of them in his head. Instead, he realized he needed time to process all that he had heard. It was time to leave.

He picked up the two envelopes, held the old, yellowed one out to Constance. "This is rightfully yours," he said.

"I'd be happier knowing it was in your possession."

Felder nodded. He slipped both envelopes into his jacket pocket. He stood up, but did not leave, hesitating a moment. One important question still remained to be resolved.

"Constance," he said.

"Yes, Doctor?"

"The, ah, arcanum. When did you stop taking it?"

"When my first guardian, Dr. Leng, was killed."

He hesitated. "Does it ever bother you?"

"What?"

"The—sorry, I can't think of a delicate way to put this—the knowledge that your own life has been artificially extended by the murder of innocent people."

Constance regarded him with her deep, inscrutable eyes. The chapel seemed to go very still.

"Are you familiar," she asked at last, "with F. Scott Fitzgerald's quotation: *The test of a first-rate intelligence is the ability to hold two opposed ideas in the mind at the same time, and still retain the ability to function?*"

"I've heard it, yes."

"Consider this. I was not merely the beneficiary of Dr. Leng's experiments. I became the ward of the man who murdered and mutilated my own sister. I spent over a *hundred* years beneath his roof, reading his books, drinking his wines, consuming his food, conversing pleasantly with him in the evenings—all the while knowing who he was and what he did to my own sister. A rare case of opposing ideas, wouldn't you say?"

She paused. Felder was struck by the unusual look in her eyes—of what? He could not say.

"So I ask you, Doctor: does that mean I have a first-rate intelligence—or that I am insane?" She paused, her deep eyes glittering. "Or ... *both*?"

And with that, she nodded her dismissal, picked up her book, and began to read.

87

D'AGOSTA WAS FEARFUL THE OLD BAR MIGHT have closed up. He hadn't been there in years. Few of his fellow officers even knew of the place—the ferns in their macramé hangers guaranteed that no self-respecting cop would be caught dead in there. But as he turned the corner from Vesey onto Church Street, feet crunching against the light dusting of snow, he saw—with relief—that the place was still there. The ferns in the window appeared, if anything, deader than ever. He descended the steps and went inside.

Laura Hayward was already there. She was sitting in the back, at the very same table—how was that for a coincidence?—a fresh, foamy Guinness in one hand. She looked up as D'Agosta approached, smiled.

"I didn't even know this place had a name," she said as he sat down.

D'Agosta nodded. "Vino Veritas."

"Maybe the owner's a wine connoisseur. Or a Harvard graduate. Or both."

D'Agosta didn't quite understand this, so instead of replying he nodded to the waiter and pointed at Hayward's drink.

"It seemed like a good place to meet," he said as his own Guinness was placed before him. "Just a stone's throw from Police Plaza."

He took a sip from the pint glass, then sat back in his chair, trying to appear nonchalant. In fact he was nervous as hell. The idea had come to him that morning, on his way to work. No big plan this time, no elaborate preparations. Instinct told him that he'd better just go for it.

"Big doings in Captain Singleton's office," Laura said, teasingly.

"So the word's already out?"

She nodded. "Midge Rawley. She's the last person you'd think. I mean, she's been Glen's confidential secretary, known every last bit of his business, for—what?—at least ten years."

"And I think she was loyal for all of them. Until just recently. At least, that's when the payments took place—according to the bank records."

"I'd heard she'd been having some personal problems. Separated from her husband, mother in a nursing home. I suppose that's why they chose her."

"Maybe they blackmailed her. Almost makes you feel sorry for her."

"Almost. Until you remember it was her tip-off that betrayed the location of the Central Park boathouse meet. Which led to the shootout, the deaths of five people, and the kidnapping and murder of Helen Pendergast." Laura paused. "Did the search warrant uncover anything?"

D'Agosta shook his head. "We're hoping to learn more from the audio and video surveillance logs. Or maybe from Rawley herself. The Internal Affairs boys have her down in the Tombs right now. Who knows? She might get talkative." He took another sip of his Guinness. He was getting more nervous by the minute—and this small talk wasn't helping any.

"Anyway, you did good, Vinnie. This will be a real feather in your cap."

"Thanks."

"And it may take Singleton down a notch or two, as well."

D'Agosta had thought of this. Having a mole discovered in his own private office would make Captain Singleton defensive, to say the least—and that, indirectly, would only help get D'Agosta off the hot seat. Although it was a damn shame—Singleton was a decent man.

"It's really Pendergast who should get the credit," he said.

"He just called you, out of the blue, and told you who to finger?"

"Not exactly. Let's say he pointed me in the right direction."

"So it was your own good police work that did it. Don't sell yourself short, Vinnie—you scored, big-time. Take the credit and run." Laura's sly smile deepened. "So does this mean you and Agent Pendergast are best buddies again?"

"He called me 'my dear Vincent,' if that's any indication."

"I see. So Pendergast is back in New York, the Hotel Killer murders have stopped, and the FBI profilers think the killer's moved on. It's Christmas Eve. God's in his heaven, all's right with the world." She raised her glass.

D'Agosta took another sip of his Guinness. He barely tasted the brew. It was all he could do to keep from squirming in his chair. This was growing intolerable. He'd have to find some way to introduce the subject, but he was damned if he knew how—

Suddenly he became aware that Laura had put down

her glass and was gazing at him intently. For a moment they looked at each other in silence. And then, she spoke.

"Yes," she said in a low voice.

D'Agosta was confused. "I'm sorry?"

She reached over, took his hand. "You big dope. Let me put you out of your misery. Of course I'll marry you."

"You...how...?" D'Agosta fell silent, at a loss for words.

"Do you think I'm a complete idiot? Why would you ask me to meet you for a drink here, of all unlikely places? You made such a big deal out of picking this particular spot—the spot where we first got to know each other. Two years ago, remember?" She squeezed his hand, then laughed. "Vino Veritas, indeed. You know what? Deep down, Lieutenant D'Agosta, you're just an old softie. A sentimentalist. And that's one of the things—one of the *many* things—I love about you."

D'Agosta looked down. He was so moved that he could not speak. "I can't believe you knew. I mean..."

"So where's the ring?"

D'Agosta stammered, trying to explain it was spontaneous, last minute, until he was interrupted by her laugh. "I'm just teasing you, Vinnie. I like spontaneous. I can wait for the ring—no problem."

Sheepishly, he reached over and took her hand. "Thanks."

Still smiling, she cocked her head. "Let's go someplace else. Some *new* place, really nice. As nostalgic as this place is, let's make a new memory of tonight. We need to celebrate—and not just because it's Christmas Eve. We've got a lot of planning to do."

She signaled the waiter for the check.

And Last

THE LARGE, ORNATELY PANELED LIBRARY OF 891 Riverside Drive was lit only by fire and candlelight. It was a late-February evening, and a light freezing rain was falling on the cars passing by on Riverside and the West Side Highway, but no sound of traffic, no *tick*, *tick* of ice upon glass panes, penetrated the barred and curtained windows. The only sound was the crackling of the fire, the scratch of Agent Pendergast's fountain pen on cream laid writing paper, and a low, infrequent conversation that was being carried out between Constance Greene and Tristram.

The two were sitting at a gaming table placed before the fire, and Constance was teaching Tristram how to play ombre, a card game that had gone out of fashion decades, if not centuries, before. Tristram stared at his cards, his young face screwed up in thought. Constance had begun introducing him to games slowly—with whist—and already Tristram's memory, concentration, and logical abilities showed remarkable improvement. Now he was immersed in the subtleties of spadilles, entradas, and estuches.

Pendergast was sitting at a writing table in the far

corner of the library, his back to a wall of leather-bound books. From time to time he glanced up from his writing, his silvery eyes moving around the room, always coming to rest at last on the two persons playing cards.

Now the quiet of the room was broken by the ringing of Pendergast's cell phone. He slipped it from his pocket, glanced at the number. "Yes?" he spoke into it.

"Pendergast? It's me. Corrie."

"Miss Swanson. How are you faring?"

"Fine. I've been swamped catching up with my coursework, that's why I'm calling only now. I've got one hell of a story to tell you...and..." Here there was a hesitation.

"Is everything all right?"

"Well, if you mean by that I'm not hearing any goose-stepping coming at me from behind, yeah. But listen: I solved a case, a real, honest-to-God case."

"Excellent. I want to apologize for having been unable to give you greater assistance when you came to me back in December—but I had great faith in your ability to look after yourself. Faith that, it would seem, was justified. And as it happens, I have a rather interesting story to tell you, as well."

A pause.

"So," Corrie went on. "Any chance of renewing that offer for lunch at Le Bernardin?"

"How remiss of me for not suggesting it immediately. We should do it soon, however—because I'm thinking of taking an extended vacation."

"Name the date."

Pendergast considered a small appointment book he plucked from his jacket pocket. "Next Thursday, one o'clock."

"That'll be great, I don't have any classes on

Thursday afternoons." Another hesitation. "Hey, Pendergast?"

"Yes?"

"Would it be all right if...if I brought my father along? He's part of the story."

"Naturally. I'll look forward to seeing the two of you next Thursday."

He put pen and paper aside and stood up. Tristram had left, and Constance was sitting at the table alone, shuffling the cards. Pendergast looked over to her.

"How is his playing coming along?"

"Quite well. Better than I expected, actually. If he continues to learn at such a rapid pace, I may move on to rubicon bezique or skat."

Pendergast remained silent a moment before speaking again. "I've been thinking about what you said. Back when I visited you in Mount Mercy, looking for advice. And you were right, of course. I *had* to go to Nova Godói. There was no choice. And I had to act— alas, with extreme violence. I've rescued Tristram, true. But the other half of the equation—the more complex and difficult part of the equation—remains unsolved."

For a moment, Constance did not reply. When she did, it was in a low voice. "So there's been no word."

"None. I've got certain, ah, assets in place, and he's been put on the watch lists of both the DEA and the local consulate officials—discreetly, of course. But he seems to have vanished into the forest."

"Do you think he might be dead?" she asked.

"Perhaps," Pendergast replied. "His injuries were grievous."

Constance put down the cards. "I've been wondering. I don't mean to offend with the question but... Do you think he could have gone through with it? Killing you, I mean."

For a moment, Pendergast did not answer, looking into the fire. Then he glanced back at her. "I've asked myself that question many times. There were times— when he was shooting at me in the lake, for example— that I felt sure he meant to do so. But then, there were so many other times when he seems to have missed his opportunity."

Constance picked up the cards again and began dealing fresh hands. "Not knowing his future intentions, not knowing whether he's dead or alive...rather disquieting."

"Indeed."

"What about the rest of the Covenant?" Constance asked. "Do they still pose a threat?"

Pendergast shook his head. "No. Their leaders are dead; their fortress destroyed; all their decades of research findings burned and gone. Their raison d'être—the twins themselves—are almost all alienated from the project. From the reports I've received, many have already begun integrating themselves into Brazilian society. Of course, the very latest 'iterations' of twins—those leading up to Alban and the beta test— were the Covenant's greatest successes, and I understand the Brazilian authorities are finding some of them too incorrigible to be rehabilitated. But their number is small, and there is simply no way for *Der Bund* to achieve a second critical mass, even..." And here his voice sank lower: "Even were Alban to resurface."

There was a brief silence. Then Constance nodded at Tristram's empty chair. "Have you decided what to do about him?"

"I was considering one idea."

"And what might that be?"

"That, in addition to being my amanuensis—and my oracle, it would seem—you might be his..."

Constance glanced up at him, one eyebrow raised ever so slightly. "His what? *Baby*sitter?"

"More than babysitter. Less than guardian. More like—older sister."

"*Older* is the operative word. A hundred and thirty years older. Aloysius, don't you think I'm a little advanced in age to start acting like a sibling again?"

"It is admittedly a novel idea. Will you at least consider it?"

Constance looked at him for a long moment. Then her gaze returned to Tristram's empty chair. "There *is* something affecting about him," she said. "So much the opposite of his brother, at least as you've described him to me. He's so young and impatient—and remarkably naive about the world. So *innocent*."

"As was someone else we both knew, once."

"The thing is, I sense in him an incredible, almost boundless empathy, a depth of compassion I haven't seen since the monastery."

At this point Tristram stepped back into the library, glass of milk in hand.

"Herr Proctor is coming," he told them. "He is bringing you—what was the word he used?— *refreshments*." He repeated the word as he sat down at the card table, as if to taste it.

Pendergast turned toward the youth. For a moment, he simply looked at him, drinking his milk with evident enjoyment. His wants were so simple, his gratitude for even the slightest kindness so boundless. He rose from his chair and walked over to his son. Tristram put down the milk and looked up at him.

He knelt, bringing himself to the boy's level, reached into a pocket of his jacket, and pulled out a ring: gold, set with a large, perfect star sapphire. Taking Tristram's hand, he pressed the ring into it. The youth stared at it, turned it over in his hands, then brought it closer to his eyes, watching the star move on the surface of the sapphire.

"This was your mother's, Tristram," he said gently. "I gave it to her on our engagement. When I feel you are ready—not yet, but perhaps in the not-too-distant future—I will tell you all about her. She was a most remarkable woman. Like all of us, she had her faults. And she...had more than her share of secrets. But I cared for her very much. Like you, she was a victim of *Der Bund*. Like you, she had a twin. It was...very difficult for her. But the years we spent together were some of the most wonderful of my life. It's those memories in particular I would like to share with you. Perhaps they will help make up, in a small way, for the memories you've been deprived of—all these years."

Tristram looked up from the ring into Pendergast's face. "I would like very much to learn about her, Father."

There was a discreet cough. Pendergast looked up to see Proctor standing in the doorway, a silver salver in one upraised hand, two glasses of sherry balanced upon it. As Pendergast rose, the chauffeur stepped forward, offering one of the glasses to the FBI agent and the other to Constance.

"Thank you, Proctor," Pendergast said. "Most kind."

"Not at all, sir," came the measured response. "Mrs. Trask has asked me to tell you that dinner will be laid on at eight o'clock."

Pendergast inclined his head.

As Proctor began to pass from the library into the great rotunda that served as the mansion's reception area, the chauffeur paused to look back over his shoulder. Pendergast had returned to his writing table in the far corner, staring rather moodily into the fire. Constance was shuffling a deck of cards and was speaking in low tones to Tristram, who was sitting across from her, listening attentively.

When Constance had been released from Mount Mercy about three weeks earlier, she'd been reserved and distant with the young man, Pendergast's son. Now, Proctor noticed, she was warming to him—at least somewhat. The fire, the candlelight, threw a mellow light over the rows of old books, the exquisite furnishings, and the three inhabitants. There was a sense of—if not peace exactly—something like equanimity in the room. Calmness and composure. Proctor was not generally given to such reflections, but the sight did, indeed, strike him almost like a family tableau.

An Addams Family tableau, he corrected himself as he exited the library, a faint smile on his lips.

Pendergast watched as the chauffeur vanished. He turned back to the letter and picked up the fountain pen. It scratched over the paper for perhaps another two minutes. Pendergast rested it on the green baize of the writing table and picked up the piece of paper to read from the beginning.

> *My dear Viola,*
>
> *I am writing you for several reasons. First, to apologize for the reception I gave you at our last meeting. You went to a great deal of trouble on my behalf, and my behavior toward you at the time was execrable. I make no excuse, save to tell you—which you no doubt already know—that I was not myself.*
>
> *I would also like to thank you for saving my life. I do not exaggerate. When you showed up on my doorstep*

nearly two months ago, I was on the very brink of com-
mitting that act I so callously described to you at the time.
Your presence, and your words, delayed my hand long
enough for other developments to take me away. In plain
words, you arrived at the Dakota in the nick of time—
and for that you have my lasting, most infinite, and deep-
est gratitude.

It is my intention to take a vacation. For how long,
or where, I do not know. If I find myself in Rome, I will
certainly contact you—as a friend. This is how it must
be, between us, from now on, forever.

There are few things that ground me to this earth,
Viola, and even fewer people. Please know that you are
one of them.

With great affection,
Aloysius

Pendergast put the letter down, signed it, folded
it, and slipped it into an envelope. Then he stared at
the card players, Constance and Tristram, engrossed
in their game. His gaze drifted to the blazing fire. He
gazed into it, motionless, sherry untasted, for a long
time—so long, in fact, that he was only roused by Proctor's returning to inform them that dinner was served.
Tristram immediately jumped to his feet and skipped
on behind the retreating butler, evidently hungry—a
youth for whom each new meal was a novelty. Constance followed at a more dignified pace. Last of all,
Special Agent Pendergast rose—let his fingertips drift
across the envelope that lay upon the writing desk—
and then glided silently out of the room, a dim shape
that grew increasingly faint as it made its way through
the secret and shadow-haunted spaces of the mansion
on Riverside Drive.

Acknowledgments

The authors wish to extend their sincere thanks to the following people for their assistance: Jamie Raab, Jaime Levine, Mitch Hoffman, Nadine Waddell, Jon Couch, Douglas Margini, Eric Simonoff, Claudia Rülke, and the two persons who suggested the book's title to us—Julia Douglas and Michael Sharp.

About the Authors

DOUGLAS PRESTON and LINCOLN CHILD are the coauthors of the famed Pendergast series, including the first two books in the Helen Trilogy, *Fever Dream* and *Cold Vengeance*. Preston and Child are also the authors of the Gideon Crew series. Preston and Child's *Relic* and *The Cabinet of Curiosities* were chosen by readers in a National Public Radio poll as being among the one hundred greatest thrillers ever written, and *Relic* was made into a number-one box office hit movie. Doug Preston's acclaimed nonfiction book, *The Monster of Florence*, is being made into a movie starring George Clooney. Lincoln Child is a former book editor who has published five novels of his own, including the huge bestsellers *Deep Storm* and *The Third Gate*. Readers can sign up for The Pendergast File, a monthly "strangely entertaining note" from the authors, at their website, www.PrestonChild.com. The authors also welcome visitors to their alarmingly active Facebook page, where they post regularly.

In the Colorado Rockies,
Special Agent Pendergast must solve
a deadly century-old mystery—before
a town goes up in flames . . .

White Fire

Please turn this page for a preview.

Prologue: A True Story

August 30, 1889

THE YOUNG DOCTOR BID HIS WIFE GOOD-BYE ON the Southsea platform, boarded the 4:15 express for London, and arrived three hours later at Victoria Station. Threading his way through the noise and bustle, he exited the station and flagged down a hansom cab.

"The Langham Hotel, if you please," he told the driver as he stepped up into the compartment, flushed with a feeling of anticipation.

He sat back in the worn leather seat as the cabbie started down Grosvenor Place. It was a fine late-summer evening, the rarest kind in London, with a dying light falling through the carriage-choked streets and sooty buildings, enchanting everything with a golden radiance. At half past seven the lamps were only just starting to be lit.

The doctor did not often get the chance to come up to London, and he looked out the window of the hansom cab with interest. As the driver turned right onto Piccadilly, he took in St. James's Palace and the Royal Academy, bathed in the afterglow of sunset. The crowds, noise, and stench of the city, so different from his home countryside, filled him with energy. Countless horseshoes rang out against the cobbles, and the sidewalks thronged with people from all walks of life: clerks, barristers, and swells rubbed shoulders with chimneysweeps, costermongers, and cat's-meat dealers.

At Piccadilly Circus, the cab took a sharp left onto Regent Street, passing Carnaby and the Oxford Circus before pulling up beneath the porte cochere of the Langham. It had been the first grand hotel erected in London, and it remained by far the most stylish. As he paid off the cabbie, the doctor glanced up at the ornate sandstone façade, with its French windows and balconies of wrought iron, its high gables and balustrades. He had a small interest in architecture, and he guessed the façade was a mixture of Beaux-Arts and North German Renaissance Revival.

As he entered the great portal, the sound of music reached him: a string quartet, hidden behind a screen of hothouse lilies, playing Schubert. He paused to take in the magnificent lobby, crowded with men seated in tall-backed chairs, reading freshly ironed copies of *The Times* and drinking port or sherry. Expensive cigar smoke hung in the air, mingling with the scent of flowers and ladies' perfume.

At the entrance to the dining room, he was met by a small, rather portly man in a broadcloth frock coat and dun-colored trousers, who approached him with brisk steps. "You must be Doyle," he said, taking his hand. He had a bright smile and a broad American accent. "I'm Joe Stoddart. So glad you could make it. Come in—the others just arrived."

The doctor followed Stoddart as the man made his way among linen-covered tables to a far corner of the room. The restaurant was even more opulent than the lobby, with wainscoting of olive-stained oak, a cream-colored frieze, and an ornate ceiling of raised plaster-work. Stoddart stopped beside a sumptuous table at which two men were already seated.

"Mr. William Gill, Mr. Oscar Wilde," Stoddart said. "Allow me to introduce Dr. A. Conan Doyle."

Gill—whom Doyle recognized as a well-known Irish MP—stood and bowed with good-humored gravitas. A heavy gold Albert watch chain swayed across his ample waistcoat. Wilde, who was in the midst of taking a glass of wine, dabbed at his rather full lips with a damask napkin and motioned Conan Doyle toward the empty chair beside him.

"Mr. Wilde was just entertaining us with the story of a tea party he attended this afternoon," Stoddart said as they took their seats.

"At Lady Featherstone's," Wilde said. "She was recently widowed. Poor dear—her hair has gone quite gold from grief."

"Oscar," Gill said with a laugh, "you really are wicked. Talking about a lady in such a manner."

Wilde waved his hand dismissively. "My lady would thank me. There is only one thing in the world worse than being talked about, and that is not being talked about." He spoke rapidly, in a low, mannered voice.

Doyle examined Wilde with a covert look. The man was striking. Almost gigantic in stature, he had unfashionably long hair parted in the middle and carelessly thrown back, his facial features heavy. His choice of clothing was of an eccentricity bordering on madness. He wore a suit of black velvet that fitted tightly to his large frame, the sleeves embroidered in flowery designs and puffed at the shoulders. Around his neck he had donned a narrow, three-rowed frill of the same brocaded material as the sleeves. He had the sartorial audacity to sport knee breeches, equally tight fitting, with stockings of black silk and slippers with grosgrain bows. A *boutonnière* of an immense white orchid drooped pendulously from his fawn-colored vest, looking as if it might dribble nectar at any moment. Heavy gold rings glittered on the fingers of his indolent hands. Despite the wild idiosyncrasy of his clothing, the expression on his face was mild, balancing the keen quality of his eager brown eyes. And for all this the man displayed a remarkable delicacy of feeling and tact. He spoke in a curious precision of statement, with a unique trick of small gestures to illustrate his meaning.

"You're most kind to be treating us out like this, Stoddart," Wilde was saying. "At the Langham, no less. I'd have been left to my own devices otherwise. It's not that I want for supper money, of course. It is only people who pay their bills who lack money, you see, and I never pay mine."

"I fear you'll find my motives are completely mercenary," Stoddart replied. "You might as well know that I'm over here to establish a British edition of *Lippincott's Monthly*."

"Philadelphia not large enough for you, then?" Gill asked.

Stoddart chuckled, then looked at Wilde and Doyle in turn. "It is my intention, before this meal is complete, to secure a new novel from each of you."

Hearing this, a current of excitement coursed through Doyle. In his telegram, Stoddart had been vague about the reasons for asking him to come to London for dinner, but the man was a well-known American publisher and this was exactly what Doyle had been hoping to hear. His medical practice had had a slower start than he would have liked. To fill the time, he'd taken to scribbling novels while waiting for patients. His last few had met with a small success. Stoddart was precisely the man he needed to further his progress. Doyle found him pleasant, even charming—for an American.

The dinner was proving delightful.

Gill was an amusing fellow, but Oscar Wilde was nothing short of remarkable. Doyle was captivated by the graceful wave of his hands; the languid expression that became quite animated when he delivered his peculiar anecdotes or amusing *bons mots*. It was almost magical, Doyle considered, that—thanks to modern technology—he'd been transported in a few short hours from a sleepy seacoast town to this elegant place, surrounded by an eminent editor, a member of Parliament, and the famous champion of aestheticism.

The dishes came thick and fast: potted shrimps, galantine of chicken, tripe fried in batter, *bisque de homard*. Red and yellow wine had appeared at the beginning of the evening, and the generous flow had never ceased. It was astonishing how much money the Americans had; Stoddart was spending a fortune.

The timing was excellent. Doyle had just begun a new novel that Stoddart would surely like. His penultimate story, *Micah Clarke*, had been favorably reviewed, although his most recent novel, about a detective, based in part on his old university professor Joseph Bell, had been rather disappointingly received after appearing in *Beeton's Christmas Annual*...He forced himself back to the conversation at hand. Gill, the Irish MP, was questioning the veracity of the maxim that the good fortune of one's friends made one discontented.

Hearing this, a gleam appeared in Wilde's eyes. "The devil," he replied, "was once crossing the desert, and he came upon a spot where a number of fiends were tormenting a holy hermit. The man easily shook off their evil suggestions. The devil watched their failure and then stepped forward to give them a lesson. 'What you do is too crude,' said he. 'Permit me for one moment.' With that he whispered to the holy man, 'Your brother has just been made bishop of Alexandria.' A scowl of malignant jealousy at once clouded the serene face of the hermit. 'That,' said the devil to his imps, 'is the sort of thing which I should recommend.'"

Stoddart and Gill laughed heartily, then began to fall into an argument about politics. Wilde turned to Doyle. "You must tell me," he said. "Will you do a book for Stoddart?"

"I was rather thinking I would. The fact is, I've started work on a new novel already. I was thinking of calling it *A Tangled Skein*, or perhaps *The Sign of the Four*."

Wilde pressed his hands together in delight. "My dear fellow, that's wonderful news. I certainly hope it will be another Holmes story."

Doyle looked at him in surprise. "You mean to say you've read *A Study in Scarlet*?"

"I didn't read it, dear boy. I *devoured* it." Reaching into his vest, Wilde pulled out a copy of the Ward Lock & Co. edition of the book, with its vaguely Oriental lettering so in vogue. "I even looked through it again when I heard you would be dining with us this evening."

"You're very kind," Conan Doyle said, at a loss for a better reply. He found himself surprised and gratified that the prince of English decadence would enjoy a humble detective novel.

"I feel you have the makings of a great character in Holmes. But..." And here Wilde stopped.

"Yes?" Doyle said.

"What I found most remarkable was the *credibility* of the thing. The details of the police work, Holmes's inquiries, were enlightening. I have much to learn from you in this way. You see, between me and life there is a mist of words always. I throw probability out of the window for the sake of a phrase, and the chance of an epigram makes me desert truth. You don't share that failing. And yet...and yet I believe you could do more with this Holmes of yours."

"I would be much obliged if you'd explain," Doyle said.

Wilde took a sip of wine. "If he's to be a truly great detective, a great *persona*, he should be more eccentric. The world doesn't need another Sergeant Cuff or Inspector Dupin. No—make his humanity aspire to the greatness of his art." He paused a moment, thinking, idly stroking the orchid that drooped from his buttonhole. "In *Scarlet*, you call Watson 'extremely lazy.' In my opinion, you should allow the virtues of dissipation and idleness to be bestowed on your hero, not his errand boy. And make Holmes more reserved. Don't have *delight shining on his features*, or have him *barking with laughter*."

Doyle colored, recognizing the infelicitous phraseology.

"You must confer on him a vice," Wilde went on. "Virtuous people are so banal; I simply cannot bear them." He paused again. "Not just a vice, Doyle—give him a *weakness*. Let me think—ah, yes! I recall." He opened his copy of *A Study in Scarlet*, leafed quickly through the pages, found a passage, and began to quote Dr. Watson: "'I might have suspected him of being addicted to the use of some narcotic, had not the temperance and cleanliness of his whole life forbidden such a notion.'" He returned the book to his vest pocket. "There—you had the perfect weakness in your hands, but you let it go. Pluck it up again! Deliver Holmes into the clutches of some addiction. Opium, say. But no: opium is so dreadfully common these days, it's become quite overrun by the lower classes." Suddenly Wilde snapped his fingers. "I have it! Cocaine hydrochloride. There's a novel and elegant vice for you."

"Cocaine," Doyle repeated a little uncertainly. As a doctor, he had sometimes prescribed a seven percent solution to patients suffering from exhaustion or depression, but the idea of making Holmes an addict was, on the face of it, quite absurd. Although Doyle had asked for Wilde's opinion, he found himself slightly put out at actually receiving criticism from the man. Across the table, the good-humored argument between Stoddart and Gill continued.

The aesthete took another sip of wine and tossed his hair back.

"And what about you?" Doyle asked. "Will you do a book for Stoddart?"

"I shall. And it shall be under your influence—or rather, Holmes's influence—that I will proceed. Do you know, I've always believed there's no such thing as a moral or immoral book. Books are well written or badly written—that's all. But I find myself taken with the idea of writing a book about both art *and* morals. I'm planning to call it *The Picture of Dorian Gray*. And do you know, I believe it will be rather a ghastly story. Not a ghost story, exactly, but one in which the protagonist comes to a beastly end. The kind of story one wishes to read by daylight—not lamplight."

"Such a story doesn't seem to be exactly in your line."

Wilde looked at Doyle with something like amusement. "Indeed? Did you think that—as one who would happily sacrifice himself on the pyre of aestheticism—I do not recognize the face of horror when I stare into it? Let me tell you: the shudder of fear is as sensual as the shudder of pleasure, if not more so." He underscored this with another wave of his hand. "Besides, I was once told a story so dreadful, so distressing in its particulars and the extent of its evil, that now I truly believe nothing I hear could ever frighten me again."

"How interesting," Doyle replied a little absently, still mulling over the criticism of Holmes.

Wilde regarded him, a small smile forming on his large, pale features. "Would you care to hear it? It is not for the faint of heart."

The way Wilde phrased this, it sounded like a challenge. "By all means."

"It was told to me during my lecture tour of America a few years back. On my way to San Francisco, I stopped at a rather squalid yet picturesque mining camp known as Roaring Fork. I gave my lecture at the bottom of their mine, and it was frightfully well received by the good gentlemen of the camp. After my lecture, one of the miners approached me, an elderly chap somewhat the worse—or, perhaps, the better—for drink. He took me aside, said he'd enjoyed my story so much that he had one of his own to share with me."

Wilde paused, wetting his thick, red lips with a delicate sip of wine. "Here, lean in a little closer, that's a good fellow, and I'll tell it you exactly as it was told to me..."

Ten minutes later, a diner at the restaurant in the Langham Hotel would have been surprised to note—amid the susurrus of genteel conversation and the tinkle of cutlery—a young man in the dress of a country doctor abruptly rise from his table, very pale. Knocking over his chair in his agitation, one hand to his forehead, the young man staggered from the room, nearly upsetting a waiter's tray of delicacies. And as he vanished in the direction of the gentlemen's toilet area, his face displayed a perfect expression of revulsion and horror.

1

Present Day

CORRIE SWANSON STEPPED INTO THE LADIES' room for the third time to check how she looked. A lot had changed with her since she'd transferred to the John Jay College of Criminal Justice at the beginning of her sophomore year. John Jay was a buttoned-down place. She had resisted it for a while, but finally realized she needed to grow up and play the game of life instead of acting the rebel forever. Gone were the purple hair, the piercings, the black leather jacket, the dark eye shadow and other Goth accoutrements. There was nothing she could do about the Möbius strip tattoo on the nape of her neck, beyond combing her hair back and wearing high collars. But someday, she realized, that would have to go as well.

If she was going to play the game, she was going to play it well.

Unfortunately, her personal transformation had taken place too late for her advisor, a former NYPD cop who had gone back to school and turned professor. She got the feeling his first impression of her had been that of a perp, and nothing she'd done in the year since she'd first met him had erased that. Clearly, he had it in for her. He had already rejected her first proposal for the Rosewell thesis, which involved a trip to Chile to do a perimortem analysis on skeletal remains discovered in a mass grave of Communist peasants murdered by the Pinochet regime back in the 1970s. Too far away, he said, too expensive for a research project, and besides it was old history. When Corrie replied that this was the point—these were old graves, requiring specialized forensic techniques— he said something about not involving herself in foreign political controversies, especially Communist ones.

Now she had another idea for her thesis, an even better one, and she was willing to do almost anything to see it happen.

Examining herself in the mirror, she rearranged a few strands of hair, touched up her conservative lipstick, adjusted her gray worsted suit jacket, and gave her nose a quick powdering. She hardly recognized herself; God, she might even be mistaken for a Young Republican. So much the better.

She exited the ladies' room and walked briskly down the hall, her conservative pumps clicking professionally against the hard linoleum. Her advisor's door was shut, as usual, and she gave it a brisk, self-confident rap. A voice inside said, "Come in."

She entered. The office was, as always, neat as a pin, the books and journals all lined up flush with the edges of the bookshelves, the comfortable, masculine leather furniture providing a cozy air. Professor Greg Carbone sat behind his large desk, its acreage of burnished mahogany unbroken by books, papers, family photographs, or knickknacks.

"Good morning, Corrie," Carbone said, rising and buttoning his blue serge suit. "Please sit down."

"Thank you, Professor." She knew he liked to be

called that. Woe to the student who called him Mister or, worse, Greg.

He settled back down as she did. Carbone was a strikingly handsome man with salt-and-pepper hair, wonderful teeth, trim and fit, a good dresser, articulate, soft-spoken, intelligent, and successful. Everything he did, he did well, and as a result he was an accomplished asshole indeed.

"Well, Corrie," Carbone began, "you are looking well today."

"Thank you, Dr. Carbone."

"I'm excited to hear about your new idea."

"Thanks." Corrie opened her briefcase (no backpacks at John Jay) and took out a manila file folder, placing it on her knee. "I'm sure you've been reading about the archaeological investigation going on down in City Hall Park. Next to the location of the old prison known as the Tombs."

"Tell me about it."

"The parks department has been excavating a small cemetery of executed criminals to make way for a new subway entrance."

"Ah yes, I did read about that," said Carbone.

"The cemetery was operational from 1858 to 1865. After 1865, all execution burials were moved to Hart Island and remain unavailable."

A slow nod from Carbone. He looked interested; she felt encouraged.

"I think this would make for a great opportunity to do an osteological study of those skeletons—to see if severe childhood malnourishment, which as you know leaves osteological markers, might correlate with later criminal behavior."

Another nod from Carbone.

"I've got it all outlined here." She laid a proposal on

the table. "Hypotheses, methodology, control group, observations, and analysis."

Carbone laid a hand on the document, drew it toward himself, opened it, and began perusing.

"There are a number of reasons why this is a great opportunity," she went on. "First, the city has good records on most of these executed criminals—names, rap sheets, and trial records. Those who were orphans raised in the Five Points House of Industry—about half a dozen—also have some childhood records. They were all executed in the same way—hanging—so the cause of death is identical. And the cemetery was used for only seven years, so all the remains come from roughly the same time period."

She paused. Carbone was slowly turning over the pages, one after another, apparently reading. There was no way to tell what he was thinking; his face was a blank.

"I made a few inquiries, and it seems the parks department would be open to having a John Jay student examine the remains."

The slow turning of the pages paused. "You already contacted them?"

"Yes. Just a feeler—"

"A feeler . . . You contacted another city agency without seeking prior permission?"

Uh-oh. "Obviously I didn't want to bring you a project that might get shot down later by outside authorities. Um, was that wrong?"

A long silence, and then: "Did you not read your undergraduate handbook?"

Corrie was seized with apprehension. She had in fact read it—when she'd been admitted. But that was over a year ago. "Not recently."

"The handbook is quite clear. Undergraduate students

are not to engage other city departments except through official channels. This is because we're a city institution, as you know, a senior college of the City University of New York." He said this mildly, almost kindly.

"I...Well, I'm sorry, I didn't recall that from the handbook." She swallowed, feeling a rising panic—and anger. This was such unbelievable bullshit. But she forced herself to keep her cool. "It was just a couple of phone calls, nothing official."

A nod. "I'm sure you didn't *deliberately* violate university regulations." He began turning the pages again, slowly, one after the other, not looking up at her. "But in any case I find other problems with this thesis proposal of yours."

"Yes?" Corrie felt sick.

"This idea that malnourishment leads to a life of crime...It's an old idea—and an unconvincing one."

"Well, it seems to me worth testing."

"Back then, almost everyone was malnourished. But not everyone became a criminal. And the idea is redolent of...how shall I put it?...of a certain philosophy that crime in general can be traced to unfortunate experiences in a person's childhood."

"But malnourishment—severe malnourishment—might cause neurological changes, actual damage. That isn't philosophy; that's science."

Carbone held up her proposal. "I can already predict the outcome: you'll discover that these executed criminals *were* malnourished as children. The real question is why, of all those hungry children, only a small percentage went on to commit capital crimes. *That's* the real question. And your research plan does not address that. I'm sorry, this won't fly. Not at all."

And, opening his fingers, he let her document drop gently to his desk.

2

THE FAMOUS—SOME MIGHT SAY INFAMOUS—
"Red Museum" at the John Jay College of Criminal
Justice had started as a simple collection of old investi-
gative files, physical evidence, prisoners' property, and
memorabilia that, almost a hundred years ago, had been
put into a display case in a hall at the old police academy. Since then, it had grown into one of the country's
largest and best collections of criminal memorabilia.
The crème de la crème of the collection was on display
in a sleek new exhibition hall in the college's Skidmore,
Owings & Merrill building on Tenth Avenue. The rest
of the collection—vast rotting archives and moldering
evidence from long-ago crimes—remained squirreled
away in the hideous basement of the old police academy
building on East Twentieth Street.

Early on at John Jay, Corrie had discovered this
archive. It was pure gold—once she'd made friends with
the archivist and figured out her way around the disorganized drawers and heaping shelves of stuff. She had
been to the Red Museum archives many times in search
of topics for papers and projects, most recently in her
hunt for a topic for her Rosewell thesis. She had spent a

great deal of time in the old unsolved-case files—those cold cases so ancient that all involved (including the possible perps) had definitely and positively died.

Corrie Swanson found herself in a creaking elevator, descending into the basement, one day after the meeting with her advisor. She was on a desperate mission to find a new thesis topic before it became too late to complete the approval process. It was mid-November already, and she was hoping to spend the winter break researching and writing up the thesis. She was on a partial scholarship, but Agent Pendergast had been making up the difference in tuition, and she was absolutely determined not to take one penny more from him than necessary. If her thesis won the Rosewell Prize, with its twenty-thousand-dollar grant, she wouldn't have to.

The elevator doors opened to a familiar smell: a mixture of dust and acidifying paper, underlain by an odor of rodent urine. She crossed the hall to a pair of dented metal doors, graced with a sign that said RED MUSEUM ARCHIVES, and pressed the bell. An unintelligible rasp came out of the antiquated speaker; she gave her name, and a buzzer sounded to let her in.

"Corrie Swanson? How good to see you again!" came the hoarse voice of the archivist, Willard Bloom, as he rose from a desk in a pool of light, guarding the recesses of the storage room stretching off into the blackness behind him. He presented a rather cadaverous figure, stick-thin, with longish gray hair, yet underneath was charming and grandfatherly. She didn't mind the fact that his eyes often wandered over various parts of her anatomy when he thought she wasn't paying attention.

Bloom came around with a veined hand extended, which she took. The hand was surprisingly hot, and it gave her a bit of a start.

"Come, sit down. Have some tea."

Some chairs had been set around the front of his desk, with a coffee table and, to the side, a battered cabinet with a hot plate, kettle, and teapot, forming an informal seating area in the midst of dust and darkness. Corrie flopped into a chair, setting her briefcase down with a thump next to her. "Ugh," she said.

Bloom raised his eyebrows in mute inquiry.

"It's Carbone. Once again he rejected my thesis idea. Now I have to start all over again."

"Carbone," Bloom said in his high-pitched voice, "is a well-known ass."

This piqued her interest. "You know him?"

"I know everyone who comes down here. Carbone! Always fussing about getting dust on his Ralph Lauren suits, wanting me to play step-n-fetchit. As a result, I can never find anything for him, poor man...You know the real reason he keeps rejecting your thesis ideas, right?"

"I figure it's because I'm a junior."

Bloom put a finger to his nose and gave her a knowing nod. "Exactly. And Carbone is old school, a stickler for protocol."

Corrie had been afraid of this. The Rosewell Prize for the year's outstanding thesis was hugely coveted at John Jay. Its winners were often senior valedictorians, who went on to highly successful law enforcement careers. As far as she knew, it had never been won by a junior—in fact, juniors were quietly discouraged from submitting theses. But there was no rule against it, and Corrie refused to be deterred by such bureaucratic baggage.

Bloom held up the pot with a yellow-toothed smile. "Tea?"

She looked at the revolting teapot, which did not appear to have been washed in a decade. "That's a teapot? I thought it was a murder weapon. You know, loaded with arsenic and ready to go."

"Always ready with a riposte. But surely you know most poisoners are women? If I were a murderer, I'd want to see my victim's blood." He poured out the tea. "So Carbone rejected your idea. Surprise, surprise. What's plan B?"

"That *was* my plan B. I was hoping you might be able to give me some fresh ideas."

Bloom sat back in his chair and sipped noisily from his cup. "Let's see. As I recall, you're majoring in forensic osteology, are you not? What, exactly, are you looking for?"

"I need to examine some human skeletons that show antemortem or perimortem damage. Got any case files that might point to something like that?"

"Hmm." His battered face screwed up in concentration.

"The problem is, it's hard to come by accessible human remains. Unless I go prehistoric. But that opens up a whole other can of worms with Native American sensitivities. And I want remains for which there are good written records. *Historic* remains."

Bloom sucked down another goodly portion of tea, a thoughtful expression on his face. "Bones. Ante- or perimortem damage. Historic. Good records. Accessible." He closed his eyes, the lids so dark and veiny they looked like he might have been punched. Corrie waited, listening to the ticking sounds in the archives, the faint sound of forced air, and a pattering noise she feared was probably rats.

The eyes sprang open again. "Just thought of something. Ever heard of the Baker Street Irregulars?"

"No."

"It's a very exclusive club of Sherlock Holmes

fanatics. They have a dinner in New York every year, and they publish all sorts of Holmesian scholarship, all the while pretending that Holmes was a real person. Well, one of these fellows died a few years back, and his widow, not knowing what to else do, shipped his entire collection of Sherlockiana to us. Perhaps she didn't know that Holmes was a *fictional* detective, and we only deal in *nonfiction* here. At any rate, I've been dipping into it now and then. Lot of rubbish, mostly. But there was a copy in there of Doyle's diary—just a photocopy, unfortunately—and it made entertaining reading for an old man stuck in a thankless job in a dusty archive."

"And what did you find, exactly?"

"There was something in there about a man-eating bear."

Corrie frowned. "A man-eating bear? I'm not sure—"

"Come with me."

Bloom went to a bank of switches and struck them all with the flat of his palm, turning the archives into a flickering sea of fluorescent light. Corrie fancied she could hear the rats scurrying and squealing away as the tubes blinked on, one aisle after another.

She followed the archivist as he made his way down the long rows between dusty shelving and wooden cabinets with yellowed, handwritten labels, finally reaching an area in the back where library tables were piled with cardboard boxes. Three large boxes sat together, labeled BSI. Bloom went to one box, rummaged through it, hauled out an expandable folder, blew off the dust, and began sorting through the papers.

"Here we are." He held up an old photocopy. "Doyle's diary. Properly, of course, the man should be referred to as 'Conan Doyle,' but that's such a mouthful, isn't it?" In the dim light, he flipped through the pages, then began to read aloud:

> *... I was in London on literary business. Stoddart, the American, proved to be an excellent fellow, and had two others to dinner. They were Gill, a very entertaining Irish MP, and Oscar Wilde ...*

He paused, his voice dying into a mumble as he passed over some material, then rising again as he reached a passage he deemed important.

> *... The highlight of the evening, if I may call it that, was Wilde's account of his lecture tour in America. Hard to believe, perhaps, but the famed champion of aestheticism attracted huge interest in America, especially in the West, where in one place a group of uncouth miners gave him a standing ovation ...*

Corrie began to fidget. She had so little time to waste. She cleared her throat. "I'm not sure Oscar Wilde and Sherlock Holmes are quite what I'm looking for," she said politely. But Bloom continued to read, holding up his finger for attention, his reedy voice riding over her objections.

> *... Towards the close of the evening, Wilde, who had indulged a great deal in Stoddart's excellent claret, told me, sotto voce, a story of such singular horror, of such grotesque hideousness, that I had to excuse myself from the table. The story involved the killing and eating of eleven miners some years previous, purportedly by a monstrous "grizzled bear" in a mining camp called Roaring Fork. The actual details are so abhorrent I cannot bring myself to commit them to paper at this time,*

although the impression left on my mind was indelible
and one that will, unfortunately, follow me to the grave.

He paused, taking a breath. "And there you have it. Eleven corpses, eaten by a grizzly bear. In Roaring Fork, no less."

"Roaring Fork? You mean the glitzy ski resort in Colorado?"

"The very one. It started life as a silver boomtown."

"When was this?"

"Wilde was there in 1881. So this business with the man-eating bear probably took place in the 1870s."

She shook her head. "And how am I supposed to turn this into a thesis?"

"Nearly a dozen skeletons, eaten by a bear? Surely they will display exquisite perimortem damage—tooth and claw marks, gnawing, crunching, biting, scraping, worrying." Bloom spoke these words with a kind of relish.

"I'm studying forensic criminology, not forensic bearology."

"Ah, but you know from your studies that many, if not most, skeletal remains from murder victims show animal damage. You should see the files we have on that. It can be very difficult to tell the difference between animal marks and those left by the murderer. As far as I can recall, no one has done a comprehensive study of perimortem bone damage of this kind. It would be a most original contribution to forensic science."

Very true, Corrie thought, surprised at Bloom's insight. *And come to think of it, what a fabulous and original subject for a thesis.*

Bloom went on. "I have little doubt at least some of the poor miners were buried in the historic Roaring Fork cemetery."

"See, that's a problem. I can't go digging up some historic cemetery looking for bear victims."

A yellow smile appeared on Bloom's face. "My dear Corrie, the only reason I brought this up at all was because of the fascinating little article in the *Times* this very morning! Didn't you see it?"

"No."

"The original 'boot hill' of Roaring Fork is now a stack of coffins in a ski equipment warehouse. You see, they're relocating the cemetery on account of development." He looked at her and winked, his smile broadening.

3

ALONG THE COTE D'AZUR IN THE SOUTH OF France, on a bluff atop Cap Ferrat, a man in a black suit, surrounded by bougainvillea, rested on a stone balcony in the afternoon sun. It was warm for the time of year, and the sunlight gilded the lemon trees that crowded the balcony and descended the steep hill to the Mediterranean, ending in a strip of deserted white beach. Beyond could be seen a field of yachts at anchor, the rocky terminus of the cape topped by an ancient castle, and the blue horizon.

The man reclined in a chaise longue covered with silk damask, beside a small table on which sat a salver. His silvery eyes were half closed. Four items sat on the tray: a copy of Spenser's *Faerie Queene*; a small glass of pastis; a beaker of water; and a single unopened letter. The salver had been brought out two hours ago by a manservant, who now awaited further orders in the shade of the portico. The man who had rented the villa rarely received mail. A few letters bore the return address of one Miss Constance Greene in New York; the rest came from what appeared to be an exclusive boarding school in Switzerland.

As time passed, the manservant began to wonder whether the sickly gentleman who had hired him at excessively high wages might have suffered a heart attack—so motionless had he been these past few hours. But no—a languid hand now moved, reaching for the beaker of water. It poured a small measure into the glass of pastis, turning the yellow liquid a cloudy yellowish green. The man then raised the glass and took a long, slow drink before replacing it on the tray.

Stillness returned, and the shadows of afternoon grew longer. More time passed. The hand moved again, as if in slow motion, again raising the cut-crystal glass to pale lips, taking another long, lingering sip of the liqueur. He then picked up the book of poetry. More silence as the man appeared to read, turning the pages at long intervals, one after another. The afternoon light blazed its last glory on the façade of the villa. From below, the sounds of life filtered upward: a distant clash of voices raised in argument, the throbbing of a yacht as it moved in the bay, birds chattering among the trees, the faint sound of a piano playing Hanon.

And now the man in the black suit closed the book of poetry, laid it upon the salver, and turned his attention to the letter. Still moving as if underwater, he plucked it up and, with a long, polished nail, slit it open, unfolded it, and began to read.

Nov. 27

Dear Aloysius,

I'm mailing this to you c/o Proctor, in hopes he'll pass it along. I know you're still traveling and probably don't want to be bothered, but you've been gone almost a year and I figured maybe you were about ready to come home. Aren't you itching by now to end your leave of absence from the FBI and start solving murders again? And anyway, I just had to tell you about my thesis project. Believe it or not, I'm off to Roaring Fork, Colorado!

I got the most amazing idea for a thesis. I'll try to be brief because I know how impatient you are, but to explain I do have to go into a little history. In 1875, silver was discovered in the mountains over the Continental Divide from Leadville, Colorado. A mining camp sprang up in the valley, called Roaring Fork after the river flowing through it, and the surrounding mountains became dotted with claims. A year later, in May of 1876, a rogue grizzly bear killed and ate a miner at a remote claim in the mountains—and for the rest of the summer the bear totally terrorized the area. The town sent out a number of hunting teams to track and kill it, to no avail, as the mountains were extremely rugged and remote. By the time the rampage stopped, eleven miners had been mauled and horribly eaten. It was a big deal at the time, with a lot of local newspaper articles (that's how I learned these details), sheriff's reports, and such. But Roaring Fork was remote and the story died pretty quickly once the killings stopped.

The miners were buried in the Roaring Fork cemetery, and their fate was pretty much forgotten. The mines closed up, Roaring Fork dwindled in population, and in time it almost became a ghost town. Then, in 1946, it was bought up by investors and turned into a ski resort—and now of course it's one of the fanciest resorts in the world—average home price over four million!

So that's the history. This fall, the original Roaring Fork cemetery was dug up to make way for development. All the remains are now stacked in an old equipment shed high up on the ski slopes while everyone argues about what to do with them. A hundred and thirty coffins—of which eight are the remains of miners killed by the grizzly. (The other three were either lost or never recovered.)

Which brings me to my thesis topic: A Comprehensive Analysis of Perimortem Trauma in the Skeletons of Eight Miners Killed by a Grizzly Bear, from a Historic Colorado Cemetery.

There has never been a large-scale study of perimortem trauma on human bones inflicted by a large carnivore. Ever! You see, it isn't often that people are eaten by animals. Mine will be the first!!

My thesis advisor, Prof. Greg Carbone, rejected my two earlier topics, and I'm glad the bastard did, if you'll excuse my language. He would have rejected this one, too, for reasons I won't bore you with, but I decided to take a page out of your book. I got my sweaty hands on Carbone's personnel file. I knew the man was too perfect to be real. Some years back, he'd been boning an undergraduate student in one of his classes—and then was dumb enough to flunk her when she broke it off. So she complained, not about the sex, but the bad grade. No laws were broken (the girl was twenty), but the scumbag gave her an F when she deserved an A. It was all hushed up, the girl got her A and had her tuition "refunded" for the year—a way of paying her off without calling it that, no doubt.

You can find anybody these days, so I tracked her down and gave her a call. Her name's Molly Denton and she's now a cop in Worcester, Mass—a decorated lieutenant in the homicide department, no less. Boy, did she give me the lowdown on my advisor! So I went into the meeting with Carbone armed with a couple of nukes, just in case.

I wish you'd been there. It was beautiful. Before I even got into my new thesis idea, I mentioned all nice and polite that we had a mutual acquaintance: Molly Denton. And I gave him a big fat smirk, just to make sure he got the message. He went all pale. He couldn't wait to change the subject back to my thesis, wanted to hear about it, listened attentively, instantly agreed it was the most marvelous thesis proposal he'd heard in years, and promised he would personally shepherd it through the faculty committee. And then—this is the best part—he suggested I leave "as soon as possible" for Roaring Fork. The guy was butter in my hands.

Winter break just started, and so I'm off to Roaring Fork in two days! Wish me well. And if you feel like it, write me back c/o your pal Proctor, who will have my forwarding address as soon as I know it.

Love,
Corrie

P.S. I almost forgot to tell you one of the best things about my thesis idea. Believe it or not, I first learned about the grizzly bear killings from the diary of Arthur Conan Doyle! Doyle heard it himself from no less than Oscar Wilde at a dinner party in London in 1889. It seems Wilde was a collector of horrible stories, and he'd picked up this one on a lecture tour of the American West.

The manservant, standing in the shadows, watched his peculiar employer finish reading the letter. The long, white fingers seemed to droop, and the letter slid to the table, as if discarded. As the hand moved to pick up the glass of pastis, the evening breeze gently lofted the papers and wafted them over the railing of the balcony, over the tops of the lemon trees; then they went gliding off into blue space, fluttering and turning aimlessly until they had vanished from view, unseen, unnoticed, and completely disregarded by the pale man in the black suit, sitting on a lonely balcony high above the blue sea.

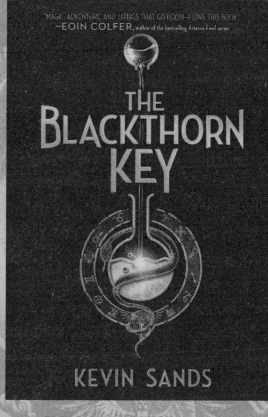
WHITE MOUNTAIN LIBRARY
SWEETWATER COUNTY LIBRARY SYSTEM
Rock Springs, WY

FRAMED!

JAMES PONTI

ALADDIN
New York London Toronto Sydney New Delhi

ALADDIN

An imprint of Simon & Schuster Children's Publishing Division
1230 Avenue of the Americas, New York, New York 10020
First Aladdin paperback edition May 2017
Text copyright © 2016 by James Ponti
Cover illustration copyright © 2016 by Paul Hoppe
Also available in an Aladdin hardcover edition.
All rights reserved, including the right of reproduction in whole or in part in any form.
ALADDIN is a trademark of Simon & Schuster, Inc., and related logo is
a registered trademark of Simon & Schuster, Inc.
For information about special discounts for bulk purchases, please contact Simon & Schuster
Special Sales at 1-866-506-1949 or business@simonandschuster.com.
The Simon & Schuster Speakers Bureau can bring authors to your live event.
For more information or to book an event contact the Simon & Schuster Speakers Bureau
at 1-866-248-3049 or visit our website at www.simonspeakers.com.
Cover designed by Laura Lyn DiSiena
Interior designed by Laura Lyn DiSiena and Steve Scott
The text of this book was set in Jansen.
Manufactured in the United States of America 1019 OFF
10 9
The Library of Congress has cataloged the hardcover edition as follows:
Names: Ponti, James, author.
Title: Framed! / by James Ponti.
Description: First Aladdin hardcover edition. | New York : Aladdin, 2016. |
Summary: In Washington, D.C., twelve-year-old Florian Bates, a consulting detective for the
FBI, and his best friend, Margaret, help thwart the biggest art heist in United States history.
Identifiers: LCCN 2015045506 (print) | LCCN 2016023737 (eBook) |
ISBN 9781481436304 (hardcover) | ISBN 9781481436328 (eBook)
Subjects: | CYAC: Mystery and detective stories. | United States. Federal Bureau of
Investigation—Fiction. | Friendship—Fiction. | Art thefts—Fiction. | Washington (D.C.)—
Fiction. | BISAC: JUVENILE FICTION / Mysteries & Detective Stories. | JUVENILE
FICTION / Action & Adventure / General. | JUVENILE FICTION / Humorous Stories.
Classification: LCC PZ7.P7726 Fr 2016 (print) | LCC PZ7.P7726 (eBook) | DDC [Fic]—dc23
LC record available at https://lccn.loc.gov/2015045506
ISBN 9781481436311 (pbk)

For Alex

1.

The (Not So) Safeway

MY NAME'S FLORIAN BATES. I'M TWELVE YEARS old and a seventh grader at Alice Deal Middle School in Washington, DC. My two favorite foods are pizza and egg rolls. I'm on the student council, I'm in the Scrabble club, and I plan to try out for soccer.

I also work for the FBI.

I know. That last one kind of comes out of the blue, doesn't it?

Technically they classify me as a "covert asset," which sounds very James Bond spylike but only means they want to keep me a secret. After all, it would be pretty embarrassing for them to admit they get help from a twelve-year-old, and

it would be even worse if one of the guys on the Ten Most Wanted list showed up at my front door in a bad mood. So the covert part is good for both of us.

Becoming a detective wasn't something I meant to do. It just sort of happened because I notice things other people don't. My brain's weird that way. It spots details that seem insignificant and snaps them together like puzzle pieces.

The only people outside the Bureau who are supposed to know my status are my parents and my best friend Margaret. But that changed the day the Romanian Mafia kidnapped me after school. I was taking a shortcut behind the Safeway supermarket, and unless they were trying to influence any upcoming student council votes, it meant my identity was no longer a secret.

It's funny because earlier that day Margaret had warned me not to take that route. Normally we walk home together. But on Thursdays she has piano, so I go alone. That's when I look for shortcuts. Not because I'm in a hurry, but because it's like another puzzle.

"There are a lot of Dumpsters back there," she pointed out when I told her about it. "And you know what Ben Franklin said about Dumpsters. 'Nothing good ever happens when you're surrounded by them.'"

"I'm pretty sure Ben Franklin was dead about a hun-

dred and fifty years before the Dumpster was invented," I countered.

"Then maybe I saw it on a poster. Either way, it's good advice. You shouldn't go back there."

"It may smell bad," I said, feeling suddenly defensive, "but it's not like it's dangerous or anything."

"Hmmm," she replied. "And how do you know that?"

I thought about it for a moment and smiled. "Because it's called the Safeway. If it was dangerous it would be called the Un-Safe Way."

She didn't find this nearly as clever as I did. So while I laughed, she just shook her head and said, "Boys are *soooo* funny." Then she leaned in close and added, "And *soooo* stupid."

Considering I was kidnapped in the exact place she warned me not to go, I'd say that little nugget belongs on a poster too. In my defense, I was going to walk the long way, but it started raining and I didn't want to get soaked.

I'd just squeezed through the gap in the fence and was hurrying behind the store holding my backpack over my head when I noticed the delivery truck. It should've been parked by the loading dock, but I was too busy worrying about getting wet to pay attention to that.

The rain was so hard I could see through its windshield only when the wipers swished across the glass. That's why

I didn't notice the driver had gotten out and left the engine running. I figured someone was just sitting inside waiting for the storm to pass.

When he stepped out from behind a Dumpster I almost crashed into him, which would have hurt because he was enormous. The sign on the truck said it belonged to a flower shop called the Happy Leprechaun, but this guy was neither. He was about six foot four, three hundred pounds, and looked like a professional wrestler. One of the villains.

He just stared at me, unconcerned about the rain pelting down on his giant bald scalp, and smiled. For a nanosecond I thought I was letting my imagination run wild. Then I looked down and noticed he wasn't wearing comfortable shoes like a delivery person would. He had on steel-toed work boots popular among factory workers, bricklayers, and international assassins.

I sprinted in the opposite direction, digging around in my backpack as I ran. I was trying to find the "panic button" the FBI had issued me. All I needed to do was push it twice and a team of agents would be put on instant alert. Unfortunately, he got to me before I got to it.

He tackled me and we skidded across the wet pavement into a pile of old fruit cartons. At first I thought I'd sliced my

knee open, but what looked like blood turned out to be rotted strawberries smushed into my jeans. I tried to scramble up onto my feet, but he wrapped his arms around my head and put me in a sleeper hold. Just before I blacked out I looked at all the Dumpsters and told myself that I really should start following Margaret's advice.

I don't know how long I was unconscious, but when I woke up, I had a throbbing headache and was lying on the floor of the truck with my feet bound together and my hands tied behind my back.

I let out a low, painful moan. "Uunnnnnffff."

"Feel better if sleep," he said with a thick accent. "Twenty minute."

For a few seconds my vision was blurry, but when things came into focus I saw something beautiful—my backpack. He must have picked it up so no one would find it and come looking for me. That meant I still had a chance to press the panic button. I just needed to distract him long enough to scoot over to it.

I'd taken a hostage survival course at Quantico, the FBI training center, but at the time I couldn't imagine anyone wanting to kidnap me, so I didn't pay as much attention as I should have. Crazy stupid, I know, but at least I remembered the basics.

SURVIVAL STEP 1—Build a Rapport
with Your Captor

"That was an impressive tackle," I said. "Are you a football player?"

"Football is baby sport," he scoffed. "Pads. Helmets. I play man sport. Rugby."

"Well, I bet you're great at it," I said. "Did you play back home in Romania?"

He looked into the rearview mirror and eyed me suspiciously. "How you know I Romanian?"

I didn't want to tell him that the FBI had warned me that the Romanians were after me or that I saw the Romanian flag tattooed on his forearm when he put me in the sleeper hold. I wanted him to like me, so I tried buttering him up.

"My grandfather is from Romania," I said. "I have a picture of him when he was a soldier and he looks just like you."

This made him smile. (For the record my papa Gio is from Italy, and my grandpa Ted grew up in New Hampshire. But I think it's okay to lie when you've been abducted.)

"By the way, as one Romanian to another," I continued, "I think you've made a mistake. I think you nabbed the wrong kid."

The smile turned into a scowl and I worried that I'd offended him.

"I'm not saying you're not good at your job," I added. "It's just that with peer pressure and our need to fit in, kids look and dress so much alike that even we have trouble telling each other apart. One time my parents drove right by me at pickup. My own parents. So there's no shame in grabbing the wrong one."

"Not wrong," he replied forcefully.

SURVIVAL STEP 2—Disrupt Your Captor's Train of Thought

"Do you mean 'not wrong' as in *I'm* not wrong in what I'm saying? Or 'not wrong' as in *you're* not wrong in whom you kidnapped?"

I waited for a response, but all I heard was a low, frustrated growl. I assumed this was his deep-thinking noise.

"If you don't use pronouns, it really makes the conversation hard to follow. You need to say '*You're* not wrong' or '*I'm* not wrong.' Especially in a situation like this with threats and demands. The wrong pronoun could have someone else ending up with your ransom money, and that wouldn't be good for either one of us."

"Not wrong!" he barked again as if saying it louder suddenly solved the grammar issues. Just then he swerved to

avoid another car, blasted his horn, and yelled what I assumed were choice Romanian curse words. I figured he was distracted enough for me to start inching toward my backpack.

"Don't feel bad," I continued. "I understand how hard it is to learn a new language. My family moves all the time. I've had to learn French and Italian. It's *molto difficile*. That's Italian for 'very difficult.'"

"Stop talk!"

"That's a perfect example of what I mean. You said 'stop talk' but it should be 'stop talking.' English is so complicated. But let's forget about grammar and get back to you kidnapping the wrong person. Like I said, it's an easy mistake and easy to fix. If you let me go, I promise not to tell anyone. Just drop me off at the nearest Metro station."

"Shut mouth or else!"

The "or else" was ominous, and combined with the continued lack of pronouns it reminded me of the third step from my training.

SURVIVAL STEP 3—Do Not Antagonize Your Captor

(When I told Margaret about the steps, she couldn't believe this wasn't first.)

So far I'd managed to get about halfway to the backpack, but I still needed one big push to reach it. When my FBI handler warned me about the Romanians, I did some studying and came across a website with phrases in different languages. I'd learned one just in case a moment like this arrived.

"Vehicolul meu aerian e plin cu maimute!"

I wasn't sure about my pronunciation, but it must have sounded Romanian enough because moments later he veered over to the side of the road and slammed on the brakes. The truck came to a screeching halt that sent me tumbling across the floor.

At this point the backpack was just beyond my fingertips. I was about to scoot the last little bit when he stood up, walked into the back of the delivery truck, and leaned over me, no regard for personal space (or dental hygiene).

"What saying you?" he demanded, his face red and splotchy.

"I said that if you let me go I won't tell anyone."

"No," he replied as he leaned even closer. "What saying you Romanian?"

I gulped and gave it another try, hoping I'd remembered it correctly. One wrong word could give the sentence a totally different meaning.

"Vehicolul meu aerian e plin cu maimute!"

Judging by his glower, I was pretty sure I'd ruined every-thing. I could just imagine the funeral, with my FBI instructor saying, "I told him not to antagonize his captor." And Margaret shaking her head and responding, "And I told him not to go behind the Safeway."

He reached down and pressed his beefy hands against the sides of my head, and I waited for the inevitable crushing of my skull. But that's not what happened. Instead he flashed a huge yellow-toothed grin and laughed.

"Hubbercraft?" he asked, mispronouncing the word as he continued to laugh.

"Yes," I replied, smiling back and repeating the phrase in English. "My hovercraft is full of monkeys." It was a silly phrase from a silly website, but it seemed to do the trick.

Rapport had finally been established.

"You're funny," he said as he helped me back into an upright position.

"Thanks," I replied. "By the way, 'You're funny' is excellent subject/verb agreement. I wonder if the fact that you were more relaxed helped . . ."

"Now shut mouth!"

Okay, so it was only limited rapport.

"Oh, and forget about backpack," he said. "I already took out what you're looking for."

He cackled and my heart sank.

"No call home for you," he added as he pulled my phone out of his shirt pocket and dangled it in the air. I tried not to show relief that he had only found my phone and not the panic button.

"Okay," I said, sounding as disappointed as I could. "No call home."

Fifteen minutes later we pulled off the highway onto a farm road and parked behind a barn. Everything was quiet for a moment until he said, "Do not joke when here. Understand?"

It was more of a warning than an order, as if the next person I met might not have a sense of humor.

"I understand," I replied. "Thank you."

He untied my feet and led me into the barn, my sneakers squishing down into the mud as we walked.

"Sit here and wait quiet," he instructed when we reached an old wooden picnic table.

SURVIVAL STEP 4—Brains Are Better Than Muscles

I knew I was about to come face-to-face with Nicolae Nevrescu, a ruthless gangster known as "Nic the Knife." He was the prime suspect in the case I was working on, and

considering his reputation, I figured I was running out of time to act. The more I thought about my situation, the more upset it made me. And the more upset I got, the harder it was to breathe.

At first my breaths were slow and labored, but then I started to gasp for air.

"Quiet!" the kidnapper told me.

My gasping intensified and I leaned forward against the table in full panic mode.

"What is wrong?" he said.

I was trying to figure out how to hyperventilate and talk at the same time when a new voice came to my rescue.

"He needs his inhaler—*inhalator*," he said, using the Romanian word.

I looked up from the table and saw that it was Nevrescu.

"Yes," I wheezed as I nodded.

"Where it is?" asked the kidnapper.

"Back . . . pack," I gasped.

"Get it now!" said Nevrescu. "We can't let him die. At least not yet."

The massive man rushed back to the truck and grabbed my backpack. Since my hands were still tied behind my back he just dumped everything onto the table and I pointed at the inhaler with my head.

"Squeeze," I gasped.

He held it up to my mouth and pressed down while I sucked in a lungful of mist.

"Again," I said, my voice returning to somewhat normal.

He squeezed a second time and I sucked down some more mist.

You've got to hand it to the FBI. It looked and worked just like an actual inhaler. You'd never guess it was really a panic button.

"Thank you," I said with a huge sigh of relief. "You just saved my life."

Help was on the way. Now I only had to drag things out until it arrived.

Nevrescu sat down across the table from me and started to look through the papers strewn across the table. I don't know what ruthless crime lords are supposed to look like, but he looked more businesslike than I expected. His hair was cut stylishly, short on the sides, but a little thicker on top. He had a neatly trimmed beard and mustache and intense blue eyes. He also spoke with an accent, but his English was perfect.

"Florian Bates," he said, reading my name off the top of some homework. "You are the one the FBI only talks about in whispers. The one they call Little Sherlock."

"I have no idea what you're talking about," I said.

He gave me a disappointed look. "Let's not play games. I know who you are, and you know who I am."

I nodded reluctantly. "I know you're the man who mastermined the robbery at the National Gallery of Art."

He chuckled. "Mastermind? I love that word. I wish it were true. No, that fact you have wrong. That's why I had you brought here. So we could set the record straight and you could tell your friends at the FBI they are looking for the wrong person."

He started to roll up his sleeves and I could see the collection of tattoos on his forearms. One was a red-and-black eel that I recognized as the symbol of the Eastern European League, a crime syndicate known as EEL. There were other assorted tough-guy phrases and symbols, but one of them didn't fit in with the others.

It was a daisy with the numbers "24/7" directly beneath it. It looked like the logo of a flower shop willing to make deliveries twenty-four hours a day, seven days a week. But Nevrescu didn't exactly seem like a florist.

He saw that I was staring at it. "What's wrong, Little Sherlock?"

"*Young* Sherlock," I corrected.

"What's that?"

"They don't call me *Little* Sherlock. They call me *Young* Sherlock."

He laughed. "I thought you had no idea what I was talking about."

I gave him a look. "I thought we weren't playing games."

"Okay. So what's wrong, Young Sherlock?"

"I'm not sure but it's right there," I said, trying to make sense of it. "I can almost see it."

I closed my eyes and tried to picture the puzzle pieces: Daisy, 24/7, EEL, FBI, Nic the Knife, Romania, Happy Leprechaun, Safeway. It just didn't make sense and then . . . *SNAP*.

I opened my eyes and smiled. The solution seemed completely impossible except for one detail. It was the only thing that made the pieces fit together.

"There's been a huge mistake," I said urgently. "You need to let me go right now."

"Is that so?" He laughed. "Why should I do that?"

I looked right at him and did not blink. "Because the FBI is going to be here in less than five minutes and that doesn't leave us much time to talk about why your tattoo changes everything."

2.

The Meaning of TOAST

Three Months Earlier

I PROMISE I'LL EXPLAIN HOW NIC THE KNIFE'S tattoo changed everything. But before I can do that, I have to explain what *everything* is. That means I have to go back three months earlier to when I first came to Washington. Back then I wasn't a covert anything, just a kid whose family moved a lot. And I wasn't looking for a criminal mastermind. I was trying to find my underwear.

"Mom!" I yelled down the stairs. "I can't find my boxers!"

You'd think that after four moves in seven years I'd be better at packing and unpacking my stuff. But after dumping three boxes of clothes onto my bed, I'd found plenty of

sweaters, jackets, and gloves (very helpful considering it was the middle of summer), but no underwear (unless you count an old pair of tighty-whities that were two sizes too small). It had reached the point where I'd had to put on a bathing suit after my shower.

"Mom!" I tried again.

There was still no response so I went looking for her. I was halfway down the stairs as I called out, "Do you know where my boxers . . ."

My words trailed off when I saw that she was at the front door talking to a girl. The last thing I wanted to do was discuss my underwear in front of some random girl, so I tried to make a save.

"Boxes," I said with a fake cough, trying to cover the change. "Do you know where my boxes are?"

Judging by the girl's smile, I had fooled exactly zero people.

"Florian, I'd like you to meet one of our new neighbors," Mom said. "This is Margaret."

The first thing that stood out about Margaret wasn't that she's African American or even that she's about three inches taller than me. It was that smile. Bright white teeth with silver braces across the bottom row. There was something so easy and friendly about it. I've always wanted a smile like that.

In pictures mine just looks like I'm scared of some creature lurking behind the camera, but hers radiated confidence.

"Welcome to the neighborhood," she said, holding up a plate of cookies.

"Thanks," I answered. "I was just looking . . . for . . . my . . ."

"Boxes," she said.

"Right, boxes."

There was an awkward silence until Mom came to the rescue. "Why don't I find them while you two have some cookies," she suggested. "In the kitchen, where there's less mess."

Margaret and I snaked our way though the unpacked chaos of the front room into the kitchen.

"Milk?" I offered.

"Yes, please."

Rather than sit down at the table, she poked around the piles of stuff stacked on the counter, more curious than snooping. "So where'd you move from?"

"Rome," I said.

She looked up. "The one in Italy?"

"Is there another?" I asked.

"I think there's one in Georgia," she said.

"It definitely wasn't Georgia," I replied. "It had the

Colosseum and lots of Italian people riding around on scooters."

"Is that where you always lived?"

"No. Before that we were in Boston, London, and Paris," I said. "We move a lot. My parents work in museums."

"That sounds cool. Mine are just lawyers," she replied as she plopped down at the kitchen table. "The boring kind, not the murder-trial kind. By the way, I love this house."

"Thanks," I said as I handed her a glass of milk. "I think yours is great, too. My mom's insanely jealous of the flowers in your front yard."

The instant I saw her reaction I realized my mistake and wished I could rewind the conversation and try it again.

"You know where I live?"

I stared at my cookie for a moment before nodding. "Four doors down and across the street. The yellow house with the brick chimney and a piano next to the big window in the front room."

She tilted her head to the side and asked, "How did you know that?"

I could have just told her that I saw her in her yard or something, but I didn't want to start with a lie. So I told her the truth. "Well, I saw the house. And just now I saw you. And I could tell that you live there."

"You could? Do I look like I live in a yellow house? Like I have a chimney and a piano?"

"Of course not," I replied. "It's just that I went for a walk this morning and . . ."

"You saw me then?" she asked.

"No, I'm pretty sure you were asleep."

"What time was it?" she asked.

"Five."

"I was definitely asleep. Do you normally go for walks that early?"

"Not *normally*. But we just got here a couple days ago and my body still thinks it's on Italy time. I woke up and couldn't fall back asleep, so I figured it would be a good opportunity to get to know the neighbors."

She laughed. "And how many neighbors did you meet at five in the morning?"

"None," I replied. "But I don't really need to meet them in order to get to know them. You can tell a lot about someone just by what you see from the sidewalk."

"And you were able to tell that the yellow house with the brick chimney and the piano is mine?"

I nodded.

"How?"

Past experience had taught me that people are turned

off by this particular skill. But I was too far along to stop now.

"There's a girl's bicycle in the side yard," I explained. "The seat is set high for someone tall, like you."

"Just because there's a girl's bike, that doesn't mean—"

"I'm not done," I said, cutting her off. "You're wearing a University of Michigan T-shirt and there is a University of Michigan Law School decal in the window of the silver station wagon in the driveway. There's also a DC Dynamo sticker on the bumper and an identical one on the bumper of the green sedan parked on the street."

"So?"

"Your soccer shorts," I said, pointing to them. "It says 'DCD' right there on your shorts. I'm guessing you play for the Dynamo."

She took another bite of her cookie as she thought through it all.

"Anything else?"

"Well, judging by the way you dip your cookie in your milk, I'd say you're left-handed. But that's about it."

She sat there for a moment with her mouth slightly open.

"That's amazing," she finally said. "I don't know if it's superfreaky amazing or unbelievably cool amazing. But it's definitely amazing."

"Usually people just think it's strange and they never talk to me again," I said. "But it would be great if you think it's cool because, from what I saw, only two other houses in the neighborhood have kids and they're way too young. You're my best bet for a friend."

"Is that so?" she said. "And did you do this with all of the houses in the neighborhood?"

I nodded.

She had a spark of an idea and I could see the wheels turning as she leaned forward and asked, "Which house belongs to the insane person who screams at you if you so much as put one toe in her front yard?"

"Easy," I replied. "Three doors to the left, blue house with the crazy perfect hedges."

"Who puts up way too many Christmas decorations?"

"Gray house across the street from you."

She gave me a look. "How could you possibly . . ."

"You can see the nails along the roofline where they hang the lights," I explained.

"Okay, let me come up with something you can't figure out from the street." She flashed an evil smile. "Where would you find a ridiculously large comic book collection?"

I toyed with her for a moment to let her think she'd stumped me. Then I answered, "The green house on the

corner with the double security bars on the basement windows and the Fantastic Four license plate holder on the car."

At this point even I thought I was weird. But she just smiled and shook her head.

"I want that," she said. "I. Want. That."

"The comic book collection or the license plate holder?"

"No, that skill," she said. "Can you teach me how to do that?"

It had never dawned on me that this was something I could actually share with someone else. "You want me to teach you TOAST?"

"Toast?" she asked. "You've tasted my cookies, which are . . . epic. Don't you think I know how to make toast?"

"Not that toast," I said. "'TOAST' stands for the Theory of All Small Things. That's how I read people and places. The idea is that if you add up a bunch of little details, it reveals the larger truth."

"And where did you learn this theory? Philosophy class? Spy school?"

"I . . . invented it . . . I guess."

This made her laugh. "You invented TOAST?"

"It's based on some things I learned from my parents," I said. "But I put it all together and came up with the name. So yes, I invented it."

"You said your parents work at museums, right?"

"My father designs security systems, and one day he explained that the key to his job is finding the tiny flaw or inconsistency that the bad guys can take advantage of."

"Like the saying that 'a chain is only as strong as its weakest link'?"

"Exactly," I said. "And my mother's an art conservator. She restores old paintings and says the best way to understand a painting is by finding the smallest detail that tells the whole story, like the smile on the *Mona Lisa*."

"And this led to TOAST?"

I nodded. "Even though their jobs are incredibly different, they both rely on the idea that tiny things can be hugely important," I explained. "Once I even used TOAST to help my dad catch a criminal."

"This I have to hear," she said as she grabbed another cookie and chomped happily. "How'd you do that?"

"There was a museum in Spain that was robbed three times in a year. The stolen items were small but extremely valuable. No one could figure out how the thief was doing it. They hired my dad and he checked everything out and was just as stumped as they were.

"But one day he had a bunch of reports spread out on the kitchen table and I started looking at them. Most of it was

technical stuff that I didn't understand, but I noticed all the robberies had two traits in common."

"What?" she asked eagerly.

"They all happened on Saturdays when it was raining."

Margaret considered this for a moment. "And you were able to figure it out from Saturday and rain?"

"No," I said. "I just noticed it. My dad was the one who figured it out. You see, museum attendance usually doubles on the weekend."

"That makes sense."

"And with that many people when it was raining, the coatroom didn't have enough space for all of the raincoats. They had to open an additional room to handle the extras. When they did that, they shut off part of the alarm system to keep it from sounding all day."

"That's brilliant," she said.

"Dad's pretty smart," I replied.

"And you'll teach me this?"

"Sure," I said. "But it will have to be some other time."

"Why?"

"Because I think you have to go somewhere right now."

"What time is it?" she asked, suddenly panicked. "I've got to get to soccer practice." She got up to go, and then stopped in her tracks and looked back at me.

"How did you know that?" she demanded. "Did you just TOAST me again?"

I laughed. "It's not a verb. But no, I didn't TOAST you. I can see the driveway through the side window. And your car just got here. My guess is that the woman headed to the front door is your mother."

Just then the doorbell rang.

"See you later," Margaret said as she rushed out of the room. When she reached the front door she turned back and added, "By the way, in case you're wondering whether I think it's cool or freaky?"

I took a nervous breath.

She flashed the smile and said, "Very, very cool."

3.

Napoleon's Candle

THERE ARE SOME THINGS, LIKE BREATHING AND walking, that you do automatically. And since you don't really think about them, they're hard to teach. For example, how would you teach somebody to breathe? Would you make up a list of step-by-step instructions?

1. Suck air through nose

2. Blow air back through nose

3. Repeat twenty thousand times every day

That might work, but it's kind of cheating because "suck air" and "blow air" are just two other ways of saying "breathe." You haven't actually explained how to do it. You've just swapped the words.

TOAST is like that for me. It's more instinct than idea. So when Margaret asked me to teach her, I wasn't sure how to break it down into something that made sense. I took her to the National Gallery of Art, the museum where my mom works, and showed her a painting of a man with red hair and a beard.

"Margaret, I'd like to introduce you to Vincent van Gogh," I said.

"Hey, Vince, how's it going?" she replied, playing along. Then she turned and asked, "Why do you want me to meet him?"

"Because he's the artist I know best," I told her. "Mom's crazy about him, so she's taught me a lot. Like for instance he only painted for about ten years but still created more than two thousand works of art."

"That's pretty amazing."

"And he usually couldn't afford to hire models, which is why he painted so many self-portraits, like this one. I love the colors: the orange beard, the blue background, the little flecks of green in his face."

Margaret studied the picture. "It's very cool, but he looks kind of sad."

"I think he was sad a lot of the time," I said.

"Is that why he cut off his ear?" she asked.

"How'd you know about that?"

"Everybody knows Van Gogh cut off his ear," she said. "It's common knowledge."

"I guess it is," I said. "But here's the funny thing: Everybody's wrong."

She gave me a curious look. "He didn't cut it off?"

"Maybe he did. Maybe he didn't. It's hard to say. But let me introduce you to someone else." I led her to a self-portrait on the opposite wall. "This is Paul Gauguin."

"Okay, this guy looks shady," she said.

"What makes you say that?"

"Because he's got a halo over his head, but he's holding a snake. So which one is he? An angel or a devil? A hero or a villain?"

"He might be a villain," I replied. "There's a chance *he's* the one who cut off Van Gogh's ear. They lived together and fought all the time. Gauguin loved to fence, and sometimes he'd grab his sword in the middle of an argument and threaten Vincent. The theory is that one time he did and accidentally cut off the ear with his sword."

"If that's what happened, why didn't Van Gogh tell anybody?" she asked. "Why did he let everyone think he'd done it to himself?"

"He worshipped Gauguin, so maybe he was embarrassed about what happened. Or maybe he wanted to make sure his friend didn't get into trouble. All we know for certain is that they never saw each other again after that night."

Margaret considered this. "It's interesting, but like you said, maybe he did or maybe he didn't. It's just a theory. If you can't know for sure, then you can't say that everybody's wrong."

"I don't think everybody's wrong because they *believe* Van Gogh cut off his own ear," I tried to explain. "I think they're wrong because they're *certain* he cut off his own ear. Once you're certain about something, you no longer question it. And if you don't question what you think you know, then you'll only ever see the big things and TOAST is worthless to you."

"Let me get this straight," she replied. "You're saying that big things, like everybody believing something, block the important details from view."

"Exactly," I said. "And now that you know that, we can get started."

We walked across the hall and I showed her a large

portrait of Napoléon standing in his study. "Okay, here's Napoléon," I said. "What time is it?"

"That's easy," she said, looking at the grandfather clock in the picture. "Four thirteen."

"A.m. or p.m.?"

She scrunched up her face and thought about it for a moment before saying, "I don't know."

"See if you can figure it out," I said. "Use TOAST."

It took her a minute, but when she did she flashed an aha smile. "A.m."

"How do you know?" I asked.

"Because the candle's lit," she said. "It's the middle of the night. Four a.m."

"That's TOAST," I told her. "Now let's try it out on some living people."

The museum turned out to be the perfect place to practice. It was filled with different types of people, so we had a broad cross-section to study. And they all moved slowly, which gave us plenty of time to observe. We started with a couple in the Rembrandt room. The woman had on a black dress, and the man wore a shirt and tie.

"What can you tell me about them?" I whispered as we stood across the room.

Margaret looked and answered quickly, "Both in their

twenties. She's got brown hair and is about five foot four. He's got black hair and is almost six feet tall."

"Let me rephrase that," I said. "What can you tell me . . . that isn't on their driver's licenses? Ignore the big things. What does TOAST tell you?"

She looked again, but after thirty seconds she turned to me, frustrated. "You know, if I already knew how to do it, I wouldn't need you to teach me."

"Fair point," I said. "How about if I ask you some questions?"

"Questions might be helpful."

"Is there anything that doesn't seem like it belongs?"

"You mean like their clothes?" she asked.

"What makes you say their clothes don't belong?"

"They're dressed for work, not for sightseeing."

"That's good," I told her. "Build on that. Do you think they work here at the museum?"

"No," she replied. "Because they're walking around and looking at the paintings like visitors, not employees."

"Give me another detail that stands out."

She looked some more and replied, "Her shoes. She's wearing a nice dress, but with sneakers. They don't go together."

"That's very good," I told her. "You've got two small

things that don't seem to fit. When you add them together, what do they tell you?"

She thought about it for a moment. "She takes the Metro and walks to work. She wants to be comfortable and she doesn't want to scuff up her nice shoes, so she keeps those in her office and wears the sneakers whenever she leaves. I bet they're on their lunch break."

"Look at that. You're a natural."

Margaret smiled. "Want to know more?"

"Sure," I said.

"Judging by their age, they're probably interns. She wanted to come and look at the pretty pictures. He wanted to come and look at the pretty girl."

I laughed. "What makes you say that?"

"Notice how she's looking at the paintings. She's wrapped up in them. But he's turned toward her."

She was absolutely right.

"Like I said, you're a natural."

We did this for another hour, going from room to room, picking up on little details and clues about people, before ending up where we started, by the self-portraits of Van Gogh and Gauguin. There we came across a man who'd nodded off to sleep while sitting on a couch, which made him an ideal subject. He wasn't moving, which made him

easy to study. And his eyes were closed, so he couldn't see us looking at him.

"Ready to take a test?" I asked.

She smiled confidently. "Ready to take it. Ready to crush it."

"Find out everything you can about Sleeping Beauty and meet me over there by Gauguin."

"It's in the bag," she replied.

I walked by him first and pretended to look at a Degas painting of ballerinas. While I did, I made some mental notes about him. Margaret was more direct. She actually sat at the other end of the couch and got a close-up look.

She stayed there for a minute and then came over to me. I was smiling because of her bold move, but she seemed unhappy.

"What's wrong?" I asked.

"I was doing great up until now, but I didn't notice anything interesting or out of place about him," she explained. "The only thing close is that he's got a scar on his chin. Does that mean anything?"

"Just that he cut himself once," I said.

"That's what I figured."

"You want me to ask you some questions like before?"

"I don't want you to," she replied. "But I guess I need you to."

"Sometimes it's not so obvious," I said. "You've got to

start small and build up. Can you tell me anything about where he lives?"

She started to give me an "are you crazy?" look, but then she realized something.

"Not in DC," she said. "He's wearing a T-shirt from the Spy Museum and he has a big, bulky camera on a strap around his neck. He's a tourist. That means he doesn't live in Washington."

"Good," I said. "So that's where he doesn't live. Do you have any idea where he does?"

"No," she said, stumped. "Do you?"

"He's from Europe. Of course, it's easier for me because two weeks ago so was I."

She turned to look back at him, and this time she saw it. "His shoes! His running shoes look funny!"

"You got it," I said, signaling her to lower her voice. "Those are called Europa trainers. They're a brand from Eastern Europe. They don't sell them in the States."

"That's cool," said Margaret. "I'll do better with the next one. Give me another test."

"We're not done with him."

"We're not?" she asked. "What else can you tell?"

"He's wearing contact lenses, he's left-handed, and he's here with his wife and baby."

"You can't possibly know that." Then she gave me a look. "Can you?"

"There are indentation marks on the bridge of his nose and on both temples that could only be made by wearing glasses on a regular basis. But there is no sign of them today, so he's wearing his contacts. There are spit-up stains on his shoulder, the kind you get from holding a baby. And since we determined that the shirt is a souvenir from the trip, it's most likely the first time he's ever worn it. That means the stains are fresh and the baby is with him today. The wedding ring tells us that he's married. The fact that he's wearing his wedding ring on the right hand is another sign that he's European, probably Eastern European. It's more of a custom there. My guess is that they're a couple making their first trip with their baby, which would explain why he's so tired."

"And how do you know he's left-handed?"

"The spit stains from the baby are on the right shoulder," I explained. "That's the side that a left-handed person would use. You're left-handed; how would you hold a baby?"

Margaret thought about this for a second and imagined she was holding a baby. Her instinct was to hold it on her right shoulder.

"It's clever, I'll give you that," she said. "But you can't be sure. It's all still guessing."

"Yes, but it's informed guessing. The whole point of TOAST is that one little thing can be misleading, but the more little things there are, the more likely the guesses are to being right. Like the shoes *and* the wedding ring both being Eastern European."

Just then a woman carrying a baby approached the man and started talking to him in a language neither of us recognized. He smiled as he placed the baby against his right shoulder and started to pat its back with his left hand. Margaret continued to watch them as the couple shared a quick kiss and started to walk together through the museum.

"One day I'll be able to do that," she said.

"What?" I asked. "Burp a baby?"

"Very funny," she replied, slugging me in the arm. "No, one day I'll be able to read people like that. Like you do."

A week later Margaret was over at my house and Mom was making her special Sunday spaghetti sauce. It's a legendary family recipe that simmers all day and fills the house with the most amazing aroma.

"That smells incredible, Mrs. B.," Margaret said as we passed through the kitchen.

"Thank you," she said. "Would you like to stay for dinner?"

"To eat that?" replied Margaret. "I would *love* to stay for dinner."

"Check with your parents," said Mom. "Florian's dad is on his way home from the airport, so we should be eating in about an hour."

Dad had been on a business trip for most of the week. When we sat down to eat, he hadn't even had a chance to tell us anything about it before Margaret asked him, "Did you have fun playing golf while you were in California?"

"I had a great time," he said, "but I played awful."

She nodded and replied, "Well, it's hard to play well when you're using somebody else's clubs. At least that's what my dad says."

She tried to play it cool, but when she turned and saw my expression, she couldn't help but break into a huge grin.

"How did you know my father had been to California?" I asked. "And how did you know he played golf when he was there? I didn't even know that, so I couldn't have told you."

"And how could you have possibly known that I used someone else's clubs?" asked Dad.

She was still beaming as she looked at our stunned faces and said, "I just used TOAST."

The Copyist

WE SAT IN SILENT AMAZEMENT UNTIL MY MOTHER
began to laugh.

"At last," she said gleefully. "Someone has done to Florian
what he does to us."

I laughed too. I couldn't believe it. Margaret had used
TOAST to figure out that my father borrowed someone
else's golf clubs during his trip to California. And I had absolutely no idea how. I kept looking back and forth between
Dad and her, trying to figure out what clues she saw.

"You better tell him how you did it," Dad said. "Before
his brain explodes."

"Please do," I said. "I'm completely stumped."

Margaret basked in a moment of glory before she explained. "First of all, the trip to California. I knew that before we even sat down. Mr. Bates put his briefcase on the hall table and there's a copy of the *Los Angeles Times* sticking out of the pocket." She turned to my father. "I'm guessing you read it on the flight home."

"I sure did," he told her. "That's good."

"Okay, but that's not enough," I said, holding up a hand to call time-out. "Just because he has a newspaper doesn't mean he was there. We get the *New York Times* every Sunday without going to New York. The *LA Times* is for sale in airports all over the country."

"True, but TOAST is about multiple small things," she replied. "And you didn't let me finish. There's also a claim tag on the briefcase's handle. It says LACMA."

"Lacma? What's that?"

"I don't know, but I'm pretty sure the LA stands for Los Angeles," she said. "Maybe the Los Angeles Contemporary Museum of Art."

"Los Angeles *County* Museum of Art," said Dad. "They're my new clients. I spent the last three days studying their security protocols."

"So that gets you to California," said my mother. "How did you know he played golf?"

"His hands gave it away."

Dad held them up, and I saw it instantly.

"His right hand is tan and his left hand is pale," I said, shaking my head. "How could I miss that?"

"Yeah, Florian, how could you miss that?" asked Mom. Then she turned to Margaret and whispered, "What did he miss?"

"You only wear one glove when you golf," she explained. "If you play enough in a short period of time, the sun only tans the one exposed hand."

Mom gave Dad a suspicious look and asked, "Exactly how much did you play while you were *studying* their security protocols?"

He grinned. "Is it my fault the museum director loves to play golf and discuss work at the same time?"

"It still doesn't explain how you knew he borrowed clubs," I said.

Margaret smiled. "That was the easiest part of all. We were all here when he came home. He had a suitcase and a briefcase . . ."

". . . but he wasn't carrying golf clubs," I said.

"Nope. That means he had to borrow some while he was out there."

It was brilliant. Actually, it was better than brilliant.

It was perfect. Margaret had taken my special thing and turned it into our special thing. Up until that moment the real value of TOAST was that it helped me figure out new things whenever my family moved. But that was the day it became something different. From that point on it became something the two of us could do together.

For example, when we rode the Metro we'd play a game where we'd try to predict who was getting off at which stop based only on what they were carrying. And one time we sat on the steps of the Lincoln Memorial and tried to figure out what state different tourists were from by the clothes they were wearing. The more we played, the better we got. But we weren't trying to develop our skills so that we could become detectives or spies or anything like that. We were just having fun.

Until we saw him.

It was July 29. I remember it because it was Margaret's birthday. As a present, my mom had arranged for us to go behind the scenes at the museum. She took us into the studio where she works, showed us all the high-tech equipment, and even let us see a newly acquired Picasso that hadn't gone on display yet. It was very cool and when we left we walked through the Impressionism galleries.

That's where we came across an artist painting a replica of Monet's *Woman with a Parasol*.

"Is he a conservator like your mom?" asked Margaret.

"No," I replied. "He's a copyist."

"You mean like a forger?"

"It's only forgery if you say it's the original," I explained. "Copyists are artists who practice by painting copies of other works. It's a great way to learn from the masters. It's how most great artists got started."

"So he doesn't work here?" asked Margaret.

"No, but he had to get a permit from the museum," I said. "I doubt it was hard because he's really good. His painting looks just like the original. "

"European too," said Margaret.

"French, to be precise," I said. "It's a Monet, *Woman with a Parasol.*"

"Not the painting," she replied. "I mean the artist is European. Check out his shoes."

He was wearing Europa trainers like the man we saw the first day I taught her about TOAST.

"Just like Sleeping Beauty," she continued.

I started to laugh, but then something caught my attention. The man we saw the first day was a young father on vacation. This man was an artist hard at work. If you stood them side by side, they'd look almost nothing alike, but the Theory of All Small Things led me to an unexpected conclusion.

"I think it's the same guy," I said.

"No way," said Margaret. "He was blond and this guy has black hair."

"I know."

"And he was a total tourist," she added. "Not a hipster art student."

"I know that, too. But I still think it's him."

"Why?"

"For one, look how he's painting: He's left-handed, just like the other guy."

"A lot of people are left-handed," she replied as she held up her left hand and wiggled her fingers. "Like me, for example."

"Only ten percent of people are left-handed," I said. "If you multiply that ten percent by the small number of people in Washington who have those shoes, and narrow that group down by men that age with that body type, the number gets ridiculously small. Then consider that they were both in this museum during the last few weeks, and it says that he's the same person we saw before."

"You're telling me that you trust TOAST more than you trust your own eyes?" she said. "The small things tell you one thing and you go with that?"

I thought about it for a moment before I answered.

"I do," I said. "I absolutely do."

She sighed. "So do I. I can't put my finger on the exact reason why, but he seems like the same guy to me, too. I wish there was a way we could tell for sure."

"Yeah," I replied, lost in thought.

We stood there for a moment, and then we both turned and looked at each other at the exact same time and said, "The scar."

"It's on his chin," she said. "And you remember who spotted that scar, don't you?"

"I believe it was you."

"Oh, you don't believe it was me," she teased. "You know it was me. You thought it was worthless, but I thought it was important. Turns out . . . I was right."

"So what's the plan?" I asked. "You want to stand here and keep congratulating yourself? Or do you want to go look for the scar?"

"I'm all for doing both," she answered. "But I guess I could take it easy on you and we could just go find out."

I figured we'd casually look at some nearby paintings and glance at his chin, but Margaret's approach was more direct. She walked right up to him and leaned over his shoulder.

"Your painting is beautiful," she said.

"Thanks," he replied with a trace of an accent. "It helps to have something beautiful like a Monet to copy."

As he talked he turned to look at her and smiled. The scar was right there across the left side of his chin.

Neither of us had any doubt. It was the same man.

5.

Foggy Bottom

"WHAT SHOULD WE DO?" MARGARET ASKED urgently.

"What do you mean?" I replied.

"Should we call the police? Alert security?"

"And tell them what?"

We'd moved into the massive hallway that runs through the middle of the National Gallery, so we could keep an eye on the copyist without him hearing us.

"We'll tell them that the man in there is not who he is pretending to be," she said in an excited whisper.

"He's not pretending to be anyone," I said. "He says he's a copyist, and judging by his painting, that's exactly what he is."

"Then he's a forger," she said. "He's making a forgery of *Woman with a Parasol* to sell on the black market. Where do you think the black market is for paintings like that? Paris? Cairo? Marrakech?"

"Definitely Marrakech," I answered with a laugh. "Except it doesn't make sense to forge a painting that's on public display. No one would be fooled because all they have to do is go online to see that the original is hanging in the museum."

"I got it. I got it. I got it," she said excitedly but still trying to keep her voice down. "He's a spy. No, even better, he's an international hit man. That makes total sense."

"How in the world does international hit man make total sense?"

"He completely changed his appearance," she said. "That means he's hiding something. Hit men hide stuff. It's like the main thing they do. You know . . . other than kill people."

"I've created a monster," I said, shaking my head. "Maybe I should have warned you sooner, but there's a trap that comes with TOAST. And I think you've fallen into it."

"What trap?" she asked.

"Crazy conspiracy theories," I said. "Just because something is unexpected doesn't mean it's suspicious. Most things are completely innocent and can be easily explained. If you

think about it, all he's done is change his hair. Have you ever changed yours?"

"Yes, but . . ." She let out a sigh and slumped a bit. "Why are you trying to take all the fun out of this?"

I laughed. "You think it would be fun if he actually was an international hit man?"

"Maybe 'fun' isn't the right word," she replied. "But you know what I mean. You're the one who taught me TOAST and all I'm doing is using it."

"Yes, but you're using it to make wild speculations," I said.

"Okay," she said. "Forget hit man. Forget forger and spy. Just tell me that you honestly don't think he's suspicious and I'll let it go."

I studied him through the doorway as he started to pack up his paints and brushes for the day. It was definitely the same guy and he looked really different. . . .

"Okay," I admitted. "He's a little suspicious. But we can't call the police or tell security that they need to arrest someone because he changed his hair. I'm pretty sure they'd want evidence of something . . . you know . . . criminal."

"I completely agree," she said to my momentary relief. Then she added, "So let's find some and give it to them."

"Find some what?"

"Evidence," she replied. "Let's follow him and see where he goes."

I thought she was joking, so I waited for her to laugh. But the laugh never came. She was serious. "That's the worst idea ever," I told her.

"Why?"

"First of all we don't know how to follow people," I responded. "We play games with TOAST. That doesn't make us spies. Also, what if he actually is a bad guy and he catches us? That would be monumentally bad."

"He's not going to catch us," she said. "I guarantee it."

"And you're so confident because . . ."

"We're going to follow him with TOAST," she answered.

"What does that even mean?" I asked with a raised eyebrow.

"We don't actually follow him; instead we make him follow us," she replied. "We read him and figure out where he's going and we get there before he does. He can't see us behind him if we're out in front."

"You mean like predicting who gets off the Metro at which stop?" I said.

"That's exactly what I mean. You see that plastic bag he's putting his supplies in?" she asked.

I looked over at him. "Sure."

"The logo is from the George Washington University

bookstore. If he's a student and lives near campus, then he's going to get off at the Foggy Bottom Metro stop. So let's get there first and keep an eye out for him."

I hesitated before answering. She'd gotten my interest, but it still sounded dangerous.

"Don't forget that it's my birthday," she reminded me. "This can be your present to me."

"I already gave you a present," I said in mock protest. "And the most dangerous part was the potential for a paper cut while gift wrapping."

"If there's anything just a little bit dangerous, I promise we'll call it off, go back to my house, and have some cake."

He was almost packed up. The copyists store their equipment in a room downstairs, so I knew this was our only chance to pull off her plan.

"Come on," she added. "Let's have an adventure."

"Adventure" was the part I couldn't resist.

"Okay," I said. "But only because it's your birthday. *And* I still want a piece of cake."

Thirty minutes later we were sitting on a bench on the edge of the GWU campus drinking sodas to fight the summer heat and keeping an eye on the exit of the Foggy Bottom Metro station. And thirty minutes after that, we were still waiting.

"How long before we give up?" I asked, only half joking.

"We're not going to give up," she replied. "This will work. We just have to be patient."

"Aren't you supposed to go out for birthday dinner with your parents?"

"I've got an hour," she said, checking the time. "That means we can wait twenty more minutes and I'll still have enough time to get home and get ready."

"Are you going someplace fancy?" I asked.

"The exact opposite. We're going to Ben's Chili Bowl. It's a hamburger-and-hot-dog place over on U Street. We go every year on my birthday."

"That's cool," I said. "We don't have any places that are traditions like that. We've moved too much."

"Not me," she replied. "I've lived in the same house my whole life." Then she hesitated for a moment and added, "Well, except for the first couple weeks."

"What do you mean?" I asked.

Margaret took a sip of soda and thought about her answer.

"Actually . . . I'm adopted," she said somewhat carefully. "We don't know the specifics of where I came from. We're not even sure if today is my actual birthday. It's just the one we picked to celebrate. My birth parents abandoned me at a firehouse when I was about ten days old. Engine House Four."

This caught me completely off guard. I think it was because she used the word "abandoned." It was so cold and sad. I sat quietly for a moment before saying, "It's amazing that one person could be so unlucky and lucky in the same week."

"How do you mean?" she asked.

"So unlucky to have parents who would do that," I explained. "So lucky to end up with the ones you did."

The corners of her mouth turned up into a tiny smile and she looked over at me. "Thanks." She took another sip and was about to say something else when we caught a glimpse of our guy coming out of the Metro station.

"There he is," I said.

He was alone and in a hurry. We froze for a second, surprised that the plan had worked.

"Don't get up," I whispered. "You talked to him earlier, so he's seen your face. Just look at me."

She turned toward me and I watched him. He got as close as twenty feet before jogging across the street.

"Okay, you can look now," I told her.

We followed him, staying across the street and about fifteen feet behind him as he walked. My pulse started racing.

He turned onto H Street and entered a ten-story brick building with a sign that read PHILIP S. AMSTERDAM HALL. It was one of the GWU dorms.

"So now we know he's a student," she said.

"Which is still not evidence of anything criminal," I countered.

"True, but we're not done yet."

"We're not?"

She shook her head. "I've still got ten more minutes before we have to leave."

We crossed the street and approached the dormitory. We tried to open the door but couldn't without a pass card. The windows were tinted, so we cupped our hands over our eyes and pressed up against the glass to see better. A flyer on the door advertised summer housing orientation.

"I think we should go," I said.

"Just give me a second," she said. She rapped her knuckles against the glass and turned to me saying, "I just want to peek inside."

She rapped again.

We were about to give up when someone opened the door.

Margaret started to say thank you but stopped when she saw it was the copyist. He looked at her with a hint of recognition.

"Do I know you?" he asked.

"No," she answered, her voice cracking.

"Actually, I think we've seen you before," I said, trying to think fast. "We were down here in the lobby the other day waiting for my brother. He lives on the fifth floor."

He looked at me for a moment and slowly nodded. "That must be it."

He held the door open for us to enter, but we were way too scared to move.

"Aren't you coming in?"

"No," I said, trying not to sound nervous. "I was just looking to see if my brother was inside. But he's not. We'll wait out front."

"Yeah," Margaret added. "Thanks."

He shrugged and said, "Okay."

He disappeared into the building, and after about twenty seconds of standing still (whether we were keeping cool or momentarily paralyzed by fear is open for debate), Margaret and I bolted toward the Metro station. We were still breathing heavily when we got on the train and plopped down into our seats. I didn't feel any relief until the doors closed and I knew he hadn't followed us.

"Okay," Margaret said. "That was officially the dumbest idea ever."

I was too shaken to speak so I just nodded my agreement.

6.

The Scene of the Crime

OVER THE NEXT TWO WEEKS MARGARET AND I avoided the National Gallery so we wouldn't bump into the copyist. We also decided not to tell security (because we didn't have any evidence) or our parents (considering following a stranger across town would definitely get us grounded). Instead we kept our *adventure* to ourselves and focused on the fast-approaching first day of school.

With all the times my family had moved, I'd developed strong new-kid survival skills. Normally I used TOAST to find pockets of potential friends and avoid the jerks and bullies. But Margaret gave me something new: advanced intelligence. She told me about the different cliques, her favorite

teachers, and what foods to avoid in the cafeteria. (Pretty much all of them.)

We even went on a scout. Her soccer team played on the field behind the school, so one day I went to practice. Afterward she introduced me to some of her teammates in our grade, and then we looked around the campus. The main building was huge: three stories of red brick with large columns at the front entrance. It was intimidating, and when I looked through a window down an endless hallway of lockers, I wondered if I'd feel lost there.

That same night my dad's ringtone woke me at 2:17. I would've gone back to sleep but when I heard him talking I could tell it was an emergency. I worried about my grandfather, who'd been sick, and wondered if there'd been a turn for the worse.

I sleepily staggered out to the hallway just as Dad hurried toward the stairs, still buttoning his shirt as he rushed.

"Is everyone okay?" I asked. "Something wrong with Grandpa Ted?"

"Grandpa's fine," he said. "I didn't mean to wake you."

"Where are you going?"

"Three paintings were stolen from the National Gallery and they want my help. Go back to sleep."

He was halfway out the door before my semiconscious brain made the connection.

"Wait!" I called out.

"I can't, buddy, this is important. We can talk in the morning."

"Were they Impressionist paintings?"

The door closed and I figured he didn't hear me. But then it slowly opened and I saw him standing there looking up the stairs at me, his head haloed by the porch light.

"Why do you ask that? What makes you think they were Impressionist?"

I took a deep breath and sighed. "I may know something."

"I don't have time for games, Florian. Something like what?"

Awkward pause.

"Like, I may know who did it."

He gave me a confused look.

"Margaret and I noticed this strange guy hanging out at the museum. . . . We kind of followed him."

"You did what?" he exclaimed.

"Yeah, I know, it was stupid," I replied. "But he was suspicious. And he was hanging out in the Impressionism section."

Dad was in too much of a hurry to analyze the whole

situation, so he trusted his gut. "Get dressed quick. I'll tell your mom you're going with me and leave out the part about you following a suspicious man across town. We'll deal with that later."

"Good idea," I said. "Although, we don't really have to ever tell her that part, do we?"

In normal traffic it takes about thirty-five minutes to get from our house to the museum. But with the streets empty, we made it in twenty. That gave me just enough time to tell Dad everything I knew about the man in the Europa trainers.

He slowed down when we turned onto Constitution Avenue and the museum came into view.

"This is going to be a zoo," he said. "An absolute zoo."

As we got closer, we could see security officers setting up wooden barricades along the sidewalks and news crews unloading camera gear from television trucks. Everything was bathed in the red and blue lights of the police cars that clogged the road.

The entrance to the underground parking lot was blocked by it all, so we parked down the street in front of the Smithsonian's Museum of Natural History and walked.

Dad flashed his security credentials at the checkpoint and we climbed the massive steps that led to the entrance.

"They're looking for clues," he said, nodding toward

some cops who were shining their flashlights into the bushes along the front of the building.

Everything was surreal.

We entered the main rotunda and the first thing I saw was a pair of detectives questioning the cleaning crew. The custodians looked nervous, as if the giant pillars that circled them formed a marble holding cell.

"You think they're witnesses or suspects?" I asked.

Dad just shrugged and said, "Good question."

I looked back over my shoulder as we continued walking, trying to make sense of it all. Skylights normally gave the hallway a bright, sunny feel, but now there were sinister shadows and pockets of total darkness.

We stopped to look into the room where Margaret and I had seen the copyist painting *Woman with a Parasol*. The plaque on the door read IMPRESSIONISM/GALLERY 85, but the entryway was blocked by bright yellow police tape. Inside, the crime scene unit searched for evidence around the huge gap on the wall where a painting had been.

"Wow," said Dad when he saw the empty space. "Just wow!"

"What's missing?" I asked.

"*Child with Toys*," he answered. "Renoir."

"Unbelievable," I said under my breath.

We could see through to more activity in another gallery.

"The other two were taken from there," he said. "*The Dance Class* by Degas and Van Gogh's *Girl in White*."

"Renoir, Degas, and Van Gogh," I said, shaking my head. "This guy isn't messing around."

"No, he isn't," said Dad.

We took an elevator three floors underground to the security center. Although the marble and limestone made the rest of the building feel like a Roman temple, this room looked like it belonged in a science fiction movie. All the furniture was black leather and silver metal, and the wall was covered with a bank of monitors playing surveillance video from throughout the building.

Two people were already there: a man in the corner with a British accent talking on a phone and another furiously typing away on the main computer console. The British man, wearing black jeans and a stylish black T-shirt, tried to sound calm but looked anything but as he paced back and forth.

"No, sir, I'm on top of things," he said unconvincingly. "We'll have it under control."

The man at the computer looked up and saw my father. "Jim, I'm glad you're here."

He was heavyset with a big moon face. His pale skin and

the circles under his eyes made it look like he hardly ever slept or stepped out into the sun. His jacket and tie had been tossed aside and his overall vibe was rumpled wreck.

"I want you to look over the data from the . . ." he stopped when he noticed me. "Who's this?"

"Earl, this is my son Florian," Dad said. "It's a long story, but . . ."

He didn't get time to explain. The door flew open and two more people stormed in. One was Serena Miller, the director of museum security and an old friend of Dad's. I recognized her because she'd stopped by the house to visit the first week we were in Washington. The other was a tall African-American man wearing a dark blue suit with a matching tie. Unlike Earl, his suit was still crisp and pressed. And unlike the British man, he wasn't trying to *appear* calm. He was completely cool and composed.

"Jim, this is Special Agent Marcus Rivers of the FBI's art crime team," Ms. Miller said, introducing him to my father.

"Nice to meet you," Dad said, shaking his hand.

"This is Jim Bates," she said, continuing the introduction. "He consults with us and I've asked him to help and . . ." Like Earl, she stopped the moment she saw me. "And for some reason he's brought along his son."

Rivers looked at me, more curious than angry, and then

turned to my dad. "It's not exactly a bring-your-kid-to-work kind of situation, is it?"

"I'm sorry about that," Dad replied. "But I think he may have seen something . . . *interesting* and I thought you should hear it."

"Interesting?" he asked. "In what way?"

"Tell them," Dad said to me. "Be as specific and accurate as possible."

Everyone was staring. Even the British man, who'd now finished his phone call. It was an intimidating group, especially considering there was a special agent in the mix. I took a deep breath and just started talking.

"About four weeks ago, my friend Margaret and I saw a man asleep on one of the couches in the gallery with Van Gogh's self-portrait. He was a tourist with blond hair. He slept for about fifteen minutes until his wife and their baby joined him."

They looked confused, but I just kept talking. "Then two weeks ago, we saw a copyist painting a replica of Monet's *Woman with a Parasol*. He had dark hair and was dressed like an art student. A total hipster. He goes to George Washington University and lives in the Philip S. Amsterdam Hall. I point that out because that residence hall does not allow married students or children. Married students are housed somewhere else. I checked online."

This was when the British man spoke up. "What's the point of this?" he asked impatiently. "Sixty-five million dollars in art is missing and we're listening to a child recount insignificant information. I've just had a very unpleasant phone call with my bosses back in England and assured them we are acting swiftly."

I ignored him and focused on the agent. "The sleeping father and the artist were the same man," I said. "A man who'd decided to completely change his appearance."

"Are we seriously letting this continue?" asked the Brit. "Every second we waste is a second the thief gets farther away."

"Why do you think they're the same person?" asked the agent.

"Both were wearing Europa trainers, a type of running shoe found only in Eastern Europe. Both were left-handed. And both had identical scars on their chins. I don't think it was the same person, I'm certain of it."

He obviously did not know what to make of me.

"Oh, and another thing," I said. "The two rooms we saw him in. Rooms in which he spent long periods of time. They're the same two rooms that just got robbed."

That's when the agent smiled. "Well, now. That does seem interesting."

7.

Seen but Not Heard

AGENT RIVERS WAS INTRIGUED BY MY STORY OF the man in the European shoes. But as far as clues and potential leads went, it was way down the list. It had been two weeks since Margaret and I had seen the man, and the museum was an active crime scene with fresh evidence to be gathered and security footage to be viewed.

Rivers let me stay because every copyist has to apply for a permit. When there was a free moment, he planned to have someone get the applications so I could look at the ID photos and see if any belonged to the man. Until then I was supposed to sit in the back of the room and wait.

Silently.

The silent part was stressed more than once, but I didn't mind. I had a front row seat to an actual mystery and my father was one of the good guys trying to solve it. It was beyond cool. I listened carefully as they re-created the events of the night.

"Start at the beginning," Rivers instructed. "How did someone take three paintings without setting off an alarm?"

"Our security software is all being updated," Ms. Miller explained. "Earl was in charge."

"That's right," he said. "We have fixes every few months, but this is the first major overhaul in years. The entire system had to be taken off-line while it rebooted. That meant we had no cameras, motion sensors, or alarms. We were totally dark."

"There are supposed to be countermeasures when you do that," said the British man.

"There were," answered Ms. Miller. "We overlapped shifts so we had extra guards along the perimeter of the building during the upgrade."

"And they didn't see anything?" asked Dad.

"Nothing out of the ordinary."

"I'm sorry," interrupted the agent, looking at the British man. "Who are you again?"

"Oliver Hobbes," he said. "I'm with the insurance company."

"And were you here during the reboot?" he asked.

"No, they called me after the paintings were found missing," he said.

"And when was that?" the agent asked.

"The system went down at one fifteen and everything was back up and running at one thirty-two," said Miller. "A custodian noticed a painting was missing and sounded the alarm at one fifty-one."

Rivers wrote down the times in a notepad he carried.

The mention of the custodian reminded me of the scene in the rotunda when we arrived. I scanned the monitors and saw that the police were still questioning the cleaning staff. There were five custodians waiting by the fountain while two others were talking to detectives off to the side. All of them wore matching blue coveralls. Their work carts were lined up in two rows of four on the far wall. I wished the monitors had sound so I could eavesdrop.

On another pair of monitors I saw the crime scene unit looking for evidence in the rooms that had been burglarized. I was amazed by how meticulously they worked. Then something struck me, and I looked back at the screen showing the rotunda.

There were two rows of four work carts, which made a total of eight, but there were only seven workers. Someone

was missing. I checked the other monitors, looking for anyone else in blue coveralls.

There were none.

"Dad," I blurted out excitedly. "Dad!"

The conversation at the table stopped abruptly and everyone glared at me.

"You really need to be quiet, Florian," my father said impatiently. "We have to focus on this."

"One of the custodians is missing," I said, pointing at the monitor.

"What do you mean?" asked Agent Rivers.

"There are eight carts but only seven custodians," I explained. "Where'd the extra cart come from?"

The agent walked right up to the monitor and tapped each person on the screen as he counted. Seven. He didn't say a thing. He just bolted out of the room with Serena and Earl right behind him.

That left me alone with my father and Hobbes, the insurance agent. Dad came over and sat next to me.

"I'm sorry," I said. "I know I wasn't supposed to talk, but . . ."

"It's okay," he assured me. "That was great that you noticed it . . . although maybe not so great for them."

On the screen we could see Rivers pull the detectives

aside and start a heated conversation. Once again I wished there were sound on the monitors.

"I owe you a huge apology," Hobbes said as he approached and offered his hand. "I was stressed and upset and I took it out on you. I hope you can forgive me."

"Of course," I said. "It's pretty crazy having a twelve-year-old interrupt your crime scene. I probably would have reacted the same way."

"Oliver Hobbes," he said as we shook.

"Florian Bates," I replied. "You said you work with the insurance company, right?"

"Yes," he answered. "The museum called me right after they called your dad."

"Oliver and I have crossed paths often," said my father.

"Yeah, your father's one of the best in the business," he replied. "I was relieved to see that he's part of the recovery team."

Before we could continue the conversation, Agent Rivers and the others returned. "What's your name?" he asked as he strode back to the main console.

"Florian Bates," I replied.

"How old are you?"

"Twelve."

"Well, twelve-year-old Florian Bates, you are officially

smarter than the detectives of the Metropolitan Police Department. They had no idea they were missing a custodian." He turned to Ms. Miller. "Can you pull up the security video starting at thirty minutes before the robbery?"

"Of course."

She nodded to Earl, who sat down and started typing. Within seconds the monitors were filled with footage from earlier in the night. The time on the bottom of each image read "12:45."

"What are we looking for?" asked Dad.

"A guilty-looking custodian," said the agent.

Even sped up, the footage was incredibly boring.

We were about halfway through it when Hobbes shook his head and complained, "They're all the same size. They're wearing identical uniforms. And they're looking down, not up at the cameras."

"I didn't say it would be easy," replied Rivers. "What were those shoes you were talking about?"

It took me a moment to realize he was asking me.

"What?" I asked.

"You said he had on a special type of shoe," he replied. "If he's our guy, he may have the same shoes on in this picture."

I hadn't even thought about that.

"Brilliant," said Oliver. "Check the shoes."

For the first time I moved over from the couch and stood next to them, examining each pair of shoes on the screen. First it was exciting. Then it was nerve-racking. And finally, it was embarrassing. We went back and forth over an hour and a half's worth of security footage and there was no sign of the man in the Europa trainers. I was so certain we'd find him. I was certain I'd be a hero. My clue was a dud.

"I guess I was wrong," I said softly.

"Don't sweat it," said the agent as he put a friendly hand on my shoulder. "I still want you to look through the applications to see if you can identify him. You never know how these things come together."

I forced a smile and nodded.

"Look there," said my dad, pointing at one of the monitors. "Who's that?"

The monitor showed the exterior of the building as a man in a blue custodian's uniform crossed Constitution Avenue and disappeared into the darkness.

"I think that's our eighth custodian," said the agent. "What's the time?"

"One forty-three," answered Earl.

"What time does the custodial shift end?"

"Not until four," he replied.

Agent Rivers turned the knob to make the video play

in reverse and stopped it at the point where we had the best view of the custodian. It still wasn't much to go by. His back was turned to the camera and he was wearing a baseball cap, so we couldn't really tell anything about him.

"So I've got a question," said Rivers. "If that's our guy leaving the scene, then where are the paintings?"

8.

Nightcrawlers

IT WAS NEARLY FOUR IN THE MORNING BUT THE
National Gallery was anything but sleepy. Since the prime
suspect left with nothing in his possession, everyone was
scouring the building to see if the paintings had been hidden in the museum. Everyone, that is, except for me and
Earl.

We stayed in the security center, where he worked on his
computer and I waited for my mom to pick me up. The mystery man in the Europa trainers was now even farther down
the list of leads. I was being sent home.

"Did you have to stay in here just to keep an eye on me?"
I asked. "If so, I'm really sorry."

"No," he said. "I'm responsible for the software upgrade and I need to keep an eye on the network while it filters through the entire system. Besides, you shouldn't apologize for anything. You saved the day."

"You think so?"

"Absolutely," he said.

"Thanks, Mr. . . ."

"No Mr.," he replied. "Just call me Earl."

I smiled. "Okay. Thanks, Earl."

"This is some show we've got tonight, isn't it?" he asked, looking at the security monitors.

On the screens we could see teams of police officers, security guards, and detectives hunting for any place the paintings could be hidden. There were people on ladders poking up into the ceiling tiles. There was a crew taking apart the couches in the galleries. A lot of attention was focused on bathrooms as well as the storage areas not open to the public. Agent Rivers was in charge of it all, and he marched up and down the main hallway giving orders and conferring with my father and Ms. Miller.

"If he hid the paintings here, that means he has to come back to get them," I said. "That seems really dangerous."

"Maybe not as dangerous as walking across the street

with them under his arm," said Earl. "He's obviously smart, so he must have figured out some way to get them without getting caught."

"And if he's smart, he must have picked those paintings on purpose," I reasoned. "Something like that wouldn't be random."

He gave me a look and smiled. "I've been thinking the same thing all night."

He typed something into the computer and the basic information about each of the three paintings came up on the screen in front of us:

The Dance Class by Edgar Degas (c. 1873)
Oil on canvas, 18 3/4″ x 24 1/2″
Gallery 83

Girl in White by Vincent van Gogh (1890)
Oil on canvas, 26 1/4″ x 18 1/16″
Gallery 83

Child with Toys by Auguste Renoir (1895–1896)
Oil on canvas, 21 3/8″ x 25 3/4″
Gallery 85

"What do they have in common?" I asked.

"The Degas and the Renoir are both French Impressionism," he said. "*Girl in White* is technically Postimpressionism. But most people don't notice the difference."

"Wow," I said. "You really know your art."

"I've spent eight of the last ten years trying to protect every painting in this building," he said. "After a while you get to know them pretty well."

"Why only eight?" I asked.

"I worked across the street at the National Archives for two years," he said. "But I missed this place too much and begged Serena for my old job."

"Since you know the paintings so well, can you think of why someone would want these three in particular?"

He shook his head. "Not really. They're not even the most valuable pieces in the rooms they were in."

"According to Mr. Hobbes, they're worth over sixty-five million dollars," I said.

"Don't get me wrong, they're incredibly valuable," he said. "But if you're going to risk stealing masterpieces, why not take the *most* valuable or at least the most important works?"

It was a good point but I reminded myself that monetary value and historical importance were big things, which can

be misleading. I thought about the small things. I thought about TOAST.

I looked at the images on the computer and tried to figure out what small things they had in common. The Renoir was a picture of a young boy and his nanny playing with toys. The Degas showed ballerinas in a dance class. And the Van Gogh had a woman in a dress walking through a field of flowers. No common themes.

I looked at the years they were painted, their previous owners, and even the frames they were in. They still had nothing in common. I was stumped until I noticed one seemingly insignificant thing.

"They're the same size!" I said.

"What?"

"They're all within a couple inches of being the same size," I said, not sure why it would be important.

Before I could come up with anything more, my mother arrived. Since she worked at the museum, her security pass let her come right in and pick me up.

"I can't believe this really happened," she said, looking at the monitors as she entered the room.

"They stole three paintings," I said. "Renoir, Degas, and Van Gogh."

"That's what your dad told me on the phone," she said,

her eyes still fixed on the monitors. "I just can't imagine."

"Florian was a big help," Earl said. "I think without him they still wouldn't have any idea what happened."

She smiled. "Well, thank you. But I think it's time that I take him home so he can get some sleep."

"Can't we stay just a little bit longer?" I asked. "I know you're just as curious as I am."

"That's not the point," she said. "They've got work to do. I'm sure your dad will fill us in on everything."

I said good-bye to Earl and we left. As we rode the elevator, I asked her, "Why would someone steal a painting because of its size instead of its value?"

"I don't know," said Mom. "Maybe the criminal has small walls and there's not enough room for bigger paintings."

We both laughed at this.

But it kind of made sense. Maybe there was some sort of size limit. I didn't figure out what it could be until we were in the rotunda and I saw the crime scene unit examining the extra work cart. That's when I noticed that unlike the others, its trash bag was empty.

"That's it!" I said to Mom. "Where's Dad?"

"What's it?"

"I know where the paintings are."

I remembered my father had been walking up and down

the main hall with Rivers. I started running toward where I'd seen them last.

"Wait for me," called Mom, trying to keep up.

I found them by the fountain in the East Garden Court. The first one to see me was Agent Rivers. Rather than being angry, he seemed amused.

"Let me guess?" he said. "You've solved the case?"

"I–I think so," I stammered, trying to catch my breath.

This caught him off guard, and I realized he'd been joking.

"All the paintings are about nineteen by twenty-five inches," I said.

"Okay," he said. "Why does that matter?"

"It's the perfect size to fit in his trash bag. That's how he went from room to room without anyone noticing. The paintings were in his trash bag on the cart. And that's how he's getting them out of the building."

"They're in the trash!" exclaimed Rivers.

"So he doesn't have to come back for them," I responded. "The garbage truck will pick them up for him."

"Where's trash collection?" he asked Ms. Miller.

"Right this way," she said, pointing.

Everyone rushed out to a loading dock, where there were three large Dumpsters, two blue and one green. Even though it was the middle of the night, a truck was backing up to pick up a

blue one. It turns out that a lot of the city's garbage is collected at night, when the tourists and government officials are gone.

"Stop. Right. Now," Rivers said, holding up his badge. "Nobody move."

A very dedicated team of FBI agents spent the next thirty minutes digging through the Dumpsters and bags of trash while detectives questioned the garbage crew to see if they might be involved. They didn't find anything until they checked the green recycling Dumpster.

All three paintings were found tucked in a stack of cardboard boxes that had been folded and bundled together. The size was the key. If they were just a few inches bigger they wouldn't have fit in the bundler.

"Twelve-year-old Florian Bates," Agent Rivers bellowed. "You are not just smarter than the officers of the Metropolitan Police Department. You are smarter than all of us."

My mom and dad laughed, but the strangest thing happened. The searchers all turned to me and gave me a round of applause.

I'd never felt anything like it before.

9.

Sunday Sauce

I WOKE UP WITH MY HEAD AT THE WRONG END OF the bed, completely unsure if the "4:15" on my clock was morning or afternoon. It was just like I was in Napoléon's portrait, only there were no candles to help me solve the mystery. The most disorienting part was the amazing aroma that filled the air. It was the unmistakable, mouthwatering smell of my mom's Sunday spaghetti sauce. But this was Saturday. Or at least I thought it was. There was a decent chance I'd slept for an entire day. Either that or I was having a smellucination. (Is there such a thing?)

"Mom?" I called into the kitchen as I walked down the stairs.

"Ah, look who's awake." Her hands were busy grating Parmesan cheese, so she bypassed the hug and leaned over to give me a kiss on the forehead. "Hello, sleepyhead."

"It's not Sunday, is it?" I asked, a bit nervous.

"No, it's still Saturday," she replied to my relief. "I figured I'd break with tradition and make your favorite meal a day early. You know, because you're such a good son. Oh, and the part about you saving over sixty-five million dollars in art from being stolen didn't hurt."

I smiled. "That really happened, huh? I thought maybe I had dreamed it."

"No, it happened," exclaimed a voice.

I turned to see Margaret sitting at the table, a big, goofy grin on her face.

"It's all over the news and I have been waiting all day to hear the inside story," she continued.

"Hey, Margaret, when did you get here?"

"After my game."

It was only then that it registered she was wearing her DC Dynamo soccer jersey. "Oh, wait! Today was the play-offs. Did I miss it?"

"Just by a couple hours," she said. "And it's a shame, because I was amazing. In fact, the reason I came over was to give you a hard time for missing it. But then your mom told

me about what happened and I figured it was an acceptable excuse. Barely acceptable. But acceptable."

"Did you win?" I asked.

"Four—nothing, remember the part about me being amazing?" she said. "But we can talk about soccer later. I want to hear about the robbery. It's all over the news, but there hasn't been anything about a twelve-year-old boy as part of the story. Start at the beginning. You know, right after the part where I had to convince you the copyist was suspicious and worth looking into. Start there."

I laughed and began to fill her in on what happened. I told her about arriving at the crime scene and telling the FBI about the copyist. I went through the details of the missing janitor and the search for the three paintings. I explained it all, and by the time I got to the discovery of the paintings, she and my mother were on the edge of their seats. (Mom had heard only bits and pieces of it before I went to sleep.)

"Mom and I were about to leave when I finally realized the importance of the size of the paintings," I said.

"I still don't get that part," Margaret said.

"They had to be small enough to fit into the garbage bag on his cart," I explained. "But more important, they had to fit into the machine that bundled all the cardboard boxes together for recycling. It was a great plan because the boxes

provided padding to protect the paintings from getting hurt. And the recycling truck would have actually taken them out of the museum. All the thief had to do was wait for them to be delivered at the recycling center."

"That. Is. Amazing," Margaret said. "After they found the paintings, did they catch the guy who stole them? Did they find the eighth janitor?"

"Actually . . . I don't know. I've been asleep. Mom?"

"Not yet," she answered. "Your dad said the FBI set up a stakeout at the recycling center, but he didn't show up. He's still out there somewhere."

That made me happy they hadn't mentioned me on the news. I was part of the reason someone lost $65 million. He was mad and the last thing I wanted was for him to even know I existed.

"So who's hungry?" asked Mom. "I think we should go ahead and eat without your dad. There's no telling when he'll get home."

The spaghetti was delicious (of course), and while we ate I tried to fill in any gaps I may have left in the story. We also got Margaret to tell us all about her soccer game, which on any other day would have been the big news.

"Does that mean you're in the WAGS championship?" I asked as I twirled some pasta onto my fork.

"We play the final next week," she said. "And I better see you there."

"I wouldn't miss it," I said. "Unless of course the FBI needs any more help with international art crimes."

"What's WAGS?" asked my mom.

"Washington Area Girls Soccer," explained Margaret. "It's made up of leagues all over the District. There are about a hundred teams in our division."

"And you're playing for the championship?"

Margaret nodded and smiled.

"That's impressive," said Mom.

Just then the front door opened and my dad hurried into the house. "Hello," he called out.

"In here," said Mom. "Sorry, we started without you. We didn't know when you'd get home."

"Actually, I'm just here for a second," he replied as he came into the kitchen. "I'd like you to meet someone."

"Hello, Mrs. Bates," said the man following Dad. "I'm Special Agent Marcus Rivers of the FBI. We didn't get a chance for an official introduction last night."

"Well, you had a lot going on," Mom joked as she stood up and shook his hand.

"He's the agent in charge," I whispered to Margaret.

Despite the fact that he probably hadn't slept at all, Agent

Rivers still looked as sharp as he did the night before. The only difference was that he'd switched from the dark blue suit to a dark gray one.

"Would you like to stay for dinner?" asked my mother.

He took a deep whiff and practically swooned. "I'd love nothing more, but I'm in something of a fluid situation at the moment." He turned his attention to Margaret and me. "Florian, is this the friend you were with when you saw the man in the museum?"

"Yes," I said. "This is Margaret."

"Nice to meet you, Margaret," he replied. "I don't mean to be rude, but how can I get in touch with your parents?"

"My parents?" she asked. "Am I in trouble of some kind?"

"Of course not," he said. "It's just that you're a minor and I'm going to need them to be involved."

"I think they're at the grocery store," she said. "But they should be back in half an hour."

Rivers checked his watch and looked back up at her. "Actually, we don't have that much time. Why don't we call them there?" He handed his phone to her. "Just dial the number."

"What's going on?" I asked him.

"I need you both to come down to the Hoover Building."

"What's the Hoover Building?" I asked.

"FBI Headquarters."

10.

The Bureau

MARGARET WAS EXCITED. HANDS-IN-THE-AIR-ON-a-roller-coaster excited. Except instead of whizzing around a theme park, we were racing down Massachusetts Avenue.

"This is so cool!" she exclaimed as the agent behind the wheel expertly maneuvered in and out of traffic. "Imagine if you could get to school this way. You'd never get another tardy."

"No, but you might get whiplash," I replied as my fingers gripped my armrest. (Did I mention that I hate roller coasters?)

We were riding in a government-issue black SUV with an armored body and bulletproof windows. "It's not like

anyone's going to shoot at us," Rivers assured us when he told us about these features. "That's just how they come."

After we'd wolfed down the rest of our spaghetti while he spoke with Margaret's parents on the phone, Margaret raced home to change. Then we all piled into the vehicle. Mom and Dad sat in the back row, Margaret and me in the middle, and Rivers in the passenger seat, while another agent drove.

Fast.

Apparently, FBI agents don't have to follow the speed limit when they're on a case.

"Look, look, look!" Margaret said, pointing at a tourist holding up her phone to take a picture. "She's taking our picture. She thinks we're important." Margaret smiled and waved even though the tinted window made it impossible for the woman to see her.

"Why exactly are we going to the Hoover Building?" I asked.

"Two reasons," said Rivers. "I want you two to look at some pictures to see if you recognize the man you saw in the museum."

"I. Told. You. So," Margaret said, poking me in the shoulder to punctuate each word. "He's an international hit man. Couldn't be more obvious."

"Actually, he's not," replied the agent. "But he may be involved with some high-end art crimes. That's what we're trying to figure out."

"What's the other reason?" asked my mother.

"Admiral Douglas wants to personally thank Florian for his help last night," he said. "We're going to stop by his office."

"Admiral Douglas?" I asked. "Who's he?"

"Admiral David Denton Douglas is the director of the FBI," explained Rivers "He's a close adviser of the president and as powerful as they get. In all his years as director, this is the first time he's ever requested a meeting with an eleven-year-old."

"Hey," I protested. "I'm twelve."

Rivers laughed.

"I'm just messing with you," he said. "I know all about you, Florian Bates. You were born at Brigham and Women's Hospital in Boston, Massachusetts, on March twenty-fourth to parents James and Francesca Bates. Most recently you attended the Castelli International School in Rome, where you got straight As except for a B in physical education."

"How do you get a B in PE?" asked Margaret.

"It's a long story," I said with a sour face, unhappy to be reminded of what I considered a miscarriage of academic justice.

"And you will soon be starting seventh grade at Alice Deal Middle School," Rivers continued. "Where you'll be part of the International Baccalaureate program. Very impressive, by the way."

"How do you know all that?"

"The I in FBI, it stands for 'investigation,'" he said. "We know things. Besides, you're about to meet the director. We don't let that happen without a thorough background check."

"Well, just for the record, it's not certain that I'll be in the IB program," I told him. "I've applied for it but won't find out if I was accepted until next week."

"Okay," Rivers replied. "Maybe I wasn't supposed to say anything about that. Just act surprised when they tell you."

Margaret and I shared a happy look. She was already in IB and this meant we'd have classes together.

"What about me?" she asked playfully. "Do you know anything about me?"

Agent Rivers opened an e-mail on his phone and started reading. "Margaret Campbell. Daughter of Paul and Denise Campbell. Both attorneys. Also a student at Alice Deal Middle School." He looked up from his phone. "Favorite color: purple."

She was blown away. "The FBI knows my favorite color?"

He shook his head. "No, I looked at the purple shirt,

the purple sneakers, and the purple nail polish and took a guess. With regard to the other stuff, I called it in as soon as Florian told me your name."

The SUV pulled into an underground parking structure where an agent was already waiting. He gave us visitor badges and within seconds we were on an elevator. I wasn't sure if we were in a rush because we were on a tight schedule or if the Bureau wanted to make sure no one saw us there.

We got out on the fifth floor, which was a maze of offices and cubicles. Because it was a Saturday, most were empty, but there were some people scattered about.

"Working on a Saturday," Margaret said. "That's just not right."

"Yeah, well, we haven't had much luck convincing the criminals to take the weekends off, but we're trying," he joked. "This area is all dedicated to major theft investigations. Cargo Theft over there. Jewelry and Gems next to that. And this is Art."

"Your office," I said.

"Home sweet home."

A few minutes later, Margaret's parents were ushered in and we all sat down on a pair of couches. Each family on a different couch with the kids in the middle.

"Now that we're all here, I'd like to officially welcome

you to the Hoover Building," Rivers said. "And I'd like to thank you for doing this on such short notice."

"Sure," said Margaret's dad. "But what exactly are we doing?"

"Margaret and Florian reported seeing a suspicious person at the National Gallery. We want to show them a photo array to see if they can identify that man."

"Is this dangerous?" asked her mother.

"Not at all," he said. "One of the reasons we're doing this on a Saturday in my office is because that way they'll be nowhere near anyone who might identify them. We're not asking them to testify in court. We've just received some surveillance footage and we want to know if we're looking at the right guy."

The four parents all shared some concerned looks but nodded their agreement.

"Great, let's start with Margaret," he said. "Why don't you and your parents come with me, while the Bates family waits here? I don't want your identification to influence Florian's."

They left the room and I sat there with my parents.

"This has been a crazy twenty-four hours," Mom said under her breath.

"You're not kidding," replied my father.

Normally, you can tell a lot about a person by looking at their office. But all I could tell about Agent Rivers was that he's neat. Extremely neat. The only personal touch on his desk was a picture of him at a graduation with his parents and a younger sister. His mom and dad looked proud. His sister looked bored. Other than that, there was no hint as to what his life outside of law enforcement might involve. The shelves of his bookcase were filled with neatly organized art books, and the walls had an impressive display of diplomas. He had a bachelor's degree from Harvard and a master's and PhD from Georgetown. No wonder his parents looked so proud.

It took less than two minutes for them to come back to the room. "All right, Florian. Your turn."

My parents and I followed him into a large room near his office.

"We call this the bullpen," he said. "It's where we brainstorm different cases."

The room had a few tables and large marker boards on each wall. Each board had information about a different case. On one board there were pictures of the interior and exterior of the National Gallery, diagrams of the crime scene, copies of each of the three paintings, and a timeline of events.

"We call this a case board," he explained. "It's where we put what we know about a case so we can all be on the same page. You see that empty space there?" he asked.

"Yeah," I said.

"That's where we'd like to have a photo of our prime suspect," he explained. "Hopefully you'll be able to help us with that."

"I'll do my best," I replied.

"I know you will," he told me. "I'm going to show you six photographs and I want you to tell me if any one of them is the man you saw at the National Gallery. Don't tell me what you think I want to hear. Don't tell me something that you *think* you might remember. Only tell me what you are exactly certain of. Understand?"

I nodded. "Yes, sir."

He put a binder in front of me and opened it to reveal two rows of three photographs. It took me all of a second and a half to point to the one in the lower right corner.

"That's him," I said. "That's how he looked the first time we saw him. When he had blond hair and a wife and a baby."

"Are you certain?"

"Without a doubt," I assured him.

"That's exactly what Margaret said."

He smiled, peeled the photo off the paper, and taped it in the empty spot on the case board. "There now, doesn't that look better?"

"It sure does," I said.

He told us to wait while he got Margaret and her parents. When they entered, she smiled the second she saw the picture taped to the case board. She knew that meant I'd identified the same person. Rivers logged on to a computer and turned the monitor toward us.

"Now I want to show you some security footage from Dulles International Airport," he said. "Tell me if you see the man again."

He pressed a key and a slideshow of images began to play. Each shot was a picture of someone going through airport security. Each one stayed up for about a second and a half. We watched carefully, trying to make sure we didn't miss anything.

"That's him," both of us said at the exact same time.

Rivers hit the space bar and stopped the slideshow so the picture froze on the screen. In this image, the man looked like he did the second time we saw him, with dark hair. He had a kind, innocent face.

"Are you certain?" asked Rivers. "He looks like a completely different person."

"There's no doubt," I said.

"That's how he looked when he was a copyist," added Margaret. "I know it's him."

"Go back two pictures," I said.

Rivers gave me a curious look, but did just that, stopping at a picture of an older man going through security.

"Look," I said, pointing at the background of the image. "You can see his feet when he was waiting in line. You can see the Europa trainers I was telling you about."

Rivers smiled. "Okay. I'm convinced."

He opened a file and referenced it while he talked to us. "We believe his name is Pavel Novak. He's from the Czech Republic and is thought to have been involved in several art crimes in Eastern Europe. We've had no record of him ever coming to the United States before, which is how we missed him."

"But he's the guy, right?" said Margaret. "He dressed up as the eighth janitor and stole the paintings."

"Actually, no," said Rivers. "These pictures were taken yesterday afternoon, about ten hours before the burglary. When the paintings were being stolen, he was in an airplane over the Atlantic Ocean."

We mulled this over for a moment.

"Are you sure?" I asked.

Rivers nodded. "That doesn't mean he wasn't involved.

He almost certainly was. He just wasn't the one who stole the paintings from the wall."

"If he didn't steal them, then what did he do?" I asked.

"My guess is that he was studying the museum, trying to get a solid feel for everything from schedules to security. Because of you, we know he was in both rooms where there were paintings stolen. That's a huge help."

"But when he was in the gallery with the Van Gogh and the Degas, he was asleep," I replied. "What could he see with his eyes shut?"

"He had a camera," said Margaret. "He had a big, bulky camera. He could have been shooting video the whole time he was pretending to be asleep. Then he could go back and look at it later."

Rivers smiled at Margaret and then her parents. "I guess only smart kids go to Alice Deal Middle," he said. "That's a very good theory."

"And we know he spent days in the other gallery while he was painting the copy of *Woman with a Parasol*," I added.

"Eight days total according to the copyist office," he said. "So now that we know Novak was the one you saw, we can start searching his known associates in Washington and among EEL."

"What's EEL?" asked my mother.

"The Eastern European League," he said. "It's a crime

syndicate with strong ties in the Czech Republic, Slovakia, Romania, and Bulgaria."

Margaret and I shook our heads in total disbelief. What had started out as a game, practicing TOAST, now involved the FBI and an international crime syndicate.

"What do we do now?" asked my dad.

"We just have to wait here for another twelve minutes," said Rivers, checking his watch. "Then we'll go up to the admiral's office. He keeps an exact schedule. Not a minute early, not a minute late."

I poked around the bullpen while we waited and looked at the case boards, including one where a man was taking down the pictures.

"Solved it?" I asked.

"More like decided it wasn't for us," he replied.

"This is Agent Crosby from Jewelry and Gems," Rivers said by way of introduction. "We go way back."

"If you're trying to catch someone smuggling diamonds from Sierra Leone, I'm your guy," he said to everyone.

Three pictures were taped to the board and numbered "1," "2," and "3." A date was written beneath each. There was also a map of Washington with corresponding locations marked with the same numbers. None of the locations were near each other.

"What's the case?" I asked.

"Three B and Es," said Agent Crosby. "That's breaking and entering. A sapphire ring was stolen from one. A pearl necklace from another. And we're not sure if anything was stolen from the third."

"A ring and a necklace?" I asked. "I know you're Jewelry and Gems, but that doesn't sound big enough for the FBI."

"It's not," he replied. "But all three victims are employed by the CIA. They asked us to look into it to make sure the cases weren't related. They aren't, so we're returning them to our friends in the Metropolitan Police Department."

I looked at the pictures and something caught my eye.

"Uh-oh," I heard Margaret whisper to my mom.

"What?" she asked.

"He just saw a clue they missed," Margaret said. "Watch this."

It wasn't really a clue yet, but there was something. All three photographs were taken in apartments. The first two in kitchens and the third in a bedroom.

I pointed to the open window in one of the kitchen shots. "Is that how the burglar got into the apartment? Through the window?"

Agent Crosby gave me a confused look, not sure why I cared.

"Yes," he said.

I studied the picture, and then the other kitchen shot.

"Can I see a picture from the third victim's kitchen?" I asked.

Now Crosby was annoyed. He was about to tell me it was none of my business when Agent Rivers joined the conversation.

"Why don't you show him?" he instructed. "Just for fun."

"The kitchen's not relevant," Crosby told us. "In that robbery, the burglar entered through the bedroom window."

"I'd still like to see it," I replied.

Rivers looked at me and smiled, which was the exact opposite reaction to Agent Crosby's.

"Show it to him," Rivers said a bit forcefully. That's when I realized he outranked him. Crosby dug through a file, pulled out a picture, and handed it to me. I saw exactly what I was looking for.

"Do any of these victims have anything to do with China?" I asked.

"As a matter of fact, two of them do," he said, surprised. "They work at the Chinese counterintelligence desk." He thought for a moment. "How could you possibly know that?"

"I think you better tell the CIA that the Chinese government is trying to spy on these employees," I said.

Rivers laughed and Crosby looked like he'd just been punched in the gut. Margaret walked over and put a friendly hand on his shoulder. "Don't feel bad. He does that to everyone. You just got TOASTed."

11.

The Admiral

I USED TO THINK THE PRINCIPAL'S OFFICE WAS intimidating.

Then I got called to the office of the director of the FBI and developed a whole new understanding of the word.

The reception area had dark paneling, antique furniture, and three massive paintings on the wall. The names beneath the paintings formed the motto of the FBI. There was *Fidelity*, featuring an eagle soaring over the Grand Canyon; *Bravery*, which showed a Civil War battle scene; and *Integrity*, with George Washington taking the oath of office.

This was the room where Mom, Dad, Margaret, and her parents sat waiting under the watchful eye of a man who

politely offered everybody bottled water but also looked like he knew seventeen different ways to kill you with a pencil.

Agent Rivers led me into a room with a large desk and a conference table. In here, one wall was covered with a map of the United States. Another was filled with photographs of the director with various world leaders. And a third contained a hidden door that opened onto a smaller, secret office.

That's where the director and Rivers talked while I waited nervously, wondering what I had gotten myself into.

"I thought I was just supposed to thank him?" the director asked. "I didn't realize we were involving him in other cases."

"Yes, sir," said Rivers. "But I think you should listen to his theory. It's compelling. Especially when you consider that his last theory helped us recover more than sixty-five million dollars in stolen art."

They lowered their voices and I couldn't hear much more until the end of the conversation when he asked, "How old is he again?"

"Twelve," responded Rivers. "But not like any twelve-year-old you've ever met."

They walked into the room and I was surprised by how tall the director was. He stood at least six foot four and wore his silver-gray hair in a crew cut. He had a thin mustache

that curled up ever so slightly at the ends, and his imposing presence was softened by the hint of a Southern accent.

"Florian, it's nice to meet you," he said. "I'm Admiral Douglas."

"It's an honor, sir," I replied as we shook hands.

"Agent Rivers says that you're some sort of superdetective. Would you say that's an accurate assessment?"

"Well . . . sir," I replied, flustered, "I don't know if I'd—"

"Son, in this room there's no need for modesty," he interrupted. "Just answer the question."

I took a breath and replied as confidently as I could manage, "I notice things that other people miss."

"What sort of things?" he asked.

It felt like a test. I knew Agent Rivers had put his reputation on the line and I wasn't about to let him down. I decided to show off.

"Well, sir, I know that you have a chronically sore back," I said. "And that you've owned that tie for more than a decade."

He checked to see which tie he was wearing and then looked at Agent Rivers for a moment before turning back to me and asking, "What makes you say that?"

"The only nongovernmental item in this room is the small pillow you keep on the bottom shelf of the bookcase behind your desk," I responded. "I assume you use it to give

your back relief when you sit for long periods. Also, your laces are tied along the inner edge of each shoe rather than the middle. Instead of leaning over and tying them while they're flat on the floor, you put your foot up on your knee to ease the strain. Finally, there is a model of a submarine on the corner of your desk with an engraving thanking you for your service as its captain. Considering your height and the low ceilings on a sub, I imagine you had to bend over much of the time, which is probably when your back troubles started in the first place."

He smiled. "And the tie?"

"There's a photograph on the wall behind me of you meeting the former prime minister of France," I said. "You're wearing the same tie in the picture and he died twelve years ago. That means the tie is at least twelve years old."

Douglas laughed and turned to Agent Rivers, who flashed a huge smile.

"Not like any other twelve-year-old indeed," he said. "Florian, why don't we have a seat and talk about what the Chinese government is up to?"

We sat at the conference table and Rivers pulled three photographs from a file, placing them in front of the director and me.

"Three apartments, each the home of a CIA employee,"

said Rivers. "And each also the scene of a relatively small break-in."

Douglas looked at the pictures for a moment and asked, "And you think each of these was committed by a spy working for the Chinese government?"

"I can't be certain he's working for the government," I replied. "He could be working for a corporation or some other organization, but the government seems most likely."

"And what makes you think this?"

"TOAST, sir."

"I see three kitchens, son," he replied. "But no toast."

"TOAST is the Theory of All Small Things," I told him. "It's how I . . . well, for lack of a better term . . . it's how I solve mysteries."

This made him smile. "Seeing as I'm just the director of the FBI and not a superdetective, why don't you explain it to me?"

"TOAST considers small, seemingly insignificant details that when added together reveal hidden truths," I said. "In this instance, the three apartments are located in entirely different parts of the city. Each is at least four miles from the other two. Yet all of them have a menu from the same Chinese restaurant on the refrigerator. That's what caught my attention."

The admiral smiled at this detail. "That's interesting, but I hardly think that—"

"It says 'Free Delivery' on the top of the menu," I continued. "Do you know a Chinese restaurant that has free delivery throughout the entire city? Normally they only deliver in a one- or two-mile radius, a mathematic impossibility for these apartments."

"Good point," he replied.

"And if you notice, identical coupons have been torn off the bottom of each menu. You can still see part of one here. It says 'half off your first order.'"

I handed the admiral the picture for him to examine.

"Imagine that you're a spy who wants to infiltrate the CIA. You can't break into headquarters. You can't hack employee records on the agency's computer servers. You can't follow workers when they head home. All of these are overt acts that run the risk of getting caught. But you're completely safe if the employees invite you to their homes."

Admiral Douglas shook his head in amazement. "You get them to order food."

"That's right," I said. "Somehow the spy got these menus into CIA headquarters. Maybe he made a delivery to the building and just stuck a bunch of menus in with the food. Maybe he got someone to innocently bring them in. But

somehow they made their way into a common area such as a break room where they were left out for anyone."

"And if only those menus have the coupon," said Rivers. "That means whenever anyone places an order and mentions the coupon, the person taking the call knows it's someone who works for the CIA."

I nodded. "So our spy delivers the food, and the person opens the door, allowing him to look inside the apartment, maybe even secretly take a picture or two. Later on he breaks in, makes it look like a burglary, and sneaks a listening device into a purse or briefcase."

Admiral Douglas looked at it all for a moment in total disbelief. "That's brilliant."

"He really thought of everything," I said.

He laughed. "I wasn't talking about the spy, Florian. I was talking about you."

This made me blush.

"How long have our men been working on this case?" he asked Agent Rivers.

"A couple of weeks," he replied.

"And how long did it take Florian to crack it wide open?"

Rivers smiled. "A couple of minutes."

"Mrs. Jenkins, can you come in here for a moment," Douglas called out to one of the secretaries. "Take-out

Chinese," he muttered to himself as he waited for her to come in. "Unbelievable."

A woman appeared at the door with a notepad in her hand.

"Yes, sir," she said.

"I need you to schedule an appointment with the director of the CIA and tell him it's urgent," he said. "And please ask Florian's parents to come in here. I'd like to discuss something with them."

I looked at Agent Rivers and he just shrugged, unsure why the director wanted to speak to my parents.

"Florian, just for fun, why don't you close your eyes?"

"Sure," I said.

"What color are my socks?" he asked. "Black or blue?"

"Neither, sir," I said with a smile. "They're burgundy."

He laughed again. "Thought I might trick you on that one."

Just then Mrs. Jenkins walked my parents into the room. Admiral Douglas jumped up from his seat and greeted them, giving each an enthusiastic handshake.

"Welcome, welcome," he said. "This is some boy you have here."

"We think so," said Mom.

"Please have a seat," he said, motioning toward the table.

"I'm going to be honest. I have to go to the White House this evening, and now, thanks to Florian, I also have to squeeze in a quick chat with the director of the CIA. So if you'll pardon me, I don't have time for any small talk. I'm just going to cut to the chase."

"Certainly," said Dad.

"I would like Florian to work with us here at the Bureau."

My eyes opened wide. "You want me to be an FBI agent?"

"Actually, I was thinking more as a consultant," he replied. "Not often. But every now and then we might call and ask you to do that TOAST thing. I still don't fully understand it, but I've only dedicated thirty-plus years to intelligence gathering."

"Mom? Dad? Can I?" I asked excitedly.

"He's joking," my father said.

"No, I'm afraid not," he replied. "The only thing crazier than me asking a twelve-year-old to join us would be me not asking. In two days he's helped us locate over sixty-five million dollars in stolen art and quite possibly uncovered a clandestine spying operation being run by the Chinese government. Imagine what he could do if we gave him another two days."

My parents were speechless, which I took as a sign that they were at least considering it.

"Would I get paid?" I asked.

The director chuckled at this. "We'd have to figure something out," he replied. "We can't put a twelve-year-old on the payroll without attracting congressional attention, but I'm sure there's a way we can compensate you for your services."

"In a college fund," blurted my mom. "We'll create a college fund and you can pay him there."

"That's a fantastic idea," said the director.

"But he can only help you when he's done with his homework," she continued.

"What's that?" asked the director.

"He can help save the country," she said. "But only after he finishes all of his schoolwork. I won't let this hurt his grades."

The director laughed. "Sounds reasonable to me. What do you think, Florian? You want to join us?"

It was the easiest question I ever answered.

12.

The New FBI

IT WAS WEDNESDAY MORNING AND MY PARENTS were at work. I'd just poured the milk on my cereal and was about to savor that perfectly crunchy first spoonful when the doorbell rang.

"This is going to change everything," Margaret announced as she entered the room tornado-style, midway through a conversation that had apparently started without me.

"What is?" I asked.

"My big idea," she answered as though it was obvious. "It's epic."

"Something tells me this isn't a brief conversation," I

replied. "Can you explain it in the kitchen? I don't want my cereal to get soggy."

"Kitchen it is," she said, trying to seem as accommodating as possible.

We sat at the table and I ate while she kept talking.

"I'm just going to say three words," she said. "The New FBI."

"What's the New FBI?" I mumbled, my mouth full of Alpha-Bits.

"Florian Bates Investigations."

I swallowed the cereal and smiled. "I get it. That's funny."

"It's not funny, it's brilliant," she said. "You're already a consultant to the actual FBI. This just takes it to the logical next step. As soon as word gets out about you, people will start knocking on your door looking for everything from stolen property to missing persons. Senators, ambassadors . . . spies. They'll come when they've run out of options because . . . Florian Bates Investigations is solving the mysteries of the world, one case at a time." (That last part she said with a ta-da kind of feeling.)

"You even came up with a slogan?"

"I told you it was epic."

"Except no one's going to come because word's not going to get out," I countered. "The only ones who'll know about

me are the FBI, my parents, and you. Admiral Douglas and Agent Rivers didn't even want me to tell you, but I told them it was deal breaker. I said that you're my best friend and I wouldn't lie to you."

"You said that?"

"Of course I did," I replied.

"That's really sweet," she said. "But trust me when I say that nothing stays secret in Washington. It may just be passed along as a whisper or rumor, but people will find out. They'll find out because they'll be desperate. Because no one else will be able to help them. That's when they'll come looking for us."

"Us?"

"Yeah, us," she said. "I'm going to be your partner. You're great with clues, but let's face it, your people skills are lacking."

"What's wrong with my people skills?" I asked incredulously.

"That's the beauty of it. You don't have to worry about what's wrong with your people skills because I've got it covered," she said. "I'll also help you with the investigating. I've gotten pretty good at TOAST. If we work together, there's no mystery we can't solve."

"I can't tell if you're joking or not."

She gave me a look. "No joke. In fact, we've already gotten our first case."

"We have? Who's the client?"

Her expression changed and she forced a little smile. "Me."

"And what mystery do you want solved? Because if you want me to spy on the team you guys are playing in the finals I'm going to have to say no."

"It's nothing like that," she said. "I don't need your help to win a soccer game."

"Then what do you need it for?"

"I want you to find my parents. My birth parents. I want you to find out who they are and why they abandoned me at the fire station."

This caught me completely off guard and the mood took a sudden turn from silly to serious. I didn't know what to say.

"When we were in the SUV with Agent Rivers, he knew everything about you," she continued. "He knew your birthday. The name of the hospital where you were born. He knew your entire history. But he skipped over those parts with me. That's because even the FBI can't figure out where I come from. But you can, Florian. If anyone can do it, it's you."

"I think it's really dangerous," I said.

"No one's going to hurt us."

"Not dangerous like that," I explained. "But you might find out something bad. You might find out something you don't really want to know."

"This isn't something I just came up with. I've wanted to know this my whole life. Believe me, I'm glad they gave me up. I love my parents, but I'm incomplete. Like a book with the first chapter torn out. I need to know. . . ."

I realized there was only one answer I could give her.

"Okay. I'll do it."

"Really?" she said excitedly.

"Yes," I said. "I'll look for your parents."

"You're not going to look for them, Florian," she said. "You're going to find them."

I didn't want to make a promise I couldn't keep, but she was persuasive. "Yes. I'll find them."

There was that big smile again. The one I saw the first day we met.

"But I can't work on it today," I added. "I've got to go back to the National Gallery. I'm still trying to figure out something about the robbery."

"Okay," she said, doing a pretty bad job of masking her disappointment. "I'll see you later then."

I swallowed my last spoonful of cereal and got up to rinse

the bowl in the sink. "Why later? Aren't you coming with me to the museum?"

"I thought the FBI stuff was all top secret."

"Yeah, well, I thought you just said we were partners."

And that's where it became official. As I rinsed my bowl in the sink. Florian Bates Investigations was born.

13.

Nerds United

"SO WHY ARE WE GOING TO THE MUSEUM?" Margaret asked as we walked from the Metro station toward the National Gallery. "What are we looking for?"

"I'm not sure . . . but something," I answered, not meaning to sound so mysterious. "It just doesn't add up for me. Like the time I built the Death Star out of Legos. It looked good. Everything fit together. But I still had pieces left over. Turns out I'd skipped an entire level with a docking bay."

She flashed a smile. "Death Stars and docking bays. You really are a nerd, aren't you?"

"Nerds make the world go round," I said proudly.

"Yes, we do," she replied. "But I don't know what leftover pieces there could possibly be. We identified Novak's picture and know that he's back in the Czech Republic. All that's here are the paintings, and you already found those."

"I just think we may have missed something."

She gave me a look. "And by 'we,' you actually mean the FBI, the crime scene unit, and museum security?"

"Yeah," I said sheepishly. "That's how it goes with TOAST. You have to look for the crumbs, too."

When we entered the museum, we saw a crush of people in the rotunda and Margaret asked, "Is it my imagination, or is it more crowded than usual?"

"It's not your imagination at all," I answered. "Today's the first day they've reopened the two rooms where the pictures were stolen. Mom said attendance is expected to be high for a couple weeks. I guess everyone's suddenly interested in art."

"Either that or they think they're smarter than the FBI and can uncover some clue the experts missed," she said with a sly grin.

"Who would be crazy enough to believe that?" I replied as we both laughed.

Unfortunately, the crowds were the biggest in the rooms where we wanted to go. Our first stop was Gallery 83, which

is where we saw Novak the first time, when he was asleep on the couch.

"Two paintings were stolen from here: *The Dance Class* by Edgar Degas and *Girl in White* by Vincent van Gogh," I said as I pointed to each, both now back where they belonged on each side of the door.

"And Novak was sleeping, or at least pretending to sleep, here," Margaret added as she sat down on the couch right where we saw him. I sat next to her and we scanned the room, looking at what he would have seen that day.

Margaret noticed a guard standing in the corner of the room.

"Was there a guard in here before?" she asked, motioning to the guard in the corner.

I leaned over and whispered to her, "I don't think he's actually a guard. I think he's FBI. Agent Rivers said they're going to keep a heightened presence here to see if anyone suspicious returns to the scene of the crime."

We both got a charge from the undercover feel of it all.

"But that day there wasn't anyone there?"

"Not permanently," I said. "Each guard normally rotates between three or four rooms, which is probably why Novak was here in the first place. He wanted to figure out the pattern."

"So he pretends to sleep and runs his video camera for about thirty minutes, which gives him a good sense of their schedule," she replied. "But how does he find out when the security system is going to be upgraded? Does he overhear someone talking about it?"

"No way," I said. "Information like that is kept secret. The guards probably didn't even know it was going to happen until a day or two before. My guess is that his partner found that out."

"Partner? You mean the guy who dressed up as the other custodian?"

"That would make sense," I replied. "He has to have some sort of inside connection to get the custodian's uniform. Maybe that same connection is how he found out about the security system."

"Which means it could be someone who works here at the museum," she said.

"That's a definite possibility. Somehow the thief knew they were going to reset the security system at exactly one fifteen in the morning."

"Does the FBI think there was an insider?"

"If so, they didn't share that with me," I said. "But I do know Agent Rivers is here investigating today. Maybe that's why."

"We should say hi."

"Covert asset," I reminded her. "If I see him in public, I'm supposed to act like I don't know him. You too."

I opened up a little notebook and drew a diagram of the room, making sure to mark where each picture hung and the locations of the three doorways. I wanted to have notes to refer to later at home.

"So explain this to me," she said.

"What?"

"If you're already on the inside and know when the entire security system is going to be reset, then why do you even need to have someone study the guards? And why do you go to the trouble of flying that person all the way from the Czech Republic and making him change his identity?"

"That's the part that doesn't make sense to me," I answered. "He's supposed to be an expert art thief, but you don't use him to actually steal the paintings. It's like having LeBron James on your basketball team but only having him sell hot dogs. If they just needed surveillance, I'm sure they could have found someone else. He must have had another job, something more specialized that made it worth bringing him here."

"I bet Paul and Vince know," she said.

"Who?"

"Gauguin and Van Gogh," she replied, pointing at their self-portraits in the room. "I bet they saw it all, but they're keeping it a secret just like they kept the secret of who cut off Van Gogh's ear."

I turned to look at her for a moment and said, "You're really a nerd too."

We shared a smile and it dawned on me that Margaret was the first friend I had with whom I could truly be myself. Next we went into Gallery 85, which is where we'd seen Novak painting the copy of *Woman with a Parasol* and where Renoir's *Child with Toys* was stolen. Like the first room, this one was more crowded than usual and had a guard (possibly an agent) stationed in the corner keeping an eye on things.

"And this is where he posed as a copyist," said Margaret.

"He wasn't posing," I reminded her. "He may have lied about his name, but his copy of the painting was amazing. He's supertalented. Agent Rivers says that he was a star student at the Academy of Fine Arts in Prague."

She gave me a confused look. "How does a talented artist get involved with criminals?"

"It's hard to make a living as a painter," I reasoned. "Maybe someone offered him too much money to pass up."

"Okay, then let's rephrase the question," she said.

"How does an art thief from the Czech Republic even meet someone with an inside connection to a museum in Washington?"

"That's a great question. It could be like my parents. After all, my mom's from Italy, and my dad's from Boston."

"How'd they meet?"

I smiled at the memory of a story I'd heard many times. "She was working at a small museum in Rome, and went to an international conference in London to give a speech about techniques in art conservation. My dad was at the same conference and was supposed to attend a presentation about motion detectors but walked into the wrong room by mistake. He was just about to leave when she stood up to give her talk."

"And when he saw her he decided to stay?" Margaret asked.

"Exactly," I replied. "A week later that small museum in Rome was really surprised when an American security expert offered an amazingly low price to come and consult about their new alarm system. It took him two weeks of consulting to finally work up the courage to ask her out."

Margaret laughed. "Nicely played, Mr. B. So do you think the same thing could have happened here? One of the conservators or curators or security people was in Europe

going to a conference and bumped into Novak by accident? They get to know each other and instead of getting married like your parents, they decide to commit a felony."

"Maybe," I said. "But here's another question for you. Why paint *Woman with a Parasol* instead of *The Japanese Footbridge*?"

"What's *The Japanese Footbridge*?" she asked.

"That picture," I said, pointing at another painting. "It's also by Monet. If you copy it, you're facing two doorways and can see who comes and goes. But *Woman with a Parasol* is in the corner. When he painted it, he was looking away from everything."

"You're right," she said. "The other picture seems like the smarter option."

"Unless it wasn't about the room," I countered. "Maybe this was about access. The copyists keep their supplies and canvases on the same floor where my mother's studio is. It's just down the hall from the security center."

"So that lets him get downstairs where the public normally can't go," Margaret says, picking up on my train of thought. "Maybe that's when he snoops around and finds out about the security system being reset."

I thought this through for a moment.

"That's good," I said. "He goes down there every morning

to pick up all his stuff and back again in the evening to put it away. He does a little spy work along the way."

"Although it's hard to sneak around carrying a canvas and all those paints," joked Margaret.

I know she was joking, but it was a good point. And it made me think of something. "Wait a second," I said, suddenly excited. "You're absolutely right. Paintings are big and bulky."

She gave me a blank look. "I hate it when I'm right and I don't know why. It means I don't get to gloat about it."

I flashed a huge grin. "How did you know my dad borrowed his golf clubs when he was in California?"

"What?" she said, now totally confused.

"The time you figured out that my dad had played golf in California. How did you know he'd borrowed somebody else's golf clubs?"

"Because he wasn't carrying any clubs when he came home," she said. "Why is that important?"

"That's the hardest clue to find," I said. "The clue that's a clue because it's missing, not because it's there."

"And . . . ?" she asked.

"What wasn't Novak carrying at the airport?" I said, piecing it together.

"I don't know," she said. "He had a suitcase, a backpack"—

she smiled and I knew she had it—"but he didn't have the painting. He didn't have his copy of *Woman with a Parasol*. Something that beautiful that you spent eight days painting, you'd bring home with you, right?"

"I would," I said.

"Although he could have just shipped it home in the mail," she said. "I don't know if you bring something like that on a plane."

"That's true," I said. "But think about what we were just saying. He had a special talent worth bringing him all the way from Eastern Europe. What if that talent was his ability to paint? What if he didn't ship it? What if he never took it out of the museum?"

We both looked at the painting on the wall.

"You think that's his copy on the wall?" she asked.

I shrugged. "I don't know. But I think it could be."

We walked over and studied the painting, looking for any hint that it might be a forgery. I leaned forward until I was just inches from it. That's when the guard cleared his throat to get my attention.

"Back up," he said firmly.

"Sorry," I replied. "It's just beautiful, isn't it?"

"Yeah," he replied. "But it's just as beautiful from farther back."

I stepped away and he turned his attention to the rest of the room.

"What do you think?" Margaret whispered. "Is it a forgery?"

"I don't know. I'm not an art expert," I said. "Luckily I know someone who is."

I started dialing as we walked toward the elevator. I called Agent Rivers and he told us to stay in my mother's studio until all of her coworkers were gone. He wanted it to look like we were just waiting for her to finish so we could go home together. It was all part of the plan to keep my involvement hidden. The last person left around five forty-five, and a few minutes later he arrived. He'd been in the security center, so there was nothing suspicious about him being at the museum.

"Okay," he said as he locked the door to assure our privacy. "What's your big discovery?"

"It's not a discovery so much as a theory," I said, trying to lower his expectations. "But I think maybe four paintings were stolen."

Rivers and my mom shared a confused look before turning their attention to me.

"What's the fourth painting?" he asked.

"*Woman with a Parasol*," I said.

"*Woman with a Parasol* is in Gallery Eighty-Five," Mom replied. "I saw it this morning."

"Yes, but what if it was a copy?" I suggested. "What if you saw the copy that Novak painted?"

I could see Rivers start to run the idea through his head.

"It would explain why they went to the trouble of bringing him here," Margaret added. "Studying the guards was just a side job. The main reason he was involved was so that he could paint the forgery."

All eyes turned to Margaret.

"I'm the partner," she said proudly. "We figured this part out together."

Rivers chuckled and shook his head.

"Why go to all that trouble?" Mom asked. "Why not just put it with the other paintings in the recycling?"

"It's too big," I said. "Even without the frame it wouldn't have fit in the recycling bundler."

"And you're basing this on what?" asked Rivers. "You can tell that it's a forgery?"

"No," I said. "It's just a theory."

He considered this for a moment. "Okay," he said. "Let's go have a look."

We all went up to the main floor, my mom carrying her bag like she was going home. If anyone noticed us it would

just look like we were leaving for the day. We stopped in Gallery 85. Rivers made sure no one was around while my mother examined the picture closely.

"So?" he asked her. "Could it be fake?"

"If so, it's an amazingly good one," she said. "I can't tell just by looking at it. I'd have to take it down, put it under the microscope, and run some tests."

Agent Rivers thought about this for a moment and said, "No. I need you to figure it out without moving the painting."

My mother gave him a quizzical look. "Why?"

"Because we think there's an employee involved," he said.

Margaret and I shared a look and a nod.

"If it's true and if this is a copy, they think they've gotten away with it. The moment it comes off the wall, we warn them that we're on to them."

Mom considered all of this for a moment and said, "I only need a tiny flake of paint to run a cesium test."

"Brilliant," he said. "How do you order a test like that?"

"It's a lot of paperwork," she answered. "And I have to allocate the expense to a certain budget."

He shook his head. "That's way too many people involved. Get me a flake and I'll have the test run. We have labs too."

He smiled at us and nodded before walking in the oppo-

site direction. Mom looked at the painting for a few more moments, and then we headed for the door.

"What's a cesium test?" I asked once we were outside.

"It's a way to see if a painting is old or modern," she said. "There's cesium in all the paint made after 1945 and none in the paint made before. So if you test a painting that was supposedly done in the 1800s and find any cesium in it, then . . ."

"You know it's a fake," I said.

"Exactly."

"What happened in 1945?" asked Margaret.

"That's when the first nuclear explosion took place," Mom explained. "Cesium was part of the radioactive fall-out."

"And that spread everywhere?" I asked.

She nodded. "Yep. All over the world including into all the dirt and plants used for making paint."

"And that can be determined just by testing a single flake?"

"You've got to love science," she said.

Margaret shook her head and added, "Nerds really do make the world go round."

14.

The Hornet's Nest

SINCE IT WAS GOING TO TAKE A FEW DAYS TO GET the results of the cesium test, Margaret and I had time to work on our other case: the search for her birth parents. This one didn't involve any Eastern European crime syndicates or million-dollar art thefts, but I knew solving it would be just as tricky. Maybe more.

"You're sure you want to do this?" I asked as we rode the Metro.

Her answer was soft but firm. "I'm positive."

She had a determined look so I didn't suggest we play the game where we try to guess who's getting off at which

stop. Instead we rode without talking much until we reached the Howard University station.

"This is our stop," I said as I stood, not that she needed to be reminded.

Even though it wasn't quite noon, the temperature was already in the nineties and rising. As we walked along the campus, the large shade trees that lined Georgia Avenue offered us a little relief from the heat.

"I understand that your adoption is a sensitive issue," I said. "But we're going to have to be able to talk about it in order for me to solve it."

"I know," she said. "What do you want to know?"

"Everything," I answered. "Tell me whatever you know."

"Not much," she replied. "On the night of August sixth somebody dropped me off at Engine House Four."

"Was it a man or a woman?" I asked.

She shrugged. "Nobody ever told me."

"Did they leave you in a crib, a stroller, or something like that?"

"The only thing I know is that I was wrapped in a blanket," she said, her eyes looking forward and not at me. "We still have it. I can show it to you later. It's yellow and has my name

embroidered on it in big block letters, 'MARGARET A.'"

"A?" I said, curious. "What's the A? A middle initial? The first letter of your birth parents' last name?"

She stopped and looked at me. "I just told you everything I know. I was left at the firehouse with a blanket that said 'Margaret A' on August sixth. That's it."

"I'm sorry," I said, worrying that I had upset her. "I didn't mean to—"

"Don't be sorry," she replied. "I'm not mad that you're asking the questions. I'm just frustrated that I don't know the answers. That's why we're doing this."

"Have you talked to your parents about what they know?"

"Not much," she said. "I always worry that if I ask them anything, they'll think I'm unhappy about them being my mom and dad. And I'm not. I love them. I don't want to upset them, so I never bring it up."

"Well, we've got some solid clues to go on," I said, trying to sound positive. "Let's see where they lead us."

The firehouse was a squat two-story building made of dark brown bricks. ENG4INE was painted on one wall and there were three red barn doors for the garage. One of them was open and we could see a red-and-white fire truck inside. Written on the front of the truck was THE HORNET'S NEST.

"What's the Hornet's Nest?" asked Margaret.

I shrugged. "Let's poke it and find out."

We were heading for the office when a firefighter saw us through the open garage door.

"Are you here about CPR training?" he asked. He was young and wore dark blue pants and a matching button-up shirt with a DCFD patch on the left shoulder.

"No," I said, unsure how best to explain exactly why we were there. "We just want to find out—"

"We're looking for information," Margaret said, taking charge. "About something that happened at this station twelve years ago."

He looked us over for a moment and said, "Then you'll want to talk to the captain. He's the only one who's been here that long."

"Is he in the office?" I asked, pointing toward the door.

"No," he answered. "He's in the kitchen . . . God help us."

We followed him through the garage door and alongside the fire truck. There were hoses, lockers, and even a pole to slide down from upstairs. On the wall were rows of pictures—one taken each year of the firefighters at the station. Someone had also painted a logo of a giant hornet wearing a fire helmet and jacket holding a hose and ax. Beneath it again was written THE HORNET'S NEST.

"It's our symbol," he said, noticing me looking at it. "Don't mess with the hive."

"Cool," I answered.

The kitchen was in the back, and there a man was frying something on the stove. He was older, but fit, his blue T-shirt tight on his biceps. He had a thin white mustache and goatee.

"Twenty-six years in the department and he can still only cook three things," joked the firefighter. "What are you making today?"

"Fish sandwiches," he said. "And if you say anything more about my cooking, you're going to go without." He looked at Margaret and me and asked, "Who do we have here?"

"These two are looking for information about something that happened here twelve years ago," he said. "I told them they needed to talk to someone old like you."

He flipped a pair of fish patties with a spatula, causing a sudden sizzle.

"What could you two possibly want to know about from twelve years ago?" he asked. "Were you even born yet?"

"I was," said Margaret. "About a week earlier. That's why I'm here."

There was something about what she said and the way she said it that caught his attention. He looked at her more

intently, and slowly a smile came over his face. "Are you her? What was her name again? Mary? Mallory?"

"Margaret," she said.

"That's it!" he replied, his face lighting up. "You're Margaret, aren't you?"

"You remember me?" she asked, small tears suddenly welling up in her eyes.

"I don't remember *you*," he said with a laugh. "I remember a baby about this big." He held up his hands like he was cupping a small baby. "Look how much you've grown."

They stood there frozen by the moment. Everything about it was perfect. Except for the smell.

"Cap," said the firefighter. "Cap. Your fish. It's burning!"

The captain snapped out of it and looked down at the pan, a plume of dark smoke suddenly rising from the patties.

"Well, you're a firefighter," he said. "Do something about it. I'm going to talk to my old friend."

He handed the younger man the spatula and walked over to Margaret. The two of them looked at each other for a moment, and he introduced himself.

"Captain Joseph Abraham, DC Fire Department," he said.

"Margaret Campbell," she replied. "It's a pleasure to meet you."

"The pleasure is all mine." They shook hands, and he

never broke eye contact and never stopped smiling. "What can I do for you?"

"I want to find out where I come from," she said. "I want to find out who my parents are."

His smile suddenly disappeared. "I'm not so sure that's a good idea. And even if it was, I don't know that I could help you."

"Can you at least tell me about that night?" she asked hopefully. "I was here in the firehouse until the next morning, right?"

He thought about this for a second and nodded. "You were. I can tell you about that."

Margaret flashed a huge grin. The captain went to say something else, but then he turned and looked at me as though it was the first time he'd noticed I was there.

"Who's this?" he asked her.

"My best friend," she answered.

"Florian," I said.

"Nice to meet you, Florian," he replied. "Why don't you two come with me?"

He led us upstairs. Most of the second story was the dormitory where everyone sleeps, but there were two big rooms, one marked LOUNGE that had a big-screen TV and seven matching recliners, and one marked LIBRARY that had a pair of couches and a bookcase. That's where he took us.

"Have a seat," he said, motioning to one couch while he sat down on the other.

"So you were actually here that night?" Margaret asked. "The night I was"—she paused for a moment looking for the right word—"left."

"Yes, I was," he replied.

"What can you remember about it?"

"It was summer, about this time, right?"

"Right," she said. "August sixth."

"Most of us were in the TV room watching a baseball game—I don't remember who was playing—and the bell rang. The doorbell, not the fire alarm. So we sent a probie to answer it."

"What's a probie?" I asked.

"A probationary firefighter," he said. "A trainee. Probies usually get stuck with all the errands. His name was Munson, Tom Munson. So he goes down there and we keep expecting him to come back, but he doesn't. Eventually the inning ends and a couple of us go downstairs to see what's what. Imagine our surprise when we find Tom holding a baby and talking to a young man, African-American, around twenty years old."

"Was it my father?" asked Margaret anxiously.

"I don't think so. But you have to realize the sanctuary

law is designed to protect the baby. And one of the ways the law protects the baby is that it doesn't allow us to ask questions. The firehouse is a safe haven, and if you can't take care of your baby, you can bring her here without getting in trouble. So we didn't ask him if he was your father. That said, I think he mentioned something about being a friend of your mother's."

All of this was new information to Margaret, and I could tell it was a little overwhelming.

"Do you remember anything about him?" I asked.

"Not really," he answered. "It was late and I was only down there with him for about a minute. But, like I said, our concern wasn't him, it was her."

He looked right at Margaret and smiled.

"You know this is where you slept that night?" he added.

"Here?" she said, looking around the library.

"Yeah, we took turns all night long," he told her. "Let me show you something."

Two bookshelves were filled with photo albums. He went over, picked one out, and started flipping through it. The pages were filled with images ranging from firefighters in action to goofy shots around the firehouse. He stopped when he found what he was looking for and turned the book around so that we could see it.

"That's you that night," he said.

He pointed to a picture of a baby wrapped in a yellow blanket being held by one firefighter and surrounded by another five. He peeled back the plastic cover, took the picture out of the album, and handed it to Margaret.

"Tom Munson is the one holding you; he's the probie who answered the door," he said.

"And is this you?" Margaret asked, pointing at a younger version of the man sitting across from us.

"Yes, it is. It's funny because back then you were the one who was bald and I was the one who had hair. That's all changed now."

She looked at the blanket and read the embroidery out loud. "MARGARET A."

"I wish we knew what the A stood for," I said.

Captain Abraham smiled. "We decided it stood for Angel. That's what we called you, Margaret Angel."

15.

Not a Buffalo

WE STAYED AND TALKED TO CAPTAIN ABRAHAM for another fifteen minutes, but most of the conversation was Margaret filling him in on her life. It was as if she'd discovered a long-lost uncle who wanted to know about everything from soccer to school. He was excited to hear her team was playing for the city championship and said that Deal was one of the best schools in the District. I just sat back and kept my mouth shut, trying to stay out of the way of the conversation but making sure to pay attention for anything that might help us find her birth parents. With regard to potential clues, we were left with two:

1. The names of everyone who was on duty that night.

2. A copy of the photo of Margaret with all the firefighters. This one was a little tricky because Abraham didn't want to let us take it for fear that the original might never come back. He promised to have a copy made and send it to her, but just to be safe, when he got up to introduce her to one of his coworkers, I secretly snapped a picture of it with my phone.

When it was time to leave, he gave her an Engine 4 shoulder patch with the Hornet's Nest logo. He also gave her some advice: "Don't look any further than this," he warned. "I know you think you want to know who your birth parents are, and that's understandable. But your life started here, that night, when Tom took you in his arms. That's when you were born. There's no need to look any earlier than that."

Whether or not she intended to follow this advice, she respected him enough to say, "I'll think about it."

I could tell he was about to make another argument, but

instead he stopped himself and said, "Don't forget to give me your address, so I can send you a copy of that picture."

He pulled a business card out of his wallet and turned it over so that she could write it on the back.

"And stop by for lunch sometime," he added.

"Let me guess," she replied. "You'll make fish sandwiches."

He laughed. "I promise not to burn yours."

He walked us to the door, and just as we were about to leave, he leaned over and whispered into my ear, "You take care of our girl, okay?"

I looked back at him and nodded. "Yes, sir. I'll do whatever it takes."

He winked and replied, "Good answer."

Margaret and I walked for nearly a block before either of us said a word. I wanted to give her a chance to think through everything that'd just happened. Finally she simply said, "Wow."

"You're not kidding," I replied. "I was completely wrong about coming here. I thought it was a bad idea, but that was awesome."

"It's weird because I've always known this story," she said. "But now, seeing the place, talking to someone who was there, for the first time it seems real."

"I'm guessing your promise to 'think about it' doesn't include you actually thinking about it," I added.

"No way," she replied. "I still want to keep looking. I'm more determined than ever."

"That's what I figured," I said.

We were walking alongside the Howard University campus again and I pulled my phone out of my pocket. "I've got a little surprise for you," I told her as I opened it to the picture of Margaret with the firefighters.

"Sneaky," she said as she took the phone. "When'd you get this?"

"When he introduced you to the paramedic," I said. "It's just a picture of a picture, so the quality's not great. But it should do until he sends you a better one."

"Thanks. It's a great picture, isn't it?"

"Actually, it's even better than you think."

"What do you mean?"

I zoomed in past the firefighters so that only the image of Margaret filled the screen.

"What do you see?" I asked.

"A baby . . . in a blanket . . . surrounded by firefighters," she answered, unsure what I was getting at.

"And what's the baby wearing?"

She looked at the picture more closely. Even though the

blanket covered most of her, you could still make out a little bit of what she was wearing.

"Looks like a onesie," she said. "With a little buffalo on it."

"That's not a buffalo," I replied. "Technically it's a bison."

She rolled her eyes. "Okay, so *technically* it's a bison. Why is that important?"

I looked up to draw her attention to the banners that hung from the streetlight we were standing near. They matched the ones on all the streetlights along Georgia Avenue. On one side was a picture of a Howard University student. On the other it said I BLEED BISON BLUE!

"The name of the team at Howard is the Bison," she said, putting it together.

"Yep," I replied. "And judging by this onesie, I wouldn't be surprised if you were born at Howard University Hospital."

Her eyes lit up. "That's a-mazing," she said, dragging out the word. "I can't believe I missed that."

"Well, you had a lot going on. That's why you hired me, remember?"

"Let's go to the hospital and look at the records from the week I was born," she said excitedly. "We can find the answer right now."

"It's not that easy," I told her. "They won't just show you

hospital records. There are privacy issues involved."

Her elation turned to frustration.

"But we can go over there and look around," I suggested. "You said that just being at the firehouse helped. Maybe visiting the hospital will help too."

The hospital was on the other side of the campus. It was nine stories tall and a couple blocks wide. According to the directory, Labor and Delivery was on the third floor. While we waited for the elevator, Margaret grabbed a brochure from an information stand in the lobby.

"'Howard University Hospital was founded in 1862 to care for freed slaves,'" she said, reading from it. "'It was originally called the Freedmen's Hospital.'"

"A hospital with history," I said. "How cool is that?"

"Yeah," she replied as we stepped onto the elevator. "The question is, am I part of that history?"

On the third floor we made it only as far as the waiting room. You have to be the family member of a patient to get beyond that. Still, we found something interesting. On one wall of the waiting room was a giant collage made up of pictures of babies who'd been born at the hospital. In some of the older-looking pictures, many of the babies were wearing the exact same onesie that Margaret had on in her picture from the firehouse.

"Look," she said, pointing at it. "It's identical. This is the place."

"That's how TOAST works," I reminded her. "One little detail at a time."

After the hospital, we went back to my house and I dug some leftover Chinese food out of the fridge for lunch. "You want chicken lo mein? Or beef and broccoli?" I asked, holding up both cartons.

"I'm not much of a broccoli girl," she said as she took the lo mein. "Got any leftover egg rolls?"

"Never," I said with a satisfied smile on my face. "I always finish off the egg rolls. It's too risky to leave them for later."

"Risky how?"

"Three reasons: One, my dad could eat them; two, the electricity could go out and they could spoil in the refrigerator; and three, in the event of the zombie apocalypse they would remain uneaten for all eternity. Total tragedy."

"Clearly you've thought this through."

"That's the kind of thoroughness you can expect from Florian Bates Investigations," I said. "So, why don't we work on the case?"

Inspired by what we'd seen at FBI Headquarters, we made a case board using an old corkboard the previous owners of the house had left in the basement. I printed a copy

of the picture of Margaret and the firefighters and pinned it in the middle. We also put up the list of the firefighters who were on duty that night and the brochure from Howard University Hospital.

"Before we continue, there's something I've been trying to figure out," I said.

"What?"

"Do you think we should give our cases numbers or names?"

"That's what you think is important?" she asked, incredulous.

"You're the one who wanted to start the New FBI," I reminded her. "We have to figure out everything. Even stupid little organizational details. And nothing helps organization more than consistency. So is this case one? Or do we give it a name?"

"We should definitely give it a name," she said. "Numbers will be hard to remember later, but names will stick out."

"I couldn't agree more. So what do we call this one?"

She took a bite of lo mein while she thought about it. "How about Hornet's Nest?"

"I like it," I said. "It's much better than the name I was thinking of."

"What name did you have?" she asked.

"The case of Finding Out Who Margaret's Birth Parents Are," I replied.

"Very clever."

"Clever is what I was going for," I joked.

She took the shoulder patch with the Hornet's Nest logo and stuck it to the top of the case board.

"Now it's official."

We went online and tried to track down the other firefighters who were on duty the night Margaret was left at Engine House Four. Their names were:

Tom Munson
Vince Jackson
Jerry Cavanaugh
Bill Baker
John Reynolds

Unfortunately, these were very normal names. It's a lot easier to find people with unusual ones like Philo T. Farnsworth (who invented the television) or Bronko Nagurski (who was one of the first-ever football stars). It turned out there were seventeen different Vincent Jacksons living in Washington and eleven Bill Bakers. Finding the right ones was going to take time. However, we did get lucky with Jerry Cavanaugh.

On the website for the DC Fire Department, we found a link to the Emerald Society, a fraternal organization made up of local firefighters of Irish descent. It's a social group that raises money for charities, and on one of their pages, we found a picture of Jerry Cavanaugh marching in the St. Patrick's Day parade. He was wearing an emerald-green beret and had a thick mustache. Even though he was older and his mustache had grayed, it was easy to recognize him from the picture we already had.

"It says he's a captain with Engine Company Twenty-One," Margaret said. "We should call."

"Nobody's stopping you," I told her.

She flashed a nervous smile and dialed the number. It turned out he was off duty, but it was still a step in the right direction. She wrote "Engine Co. 21" by his name on the case board.

The least common name on the list also turned out to be the most frustrating. None of the Tom Munsons we found in the DC area had any connection to the fire department. After the seventh one, Margaret stood up and stretched.

"You want to call it a day and start up again tomorrow?" she asked.

"I can't tomorrow," I said. "I got a text from Agent Rivers. I've got training."

"What type?"

I shrugged. "FBI training, I guess."

"Well, we'll get to it soon," she said. "Thanks for today."

"My pleasure," I replied. "And we're going to find them. You know why?"

"Why?"

"Because Florian Bates Investigations uncovers the mysteries of the world, one case at a time."

She smiled. "You see? It's catchy."

16.

Quantico

AGENT RIVERS PICKED ME UP AT PRECISELY seven fifteen in the morning, just like he said he would. This time there was no black, armored-plated SUV with bullet-proof windows. Instead he drove a maroon hybrid with a parking permit for the Harvard Club of Washington, DC. So, while we didn't have any extra protection from random gunfire, we were well prepared should an emergency philosophy discussion break out. His usual uniform of dark suit and matching tie had been replaced by sweatpants and a T-shirt, both neatly ironed and bearing the shield of the FBI.

"Ready for your big day?" he asked as we merged into the traffic heading south on the interstate.

"As ready as I can be considering I don't really know what I'm doing," I replied. Beyond the pickup time and the instruction to bring gym clothes, the text was pretty vague on details.

"It's just some introductory training," he replied. "If you're going to be a consultant with the Bureau, you'll need to do this every now and then. It's what we call a necessary evil."

"And we're training together?"

"No. I have to take a couple recertification courses," he said. "I'd already scheduled them about a month ago and figured we might as well take care of yours at the same time. And this way your parents don't have to drive you down to Quantico and wait in the lobby all day."

Quantico is a Marine Corps base in rural Virginia that's home to the FBI training center. It took us about an hour and a half to get there, and during that time I learned the following things about Agent Rivers:

1. Although his car was almost as clean as his office, a pair of empty cups in the cup holders indicated he's a fan of gourmet coffee.

2. Unlike the agent who drove us in the SUV, he never goes so much as one mile over the speed limit.

3. Judging by his reactions to sports talk radio, he's an avid fan of the Washington Nationals baseball team.

4. When I asked him about a trumpet case in the backseat, he told me he plays in a band called Funk Brothers Incorporated that performs at Bureau parties and weddings and is made up entirely of fellow agents.

We got off the interstate at a town named Garrisonville, and I started to get a little . . . I don't know if "anxious" is the right word, but I was definitely curious about the day ahead.

"Can you tell me what kind of training it is?" I asked. "Or is it top secret?"

"It's not a secret from you," he said. "Your schedule is sticking out of the briefcase behind my seat."

I reached back and grabbed the paper.

As I read it, my mood turned to instant excitement. "Are you serious?" I exclaimed. "This is going to be epic. We're talking the best day of my life."

"See, I told you," he answered.

"Tactical and evasive driving. Weapons training. Explosives!" I shook my head in amazement. "Explosives?!"

"Oops," he said. "That sounds like *my* schedule. Yours must be the other sheet."

I reached back and grabbed another piece of paper, and when I saw it I came straight back to reality. "Classroom study. Self-defense. Hostage preparedness."

"That sounds more like it," he said.

"Don't you mean that sounds more boring?" I replied.

"Trust me," he said. "It may not be the most exciting day of your life, but it'll be more fun than you think. Besides, you'll probably be able to hear the explosives go off, and the boom is half the fun."

"Who's Johan Blankvort of Bethesda, Maryland?" I asked, reading the name off the top of the schedule.

"You are," he said. "Which reminds me. There's a present for you in the glove compartment."

I opened it but didn't see anything presentlike. "What am I looking for?" I asked.

"The wallet," he said.

"You're giving me money?" I asked, confused.

"No, the wallet is the present," he said. "It's one of those recycled deals. They're very hip right now."

Normally, when adults say something's hip, it definitely isn't. But the wallet was kind of cool. Inside there was a student ID from North Bethesda Middle School, a Montgomery

County library card, and a summer YMCA pool pass, all made in the name of Johan Blankvort, but with my picture. There was also a Scooper-Star loyalty club card from the Wow Cow ice cream shop.

"Am I going undercover?" I asked.

"Kind of," he said. "But not like you think. You're only lying to the rest of the FBI. We don't want the name Florian Bates to appear anywhere in the Bureau's records. For you to be a true covert asset, we need to fully protect your identity."

"Then how do we explain why Johan Blankvort is getting a day of FBI training? Won't people find that suspicious?"

"He—I mean you—won an essay contest about 'What America Means to Me.' This is first prize."

"Nice," I said. "I hope my essay was good."

"Moved me to tears," he replied with a laugh. "You should be very proud. Also, one more cone at Wow Cow and your next one's free. So you've got that going for you."

I'd never been on a military base before and it took a bit to get used to the Marines carrying guns, but the training center had its own little section and looked like a small college. I checked in, as Johan Blankvort, and was told to go to Gymnasium 4. Rivers had time before his first class so he showed me the way.

There were already several training sessions under way once we got to the gym, and it didn't take a detective to notice what the instructors had in common. Each looked like he belonged in a mixed-martial-arts cage match.

Except for mine.

My instructor looked like she taught kindergarten. She was barely five feet tall, had her hair pulled back in a ponytail, and wore knee-length black workout pants and a gray T-shirt with FBI written in big black letters across the chest. She was doing some stretches and smiled when she saw us.

Agent Rivers talked to her off to the side so no one could hear what they were saying. Judging by her expression and the way he put his hand on her shoulder, I got the impression they knew each other well. Once they were done, he took care of the introductions.

"I'd like you to meet Agent Cross," he said.

"Just call me Kayla," she added, offering her hand.

"Nice to meet you, Kayla," I answered as we shook. "I'm . . . Johan."

They laughed. "Actually, Kayla's the one person here today who knows who you really are. But that's good. Keep it up," said Agent Rivers. Then he turned to her and added, "I told you he was sharp."

"Good to know," she said. "Come on, Johan. Let's see how sharp you are on the mat."

I already felt self-conscious because of my age and the elementary-school feel of my instructor. But then we started doing yoga poses and it became downright ridiculous. I noticed guys smirking as they did their push-ups nearby.

"Ignore them," she said, reading my reaction. "Training tip number one: Do your thing and don't worry about what anyone else thinks. You only need to worry about you."

I nodded. "Got it."

"Now here's the scenario," she said once we were limbered up. "I'm the victim and you're the perp. That's what we call the bad guy. I'm walking home all alone on a dark street and you attack me. Show me how you do it?"

My specific memory of what happened next is sketchy. I do recall approaching her from behind and trying to wrap my arms around her. There was an iron grip around my wrist and a high-pitched scream. I'm pretty sure the scream was me. (Okay, I'm positive the scream was me.) Then I remember flying through the air upside down. When I landed on the mat, the image that ran through my head was that of my mother slamming dough against the counter when she makes homemade pizza.

"Unfff," I said as the air rushed out of my body. It took

me a second to catch my breath, and when I opened my eyes I saw Agent Rivers. He'd leaned over to look at me, and from my point of view he was upside down.

"Oh, by the way, don't let her appearance fool you," he said. "She's kinda like a ninja."

He cackled and walked away promising, "I'll pick you up at four. Try to stay in one piece."

Kayla was my instructor for the entire day and somehow maintained her cheery disposition, no matter what we were doing. We spent another hour and a half practicing self-defense, and my biggest accomplishment was that I went the last twenty-five minutes of that exercise without going airborne. The classroom session was all about standard FBI protocols and procedures, and while it was beyond boring, my aching body needed the rest. Lunch was in a massive cafeteria called a "mess." I had a sub sandwich and chips. She had quinoa salad and a bowl of soup.

"Let me guess," I said halfway through the meal. "You're a vegetarian and you grew up in Philadelphia."

She smiled. "That's right. How'd you know? I still have the accent?"

"Not really," I answered. "But you called my sandwich a hoagie, and that's a total Philly thing."

"And you guessed vegetarian because it was the only way

to explain why I'd pass up everything else for quinoa and vegetable soup?"

I nodded. "Pretty much."

"You're good, Johan Blankvort," she joked. "Very, very good."

Hostage preparedness class involved a lot of role-playing scenarios. Each one had an exotic name like Tokyo Takeaway or Stockholm Surprise. Kayla would put me in a situation—such as tying my hands behind my back and placing a hood over my head—and ask me what I should do next. I'll admit that I didn't pay as much attention as I should have, but at the time, getting kidnapped seemed about as likely as going to the moon. (I know, crazy stupid.)

Our final session was my favorite. We went to Hogan's Alley, which is a fake town located on the base. It has houses, a diner, a post office, and other small businesses, and it's populated by real people, except they're actors. You're supposed to interact with them like you're an FBI agent.

The exercise was a team competition. Kayla and I were paired as partners and put up against two cadets from the academy. I don't know for sure if they were smirking during yoga, but they totally seemed like the type.

A senior agent was in charge and explained the situation. "The Bank of Hogan has just been robbed. You two are the

lead team," he said, pointing at the others. "And you two are support," he said, pointing at us. "I want you to go inside, inspect the scene, and question witnesses. You've only got ten minutes. When the time is up, you need to give me a full rundown of what the next steps should be."

Before we started, Kayla pulled me to the side for a little pep talk. "The key to any team is knowing its greatest strength. What's ours?"

I thought about it for a second. "The fact that these two guys don't think there's a chance in the world that a woman and a kid can beat them."

She flashed a devious grin. "That's exactly right. And what are we going to do?"

"Destroy them."

"I like you more and more all the time, Johan Blankvort."

We entered the bank, and the two other agents instantly took charge. Just by the way they talked it was obvious they'd seen way too many cop movies and pictured themselves as action heroes. Every now and then Kayla and I shared a conspiratorial smirk and shook our heads.

Still, we had to work together, so we took statements and did our best to establish the facts of the robbery. The eyewitnesses all told the same basic story with each providing a unique detail or two.

Here's what they said:

Two men wearing masks entered the bank with shotguns drawn. They forced all the employees and customers into the vault and locked them inside while they raided the cash drawers. One of the customers saw the robbers getting out of a dark blue pickup truck. A teller noticed that one of them had a star tattooed on the back of his hand. And the bank manager said that, when they left, they sped away south on Oak Street, which is the direction of the train station.

When our time was up, the agent in charge instructed us all to stop.

"It took five minutes for the victims to get released from the vault, five minutes for the FBI to arrive, and ten minutes for you to examine the scene," he said. "That means your perps have at least a twenty-minute head start and time is at a premium. What do you do next?"

As the lead detectives, the cadets went first, still in full Hollywood mode.

"Roadblocks are pointless; they've had too much of a head start," said one. "Still, we need to put out a BOLO." He stopped, looked straight at me, and smugly added, "That means 'Be on the lookout.'" Then he turned to the others and resumed. "For a blue pickup truck and a man with a star tattoo on the back of his hand. We should access security footage from any businesses

along this road and reach out to our friends in the armed forces because there's a good chance these two are ex-military."

"Why do you say that?" asked the man in charge.

"Gut feeling, sir."

"On top of that," added the other, "a train left the station at three twenty-seven. We should stop it and perform a hard target search of each car in case they ditched the truck and are taking the train to some sort of rendezvous point."

"How do you know there was a train at three twenty-seven?" asked the agent in charge.

The cadet smiled, proud of this discovery. "There's a schedule on the counter. I checked it as soon as I heard what direction they'd headed."

"Very impressive," said the agent in charge. "And you both agree with this course of action?"

They nodded with supreme confidence.

"What about you two?" he asked Kayla and me.

We shared a look, and I could tell by her expression that we'd both come up with the same solution.

"Go ahead," she said to me. "You tell him."

"Well, that all sounds very good and official," I said, referring to the other agents' response. "Especially that BOLO thing. But I think it would require a lot of manpower and resources."

"You can't cut corners when it comes to a bank robbery," one of them said to me.

"All that matters is putting cuffs on the bad guy," said the other.

"That's what I figured," I replied. "So shouldn't we just arrest the bank manager?"

Kayla and the agent in charge both started laughing, and the two cadets just looked at me like I was speaking some foreign language.

"If he was locked in the vault with everybody else, then he couldn't have seen which direction they drove off," I explained. "Unless he's part of the team and trying to send us chasing the wrong leads. I say we arrest him and put the pressure on him to give up his partners."

"How old are you, son?" asked the agent in charge.

"Twelve and a half, sir," I replied.

"Great job," he said. "I'm pretty sure we'll all be working for you one day." Then he stopped and looked at the other two. "Well, maybe not all of us."

I kind of felt bad for the other two, but Kayla was in heaven as we walked back to the main complex. When we were halfway there we met up with Agent Rivers, who was returning from explosives class.

"It was bee-yoou-ti-ful," she told him. "These two

Hollywood guys are running around all macho, and then Florian solves the case in a second. I think they're still sitting there with their mouths open trying to figure out what just happened."

Agent Rivers smiled, a hint of pride on his face.

"I told you," he said to her.

"You sure did," she replied.

"Nicely done, Florian," he said. "So what did you think about your day at the FBI Academy?"

"I liked it. A lot," I said. "Except for the part about being thrown through the air. That hurt. But I liked the rest."

"And Kayla?"

"Kayla's the best," I said. Then I looked at him for a moment and decided to show off a little. "Of course, you already know that, considering she's your girlfriend."

They both stopped walking and gave me a dumbfounded look. I basked in the moment without saying much. It really is my favorite part of solving a mystery—the instant you get to share what you've figured out and everybody else gives you that look.

"H-How did . . . ?" he stammered.

"What?" I asked. "Was I not supposed to know?"

17.

The Trouble with Secrets

AS WE WALKED TOWARD THE MAIN COMPLEX from Hogan's Alley, I had a bounce in my step. Not only had I done well in the bank robbery exercise, but I'd also figured out that Agent Rivers and Kayla were boyfriend and girlfriend.

"How did you know that?" asked Rivers.

I smiled broadly and began to reconstruct.

"Well, there were about four clues in all," I said. "The first was when I got in the car. I'm not exactly tall, but even I had to move the seat back. That means the person who normally sits in that seat is shorter than I am."

I looked over at Kayla, who stood no more than five feet tall.

"Then I saw the way you talked to her when we first arrived," I said. "You put your hand on her shoulder and she lit up when she saw you. I could tell you were friends. Maybe even good friends."

"See what I mean?" Rivers said to her. "He sees everything."

"It's good," she replied. "But it's not enough. Like you said, we might just be friends. What are the other clues?"

"The biggest one was your name," I explained.

"How was my name a clue?" she wondered.

"There were two coffee cups in Agent Rivers's car," I said. "One had 'Marcus' written on it and the other . . ."

". . . had 'Kayla.'"

"But that wasn't even the clincher," I added.

"No?" she asked, smiling, playing along for my benefit. "What was the clincher?"

Before I could answer, Agent Rivers interrupted and said, "The nail polish."

Now I was the one caught off guard.

"That's right," I said, confused. "There was a small bottle of nail polish in the glove compartment. It's the same color you're wearing now." I turned to Agent Rivers, surprised that he had figured this out. "How did you know I'd seen it?"

"Well, that's the reason I put it there in the first place,"

he said. "And the reason I had you look for your wallet in my glove compartment. I wanted you to see it."

Now I was totally confused. "I don't understand. Why?"

"It's part of your training, Florian. Maybe the most important part. The truth is, Kayla's not my girlfriend. I planted those clues to see if you would put them together. You're clever, so I had to make them obscure. But I knew you couldn't resist snapping the pieces together."

"Oh," I said, embarrassed. "You were trying to make fun of me?"

"No, no, no," he said. "I would never do that. Florian, I am totally in awe of you. You have a once-in-a-generation gift. There aren't three agents in the Bureau who would have put all of that together."

I was still confused by it all. "How was that part of my training?"

"It was a test to see if you could be led in a direction. It's one reason why it's so important we keep your identity secret. No one will ever see you coming, which makes your talent that much more valuable. But if anyone knows you're working for us, they can set traps for you. Just like I did. They can misdirect you."

I didn't know how to respond. I couldn't believe I'd fallen for it.

"I still say it's incredible," added Kayla. "Absolutely incredible."

She put her finger under my chin and lifted it up so that I looked up from the ground. "It was a total pleasure, Florian."

"Thank you," I said, trying to shake my suddenly sour mood. "I really appreciate your help."

She smiled and stared into my eyes until I finally smiled back. Then she turned to Rivers. "It was fun being your pretend girlfriend for a day. You know, if you wanted, you could always ask me out on a date and we could see what it would be like without the pretend part."

I couldn't tell how serious she was, but it was the first time I'd seen Rivers flustered.

"I'll put that under advisement," he said.

She gave him a hug and headed toward the locker room.

Rivers and I continued walking.

"I'm really sorry, Florian."

"About what?" I asked.

"About setting you up," he said. "It didn't really turn out like I meant. To be honest, I began to think you couldn't put it together because it was too hard. And when you did, I didn't consider how it'd make you feel."

"No, it's a good lesson for me," I replied. "Are we going home now?"

"Not yet," he said. "We still have to stop by the lab."

The FBI lab was located on the edge of the campus. Rivers flashed a badge to get us past two security points, and we took an elevator to the fifth floor.

"What's up here?" I asked.

"Ancillary field equipment and devices."

I gave him a raised-eyebrow look. "You guys really hate English, don't you?"

"Gadgets," he said with a laugh. "Very cool gadgets."

This was where I got my panic button disguised as an asthma inhaler as well as a pair of sunglasses that had a small camera built into the frames.

"What do I need that for?" I asked him.

"You don't," he said. "But they're cool and I thought you might like them."

I smiled. "That works for me."

"I also want you to have this SmarTrip card," he said. "It's good to ride on any Metro or bus in and around the District."

"I've already got one," I said. "I use it all the time."

"Well, this one's a little different," he said. "First of all, you never have to put any money on it. It resets automatically, so you ride free forever."

"Cool," I said.

"Even cooler is the chip that's in it. We can track wherever it goes. Like those chips you put into a dog collar in case your dog gets away."

"Isn't that what the panic button's for?" I asked.

"No," he said. "You press the panic button when you're having trouble. If you do, we come crashing through the door, so your cover's blown. This just lets us keep track of where you are."

"Okay," I said. "I guess that's a good thing."

"Don't worry, we're not going to spy on you," he assured me. "We just want you to be safe. Now let's go down to the basement to see a friend."

We rode the elevator to sublevel four and walked against the tide of people leaving for the day until we reached a door.

"Who's the friend?" I asked.

"His name is Dr. Eduardo Gonzalez and he's one of the world's preeminent forensic scientists." He went to open the door but stopped right as his hand reached the handle and turned to me. "He's also a little . . . strange . . . but in a good way."

We stepped into a room filled with the sound of Spanish music and where numbers were scribbled all over the walls. I got the impression the doctor didn't waste time looking for paper when an idea struck. Experiments appeared to be

under way on three different tables, and he was working on the one in the middle. He had wild curly hair and sang along with the music. What he lacked in vocal ability he more than made up for in volume. He was so focused on the experiment (and the music) that it took him about twenty seconds to notice us.

"Old Man Rivers," he said, looking up from his microscope. "Qué pasa?"

"Not much. How you doing, Gonzo?"

The scientist's happy mood disappeared the instant he noticed that I was in the room too.

"Who's this?"

"A friend," said Agent Rivers. "Johan Blankvort."

"*Buenas tardes*," I said, trying to win him over.

"*Buenas tardes*," he said skeptically.

"He's the one whose grandmother I told you about," Rivers said to him.

I had absolutely no idea what he was talking about, and reading my confusion, Rivers turned to me and explained.

"I told him that your grandmother found a painting in her attic and didn't know if it was an antique or a fake," he said to me. "I hope you don't mind."

"No," I said, still unsure what was going on.

"You see, I wanted Gonzo here to run a test to tell us if

the paint was old or new. That way we'll know what we've got on our hands."

I finally realized that this was what he'd done with the paint chip from *Woman with a Parasol.*

"Except I told him I'm not supposed to use the equipment for unauthorized jobs," Gonzalez said. "A test like that costs the taxpayers."

Now I realized that this was also a negotiation.

"How much did it cost the taxpayers?" asked Rivers. "Box seats for the Nationals game?" He pulled a pair of tickets out of his pocket and put them on the table. Gonzalez didn't pick up the tickets, but he did look at them.

"Yankees game, Sunday afternoon," he said admiringly. "That might cover the cost of the test. But when you dropped off the paint chip, you also said you wanted the job rushed. The rush costs extra."

"I thought it might," said Rivers. "That's why I brought another pair for the following Sunday."

He laid another pair of tickets on the table. Gonzalez scooped them up and slipped them into the pocket of his lab coat. "Let me see if the results are in."

When the scientist ducked into a little office, Rivers turned to me and whispered, "He doesn't even use the tickets for himself. He gives them to the Boys and Girls Club.

He likes to act like he's tough, but he's one of the good guys."

Two minutes later, Gonzalez came back with a printout and handed it to Rivers, who looked at it with total confusion.

"You know, of the three people in this room, only one of us is actually a nuclear scientist," he said. "You mind translating?"

Gonzalez pointed at some of the numbers on the printout. "See that? It's strontium." He pointed to another and added, "And that's cesium."

"What does that mean?" I asked.

He looked at me over the top of his glasses and said, "It means your grandmother's picture is no antique. It was definitely painted after 1945."

Rivers and I shared a look. The *Woman with a Parasol* hanging in the museum was a fake.

18.

The Dinner Party

THAT NIGHT MY PARENTS HELD A HASTILY arranged dinner party at our house. Since the get-together was his idea, Agent Rivers wanted to buy and bring the food, but Mom refused, insisting that cooking for six was no trouble.

"All I have to do is double the ingredients of what I was already going to make," she explained. "Besides, anyone who knows me knows I always cook for the guests in my house. If we brought food in, people would instantly suspect we were up to something. And we don't want that, do we?"

"No, we don't," agreed Agent Rivers.

(Of course that's because they were definitely up to something.)

He'd come up with his plan on the way back from Quantico and spent most of the drive on the phone with my parents and his boss. He wanted to meet with a small team that he could trust and needed to do it away from the Bureau and the National Gallery. Right now the only other people who knew the Monet hanging in the museum was a fake were the people responsible for taking it. He didn't want to do anything that might attract attention or indicate that there'd been a development in the case. So rather than meet around a conference table at the Hoover Building, everyone sat around the kitchen table at our house.

The other guests were Serena Miller, director of security at the National Gallery, and Oliver Hobbes, the representative from the insurance company. Luckily, both lived near us, so they were able to come on short notice. They were under the impression it was a social gathering until we were about half way through my mom's chicken risotto. That's when Agent Rivers stepped into another room to take a phone call.

"Sorry for the interruption," he said when he returned. "But there are some important things we have to discuss and I had to wait for approval before I could move forward."

"Does that mean there are new developments in the case?" asked Hobbes.

"You could say that," answered Rivers. He hesitated for a moment before dropping the bombshell. "A fourth painting has been stolen."

There was silence around the table as they waited to see if this was some sort of joke. Even my parents, who'd already heard the news, looked shocked all over again.

"You can't be serious," gasped Hobbes.

"I'm sorry to say that I am."

"Then what are we doing here?" asked Miller urgently. "We need to get to the museum."

"No, we don't," said the agent, making a calming motion with his hands. "That's why I asked Francesca and Jim to invite you here. *This* is where we need to be. This is where we need to develop our strategy."

"When did this even happen?" asked Miller.

"It was stolen the same night as the others," he said. "Except, unlike them, this one was swapped with a forgery."

"Which painting?" Hobbes asked.

"*Woman with a Parasol*," answered Rivers.

Hobbes and Miller looked like they were going to faint. "That's one of the signature pieces in the entire collection," he said. "It's irreplaceable."

"I know," replied Rivers. "Which is why we're going to get it back."

He went step-by-step through everything he knew, careful to speak only in facts, not theories. He minimized my role in the discovery of the fraud, because although we were all on the same side, as far as Hobbes and Miller knew, my involvement was limited to the night of the burglary. They weren't supposed to find out about my relationship with the FBI. In fact, that's one of the reasons we had the meeting at our house. It gave me a good excuse to be there. I was in listening mode, not speaking up.

"Now comes the tricky part," said the agent as the others looked through the report from Dr. Gonzalez. "We're going to keep it a secret from everybody who's not in this room. We're all going to act like the painting on display in Gallery Eighty-Five is the masterpiece by Monet."

"That's unacceptable," exclaimed Miller. "I'm the museum's director of security and have a responsibility to my board of trustees and executive officers. If one of the most important paintings in our collection has been stolen, I have to tell them about it."

"The same goes for my supervisors," said Hobbes. "Our company is financially liable for this painting upwards of forty million dollars. They'll want to know as much as they can, as soon as they can."

"Actually," said Rivers. "I'm pretty sure they'll want the

painting recovered. That's true of your supervisors and of the trustees. Still, I understand the difficulty of your situations, which is why the director of the FBI is personally calling the chairman of the museum's board and the president of the insurance company. He's informing them about the theft and asking them, in his very convincing way, to keep it quiet so that we are in a better situation to capture the bad guys."

He waited to make sure there were no more complaints, but the mention of the director's involvement seemed to put an end to the protests.

"All right, then," he said. "This food's delicious, so let's keep eating and figure this out."

"Why do you want to keep it a secret?" asked Mom. "Wouldn't people knowing about it help put pressure on the thief?"

"Yes, but pressure's not what we want," he explained. "I want the opposite of pressure. Right now he thinks he's gotten away with the crime of the century. That's good. We didn't catch him at the recycling center because word had already gotten out that the other paintings were recovered. As long as he thinks we don't know about the Monet, he's far more likely to make a mistake. "

"What's the latest on the artist who painted it?" asked my father.

"According to our counterparts at Interpol, Pavel Novak has not been seen since he flew from Washington to Prague the night of the burglary. We suspect he's somewhere in the Czech Republic, but realistically he could be almost anywhere in Eastern Europe. We're working with local police agencies and also trying to check with sources who have connections inside EEL."

"That's the crime syndicate you mentioned at FBI Headquarters," said Mom.

"That's right," he replied. "The Eastern European League is involved in illegal activity throughout the region. Even if it wasn't involved in this particular case, it's almost certain to have a history with Novak or any associates he may have."

"What about the burglar?" asked Hobbes. "The custodian who went missing?"

"We're still following multiple leads, but so far we're frustrated by our lack of results," he admitted. "We've looked at all the custodians who've worked in the National Gallery in the last year and each one has a solid alibi. The same cleaning company provides custodial services to the Department of Labor, the Bureau of Engraving and Printing, and the National Archives, so we're looking into all of those employees as well, but there are hundreds of names."

The mention of the National Archives caught my attention, and I must have reacted because Agent Rivers stopped talking and looked at me.

"Florian? Is there something you'd like to say?"

"Not really," I replied. "It's just that when you mentioned the National Archives, it made me think of something. Actually, someone."

"Who?" my father asked.

"Earl," I replied. "I don't know his last name."

"Earl Jackson?" asked Serena. "The man who was working in the security center the night of the burglary?"

I nodded.

"He's been with the museum for ten years," she said. "I guarantee he had nothing to do with this."

"I didn't think he did," I replied. "It's just that he came to mind and I guess I made a face."

"Why?" asked Agent Rivers. "What does he have to do with the National Archives?"

"He told me he used to work there," I said. "He left for two years and said he begged Ms. Miller for his job back."

"Is that true?" asked Rivers.

"Yes," said Miller. "But I mean it when I say there's no way he's involved."

"Well, someone from your department is," said Hobbes.

"What's that supposed to mean?" she replied angrily.

"It's obvious," he answered.

"Let's not get into finger-pointing and accusations," said Rivers.

"Someone from your department has to be involved," Hobbes reiterated, ignoring the agent. "Someone had to tell the thief that the security system was going to be reset at precisely one fifteen."

"And you think it was Earl?" she replied.

"I have no idea if it was him," replied Hobbes. "I've only met him a few times so I don't know him. But I do know that he was in charge of the security upgrade the night the paintings were stolen. And now it turns out he has a connection to the National Archives, which may be important."

It was about to erupt into a full-fledged argument when my mother came to the rescue. "Who wants dessert?" she said. "Agent Rivers brought an apple crumb pie that looks delicious."

At first no one responded, so I jumped in.

"Do we have any ice cream to go with it?"

"Of course we do," she said.

"Sounds good to me," said Agent Rivers.

The pie did the trick and the argument was averted, although Hobbes and Miller exchanged angry looks with

each other the rest of the evening. The focus of the conversation turned to the different types of people behind most art thefts.

"There are three basic types," said Rivers. "Knuckleheads, masterminds, and extortionists."

"What are knuckleheads?" I asked.

"Basic criminals, usually not so bright, who see an opportunity to steal a piece of art and take it," explained my father. "They're usually short on planning and have no idea what to do with what they take."

"They're also responsible for most of the art stolen throughout the world," added Ms. Miller.

"But I don't think that's what we're dealing with here," said Rivers. "Breaking a window and grabbing a picture off the wall is one thing. But creating a high-level forgery and swapping it with the original takes meticulous planning."

"Which leads us to mastermind," said Hobbes. "A crime in which a very rich person targets a specific piece of art to add to his collection."

"That could be the case here," speculated my mother. "*Woman with a Parasol* is iconic."

"No doubt," said Rivers. "But the truth is, the mastermind art thefts tend to be more of what you see in movies and less of what happens in real life."

"So you suspect extortion?" said Serena.

"I'm leaning that way," he said. "But I want to stay open-minded."

"What's extortion?" I asked.

Agent Rivers turned to Oliver Hobbes. "You want to tell him?"

"That's when criminal syndicates like EEL acquire a painting and then try to ransom it back to the insurance company or museum," he said. "Officially, insurance companies do not pay ransoms. But unofficially, they do offer rewards for information leading to the return of stolen paintings, which some people claim is really the same thing."

"Why would an insurance company pay that?" I asked.

"*Woman with a Parasol* is valued at roughly forty million dollars," he said. "That's what my company will have to pay the National Gallery if it's not recovered so that they can purchase something of equal value to replace it. But who-ever has it can't sell it for that much on the black market because of its history. It's toxic. So if they offer to 'help find it' for two million, then they make a lot of money and we save thirty-eight million dollars."

"But that's not going to happen in this situation because we're going to catch the bad guys and get it back ourselves," Rivers claimed.

"I like your thinking," said Hobbes. "So will my bosses."

"How do we do it?" asked Ms. Miller.

"Each of us has to work a specific lead," he said. "I know you don't want to think that anyone at the museum might be involved, but it has to be considered. The thief did know that the security system was going to be shut down. Isolate who had that information and see how word might have gotten out. Also, keep an eye on your staff and watch for suspicious behavior. Remember, the thief thinks he's gotten away with it, so see if anyone is making big life changes with an eye on sudden money coming in."

She nodded. "Fine. I can do that."

I caught his eye as a signal to remind him of a conversation we had during the car ride home. "Oh, and can I get a record of who on the staff has traveled to Europe in the last three years?"

She gave him a confused look. "Why?"

"If there is someone from the museum involved, we have to figure out how he might have met Pavel Novak in the first place," he said. "He's never been to the US, so the odds are that meeting took place in Europe."

"Europe is an entire continent," she pointed out. "How can you possibly figure out if two people met each other?"

"I can't," he said. "But we have this genius at the Bureau. If

anyone can figure it out, he can. His name is Johan Blankvort."

As he said it, he shot me a look.

"What do you want me to do?" asked Hobbes.

"You've dealt with extortionists before and know about the black market," Rivers said. "Put feelers out to see if there's been any chatter that might seem even the slightest bit connected to what we're dealing with."

"I've also got a database of every major art auction in the past twenty years," Hobbes said. "I'll dig around and see if anyone has expressed particular interest in Monet or the major Impressionist works."

"That's a great idea," Rivers said. "I'd love to get a copy if I could. I might show it to Johan."

"Of course."

Now Rivers turned to my parents.

"I know you don't have an official role in this investigation, but your brainpower and breadth of knowledge are greatly appreciated. If you think of anything, please let me know."

"Our pleasure," said Mom.

"Absolutely," said Dad.

"And remember," he said to everyone, "the key to this is that we keep it a secret. If word gets out, everything changes."

19.

Capitol Crush

THE NEXT MORNING I RODE MY BIKE TO DEAL Middle to watch the championship game of the U13 Washington Area Girls Soccer League. The match was played on the big field behind the school and when I got there I was amazed by how many people had turned out.

Margaret had already told me all about the team they were facing. The Capitol Crush had won back-to-back city championships and was looking to become the first team ever to win three in a row. They wore red-and-white-striped jerseys and their supporters hung a huge banner on the fence that read CRUSH IT!

I headed for the opposite sideline and found Margaret's

parents in a cluster of Dynamo fans. "Did I miss anything?" I asked.

"No," said Mrs. Campbell. "Your timing's perfect. They're just about to do the Tornado."

The Tornado.

Margaret had told me all about that too, but I didn't fully appreciate how cool it was until I saw it in person. It started with the team forming a tight circle in front of their goal. Their arms were wrapped around each other's shoulders and they swayed side to side and started chanting, "D-C-D, D-C-D," for DC Dynamo. They got louder and louder and swayed more and more until the circle looked like it was about to spiral out of control. Finally one of the girls let out a piercing yell and they scattered from the huddle and ran to their positions.

Everyone on our sideline went nuts.

"That was impressive. I'm glad I didn't miss that," I said when the noise died down. "Although I meant to get here earlier so I could give her a pep talk."

Her dad laughed. "It's probably best that you didn't."

"Why's that?" I asked.

"Margaret's not exactly . . . chatty . . . before a big game," he explained.

When I saw her face I instantly realized what he meant.

The girl I normally hung out with, the goofy, brainy girl who was always smiling, bore little resemblance to the one who lined up to play center midfielder. This one was oblivious to the world beyond the sidelines. She focused an intense stare straight ahead at her opponent while she loosened up her shoulders and gently rocked up and down on the balls of her feet. It was unnerving.

"Where have I seen that look before?" I asked.

"The zoo," replied her mother. "It's the same expression the tiger has right before feeding time."

We all laughed because it was true.

The game was exciting from start to finish, and both teams played great. The Crush scored early, but the Dynamo tied it up right before halftime. It was still 1–1 when Margaret moved up out of position, stole a pass between two defenders, and sprinted all alone toward the goal. Their keeper, who played brilliantly all game long, charged out to challenge her, but Margaret put on the brakes and chipped the ball over her head and sent it fluttering into the net.

"Did you see that?" Mrs. Campbell squealed, jumping up and down. "Did you see that?"

It was a memorable play, but nothing like the one the Capitol Crush pulled off in the final moments of the game.

They were awarded a free kick, and, desperate to tie the score and force overtime, all of their players moved forward and flooded the penalty area. Two of them even started arguing about who should take the kick. Then, in the middle of the argument, another player sneaked in and kicked the ball to the other side of the field.

It was a trick play designed to give one of their players an open shot and it worked perfectly. No one was near her as she got the ball and volleyed it to the top left corner of the goal. Everyone on the DC Dynamo had been caught off guard watching the argument.

Except for Margaret.

She'd slipped in behind the keeper and taken a spot on the goal line. As the ball rocketed toward the net, she jumped up and headed it just enough to send it over the crossbar. Both sidelines went bananas, while Mr. Campbell and I did so many high fives the palm of my hand turned red. Two minutes later the referee blew the whistle, ending the game, and Margaret's teammates swarmed around her.

Somewhere in the middle of the celebration, she looked toward the sideline and we locked eyes. It was the first time I saw her smile that day. It lasted only a second because two more players piled on top of her and they all tumbled to the ground. I knew the team was going to their coach's house for

a party, so I said good-bye to Margaret's parents and headed for the bike rack.

The school is a massive, three-story brick building that seems even larger because it sits on the top of a hill. I walked around to the front and was unlocking my bike when I heard someone coming toward me. I looked up and saw that it was Margaret. Despite being exhausted from a grueling game in the summer heat, she had run all the way up the hill after me.

"Where are you going?" she asked in between deep breaths.

"Home," I said.

"Without saying anything to me?"

"I didn't want to interrupt the celebration," I explained. "I figured we'd talk later."

"You're my best friend, Florian. By definition that means you can't interrupt me. You're always a part of whatever I'm a part of."

It was, without a doubt, the nicest thing anyone had ever said to me.

"I'll remember that in the future," I said. "By the way. You were . . . Amazing . . . Incredible . . . Unbelievable. It took my breath away."

She grinned. "It was a good game, wasn't it?"

I laughed. "You could say that."

"Thanks for saving that last goal," she said. "I don't know if we could've held them off in extra time."

"What are you talking about?" I asked.

"Without you I never would have headed that ball over the crossbar."

"Yeah right."

"I mean it," she replied. "The two players who got into the argument, I'd noticed them whispering to each other right before that. I thought that was strange. Then I realized their best goal scorer was in the absolute wrong place, totally away from the play. So I ignored the big thing, which was the argument, and added up the little things."

"You mean you used . . ."

"TOAST," she said, finishing my sentence. "TOAST absolutely won that game."

Now I was the one who was grinning.

"I'm going to keep the trophy and all," she continued. "But I couldn't have done it without you."

I looked up at the entrance to the school. It was imposing with tall white columns and three pairs of dark blue doors.

"Two more days until we start," I said.

"You're not worried about Deal, are you?"

"I always worry about new schools," I answered.

"Don't. You're going to do great," she assured me.

"Why? Because the school's loaded with geeky kids who have mad mystery-solving skills?"

"No," she answered. "Because I'll be there."

"That should take care of it," I replied. "Now go back and get your trophy and have fun at the party."

"Okay. I'll see you later." She jogged back down the hill to where her teammates were waiting. When she reached them, they swarmed her all over again.

Despite her assurance, I was still a little nervous about starting at a new school. Again. Each time presented new challenges.

I was in no rush to get home, so I rode around the neighborhood for a while to get a better feel for it. First I went to a castle-looking building right by the campus called Fort Reno. It was used to defend Washington during the Civil War, and now it's a park. According to one of the information plaques, it's the highest point in the city. After that I had a couple slices of pepperoni and sausage at a pizzeria with free Ping-Pong and foosball.

I was just about to play a kid in foosball when I noticed a man watching me as he talked on a cell phone. He was thin and muscular with short red hair and aviator sunglasses. He was also the only person in the building who wasn't working, eating, or playing.

"You going to play?" the boy asked me.

"No," I said. "I just realized what time it is and have to get home."

Since the red-haired man was between the front door and me, I decided to slip out the back. Unfortunately, it opened onto an alley where there was another man waiting for me. He was tall and lean and wore the same sunglasses as the guy inside.

"Stop right there," he said.

I instantly thought back to Kayla's self-defense training and tried to get into position.

"Are you Johan Blankvort?" he asked.

At first I didn't recognize the fake identity I'd been given, so I barked, "No."

Then I thought about it for a second and said, "I mean, yes. I mean, who wants to know?"

"I'm Agent Chaffee of the Federal Bureau of Investigation," he said in that direct FBI way.

"And I'm Agent Kendall," said a voice from behind.

I turned and saw that the redhead had followed me out.

"Agent Rivers asked us to come and get you and bring you straight home."

Just then I heard a text signal on my phone.

"That's him telling you to trust us," said Kendall. "I was just speaking to him on the phone."

I pulled my phone out of my pocket and indeed there was a text from Rivers: *It's okay. Go with them.*

"Okay," I said. "So what's going on?"

"He didn't tell us that," replied Chaffee. "He just said to get you."

They led me to a black SUV, and when I got in I saw that they'd already loaded my bike into the back.

"Hey, that was locked," I protested.

"You might want to get a new one," Chaffee said, tossing the lock to me. "This one was pretty easy to pick."

I started to ask how they found me when I remembered the tracking chip inside the SmarTrip card for the Metro. It took only a few minutes to make it to the house, and when we pulled up I saw the maroon hybrid parked in front. I was excited because I thought there might have been a big break in the case, so I hurried up the front steps and went inside.

"Florian?" my mother called out. "We're in the kitchen."

I found my parents sitting around the table with Agent Rivers and another agent I didn't recognize. They all looked worried.

"What's the matter?" I asked.

"Were you at a soccer game today?" Rivers asked. "On the field behind your school?"

"Yes," I said. "It was great. Margaret's team won the championship and—"

"Did you see this man when you were there?" he said, cutting me off as he placed a photograph on the table.

I picked it up and studied it. It looked like a surveillance picture taken from a distance with a long lens. The man looked both stylish and menacing at the same time. He had on a nice suit, but his face was tight and muscular.

"Not that I remember," I said. "But there were a lot of people."

"Well, he was there," he said. "And we think he may have been there because of you."

"Who is he?" I asked.

Rivers sighed before answering. "He's an EEL crime boss named Nicolae Nevrescu. But his enemies call him 'Nic the Knife.'"

"That sounds bad," I said with a gulp. "What do his friends call him?"

"He doesn't have any friends."

20.

The Underground

MY PARENTS AND I SPENT THE NEXT HALF HOUR learning all about Nicolae Nevrescu from Rivers and his fellow agent Martin Kellogg.

"Marty's really our expert on him," Rivers explained. "So I want him to tell you the basics."

Kellogg was about ten years older, and unlike the always-sharp Rivers, he was somewhat wrinkled and unkempt. He'd spent years sitting in the backs of surveillance vans tracking criminals and was a little worse for the wear.

"Although he's the son of a prominent Romanian mobster, the plan seems to have been to keep Nic out of the family business," he said with his New York accent. "He was

smart, had a bright future, and his parents wanted him to go to America and start a new chapter in the family's history. He came to Washington as a student at Georgetown, majored in international business, made good grades, and was headed to law school."

"So how did he end up a gangster?" asked Dad.

"The how we don't know," he answered. "We just know that he did. With money from his dad, he opened a construction company that was corrupt from the beginning. In little over a decade, his businesses have grown to include everything from sanitation and recycling centers to demolition and dry-cleaning companies. All of them launder money for his father and other EEL crime lords."

"How do you launder money?" I asked.

"You take money earned through illegal activities and pass it through a legitimate business so it becomes clean," he explained.

"If you know all this," asked my mother, "then why don't you arrest him?"

"We want to," he answered. "But what we know and what we can prove in court are two different things. We've had him under surveillance for two years, and we're building a case against him."

"Which brings us to today," said Rivers. "The surveillance

team followed him to the soccer game at Deal."

"That's all?" I asked. "That's why you grabbed me off the street and terrified my parents? Because both of us were at a soccer game? There were a lot of people there. What makes you think he was there because of me? He could have been there to watch his kid. Or watch his friend's kid. It was a big game, the city championship."

"He doesn't have any kids, and he doesn't have any friends," said Kellogg. "All of his family is in Romania, and in two years he's never once shown the slightest interest in soccer or youth sports. But he did show an interest in you."

"What do you mean?" asked Dad.

"After the game, he walked around the school and watched Florian get on his bike and leave." Kellogg handed a photograph to my mom and dad, and I leaned over from my seat to look at it. In the picture, I was watching Margaret as she ran back down the hill to her team, and he was about twenty-five yards behind me. It was weird seeing a picture of myself that I hadn't known was being taken.

"I still think you're taking a big leap," I replied. "The parking lot in front of the school was full of cars. He could have been looking at anything. He may not have even noticed me and just happened to be facing that direction."

"You're absolutely right," said Rivers. "This may well be

an overreaction. In fact, it probably is. But we'd rather over-react and err on the side of safety than make a mistake and put you in jeopardy."

"We agree," said Mom.

"Definitely," added Dad.

I turned to Kellogg and asked, "How did you even know I was there? I thought I was a covert asset."

"The chip on your SmarTrip card," answered Rivers. "There's always the worry that a surveillance op might blow someone's cover. So there's a monitor in the van that picks up the signal from anyone with a chip like yours."

"I still didn't know who you were," added Kellogg. "But when the monitor displayed a number, I called it in to the covert asset desk to let them know our two situations had overlapped. They called Rivers."

"And when I heard it involved Nevrescu and EEL, it set off the alarm in the little monitor in my head," he said. "Since we suspect that EEL is involved in the theft, we decided to act."

The pieces may have snapped together for them, but they didn't for me. It seemed like a total stretch. Although I will admit that may have been because I didn't want to think that the Romania Mafia might be coming after me. But it still seemed unlikely.

"Does it make sense that he'd be interested in art?" I asked Kellogg.

"He's not your average criminal," he replied. "He graduated from Georgetown and is intellectual. He supports various cultural activities in the Romanian-American community. He even created a scholarship fund, totally legitimate, that helps inner-city DC kids go to college. So a Monet might appeal to him a great deal."

"Besides, his interest wouldn't necessarily be in the artistic value of the painting," added Rivers. "In the world of organized crime, stolen art is often used in place of money to pay off one group or another."

"So what do we do about it?" asked Mom as she reached over and put a protective hand on my knee.

"First of all, Florian's off the case," he said.

"What?" I protested.

"Stay away from any place and anyone associated with the crime or the investigation," he continued. "If he was there to see you, he most likely just heard a rumor that you were involved and was curious to find out how. We don't want to give him any reason to believe that rumor's true. If you stay away from the museum and the investigation, he'll lose interest quickly."

"If Florian's a covert asset, then how could Nevrescu

even hear a rumor about him?" asked Mom.

"That night at the museum, there were a lot of people there when Florian figured out where the paintings were hidden," he said. Then he turned to me and asked, "Do you want to tell them which ones might have told Nevrescu?"

"How would I know?" I replied.

He gave me a look and leaned in. "Do you want to tell them, Florian? Because I think you know."

"You haven't told anyone, have you?" Dad asked me.

"No. Of course not," I replied. "He's talking about the guys on the garbage truck."

"I figured you caught that," Rivers said with a smile.

"Okay, for those of us who aren't detectives?" asked my mom.

"The garbage truck drivers were there on the scene being questioned as the agents dug through the Dumpsters looking for the paintings," I reminded her. "They were there when the agents gave me the standing ovation. And Agent Kellogg said that Nevrescu owns sanitation and recycling centers. So there's a possible connection."

"Impressive," said Agent Kellogg.

"I told you," replied Rivers.

"What about the stuff from the dinner party?" I asked. "You said you wanted me to use TOAST to analyze the travel

records from the museum to see who had traveled to Europe on business and to look over the information Oliver Hobbes had about auctions involving Monet and the Impressionists. Neither of those involves Nevrescu. Can I still do that?"

Rivers looked at my parents as if to gauge their response.

"I can look at them here at the house," I added. "The sooner this case is solved, the better all of this will be."

"I guess that would be all right with me," said Rivers. "If it's okay with your parents."

Dad nodded. "That would be okay. He's safe here."

One of the advantages of having a father who designs security systems is that our house is super well protected. We had video surveillance, door and window sensors, motion detectors, exterior lighting, alarms, and anything else you could think of. We even had special high-security cables for Internet access, which was necessary because my dad runs his business from home.

They stayed for a little while more and reminded me about fifteen times to make sure I always carried my panic button with me. The next morning I went down into the unfinished room in our basement and started turning it into the world headquarters of Florian Bates Investigations. If I was going to have to work out of the house, then I wanted to at least have a good place to do it.

I was staring at one of the walls when I heard a voice behind me.

"What are you doing?"

I turned to see that it was Margaret. "Interior decorating."

She laughed. "Well, now I know."

"What?" I asked.

"Now I know the thing you're really bad at is interior decorating."

I nodded. "I am, aren't I?"

"Terrible," she said.

I had just been trying to squeeze as much into each corner as I could, but then Margaret took over and started "using the negative space," as she said. Over the next four hours it went from a room with boxes to a cool environment where we could brainstorm and work cases together. She made one wall into a giant case board and turned the gaps under the stairs into funky staggered shelving.

While we worked I told her all about Nic the Knife, stressing my belief that he wasn't involved and accusing my parents and Agent Rivers of overreacting.

"They're not overreacting," she retorted. "They're being careful and that's smart."

She got onto the computer, which sat on a desk we made out of an old door and some wooden boxes, and started

looking up everything she could about Nevrescu. I'd done the same thing the night before so I'd already seen most of what she came across.

"Here's an article about his scholarship fund," she said. "He looks intense."

"Is that the picture of him by the bridge with his arms crossed?" I asked as I tried to figure out the best place to put a floor lamp.

"That's the one," she said.

"He definitely has a don't-mess-with-me vibe," I said.

"And that's in an article about him helping kids go to college," she joked. "Imagine how he looks when he's trying to be intimidating."

"How's this?" I moved out of the way so she could see where I'd put the lamp.

"Uh-uh," she replied, shaking her head. "Over there."

She pointed at the other corner.

I moved the lamp and she kept looking online.

"*Mi-ar placea sa vizitez Romania,*" she said. Well, that's what she tried to say. What she actually said was a much-butchered version of that.

"What's that?" I asked.

"It's Romanian for 'I'd like to visit Romania one day,'" she answered. "Here's a website of Romanian phrases. It might

help if you learned some in case you two come face-to-face someday. I wonder how you say 'No, I didn't have anything to do with uncovering your plot to steal tens of millions of dollars of paintings. Please don't hurt me.'" She pretended to look at the list and said, "No, I guess that's not a common enough phrase."

"Let me look at that," I said.

I looked over her shoulder at the phrases. It's funny because Romanian has a lot in common with Italian, so I could actually make sense of most of the phrases.

"Check this one out," she said, pointing to one at the bottom. "My hovercraft is full of monkeys." She laughed when she read that. "You definitely have to learn that one. You never know when that'll come in handy."

We both got up to leave, and when we reached the door, we turned around to look at the room. It was much cooler than I would have imagined.

"What do you think?" she asked.

"I love it," I replied. "How about you?"

"Almost," she said. "But it's missing something."

She knelt down and started looking through a box filled with odds and ends from our many moves.

"Should we give it a name?" I asked.

"What? The room?"

"Yeah, should we give it a name? In London, the police work out of Scotland Yard."

"And in Gotham City, Bruce Wayne's got the Batcave," she offered.

"Exactly," I answered, going with it. "We need a name like that."

I tried to brainstorm, and she kept digging through the box.

"Wait a minute, I think I've got it," she said.

She pulled out a metal sign that had the symbol of the London subway system. It was classic and simple. A red circle with a blue bar across the middle. The word "Underground" was written in the bar.

"I like it," I said.

She hung it from an old nail in the wall and stepped back to look at everything.

"It's perfect," she said. "Welcome to the Underground."

21.

Back to School

IT WAS THE FIRST DAY OF SCHOOL AND MOM wanted to drive. This had nothing to do with her being worried about Nicolae Nevrescu, and everything to do with the fact that she's a mom and thinks I'm still in kindergarten.

"It's less than a mile away," I said. "I can just walk with Margaret."

"Why don't I drive Margaret, too?" she offered.

"Because then her mother will feel left out and she'll want to drive," I answered. "We'd end up with two cars when we don't need any."

"Okay, but if I don't drive, then I get to take a first-day-of-school picture in front of the house," she said, suddenly

turning it into a negotiation. "And one with a real smile, not the I'm-twelve-and-hate-having-my-picture-taken pretend smile."

I carefully considered her offer. "Are you going to post the picture online?"

"I'm going to post some picture online," she said. "It will either be this one or that adorable one of you as a baby dancing in a diaper. I'll let you pick."

She's a tough negotiator, my mother.

"All right, then," I said, cutting my losses. "Let's take some pictures."

I posed for a few solo shots and a couple more with Margaret. Once Mom was satisfied, Margaret and I started walking. We'd made it to the end of the driveway when Mom called out random encouragement: "Seventh grade will be seventh heaven! Be your true self! I love you!"

I turned to face her. "That's why you can't drive me on the first day, Mom. Because you say stuff like that. Out loud. Where people can hear."

"I know. It's just that I care so much."

"I know you do, Mom."

"Don't worry, Mrs. B.," Margaret said. "I'll keep an eye on him."

We waved good-bye and started down the sidewalk—

although I can't be certain Mom didn't secretly follow us in her car.

"Sorry about that," I said to Margaret once we were far enough away.

"Are you kidding?" she replied. "At seven fifteen I was in the middle of a video chat with my grandmother so she could see my outfit."

It's always hard to start at a new school, but at least it wasn't in the middle of the year. We moved to London in February and that was a total nightmare. I got the worst seat in every classroom and never really found a group of friends.

This time I had high hopes. I also had Margaret helping guide the way and answering any questions. Like when we walked through the front door and I saw the security setup.

"Metal detectors and X-ray machines?" I asked. "Is this an everyday thing?"

She shrugged like it was no big deal. "You get used to it. They use them throughout the District."

"The school's safe, isn't it?"

"Totally," she said. "Besides, this will help keep out any strangers, you know, like the Romanian Mafia."

I laughed. "Well, when you put it that way, I guess it's a good thing."

Because Deal was so large, each grade was split into

teams of five teachers and about a hundred students. The teams were named after major international cities and we were assigned to Team Cairo.

Margaret and I had three classes together: English, ancient history, and algebra. But more important, we were both in the same lunch. Breakfast may be the most important meal of the day nutritionally speaking, but lunch is the one that matters the most when it comes to socializing. It really helps to have a friend.

The biggest struggle I had that first week had nothing to do with schoolwork or making friends, and everything to do with coming back to reality. I'd just spent a summer during which I went to the FBI training academy, helped discover a spy ring trying to infiltrate the CIA, and been part of the investigation into nearly $100 million in stolen paintings. And now I was a seventh grader.

Just a seventh grader.

I was a normal kid in a class full of normal kids, and I couldn't even tell anyone about all the cool adventures. My English teacher asked us to write about what happened over the summer and I couldn't think of anything interesting that hadn't been classified by the government.

The most exciting moment came on Tuesday afternoon when Margaret and I were walking home from school. She

kept a constant lookout for anyone suspicious and was certain the man in the slow-moving Volkswagen was an EEL operative. When he stopped and got out of his car, she was prepared to, as she put it, "unleash the fury of my kung fu." Luckily she managed to stop herself when we realized he was delivering a pizza to the house we were standing in front of.

"Do you normally unleash that power with or without pepperoni?" I asked as we both struggled to keep a straight face.

By Friday even she was no longer concerned about the Romanian Mafia. On Saturday afternoon I was in full sprawl on the couch watching television when Mom asked me if I had any homework.

"Five pages of algebra and five hundred words about my summer," I said.

"How close are you to being done?" she asked.

I smiled. "I've got the whole weekend to do it. I haven't even started."

She gave me that Mom look and said, "Too bad."

"Why?" I asked.

"Because our deal was that you couldn't save the country until after you'd finished your homework."

I shot upright on the couch. "What? Is there work for me to do? Detective work?"

She held up two manila envelopes. "Agent Rivers had these dropped off today."

"Let me see them," I said.

She held them out for me, but then snapped them back as I reached for them. "Let me see your homework."

I got the point and instantly turned off the television and rushed upstairs to get my backpack. "I'll have it done right away," I promised.

"No, you'll have it done *right*," she corrected. "Do not rush your homework. I'm going to check everything before I consider it done."

The algebra went pretty quickly, but the five hundred words were a different story. I didn't know what to write. Like I said, all the cool stuff was classified, so I decided to write about our move to America and the change of culture.

"Pffftt," Mom said after she read it. "There's nothing there."

"That's because nothing happened," I said. "Except for the FBI stuff, but I can't write about that."

"Nothing happened, huh?" she said. "Well, this is your first chance to let anyone at the school get to know you."

"Not really," I replied. "Margaret knows me."

"She does?" said my mother. "When did she get to know you?"

"This summer . . ." My words trailed off when I realized what she was trying to do.

"I guess something did happen," she replied.

I went back upstairs and wrote about my friendship with Margaret. I didn't make it all gushy. I just started writing about things we did, and by the time I stopped to take a look, I'd already finished 627 words.

"*Magnifico*," Mom said when she read it. "If you'd like I can give you one of the pictures I took of the two of you and you can turn it in with the essay."

"Thanks, but no thanks, Mom."

Margaret came over the next morning and we went down into the basement to start working. Agent Rivers had sent two envelopes. One had a record of every museum employee who had traveled to Europe on official business over the past three years. The other had records of all the auctions for major works of Impressionism going back five years.

"Which do you want to do first?" I asked.

"Let's start with the travel," she said.

Our goal with the travel was to figure out how someone at the museum might have met Pavel Novak.

"Let's look at who went to conventions and expositions," I said. "That's the most likely place for them to have bumped into each other."

"Sounds good," said Margaret.

"I got this list of them from my mom," I said. "She's a member of some art group and gets invited to all of them."

The fact that the room was unfinished is what made the Underground such a great place to work. We didn't have to worry about ruining anything like the paint on the wall, because there wasn't any paint on the wall. So Margaret wrote the name and date of each convention on separate index cards and taped them to the walls.

"Now let's see which of these dates and places line up with trips by museum staff," she said.

At first none of the dates lined up, which didn't make any sense. After all, someone had to at least go to some meeting.

"I got it," I said when I realized what we'd done wrong. "The dates on the travel documents are in the American style and the dates on the events are European."

"We use different dates?" she asked.

"Americans write the month first and then the day, while Europeans write the day first and then the month. So June thirteenth is 6/13 in America, and it's 13/6 in Europe."

When we fixed this, all of the trips lined up perfectly.

"So in the last three years, there were seven conventions where museum staff went to Europe," Margaret said, looking at our wall.

"Any of them in the Czech Republic?" I asked hopefully.

"No," she said. "Two of them were in London, and the others were in Munich, Copenhagen, Florence, Budapest, and Warsaw."

"Okay, so that's where the staff went," I said, thinking out loud. "Which ones would Pavel Novak go to? He was a star student at the Academy of Fine Arts in Prague. He wants to find a job. He wants to get hired to paint."

"Then that knocks out Copenhagen," said Margaret. "Because it's a forum for fund-raising, and Munich, because it's just for security people."

"That's good," I said as I took those lists down. "Now we're down to five."

"And we can eliminate Florence, too," said Margaret.

"How?"

"Because the only person to go to that one was a curator named Michael Jennings," she said. "And according to the museum's website, he left to work at the Metropolitan Museum of Art in New York over a year ago."

We'd cut the list to four, but it still felt a little needle-in-a-haystack-ish. We just sat there stumped and stared at the wall.

"By the way," I said, "I wanted to warn you that my mother posted those first-day-of-school pictures of us online

and now all my relatives want to meet you when they visit. So be prepared to get swarmed at the holidays."

"I can handle it," she said. "That's the danger of social media."

That gave me an idea. I hopped up and went over to the computer.

"What are you doing?"

"Checking social media," I answered.

"I thought we were working," she protested.

"This is work," I told her. "Maybe mothers aren't the only ones who share too much. What if schools do too?"

I typed in "Academy of Fine Arts in Prague."

"Check it out," I said when the results filled the screen.

We spent the next twenty minutes scrolling through all of the pictures, posts, tweets, and mentions the academy had put up. We found what we were looking for in a picture posted fifteen months earlier.

"Alumni get-together at ArtFest in Budapest," said the caption.

"Top row, third from the left," I said. "I think that's our boy."

Margaret leaned in close to get a good look, and when she turned to face me, she had a big smile. "Got him!"

I got up and went to the wall where we'd taped the roster for the ArtFest in Budapest.

"Who do we have?" she asked.

I started reading off the names. "Michael Jennings, Kendra May, Ryan Thigpen . . ."

The bottom two took my breath away.

"Who is it?"

I held up the paper and said, "Serena Miller and Earl Jackson."

22.

Extra-Credit Algebra

I COULDN'T BELIEVE THAT SERENA MILLER AND Earl Jackson could possibly be involved in the theft of *Woman with a Parasol.*

Or maybe I just didn't want to believe it.

Miller was a family friend and Jackson was so nice and unassuming he insisted I call him by his first name. But I also couldn't ignore the fact that both were at ArtFest in Budapest at the same time as Pavel Novak.

"It could just be a coincidence," offered Margaret. "Remember when you were first teaching me about TOAST? You warned me that just because something is unexpected, doesn't mean it's suspicious."

"Yes, but it's the closest we've come to connecting Novak with anyone at the museum," I said. "Even worse, they were both directly involved with updating the security software. You couldn't pick anyone in a better position to orchestrate the whole burglary."

I sat down in my chair and slumped.

"I haven't met either one of them, so I don't know what they're like," she said. "But there were three other people from the museum at that convention. What about them?"

These were the names and titles listed on the itinerary:

Michael Jennings, PhD, Curator
Kendra May, Conservator
Ryan Thigpen, Project Manager
Serena Miller, Director of Security
Earl Jackson, Security Manager

"We know it's not Jennings because he moved to New York over a year ago to work at the Metropolitan Museum of Art," I said.

"What about the other two?" Margaret asked. "If Kendra May is a conservator, then she probably works with your mom."

"You're right," I said. "Let's find out."

We headed upstairs and found Mom in the front yard

painting a picture of the house. It's a tradition she's done of every home we've lived in.

"Wow," Margaret said, admiring it. "That's beautiful, Mrs. B."

Mom smiled. "Thanks. It may not be nice enough for the National Gallery, but we should be able to find a spot for it somewhere in the house."

"Don't let her modesty fool you," I said. "She's sold paintings in some really nice galleries."

"And don't let sales fool you," she responded. "Van Gogh only sold two paintings in his entire life. We could talk for hours about the difference between what's true art and what sells. But I don't think that's why you came up here. You look like you have a question."

"Two actually," I said. "Do you know a project manager named Ryan Thigpen?"

She thought about it for a moment. "The name's familiar. But I don't know him. I think he oversees modern-art installations in the East Building."

"What about Kendra May?"

"Of course," said Mom. "Kendra's extremely talented. She specializes in the Impressionists and the Postimpressionists, like I do. She did an amazing job repairing a Degas that had been damaged in storage."

"So if her specialty is the Impressionists, then she'd be a fan of Monet, right?" reasoned Margaret.

"Who isn't a fan of Monet?" answered Mom. "But sure. In fact, I think she did some academic research about him for her PhD."

So far, so good.

"What's she like as a person?" I asked. "Is she nice?"

Mom laughed a little as she considered this. "She's not mean. But she's also not too friendly. She likes to do her own thing. And she really gets upset if anyone moves her lunch in the break room refrigerator."

Margaret and I shared a look. I already liked her much more as a candidate than Serena and Earl.

"Why do you ask?" Mom wanted to know.

"It's part of what I'm looking into for Agent Rivers," I said. "It turns out she was at a convention in Hungary at the same time as the man who painted the forgery of *Woman with a Parasol.*"

"And you think she might be involved?" asked Mom.

I shrugged. "Maybe."

"Well then, I have bad news," she said. "Kendra had a baby a few days before the burglary. A boy named Vincent."

Suddenly, Kendra May seemed much less likely to be the one we were looking for. I can't imagine anyone planning a

major museum heist to coincide with giving birth. It would just make everything too unpredictable.

Margaret and I grabbed some apples from the kitchen and headed back to the basement.

"Here's what I'm thinking," Margaret said as we got back to work. "You're not going to meet someone and instantly hatch a plan to rob the National Gallery. You'd want to meet at least another time or two."

"That's true," I said. "So let's go back to all the records and see who went back to Europe."

This time we didn't consider only convention and trade show trips. We looked at all travel involving any of our potential candidates.

"Here's one for Ryan Thigpen," said Margaret. "Stockholm, Sweden, in January of this year."

"That sounds unbearably cold," I replied. "Anything for Kendra May?"

"No," she said. "I'm thinking that and the baby give her a pretty good alibi."

I was scanning through the papers when I came across a trip to Berlin by Earl Jackson. "Four days meeting with consultants," I said, reading off the description on the trip.

"Oh no," said Margaret.

"What is it?"

"Two trips by Serena Miller," she said, looking up at me. "One last September and one just a few weeks before we saw Novak in the museum."

"Where to?" I asked.

"The first one to Paris and the second Prague."

TOAST is about the accumulation of many little details, and for the moment at least, those details weren't looking too good for Serena. I was bummed, so Margaret reminded me that we had an entirely different lead to follow.

"You never know how it all might shake out," she said. "Let's see if the auctions show us anything interesting."

Because his insurance company worked with all the prestigious auction houses, Oliver Hobbes had been able to access complete bidding records for major auctions involving the big names of Impressionism. Normally, the public only finds out who winds up with the painting. But this gave us a much bigger picture of who was interested in the paintings the burglar targeted. We hoped we could find a mastermind hidden among the bidders.

"Each auction is printed on a separate piece of paper," I said to Margaret. "So let's line them up in chronological order."

Just like we'd done with the names of the conventions, we taped the results of each auction on the wall. This way

we could walk along the evidence and look at the big picture instead of only bit by bit on a computer screen.

"I want to put pictures of the paintings up too," said Margaret. "That'll help me keep track of them in my brain."

"Good idea," I said.

Margaret got the images off the web and printed thumbnail copies of each. "There," she said as she taped the last one up. "It's like Gallery Eighty-Five has come to the Underground."

At first it was hard to look past anything but the massive sums of money paid out at the auctions. One of Monet's water lily paintings sold for $47 million to a private collector, while a museum paid $32 million for a portrait by Renoir.

"We're talking mad, crazy money," said Margaret. "And we think one of these people may be the mastermind?"

"Not one of the winners," I said. "Someone who can pay forty-seven million dollars for a painting doesn't need to steal one. We're looking for one of the losers. Someone who keeps trying to get one but gets outbid."

"So, if you can't beat 'em, cheat 'em?" she said.

"You got it."

Basically there were four different types of bidders: institutions such as museums looking to add the paintings to their collections, monetary funds and banks buying them

as financial investments, private collectors, and what were called "anonymous entities."

"Why be an anonymous entity?" asked Margaret.

"A lot of reasons, I guess. Maybe you don't want anyone to know how much money you have. Maybe you don't want the art world to know which artists you're interested in. Or maybe . . ."

". . . you're a criminal who wants to keep his identity hidden," she said.

"Yeah," I agreed. "Maybe that."

We decided to focus on the anonymous bids.

"In order to stay anonymous, you have to hire a representative to do the actual bidding and communicating with the auction house," I explained to Margaret. "So what you do is give your representative a limit—say five million dollars— and the representative stays in the bidding until the price goes over the limit."

"That's why so many of these end on nice round numbers," she said pointing at one of the bid sheets. "This bidder stopped at ten million dollars. And this one stopped at fifteen million. Those must have been the limits their client gave them."

"Exactly," I said.

"So why did this one stop at 12,457,493 dollars?" she asked, pointing at a bid for a Monet.

I looked at it for a moment and said, "I have no idea."

She looked at an auction six months later. "Here's the same representative, American Art and Antique Acquisitions, trying to get another painting, also a Monet. The final bid is 12,629,127 dollars."

"Those are such random numbers," I said, completely baffled.

We looked through all the auctions and found nine instances when American Art and Antique Acquisitions tried to purchase a painting. Each time the painting was either a Monet or a Renoir. And each time the bidding stopped at a seemingly random number.

We wrote the bids on a separate sheet of paper and hung it on the wall, too. Then we just sat there and stared at it. And stared. And stared. As if the answer might jump out at us.

"Argghhh," Margaret said, rubbing her temples. "It's like I'm doing extra-credit algebra homework."

"Maybe that's it," I said. "Maybe it's algebra."

"What type of algebra?"

I got on the computer to search for something. "Here it is. Write this down: 'Amount to' equals 'amount from' times 'rate from' over 'rate to.'"

I looked up and she was giving me a total stink eye.

"I speak English, not equations," she said. "Why don't you just copy down what you see on the screen? And then explain what the heck you're talking about."

"Exchange rates. I dealt with them all the time when I lived in Europe. We'd have to figure out how many dollars are in a euro. Or if we went to London we'd have to convert euros into pounds. Maybe these actually are nice round numbers," I said, pointing at the list. "Just not in dollars."

I tried doing the math on paper until Margaret reminded me that the computer would be quicker. I started entering numbers into the equations, and then I compared those amounts with currency rates from the days of each auction. It was complicated, but when I was done it couldn't have been more basic. Each number equaled the exact same amount.

"Fifty million leu," I said.

"Fifty-million what?" she asked, confused.

"Leu. It's a type of money."

"Oh," she said. "Which country uses the leu?"

That's when I grinned. "Romania."

23.

An Actor Named
John Wilkes Booth

ONCE NICOLAE NEVRESCU ENTERED THE STORY, preserving my covert status became more essential. I wasn't allowed to call or text Agent Rivers, and I certainly couldn't just show up at the Hoover Building and ask to see him. If I wanted to make contact, he told me I needed to do so by way of a website made especially for people like me.

"You mean secret agents?" I asked, charged with excitement.

"No, I mean middle schoolers," he answered, bringing me back to earth.

The FBI Kids Page is a site for students who want to learn about the Bureau. It has video clips, interactive games, animations, and a link called "Ask an Agent."

I clicked the link and signed in as twelve-year-old Johan Blankvort of Bethesda, Maryland. My question: "How can you meet an agent in person?" Soon I received a standard response that told me about community outreach programs, such as the demonstrations put on by the FBI's K-9 Explosives Detection team, where agents were available to the public. Then, the next morning while Margaret and I were walking to school, I got a text from a phone number I didn't recognize. It read:

Tell Johan to visit Our American Cousin after school today.

That was it. I waited for another text that might, you know, explain what that one meant, but none came.

"Who's that from?" Margaret asked.

"Agent Rivers."

"What's he have to say?"

Sigh. "I have absolutely no idea."

She read the text and asked, "Who's Johan?"

"I am. Johan Blankvort is my secret identity with the Bureau."

"Get out!" She stopped in her tracks and turned to face me. "You have an actual government-issued secret identity?"

"I've even got fake IDs," I said, fighting back an ear-to-ear grin.

"That may be the coolest thing I've ever heard," she replied. "But if you're Johan, then who's your American cousin?"

I spent most of the day trying to figure that out. I must have reread the text a hundred times. Including once during life science, which cost me three class-participation points. But it wasn't until lunch that I paid attention to the fact that the words "Our American Cousin" were all capitalized.

"You think that's important?" Margaret asked when I pointed it out to her. "People are kind of random when it comes to punctuation in texts."

"Agent Rivers isn't random about anything," I countered. "If it's capitalized, it must be the title of something."

I googled "Our American Cousin" and found that it was the name of the play Abraham Lincoln was watching the night he was assassinated.

Now I knew what I was supposed to do.

After school, I got on the Metro and took the Red Line to Gallery Place. (I'm guessing the instant I used my SmarTrip card a message alerted Agent Rivers I was on my way.) From the subway station it was just a short walk to Ford's Theatre.

On April 14, 1865, Abraham Lincoln went to Ford's to watch a performance of *Our American Cousin*. During the

play's third act, he was shot by John Wilkes Booth. Now it was a historic site run by the National Park Service.

It also happened to be right around the corner from FBI Headquarters.

I got my ticket and blended in with all the tourists walking through the exhibits that detailed the events leading up to the president's death. I was looking at the actual derringer pistol Booth used to kill him when the man standing next to me asked a question.

"How long did it take you to figure out where we were meeting?"

I glanced up and saw that it was Agent Rivers.

"Most of the day," I said. "And I got in trouble for looking at my phone during class."

"Sorry about that," he said. "But I knew you'd solve it."

If anyone happened to notice us, we just looked like tourists on vacation. He'd swapped his normal suit and tie for a Nationals T-shirt and a pair of jeans. For the most part, we didn't even look at each other. We just kept our eyes on the exhibits and talked quietly.

"So, what did you find out?" he asked.

"A lot," I replied. "Last year Pavel Novak and five staff members from the National Gallery were at the same trade show in Budapest."

"Anyone we know on that trip?" he asked.

"Earl Jackson . . . and Serena Miller."

I could see his reflection in the exhibit glass and his reaction was as surprised as mine had been.

"Really? Earl and Serena?"

"It gets worse. Miller took two more trips to Europe, including one to Prague two weeks before Novak entered the country."

"That's . . . interesting."

"I keep thinking back to when Earl's name came up at the dinner party. She was so adamant that he couldn't be involved. I thought it was because she trusted him. But maybe she was just worried that if we pursued him, it would lead to her as well."

"What about the auctions?"

"More good news," I said. "It turns out an anonymous bidder has tried—and failed—to acquire a major Impressionist work at nine different auctions. He's put up a lot of money and is no doubt frustrated that he keeps losing."

"If the bidder's anonymous, how does it help us?" asked Rivers.

"Well, we know that the money is coming from Romania," I said. "And also that the bids were placed by a company here in Washington."

"So it could be Nevrescu laundering the money for his father?"

I nodded.

"I looked him up some more," I said. "He really likes to get involved in cultural events. Especially ones in the Romanian-American community."

"Right."

"So in two weeks there's an open house at the Romanian embassy. They're calling it a festival of food and family. He's one of the sponsors of the event. He'll be there."

"Maybe," said Rivers. "But we sure won't."

"Why not?" I asked. "It's a chance to interact with him in public. A chance to see who he's meeting with."

"We already have him under surveillance a lot of the time," he reminded me. "So we know most of the people he meets with. But more important, we're not allowed to go inside an embassy."

"You're the FBI. You can go anywhere you want."

"In America," he said. "But as soon as you set foot onto embassy grounds, by law you are in that country. If I tried to investigate someone while they were in that building, it would be seen as a violation of their sovereignty. Before you know it, the State Department's involved and there's an international incident."

"Oh," I said, slightly embarrassed. "I didn't realize the legal part of it."

"That's okay. You're the kid and I'm the FBI agent. I'm the one who's *supposed* to know that," he told me. "But you've done an amazing job, Florian. You've given us a lot to build on."

"I love doing it," I told him. "What can I work on next?"

He looked at me, sighed, and put his hand on my shoulder. Past experience told me I wasn't going to like what he said next.

"Nothing," he answered. "You can't do anything involving the *Woman with a Parasol* case. I don't even want you working on it at home."

I was devastated.

"But you just said I'd done an amazing job."

"You have," he said. "But we can't risk your safety. The more likely it is that Nevrescu is involved, the more likely it is that you're in danger."

"Why? Just because we were both at the same soccer game?"

"I'm sorry, Florian. But that's more than enough for me."

"But it was just a coincidence," I argued. "There were tons of people there. Besides, if he wanted to do anything to me, don't you think he would have just done it then, when he had the chance?"

Rather than answer, Rivers turned toward the enlarged picture on display in front of us. "This photograph was taken at Abraham Lincoln's second inauguration," he said, "six weeks before he was killed."

The photo was of a massive crowd on the steps of the Capitol Building. In the middle of them all, you could see Abraham Lincoln, standing behind a podium reading his speech.

"Lincoln's in the middle, but do you know who this is?"

He pointed to a man in the crowd of people looking down on the president from behind.

"No. Who is it?"

"He's an actor named John Wilkes Booth," he said. "But there were tons of people there. And besides, if he wanted to hurt the president, don't you think he would have done it when he had a chance?"

I stood there silently and considered what he was saying.

"You tell me," said Rivers. "You think him being there was a coincidence?"

24.

Let's Play TOAST

WHEN AGENT RIVERS SAID I WAS OFF THE CASE, he meant it. As soon as I started to leave Ford's Theatre, it was as if we'd never met. I turned back to say good-bye, but he'd already disappeared through some unseen exit.

As the days passed, I had no idea if the leads I'd given him helped or if the case had taken a dramatic turn or maybe even hit a dead end. I constantly checked news sites to see if there were any breaking stories about Romanian mobsters being arrested, and every day I'd wait anxiously for my mother to get home from work, just in case she might have heard a rumor or maybe seen federal agents sealing off Serena Miller's office.

My only connection to the investigation was in the Underground, where I still had my own case board on the wall. I tinkered with it all the time, straightening the cards, reorganizing them. Hoping I might stumble onto some perfect alignment that revealed the mastermind.

I was trying out a color-coding system for the cards when I heard someone hustling down the stairs to the basement. Seconds later, Margaret burst into the room in full-Margaret mode.

"I just had a genius idea!"

"What is it?" I asked expectantly. "Does it have to do with *Woman with a Parasol*? Finding your birth parents? Did you figure out how to find one of the long-lost firefighters?"

"No, no, and no. It has to do with you."

"Okay," I said, my enthusiasm slightly dampened. After all, I'm far less interesting than all those things. Still, I was happy that something was about to break the boredom. "What's your idea?"

"You're running for student council."

I waited to see if there was any more to this brainstorm, but I could tell by her expression and the awkward silence that she had put it all out there.

"What's . . . student council?" I asked warily.

"What do you mean, 'what's student council?'?"

"I think the question's pretty self-explanatory," I said.

"Have you been living under a rock or something?" she asked.

"No, but I have been living in Europe for the last eight years," I reminded her. "I don't think they have student council there. At least not at the schools where I went."

"That's too bad, because it's really cool. There are two representatives from each homeroom and they get to help plan the school dances and organize fund-raisers, and at the end of the year they take a trip to Kings Dominion. We're talking epic roller coasters."

"Dances, fund-raisers, roller coasters?" I said, listing three things I considered far more terrifying than the Romanian Mafia. Although, for the record, I had yet to confess any of these fears to Margaret.

"So what do you think?" she asked expectantly.

"I . . . don't know." I tried to fake a little enthusiasm but the best I could do was "Maybe?"

"Why *maybe*? It'll be a great way to make new friends and it's a lot of fun."

"Really? Because it doesn't sound like a lot of fun. It sounds like . . . a lot of work."

She plopped into a chair and all the oomph seemed to drain from her body. "I don't know how to break this to you,

Florian, but in the world of twelve-year-olds, that stuff is fun. I know you got to be a part of something huge. And I think there are going to be times when you get to do that again. I mean, you're a consulting detective with the FBI! That's amazing. But it's also a part-time job. You can't just sit around rearranging the cards on your case board, waiting for a mysterious text."

She looked up at the case board for a moment and smiled. "Although I see what you're doing with the color coding and I think it may be game changing."

"It works, doesn't it?" I said, glad that she saw it too. "It helps your eye pull everything together."

"Even so," she replied, getting back on the subject. "You have to embrace the fact that you're a seventh grader. Middle school has to be enough, because that's your full-time job. That's your life. So, you can either run for student council tomorrow. Or I can have your mom come down here and start giving you pep talks about how 'seventh grade will be seventh heaven' and why you 'need to be your true self.'"

"You'd never do that to me," I said.

She gave me a sly smile and said, "I think you know me well enough to know that's exactly what I'd do."

"Fine," I said in full surrender. "Anything but that."

"So you're telling me you'll run?"

"Yes," I answered reluctantly, trying to convince myself at the same time. "If you say it's great, then it must be great."

The next day Jennifer Damon and I were elected to be the student council representatives for Mr. White's homeroom. Three other girls ran, and I think I squeaked in because they split the popular-girl vote, thereby leaving the geeky-boy superhero-fan-club constituency all for me.

Slowly but surely, I was taking baby steps into accepting my middle school–ness.

When I woke up Saturday morning, it had been twelve days since I'd left Ford's Theatre. Twelve days with no connection to the mystery. Twelve days for my mind to reboot, just like they rebooted the security system at the National Gallery.

That's when I had my revelation.

Maybe I needed those twelve days off because, when I finally saw it, it seemed as clear as day. And I marched right across the street to Margaret's house to tell her all about it.

"We have betrayed our core beliefs!" I exclaimed when she answered the door. "I have just had an epic realization."

I blustered into her house, only to stop when I saw myself in a hallway mirror. "This is what it's like to be you, isn't it?" I said. "This is what it's like to burst into a room half-way through a conversation that the other person didn't even know had started."

She looked at me and shook her head in total confusion. "I have absolutely no idea what you're talking about."

"Ha!" I said, pointing at her. "And that's what it's like to be me. I never know either. You get used to it."

"How have we betrayed our core beliefs?"

"By ignoring TOAST," I told her. "What is it? Give me your best definition."

"Okay," she said, getting into the spirit of it. "The Theory of All Small Things ignores the seemingly obvious to consider only small details so that when they're added together they reveal an undeniable truth."

I stopped and smiled. "That's a really good way to put it."

"Thanks, I may have practiced it in my head a couple thousand times. You know . . . because I'm me."

"Unfortunately, that's not what we've been doing," I said. "We haven't been ignoring the obvious to focus on the details. We've only been looking for the details that make the big things more likely to seem true."

"I think you may have lost me for part of that," she said.

"I know. I'm not expressing it nearly as well as you, but I think we've been looking at this all wrong. I think we need to go back to playing TOAST again. That's how we got as far as we did."

She looked at me as she considered this before finally saying, "Okay. Where do you want to play?"

I did not hesitate with my answer. "The Romanian embassy."

"You can't be serious," she said. "Agent Rivers specifically said that you couldn't go near there. It's against the law."

"No," I corrected. "He said that the FBI couldn't investigate there. And when it comes to this case, I no longer have anything to do with the FBI. I am a civilian. The Romanian embassy is holding an open house to share its culture with the people of Washington. That's us."

"Really?" she asked. "This is what you want to do?"

"When will we ever get a chance to look at Nevrescu using TOAST?" I said. "This is our one shot. He'll be there schmoozing and mingling and we'll be able to see him in action. And we're the only ones who can do it. The FBI can't go in. Only we can find these clues. Only we can ignore the version of him that's in the papers, and look for the little details that will tell us the truth."

"And what if he recognizes you?"

"He won't," I said confidently. "It was just a coincidence that we both were at your soccer game."

"Why do I have a feeling that if I don't agree to go, you're going to go without me?"

"Because you're smart and that's exactly what I'm going to do."

"Okay, then I'll do it," she said. "Just let me get my sneakers. You know, in case we end up having to run out of there."

A few minutes later we were on our way.

I used cash to ride the Metro because I'd purposely left my SmarTrip card home. I didn't want any alarms to let Agent Rivers know what I was doing. We got off at the Dupont Circle station and walked up Massachusetts Avenue for about half a mile.

"There it is," I said, pointing across the street as we neared the embassy.

The building was three stories tall and had a massive antenna on the roof. The front doors were open and the sound of music could be heard from inside.

"Once we set foot on the driveway, we're no longer in America," I reminded her as we crossed the street. "So let's make sure we don't do anything stupid."

"Good tip," she said. "I don't suppose you memorized any of those Romanian phrases?"

"Just one."

"Let me guess," she replied. "My hovercraft is full of monkeys."

"That's the one."

We walked along the circular driveway until we reached the front door, where a bearlike man with a huge smile and a booming voice greeted us. *"Bine ati venit."*

I smiled back at him and said, *"Multumesc."*

"What just happened there?" Margaret asked once we stepped inside the entryway, where there was a grand staircase.

"He said, 'Welcome,' and I said, 'Thank you,'" I explained.

"I thought you didn't speak Romanian," she said.

"I don't," I answered. "But I can fake a little here and there. Like I said, it's similar to Italian."

The festival was limited to the bottom floor, and while most of the rooms were open to the public, they were very specific about not going into any rooms with closed doors. In one room a violinist performed traditional folk music, while in another a stereo pulsated with Romanian dance pop. And everywhere we went, there was food.

"You have got to try these cabbage rolls," Margaret told me in between bites. "De-licious."

"Do you see any sign of Nevrescu?" I asked.

"No," she said. "But I can take a look over there by that table full of fried dough and sweet cheese."

A pattern quickly emerged as we went from room to room. Wherever we'd go, I'd look for Nevrescu, and Margaret would

look for food. Her search had a much better success rate than mine until we reached the library.

The room was beautiful with antique furniture and dark wood bookcases that went from floor to ceiling. It was packed with people and I spied Nevrescu in the opposite corner doing the meet and greet with everyone.

"There he is," I said, nodding toward him.

"Excellent," mumbled Margaret as she finished swallowing a dessert known as *papanash*. "And with 'excellent' I'm referring to both the fact that you found Nevrescu and this dessert. OMG, it's delicious."

Nic the Knife's social swirl seemed to stay in that particular area, so I found a spot where we were somewhat shielded from his view by a large cabinet.

"If he has no idea who you are, then why are you hiding?" she asked.

I didn't really have an answer for that one, so all I did was smile.

"That's what I thought," she said.

Then I pulled out a pair of glasses and put them on.

"What are those?" asked Margaret.

"Glasses," I answered as if it were beyond obvious.

"Yes, but you don't wear glasses," she said. "So I repeat, 'what are those?'"

"Okay," I whispered. "Maybe they're spy glasses with a built-in camera that Agent Rivers gave me at Quantico."

She shook her head and let out a sigh of resignation. "I can tell this is going to turn out really well."

"All we're doing is playing TOAST," I reminded her. "The glasses are so we can go back to the instant replay if we need to. All systems are go."

Seeing Nevrescu in action completely changed my perception of him. Despite the intense death stare that was on display in all the photos we came across, in person he seemed charming, even from a distance. For example, when he'd meet someone, he'd always make sure to shake with one hand, and clasp them on the arm with the other. It was friendly and warm. And definitely not what I expected. We watched him for about fifteen minutes, making sure he never caught sight of us.

The plan worked really well until I saw someone totally unexpected. There was a swinging door that led to the kitchen and when it opened I got a quick glimpse of a man loading a trash can. The door swung shut again before I could be certain, but he seemed to be wearing the same blue coveralls as the custodians who worked at the National Gallery.

"Did you see that?" I asked Margaret.

"Did I see what?"

I headed for the kitchen and pressed the door just enough to look inside.

"Florian, where are you going?" asked Margaret, a hint of desperation in her voice.

"I just want to take a peek," I said, pushing it more.

"They were pretty specific about where we could and couldn't go," she reminded me. "The key detail was that closed doors were a no-go."

I pushed the door all the way open and said, "But this door isn't closed anymore."

"Why are boys always this way?" she said, shaking her head.

I didn't stay to answer. I looked into the kitchen, and when I saw that no one was in there, I went all the way in. The only way I was going to get a decent look was to go into the next room.

"And now he's totally gone off the deep end," I heard Margaret say as the door swung shut behind me.

I don't know what came over me, but I wasn't scared in the least. I was determined to find him. I strode right across the kitchen and entered a pantry . . . where two security guards were taking a cigarette break.

"What's this?" demanded one of the guards.

I stammered for a moment and failed miserably as I tried to use the Romanian phrase for "where is the bathroom?" I can't be certain but I'm pretty sure I asked for the hovercraft.

"Speak in English," said the other guard.

"Oh, great, you speak English," I replied, my brain a total blank as to what to say. "That means I can speak in English to you."

I was still stammering away when a voice called out from behind.

"Johan, what are you doing?"

Agent Rivers had come to my rescue. He was dressed kind of nerdy in a plaid shirt with a name tag that read, MR. MIKE EVANS, NORTH BETHESDA MIDDLE SCHOOL. And when he talked, his voice had an excitable quality to it.

"I'm so sorry," he said to the guards. "My name's Mike Evans. I'm the art teacher at North Bethesda Middle. Go Firebirds! Anyway, I brought two of my best students here to fully immerse themselves in the culture of another country. Unfortunately, Johan here has a tendency to wander off where he shouldn't. What have I told you about that, Johan?"

"Not to do it," I said, still totally confused as to how he got here but so grateful that he did.

"Anyway, I was led to believe that there would be a display of traditional Romanian painted eggs that we could

look at. As an artist, I feel they truly capture the spirit and heritage of your country. I'd really like to show my students those eggs because next month we're going to be painting similar ones in class, and I think yours would give them an excellent target, creatively speaking. They are just exquisite."

By the time he stopped talking long enough to take a breath, the guards had practically forgotten about me and were just looking to get back to their cigarettes.

"So can you tell me where they are?" Rivers asked.

"Where what are?" one guard asked, confused.

"The eggs. The painted Romanian eggs. I'd like to show them to the students."

"Fine, fine," he replied. "The eggs are in the library. But no more wandering, okay?"

All eyes turned to me.

"I promise," I said.

We left the kitchen and beelined for the front door.

"How'd you know I was here?" I asked under my breath once we'd gotten clear of the guards.

"Johan Blankvort sent a message to 'Ask an Agent' wanting to know 'Where is the Embassy of Romania?' An odd question for an FBI agent, but certainly one that caught my attention."

"But I didn't send in any question," I said, even more confused.

"That was me," said Margaret. "When I went to get my sneakers."

"You went behind my back?"

"No, she saved your butt," Rivers corrected. "Although, it may be short-lived because there's a decent chance I'm going to kill you when we get out of here."

We made it to the entryway and were almost to the grand staircase when I saw Nicolae Nevrescu talking to a young woman in a blue dress. He seemed to be flirting with her. Right up until the point he looked our way.

"Um, we may have a problem."

When I saw Nevrescu signal a humongous bodyguard to come over to him, I corrected that statement.

"Oh yeah, we definitely have a problem."

25.

The Getaway

MARGARET, AGENT RIVERS, AND I WERE ABOUT twenty-five feet from the front door when Nicolae Nevrescu saw me. The look of recognition and surprise on his face was unmistakable. And worst of all, there was no way I could beat him to the door.

"He knows me," I said under my breath to Rivers. "He just spotted me."

"He may know you," said Marcus, "but he doesn't know me. You two do not stop walking until you make it to the sidewalk. Kayla's waiting for you."

"Kayla who taught me self-defense at Quantico?"

"She'll be off to the right when you get through the door,"

he said. "She's standing on the line that marks the end of their jurisdiction. Do not stop walking until you reach her."

Now Nevrescu was headed right to us, but there was no way to know if he could tell that Rivers was with us or not.

"What about you?" I asked Rivers nervously. "What are you going to do?"

He didn't answer. Instead he just resumed playing the role of the very excitable middle school teacher.

"Mr. Nevrescu," he said as he cut him off and blocked him from reaching us. "My name is Mike Evans and I'm the art teacher at North Bethesda Middle. I just want to say that I am a huge fan of your scholarship program. I just think it's amazing that you've helped so many deserving kids."

He kept talking but I could no longer make out what he was saying once we got to the door.

"Go, go, go," said Margaret as she took me by the arm and hurried me along.

I turned to look back over my shoulder but couldn't see Rivers in the crush of people and had no way of knowing if his act was working or if things were going to go very wrong for him. Margaret kept pulling me along.

Then another voice called out, "Wait one second. Come back."

It was the bodyguard Nevrescu had signaled inside the

embassy. He was about six foot six, so his strides were long and he was catching up.

"Sorry," I called back to him, picking up the pace. "But we're running late."

I looked to the right and saw Kayla, all bright and smiley. She had on jeans, a tank top, and a pair of boots that maybe nudged her over the five-foot mark.

"There's our rescue team," I told Margaret.

"Seriously?" she replied uneasily. "The kindergarten teacher?"

"Don't be fooled," I assured her.

"Come back or else," the bodyguard demanded as he closed the gap some more.

Kayla was careful to stay beyond the sidewalk, but she reached out and signaled us to hurry. "Come on, you two," she said in her cheery voice. "Right over here."

We reached her just as the bodyguard reached us, and she swept us with her arm so that we were directly behind her.

"You two need to come back," he said, ignoring her. "It's important."

"Actually," Kayla said. "They don't need to do anything. You see, they're with me."

The man laughed. "And who are you? Their babysitter?"

"You know, I did babysit back home in Pennsylvania," she said as she took his hand. It looked as if she was going to shake it, but instead she started to twist his pinkie and ring fingers and practically brought him to his knees. "But today I'm not a babysitter. Today I'm your worst nightmare."

The amazing thing was that even as she was physically destroying and taunting him, she kept talking in that upbeat kindergarten teacher's voice. She continued to twist his fingers and he grimaced in agony, a line of sweat forming on his forehead.

"Now, I'm wearing my favorite boots," she continued. "And I don't want to mess them up. But if you so much as make another move toward either of these children, I will not hesitate to use them in ways that you will find excruciatingly uncomfortable."

Just then a black SUV pulled up next to us.

"You two get in," Kayla instructed us without turning her attention from the bodyguard.

I opened the door and we both jumped in. Once we were safely inside, Kayla finished her conversation with the man.

"So do we understand each other?"

He didn't respond at first, which caused her to twist the fingers even more.

"Yes," he said. "We understand each other."

She flashed a smile and said, "It was a pleasure to meet you."

She let go and he pulled back his injured hand and clutched it with the other. Kayla literally had to jump up to get into the backseat with us. Once she did, she slammed the door shut, the power locks closed, and the SUV was moving down Massachusetts Avenue.

She looked over at Margaret and smiled. "Hey, I'm Kayla."

"Hi," Margaret said. "You're my hero."

Kayla laughed. "You'd be surprised, but I get that a lot."

As we drove away, I turned around in my seat so I could look out the rear window to see if Agent Rivers had made it out of the embassy. I didn't see any sign of him.

"We have a covert asset," Kayla instructed the agent behind the wheel. "Drive accordingly."

"Roger that," said the driver as he picked up the pace.

We stayed on Massachusetts Avenue, which is also known as Embassy Row, for about a mile. Then we started making some sudden turns onto little side roads. I could feel car sickness coming on.

"He's just making sure no one's following," explained Kayla.

"That's good," I said. "That man you destroyed. Is he going to cause trouble for you?"

She laughed. "He is going to go to his grave without admitting to anybody that he was outmuscled by little ol' me."

Margaret laughed.

Kayla looked at me and shook her head. "Florian, what were you thinking?"

"I don't know," I admitted.

"You are unbelievably smart," she said. "This was anything but."

"I know."

That was the entire lecture I got from her, but I was certain there were more to come.

"Are we clear?" she asked the driver.

"Absolutely," he replied. "No one's following."

"Great, take us to the Washington Field Office.

"I'm stationed there and not at the Hoover," she said to me.

"I'm worried about Agent Rivers," I said. "I didn't see him come out of the embassy."

"Yeah, well, he was sure worried about you," she replied. "Thank goodness you had enough sense to send a distress signal."

"Actually that was Margaret," I said. "Thanks, Margaret."

"It's okay," she said. "That's what BFs do, right?"

Ten minutes later we pulled into the underground garage

at the FBI Washington Field Office. It was large and non-descript, about a half mile from the Hoover Building. A few minutes after we got there, another car pulled up beside us. It was a maroon hybrid. Agent Rivers was behind the wheel.

I let out a huge sigh of relief.

"Looks like your ride is here," she said. "So it's time for me to say good-bye. You two stay out of trouble, okay?"

"Okay," I said.

"Definitely," said Margaret.

"And, Florian," she said, looking me right in the eyes. "That big brain of yours . . . don't forget to use it."

We got out of the SUV and Agent Rivers came right to me.

"Florian, I can't believe you did that," he said. "I am so angry with you."

"I know," I replied.

"But we are going to deal with the anger a little later," he said.

That's when he wrapped me up in a hug. It was tight and comforting and long.

"I'm sorry, Agent Rivers," I said, looking up at him.

"You call me Marcus."

I nodded. "I'm sorry, Marcus."

26.

Black Tuesday

"EPIC" IS ONE OF MARGARET'S FAVORITE WORDS. It's also a good way to describe the scope of the grounding my parents gave me after Agent Rivers drove us home and told them what happened.

I made a point of explaining to Margaret's mom and dad how I'd put her in an impossible situation. And Marcus followed up by pointing out that she was the one who saved the day, so we were able to help her a little. But my world was limited to the campus of Alice Deal Middle School and the walls of my house for as far as the eye could see. And while at home, the computer was limited only to its role in helping with homework, and the tele-

vision was banished as though Philo T. Farnsworth had never invented it.

And I totally deserved the punishment. Every bit of it.

The one exception was that I was allowed to keep participating in after-school activities. Suddenly I became the most active member in student council history, volunteering for any subcommittee or planning board I could get on.

Two weeks after our little adventure to Romania, I came out of an oversight committee that considered possible changes in the school dress code—like I said, I volunteered for *everything*—and was surprised to see my dad waiting for me in front of the school.

"What's wrong? Mom's worried I'm having too much fun on my walk home?" I joked as I got in the car.

"Worse," he said, a serious look on his face. "There's been a new development. The story broke. All of it. A writer at the *Post* published it online about two hours ago. TV news jumped on board and now it's a circus."

"I don't understand—what story?"

"They're reporting that *Woman with a Parasol* was stolen, and claiming the FBI and National Gallery kept it a secret out of embarrassment. Nicolae Nevrescu was identified as the prime suspect." He turned to look at me. "And there've been mentions that a boy has been part of the investigation."

"Did they use my name?"

"Not yet," he said. "But there are so many bigger parts of the story right now. It's really going to cause problems for Agent Rivers."

"It'll put pressure on Nevrescu, too," I said.

"One of the news stations ambushed him outside his construction company," said Dad. "There was a lot of shouting and yelling."

When I got home the television and computer bans were temporarily lifted so that we could watch the story unfold. Margaret came over and joined Dad and me.

"How'd the story even get out?" I asked as we watched a reporter do a live update from the sidewalk in front of the museum.

"It's like I told you," Margaret replied. "Nothing stays secret in Washington."

As far as names, the only ones mentioned much were Marcus Rivers as the agent in charge and Nicolae Nevrescu as the prime suspect. A few reporters revealed that there may have been involvement in the crime by museum staff, but no one referred directly to Serena Miller or Earl Jackson.

Oliver Hobbes, however, was all over the news. Not as a suspect but as someone to be interviewed. We saw him on

two national broadcasts as an industry expert with a working knowledge of the situation.

"I bet he's your leak right there," said Dad.

"Oliver?"

"He's always had a shady side."

"But why would he leak the story?" asked Margaret.

"I'm sure he's getting pressure from the insurance company," Dad said. "They probably think the FBI is moving too slowly and wanted to put them in the hot seat."

"My company was against keeping the theft a secret right from the beginning," Hobbes said during his interview. "We believe that the best policy is total honesty with the public. But the FBI insisted and we were forced into silence."

"That's pretty harsh," interjected Margaret.

"And why do you think the FBI kept it a secret?" asked the interviewer.

"Isn't it obvious?" said Hobbes. "They don't want the public to know how much they've messed up."

When Mom got home from work, she gave us a behind-the-scenes account of the National Gallery.

"Everyone was running around crazy," she said. "Reporters kept trying to come inside with their television crews. Serena Miller went in for a closed-door meeting with the director that lasted over an hour. Eventually my boss came

into our studio and told us to leave early and not speak to the press."

"Does anyone there know that you already knew?"

Mom shook her head. "I'm good at keeping secrets. I played dumb like everybody else."

As far as my participation, a few reporters mentioned a rumor about a kid being involved, but it seemed so far-fetched and strange that no one gave it much thought. I had my fingers crossed that things would stay that way.

"Wait a second," said Margaret, holding her hands up to signal stop. "Where's Pavel Novak?"

"In the Czech Republic," I said, unsure what she was going for.

"No, I don't mean where is he on the planet. I mean, where is he in the story?" she asked. "He's the one person that we definitely know is involved in the crime, and no one has mentioned his name."

"That's true," I said.

"They must not know," said Dad. "Whoever leaked the story must not know about Novak's involvement."

"Then it's not Hobbes," I said. "He's known from the beginning."

"Then who could it be?" Margaret asked, thinking out loud.

"Oh no," said Mom. "This does not look good."

We looked over to her and she was glued to the monitor.

"What's the matter?" I asked.

"Marcus is in trouble."

We all quieted and turned up the volume and listened as a news anchor held up a piece of paper and began to read from it.

"According to this statement from Nevrescu's attorney, the businessman categorically denies any involvement," she said. "In a troubling twist, there are reports Special Agent Marcus Rivers may have entered the Romanian embassy under a false identity two weeks ago."

The anchor next to her shook his head as though this was an earth-shattering development. "If that's true, it would be a clear violation of international law," said the anchor. "I'm sure the State Department will be getting involved now."

I couldn't believe it. On top of everything else, Marcus was going to get in trouble because of something I did. It was my fault and he was going to pay the price.

"They're going to fire him, aren't they?" I said. "It's going to cost him his career."

"You may be right," said Dad.

Then Mom reached over and put her hand on my shoulder. "Unless you solve it first."

"Seriously?" I said.

Mom and Dad shared a look for a moment and then both of them turned to me. "There is a temporary lifting of the restriction within the confines of the Underground. Just downstairs. You can't talk to anyone. You can't go anywhere."

"We don't need to go anywhere. The TV's bringing it all to us." I looked right at Margaret. "This is our test. Are you ready?"

"Ready to take it. Ready to crush it."

27.

Kidnapped

MARGARET AND I SPENT TUESDAY EVENING AND all day after school Wednesday in the Underground trying to break the case. We were in total TOAST mode, ignoring the big things to focus on little details that didn't quite fit.

Here were some of the things we wanted to figure out:

1. Who leaked the story? We filled an entire wall with cards that listed who knew what and when. Then we started comparing those names with what information did and did not become public.

2. What was the importance of the cleaning crew? When we looked back at the video my secret-agent glasses recorded at the Romanian embassy, we were able to identify that the custodian there worked for the same company as the custodians at the National Gallery.

3. How did the burglar find out about the security upgrade? If neither Serena nor Earl was involved—which we believed in our hearts to be true—then someone else had to pass along the information about the upgrade. Who could have known about it?

4. Who else crossed paths with Pavel Novak?

"Okay," Margaret said, staring at the evidence on the wall. "I've got one more for you. But I warn you, it's really TOASTy."

"What does 'really TOASTy' mean?" I asked.

"I mean in the Theory of All Small Things, this is smaller than small. It's tiny. But it doesn't make sense," she explained.

"Lay it on me," I said.

"How'd he know about the soccer game?"

She just let it sit there for a moment.

"What do you mean?"

"We know there's a Romanian connection."

"Right."

"And it all points to Nevrescu as the mastermind."

"Yes, but we can't prove it."

"Nevrescu recognized you at the embassy because he had seen you at the soccer game."

"Right," I said.

"But how did he know you would be at the soccer game in the first place? He didn't follow you from your house. The FBI would have mentioned that. But they just said he went to the soccer game and watched you there."

I considered this and smiled.

"You're absolutely right," I said. "It's tiny, but that may be the piece."

That question kept me up all night and bothered me all through the next school day. How could Nevrescu have known where I was going?

"Your SmarTrip card!" Margaret said the instant she saw me in the cafeteria on Thursday. "The agent knew you were there because your SmarTrip card set off some kind of alarm. Nevrescu must have access to the same information or equipment."

I thought this through for a minute. "You might be right. But that would mean he has some sort of connection inside the FBI. We've got to reach out to Marcus."

"He can't talk to you," she said. "He's all over the news. I'm sure he's in the admiral's office fighting for his job. You can't just have Johan Blankvort send a question into 'Ask an Agent.'"

"Well, we've got to do something," I said. "Let's go straight to my house after school."

"I can't. I have my piano lesson."

"Oh yeah, I forgot," I told her. "I'll run home and start trying to figure out a connection between Nevrescu and the FBI. You come over as soon as you can."

"Okay, and I know you're in a hurry. But don't take all your little shortcuts."

"What's wrong with my shortcuts?"

"Like the one behind the Safeway. It's gross back there. And you know what I say about Dumpsters."

"You don't have to worry about me," I said. "You just get to the Underground as soon as you can."

It was pouring when school got out, and I tried to reach both of my parents to see if either could pick me up. They couldn't, so I decided to run through the rain, and despite Margaret's warnings, I planned to take every shortcut I knew.

I ran down the street and squeezed between the fence to get behind the Safeway. I held my backpack over my head to try to keep dry as I hurried along the Dumpsters.

And that brings the story back to where I started—my kidnapping. A lot has happened since then, so I'll recap some of the highlights.

The giant man from the Happy Leprechaun Flower Shop knocked me unconscious, threw me into the back of the truck, and drove me to a farm in rural Virginia. Along the way we semibonded over the joke about monkeys in my hovercraft, and then I was able to trick him into triggering my panic button, which was disguised as an asthma inhaler.

Oh, and I was seated at a table across from Nicolae Nevrescu, crime lord and art-theft mastermind.

"You are the one the FBI only talks about in whispers. The one they call Little Sherlock," he said.

"I have no idea what you're talking about," I said.

He gave me a disappointed look. "Let's not play games. I know who you are and you know who I am."

I nodded reluctantly. "I know you're the man who master-minded the robbery at the National Gallery of Art."

He chuckled. "Mastermind? I love that word. I wish it were true. No, that fact you have wrong. That's why I had you brought here. So we could set the record straight and

you could tell your friends at the FBI they are looking for the wrong suspect."

That's when he rolled up his sleeves and I saw the tattoos. The one that caught my eye was the tattoo of the daisy with the numbers "24/7" directly beneath it. Nothing about that made sense. It just didn't fit.

Until it did. Until it answered Margaret's question: How did he know I'd be at the soccer game?

"There's been a huge mistake," I said urgently. "You need to let me go right now."

"Is that so?" He laughed. "Why should I do that?"

I looked right at him and did not blink. "Because the FBI is going to be here in less than five minutes and that doesn't leave us much time to talk about why your tattoo changes everything."

This caught him off guard.

"That inhaler," I said. "That's really a panic button. The FBI has been alerted and they are going to come crashing through the door. And we have to talk about your tattoo before that happens, don't we?"

His eyes narrowed and his lips tightened. And then he answered, "Yes, we do."

Nevrescu barked at everybody else, telling them to leave as he untied my hands. Both of us had to think fast. As the

others scurried out of the barn and rushed to their vehicles, Nevrescu and I sat back down.

"How did you know?" he asked.

"Your tattoo doesn't make sense. You're a tough guy, not a flower guy. Then I remembered the Romanian word for daisy—*margareta*, MARGARET A. The twenty-four/seven is the European style for the twenty-fourth of July. That's her real birthday, right? July twenty-fourth?"

I looked across the table and saw him turn into an entirely different man.

"You're Margaret's father."

28.

The Cavalry Arrives

THE FBI WAS COMING TO RESCUE ME, NEVRESCU'S henchmen were scrambling to get away from the barn, chaos was everywhere, but I didn't hear a thing. I was so focused on Nevrescu's tattoo and the realization that he was Margaret's birth father.

"You weren't at the soccer game to see *me*," I said. "You were there to see *her*."

"She was amazing in that game, wasn't she?" he said.

"She's amazing in everything she does," I told him.

I ran through the timeline in my head. "And when we were at the embassy, I wasn't the one you recognized, it was her. She was standing right next to me."

"You must understand that I'm a bad person," he said. "But she is not. She is only good. Nothing can ever connect her to me. That's for her safety."

All the pieces started coming together.

"Twelve years ago, you weren't a criminal, you were a student at Georgetown. Is that where you met her mother, her birth mother?"

"My family would not accept the relationship. They would not accept an African-American daughter-in-law, an African-American granddaughter. So I had to make a choice. I had to become this man, in exchange for my family looking away from them. I tell you this so you understand how far I will go to protect Margaret. You cannot tell anyone."

"Well, then you're going to have to help me come up with an explanation as to what we're doing here," I said. "Because the FBI's going to want to know how we ended up together."

Both of us sat there for a moment, breathing heavily, trying to figure out a solution. I knew the FBI would be there any moment. I pictured my case board in my mind and I drew a line through all the dots. I connected all the small pieces, and then I saw it.

"I know who did it!" I exclaimed. "I know who stole *Woman with a Parasol*!"

"It was not me," he said.

"No, it wasn't," I said. "You had nothing to do with it. That's how I know who did it."

We could now hear cars arriving outside the barn. It was only a matter of seconds before the agents burst into the barn.

"You can help me in a way that will help both of us."

Nevrescu lay facedown on the ground and put his hands behind his head, so there'd be no trouble when the agents entered.

"What do I do?" he asked.

"You get EEL to force Pavel Novak to return to America," I said. "And you tell everybody that Agent Rivers was not the man at the Romanian embassy. Tell them that you saw a man who looked like him, but that it was someone else. That one's a deal breaker. You don't do that and I'll tell everybody everything. Including Margaret."

"You care about her too much to tell her," he said. "But I still agree."

The barn door flew open and a team of federal agents burst in. They wore black riot gear and helmets and had their guns drawn. It was terrifying. In the middle of them all was Agent Rivers.

"Nicolae Nevrescu, keep your hands behind your head and do not move!" he barked as an agent approached Nevrescu and cuffed him behind his back.

Rivers walked straight to me.

"Are you okay?" he said.

"Don't worry, Marcus, I'm fine."

He wrapped me in another hug.

"This is going to have to stop," he said with a nervous laugh. "I signed up for Art Crime because it was supposed to keep me mellow."

"Yeah," I agreed. "But we've got a lot to talk about."

After the dust settled (literally) and the scene had been fully secured by the agents, Nicolae, Marcus, and I were all seated around the wooden picnic table, only now it was Nic the Knife, whose hands were tied behind his back.

"You're telling me that it was all a misunderstanding?" Rivers asked incredulously after we'd started to fill him in on our version of events.

"Not all of it," Nicolae said. "I asked Gregor to get Florian so that I could help explain that I was innocent but willing to help solve the mystery. Gregor mistook the request and was too forceful in the manner in which he got Florian. But he was never in danger. This is a special boy and I would not let anything happen to him." He looked at me and added, "I *will* not let anything ever happen to him."

I realized that he meant what he was saying. I was important to Margaret; he would never have hurt her by hurting me.

"But the important thing is that we solved the mystery," I said. "We know who stole *Woman with a Parasol*, and Nicolae can help us get Pavel Novak."

"Of course," Nic said. "I have friends in the Czech Republic who owe me a favor. Novak will be on a plane to the United States within three days. I guarantee that he'll surrender to the authorities."

"You know who did it?" Rivers asked me.

I nodded.

"Who?"

"I'll tell you when we're alone, but there's one more thing we have to take care of."

"What's that?"

"Nicolae, do you know this man?" I asked as I pointed at Agent Rivers. "Did you see him two Saturdays ago at the Romanian embassy?"

Nevrescu gave a performance worthy of an Oscar as he said, "I have never seen this man before in my life. And I would testify to that in any court in the land."

29.

A Tiny Piece of TOAST

MARCUS AND I RODE ALONG THE HIGHWAY ON our way back to Washington. I was still overwhelmed by everything as I looked out at the farms.

"It's a lot prettier when you're not tied up in the back of a truck," I said.

"Funny how that works," he replied.

"I still can't believe I pushed my panic button and you came to rescue me in a *hybrid*. I was expecting something like a helicopter, or at least one of those bulletproof SUVs."

"I didn't come because of the panic button," he said.

"What do you mean?"

"When you didn't show up at home, I started looking

for you on my own, tracking you with your SmarTrip card," he explained. "You got everybody else when you pushed the panic button. I was already on my way."

"I bet you didn't even go over the speed limit," I said.

"Speed limits are there for a reason," he said. "Safety's important." Then he cracked a smile and added, "Although I may have gone over it, by like forty miles an hour."

"Well, thanks," I said. "You've rescued me twice in two weeks. That's got to be some sort of record."

"And you said you were going to tell me who did it," he reminded me. "So spill."

"I need to explain something first. And you have to promise that you won't tell anyone."

"I promise no such thing," he said.

"Forty-five minutes ago, I told a very scary man that I wouldn't tell this to anybody, so I need to make sure it stays a secret. You have to promise."

"Let me explain how this works," Marcus said to me. "If you trust me with a secret, that means you trust my judgment with regard to the information. Not that you get to dictate that judgment for me. If we're going to work together, we're going to have to be able to think along those lines."

"You still want to work with me?" I asked. "Even after all this?"

"I know, crazy, isn't it?"

"Okay, you don't have to promise, but please use your best judgment."

"Always," he said.

"It all starts with Margaret's soccer game . . ."

I explained to him all about the search for Margaret's birth parents and the fact that Nevrescu was her father. When I was done he shook his head in amazement.

"Wow," he said. "That's a secret I can keep. That's something we need to protect her from."

"Agreed," I said.

"And from that you were able to determine who stole *Woman with a Parasol*?"

"Yes, thanks to you."

"What did I do?"

"That day at Quantico you set a trap for me."

I reached into the glove compartment and saw that the nail polish was still there. I took it out and held it up for him to see.

"You left clues like this that were too irresistible for me to ignore," I said. "Then you told me that my biggest vulnerability was that if someone knew I was on a case, they could set a trap. And that's exactly what someone did."

We continued to drive as I laid it all out for him. . . .

30.

The Solution

I WON'T GET INTO ALL THE MUSHY DETAILS, BUT IT was pretty emotional when I got home. At one point I think my mother literally hugged me for thirty consecutive minutes without letting go. After repeated assurances that I was completely fine, she slowly loosened her grip long enough so that we could eat dinner.

Afterward Margaret came over and we all sat around the front room and ate rocky road ice cream. That's when I got the text from Marcus.

"What?" asked Margaret when she saw my grin.

"The case is closed," I declared triumphantly.

"How?" asked Mom.

"Did I forget to tell you guys the part where I figured out who stole *Woman with a Parasol*?"

"Yes!" exclaimed Margaret.

"Well, I wanted to wait to make sure I was right," I said. "And apparently I was, because he's about to make an arrest."

"Who is it?" asked Dad.

"Let's turn on the TV, so we can see the press conference," I said.

When I turned it on, Oliver Hobbes was on yet another talk show complaining about the FBI and National Gallery. "It's almost criminal that such cultural treasures are protected so poorly," he said.

"Ugh," said my mom. "I cannot listen to that man say another word. Please shut him up."

"Okay," I said, pressing the mute button.

"Now tell us everything," added Margaret. "How did you solve it?"

"By answering your question," I told her. "How did Nic the Knife know that I'd be at the soccer game? And the answer is, he didn't."

"What do you mean?" asked Dad.

"He didn't know I'd be there because he didn't care," I said. "It turns out the FBI was wrong about one thing. He did have a relative playing in the game. Some girl on the

Capitol Crush was a second niece or something. He was there to see her, not me."

"Then why did he kidnap you?" asked my mother.

"Because he wanted to explain it to me, so that I could explain it to the FBI," I continued. "You see, once we suspected him, we tried to make the clues fit our suspicions. He kept intersecting the case. Clues kept pointing to him. But once you realize that he's not involved, then those clues disappear. All except for one."

"The auction bids," said Margaret. "Those all pointed back to Romania."

"Yes, they did," I replied. "And that was the final piece of TOAST. If Nevrescu is innocent, that means the bids are fake. They have to be. It's the only solution that works."

"It's Oliver Hobbes!" said Margaret.

I smiled. "You got it. He needed to pin it on somebody, and when Nic the Knife came onto the scene he had the perfect culprit. Nic was already making himself look guilty. All Oliver needed to do was set him up just a little bit more. Since the bidding records he showed us were confidential, he knew we'd never be able to compare them to the originals. All he had to do was leave the clues for us to find."

"And once you figured that out . . ." said Margaret.

"Everything else fell into place," I said. "When we were looking for an insider, we assumed that meant an employee of the museum, so we didn't consider him. But as the insurance representative, he knew exactly when the upgrade was going to take place."

"What about ArtFest in Budapest?" asked Margaret.

"He was there too," I said. "Marcus confirmed it with someone at Interpol. And, Dad, remember how fast you drove to the museum the night the paintings were stolen?"

Mom shot him a look. "Not too fast," he said. "But it was an emergency."

"But when we got to the security center, Oliver was already there on the telephone," I pointed out. "How could he beat us? He lives just down the street from us."

"He was already nearby waiting for the call," said Dad.

"You got it," I said.

"Look at him," Mom said, pointing at Hobbes on the television. "Do you think he has any idea that he's been discovered?"

"No," I said, turning up the volume. "But he's about to."

We watched as Hobbes continued to rant about the FBI, and then in a moment of perfect television, Special Agent Marcus Rivers of the FBI's Art Crime team walked onto the set during the middle of the broadcast.

There were a few seconds of confusion, until the interviewer recognized him.

"Agent Rivers, have you come down here to dispute Mr. Hobbes's claims?" she asked.

"No, I haven't," he said.

"Then why are you here?"

"Just doing my job," he said.

And he arrested Oliver right there on live television. We all cheered. And when it was over, the interviewer tried to switch sides as though she'd always been a supporter.

"Great job," she said, thrusting a microphone into his face. "How did you solve it?"

He looked right into the camera, winked, and said, "No comment."

Two days later Pavel Novak was greeted at Dulles International Airport, where he surrendered to authorities and began talking in exchange for a reduced sentence. He told them that Oliver Hobbes, whom he'd met at ArtFest in Budapest, had approached a Czech crime boss with the idea. Hobbes provided them with the information about the security reset and in return was to receive *Woman with a Parasol*. The Czechs, meanwhile, were supposed to keep the three paintings that we'd discovered in the recycling Dumpster.

Armed with this information, the FBI was able to get

Hobbes to confess. He had dressed up as the extra custodian, and his plan was to sneak the Monet out of the museum in his car that night. But he was too slow and the police had managed to block the scene before he could escape. So instead, he hid the masterpiece in a secured locker that the insurance company maintained at the museum. Like the first three paintings, it never actually ventured outside of the building. It had been so close to us the entire time we were looking for it.

Special Agent Marcus Rivers was hailed as a hero, and despite numerous media requests, he granted only one interview.

It was with *Viking Journal*, the student newspaper at Alice Deal Middle School.

31.

The (Sort Of) Safeway

MY NAME IS FLORIAN BATES. I'M TWELVE YEARS old and a seventh grader at Alice Deal Middle School in Washington, DC. I'm a consulting detective for the FBI, I'm a rabid fan of the DC Dynamo girls soccer team, and I never leave leftover egg rolls for fear that they'd remain uneaten in the event of a zombie apocalypse.

I also helped thwart the biggest art heist in US history.

And nobody knows about it. Well, almost no one.

And that's okay because the people who do know are the only ones that matter to me. My parents, who despite taking too many pictures, are pretty great; my FBI handler, who somehow manages to be cool and geeky, old-school

and cutting-edge, all at the same time; and my best friend, who's . . . well . . . who's the best person I've ever known. And it really sucks, because I know the answer to the one question that matters the most to her, and I can't tell her. I have to lie.

But other than that, life's pretty great.

Margaret and I are walking home from school, and I jokingly nod toward the rear of the Safeway.

"What do you say?" I ask. "Want to take a shortcut?"

She gives me a look—that trademark Margaret look—and asks, "Do I have to remind you what Ben Franklin said?"

"Ben Franklin did not say, 'Nothing good ever happens when you're surrounded by Dumpsters.' I guarantee it."

"I'm pretty sure he did," she replies. "I think it was in *Poor Richard's Almanack.*"

"Ben Franklin was dead long before the Dumpster was even invented. End of story."

She flashes a big smile and admits, "Maybe. But it's still pretty good advice."

"I cannot argue with that," I say, reflecting back on my recent experiences. "I'd have to rate that as 'very strong' on the advice meter."

"So, what are you going to do now that the case is solved, and you're back to being a lowly seventh grader again?"

"Well, seventh grade does have its perks," I say. "For example, you never get kidnapped in the halls."

"You see, and you didn't like those metal detectors at first, but they keep things safe," she jokes.

"And while Florian Bates Investigations is small, we're hoping to grow," I continue.

"That's right, we still have an open case: Hornet's Nest."

The mention of the search for her birth parents fills me with guilt. "I'm really sorry that I haven't found them yet," I say, and I mean it. "I know I promised but . . ."

"It will take as long as it takes," she says, cutting me off. "If there's one thing I know, it's that you'll find them, Florian. I believe in you. Completely."

I'm tempted to tell her everything on the spot. Best friends are truthful with each other, right? But before I can respond, it starts to rain. And not just a little sprinkle but fully drenching rain. I give her a look, and then I look back toward the Safeway.

"You sure you don't want to take the shortcut?" I ask. "It's the fastest way to someplace dry."

She weighs her options for a moment and nods, streams of water already running down her face. "But let's go around that way," she says, pointing to a slightly different route than I took before.

"We'll call that the 'Sort of' Safe Way," I suggest.

We sprint across the street and I hold up the bottom of the chain link fence so that she can get under it. When she reaches the other side, she does the same for me.

"If we run into any shady characters, remember to unleash the fury of your kung fu," I joke.

We run alongside the line of Dumpsters, trying to use our backpacks to shield us from the rain, and when we turn the corner, we run right up against a black, unmarked van, its engine loudly vibrating, its wipers furiously pumping across the windshield.

"I don't believe it!" I say.

"Oh my God," says Margaret. "What have I done?"

The door slides open, and there he is, a massive smile on his face.

"Haven't you learned your lesson yet?" says Special Agent Marcus Rivers. "It's just like Mark Twain said, 'Nothing good ever happens when you're surrounded by Dumpsters.'"

"That's who said it," says Margaret. "Mark Twain."

"It was not Mark Twain!" I protest. "It was Margaret. Margaret made up that quote. Margaret is who said it."

"Well," he says. "Margaret must be pretty smart because it's good advice."

"Yes, it is. She and I have already agreed to that. Is that

why you did this? You came back here to terrify us so you could make up fake quotes about Dumpsters while we stand in the rain?"

"Actually, no," he says.

"Then what are you doing here?"

"It seems as though we have a situation and we need your help." He turns to look right at Margaret and adds, "Both of you. The admiral sent me. So what do you say? You interested?"

Margaret and I share a look, now totally oblivious to the rain pummeling us. Adventure is calling. Who are we to say no?

Acknowledgments

It does not take a superdetective to uncover the fact that a book is the product of many people's hard work. I would like to thank the ones who helped bring Florian and Margaret's adventure into print. First and foremost are my editor, Fiona Simpson, and publisher, Mara Anastas. They combine kindness, creativity, and enduring patience to make Aladdin an author's dream workplace. Like the master criminals Florian tries to expose, they do their handiwork without leaving fingerprints or clues to their involvement, but trust me when I say that it is extensive and essential.

They are part of a much larger Simon & Schuster team that has been part of my writing career from the very beginning. There I would like to thank Katherine Devendorf, Laura Lyn DiSiena, Sara Berko, Carolyn Swerdloff, Emma Sector, Tara Grieco, Shifa Kapadwala, Michelle Leo,

Candace Greene, Anthony Parisi, Betsy Bloom, and Matt Pantoliano.

Just as Florian has Margaret helping him, I have a professional partner in crime, my agent, Rosemary Stimola. She's the one who warns me not to sneak through the Dumpsters, and she's the one who comes to my rescue when I do it anyway. She's also like Margaret in that she's amazing, funny, and a friend for life.

Besides Fiona, Mara, and Rosemary, perhaps no one else helps my books more than the librarians, media specialists, reading specialists, and teachers who every day fight the battle to get books into the hands of kids. It is noble work, and they are my rock stars. I would especially like to thank the librarians of Texas and Florida, who have been among my biggest supporters.

Finally, I want to thank my family. They are the world to me. They inspire me to write. They make me laugh. They make every single day special. Growing up, I always wanted to be a writer. But even more, I wanted to be a husband and a father. I am eternally blessed in that I get to be all three.

Florian and Margaret are back on the case.
This time they're investigating a series of
middle-school pranks . . . wait, what? But
when the president's daughter is involved, the
stakes are high, so it's time for some TOAST!

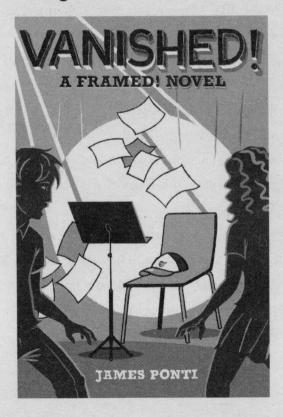

MIDDLE SCHOOL IS HARD.

Solving cases for the FBI is even harder.

Doing both at the same time, well, that's just crazy.

Trust me, I know. My name's Florian Bates, I'm twelve years old, and along with my best friend, Margaret, I'm a consulting detective for the Bureau's Special Projects Team. We assist the FBI, the same way Sherlock Holmes helped Scotland Yard; only Sherlock never had to close a case *and* write a book report on the same night.

He also didn't have to deal with all the other seventh-grade headaches like locker room bullies, nine o'clock curfews, or figuring out what to wear. All he had

to do was put on his coat and deerstalker hat. Instant detective.

Me? It seems like I'm always dressed for the wrong occasion. Like when we had to interrogate a witness while I was still in my soccer uniform. Or the time I was wearing my I'M WITH CHEWBACCA T-shirt and we ended up going undercover at the reception for the French ambassador. (In case you're wondering, "*Que la Force soit avec toi*" is how you say "May the Force be with you" in French.)

So when we arrived at the harbor patrol's maintenance-and-repair yard it shouldn't have been a surprise that I was the only one wearing a double-breasted blazer and herringbone tie. My mistake was that when I dressed for the symphony, I forgot to factor in the possibility of racing down the Potomac in a police boat. (I know, you'd think I'd learn.)

The boat was Marcus's idea. He oversees the Special Projects Team and it was a good plan except for one little detail: None of us actually had access to a boat. That meant we had to borrow one.

Margaret and I waited outside the harbormaster's office while he went in to see if he could get the duty sergeant to help us out. The stench of diesel was overwhelming, engine grease was everywhere, and when I saw my reflection in the window, I noticed my tie was crooked.

"What are you doing?" Margaret asked when she saw me fidget with it.

"Trying to straighten the knot," I explained. "It's a Windsor. It's supposed to be perfectly centered."

She gave me a look. That Margaret "you've got to be kidding me" look. "We're standing on a wharf surrounded by gas and grime and you're worried about your tie being crooked. Why don't you try to relax? No one's going to notice."

"Technically it's not a wharf," I corrected. "We're standing on a *dock*. And the dock is part of a *marina*. A wharf is an entirely different thing."

"Seriously?" she replied, shaking her head. "That's your takeaway from what I just said? Correcting my vocabulary?"

I gave her a sheepish smile and apologized. Then I tried to follow her advice and relax. But it wasn't easy. I'm not that good at relaxing on a normal day when nothing's going on, and this was no normal day. We were in the middle of a missing persons case that was beyond baffling.

That morning we'd boarded a school bus for a field trip to the Kennedy Center for the Performing Arts. At the time, our biggest worry was finding a seat just the right distance from the bullies in back and the chaperones in front. Then one of our classmates disappeared into thin air. That might

have been okay if it had been a magic show, but like I said, we were there for the symphony. So it was bad.

Suddenly bullies and chaperones didn't seem like such a big deal. We had a case to solve and we weren't having much luck figuring it out. Each clue seemed to lead us further away from the answer. And now, on top of that, I had an additional obstacle to overcome.

"Can I be honest with you?" I asked Margaret.

"This far into the friendship and you don't know?" she said. "You can always be honest with me. In fact, that's all you can be."

That made me smile.

"Okay, so here's the deal," I replied. "I'm not exactly *comfortable* when it comes to boats."

She gave me a curious look. "What does 'not exactly comfortable' mean?"

"They terrify me," I admitted. "They have ever since I saw that movie about the *Titanic*."

"You know it's at least eighty degrees today," she said. "I'm pretty sure we're not going to run into any icebergs."

"I'm not worried about sinking," I explained. "It's just that I got . . . seasick."

"You got seasick *watching* a movie?"

I nodded reluctantly.

"Were you at least on a boat while you were watching it?"

"No. We were home. I'll skip the vivid details, but we ended up having to rent one of those industrial-sized steam cleaners for the carpet and couch."

My thoughts wafted back to the salami sandwich and jalapeño-flavored tortilla chips that began the day in my lunch bag and I wondered if they would soon be reintroduced to the world.

"Well, you might not have to worry about it," Margaret said, looking through the window into the office. "I think Marcus is striking out in there."

Even though we weren't inside, it wasn't hard to guess what the problem was. The harbor patrol was part of the Metropolitan Police Department and Marcus was with the FBI. Those two groups are very protective of their turf and almost never work well together.

"Think we should help out?"

She asked it like a question, but considering she didn't wait for me to answer before she opened the door and went inside, I didn't really have much of a chance to say no.

The sergeant was big with ruddy skin, chubby cheeks, and a mustache that looked like it belonged on a walrus. He stood behind a counter similar to the check-in desk at a hotel and looked as though his patience was gone.

"But this is an emergency," Marcus said, frustrated.

"You keep saying that," replied the cop. "But I haven't heard a thing about it on my radio." He nodded to the police scanner on his desk.

"That's because we're trying to keep it contained to the Secret Service and the FBI," answered Marcus. "We haven't involved the local police yet."

The sergeant flashed a smug smile. "There, you just said it yourself. You don't want to involve the local police. Well, unfortunately for you, these boats belong to the local police. So have a nice day."

Despite my dread of seasickness, I knew we needed the boat, so I tried to help out.

"What if Frankie was missing?" I asked, interrupting. "You'd want us to look for him, wouldn't you?"

The sergeant turned his attention to me and shot me with a laser stare.

"Or imagine your daughter went camping with her Girl Scout troop and got lost in a national park."

"How do you know about my kids?"

I ignored his question. "How would you feel if the park rangers wouldn't help the police who were trying to rescue her because they were from different agencies? How would you feel if they did to you what you're doing to us right now?"

By this point he was really angry, his fat cheeks turning crimson. "I said, how do you know about my kids?" he demanded.

"The nameplate on your desk says you're Frank Bergen Sr.," I explained. "That means there's a junior. I know you call him Frankie because that's how he signed the drawing you taped to the window over there. I know your daughter's in Girl Scouts because you've got five cases of Girl Scout cookies stacked behind your desk so you can deliver them to your coworkers."

He started to say something, but I just kept talking.

"I don't know your kids at all, but I know you're the kind of dad who tapes his son's pictures up at work and tries to help his daughter sell cookies. It's the best kind of dad to be. That's why I know that eventually you're going to give Agent Rivers the keys to a boat so we can try to rescue my friend. I just don't know if you're going to do it soon enough to save him."

For a moment the room was silent except for the sound of the sergeant taking a deep breath while he considered what I'd said. His nostrils flared as he inhaled and he studied me for a moment before begrudgingly slapping a set of keys down onto the counter.

"If there's so much as a scratch . . ."

"There won't be," Marcus said as he snatched them up. "You're a good cop, Frank. And a good father. Thank you."

"Just do me a favor and find the kid," he said.

"That we will," Marcus said as he grabbed a pair of dingy orange life vests from a rack and handed them to us. "That we will."

We followed Marcus outside and had to hurry to keep up. "That was great work in there, Florian," he said, taking quick long strides. "Our boat's at the end of the dock."

I looked out at the water and felt a wave of uneasiness. "We're sure this is the best way to go, right?" I asked, hoping it sounded more like a question of strategy than a fear of barfing.

"Yes, for two reasons," he said. "First of all, it's our only chance to get close to the bridge without anyone noticing us."

This was the part he hadn't mentioned to the police officer—or anyone in the Bureau for that matter. We'd been taken off the case. A Child Abduction Rapid Deployment (CARD) team was in charge and they didn't want any help from us.

Our problem was that we were pretty sure they had it wrong.

"Secondly, they're going to put the bridge under surveillance and check all the roads and sidewalks leading to it," he said. "So they'll have everything fully covered up there. But I don't think they'll be checking the river traffic, and if you're right, that's where we need to be."

I gulped, realizing my theory had set this little adventure into motion, and wrestled my way into the life vest. The boat

didn't have one of those clever names like *Oh, Say Can You Sea* or *When You Fish Upon a Star*. Instead, it was just called *MPDC-4*. But what it lacked in creativity, it made up for in stability. I was relieved by how solid it felt beneath my feet.

"You know, this isn't so bad," I said as I plopped down on a thickly padded seat. "It's actually kind of comfy."

"Too bad it's not ours." Marcus chuckled. "We're taking the *Zodiac*."

"The what-iac?"

"The *Zodiac*," he repeated. "It's the boat tied to the back of this one."

"You know," Margaret added as she pulled me back up by my life jacket and turned me toward a small inflatable tied to *MPDC-4*. "The teeny-tiny one."

Up until that point the only zodiac I knew was the collection of astrological signs like Capricorn and Aquarius. But apparently it was also the name of the world's most terrifyingly inadequate water vessel. My horoscope: rough seas ahead.

"Shouldn't we take one of the ones with, you know, sides?" (I was no longer concerned with sounding scared.)

"Remember the part about us trying not to attract attention?" Marcus said. "If the CARD team sees a boat with police markings invade their crime scene they'll go nuts. This one's completely unmarked. Besides, it's a whole lot faster."

"So you're telling me it's supersmall *and* superfast?" I said, trying to force a smile. "That's just . . ."

"Super?" joked Margaret.

I started to climb down into the *Zodiac*, but Marcus took me by the shoulders and stopped me. "You don't have to go, Florian. I mean it. You can stay right here and I'll have someone give you a ride home. In fact, it might be a good idea for both of you to stay. Even without the markings, there's a decent chance they'll spot us. And if they do there's no telling what kind of trouble there'll be for encroaching on someone else's case."

"No way," I answered. "A kid is missing. A kid I consider a friend. I'll go wherever the clues lead. Even if it means I have to take a submarine or ride in a helicopter."

"Me too," said Margaret. "Besides, if any one of us is getting in trouble, then all of us are."

He didn't say it but I could tell he was happy with our responses. We were in every way a team.

Once we were on board, Marcus untied the boat, maneuvered it out onto the river, and opened the throttle to full speed. As we raced toward the Key Bridge, the wind made it so my tie flapped in the air and kept slapping me in the face. I was too busy double clutching the safety rope that ran along our seat to do anything about it, so Margaret leaned over and tucked the tie into my life vest.

"You okay?" she asked, her voice barely audible over the whine of the engine.

I almost answered, but stopped when I realized that I wasn't sure if words or lunch would come out. Instead I just nodded and gripped the rope tighter.

"Look for anything suspicious," Marcus shouted so we could hear him.

"You mean more suspicious than the three of us?" Margaret responded.

There was so much mist spraying my face, I had to close my eyes as I tried to picture the crime scene in my head. A thirteen-year-old had disappeared despite being surrounded by dozens of people. There were no signs of foul play, no signs of anything out of the ordinary. The only clue we found was a sticky note with three words written in pen: "HELP KEY BRIDGE."

The boat slowed down and I opened my eyes to see the Francis Scott Key Bridge come into view. Spanning the Potomac between Washington and Rosslyn, Virginia, it looked much bigger from the river than it did from the land. Whenever we drove over it in our car, it just seemed like a road that happened to pass over water. There were no towers or cables holding it up. But from this vantage point, you could see the six massive arches supporting it.

Marcus continued to slow the engine until we were basically floating along with the current. He turned on his walkie-talkie and clicked through the channels until he heard some agents communicating up above.

"They're up there," he said. "Let's hope they won't notice us."

"What are we looking for?" asked Margaret.

"Anything suspicious," he replied. "On the water or along the riverside."

He nodded to the jogging-and-bike path that ran along the water.

We saw a couple of kayaks and a man riding a stand-up paddleboard, but none of them was suspicious. A pair of sightseeing cruisers approached. One was named the *General Washington* and the other the *President Jefferson*. Both were decorated with red, white, and blue banners, as well as a sign that advertised STAR-SPANGLED TOURS.

I scanned the decks of the first one but saw only tourists taking pictures. When it passed us, our boat started bobbing up and down in its wake and my stomach gurgled even more. I closed my eyes and tried not to give the second boat a show. (Imagine dozens of tourists snapping pictures as I puked over the edge of the *Zodiac*.) I focused all my mental energy on my stomach, trying to calm the storm inside me. Trying to ignore the motion and my

sense of uselessness. Trying to block out everything.

And that's when I noticed the music playing over the speakers on the boat. My mind was so busy concentrating on my seasickness that my subconscious brain was free to identify that something was out of place.

I looked up at Marcus and Margaret and asked, "Why's a sightseeing boat in the capital of the United States and named after an American president playing the British national anthem?"

They both gave me a confused look.

"What are you talking about?" she asked.

I worried I might be hallucinating. "Don't you hear the song?"

They listened for a moment and Margaret began to sing along:

> *My country, 'tis of thee,*
> *Sweet land of liberty,*
> *Of thee I sing.*

"No, no, no," I said. "Those aren't the lyrics. The song is 'God Save the Queen.'" Having grown up in Europe, including three years spent in England, I was quite familiar with it. I started to sing the version that I knew:

God save our gracious Queen,
Long live our noble Queen,
God save the Queen.

Marcus smiled when he realized why I was confused. "I forgot that they both have the same tune," he said. "The Americans kept the music and wrote new lyrics to give it a completely different meaning."

I don't know if it was the dizziness, my stomach, the case, the clues, the music, or all of it. But in that moment I felt a surge moving up through my body. I couldn't tell if I was going to get sick, if my head was going to explode, or if I was going to solve the mystery right then and there. It just bubbled up through me. And then . . .

"I need to get off the boat," I said urgently.

"What's the matter?" asked Marcus. "Are you going to get sick?"

"No," I answered, my nausea instantly cured by my realization. "I told you I'd follow the clues wherever they lead, and they're not in the water."

"How do you know?" asked Margaret.

"It's complicated," I replied. "But the first thing you have to understand is that 'God Save the Queen' changes everything."

Molly Bigelow is NOT your average girl. She's one of an elite crew assigned the task of policing and protecting the zombie population of New York. *The Hunger Games* author Suzanne Collins says *Dead City* "breathes new life into the zombie genre."

EBOOK EDITIONS
ALSO AVAILABLE